E.M. FORSTER

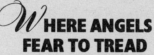

WHERE ANGELS FEAR TO TREAD

A ROOM WITH A VIEW

HOWARDS END

A PASSAGE TO INDIA

PEERAGE BOOKS

Where Angels Fear to Tread first published in Great Britain
in 1905 by Edward Arnold Ltd
A Room With a View first published in Great Britain in 1908
by Edward Arnold Ltd
Howards End first published in Great Britain in 1910 by
Edward Arnold Ltd
A Passage to India first published in Great Britain in 1924
by Edward Arnold Ltd

This edition first published in Great Britain in 1991 by
Peerage Books
an imprint of
Reed International Books Limited
Michelin House
81 Fulham Road
London SW3 6RB

ISBN 1 85052 190 5

Printed and bound in the United Kingdom by the Bath Press

ONTENTS

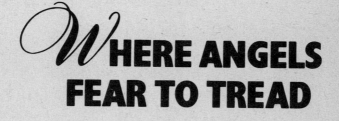

WHERE ANGELS FEAR TO TREAD

Chapter One

They were all at Charing Cross to see Lilia off–Philip, Harriet, Irma, Mrs Herriton herself. Even Mrs Theobald, squired by Mr Kingcroft, had braved the journey from Yorkshire to bid her only daughter good-bye. Miss Abbott was likewise attended by numerous relatives, and the sight of so many people talking at once and saying such different things caused Lilia to break into ungovernable peals of laughter.

'Quite an ovation,' she cried, sprawling out of her first-class carriage. 'They'll take us for royalty. Oh, Mr Kingcroft, get us foot-warmers.'

The good-natured young man hurried away, and Philip, taking his place, flooded her with a final stream of advice and injunctions–where to stop, how to learn Italian, when to use mosquito-nets, what pictures to look at. 'Remember,' he concluded, 'that it is only by going off the track that you get to know the country. See the little towns–Gubbio, Pienza, Cortona, San Gimignano, Monteriano. And don't, let me beg you, go with that awful tourist idea that Italy's only a museum of antiquities and art. Love and understand the Italians, for the people are more marvellous than the land.'

'How I wish you were coming, Philip,' she said, flattered at the unwonted notice her brother-in-law was giving her.

'I wish I were.' He could have managed it without great difficulty, for his career at the Bar was not so intense as to prevent occasional holidays. But his family disliked his continual visits to the Continent, and he himself often found pleasure in the idea that he was too busy to leave town.

'Good-bye, dear every one. What a whirl!' She caught sight of her little daughter Irma, and felt that a touch of maternal solemnity was required. 'Good-bye, darling. Mind you're always good, and do what Granny tells you.'

She referred not to her own mother, but to her mother-in-law, Mrs Herriton, who hated the title of Granny.

Irma lifted a serious face to be kissed, and said cautiously, 'I'll do my best.'

'She is sure to be good,' said Mrs Herriton, who was standing pensively a little out of the hubbub. But Lilia was already calling to Miss Abbott, a tall, grave, rather nice-looking young lady who was conducting her adieus in a more decorous manner on the platform.

'Caroline, my Caroline! Jump in, or your chaperon will go off without you.'

And Philip, whom the idea of Italy always intoxicated, had started again, telling her of the supreme moments of her coming journey–the Campanile of Airolo, which would burst on her when she emerged from the St Gotthard tunnel, presaging the future; the view of the Ticino and Lago Maggiore as the train climbed the slopes of Monte Cenere; the view of Lugano, the view of Como—Italy gathering thick around her now—the arrival at her first resting-place, when, after long driving through dark and dirty streets, she should at last behold, amid the roar of trams and the glare of arc lamps, the buttresses of the cathedral of Milan.

'Handkerchiefs and collars,' screamed Harriet, 'in my inlaid box! I've lent you my inlaid box.'

'Good old Harry!' She kissed every one again, and there was a moment's silence. They all smiled steadily, excepting Philip, who was choking in the fog, and old Mrs Theobald, who had begun to cry. Miss Abbot got into the carriage. The guard himself shut the door, and told Lilia that she would be all right. Then the train moved, and they all moved with it a couple of steps, and waved their handkerchiefs, and uttered cheerful little cries. At that moment Mr Kingcroft reappeared, carrying a foot-warmer by both ends, as if it was a tea-tray. He was sorry that he was too late, and called out in a quavering voice, 'Good-bye, Mrs Charles. May you enjoy yourself, and may God bless you.'

Lilia smiled and nodded, and then the absurd position of the foot-warmer overcame her, and she began to laugh again.

'Oh, I am so sorry,' she cried back, 'but you do look so funny. Oh, you all look so funny waving! Oh, pray!' And laughing helplessly, she was carried out into the fog.

'High spirits to begin so long a journey,' said Mrs Theobald, dabbing her eyes.

Mr Kingcroft solemnly moved his head in token of agreement. 'I wish,' said he, 'that Mrs Charles had gotten the foot-warmer. These London porters won't take heed to a country chap.'

'But you did your best,' said Mrs Herriton. 'And I think it simply noble of you to have brought Mrs Theobald all the way here on such a day as this.' Then, rather hastily, she shook hands, and left him to take Mrs Theobald all the way back.

Sawston, her own home, was within easy reach of London, and they were not late for tea. Tea was in the dining-room, with an egg for Irma, to keep up the child's spirits. The house seemed strangely quiet after a fortnight's bustle, and their conversation was spasmodic and subdued. They wondered whether the travellers had got to Folkestone, whether it would be at all rough, and if so what would happen to poor Miss Abbott.

'And, Granny, when will the old ship get to Italy?' asked Irma.

'"Grandmother," dear; not "Granny,"' said Mrs Herriton, giving her a kiss. 'And we say "a boat" or "a steamer," not "a ship." Ships have sails. And mother won't go all the way by sea. You look at the map of Europe, and you'll see why. Harriet, take her. Go with Aunt Harriet, and she'll show you the map.'

'Right-o!' said the little girl, and dragged the reluctant Harriet into the library. Mrs Herriton and her son were left alone. There was immediately confidence between them.

'Here beginneth the New Life,' said Philip.

'Poor child, how vulgar!' murmured Mrs Herriton. 'It's surprising that she isn't worse. But she has got a look of poor Charles about her.'

'And—alas, alas!—a look of old Mrs Theobald. What appalling apparition was that? I did think the lady was bedridden as well as imbecile. Why ever did she come?'

'Mr Kingcroft made her. I am certain of it. He wanted to see Lilia again, and this was the only way.'

'I hope he is satisfied. I did not think my sister-in-law distinguished herself in her farewells.'

Mrs Herriton shuddered. 'I mind nothing, so long as she has gone—and gone with Miss Abbott. It is mortifying to think that a widow of thirty-three requires a girl ten years younger to look after her.'

'I pity Miss Abbott. Fortunately one admirer is chained to England. Mr Kingcroft cannot leave the crops or the climate or something. I don't think, either, he improved his chances to-day. He, as well as Lilia, has the knack of being absurd in public.'

Mrs Herriton replied, 'When a man is neither well-bred, nor well-connected, nor handsome, nor clever, nor rich, even Lilia may discard him in time.'

'No. I believe she would take anyone. Right up to the last, when her boxes were packed, she was "playing" the chinless curate. Both the curates are chinless, but hers had the dampest hands. I came on them in the Park. They were speaking of the Pentateuch.'

'My dear boy! If possible, she has got worse and worse. It was your idea of Italian travel that saved us!'

Philip brightened at the little compliment. 'The odd part is that she was quite eager—always asking me for information; and of course I was very glad to give it. I admit she is a Philistine, appallingly ignorant, and her taste in art is false. Still, to have any taste at all is something. And I do believe that Italy really purifies and ennobles all who visit her. She is the school as well as the playground of the world. It is really to Lilia's credit that she wants to go there.'

'She would go anywhere,' said his mother, who had heard enough of the praises of Italy. 'I and Caroline Abbot had the greatest difficulty in dissuading her from the Riviera.'

'No, mother; no. She was really keen on Italy. This travel is quite a crisis for her.' He found the situation full of whimsical romance: there was something half-attractive, half-repellent in the thought of this vulgar woman journeying to places he loved and revered. Why should she not be transfigured? The same had happened to the Goths.

Mrs Herriton did not believe in romance, nor in transfiguration, nor in parallels from history, nor in anything else that may disturb domestic life. She adroitly changed the subject before Philip got excited. Soon Harriet returned, having given her lesson in geography. Irma went to bed early, and was tucked up by her grandmother. Then the two ladies worked and played cards. Philip read a book. And so they all settled down to their quiet profitable existence, and continued it without interruption through the winter.

It was now nearly ten years since Charles had fallen in love with Lilia Theobald because she was pretty, and during that time Mrs Herriton had hardly known a moment's rest. For six months she schemed to prevent the match, and when it had taken place she turned to another task—the supervision of her daughter-in-law. Lilia must be pushed through life without bringing discredit on the family into which she had married. She was aided by Charles, by her daughter Harriet, and, as soon as he was old enough, by the clever one of the family, Philip. The birth of Irma made things still more difficult. But fortunately old Mrs Theobald, who had attempted interference, began to break up. It was an effort to her to leave Whitby, and Mrs Herriton discouraged the effort as far as possible. That curious duel which is fought over every baby was fought and decided early. Irma belonged to her father's family, not to her mother's.

Charles died, and the struggle recommenced. Lilia tried to assert herself, and said that she should go to take care of Mrs Theobald. It required all Mrs Herriton's kindness to prevent her. A house was finally taken for her at Sawston, and there for three years she lived with Irma, continually subject to the refining influences of her late husband's family.

During one of her rare Yorkshire visits trouble began again. Lilia confided to a friend that she liked a Mr Kingcroft extremely, but that she was not exactly engaged to him. The news came round to Mrs Herriton, who at once wrote, begging for information, and pointing out that Lilia must either be engaged or not, since no intermediate state existed. It was a good letter, and flurried Lilia extremely. She left Mr Kingcroft without even the pressure of a rescue-party. She cried a great deal on her return to Sawston, and said she was very sorry. Mrs Herriton took the opportunity of speaking more seriously about the duties of widowhood and motherhood than she had ever done before. But somehow things never went easily after. Lilia would not settle down in her place among Sawston matrons. She was a bad house-keeper, always in the throes of some domestic crisis, which Mrs Herriton, who kept her servants for years, had to step across and adjust. She let Irma stop away from school for insufficient reasons, and she allowed her to wear rings. She learnt to bicycle, for the purpose of waking the place up, and coasted down the High Street one Sunday evening, falling off at the turn by the church. If she had not been a relative, it would have been entertaining. But even Philip, who in theory loved outraging English conventions, rose to the occasion, and gave her a talking which she remembered to her dying day. It was just then, too, that they discovered that she still allowed Mr Kingcroft to write to her 'as a gentleman friend,' and to send presents to Irma.

Philip thought of Italy, and the situation was saved. Caroline, charming sober Caroline Abbott, who lived two turnings away, was seeking a companion for a year's travel. Lilia gave up her house, sold half her furniture, left the other half and Irma with Mrs Herriton, and had now departed, amid universal approval, for a change of scene.

She wrote to them frequently during the winter—more frequently than she wrote to her mother. Her letters were always prosperous. Florence she found perfectly sweet, Naples a dream, but very whiffy. In Rome one had simply to sit still and feel. Philip, however, declared that she was improving. He was particularly gratified when in the early spring she began to visit the smaller towns that he had recommended. 'In a place like this,' she wrote, 'one really does feel in the heart of things, and off the beaten track. Looking out of a Gothic window every morning, it seems impossible that the Middle Ages have passed away.' The letter was from Monteriano, and concluded with a not unsuccessful description of the wonderful little town.

'It is something that she is contented,' said Mrs Herriton. 'But no one could live three months with Caroline Abbott and not be the better for it.'

Just then Irma came in from school, and she read her mother's letter to her, carefully correcting any grammatical errors, for she was a loyal supporter of parental authority. Irma listened politely, but soon changed the subject to hockey, in which her whole being was absorbed. They were to vote for colours that afternoon—yellow and white or yellow and green. What did her grandmother think?

Of course Mrs Herriton had an opinion, which she sedately expounded, in spite of Harriet, who said that colours were unnecessary for children, and of Philip, who said that they were ugly. She was getting proud of Irma, who had certainly greatly improved, and could no longer be called that most appalling of things—a vulgar child. She was anxious to form her before her mother returned. So she had no objection to the leisurely movements of the travellers, and even suggested that they should overstay their year if it suited them.

Lilia's next letter was also from Monteriano, and Philip grew quite enthusiastic.

'They've stopped there over a week!' he cried. 'Why! I shouldn't have done as much myself. They must be really keen, for the hotel's none too comfortable.'

'I cannot understand people,' said Harriet. 'What can they be doing all day? And there is no church there, I suppose.'

'There is Santa Deodata, one of the most beautiful churches in Italy.'

'Of course I mean an English church,' said Harriet stiffly. 'Lilia promised me that she would always be in a large town on Sundays.'

'If she goes to a service at Santa Deodata's, she will find more beauty and sincerity than there is in all the Back Kitchens of Europe.'

The Back Kitchen was his nickname for St James's, a small and depressing edifice much patronised by his sister. She always resented any slight on it, and Mrs Herriton had to intervene.

'Now, dears, don't. Listen to Lilia's letter. "We love this place, and I do not know how I shall ever thank Philip for telling me it. It is not only so quaint, but one sees the Italians unspoiled in all their simplicity and charm here. The frescoes are wonderful. Caroline, who grows sweeter every day, is very busy sketching."'

'Every one to his taste!' said Harriet, who always delivered a platitude as if it was an epigram. She was curiously virulent about Italy, which she had never visited, her only experience of the Continent being an occasional six weeks in the Protestant parts of Switzerland.

'Oh, Harriet is a bad lot!' said Philip as soon as she left the room. His mother laughed, and told him not to be naughty; and the appearance of Irma, just off to school, prevented further discussion. Not only in Tracts is a child a peacemaker.

'One moment, Irma,' said her uncle. 'I'm going to the station. I'll give you the pleasure of my company.'

They started together. Irma was gratified; but conversation flagged, for Philip had not the art of talking to the young. Mrs Herriton sat a little longer at the breakfast-table, re-reading Lilia's letter. Then she helped the cook to clear, ordered dinner, and started the housemaid turning out the drawing-room, Tuesday being its day. The weather was lovely, and she thought she would do a little gardening, as it was quite early. She called Harriet, who had recovered from the insult to St James's, and together they went to the kitchen garden and began to sow some early vegetables.

'We will save the peas to the last; they are the greatest fun,' said Mrs Herriton, who had the gift of making work a treat. She and her elderly daughter always got on very well, though they had not a great deal in common. Harriet's education had been almost too successful. As Philip once said, she had 'bolted all the cardinal virtues and couldn't digest them.' Though pious and patriotic, and a great moral asset for the house, she lacked that pliancy and tact which her mother so much valued, and had expected her to pick up for herself. Harriet, if she had been allowed, would have driven Lilia to an open rupture, and, what was worse, she would have done the same to Philip two years before, when he returned full of passion for Italy, and ridiculing Sawston and its ways.

'It's a shame, mother!' she had cried. 'Philip laughs at everything–the Book Club, the Debating Society, the Progressive Whist, the bazaars. People won't like it. We have our reputation. A house divided against itself cannot stand.'

Mrs Herriton replied in the memorable words, 'Let Philip say what he likes, and he will let us do what we like.' And Harriet had acquiesced.

They sowed the duller vegetables first, and a pleasant feeling of righteous fatigue stole over them as they addressed themselves to the peas. Harriet stretched a string to guide the row straight, and Mrs Herriton scratched a furrow with a pointed stick. At the end of it she looked at her watch.

'It's twelve! The second post's in. Run and see if there are any letters.'

Harriet did not want to go. 'Let's finish the peas. There won't be any letters.'

'No, dear; please go. I'll sow the peas, but you shall cover them up–and mind the birds don't see 'em!'

Mrs Herriton was very careful to let those peas trickle evenly from her hand, and at the end of the row she was conscious that she had never sown better. They were expensive too.

'Actually old Mrs Theobald!' said Harriet, returning.

'Read me the letter. My hands are dirty. How intolerable the crested paper is.'

Harriet opened the envelope.

'I don't understand,' she said; 'it doesn't make sense.'

'Her letters never did.'

'But it must be sillier than usual,' said Harriet, and her voice began to quaver. 'Look here, read it, mother; I can't make head or tail.'

Mrs Herriton took the letter indulgently. 'What is the difficulty?' she said after a long pause. 'What is it that puzzles you in this letter?'

'The meaning—' faltered Harriet. The sparrows hopped nearer and began to eye the peas.

'The meaning is quite clear—Lilia is engaged to be married. Don't cry, dear; please me by not crying—don't talk at all. It's more than I could bear. She is going to marry some one she has met in an hotel. Take the letter and read for yourself.' Suddenly she broke down over what might seem a small point. 'How dare she not tell me direct! How dare she write first to Yorkshire! Pray, am I to hear through Mrs Theobald—a patronising, insolent letter like this? Have I no claim at all? Bear witness, dear'—she choked with passion—'bear witness that for this I'll never forgive her!'

'Oh, what is to be done?' moaned Harriet. 'What is to be done?'

'This first!' She tore the letter into little pieces and scattered it over the mould. 'Next a telegram for Lilia! No! a telegram for Miss Caroline Abbott. She, too, has something to explain.'

'Oh, what is to be done?' repeated Harriet, as she followed her mother to the house. She was helpless before such effrontery. What awful thing—what awful person had come to Lilia? 'Some one in the hotel.' The letter only said that. What kind of person? A gentleman? An Englishman? The letter did not say.

'Wire reason of stay at Monteriano. Strange rumours,' read Mrs Herriton, and addressed the telegram to Abbott, Stella d'Italia, Monteriano, Italy. 'If there is an office there,' she added, 'we might get an answer this evening. Since Philip is back at seven, and the eight-fifteen catches the midnight boat at Dover—Harriet, when you go with this, get £100 in £5 notes at the bank.'

'But why—what—'

'Go, dear, at once; do not talk. I see Irma coming back; go quickly. . . . Well, Irma dear, and whose team are you in this afternoon—Miss Edith's or Miss May's?'

But as soon as she had behaved as usual to her granddaughter, she went to the library and took out the large atlas, for she wanted to know about Monteriano. The name was in the smallest print, in the midst of a woolly-brown tangle of hills which were called the 'Sub-Apennines.' It was not so very far from Siena, which she had learnt at school. Past it there wandered a thin black line, notched at intervals like a saw, and she knew that this was a railway. But the map left a good deal to imagination, and she had not got any. She looked up the place in 'Childe Harold,' but Byron had not been there. Nor did Mark Twain visit it in the 'Tramp Abroad.' The resources of literature were exhausted: she must wait till Philip came home. And the thought of Philip made her try Philip's room, and there she found 'Central Italy,' by Baedeker, and opened it for the first time in her life and read in it as follows:

> *Monteriano* (pop. 4,800). Hotels: Stella d'Italia, moderate only; Globo, dirty. *Caffè Garibaldi. Post and Telegraph office in Corso Vittorio Emmanuele, next to theatre. Photographs at Seghena's (cheaper in Florence). Diligence (1 lira) meets principal trains.
>   Chief attractions (2–3 hours): Santa Deodata, Palazzo Pubblico, Sant' Agostino, Santa Caterina, Sant' Ambrogio, Palazzo Capocchi. Guide (2 lire) unnecessary. A walk round the Walls should on no account be omitted. The view from the Rocca (small gratuity) is finest at sunset.
>   History: Monteriano, the Mons Rianus of Antiquity, whose Ghibelline tendencies are noted by Dante (Purg. xx.), definitely emancipated itself from Poggibonsi in 1261. Hence the distich, '*Poggibonizzi, fatti in là, che Monteriano si fa città!'* till recently inscribed over the Siena gate. It remained independent till 1530, when it was sacked by the Papal troops and became part of the Grand Duchy of Tuscany. It is now of small importance, and seat of the district prison. The inhabitants are still noted for their agreeable manners.

> The traveller will proceed direct from the Siena gate to the Collegiate Church of Santa Deodata, and inspect (5th chapel on right) the charming *Frescoes. . . .

Mrs Herriton did not proceed. She was not one to detect the hidden charms of Baedeker. Some of the information seemed to her unnecessary, all of it was dull. Whereas Philip could never read 'The view from the Rocca (small gratuity) is finest at sunset' without a catching at the heart. Restoring the book to its place, she went downstairs, and looked up and down the asphalt paths for her daughter. She saw her at last, two turnings away, vainly trying to shake off Mr Abbott, Miss Caroline Abbott's father. Harriet was always unfortunate. At last she returned, hot, agitated, crackling with bank-notes, and Irma bounced to greet her, and trod heavily on her corn.

'Your feet grow larger every day,' said the agonised Harriet, and gave her niece a violent push. Then Irma cried, and Mrs Herriton was annoyed with Harriet for betraying irritation. Lunch was nasty; and during pudding news arrived that the cook, by sheer dexterity, had broken a very vital knob off the kitchen-range. 'It is too bad,' said Mrs Herriton. Irma said it was three bad, and was told not to be rude. After lunch Harriet would get out Baedeker, and read in injured tones about Monteriano, the Mons Rianus of Antiquity, till her mother stopped her.

'It's ridiculous to read, dear. She's not trying to marry any one in the place. Some tourist, obviously, who's stopping in the hotel. The place has nothing to do with it at all.'

'But what a place to go to! What nice person, too, do you meet in a hotel?'

'Nice or nasty, as I have told you several times before, is not the point. Lilia has insulted our family, and she shall suffer for it. And when you speak against hotels, I think you forget that I met your father at Chamonix. You can contribute nothing, dear, at present, and I think you had better hold your tongue. I am going to the kitchen, to speak about the range.'

She spoke just too much, and the cook said that if she could not give satisfaction she had better leave. A small thing at hand is greater than a great thing remote, and Lilia, misconducting herself upon a mountain in Central Italy, was immediately hidden. Mrs Herriton flew to a registry office, failed; flew to another, failed again; came home, was told by the housemaid that things seemed so unsettled that she had better leave as well; had tea, wrote six letters, was interrupted by cook and housemaid, both weeping, asking her pardon, and imploring to be taken back. In the flush of victory the doorbell rang, and there was the telegram: 'Lilia engaged to Italian nobility. Writing. Abbott.'

'No answer,' said Mrs Herriton. 'Get down Mr Philip's Gladstone from the attic.'

She would not allow herself to be frightened by the unknown. Indeed, she knew a little now. The man was not an Italian noble, otherwise the telegram would have said so. It must have been written by Lilia. None but she would have been guilty of the fatuous vulgarity of 'Italian nobility.' She recalled phrases of this morning's letter: 'We love this place—Caroline is sweeter than ever, and busy sketching—Italians full of simplicity and charm.' And the remark of Baedeker, 'The inhabitants are still noted for their agreeable manners,' had a baleful meaning now. If Mrs Herriton had no imagination, she had intuition, a more useful quality, and the picture she made to herself of Lilia's fiancé did not prove altogether wrong.

So Philip was received with the news that he must start in half an hour for Monteriano. He was in a painful position. For three years he had sung the praises of the Italians, but he had never contemplated having one as a relative. He tried to soften the thing down to his mother, but in his heart of hearts he agreed with her when she said, 'The man may be a duke or he may be an organ-grinder. That is not the point. If Lilia marries him she insults the memory of Charles, she insults Irma, she insults us. Therefore I forbid her, and if she disobeys we have done with her for ever.'

'I will do all I can,' said Philip in a low voice. It was the first time he had had anything to do. He kissed his mother and sister and puzzled Irma. The hall was warm and attractive as he looked back into it from the cold March night, and he departed for Italy reluctantly, as for something common-place and dull.

Before Mrs Herriton went to bed she wrote to Mrs Theobald, using plain language about Lilia's conduct, and hinting that it was a question on which every one must definitely choose sides. She added, as if it was an afterthought, that Mrs Theobald's letter had arrived that morning.

Just as she was going upstairs she remembered that she never covered up those peas. It upset her more than anything, and again and again she struck the banisters with vexation. Late as it was, she got a lantern from the tool-shed and went down the garden to rake the earth over them. The sparrows had taken every one. But countless fragments of the letter remained, disfiguring the tidy ground.

Chapter Two

When the bewildered tourist alights at the station of Monteriano, he finds himself in the middle of the country. There are a few houses round the railway, and many more dotted over the plain and the slopes of the hills, but of a town, mediæval or otherwise, not the slightest sign. He must take what is suitably termed a 'legno'—a piece of wood—and drive up eight miles of excellent road into the Middle Ages. For it is impossible, as well as sacrilegious, to be as quick as Baedeker.

It was three in the afternoon when Philip left the realms of common sense. He was so weary with travelling that he had fallen asleep in the train. His fellow-passengers had the usual Italian gift of divination, and when Monteriano came they knew he wanted to go there, and dropped him out. His feet sank into the hot asphalt of the platform, and in a dream he watched the train depart, while the porter who ought to have been carrying his bag ran up the line playing touch-you-last with the guard. Alas! he was in no humour for Italy. Bargaining for a legno bored him utterly. The man asked six lire; and though Philip knew that for eight miles it should scarcely be more than four, yet he was about to give what he was asked, and so make the man discontented and unhappy for the rest of the day. He was saved from this social blunder by loud shouts, and looking up the road saw one cracking his whip and waving his reins and driving two horses furiously, and behind him there appeared the swaying figure of a woman, holding star-fish fashion on to anything she could touch. It was Miss Abbott, who had just received his letter from Milan announcing the time of his arrival, and had hurried down to meet him.

He had known Miss Abbott for years, and had never had much opinion about her one way or the other. She was good, quiet, dull, and amiable, and young only because she was twenty-three: there was nothing in her appearance or manner to suggest the fire of youth. All her life had been spent at Sawston with a dull and amiable father, and her pleasant, pallid face, bent on some respectable charity, was a familiar object of the Sawston streets. Why she had ever wished to leave them was surprising; but as she truly said, 'I am John Bull to the backbone, yet I do want to see Italy, just once. Everybody says it is marvellous, and that one gets no idea of it from books at all.' The curate suggested that a year was a long time; and Miss Abbott, with decorous playfulness, answered him, 'Oh, but you must let me have my fling! I promise to have it once, and once only. It will give me things to think about and talk about for the rest of my life.' The curate had consented; so had Mr Abbott. And here she was in a legno, solitary, dusty, frightened, with as much to answer for as the most dashing adventuress could desire.

They shook hands without speaking. She made room for Philip and his luggage amidst the loud indignation of the unsuccessful driver, whom it required the combined eloquence of the station-master and the station beggar to confute. The silence was prolonged until they started. For three days he had been considering what he should do, and still more what he should say. He had invented a dozen imaginary conversations, in all of which his logic and eloquence procured him certain victory. But how to begin? He was in the enemy's country, and everything—the hot sun, the cold air behind the heat, the endless rows of olives, regular yet mysterious—seemed hostile to the placid atmosphere of Sawston in which his thoughts took birth. At the outset he made one great concession. If the match was really suitable, and Lilia were bent on it, he would give in, and trust to his influence with his mother to set things right. He would not have made the concession in England; but here in Italy, Lilia, however wilful and silly, was at all events growing to be a human being.

'Are we to talk it over now?' he asked.

'Certainly, please,' said Miss Abbott, in great agitation. 'If you will be so very kind.'

'Then how long has she been engaged?'

Her face was that of a perfect fool—a fool in terror.

'A short time—quite a short time,' she stammered, as if the shortness of the time would reassure him.

'I should like to know how long, if you can remember.'

She entered into elaborate calculations on her fingers. 'Exactly eleven days,' she said at last.

'How long have you been here?'

More calculations, while he tapped irritably with his foot. 'Close on three weeks.'

'Did you know him before you came?'

'No.'

'Oh! Who is he?'

'A native of the place.'

The second silence took place. They had left the plain now and were climbing up the outposts of the hills, the olive-trees still accompanying. The driver, a jolly fat man, had got out to ease the horses, and was walking by the side of the carriage.

'I understood they met at the hotel.'

'It was a mistake of Mrs Theobald's.'

'I also understand that he is a member of the Italian nobility.'

She did not reply.

'May I be told his name?'

Miss Abbott whispered 'Carella.' But the driver heard her, and a grin split over his face. The engagement must be known already.

'Carella? Conte or Marchese, or what?'

'Signor,' said Miss Abbott, and looked helplessly aside.

'Perhaps I bore you with these questions. If so, I will stop.'

'Oh no, please; not at all. I am here—my own idea—to give all information which you very naturally—and to see if somehow—please ask anything you like.'

'Then how old is he?'

'Oh, quite young. Twenty-one, I believe.'

There burst from Philip the exclamation, 'Good Lord!'

'One would never believe it,' said Miss Abbott, flushing. 'He looks much older.'

'And is he good-looking?' he asked, with gathering sarcasm.

She became decisive. 'Very good-looking. All his features are good, and he is well built—though I dare say English standards would find him too short.'

Philip, whose one physical advantage was his height, felt annoyed at her implied indifference to it.

'May I conclude that you like him?'

She replied decisively again, 'As far as I have seen him, I do.'

At that moment the carriage entered a little wood, which lay brown and sombre across the cultivated hill. The trees of the wood were small and leafless, but noticeable for this—that their stems stood in violets as rocks stand in the summer sea. There are such violets in England, but not so many. Nor are there so many in Art, for no painter has the courage. The cart-ruts were channels, the hollows lagoons; even the dry white margin of the road was splashed, like a causeway soon to be submerged under the advancing tide of spring. Philip paid no attention at the time: he was thinking what to say next. But his eyes had registered the beauty, and next March he did not forget that the road to Monteriano must traverse innumerable flowers.

'As far as I have seen him, I do like him,' repeated Miss Abbott, after a pause.

He thought she sounded a little defiant, and crushed her at once.

'What is he, please? You haven't told me that. What's his position?'

She opened her mouth to speak, and no sound came from it. Philip waited patiently. She tried to be audacious, and failed pitiably.

'No position at all. He is kicking his heels, as my father would say. You see, he has only just finished his military service.'

'As a private?'

'I suppose so. There is general conscription. He was in the Bersaglieri, I think. Isn't that the crack regiment?'

'The men in it must be short and broad. They must also be able to walk six miles an hour.'

She looked at him wildly, not understanding all that he said, but feeling that he was very clever. Then she continued her defence of Signor Carella.

'And now, like most young men, he is looking out for something to do.'

'Meanwhile?'

'Meanwhile, like most young men, he lives with his people—father, mother, two sisters, and a tiny tot of a brother.'

There was a grating sprightliness about her that drove him nearly mad. He determined to silence her at last.

'One more question, and only one more. What is his father?'

'His father,' said Miss Abbott. 'Well, I don't suppose you'll think it a good match. But that's not the point. I mean the point is not–I mean that social differences–love, after all–not but what–'

Philip ground his teeth together and said nothing.

'Gentlemen sometimes judge hardly. But I feel that you, and at all events your mother–so really good in every sense, so really unworldly–after all, love–marriages are made in heaven.'

'Yes, Miss Abbott, I know. But I am anxious to hear heaven's choice. You arouse my curiosity. Is my sister-in-law to marry an angel?'

'Mr Herriton, don't–please, Mr Herriton–a dentist. His father's a dentist.'

Philip gave a cry of personal disgust and pain. He shuddered all over, and edged away from his companion. A dentist! A dentist at Monteriano. A dentist in fairyland! False teeth and laughing gas and the tilting chair at a place which knew the Etruscan League, and the Pax Romana, and Alaric himself, and the Countess Matilda, and the Middle Ages, all fighting and holiness, and the Renaissance, all fighting and beauty! He thought of Lilia no longer. He was anxious for himself: he feared that Romance might die.

Romance only dies with life. No pair of pincers will ever pull it out of us. But there is a spurious sentiment which cannot resist the unexpected and the incongruous and the grotesque. A touch will loosen it, and the sooner it goes from us the better. It was going from Philip now, and therefore he gave the cry of pain.

'I cannot think what is in the air,' he began. 'If Lilia was determined to disgrace us, she might have found a less repulsive way. A boy of medium height with a pretty face, the son of a dentist at Monteriano. Have I put it correctly? May I surmise that he has not got one penny? May I also surmise that his social position is nil? Furthermore—'

'Stop! I'll tell you no more.'

'Really, Miss Abbott, it is a little late for reticence. You have equipped me admirably!'

'I'll tell you not another word!' she cried, with a spasm of terror. Then she got out her handkerchief, and seemed as if she would shed tears. After a silence, which he intended to symbolise to her the dropping of a curtain on the scene, he began to talk of other subjects.

They were among olives again, and the wood with its beauty and wildness had passed away. But as they climbed higher the country opened out, and there appeared, high on a hill to the right, Monteriano. The hazy green of the olives rose up to its walls, and it seemed to float in isolation between trees and sky, like some fantastic ship city of a dream. Its colour was brown, and it revealed not a single house–nothing but the narrow circle of the walls, and behind them seventeen towers–all that was left of the fifty-two that had filled the city in her prime. Some were only stumps, some were inclining stiffly to their fall, some were still erect, piercing like masts into the blue. It was impossible to praise it as beautiful, but it was also impossible to damn it as quaint.

Meanwhile Philip talked continually, thinking this to be great evidence of resource and tact. It showed Miss Abbott that he had probed her to the bottom, but was able to conquer his disgust, and by sheer force of intellect continue to be as agreeable and amusing as ever. He did not know that he talked a good deal of nonsense, and that the sheer force of his intellect was weakened by the sight of Monteriano, and by the thought of dentistry within those walls.

The town above them swung to the left, to the right, to the left again, as the road wound upward through the trees, and the towers began to glow in the descending sun. As they drew near, Philip saw the heads of people gathering black upon the walls, and he knew well what was happening–how the news was spreading that a stranger was in sight, and the beggars were aroused from their content and bid to adjust their deformities; how the alabaster man was running for his wares, and the Authorised Guide running for his peaked cap and his two cards of recommendation–one from Miss M'Gee, Maida Vale, the other, less valuable, from an Equerry to the Queen of Peru; how some one else was running to tell the landlady of the Stella d'Italia to put on her pearl necklace and brown boots and empty the slops from the spare bedroom; and how the landlady was running to tell Lilia and her boy that their fate was at hand.

Perhaps it was a pity Philip had talked so profusely. He had driven Miss Abbott half demented, but he had given himself no time to concert a plan. The end came so suddenly. They emerged from the trees on to the terrace before the walk, with the vision of half Tuscany radiant in the sun behind them, and then they turned in through the Siena gate, and their journey was over. The Dogana men admitted them with an air of gracious welcome, and they clattered up the narrow dark street, greeted by that mixture of curiosity and kindness which makes each Italian arrival so wonderful.

He was stunned and knew not what to do. At the hotel he received no ordinary reception. The landlady wrung him by the hand; one person snatched his umbrella, another his bag; people pushed each other out of his way. The entrance seemed blocked with a crowd. Dogs were barking, bladder whistles being blown, women waving their handkerchiefs, excited children screaming on the stairs, and at the top of the stairs was Lilia herself, very radiant, with her best blouse on.

'Welcome!' she cried. 'Welcome to Monteriano!' He greeted her, for he did not know what else to do, and a sympathetic murmur rose from the crowd below.

'You told me not to come here,' she continued, 'and I don't forget it. Let me introduce Signor Carella!'

Philip discerned in the corner behind her a young man who might eventually prove handsome and well-made, but certainly did not seem so then. He was half-enveloped in the drapery of a cold dirty curtain, and nervously stuck out a hand, which Philip took and found thick and damp. There were more murmurs of approval from the stairs.

'Well, din-din's nearly ready,' said Lilia. 'Your room's down the passage, Philip. You needn't go changing.'

He stumbled away to wash his hands, utterly crushed by her effrontery.

'Dear Caroline!' whispered Lilia as soon as he had gone. 'What an angel you've been to tell him! He takes it so well. But you must have had a *mauvais quart d'heure*.'

Miss Abbott's long terror suddenly turned into acidity. 'I've told nothing,' she snapped. 'It's all for you—and if it only takes a quarter of an hour you'll be lucky!'

Dinner was a nightmare. They had the smelly dining-room to themselves. Lilia, very smart and vociferous, was at the head of the table; Miss Abbott, also in her best, sat by Philip, looking, to his irritated nerves, more like the tragedy confidante every moment. That scion of the Italian nobility, Signor Carella, sat opposite. Behind him loomed a bowl of goldfish, who swam round and round, gaping at the guests.

The face of Signor Carella was twitching too much for Philip to study it. But he could see the hands, which were not particularly clean, and did not get cleaner by fidgeting amongst the shining slabs of hair. His starched cuffs were not clean either, and as for his suit, it had obviously been bought for the occasion as something really English—a gigantic check, which did not even fit. His handkerchief he had forgotten, but never missed it. Altogether, he was quite unpresentable, and very lucky to have a father who was a dentist in Monteriano. And why, even Lilia— But as soon as the meal began it furnished Philip with an explanation.

For the youth was hungry, and his lady filled his plate with spaghetti, and when those delicious slippery worms were flying down his throat, his face relaxed and became for a moment unconscious and calm. And Philip had seen that face before in Italy a hundred times—seen it and loved it, for it was not merely beautiful, but had the charm which is the rightful heritage of all who are born on that soil. But he did not want to see it opposite him at dinner. It was not the face of a gentleman.

Conversation, to give it that name, was carried on in a mixture of English and Italian. Lilia had picked up hardly any of the latter language, and Signor Carella had not yet learnt any of the former. Occasionally Miss Abbott had to act as interpreter between the lovers, and the situation became uncouth and revolting in the extreme. Yet Philip was too cowardly to break forth and denounce the engagement. He thought he should be more effective with Lilia if he had her alone, and pretended to himself that he must hear her defence before giving judgment.

Signor Carella, heartened by the spaghetti and the throat-rasping wine, attempted to talk, and, looking politely towards Philip, said, 'England is a great country. The Italians love England and the English.'

Philip, in no mood for international amenities, merely bowed.

'Italy too,' the other continued a little resentfully, 'is a great country. She has produced many famous men—for example, Garibaldi and Dante. The latter wrote the "Inferno," the "Purgatorio," the "Paradiso." The "Inferno" is the most beautiful.' And with the complacent tone of one who has received a solid education, he quoted the opening lines—

> *'Nel mezzo del cammin di nostra vita*
> *Mi ritrovai per una selva oscura,*
> *Chè la diritta via era smarrita'*—

a quotation which was more apt than he supposed.

Lilia glanced at Philip to see whether he noticed that she was marrying no ignoramus. Anxious to exhibit all the good qualities of her betrothed, she abruptly introduced the subject of Pallone, in which, it appeared, he was a proficient player. He suddenly became shy, and developed a conceited grin—the grin of the village yokel whose cricket score is mentioned before a stranger. Philip himself had loved to watch Pallone, that entrancing combination of lawn-tennis and fives. But he did not expect to love it quite so much again.

'Oh, look!' exclaimed Lilia, 'the poor wee fish!'

A starved cat had been worrying them all for pieces of the purple quivering beef they were trying to swallow. Signor Carella, with the brutality so common in Italians, had caught her by the paw and flung her away from him. Now she had climbed up to the bowl and was trying to hook out the fish. He got up, drove her off, and finding a large glass stopper by the bowl, entirely plugged up the aperture with it.

'But may not the fish die?' said Miss Abbott. 'They have no air.'

'Fish live on water, not on air,' he replied in a knowing voice, and sat down. Apparently he was at his ease again, for he took to spitting on the floor. Philip glanced at Lilia, but did not detect her wincing. She talked bravely till the end of the disgusting meal, and then got up saying, 'Well, Philip, I am sure you are ready for bye-bye. We shall meet at twelve o'clock lunch to-morrow, if we don't meet before. They give us *caffè latte* in our rooms.'

It was a little too impudent. Philip replied, 'I should like to see you now, please, in my room, as I have come all the way on business.' He heard Miss Abbott gasp. Signor Carella, who was lighting a rank cigar, had not understood.

It was as he expected. When he was alone with Lilia he lost all nervousness. The remembrance of his long intellectual supremacy strengthened him, and he began volubly—

'My dear Lilia, don't let's have a scene. Before I arrived I thought I might have to question you. It is unnecessary. I know everything. Miss Abbott has told me a certain amount, and the rest I see for myself.'

'See for yourself?' she exclaimed, and he remembered afterwards that she had flushed crimson.

'That he is probably a ruffian and certainly a cad.'

'There are no cads in Italy,' she said quickly.

He was taken aback. It was one of his own remarks. And she further upset him by adding, 'He is the son of a dentist. Why not?'

'Thank you for the information. I know everything, as I told you before. I am also aware of the social position of an Italian who pulls out teeth in a minute provincial town.'

He was not aware of it, but he ventured to conclude that it was pretty low. Nor did Lilia contradict him. But she was sharp enough to say, 'Indeed, Philip, you surprise me. I understood you went in for equality and so on.'

'And I understood that Signor Carella was a member of the Italian nobility.'

'Well, we put it like that in the telegram so as not to shock dear Mrs Herriton. But it is true. He is a younger branch. Of course families ramify—just as in yours there is your cousin Joseph.' She adroitly picked out the only undesirable member of the Herriton clan. 'Gino's father is courtesy itself, and rising rapidly in his profession. This very month he leaves Monteriano, and sets up at Poggibonsi. And for my own poor part, I think what people *are* is what matters, but I don't suppose you'll agree. And I should like you to know that Gino's uncle is a priest—the same as a clergyman at home.'

Philip was aware of the social position of an Italian priest, and said so much about it that Lilia interrupted him with, 'Well, his cousin's a lawyer at Rome.'

'What kind of "lawyer"?'

'Why, a lawyer just like you are—except that he has lots to do and can never get away.'

The remark hurt more than he cared to show. He changed his method, and in a gentle, conciliating tone delivered the following speech:

'The whole thing is like a bad dream—so bad that it cannot go on. If there was one redeeming feature about the man I might be uneasy. As it is I can trust to time. For the moment, Lilia, he has taken you in, but you will find him out soon. It is not possible that you, a lady, accustomed to ladies and gentlemen, will tolerate a man whose position is—well, not equal to the son of the servants' dentist in Coronation Place. I am not blaming you now. But I blame the glamour of Italy—I have felt it myself, you know—and I greatly blame Miss Abbott.'

'Caroline! why blame her? What's all this to do with Caroline?'

'Because we expected her to—' He saw that the answer would involve him in difficulties, and, waving his hand, continued, 'So I am confident, and you in your heart agree, that this engagement will not last. Think of your life at home—think of Irma! And I'll also say think of us; for you know, Lilia, that we count you more than a relation. I should feel I was losing my own sister if you did this, and my mother would lose a daughter.'

She seemed touched at last, for she turned away her face and said, 'I can't break it off now!'

'Poor Lilia,' said he, genuinely moved. 'I know it may be painful. But I have come to rescue you, and, book-worm though I may be, I am not frightened to stand up to a bully. He's merely an insolent boy. He thinks he can keep you to your word by threats. He will be different when he sees he has a man to deal with.'

What follows should be prefaced with some simile—the simile of a powder-mine, a thunder-bolt, an earthquake—for it blew Philip up in the air and flattened him on the ground and swallowed him up in the depths. Lilia turned on her gallant defender and said:

'For once in my life I'll thank you to leave me alone. I'll thank your mother too. For twelve years you've trained me and tortured me, and I'll stand it no more. Do you think I'm a fool? Do you think I never felt? Ah! when I came to your house a poor young bride, how you all looked me over—never a kind word—and discussed me, and thought I might just do; and your mother corrected me, and your sister snubbed me, and you said funny things about me to show how clever you were! And when Charles died I was still to run in strings for the honour of your beastly family, and I was to be cooped up at Sawston and learn to keep house, and all my chances spoilt of marrying again. No, thank you! No, thank you! "Bully"? "Insolent boy"? Who's that, pray, but you? But, thank goodness, I can stand up against the world now, for I've found Gino, and this time I marry for love!'

The coarseness and truth of her attack alike overwhelmed him. But her supreme insolence found him words, and he too burst forth.

'Yes! and I forbid you to do it! You despise me, perhaps, and think I'm feeble. But you're mistaken. You are ungrateful and impertinent and contemptible, but I will save you in order to save Irma and our name. There is going to be such a row in this town that you and he'll be sorry you came to it. I shall shrink from nothing, for my blood is up. It is unwise of you to laugh. I forbid you to marry Carella, and I shall tell him so now.'

'Do,' she cried. 'Tell him so now. Have it out with him. Gino! Gino! Come in! Avanti! Fra Filippo forbids the banns!'

Gino appeared so quickly that he must have been listening outside the door.

'Fra Filippo's blood's up. He shrinks from nothing. Oh, take care he doesn't hurt you!' She swayed about in vulgar imitation of Philip's walk, and then, with a proud glance at the square shoulders of her betrothed, flounced out of the room.

Did she intend them to fight? Philip had no intention of doing so; and no more, it seemed, had Gino, who stood nervously in the middle of the room with twitching lips and eyes.

'Please sit down, Signor Carella,' said Philip in Italian. 'Mrs Herriton is rather agitated, but there is no reason we should not be calm. Might I offer you a cigarette? Please sit down.'

He refused the cigarette and the chair, and remained standing in the full glare of the lamp. Philip, not averse to such assistance, got his own face into shadow.

For a long time he was silent. It might impress Gino, and it also gave him time to collect himself. He would not this time fall into the error of blustering, which he had caught so unaccountably from Lilia. He would make his power felt by restraint.

Why, when he looked up to begin, was Gino convulsed with silent laughter? It vanished immediately; but he became nervous, and was even more pompous than he intended.

'Signor Carella, I will be frank with you. I have come to prevent you marrying Mrs Herriton, because I see you will both be unhappy together. She is English, you are Italian; she is accustomed to one thing, you to another. And–pardon me if I say it–she is rich and you are poor.'

'I am not marrying her because she is rich,' was the sulky reply.

'I never suggested that for a moment,' said Philip courteously. 'You are honourable, I am sure; but are you wise? And let me remind you that we want her with us at home. Her little daughter will be motherless, our home will be broken up. If you grant my request you will earn our thanks–and you will not be without a reward for your disappointment.'

'Reward–what reward?' He bent over the back of a chair and looked earnestly at Philip. They were coming to terms pretty quickly. Poor Lilia!

Philip said slowly, 'What about a thousand lire?'

His soul went forth into one exclamation, and then he was silent, with gaping lips. Philip would have given double: he had expected a bargain.

'You can have them to-night.'

He found words, and said, 'It is too late.'

'But why?'

'Because—' His voice broke. Philip watched his face–a face without refinement, perhaps, but not without expression–watched it quiver and re-form and dissolve from emotion into emotion. There was avarice at one moment, and insolence, and politeness, and stupidity, and cunning–and let us hope that sometimes there was love. But gradually one emotion dominated, the most unexpected of all; for his chest began to heave and his eyes to wink and mouth to twitch, and suddenly he stood erect and roared forth his whole being in one tremendous laugh.

Philip sprang up, and Gino, who had flung wide his arms to let the glorious creature go, took him by the shoulders and shook him, and said, 'Because we are married–married–married as soon as I knew you were coming. There was no time to tell you. Oh, oh! You have come all the way for nothing. Oh! And oh, your generosity!' Suddenly he became grave, and said, 'Please pardon me; I am rude. I am no better than a peasant, and I–' Here he saw Philip's face, and it was too much for him. He gasped and exploded and crammed his hands into his mouth and spat them out in another explosion, and gave Philip an aimless push, which toppled him on to the bed. He uttered a horrified oh! and then gave up, and bolted away down the passage, shrieking like a child, to tell the joke to his wife.

For a time Philip lay on the bed, pretending to himself that he was hurt grievously. He could scarcely see for temper, and in the passage he ran against Miss Abbott, who promptly burst into tears.

'I sleep at the Globo,' he told her, 'and start for Sawston to-morrow morning early. He has assaulted me. I could prosecute him. But shall not.'

'I can't stop here,' she sobbed. 'I daren't stop here. You will have to take me with you!'

Chapter Three

Opposite the Volterra gate of Monteriano, outside the city, is a very respectable whitewashed mud wall, with a coping of red crinkled tiles to keep it from dissolution. It would suggest a gentleman's garden if there was not in its middle a large hole, which grows larger with every rainstorm. Through the hole is visible, firstly, the iron gate that is intended to close it; secondly, a square piece of ground which, though not quite mud, is at the same time not exactly grass; and finally, another wall, stone this time, which has a wooden door in the middle and two wooden-shuttered windows each side, and apparently forms the façade of a one-storey house.

This house is bigger than it looks, for it slides for two storeys down the hill behind, and the wooden door, which is always locked, really leads into the attic. The knowing person prefers to follow the precipitous mule-track round the turn of the mud wall till he can take the edifice in the rear. Then—being now on a level with the cellars—he lifts up his head and shouts. If his voice sounds like something light—a letter, for example, or some vegetables, or a bunch of flowers—a basket is let out of the first-floor windows by a string, into which he puts his burden and departs. But if he sounds like something heavy, such as a log of wood, or a piece of meat, or a visitor, he is interrogated, and then bidden or forbidden to ascend. The ground floor and the upper floor of that battered house are alike deserted, and the inmates keep to the central portion, just as in a dying body all life retires to the heart. There is a door at the top of the first flight of stairs, and if the visitor is admitted, he will find a welcome which is not necessarily cold. There are several rooms, some dark and mostly stuffy—a reception-room adorned with horse-hair chairs, wool-work stools, and a stove that is never lit—German bad taste without German domesticity broods over that room; also a living-room, which insensibly glides into a bedroom when the refining influence of hospitality is absent, and real bedrooms; and last, but not least, the loggia, where you can live day and night if you feel inclined, drinking vermouth and smoking cigarettes, with leagues of olive-trees and vineyards and blue-green hills to watch you.

It was in this house that the brief and inevitable tragedy of Lilia's married life took place. She made Gino buy it for her, because it was there she had first seen him sitting on the mud wall that faced the Volterra gate. She remembered how the evening sun had struck his hair, and how he had smiled down at her, and being both sentimental and unrefined, was determined to have the man and the place together. Things in Italy are cheap for an Italian, and, though he would have preferred a house in the piazza, or better still a house at Siena, or, bliss above bliss, a house at Leghorn, he did as she asked, thinking that perhaps she showed her good taste in preferring so retired an abode.

The house was far too big for them, and there was a general concourse of his relatives to fill it up. His father wished to make it a patriarchal concern, where all the family should have their rooms and meet together for meals, and was perfectly willing to give up the new practice at Poggibonsi and preside. Gino was quite willing too, for he was an affectionate youth who liked a large home-circle, and he told it as a pleasant bit of news to Lilia, who did not attempt to conceal her horror.

At once he was horrified too; saw that the idea was monstrous; abused himself to her for having suggested it; rushed off to tell his father that it was impossible. His father complained that prosperity was already corrupting him and making him unsympathetic and hard; his mother cried; his sisters accused him of blocking their social advance. He was apologetic, and even cringing, until they turned on Lilia. Then he turned on them, saying that they could not understand, much less associate with, the English lady who was his wife; that there should be one master in that house—himself.

Lilia praised and petted him on his return, calling him brave and a hero and other endearing epithets. But he was rather blue when his clan left Monteriano in much dignity—a dignity which was not at all impaired by the acceptance of a cheque. They took the cheque not to Poggibonsi, after all, but to Empoli—a lively, dusty town some twenty miles off. There they settled down in comfort; and the sisters said they had been driven to it by Gino.

The cheque was, of course, Lilia's, who was extremely generous, and was quite willing to know anybody so long as she had not to live with them, relations-in-law being on her nerves. She liked nothing better than finding out some obscure and distant connection—there were several of them—and acting the lady bountiful, leaving behind her bewilderment, and too often discontent. Gino wondered how it was that all his people, who had formerly seemed so pleasant, had suddenly become plaintive and disagreeable. He put it down to his lady-wife's magnificence, in comparison with which all seemed common. Her money flew apace, in spite of the cheap living. She was even richer than he expected; and he remembered with shame how he had once regretted his inability to accept the thousand lire that Philip Herriton offered him in exchange for her. It would have been a short-sighted bargain.

Lilia enjoyed settling into the house, with nothing to do except give orders to smiling workpeople, and a devoted husband as interpreter. She wrote a jaunty account of her happiness to Mrs Herriton, and Harriet answered the letter, saying (1) that all future communications should be addressed to the solicitors; (2) would Lilia return an inlaid box which Harriet had lent her—but not given—to keep handkerchiefs and collars in?

'Look what I am giving up to live with you!' she said to Gino, never omitting to lay stress on her condescension. He took her to mean the inlaid box, and said that she need not give it up at all.

'Silly fellow, no! I mean the life. Those Herritons are very well connected. They lead Sawston society. But what do I care, so long as I have my silly fellow!' She always treated him as a boy, which he was, and as a fool, which he was not, thinking herself so immeasurably superior to him that she neglected opportunity after opportunity of establishing her rule. He was good-looking and indolent; therefore he must be stupid. He was poor; therefore he would never dare to criticise his benefactress. He was passionately in love with her; therefore she could do exactly as she liked.

'It mayn't be heaven below,' she thought, 'but it's better than Charles.'

And all the time the boy was watching her, and growing up.

She was reminded of Charles by a disagreeable letter from the solicitors, bidding her disgorge a large sum of money for Irma, in accordance with her late husband's will. It was just like Charles's suspicious nature to have provided against a second marriage. Gino was equally indignant, and between them they composed a stinging reply, which had no effect. He then said that Irma had better come out and live with them. 'The air is good, so is the food; she will be happy here, and we shall not have to part with the money.' But Lilia had not the courage even to suggest this to the Herritons, and an unexpected terror seized her at the thought of Irma or any English child being educated at Monteriano.

Gino became terribly depressed over the solicitors' letter, more depressed than she thought necessary. There was no more to do in the house, and he spent whole days in the loggia leaning over the parapet or sitting astride it disconsolately.

'Oh, you idle boy!' she cried, pinching his muscles. 'Go and play pallone.'

'I am a married man,' he answered, without raising his head. 'I do not play games any more.'

'Go and see your friends then.'

'I have no friends now.'

'Silly, silly, silly! You can't stop indoors all day!'

'I want to see no one but you.' He spat on to an olive-tree.

'Now, Gino, don't be silly. Go and see your friends, and bring them to see me. We both of us like society.'

He looked puzzled, but allowed himself to be persuaded, went out, found that he was not as friendless as he supposed, and returned after several hours in altered spirits. Lilia congratulated herself on her good management.

'I'm ready, too, for people now,' she said. 'I mean to wake you all up, just as I woke up Sawston. Let's have plenty of men—and make them bring their womenkind. I mean to have real English tea-parties.'

'There is my aunt and her husband; but I thought you did not want to receive my relatives.'

'I never said such a—'

'But you would be right,' he said earnestly. 'They are not for you. Many of them are in trade, and even we are little more; you should have gentlefolk and nobility for your friends.'

'Poor fellow,' thought Lilia. 'It is sad for him to discover that his people are vulgar.' She began to tell him that she loved him just for his silly self, and he flushed and began tugging at his moustache.

'But besides your relatives I must have other people here. Your friends have wives and sisters, haven't they?'

'Oh yes; but of course I scarcely know them.'

'Not know your friends' people?'

'Why, no. If they are poor and have to work for their living I may see them—but not otherwise. Except—' He stopped. The chief exception was a young lady, to whom he had once been introduced for matrimonial purposes. But the dowry had proved inadequate, and the acquaintance terminated.

'How funny! But I mean to change all that. Bring your friends to see me, and I will make them bring their people.'

He looked at her rather hopelessly.

'Well, who are the principal people here? Who leads society?'

The governor of the prison, he supposed, and the officers who assisted him.

'Well, are they married?'

'Yes.'

'There we are. Do you know them?'

'Yes—in a way.'

'I see,' she exclaimed angrily. 'They look down on you, do they, poor boy? Wait!' He assented. 'Wait! I'll soon stop that. Now, who else is there?'

'The marchese, sometimes, and the canons of the Collegiate Church.'

'Married?'

'The canons—' he began with twinkling eyes.

'Oh, I forgot your horrid celibacy. In England they would be the centre of everything. But why shouldn't I know them? Would it make it easier if I called all round? Isn't that your foreign way?'

He did not think it would make it easier.

'But I must know some one! Who were the men you were talking to this afternoon?'

Low-class men. He could scarcely recollect their names.

'But, Gino dear, if they're low class, why did you talk to them? Don't you care about your position?'

All Gino cared about at present was idleness and pocket-money, and his way of expressing it was to exclaim, 'Ouf—pouf! How hot it is in here. No air; I sweat all over. I expire. I must cool myself, or I shall never get to sleep.' In his funny abrupt way he ran out on to the loggia, where he lay full length on the parapet, and began to smoke and spit under the silence of the stars.

Lilia gathered somehow from this conversation that Continental society was not the go-as-you-please thing she had expected. Indeed, she could not see where Continental society was. Italy is such a delightful place to live in if you happen to be a man. There one may enjoy that exquisite luxury of Socialism—that true Socialism which is based not on equality of income or character, but on the equality of manners. In the democracy of the *caffè* or the street the great question of our life has been solved, and the brotherhood of man is a reality. But it is accomplished at the expense of the sisterhood of women. Why should you not make friends with your neighbour at the theatre or in the train, when you know and he knows that feminine criticism and feminine insight and feminine prejudice will never come between you! Though you become as David and Jonathan, you need never enter his home, nor he yours. All your lives you will meet under the open air, the only roof-tree of the South, under which he will spit and swear, and you will drop your h's, and nobody will think the worse of either.

Meanwhile the women—they have, of course, their house and their church, with its admirable and frequent services, to which they are escorted by the maid. Otherwise they do not go out much, for it is not genteel to walk, and you are too poor to keep a carriage. Occasionally you will take them to the *caffè* or theatre, and immediately all your wonted acquaintance there desert you, except those few who are expecting and expected to marry into your family. It is all very sad. But one consolation emerges—life is very pleasant in Italy if you are a man.

Hitherto Gino had not interfered with Lilia. She was so much older than he was, and so much richer, that he regarded her as a superior being who answered to other laws. He was not wholly surprised, for strange rumours were always blowing over the Alps of lands where men and women had the same amusements and interests, and he had often met that privileged maniac, the lady tourist, on her solitary walks. Lilia took solitary walks, too, and only that week a tramp had grabbed at her watch—an episode which is supposed to be indigenous in Italy, though really less frequent there than in Bond Street. Now that he knew her better, he was inevitably losing his awe: no one could live with her and keep it, especially when she had been so silly as to lose a gold watch and chain. As he lay thoughtful along the parapet, he realised for the first time the responsibilities of married life. He must save her from dangers, physical and social, for after all she was a woman. 'And I,' he reflected, 'though I am young, am at all events a man, and know what is right.'

He found her still in the living-room, combing her hair, for she had something of the slattern in her nature, and there was no need to keep up appearances.

'You must not go out alone,' he said gently. 'It is not safe. If you want to walk, Perfetta shall accompany you.' Perfetta was a widowed cousin, too humble for social aspirations, who was living with them as factotum.

'Very well,' smiled Lilia, 'very well'—as if she were addressing a solicitous kitten. But for all that she never took a solitary walk again, with one exception, till the day of her death.

Days passed, and no one called except poor relatives. She began to feel dull. Didn't he know the Sindaco or the bank manager? Even the landlady of the Stella d'Italia would be better than no one. She, when she went into the town, was pleasantly received; but people naturally found a difficulty in getting on with a lady who could not learn their language. And the tea-party, under Gino's adroit management, receded ever and ever before her.

He had a good deal of anxiety over her welfare, for she did not settle down in the house at all. But he was comforted by a welcome and unexpected visitor. As he was going one afternoon for the letters—they were delivered at the door, but it took longer to get them at the office—some one humorously threw a cloak over his head, and when he disengaged himself he saw his very dear friend Spiridione Tesi of the custom-house at Chiasso, whom he had not met for two years. What joy! what salutations! so that all the passers-by smiled with approval on the amiable scene. Spiridione's brother was now station-master at Bologna, and thus he himself could spend his holiday travelling over Italy at the public expense. Hearing of Gino's marriage, he had come to see him on his way to Siena, where lived his own uncle, lately married too.

'They all do it,' he exclaimed, 'myself excepted.' He was not quite twenty-three. 'But tell me more. She is English. That is good, very good. An English wife is very good indeed. And she is rich?'

'Immensely rich.'

'Blonde or dark?'

'Blonde.'

'Is it possible!'

'It pleases me very much,' said Gino simply. 'If you remember, I always desired a blonde. Three or four men had collected, and were listening.

'We all desire one,' said Spiridione. 'But you, Gino, deserve your good fortune, for you are a good son, a brave man, and a true friend, and from the very first moment I saw you I wished you well.'

'No compliments, I beg,' said Gino, standing with his hands crossed on his chest and a smile of pleasure on his face.

Spiridione addressed the other men, none of whom he had ever seen before. 'Is it not true? Does not he deserve this wealthy blonde?'

'He does deserve her,' said all the men.

It is a marvellous land, whether you love it or hate it.

There were no letters, and of course they sat down at the Caffè Garibaldi, by the Collegiate Church—quite a good *caffè* that for so small a city. There were marble-topped tables, and pillars terra-cotta below and gold above, and on the ceiling was a fresco of the battle of Solferino. One could not have desired a prettier room. They had vermouth and little cakes with sugar on the top, which they chose gravely at the counter, pinching them first to be sure they were fresh. And though vermouth is barely alcoholic, Spiridione drenched his with soda-water to be sure that it should not get into his head.

They were in high spirits, and elaborate compliments alternated curiously with gentle horseplay. But soon they put up their legs on a pair of chairs and began to smoke.

'Tell me,' said Spiridione—'I forgot to ask—is she young?'

'Thirty-three.'

'Ah, well, we cannot have everything.'

'But you would be surprised. Had she told me twenty-eight, I should not have disbelieved her.'

'Is she *simpatica*?' (Nothing will translate that word.)

Gino dabbed at the sugar and said after a silence, 'Sufficiently so.'

'It is a most important thing.'

'She is rich, she is generous, she is affable, she addresses her inferiors with haughtiness.'

There was another silence. 'It is not sufficient,' said the other. 'One does not define it thus.' He lowered his voice to a whisper. 'Last month a German was smuggling cigars. The custom-house was dark. Yet I refused because I did not like him. The gift of such men do not bring happiness. Non era simpatico. He paid for every one, and the fine for deception besides.'

'Do you gain much beyond your pay?' asked Gino, diverted for an instant.

'I do not accept small sums now. It is not worth the risk. But the German was another matter. But listen, my Gino, for I am older than you and more full of experience. The person who understands us at first sight, who never irritates us, who never bores, to whom we can pour forth every thought and wish, not only in speech but in silence—that is what I mean by simpatico.'

'There are such men, I know,' said Gino. 'And I have heard it said of children. But where will you find such a woman?'

'That is true. Here you are wiser than I. Sono poco simpatiche le donne. And the time we waste over them is much.' He sighed dolefully, as if he found the nobility of his sex a burden.

'One I have seen who may be so. She spoke very little, but she was a young lady—different to most. She, too, was English, the companion of my wife here. But Fra Filippo, the brother-in-law, took her back with him. I saw them start. He was very angry.'

Then he spoke of his exciting and secret marriage, and they made fun of the unfortunate Philip, who had travelled over Europe to stop it.

'I regret though,' said Gino, when they had finished laughing, 'that I toppled him on to the bed. A great tall man! And when I am really amused I am often impolite.'

'You will never see him again,' said Spiridione, who carried plenty of philosophy about him. 'And by now the scene will have passed from his mind.'

'It sometimes happens that such things are recollected longest. I shall never see him again, of course; but it is no benefit to me that he should wish me ill. And even if he has forgotten, I am still sorry that I toppled him on to the bed.'

So their talk continued, at one moment full of childishness and tender wisdom, the next moment scandalously gross. The shadows of the terra-cotta pillars lengthened, and tourists, flying through the Palazzo Pubblico opposite, could observe how the Italians wasted time.

The sight of tourists reminded Gino of something he might say. 'I want to consult you since you are so kind as to take an interest in my affairs. My wife wishes to take solitary walks.'

Spiridione was shocked.

'But I have forbidden her.'

'Naturally.'

'She does not yet understand. She asked me to accompany her sometimes—to walk without object! You know, she would like me to be with her all day.'

'I see, I see.' He knitted his brows and tried to think how he could help his friend. 'She needs employment. Is she a Catholic?'

'No.'

'That is a pity. She must be persuaded. It will be a great solace to her when she is alone.'

'I am a Catholic, but of course I never go to church.'

'Of course not. Still, you might take her at first. That is what my brother has done with his wife at Bologna, and he has joined the Free Thinkers. He took her once or twice himself, and now she has acquired the habit and continues to go without him.'

'Most excellent advice, and I thank you for it. But she wishes to give tea-parties—men and women together whom she has never seen.'

'Oh, the English! they are always thinking of tea. They carry it by the kilogramme in their trunks, and they are so clumsy that they always pack it at the top. But it is absurd!'

'What am I to do about it?'

'Do nothing. Or ask me!'

'Come!' cried Gino, springing up. 'She will be quite pleased.'

The dashing young fellow coloured crimson. 'Of course I was only joking.'

'I know. But she wants me to take my friends. Come now! Waiter!'

'If I do come,' cried the other, 'and take tea with you, this bill must be my affair.'

'Certainly not; you are in my country!'

A long argument ensued, in which the waiter took part, suggesting various solutions. At last Gino triumphed. The bill came to eightpence-halfpenny, and a halfpenny for the waiter brought it up to ninepence. Then there was a shower of gratitude on one side and of deprecation on the other, and when courtesies were at their height they suddenly linked arms and swung down the street, tickling each other with lemonade straws as they went.

Lilia was delighted to see them, and became more animated than Gino had known her for a long time. The tea tasted of chopped hay, and they asked to be allowed to drink it out of a wineglass, and refused milk; but, as she repeatedly observed, this was something like. Spiridione's manners were very agreeable. He kissed her hand on introduction, and as his profession had taught him a little English, conversation did not flag.

'Do you like music?' she asked.

'Passionately,' he replied. 'I have not studied scientific music, but the music of the heart, yes.'

So she played on the humming piano very badly, and he sang, not so badly. Gino got out a guitar and sang too, sitting out on the loggia. It was a most agreeable visit.

Gino said he would just walk his friend back to his lodgings. As they went he said, without the least trace of malice or satire in his voice, 'I think you are quite right. I shall not bring people to the house any more. I do not see why an English wife should be treated differently. This is Italy.'

'You are very wise,' exclaimed the other; 'very wise indeed. The more precious a possession the more carefully it should be guarded.'

They had reached the lodging, but went on as far as the Caffè Garibaldi, where they spent a long and most delightful evening.

Chapter Four

The advance of regret can be so gradual that it is impossible to say 'yesterday I was happy, to-day I am not.' At no one moment did Lilia realise that her marriage was a failure; yet during the summer and autumn she became as unhappy as it was possible for her nature to be. She had no unkind treatment, and few unkind words, from her husband. He simply left her alone. In the morning he went out to do 'business,' which, as far as she could discover, meant sitting in the Farmacia. He usually returned to lunch, after which he retired to another room and slept. In the evening he grew vigorous again, and took the air on the ramparts, often having his dinner out, and seldom returning till midnight or later. There were, of course, the times when he was away altogether—at Empoli, Siena, Florence, Bologna—for he delighted in travel, and seemed to pick up friends all over the country. Lilia often heard what a favourite he was.

She began to see that she must assert herself, but she could not see how. Her self-confidence, which had overthrown Philip, had gradually oozed away. If she left the strange house there was the strange little town. If she were to disobey her husband and walk in the country, that would be stranger still—vast slopes of olives and vineyards, with chalk-white farms, and in the distance other slopes, with more olives and more farms, and more little towns outlined against the cloudless sky. 'I don't call this country,' she would say. 'Why, it's not as wild as Sawston Park!' And, indeed, there was scarcely a touch of wildness in it—some of those slopes had been under cultivation for two thousand years. But it was terrible and mysterious all the same, and its continued presence made Lilia so uncomfortable that she forgot her nature and began to reflect.

She reflected chiefly about her marriage. The ceremony had been hasty and expensive, and the rites, whatever they were, were not those of the Church of England. Lilia had no religion in her; but for hours at a time she would be seized with a vulgar fear that she was not 'married properly.' And that her social position in the next world might be as obscure as it was in this. It might be safer to do the thing thoroughly, and one day she took the advice of Spiridione and joined the Roman Catholic Church, or as she called it, 'Santa Deodata's.' Gino approved; he, too, thought it safer, and it was fun confessing, though the priest was a stupid old man, and the whole thing was a good slap in the face for the people at home.

The people at home took the slap very soberly; indeed, there were few left for her to give it to. The Herritons were out of the question; they would not even let her write to Irma, though Irma was occasionally allowed to write to her. Mrs Theobald was rapidly subsiding into dotage, and, as far as she could be definite about anything, had definitely sided with the Herritons. And Miss Abbott did likewise. Night after night did Lilia curse this false friend, who had agreed with her that the marriage would 'do,' and that the Herritons would come round to it, and then, at the first hint of opposition, had fled back to England shrieking and distraught. Miss Abbott headed the long list of those who should never be written to, and who should never be forgiven. Almost the only person who was not on that list was Mr Kingcroft, who had unexpectedly sent an affectionate and inquiring letter. He was quite sure never to cross the Channel, and Lilia drew freely on her fancy in the reply.

At first she had seen a few English people, for Monteriano was not the end of the earth. One or two inquisitive ladies, who had heard at home of her quarrel with the Herritons, came to call. She was very sprightly, and they thought her quite unconventional, and Gino a charming boy, so all that was to the good. But by May the season, such as it was, had finished, and there would be no one till next spring. As Mrs Herriton had often observed, Lilia had no resources. She did not like music, or reading, or work. Her one qualification for life was rather blowsy high spirits, which turned querulous or boisterous according to circumstances. She was not obedient, but she was cowardly, and in the most gentle way, which Mrs Herriton might have envied, Gino made her do what he wanted. At first it had been rather fun to let him get the upper hand. But it was galling to discover that he could not do otherwise. He had a good strong will when he chose to use it, and would not have had the least scruple in using bolts and locks to put it into effect. There was plenty of brutality deep down in him, and one day Lilia nearly touched it.

It was the old question of going out alone.

'I always do it in England.'

'This is Italy.'

'Yes, but I'm older than you, and I'll settle.'

'I am your husband,' he said smiling. They had finished their midday meal, and he wanted to go and sleep. Nothing would rouse him up, until at last Lilia, getting more and more angry, said, 'And I've got the money.'

He looked horrified.

Now was the moment to assert herself. She made the statement again. He got up from his chair.

'And you'd better mend your manners,' she continued, 'for you'd find it awkward if I stopped drawing cheques.'

She was no reader of character, but she quickly became alarmed. As she said to Perfetta afterwards, 'None of his clothes seemed to fit—too big in one place, too small in another.' His figure rather than his face altered, the shoulders falling forward till his coat wrinkled across the back and pulled away from the wrists. He seemed all arms. He edged round the table to where she was sitting, and she sprang away and held the chair between them, too frightened to speak or to move. He looked at her with round expressionless eyes, and slowly stretched out his left hand.

Perfetta was heard coming up from the kitchen. It seemed to wake him up, and he turned away and went to his room without a word.

'What has happened?' cried Lilia, nearly fainting. 'He is ill—ill.'

Perfetta looked suspicious when she heard the account. 'What did you say to him?' She crossed herself.

'Hardly anything,' said Lilia, and crossed herself also. Thus did the two women pay homage to their outraged male.

It was clear to Lilia at last that Gino had married her for money. But he had frightened her too much to leave any place for contempt. His return was terrifying, for he was frightened too, imploring her pardon, lying at her feet, embracing her, murmuring 'It was not I,' striving to define things which he did not understand. He stopped in the house for three days, positively ill with physical collapse. But for all his suffering he had tamed her, and she never threatened to cut off supplies again.

Perhaps he kept her even closer than convention demanded. But he was very young, and he could not bear it to be said of him that he did not know how to treat a lady—or to manage a wife. And his own social position was uncertain. Even in England a dentist is a troublesome creature, whom careful people find difficult to class. He hovers between the professions and the trades; he may be only a little lower than the doctors, or he may be down among the chemists, or even beneath them. The son of the Italian dentist felt this too. For himself nothing mattered; he made friends with the people he liked, for he was that glorious invariable creature, a man. But his wife should visit nowhere rather than visit wrongly: seclusion was both decent and safe. The social ideals of North and South had had their brief contention, and this time the South had won.

It would have been well if he had been as strict over his own behaviour as he was over hers. But the incongruity never occurred to him for a moment. His morality was that of the average Latin, and as he was suddenly placed in the position of a gentleman, he did not see why he should not behave as such. Of course, had Lilia been different—had she asserted herself and got a grip on his character—he might possibly—though not probably—have been made a better husband as well as a better man, and at all events he could have adopted the attitude of the Englishman, whose standard is higher even when his practice is the same. But had Lilia been different she might not have married him.

The discovery of his infidelity—which she made by accident—destroyed such remnants of self-satisfaction as her life might yet possess. She broke down utterly, and sobbed and cried in Perfetta's arms. Perfetta was kind and even sympathetic, but cautioned her on no account to speak to Gino, who would be furious if he was suspected. And Lilia agreed, partly because she was afraid of him, partly because it was, after all, the best and most dignified thing to do. She had given up everything for him—her daughter, her relatives, her friends, all the little comforts and luxuries of a civilised life—and even if she had the courage to break away, there was no one who would receive her now. The Herritons had been almost malignant in their efforts against her, and all her friends had one by one fallen off. So it was better to live on humbly, trying not to feel, endeavouring by a cheerful demeanour to put things right. 'Perhaps,' she thought, 'if I have a child he will be different. I know he wants a son.'

Lilia had achieved pathos despite herself, for there are some situations in which vulgarity counts no longer. Not Cordelia nor Imogen more deserve our tears.

She herself cried frequently, making herself look plain and old, which distressed her husband. He was particularly kind to her when he hardly ever saw her, and she accepted his kindness without resentment, even with gratitude, so docile had she become. She did not hate him, even as she had never loved him; with her it was only when she was excited that the semblance of either passion arose. People said she was headstrong, but really her weak brain left her cold.

Suffering, however, is more independent of temperament, and the wisest of women could hardly have suffered more.

As for Gino, he was quite as boyish as ever, and carried his iniquities like a feather. A favourite speech of his was, 'Ah, one ought to marry! Spiridione is wrong; I must persuade him. Not till marriage does one realise the pleasures and the possibilities of life.' So saying, he would take down his felt hat, strike it in the right place as infallibly as a German strikes his in the wrong place, and leave her.

One evening, when he had gone out thus, Lilia could stand it no longer. It was September. Sawston would be just filling up after the summer holidays. People would be running in and out of each other's houses all along the road. There were bicycle gymkhanas, and on the 30th Mrs Herriton would be holding the annual bazaar in her garden for the C.M.S. It seemed impossible that such a free, happy life could exist. She walked out on to the loggia. Moonlight and stars in a soft purple sky. The walls of Monteriano should be glorious on such a night as this. But the house faced away from them.

Perfetta was banging in the kitchen, and the stairs down led past the kitchen door. But the stairs up to the attic—the stairs no one ever used—opened out of the living-room, and by unlocking the door at the top one might slip out on to the square terrace above the house, and thus for ten minutes walk in freedom and peace.

The key was in the pocket of Gino's best suit—the English check—which he never wore. The stairs creaked and the keyhole screamed; but Perfetta was growing deaf. The walls were beautiful, but as they faced west they were in shadow. To see the light upon them she must walk round the town a little, till they were caught by the beams of the rising moon. She looked anxiously at the house, and started.

It was easy walking, for a little path ran all outside the ramparts. The few people she met wished her a civil good night, taking her, in her hatless condition, for a peasant. The walls trended round towards the moon; and presently she came into its light, and saw all the rough towers turn into pillars of silver and black, and the ramparts into cliffs of pearl. She had no great sense of beauty, but she was sentimental, and she began to cry; for here, where a great cypress interrupted the monotony of the girdle of olives, she had sat with Gino one afternoon in March, her head upon his shoulder, while Caroline was looking at the view and sketching. Round the corner was the Siena gate, from which the road to England started, and she could hear the rumble of the diligence which was going down to catch the night train to Empoli. The next moment it was upon her, for the high road came towards her a little before it began its long zigzag down the hill.

The driver slackened, and called to her to get in. He did not know who she was. He hoped she might be coming to the station.

'Non vengo!' she cried.

He wished her good night, and turned his horses down the corner. As the diligence came round she saw that it was empty.

'Vengo . . .'

Her voice was tremulous, and did not carry. The horses swung off.

'Vengo! Vengo!'

He had begun to sing, and heard nothing. She ran down the road screaming to him to stop—that she was coming; while the distance grew greater and the noise of the diligence increased. The man's back was black and square against the moon, and if he would but turn for an instant she would be saved. She tried to cut off the corner of the zigzag, stumbling over the great clods of earth, large and hard as rocks, which lay between the eternal olives. She was too late; for, just before she regained the road, the thing swept past her, thunderous, ploughing up choking clouds of moonlit dust.

She did not call any more, for she felt very ill, and fainted; and when she revived she was lying in the road, with dust in her eyes, and dust in her mouth, and dust down her ears. There is something very terrible in dust at night-time.

'What shall I do?' she moaned. 'He will be so angry.'

And without further effort she slowly climbed back to captivity, shaking her garments as she went.

Ill-luck pursued her to the end. It was one of the nights when Gino happened to come in. He was in the kitchen, swearing and smashing plates, while Perfetta, her apron over her head, was weeping violently. At the sight of Lilia he turned upon her and poured forth a flood of miscellaneous abuse. He was far more angry but much less alarming than he had been that day when he edged after her round the table. And Lilia gained more courage from her bad conscience than she ever had from her good one, for as he spoke she was seized with indignation and feared him no longer, and saw him for a cruel, worthless, hypocritical, dissolute upstart, and spoke in return.

Perfetta screamed, for she told him everything—all she knew and all she thought. He stood with open mouth, all the anger gone out of him, feeling ashamed, and an utter fool. He was fairly and rightfully cornered. When had husband so given himself away before? She finished; and he was dumb, for she had spoken truly. Then, alas! the absurdity of his own position grew upon him, and he laughed—as he would have laughed at the same situation on the stage.

'You laugh?' stammered Lilia.

'Ah!' he cried, 'who could help it? I, who thought you knew and saw nothing–I am tricked–I am conquered. I give in. Let us talk of it no more.'

He touched her on the shoulder like a good comrade, half-amused and half-penitent, and then, murmuring and smiling to himself, ran quietly out of the room.

Perfetta burst into congratulations. 'What courage you have!' she cried; 'and what good fortune! He is angry no longer! He has forgiven you!'

Neither Perfetta, nor Gino, nor Lilia herself knew the true reason of all the misery that followed. To the end he thought that kindness and a little attention would be enough to set things straight. His wife was a very ordinary woman, and why should her ideas differ from his own? No one realised that more than personalities were engaged; that the struggle was national; that generations of ancestors, good, bad, or indifferent, forbade the Latin man to be chivalrous to the northern woman, the northern woman to forgive the Latin man. All this might have been foreseen: Mrs Herriton foresaw it from the first.

Meanwhile Lilia prided herself on her high personal standard, and Gino simply wondered why she did not come round. He hated discomfort, and yearned for sympathy, but shrank from mentioning his difficulties in the town in case they were put down to his own incompetence. Spiridione was told, and replied in a philosophical but not very helpful letter. His other great friend, whom he trusted more, was still serving in Eretrea or some other desolate outpost. It would take too long to explain everything to him. And, besides, what was the good of letters? Friends cannot travel through the post.

Lilia, so similar to her husband in many ways, yearned for comfort and sympathy too. The night he laughed at her she wildly took up paper and pen and wrote page after page, analysing his character, enumerating his iniquities, reporting whole conversations, tracing all the causes and the growth of her misery. She was beside herself with passion, and though she could hardly think or see, she suddenly attained to magnificence and pathos which a practised stylist might have envied. It was written like a diary, and not till its conclusion did she realise for whom it was meant.

'Irma, darling Irma, this letter is for you. I almost forget I have a daughter. It will make you unhappy, but I want you to know everything, and you cannot learn things too soon. God bless you, my dearest, and save you. God bless your miserable mother.'

Fortunately Mrs Herriton was in when the letter arrived. She seized it and opened it in her bedroom. Another moment, and Irma's placid childhood would have been destroyed for ever.

Lilia received a brief note from Harriet, again forbidding direct communication between mother and daughter, and concluding with formal condolences. It nearly drove her mad.

'Gently! gently!' said her husband. They were sitting together on the loggia when the letter arrived. He often sat with her now, watching her for hours, puzzled and anxious, but not contrite.

'It's nothing.' She went in and tore it up, and then began to write—a very short letter, whose gist was 'Come and save me.'

It is not good to see your wife crying when she writes—especially if you are conscious that, on the whole, your treatment of her has been reasonable and kind. It is not good, when you accidentally look over her shoulder, to see that she is writing to a man. Nor should she shake her fist at you when she leaves the room, under the impression that you are engaged in lighting a cigar and cannot see her.

Lilia went to the post herself. But in Italy so many things can be arranged. The postman was a friend of Gino's and Mr Kingcroft never got his letter.

So she gave up hope, became ill, and all through the autumn lay in bed. Gino was distracted. She knew why: he wanted a son. He could talk and think of nothing else. His one desire was to become the father of a man like himself, and it held him with a grip he only partially understood, for it was the first great desire, the first great passion of his life. Falling in love was a mere physical triviality, like warm sun or cool water, beside this divine hope of immortality: 'I continue.' He gave candles to Santa Deodata, for he was always religious at a crisis, and sometimes he went to her himself and prayed the crude uncouth demands of the simple. Impetuously he summoned all his relatives back to bear him company in his time of need, and Lilia saw strange faces flitting past her in the darkened room.

'My love!' he would say, 'my dearest Lilia! Be calm. I have never loved anyone but you.'

She, knowing everything, would only smile gently, too broken by suffering to make sarcastic repartees.

Before the child was born he gave her a kiss, and said, 'I have prayed all night for a boy.'

Some strangely tender impulse moved her, and she said faintly, 'You are a boy yourself, Gino.'

He answered, 'Then we shall be brothers.'

He lay outside the room with his head against the door like a dog. When they came to tell him the glad news they found him half-unconscious, and his face was wet with tears.

As for Lilia, some one said to her, 'It is a beautiful boy!' But she had died in giving birth to him.

Chapter Five

At the time of Lilia's death Philip Herriton was just twenty-four years of age—indeed, the news reached Sawston on his birthday. He was a tall, weakly-built young man, whose clothes had to be judiciously padded on the shoulder in order to make him pass muster. His face was plain rather than not, and there was a curious mixture in it of good and bad. He had a fine forehead and a good large nose, and both observation and sympathy were in his eyes. But below the nose and eyes all was confusion, and those people who believe that destiny resides in the mouth and chin shook their heads when they looked at him.

Philip himself, as a boy, had been keenly conscious of these defects. Sometimes when he had been bullied or hustled about at school he would retire to his cubicle and examine his features in a looking-glass, and he would sigh and say, 'It is a weak face. I shall never carve a place for myself in the world.' But as years went on he became either less self-conscious or more self-satisfied. The world, he found, made a niche for him as it did for every one. Decision of character might come later—or he might have it without knowing. At all events he had got a sense of beauty and a sense of humour, two most desirable gifts. The sense of beauty developed first. It caused him at the age of twenty to wear parti-coloured ties and a squashy hat, to be late for dinner on account of the sunset, and to catch art from Burne-Jones to Praxiteles. At twenty-two he went to Italy with some cousins, and there he absorbed into one æsthetic whole olive-trees, blue sky, frescoes, country inns, saints, peasants, mosaics, statues, beggars. He came back with the air of a prophet who would either remodel Sawston or reject it. All the energies and enthusiasms of a rather friendless life had passed into the championship of beauty.

In a short time it was over. Nothing had happened either in Sawston or within himself. He had shocked half a dozen people, squabbled with his sister, and bickered with his mother. He concluded that nothing could happen, not knowing that human love and love of truth sometimes conquer where love of beauty fails.

A little disenchanted, a little tired, but æsthetically intact, he resumed his placid life, relying more and more on his second gift, the gift of humour. If he could not reform the world, he could at all events laugh at it, thus attaining at least an intellectual superiority. Laughter, he read and believed, was a sign of good moral health, and he laughed on contentedly, till Lilia's marriage toppled contentment down for ever. Italy, the land of beauty, was ruined for him. She had no power to change men and things who dwelt in her. She, too, could produce avarice, brutality, stupidity—and, what was worse, vulgarity. It was on her soil and through her influence that a silly woman had married a cad. He hated Gino, the betrayer of his life's ideal, and now that the sordid tragedy had come, it filled him with pangs, not of sympathy, but of final disillusion.

The disillusion was convenient for Mrs Herriton, who saw a trying little period ahead of her, and was glad to have her family united.

'Are we to go into mourning, do you think?' She always asked her children's advice where possible.

Harriet thought that they should. She had been detestable to Lilia while she lived, but she always felt that the dead deserve attention and sympathy. 'After all she has suffered. That letter kept me awake for nights. The whole thing is like one of those horrible modern plays where no one is in the right. But if we have mourning, it will mean telling Irma.'

'Of course we must tell Irma!' said Philip.

'Of course,' said his mother. 'But I think we can still not tell her about Lilia's marriage.'

'I don't think that. And she must have suspected something by now.'

'So one would have supposed. But she never cared for her mother, and little girls of nine don't reason clearly. She looks on it as a long visit. And it is important, most important, that she should not receive a shock. All a child's life depends on the ideal it has of its parents. Destroy that and everything goes–morals, behaviour, everything. Absolute trust in some one else is the essence of education. That is why I have been so careful about talking of poor Lilia before her.'

'But you forget this wretched baby. Waters and Adamson write that there is a baby.'

'Mrs Theobald must be told. But she doesn't count. She is breaking up very quickly. She doesn't even see Mr Kingcroft now. He, thank goodness, I hear, has at last consoled himself with some one else.'

'The child must know some time,' persisted Philip, who felt a little displeased, though he could not tell with what.

'The later the better. Every moment she is developing.'

'I must say it seems rather hard luck, doesn't it?'

'On Irma? Why?'

'On us, perhaps. We have morals and behaviour also, and I don't think this continual secrecy improves them.'

'There's no need to twist the thing round to that,' said Harriet, rather disturbed.

'Of course there isn't,' said her mother. 'Let's keep to the main issue. This baby's quite beside the point. Mrs Theobald will do nothing, and it's no concern of ours.'

'It will make a difference in the money, surely,' said he.

'No, dear; very little. Poor Charles provided for every kind of contingency in his will. The money will come to you and Harriet, as Irma's guardians.'

'Good. Does the Italian get anything?'

'He will get all hers. But you know what that is.'

'Good. So those are our tactics–to tell no one about the baby, not even Miss Abbott.'

'Most certainly this is the proper course,' said Mrs Herriton, preferring 'course' to 'tactics' for Harriet's sake. 'And whyever should we tell Caroline?'

'She was so mixed up in the affair.'

'Poor silly creature. The less she hears about it the better she will be pleased. I have come to be very sorry for Caroline. She, if anyone, has suffered and been penitent. She burst into tears when I told her a little, only a little, of that terrible letter. I never saw such genuine remorse. We must forgive her and forget. Let the dead bury their dead. We will not trouble her with them.'

Philip saw that his mother was scarcely logical. But there was no advantage in saying so. 'Here beginneth the New Life, then. Do you remember, mother, that was what we said when we saw Lilia off?'

'Yes, dear; but now it is really a New Life, because we are all at accord. Then you were still infatuated with Italy. It may be full of beautiful pictures and churches, but we cannot judge a country by anything but its men.'

'That is quite true,' he said sadly. And as the tactics were now settled, he went out and took an aimless and solitary walk.

By the time he came back two important things had happened. Irma had been told of her mother's death, and Miss Abbott, who had called for a subscription, had been told also.

Irma had wept loudly, had asked a few sensible questions and a good many silly ones, and had been content with evasive answers. Fortunately the school prizegiving was at hand, and that, together with the prospect of new black clothes, kept her from meditating on the fact that Lilia, who had been absent so long, would now be absent for ever.

'As for Caroline,' said Mrs Herriton, 'I was almost frightened. She broke down utterly. She cried even when she left the house. I comforted her as best I could, and I kissed her. It is something that the breach between her and ourselves is now entirely healed.'

'Did she ask no questions—as to the nature of Lilia's death, I mean?'

'She did. But she has a mind of extraordinary delicacy. She saw that I was reticent, and she did not press me. You see, Philip, I can say to you what I could not say before Harriet. Her ideas are so crude. Really we do not want it known in Sawston that there is a baby. All peace and comfort would be lost if people came inquiring after it.'

His mother knew how to manage him. He agreed enthusiastically. And a few days later, when he chanced to travel up to London with Miss Abbott, he had all the time the pleasant thrill of one who is better informed. Their last journey together had been from Monteriano back across Europe. It had been a ghastly journey, and Philip, from the force of association, rather expected something ghastly now.

He was surprised. Miss Abbott, between Sawston and Charing Cross, revealed qualities which he had never guessed her to possess. Without being exactly original, she did show a commendable intelligence, and though at times she was gauche and even uncourtly, he felt that here was a person whom it might be well to cultivate.

At first she annoyed him. They were talking, of course, about Lilia, when she broke the thread of vague commiseration and said abruptly, 'It is all so strange as well as so tragic. And what I did was as strange as anything.'

It was the first reference she had ever made to her contemptible behaviour. 'Never mind,' he said. 'It's all over now. Let the dead bury their dead. It's fallen out of our lives.'

'But that's why I can talk about it and tell you everything I have always wanted to. You thought me stupid and sentimental and wicked and mad, but you never really knew how much I was to blame.'

'Indeed, I never think about it now,' said Philip gently. He knew that her nature was in the main generous and upright: it was unnecessary of her to reveal her thoughts.

'The first evening we got to Monteriano,' she persisted, 'Lilia went out for a walk alone, saw that Italian in a picturesque position on a wall, and fell in love. He was shabbily dressed, and she did not even know he was the son of a dentist. I must tell you I was used to this sort of thing. Once or twice before I had had to send people about their business.'

'Yes; we counted on you,' said Philip, with sudden sharpness. After all, if she would reveal her thoughts, she must take the consequences.

'I know you did,' she retorted with equal sharpness. 'Lilia saw him several times again, and I knew I ought to interfere. I called her to my bedroom one night. She was very frightened, for she knew what it was about and how severe I could be. "Do you love this man?" I asked. "Yes or no?" She said "Yes." And I said, "Why don't you marry him if you think you'll be happy?"'

'Really—really,' exploded Philip, as exasperated as if the thing had happened yesterday. 'You knew Lilia all your life. Apart from everything else—as if she could choose what could make her happy!'

'Had you ever let her choose?' she flashed out. 'I'm afraid that's rude,' she added, trying to calm herself.

'Let us rather say unhappily expressed,' said Philip, who always adopted a dry satirical manner when he was puzzled.

'I want to finish. Next morning I found Signor Carella and said the same to him. He—well, he was willing. That's all.'

'And the telegram?' He looked scornfully out of the window.

Hitherto her voice had been hard, possibly in self-accusation, possibly in defiance. Now it became unmistakably sad. 'Ah, the telegram! That was wrong. Lilia there was more cowardly than I was. We should have told the truth. It lost me my nerve, at all events. I came to the station meaning to tell you everything then. But we had started with a lie, and I got frightened. And at the end, when you left, I got frightened again and came with you.'

'Did you really mean to stop?'

'For a time, at all events.'

'Would that have suited a newly married pair?'

'It would have suited them. Lilia needed me. And as for him—I can't help feeling I might have got influence over him.'

'I am ignorant of these matters,' said Philip; 'but I should have thought that would have increased the difficulty of the situation.'

The crisp remark was wasted on her. She looked hopelessly at the raw over-built country, and said, 'Well, I have explained.'

'But pardon me, Miss Abbott; of most of your conduct you have given a description rather than an explanation.'

He had fairly caught her, and expected that she would gape and collapse. To his surprise she answered with some spirit, 'An explanation may bore you, Mr Herriton: it drags in other topics.'

'Oh, never mind.'

'I hated Sawston, you see.'

He was delighted. 'So did and do I. That's splendid. Go on.'

'I hated the idleness, the stupidity, the respectability, the petty unselfishness.'

'Petty selfishness,' he corrected. Sawston psychology had long been his speciality.

'Petty unselfishness,' she repeated. 'I had got an idea that every one here spent their lives in making little sacrifices for objects they didn't care for, to please people they didn't love; that they never learnt to be sincere—and, what's as bad, never learnt how to enjoy themselves. That's what I thought—what I thought at Monteriano.'

'Why, Miss Abbott,' he cried, 'you should have told me this before! Think it still! I agree with lots of it. Magnificent!'

'Now Lilia,' she went on, 'though there were things about her I didn't like, had somehow kept the power of enjoying herself with sincerity. And Gino, I thought, was splendid, and young, and strong not only in body, and sincere as the day. If they wanted to marry, why shouldn't they do so? Why shouldn't she break with the deadening life where she had got into a groove, and would go on in it, getting more and more—worse than unhappy—apathetic till she died? Of course I was wrong. She only changed one groove for another—a worse groove. And as for him—well, you know more about him than I do. I can never trust myself to judge characters again. But I still feel he cannot have been quite bad when we first met him. Lilia—that I should dare to say it!—must have been cowardly. He was only a boy—just going to turn into something fine, I thought—and she must have mismanaged him. So that is the one time I have gone against what is proper, and there are the results. You have an explanation now.'

'And much of it has been most interesting, though I don't understand everything. Did you never think of the disparity of their social position?'

'We were mad—drunk with rebellion. We had no common sense. As soon as you came, you saw and foresaw everything.'

'Oh, I don't think that.' He was vaguely displeased at being credited with common sense. For a moment Miss Abbott had seemed to him more unconventional than himself.

'I hope you see,' she concluded, 'why I have troubled you with this long story. Women—I heard you say the other day—are never at ease till they tell their faults out loud. Lilia is dead and her husband gone to the bad—all through me. You see, Mr Herriton, it makes me specially unhappy; it's the only time I've ever gone into what my father calls "real life"—and look what I've made of it! All that winter I seemed to be waking up to beauty and splendour and I don't know what; and when the spring came, I wanted to fight against the things I hated—mediocrity and dullness and spitefulness and society. I actually hated society for a day or two at Monteriano. I didn't see that all these things are invincible, and that if we go against them they will break us to pieces. Thank you for listening to so much nonsense.'

'Oh, I quite sympathise with what you say,' said Philip encouragingly; 'it isn't nonsense, and a year or two ago I should have been saying it too. But I feel differently now, and I hope that you also will change. Society *is* invincible—to a certain degree. But your real life is your own, and nothing can touch it. There is no power on earth that can prevent your criticising and despising mediocrity—nothing that can stop you retreating into splendour and beauty—into the thoughts and beliefs that make the real life—the real you.'

'I have never had that experience yet. Surely I and my life must be where I live.'

Evidently she had the usual feminine incapacity for grasping philosophy. But she had developed quite a personality, and he must see more of her. 'There is another great consolation against invincible mediocrity,' he said—'the meeting a fellow-victim. I hope that this is only the first of many discussions that we shall have together.'

She made a suitable reply. The train reached Charing Cross, and they parted—he to go to a matinée, she to buy petticoats for the corpulent poor. Her thoughts wandered as she bought them: the gulf between herself and Mr Herriton, which she had always known to be great, now seemed to her immeasurable.

These events and conversations took place at Christmas-time. The New Life initiated by them lasted some seven months. Then a little incident—a mere little vexatious incident—brought it to its close.

Irma collected picture post cards, and Mrs Herriton or Harriet always glanced first at all that came, lest the child should get hold of something vulgar. On this occasion the subject seemed perfectly inoffensive—a lot of ruined factory chimneys—and Harriet was about to hand it to her niece when her eye was caught by the words on the margin. She gave a shriek and flung the card into the grate. Of course no fire was alight in July, and Irma only had to run and pick it out again.

'How dare you!' screamed her aunt. 'You wicked girl! Give it here!'

Unfortunately Mrs Herriton was out of the room. Irma, who was not in awe of Harriet, danced round the table, reading as she did so, 'View of the superb city of Monteriano—from your lital brother.'

Stupid Harriet caught her, boxed her ears, and tore the post card into fragments. Irma howled with pain, and began shouting indignantly, 'Who is my little brother? Why have I never heard of him before? Grandmamma! Grandmamma! Who is my little brother? Who is my—'

Mrs Herriton swept into the room, saying, 'Come with me, dear, and I will tell you. Now it is time for you to know.'

Irma returned from the interview sobbing, though, as a matter of fact, she had learnt very little. But that little took hold of her imagination. She had promised secrecy—she knew not why. But what harm in talking of the little brother to those who had heard of him already?

'Aunt Harriet!' she would say. 'Uncle Phil! Grandmamma! What do you suppose my little brother is doing now? Has he begun to play? Do Italian babies talk sooner than us, or would he be an English baby born abroad? Oh, I do long to see him, and be the first to teach him the Ten Commandments and the Catechism.'

The last remark always made Harriet look grave.

'Really,' exclaimed Mrs Herriton, 'Irma is getting too tiresome. She forgot poor Lilia soon enough.'

'A living brother is more to her than a dead mother,' said Philip dreamily. 'She can knit him socks.'

'I stopped that. She is bringing him in everywhere. It is most vexatious. The other night she asked if she might include him in the people she mentions specially in her prayers.'

'What did you say?'

'Of course I allowed her,' she replied coldly. 'She has a right to mention any one she chooses. But I was annoyed with her this morning, and I fear that I showed it.'

'And what happened this morning?'

'She asked if she could pray for her "new father"—for the Italian!'

'Did you let her?'

'I got up without saying anything.'

'You must have felt just as you did when I wanted to pray for the devil.'

'He is the devil,' cried Harriet.

'No, Harriet; he is too vulgar.'

'I will thank you not to scoff against religion!' was Harriet's retort. 'Think of that poor baby. Irma is right to pray for him. What an entrance into life for an English child!'

'My dear sister, I can reassure you. Firstly, the beastly baby is Italian. Secondly, it was promptly christened at Santa Deodata's, and a powerful combination of saints watch over—'

'Don't, dear. And, Harriet, don't be so serious—I mean not so serious when you are with Irma. She will be worse than ever if she thinks we have something to hide.'

Harriet's conscience could be quite as tiresome as Philip's unconventionality. Mrs Herriton soon made it easy for her daughter to go for six weeks to the Tirol. Then she and Philip began to grapple with Irma alone.

Just as they had got things a little quiet the beastly baby sent another picture post card—a comic one, not particularly proper. Irma received it while they were out, and all the trouble began again.

'I cannot think,' said Mrs Herriton, 'what his motive is in sending them.'

Two years before, Philip would have said that the motive was to give pleasure. Now he, like his mother, tried to think of something sinister and subtle.

'Do you suppose that he guesses the situation—how anxious we are to hush the scandal up?'

'That is quite possible. He knows that Irma will worry us about the baby. Perhaps he hopes that we shall adopt it to quiet her.'

'Hopeful indeed.'

'At the same time he has the chance of corrupting the child's morals.' She unlocked a drawer, took out the post card, and regarded it gravely. 'He entreats her to send the baby one,' was her next remark.

'She might do it too!'

'I told her not to; but we must watch her carefully, without, of course, appearing to be suspicious.'

Philip was getting to enjoy his mother's diplomacy. He did not think of his own morals and behaviour any more.

'Who's to watch her at school, though? She may bubble out any moment.'

'We can but trust to our influence,' said Mrs Herriton.

Irma did bubble out, that very day. She was proof against a single post card, not against two. A new little brother is a valuable sentimental asset to a schoolgirl, and her school was then passing through an acute phase of baby-worship. Happy the girl who had her quiver full of them, who kissed them when she left home in the morning, who had the right to extricate them from mail-carts in the interval, who dangled them at tea ere they retired to rest! That one might sing the unwritten song of Miriam, blessed above all schoolgirls, who was allowed to hide her baby brother in a squashy place, where none but herself could find him!

How could Irma keep silent when pretentious girls spoke of baby cousins and baby visitors—she who had a baby brother, who wrote her post cards through his dear papa? She had promised not to tell about him—she knew not why—and she told. And one girl told another, and one girl told her mother, and the thing was out.

'Yes, it is all very sad,' Mrs Herriton kept saying. 'My daughter-in-law made a very unhappy marriage, as I dare say you know. I suppose that the child will be educated in Italy. Possibly his grandmother may be doing something, but I have not heard of it. I do not expect that she will have him over. She disapproves of the father. It is altogether a painful business for her.'

She was careful only to scold Irma for disobedience—that eighth deadly sin, so convenient to parents and guardians. Harriet would have plunged into needless explanations and abuse. The child was ashamed, and talked about the baby less. The end of the school year was at hand, and she hoped to get another prize. But she also had put her hand to the wheel.

It was several days before they saw Miss Abbott. Mrs Herriton had not come across her much since the kiss of reconciliation, nor Philip since the journey to London. She had, indeed, been rather a disappointment to him. Her creditable display of originality had never been repeated: he feared she was slipping back. Now she came about the Cottage Hospital—her life was devoted to dull acts of charity—and though she got money out of him and out of his mother, she still sat tight in her chair, looking graver and more wooden than ever.

'I dare say you have heard,' said Mrs Herriton, well knowing what the matter was.

'Yes, I have. I came to ask you; have any steps been taken?'

Philip was astonished. The question was impertinent in the extreme. He had a regard for Miss Abbott, and regretted that she had been guilty of it.

'About the baby?' asked Mrs Herriton pleasantly.

'Yes.'

'As far as I know, no steps. Mrs Theobald may have decided on something, but I have not heard of it.'

'I was meaning, had you decided on anything?'

'The child is no relation of ours,' said Philip. 'It is therefore scarcely for us to interfere.'

His mother glanced at him nervously. 'Poor Lilia was almost a daughter to me once. I know what Miss Abbott means. But now things have altered. Any initiative would naturally come from Mrs Theobald.'

'But does not Mrs Theobald always take any initiative from you?' asked Miss Abbott.

Mrs Herriton could not help colouring. 'I sometimes have given her advice in the past. I should not presume to do so now.'

'Then is nothing to be done for the child at all?'

'It is extraordinarily good of you to take this unexpected interest,' said Philip.

'The child came into the world through my negligence,' replied Miss Abbott. 'It is natural I should take an interest in it.'

'My dear Caroline,' said Mrs Herriton, 'you must not brood over the thing. Let bygones be bygones. The child should worry you even less than it worries us. We never even mention it. It belongs to another world.'

Miss Abbott got up without replying, and turned to go. Her extreme gravity made Mrs Herriton uneasy. 'Of course,' she added, 'if Mrs Theobald decides on any plan that seems at all practicable—I must say I don't see any such—I shall ask if I may join her in it, for Irma's sake, and share in any possible expenses.'

'Please would you let me know if she decides on anything. I should like to join as well.'

'My dear, how you throw about your money! We would never allow it.'

'And if she decides on nothing, please also let me know. Let me know in any case.'

Mrs Herriton made a point of kissing her.

'Is the young person mad?' burst out Philip as soon as she had departed. 'Never in my life have I seen such colossal impertinence. She ought to be well smacked, and sent back to Sunday-school.'

His mother said nothing.

'But don't you see—she is practically threatening us? You can't put her off with Mrs Theobald; she knows as well as we do that she is a nonentity. If we won't do anything she's going to raise a scandal—that we neglect our relatives, etc., which is, of course, a lie. Still, she'll say it. Oh dear, sweet, sober Caroline Abbott has a screw loose! We knew it at Monteriano. I had my suspicions last year one day in the train; and here it is again. The young person is mad.'

She still said nothing.

'Shall I go round at once and give it her well? I'd really enjoy it.'

In a low, serious voice—such a voice as she had not used to him for months—Mrs Herriton said, 'Caroline has been extremely impertinent. Yet there may be something in what she says after all. Ought the child to grow up in that place—and with that father?'

Philip started and shuddered. He saw that his mother was not sincere. Her insincerity to others had amused him, but it was disheartening when used against himself.

'Let us admit frankly,' she continued, 'that after all we may have responsibilities.'

'I don't understand you, mother. You are turning absolutely round. What are you up to?'

In one moment an impenetrable barrier had been erected between them. They were no longer in smiling confidence. Mrs Herriton was off on tactics of her own—tactics which might be beyond or beneath him.

His remark offended her. 'Up to? I am wondering whether I ought not to adopt the child. Is that sufficiently plain?'

'And this is the result of half a dozen idiocies of Miss Abbott?'

'It is. I repeat, she has been extremely impertinent. None the less she is showing me my duty. If I can rescue poor Lilia's baby from that horrible man, who will bring it up either as Papist or infidel—who will certainly bring it up to be vicious—I shall do it.'

'You talk like Harriet.'

'And why not?' said she, flushing at what she knew to be an insult. 'Say, if you choose, that I talk like Irma. That child has seen the thing more clearly than any of us. She longs for her little brother. She shall have him. I don't care if I am impulsive.'

He was sure that she was not impulsive, but did not dare to say so. Her ability frightened him. All his life he had been her puppet. She had let him worship Italy, and reform Sawston—just as she had let Harriet be Low Church. She had let him talk as much as he liked. But when she wanted a thing she always got it.

And though she was frightening him, she did not inspire him with reverence. Her life, he saw, was without meaning. To what purpose was her diplomacy, her insincerity, her continued repression of vigour? Did they make anyone better or happier? Did they even bring happiness to herself? Harriet with her gloomy peevish creed, Lilia with her clutches after pleasure, were after all more divine than this well-ordered, active, useless machine.

Now that his mother had wounded his vanity he could criticise her thus. But he could not rebel. To the end of his days he would probably go on doing what she wanted. He watched with a cold interest the duel between her and Miss Abbott. Mrs Herriton's policy only appeared gradually. It was to prevent Miss Abbott interfering with the child at all costs, and if possible to prevent her at a small cost. Pride was the only solid element in her disposition. She could not bear to seem less charitable than others.

'I am planning what can be done,' she would tell people, 'and that kind Caroline Abbott is helping me. It is no business of either of us, but we are getting to feel that the baby must not be left entirely to that horrible man. It would be unfair to little Irma; after all, he is her half-brother. No, we have come to nothing definite.'

Miss Abbott was equally civil, but not to be appeased by good intentions. The child's welfare was a sacred duty to her, not a matter of pride or even of sentiment. By it alone, she felt, could she undo a little of the evil that she had permitted to come into the world. To her imagination Monteriano had become a magic city of vice, beneath whose towers no person could grow up happy or pure. Sawston, with its semi-detached houses and snobby schools, its book teas and bazaars, was certainly petty and dull; at times she found it even contemptible. But it was not a place of sin, and at Sawston, either with the Herritons or with herself, the baby should grow up.

As soon as it was inevitable, Mrs Herriton wrote a letter for Waters and Adamson to send to Gino—the oddest letter; Philip saw a copy of it afterwards. Its ostensible purpose was to complain of the picture post cards. Right at the end, in a few nonchalant sentences, she offered to adopt the child, provided that Gino would undertake never to come near it, and would surrender some of Lilia's money for its education.

'What do you think of it?' she asked her son. 'It would not do to let him know that we are anxious for it.'

'Certainly he will never suppose that.'

'But what effect will the letter have on him?'

'When he gets it he will do a sum. If it is less expensive in the long run to part with a little money and to be clear of the baby, he will part with it. If he would lose, he will adopt the tone of the loving father.'

'Dear, you're shockingly cynical.' After a pause she added, 'How would the sum work out?'

'I don't know, I'm sure. But if you wanted to ensure the baby being posted by return, you should have sent a little sum to *him*. Oh, I'm not cynical—at least I only go by what I know of him. But I am weary of the whole show. Weary of Italy. Weary, weary, weary. Sawston's a kind, pitiful place, isn't it? I will go walk in it and seek comfort.'

He smiled as he spoke, for the sake of not appearing serious. When he had left her she began to smile also.

It was to the Abbotts' that he walked. Mr Abbott offered him tea, and Caroline, who was keeping up her Italian in the next room, came in to pour it out. He told them that his mother had written to Signor Carella, and they both uttered fervent wishes for her success.

'Very fine of Mrs Herriton, very fine indeed,' said Mr Abbott, who, like every one else, knew nothing of his daughter's exasperating behaviour. 'I'm afraid it will mean a lot of expense. She will get nothing out of Italy without paying.'

'There are sure to be incidental expenses,' said Philip cautiously. Then he turned to Miss Abbott and said, 'Do you suppose we shall have difficulty with the man?'

'It depends,' she replied, with equal caution.

'From what you saw of him, should you conclude that he would make an affectionate parent?'

'I don't go by what I saw of him, but by what I know of him.'

'Well, what do you conclude from that?'

'That he is a thoroughly wicked man.'

'Yet thoroughly wicked men have loved their children. Look at Rodrigo Borgia, for example.'

'I have also seen examples of that in my district.'

With this remark the admirable young woman rose, and returned to keep up her Italian. She puzzled Philip extremely. He could understand enthusiasm, but she did not seem the least enthusiastic. He could understand pure cussedness, but it did not seem to be that either. Apparently she was deriving neither amusement nor profit from the struggle. Why, then, had she undertaken it? Perhaps she was not sincere. Perhaps, on the whole, that was most likely. She must be professing one thing and aiming at another. What the other thing could be he did not stop to consider. Insincerity was becoming his stock explanation for anything unfamiliar, whether that thing was a kindly action or a high ideal.

'She fences well,' he said to his mother afterwards.

'What had you to fence about?' she said suavely. Her son might know her tactics, but she refused to admit that he knew. She still pretended to him that the baby was the one thing she wanted, and had always wanted, and that Miss Abbott was her valued ally.

And when, next week, the reply came from Italy, she showed him no face of triumph. 'Read the letters,' she said. 'We have failed.'

Gino wrote in his own language, but the solicitors had sent a laborious English translation, where 'Pregiatissima Signora' was rendered as 'Most Praiseworthy Madam,' and every delicate compliment and superlative—superlatives are delicate in Italian—would have felled an ox. For a moment Philip forgot the matter in the manner; this grotesque memorial of the land he had loved moved him almost to tears. He knew the originals of these lumbering phrases; he also had sent 'sincere auguries'; he also had addressed letters—who writes at home?—from the Caffè Garibaldi. 'I didn't know I was still such an ass,' he thought. 'Why can't I realise that it's merely tricks of expression? A bounder's a bounder, whether he lives in Sawston or Monteriano.'

'Isn't it disheartening?' said his mother.

He then read that Gino could not accept the generous offer. His paternal heart would not permit him to abandon this symbol of his deplored spouse. As for the picture post cards, it displeased him greatly that they had been obnoxious. He would send no more. Would Mrs Herriton, with her notorious kindness, explain this to Irma, and thank her for those which Irma (courteous Miss!) had sent to him?

'The sum works out against us,' said Philip. 'Or perhaps he is putting up the price.'

'No,' said Mrs Herriton decidedly. 'It is not that. For some perverse reason he will not part with the child. I must go and tell poor Caroline. She will be equally distressed.'

She returned from the visit in the most extraordinary condition. Her face was red, she panted for breath, there were dark circles round her eyes.

'The impudence!' she shouted. 'The cursed impudence! Oh, I'm swearing. I don't care. That beastly woman—how dare she interfere—I'll—Philip, dear, I'm sorry. It's no good. You must go.'

'Go where? Do sit down. What's happened?' This outburst of violence from his elegant ladylike mother pained him dreadfully. He had not known that it was in her.

'She won't accept—won't accept the letter as final. You must go to Monteriano!'

'I won't!' he shouted back. 'I've been and I've failed. I'll never see the place again. I hate Italy.'

'If you don't go, she will.'

'Abbott?'

'Yes. Going alone; would start this evening. I offered to write; she said it was "too late!" Too late! The child, if you please—Irma's brother—to live with her, to be brought up by her and her father at our very gates, to go to school like a gentleman, she paying. Oh, you're a man! It doesn't matter for you. You can laugh. But I know what people say; and that woman goes to Italy this evening.'

He seemed to be inspired. 'Then let her go! Let her mess with Italy by herself. She'll come to grief somehow. Italy's too dangerous, too—'

'Stop that nonsense, Philip. I will not be disgraced by her. I *will* have the child. Pay all we've got for it. I will have it.'

'Let her go to Italy!' he cried. 'Let her meddle with what she doesn't understand! Look at this letter! The man who wrote it will marry her, or murder her, or do for her somehow. He's a bounder, but he's not an English bounder. He's mysterious and terrible. He's got a country behind him that's upset people from the beginning of the world.'

'Harriet!' exclaimed his mother. 'Harriet shall go too. Harriet, now, will be invaluable!' And before Philip had stopped talking nonsense, she had planned the whole thing and was looking out the trains.

Chapter Six

Italy, Philip had always maintained, is only her true self in the height of the summer, when the tourists have left her, and her soul awakes under the beams of a vertical sun. He now had every opportunity of seeing her at her best, for it was nearly the middle of August before he went out to meet Harriet in the Tirol.

He found his sister in a dense cloud five thousand feet above the sea, chilled to the bone, overfed, bored, and not at all unwilling to be fetched away.

'It upsets one's plans terribly,' she remarked, as she squeezed out her sponges, 'but obviously it is my duty.'

'Did mother explain it all to you?' asked Philip.

'Yes, indeed! Mother has written me a really beautiful letter. She describes how it was that she gradually got to feel that we must rescue the poor baby from its terrible surroundings, how she has tried by letter, and it is no good—nothing but insincere compliments and hypocrisy came back. Then she says, "There is nothing like personal influence; you and Philip will succeed where I have failed." She says, too, that Caroline Abbott has been wonderful.'

Philip assented.

'Caroline feels it as keenly almost as us. That is because she knows the man. Oh, he must be loathsome! Goodness me! I've forgotten to pack the ammonia! . . . It has been a terrible lesson for Caroline, but I fancy it is her turning-point. I can't help liking to think that out of all this evil good will come.'

Philip saw no prospect of good, nor of beauty either. But the expedition promised to be highly comic. He was not averse to it any longer; he was simply indifferent to all in it except the humours. These would be wonderful. Harriet, worked by her mother; Mrs Herriton, worked by Miss Abbott; Gino, worked by a cheque;—what better entertainment could he desire? There was nothing to distract him this time; his sentimentality had died, so had his anxiety for the family honour. He might be a puppet's puppet, but he knew exactly the disposition of the strings.

They travelled for thirteen hours downhill, whilst the streams broadened and the mountains shrank, and the vegetation changed, and the people ceased being ugly and drinking beer, and began instead to drink wine and to be beautiful. And the train which had picked them at sunrise out of a waste of glaciers and hotels was waltzing at sunset round the walls of Verona.

'Absurd nonsense they talk about the heat,' said Philip, as they drove from the station. 'Supposing we were here for pleasure, what could be more pleasurable than this?'

'Did you hear, though, they are remarking on the cold?' said Harriet nervously. 'I should never have thought it cold.'

And on the second day the heat struck them, like a hand laid over the mouth, just as they were walking to see the tomb of Juliet. From that moment everything went wrong. They fled from Verona. Harriet's sketch-book was stolen, and the bottle of ammonia in her trunk burst over her prayer book, so that purple patches appeared on all her clothes. Then, as she was going through Mantua at four in the morning, Philip made her look out of the window because it was Virgil's birthplace, and a smut flew in her eye, and Harriet with a smut in her eye was notorious. At Bologna they stopped twenty-four hours to rest. It was a festa, and children blew bladder whistles night and day. 'What a religion!' said Harriet. The hotel smelt, two puppies were asleep on her bed, and her bedroom window looked into a belfry, which saluted her slumbering form every quarter of an hour. Philip left his walking-stick, his socks, and the Baedeker at Bologna; she only left her sponge-bag. Next day they crossed the Apennines with a train-sick child and a hot lady, who told them that never, never before had she sweated so profusely. 'Foreigners are a filthy nation,' said Harriet. 'I don't care if there are tunnels; open the windows.' He obeyed, and she got another smut in her eye. Nor did Florence improve matters. Eating, walking, even a cross word would bathe them both in boiling water. Philip, who was slighter of build, and less conscientious, suffered less. But Harriet had never been to Florence, and between the hours of eight and eleven she crawled like a wounded creature through the streets, and swooned before various masterpieces of art. It was an irritable couple who took tickets to Monteriano.

'Single or returns?' said he.

'A single for me,' said Harriet peevishly; 'I shall never get back alive.'

'Sweet creature!' said her brother, suddenly breaking down. 'How helpful you will be when we come to Signor Carella!'

'Do you suppose,' said Harriet, standing still among a whirl of porters— 'do you suppose I am going to enter that man's house?'

'Then what have you come for, pray? For ornament?'

'To see that you do your duty.'

'Oh, thanks!'

'So mother told me. For goodness' sake get the tickets; here comes that hot woman again! She has the impudence to bow.'

'Mother told you, did she?' said Philip wrathfully, as he went to struggle for tickets at a slit so narrow that they were handed to him edgeways. Italy was beastly, and Florence station is the centre of beastly Italy. But he had a strange feeling that he was to blame for it all; that a little influx into him of virtue would make the whole land not beastly but amusing. For there was enchantment, he was sure of that; solid enchantment, which lay behind the porters and the screaming and the dust. He could see it in the terrific blue sky beneath which they travelled, in the whitened plain which gripped life tighter than a frost, in the exhausted reaches of the Arno, in the ruins of brown castles which stood quivering upon the hills. He could see it, though his head ached and his skin was twitching, though he was here as a puppet, and though his sister knew how he was here. There was nothing pleasant in that journey to Monteriano station. But nothing—not even the discomfort— was common-place.

'But do people live inside?' asked Harriet. They had exchanged the railway carriage for the legno, and the legno had emerged from the withered trees, and had revealed to them their destination.

Philip, to be annoying, answered 'No.'

'What do they do there?' continued Harriet, with a frown.

'There is a caffè. A prison. A theatre. A church. Walls. A view.'

'Not for me, thank you,' said Harriet after a weighty pause.

'Nobody asked you, Miss, you see. Now Lilia was asked by such a nice young gentleman, with curls all over his forehead, and teeth just as white as father makes them.' Then his manner changed. 'But, Harriet, do you see nothing wonderful or attractive in that place—nothing at all?'

'Nothing at all. It's frightful.'

'I know it is. But it's old—awfully old.'

'Beauty is the only test,' said Harriet. 'At least so you told me when I sketched old buildings—for the sake, I suppose, of making yourself unpleasant.'

'Oh, I'm perfectly right. But at the same time—I don't know—so many things have happened here—people have lived so hard and so splendidly—I can't explain.'

'I shouldn't think you could. It doesn't seem the best moment to begin your Italy mania. I thought you were cured of it by now. Instead, will you kindly tell me what you are going to do when you arrive. I do beg you will not be taken unawares this time.'

'First, Harriet, I shall settle you at the Stella d'Italia, in the comfort that befits your sex and disposition. Then I shall make myself some tea. After tea I shall take a book into Santa Deodata's, and read there. It is always fresh and cool.'

The martyred Harriet exclaimed, 'I'm not clever, Philip. I don't go in for it, as you know. But I know what's rude. And I know what's wrong.'

'Meaning—?'

'You!' she shouted, bouncing on the cushions of the legno and startling all the fleas. 'What's the good of cleverness if a man's murdered a woman?'

'Harriet, I am hot. To whom do you refer?'

'He. Her. If you don't look out he'll murder you. I wish he would.'

'Tut, tut, tutlet! You'd find a corpse extraordinarily inconvenient.' Then he tried to be less aggravating. 'I heartily dislike the fellow, but we know he didn't murder her. In that letter, though she said a lot, she never said he was physically cruel.'

'He has murdered her. The things he did—things one can't even mention—'

'Things which one must mention if one's to talk at all. And things which one must keep in their proper place. Because he was unfaithful to his wife, it doesn't follow that in every way he's absolutely vile.' He looked at the city. It seemed to approve his remark.

'It's the supreme test. The man who is unchivalrous to a woman—'

'Oh, stow it! Take it to the Back Kitchen. It's no more a supreme test than anything else. The Italians never were chivalrous from the first. If you condemn him for that, you'll condemn the whole lot.'

'I condemn the whole lot.'

'And the French as well?'

'And the French as well.'

'Things aren't so jolly easy,' said Philip, more to himself than to her.

But for Harriet things were easy, though not jolly, and she turned upon her brother yet again. 'What about the baby, pray? You've said a lot of smart things and whittled away morality and religion and I don't know what; but what about the baby? You think me a fool, but I've been noticing you all to-day, and you haven't mentioned the baby once. You haven't thought about it, even. You don't care. Philip! I shall not speak to you. You are intolerable.'

She kept her promise, and never opened her lips all the rest of the way. But her eyes glowed with anger and resolution. For she was a straight, brave woman, as well as a peevish one.

Philip acknowledged her reproof to be true. He did not care about the baby one straw. Nevertheless, he meant to do his duty, and he was fairly confident of success. If Gino would have sold his wife for a thousand lire, for how much less would he not sell his child? It was just a commercial transaction. Why should it interfere with other things! His eyes were fixed on the towers again, just as they had been fixed when he drove with Miss Abbott. But this time his thoughts were pleasanter, for he had no such grave business on his mind. It was in the spirit of the cultivated tourist that he approached his destination.

One of the towers, rough as any other, was topped by a cross—the tower of the Collegiate Church of Santa Deodata. She was a holy maiden of the Dark Ages, the city's patron saint, and sweetness and barbarity mingle strangely in her story. So holy was she that all her life she lay upon her back in the house of her mother, refusing to eat, refusing to play, refusing to work. The devil, envious of such sanctity, tempted her in various ways. He dangled grapes above her, he showed her fascinating toys, he pushed soft pillows beneath her aching head. When all proved vain he tripped up the mother and flung her downstairs before her very eyes. But so holy was the saint that she never picked her mother up, but lay upon her back through all, and thus assured her throne in Paradise. She was only fifteen when she died, which shows how much is within the reach of any schoolgirl. Those who think her life was unpractical need only think of the victories upon Poggibonsi, San Gimignano, Volterra, Siena itself—all gained through the invocation of her name; they need only look at the church which rose over her grave. The grand schemes for a marble façade were never carried out, and it is brown unfinished stone until this day. But for the inside Giotto was summoned to decorate the walls of the nave. Giotto came—that is to say, he did not come, German research having decisively proved—but at all events the nave is covered with frescoes, and so are two chapels in the left transept, and the arch into the choir, and there are scraps in the choir itself. There the decoration stopped, till in the full spring of the Renaissance, a great painter came to pay a few weeks' visit to his friend the Lord of Monteriano. In the intervals between the banquets and the discussions on Latin etymology and the dancing, he would stroll over to the church, and there in the fifth chapel to the right he has painted two frescoes of the death and burial of Santa Deodata. That is why Baedeker gives the place a star.

Santa Deodata was better company than Harriet, and she kept Philip in a pleasant dream until the legno drew up at the hotel. Every one there was asleep, for it was still the hour when only idiots were moving. There were not even any beggars about. The cabman put their bags down in the passage—they had left heavy luggage at the station—and strolled about till he came on the landlady's room and woke her, and sent her to them.

Then Harriet pronounced the monosyllable 'Go!'

'Go where?' asked Philip, bowing to the landlady, who was swimming down the stairs.

'To the Italian. Go.'

'Buona sera, signora padrona. Si ritorna volontieri a Monteriano!' (Don't be a goose. I'm not going now. You're in the way, too.) 'Vorrei due camere—'

'Go. This instant. Now. I'll stand it no longer. Go!'

'I'm damned if I'll go. I want my tea.'

'Swear if you like!' she cried. 'Blaspheme! Abuse me! But understand, I'm in earnest.'

'Harriet, don't act. Or act better.'

'We've come here to get the baby back, and for nothing else. I'll not have this levity and slackness, and talk about pictures and churches. Think of mother; did she send you out for *them*?'

'Think of mother and don't straddle across the stairs. Let the cabman and the landlady come down, and let me go up and choose rooms.'

'I shan't.'

'Harriet, are you mad?'

'If you like. But you will not come up till you have seen the Italian.'

'La signorina si sente male,' said Philip. 'È il sole.'

'Poveretta!' cried the landlady and the cabman.

'Leave me alone!' said Harriet, snarling round at them. 'I don't care for the lot of you. I'm English, and neither you'll come down nor he up till he goes for the baby.'

'La prego—piano—piano—è un' altra signorina che dorme—'

'We shall probably be arrested for brawling, Harriet. Have you the very slightest sense of the ludicrous?'

Harriet had not; that was why she could be so powerful. She had concocted this scene in the carriage, and nothing should baulk her of it. To the abuse in front and the coaxing behind she was equally indifferent. How long she would have stood like a glorified Horatius, keeping the staircase at both ends, was never to be known. For the young lady, whose sleep they were disturbing, awoke and opened her bedroom door, and came out on to the landing. She was Miss Abbott.

Philip's first coherent feeling was one of indignation. To be run by his mother and hectored by his sister was as much as he could stand. The intervention of a third female drove him suddenly beyond politeness. He was about to say exactly what he thought about the thing from beginning to end. But before he could do so Harriet also had seen Miss Abbott. She uttered a shrill cry of joy.

'You, Caroline, here of all people!' And in spite of the heat she darted up the stairs and imprinted an affectionate kiss upon her friend.

Philip had an inspiration. 'You will have a lot to tell Miss Abbott, Harriet, and she may have as much to tell you. So I'll pay my call on Signor Carella, as you suggested, and see how things stand.'

Miss Abbott uttered some noise of greeting or alarm. He did not reply to it or approach nearer to her. Without even paying the cabman, he escaped into the street.

'Tear each other's eyes out!' he cried, gesticulating at the façade of the hotel. 'Give it her, Harriet! Teach her to leave us alone. Give it her, Caroline! Teach her to be grateful to you. Go it, ladies; go it!'

Such people as observed him were interested, but did not conclude that he was mad. This aftermath of conversation is not unknown in Italy.

He tried to think how amusing it was; but it would not do--Miss Abbott's presence affected him too personally. Either she suspected him of dishonesty, or else she was being dishonest herself. He preferred to suppose the latter. Perhaps she had seen Gino, and they had prepared some elaborate mortification for the Herritons. Perhaps Gino had sold the baby cheap to her for a joke: it was just the kind of joke that would appeal to him. Philip still remembered the laughter that had greeted his fruitless journey, and the uncouth push that had toppled him on to the bed. And whatever it might mean, Miss Abbott's presence spoilt the comedy: she would do nothing funny.

During this short meditation he had walked through the city, and was out on the other side. 'Where does Signor Carella live?' he asked the men at the Dogana.

'I'll show you!' cried a little girl, springing out of the ground as Italian children will.

'She will show you,' said the Dogana men, nodding reassuringly. 'Follow her always, always, and you will come to no harm. She is a trust-worthy guide. She is my ⎧ daughter.'
⎨ cousin.'
⎩ sister.'

Philip knew these relatives well: they ramify, if need be, all over the peninsula.

'Do you chance to know whether Signor Carella is in?' he asked her.

She had just seen him go in. Philip nodded. He was looking forward to the interview this time: it would be an intellectual duel with a man of no great intellect. What was Miss Abbott up to? That was one of the things he was going to discover. While she had it out with Harriet, he would have it out with Gino. He followed the Dogana's relative softly, like a diplomatist.

He did not follow her long, for this was the Volterra gate, and the house was exactly opposite to it. In half a minute they had scrambled down the mule-track and reached the only practicable entrance. Philip laughed, partly at the thought of Lilia in such a building, partly in the confidence of victory. Meanwhile the Dogana's relative lifted up her voice and gave a shout.

For an impressive interval there was no reply. Then the figure of a woman appeared high up on the loggia.

'That is Perfetta,' said the girl.

'I want to see Signor Carella,' cried Philip.

'Out!'

'Out,' echoed the girl complacently.

'Why on earth did you say he was in?' He could have strangled her for temper. He had been just ripe for an interview—just the right combination of indignation and acuteness: blood hot, brain cool. But nothing ever did go right in Monteriano. 'When will he be back?' he called to Perfetta. It really was too bad.

She did not know. He was away on business. He might be back this evening, he might not. He had gone to Poggibonsi.

At the sound of this word the little girl put her fingers to her nose and

swept them at the plain. She sang as she did so, even as her foremothers had
sung seven hundred years back–

> '*Poggibonizzi, fatti in là,*
> *Che Monteriano si fa città!'*

Then she asked Philip for a halfpenny. A German lady, friendly to the Past,
had given her one that very spring.

'I shall have to leave a message,' he called.

'Now Perfetta has gone for her basket,' said the little girl. 'When she
returns she will lower it–so. Then you will put your card into it. Then she
will raise it–thus. By this means–'

When Perfetta returned, Philip remembered to ask after the baby. It took
longer to find than the basket, and he stood perspiring in the evening sun,
trying to avoid the smell of the drains and to prevent the little girl from
singing against Poggibonsi. The olive-trees beside him were draped with the
weekly–or more probably the monthly–wash. What a frightful spotty
blouse! He could not think where he had seen it. Then he remembered that it
was Lilia's. She had brought it 'to hack about in' at Sawston, and had taken it
to Italy because 'in Italy anything does.' He had rebuked her for the
sentiment.

'Beautiful as an angel!' bellowed Perfetta, holding out something which
must be Lilia's baby. 'But who am I addressing?'

'Thank you–here is my card.' He had written on it a civil request to Gino
for an interview next morning. But before he placed it in the basket and
revealed his identity, he wished to find something out. 'Has a young lady
happened to call here lately–a young English lady?'

Perfetta begged his pardon: she was a little deaf.

'A young lady–pale, large, tall.'

She did not quite catch.

'A YOUNG LADY!'

'Perfetta is deaf when she chooses,' said the Dogana's relative. At last
Philip admitted the peculiarity and strode away. He paid off the detestable
child at the Volterra gate. She got two nickel pieces and was not pleased,
partly because it was too much, partly because he did not look pleased when
he gave it to her. He caught her fathers and cousins winking at each other as
he walked past them. Monteriano seemed in one conspiracy to make him
look a fool. He felt tired and anxious and muddled, and not sure of anything
except that his temper was lost. In this mood he returned to the Stella
d'Italia, and there, as he was ascending the stairs, Miss Abbott popped out of
the dining-room on the first floor and beckoned to him mysteriously.

'I was going to make myself some tea,' he said, with his hand still on the
banisters.

'I should be grateful—'

So he followed her into the dining-room and shut the door.

'You see,' she began, 'Harriet knows nothing.'

'No more do I. He was out.'

'But what's that to do with it?'

He presented her with an unpleasant smile. She fenced well, as he had noticed before. 'He was out. You find me as ignorant as you have left Harriet.'

'What do you mean? Please, please, Mr Herriton, don't be mysterious: there isn't the time. Any moment Harriet may be down, and we shan't have decided how to behave to her. Sawston was different: we had to keep up appearances. But here we must speak out, and I think I can trust you to do it. Otherwise we'll never start clear.'

'Pray let us start clear,' said Philip, pacing up and down the room. 'Permit me to begin by asking you a question. In which capacity have you come to Monteriano–spy or traitor?'

'Spy!' she answered, without a moment's hesitation. She was standing by the little Gothic window as she spoke–the hotel had been a palace once–and with her finger she was following the curves of the moulding as if they might feel beautiful and strange. 'Spy,' she repeated, for Philip was bewildered at learning her guilt so easily, and could not answer a word. 'Your mother has behaved dishonourably all through. She never wanted the child: no harm in that; but she is too proud to let it come to me. She has done all she could to wreck things; she did not tell you everything; she has told Harriet nothing at all; she has lied or acted lies everywhere. I cannot trust your mother. So I have come here alone–all across Europe; no one knows it; my father thinks I am in Normandy–to spy on Mrs Herriton. Don't let's argue!' for he had begun, almost mechanically, to rebuke her for impertinence. 'If you are here to get the child, I will help you; if you are here to fail, I shall get it instead of you.'

'It is hopeless to expect you to believe me,' he stammered. 'But I can assert that we are here to get the child, even if it costs us all we've got. My mother has fixed no money limit whatever. I am here to carry out her instructions. I think that you will approve of them, as you have practically dictated them. I do not approve of them. They are absurd.'

She nodded carelessly. She did not mind what he said. All she wanted was to get the baby out of Monteriano.

'Harriet also carries out your instructions,' he continued. 'She, however, approves of them, and does not know that they proceed from you. I think, Miss Abbott, you had better take entire charge of the rescue party. I have asked for an interview with Signor Carella to-morrow morning. Do you acquiesce?'

She nodded again.

'Might I ask for details of your interview with him? They might be helpful to me.'

He had spoken at random. To his delight she suddenly collapsed. Her hand fell from the window. Her face was red with more than the reflection of evening.

'My interview–how do you know of it?'

'From Perfetta, if it interests you.'

'Whoever is Perfetta?'

'The woman who must have let you in.'

'In where?'

'Into Signor Carella's house.'

'Mr Herriton!' she exclaimed. 'How could you believe her? Do you suppose that I would have entered that man's house, knowing about him all that I do? I think you have very odd ideas of what is possible for a lady. I hear you wanted Harriet to go. Very properly she refused. Eighteen months ago I might have done such a thing. But I trust I have learnt how to behave by now.'

Philip began to see that there were two Miss Abbotts–the Miss Abbott who could travel alone to Monteriano, and the Miss Abbott who could not enter Gino's house when she got there. It was an amusing discovery. Which of them would respond to his next move?

'I suppose I misunderstood Perfetta. Where did you have your interview, then?'

'Not an interview–an accident–I am very sorry–I meant you to have the chance of seeing him first. Though it is your fault. You are a day late. You were due here yesterday. So I came yesterday, and, not finding you, went up to the Rocca–you know that kitchen-garden where they let you in, and there is a ladder up to a broken tower, where you can stand and see all the other towers below you and the plain and all the other hills?'

'Yes, yes. I know the Rocca: I told you of it.'

'So I went up in the evening for the sunset: I had nothing to do. He was in the garden: it belongs to a friend of his.'

'And you talked.'

'It was very awkward for me. But I had to talk: he seemed to make me. You see he thought I was here as a tourist; he thinks so still. He intended to be civil, and I judged it better to be civil also.'

'And of what did you talk?'

'The weather–there will be rain, he says, by to-morrow evening–the other towns, England, myself, about you a little, and he actually mentioned Lilia. He was perfectly disgusting; he pretended he loved her; he offered to show me her grave–the grave of the woman he has murdered!'

'My dear Miss Abbott, he is not a murderer. I have just been driving that into Harriet. And when you know the Italians as well as I do, you will realise that in all that he said to you he was perfectly sincere. The Italians are essentially dramatic: they look on death and love as spectacles. I don't doubt that he persuaded himself, for the moment, that he had behaved admirably, both as husband and widower.'

'You may be right,' said Miss Abbott, impressed for the first time. 'When I tried to pave the way, so to speak–to hint that he had not behaved as he ought–well, it was no good at all. He couldn't or wouldn't understand.'

There was something very humorous in the idea of Miss Abbott approaching Gino, on the Rocca, in the spirit of a district visitor. Philip, whose temper was returning, laughed.

'Harriet would say he has no sense of sin.'

'Harriet may be right, I am afraid.'

'If so, perhaps he isn't sinful!'

Miss Abbott was not one to encourage levity. 'I know what he has done,' she said. 'What he says and what he thinks is of very little importance.'

Philip smiled at her crudity. 'I should like to hear, though, what he said about me. Is he preparing a warm reception?'

'Oh no, not that. I never told him that you and Harriet were coming. You could have taken him by surprise if you liked. He only asked for you, and wished he hadn't been so rude to you eighteen months ago.'

'What a memory the fellow has for little things!' He turned away as he spoke, for he did not want her to see his face. It was suffused with pleasure. For an apology, which would have been intolerable eighteen months ago, was gracious and agreeable now.

She would not let this pass. 'You did not think it a little thing at the time. You told me he had assaulted you.'

'I lost my temper,' said Philip lightly. His vanity had been appeased, and he knew it. This tiny piece of civility had changed his mood. 'Did he really—what exactly did he say?'

'He said he was sorry—pleasantly, as Italians do say such things. But he never mentioned the baby once.'

What did the baby matter when the world was suddenly right way up? Philip smiled, and was shocked at himself for smiling, and smiled again. For romance had come back to Italy; there were no cads in her; she was beautiful, courteous, lovable, as of old. And Miss Abbott—she, too, was beautiful in her way, for all her gaucheness and conventionality. She really cared about life, and tried to live it properly. And Harriet—even Harriet tried.

This admirable change in Philip proceeds from nothing admirable, and may therefore provoke the gibes of the cynical. But angels and other practical people will accept it reverently, and write it down as good.

'The view from the Rocca (small gratuity) is finest at sunset,' he murmured, more to himself than to her.

'And he never mentioned the baby once,' Miss Abbott repeated. But she had returned to the window, and again her finger pursued the delicate curves. He watched her in silence, and was more attracted to her than he had ever been before. She really was the strangest mixture.

'The view from the Rocca—wasn't it fine?'

'What isn't fine here?' she answered gently, and then added, 'I wish I was Harriet,' throwing an extraordinary meaning into the words.

'Because Harriet——?'

She would not go further, but he believed that she had paid homage to the complexity of life. For her, at all events, the expedition was neither easy nor jolly. Beauty, evil, charm, vulgarity, mystery—she also acknowledged this tangle, in spite of herself. And her voice thrilled him when she broke silence with 'Mr Herriton—come here—look at this!'

She removed a pile of plates from the Gothic window, and they leant out of it. Close opposite, wedged between mean houses, there rose up one of the great towers. It is your tower: you stretch a barricade between it and the hotel, and the traffic is blocked in a moment. Farther up, where the street empties out by the church, your connections, the Merli and the Capocchi, do likewise. They command the Piazza, you the Siena gate. No one can move in either but he shall be instantly slain, either by bows or by cross-bows, or by Greek fire. Beware, however, of the back bedroom windows. For they are menaced by the tower of the Aldobrandeschi, and before now arrows have stuck quivering over the washstand. Guard these windows well, lest there be a repetition of the events of February 1338, when the hotel was surprised from the rear, and your dearest friend—you could just make out that it was he—was thrown at you over the stairs.

'It reaches up to heaven,' said Philip, 'and down to the other place.' The summit of the tower was radiant in the sun, while its base was in shadow and pasted over with advertisements. 'Is it to be a symbol of the town?'

She gave no hint that she understood him. But they remained together at the window because it was a little cooler and so pleasant. Philip found a certain grace and lightness in his companion which he had never noticed in England. She was appallingly narrow, but her consciousness of wider things gave to her narrowness a pathetic charm. He did not suspect that he was more graceful too. For our vanity is such that we hold our own characters immutable, and we are slow to acknowledge that they have changed, even for the better.

Citizens came out for a little stroll before dinner. Some of them stood and gazed at the advertisements on the tower.

'Surely that isn't an opera-bill?' said Miss Abbott.

Philip put on his pince-nez. '"Lucia di Lammermoor. By the Master Donizetti. Unique representation. This evening."'

'But is there an opera? Right up here?'

'Why, yes. These people know how to live. They would sooner have a thing bad than not have it at all. That is why they have got to have so much that is good. However bad the performance is to-night, it will be alive. Italians don't love music silently, like the beastly Germans. The audience takes its share—sometimes more.'

'Can't we go?'

He turned on her, but not unkindly. 'But we're here to rescue a child!'

He cursed himself for the remark. All the pleasure and the light went out of her face, and she became again Miss Abbott of Sawston—good, oh, most undoubtedly good, but most appallingly dull. Dull and remorseful: it is a deadly combination, and he strove against it in vain till he was interrupted by the opening of the dining-room door.

They started as guiltily as if they had been flirting. Their interview had taken such an unexpected course. Anger, cynicism, stubborn morality—all had ended in a feeling of good-will towards each other and towards the city which had received them. And now Harriet was here—acrid, indissoluble, large; the same in Italy as in England—changing her disposition never, and her atmosphere under protest.

Yet even Harriet was human, and the better for a little tea. She did not scold Philip for finding Gino out, as she might reasonably have done. She showered civilities on Miss Abbott, exclaiming again and again that

Caroline's visit was one of the most fortunate coincidences in the world. Caroline did not contradict her.

'You see him to-morrow at ten, Philip. Well, don't forget the blank cheque. Say an hour for the business. No, Italians are so slow; say two. twelve o'clock. Lunch. Well–then it's no good going till the evening train. I can manage the baby as far as Florence—'

'My dear sister, you can't run on like that. You don't buy a pair of gloves in two hours, much less a baby.'

'Three hours, then, or four; or make him learn English ways. At Florence we get a nurse—'

'But, Harriet,' said Miss Abbott, 'what if at first he was to refuse?'

'I don't know the meaning of the word,' said Harriet impressively. 'I've told the landlady that Philip and I only want our rooms one night, and we shall keep to it.'

'I dare say it will be all right. But, as I told you, I thought the man I met on the Rocca a strange, difficult man.'

'He's insolent to ladies, we know. But my brother can be trusted to bring him to his senses. That woman, Philip, whom you saw will carry the baby to the hotel. Of course you must tip her for it. And try, if you can, to get poor Lilia's silver bangles. They were nice quiet things, and will do for Irma. And there is an inlaid box I lent her–lent, not gave–to keep her handkerchiefs in. It's of no real value; but this is our only chance. Don't ask for it; but if you see it lying about, just say—'

'No, Harriet; I'll try for the baby, but for nothing else. I promise to do that to-morrow, and to do it in the way you wish. But to-night, as we're all tired, we want a change of topic. We want relaxation. We want to go to the theatre.'

'Theatres here? And at such a moment?'

'We should hardly enjoy it, with the great interview impending,' said Miss Abbott, with an anxious glance at Philip.

He did not betray her, but said, 'Don't you think it's better than sitting in all the evening and getting nervous?'

His sister shook her head. 'Mother wouldn't like it. It would be most unsuitable–almost irreverent. Besides all that, foreign theatres are notorious. Don't you remember those letters in the "Church Family Newspaper"?'

'But this is an opera–"Lucia di Lammermoor"–Sir Walter Scott–classical, you know.'

Harriet's face grew resigned. 'Certainly one has so few opportunities of hearing music. It is sure to be very bad. But it might be better than sitting idle all the evening. We have no book, and I lost my crochet at Florence.'

'Good. Miss Abbott, you are coming too?'

'It is very kind of you, Mr Herriton. In some ways I should enjoy it; but–excuse the suggestion–I don't think we ought to go to cheap seats.'

'Good gracious me!' cried Harriet, 'I should never have thought of that. As likely as not, we should have tried to save money and sat among the most awful people. One keeps on forgetting this is Italy.'

'Unfortunately I have no evening dress; and if the seats—'

'Oh, that'll be all right,' said Philip, smiling at his timorous, scrupulous women-kind. 'We'll go as we are, and buy the best we can get. Monteriano is not formal.'

So this strenuous day of resolutions, plans, alarms, battles, victories, defeats, truces, ended at the opera. Miss Abbott and Harriet were both a little shamefaced. They thought of their friends at Sawston, who were supposing them to be now tilting against the powers of evil. What would Mrs Herriton, or Irma, or the curates at the Back Kitchen say if they could see the rescue party at a place of amusement on the very first day of its mission? Philip, too, marvelled at his wish to go. He began to see that he was enjoying his time in Monteriano, in spite of the tiresomeness of his companions and the occasional contrariness of himself.

He had been to this theatre many years before, on the occasion of a performance of 'La Zia di Carlo.' Since then it had been thoroughly done up, in the tints of the beetroot and the tomato, and was in many other ways a credit to the little town. The orchestra had been enlarged, some of the boxes had terra-cotta draperies, and over each box was now suspended an enormous tablet, neatly framed, bearing upon it the number of that box. There was also a drop-scene, representing a pink and purple landscape, wherein sported many a lady lightly clad, and two more ladies lay along the top of the proscenium to steady a large and pallid clock. So rich and so appalling was the effect, that Philip could scarcely suppress a cry. There is something majestic in the bad taste of Italy; it is not the bad taste of a country which knows no better; it has not the nervous vulgarity of England, or the blinded vulgarity of Germany. It observes beauty, and chooses to pass it by. But it attains to beauty's confidence. This tiny theatre of Monteriano spraddled and swaggered with the best of them, and these ladies with their clock would have nodded to the young men on the ceiling of the Sistine.

Philip had tried for a box, but all the best were taken: it was rather a grand performance, and he had to be content with stalls. Harriet was fretful and insular. Miss Abbott was pleasant, and insisted on praising everything: her only regret was that she had no pretty clothes with her.

'We do all right,' said Philip, amused at her unwonted vanity.

'Yes, I know; but pretty things pack as easily as ugly ones. We had no need to come to Italy like guys.'

This time he did not reply 'But we're here to rescue a baby.' For he saw a charming picture, as charming a picture as he had seen for years—the hot red theatre; outside the theatre, towers and dark gates and mediæval walls; beyond the walls olive-trees in the starlight and white winding roads and fireflies and untroubled dust; and here in the middle of it all, Miss Abbott, wishing she had not come looking like a guy. She had made the right remark. Most undoubtedly she had made the right remark. This stiff suburban woman was unbending before the shrine.

'Don't you like it at all?' he asked her.

'Most awfully.' And by this bald interchange they convinced each other that Romance was here.

Harriet, meanwhile, had been coughing ominously at the drop-scene,

which presently rose on the grounds of Ravenswood, and the chorus of
Scotch retainers burst into cry. The audience accompanied with tappings
and drummings, swaying in the melody like corn in the wind. Harriet,
though she did not care for music, knew how to listen to it. She uttered an
acid 'Shish!'

'Shut it,' whispered her brother.

'We must make a stand from the beginning. They're talking.'

'It is tiresome,' murmured Miss Abbott; 'but perhaps it isn't for us to
interfere.'

Harriet shook her head and shished again. The people were quiet, not
because it is wrong to talk during a chorus, but because it is natural to be civil
to a visitor. For a little time she kept the whole house in order, and could
smile at her brother complacently.

Her success annoyed him. He had grasped the principle of opera in
Italy—it aims not at illusion but at entertainment—and he did not want this
great evening-party to turn into a prayer-meeting. But soon the boxes began
to fill, and Harriet's power was over. Families greeted each other across the
auditorium. People in the pit hailed their brothers and sons in the chorus,
and told them how well they were singing. When Lucia appeared by the
fountain there was loud applause, and cries of 'Welcome to Monteriano!'

'Ridiculous babies!' said Harriet, settling down in her stall.

'Why, it is the famous hot lady of the Apennines,' cried Philip; 'the one
who had never, never before—'

'Ugh! Don't. She will be very vulgar. And I'm sure it's even worse here
than in the tunnel. I wish we'd never—'

Lucia began to sing, and there was a moment's silence. She was stout and
ugly; but her voice was still beautiful, and as she sang the theatre murmured
like a hive of happy bees. All through the coloratura she was accompanied by
sighs, and its top note was drowned in a shout of universal joy.

So the opera proceeded. The singers drew inspiration from the audience,
and the two great sextetts were rendered not unworthily. Miss Abbott fell
into the spirit of the thing. She, too, chatted and laughed and applauded and
encored, and rejoiced in the existence of beauty. As for Philip, he forgot
himself as well as his mission. He was not even an enthusiastic visitor. For he
had been in this place always. It was his home.

Harriet, like M. Bovary on a more famous occasion, was trying to follow
the plot. Occasionally she nudged her companions, and asked them what
had become of Walter Scott. She looked round grimly. The audience
sounded drunk, and even Caroline, who never took a drop, was swaying
oddly. Violent waves of excitement, all arising from very little, went
sweeping round the theatre. The climax was reached in the mad scene. Lucia
clad in white, as befitted her malady, suddenly gathered up her streaming
hair and bowed her acknowledgments to the audience. Then from the back
of the stage—she feigned not to see it—there advanced a kind of bamboo
clothes-horse, stuck all over with bouquets. It was very ugly, and most of the
flowers in it were false. Lucia knew this, and so did the audience; and they all
knew that the clothes-horse was a piece of stage property, brought in to make

the performance go year after year. None the less did it unloose the great
deeps. With a scream of amazement and joy she embraced the animal, pulled
out one or two practicable blossoms, pressed them to her lips, and flung
them into her admirers. They flung them back, with loud melodious cries,
and a little boy in one of the stage-boxes snatched up his sister's carnations
and offered them. 'Che carino!' exclaimed the singer. She darted at the little
boy and kissed him. Now the noise became tremendous. 'Silence! silence!'
shouted many old gentlemen behind. 'Let the divine creature continue!' But
the young men in the adjacent box were imploring Lucia to extend her
civility to them. She refused, with a humorous expressive gesture. One of
them hurled a bouquet at her. She spurned it with her foot. Then,
encouraged by the roars of the audience, she picked it up and tossed it to
them. Harriet was always unfortunate. The bouquet struck her full in the
chest, and a little *billet-doux* fell out of it into her lap.

'Call this classical?' she cried, rising from her seat. 'It's not even
respectable! Philip! take me out at once.'

'Whose is it?' shouted her brother, holding up the bouquet in one hand
and the *billet-doux* in the other. 'Whose is it?'

The house exploded, and one of the boxes was violently agitated, as if
some one was being hauled to the front. Harriet moved down the gangway,
and compelled Miss Abbott to follow her. Philip, still laughing and calling
'Whose is it?' brought up the rear. He was drunk with excitement. The heat,
the fatigue, and the enjoyment had mounted into his head.

'To the left!' the people cried. 'The innamorato is to the left.'

He deserted his ladies and plunged towards the box. A young man was
flung stomach downwards across the balustrade. Philip handed him up the
bouquet and the note. Then his own hands were seized affectionately. It all
seemed quite natural.

'Why have you not written?' cried the young man. 'Why do you take me
by surprise?'

'Oh, I've written,' said Philip hilariously. 'I left a note this afternoon.'

'Silence! silence!' cried the audience, who were beginning to have enough.
'Let the divine creature continue.' Miss Abbott and Harriet had
disappeared.

'No! no!' cried the young man. 'You don't escape me now.' For Philip was
trying feebly to disengage his hands. Amiable youths bent out of the box and
invited him to enter it.

'Gino's friends are ours—'

'Friends?' cried Gino. 'A relative! A brother! Fra Filippo, who has come
all the way from England and never written.'

'I left a message.'

The audience began to hiss.

'Come in to us.'

'Thank you—ladies—there is not time—'

The next moment he was swinging by his arms. The moment after he shot
over the balustrade into the box. Then the conductor, seeing that the
incident was over, raised his baton. The house was hushed, and Lucia di

Lammermoor resumed her song of madness and death.

Philip had whispered introductions to the pleasant people who had pulled him in—tradesmen's sons perhaps they were, or medical students, or solicitors' clerks, or sons of other dentists. There is no knowing who is who in Italy. The guest of the evening was a private soldier. He shared the honour now with Philip. The two had to stand side by side in the front, and exchange compliments, whilst Gino presided, courteous, but delightfully familiar. Philip would have a spasm of horror at the muddle he had made. But the spasm would pass, and again he would be enchanted by the kind, cheerful voices, the laughter that was never vapid, and the light caress of the arm across his back.

He could not get away till the play was nearly finished, and Edgardo was singing amongst the tombs of his ancestors. His new friends hoped to see him at the Garibaldi to-morrow evening. He promised; then he remembered that if they kept to Harriet's plan he would have left Monteriano. 'At ten o'clock, then,' he said to Gino. 'I want to speak to you alone. At ten.'

'Certainly!' laughed the other.

Miss Abbott was sitting up for him when he got back. Harriet, it seemed, had gone straight to bed.

'That was he, wasn't it?' she asked.

'Yes, rather.'

'I suppose you didn't settle anything?'

'Why, no; how could I? The fact is—well, I got taken by surprise, but after all, what does it matter? There's no earthly reason why we shouldn't do the business pleasantly. He's a perfectly charming person, and so are his friends. I'm his friend now—his long-lost brother. What's the harm? I tell you, Miss Abbott, it's one thing for England and another for Italy. There we plan and get on high moral horses. Here we find what asses we are, for things go off quite easily, all by themselves. My hat, what a night! Did you ever see a really purple sky and really silver stars before? Well, as I was saying, it's absurd to worry; he's not a porky father. He wants that baby as little as I do. He's been ragging my dear mother—just as he ragged me eighteen months ago, and I've forgiven him. Oh, but he has a sense of humour!'

Miss Abbott, too, had a wonderful evening, nor did she ever remember such stars or such a sky. Her head, too, was full of music, and that night when she opened the window her room was filled with warm sweet air. She was bathed in beauty within and without; she could not go to bed for happiness. Had she ever been so happy before? Yes, once before, and here, a night in March, the night Gino and Lilia had told her of their love—the night whose evil she had come now to undo.

She gave a sudden cry of shame. 'This time—the same place—the same thing,'—and she began to beat down her happiness, knowing it to be sinful. She was here to fight against this place, to rescue a little soul who was innocent as yet. She was here to champion morality and purity, and the holy life of an English home. In the spring she had sinned through ignorance; she was not ignorant now. 'Help me!' she cried, and shut the window as if there was magic in the encircling air. But the tunes would not go out of her head, and all night long she was troubled by torrents of music, and by applause and laughter, and angry young men who shouted the distich out of Baedeker:

> *'Poggibonizzi fatti in lá,*
> *Che Monteriano si fa città!'*

Poggibonsi was revealed to her as they sang—a joyless, straggling place, full of people who pretended. When she woke up she knew that it had been Sawston.

Chapter Seven

At about nine o'clock next morning Perfetta went out on to the loggia, not to look at the view, but to throw some dirty water at it. 'Scuse tante!' she wailed, for the water spattered a tall young lady who had for some time been tapping at the lower door.

'Is Signor Carella in?' the young lady asked. It was no business of Perfetta's to be shocked, and the style of the visitor seemed to demand the reception-room. Accordingly she opened its shutters, dusted a round patch on one of the horse-hair chairs, and bade the lady do herself the inconvenience of sitting down. Then she ran into Monteriano and shouted up and down its streets until such time as her young master should hear her.

The reception-room was sacred to the dead wife. Her shiny portrait hung upon the wall—similar, doubtless, in all respects to the one which would be pasted on her tombstone. A little piece of black drapery had been tacked above the frame to lend a dignity to woe. But two of the tacks had fallen out, and the effect was now rakish, as of a drunkard's bonnet. A coon song lay open on the piano, and of the two tables one supported Baedeker's 'Central Italy,' the other Harriet's inlaid box. And over everything there lay a deposit of heavy white dust, which was only blown off one memento to thicken on another. It is well to be remembered with love. It is not so very dreadful to be forgotten entirely. But if we shall resent anything on earth at all, we shall resent the consecration of a deserted room.

Miss Abbott did not sit down, partly because the antimacassars might harbour fleas, partly because she had suddenly felt faint, and was glad to cling on to the funnel of the stove. She struggled with herself, for she had need to be very calm; only if she was very calm might her behaviour be justified. She had broken faith with Philip and Harriet: she was going to try for the baby before they did. If she failed she could scarcely look them in the face again.

'Harriet and her brother,' she reasoned, 'don't realise what is before them. She would bluster and be rude; he would be pleasant and take it as a joke. Both of them—even if they offered money—would fail. But I begin to understand the man's nature: he does not love the child, but he will be touchy about it—and that is quite as bad for us. He's charming, but he's no fool; he conquered me last year; he conquered Mr Herriton yesterday, and if I am not careful he will conquer us all to-day, and the baby will grow up in Monteriano. He is terribly strong; Lilia found that out, but only I remember it now.'

This attempt, and this justification of it, were the results of the long and restless night. Miss Abbott had come to believe that she alone could do battle with Gino, because she alone understood him; and she had put this, as nicely as she could, in a note which she had left for Philip. It distressed her to write such a note, partly because her education inclined her to reverence the male, partly because she had got to like Philip a good deal after their last strange interview. His pettiness would be dispersed, and as for his 'unconventionality,' which was so much gossiped about at Sawston, she began to see that it did not differ greatly from certain familiar notions of her own. If only he would forgive her for what she was doing now, there might perhaps be before them a long and profitable friendship. But she must succeed. No one would forgive her if she did not succeed. She prepared to do battle with the powers of evil.

The voice of her adversary was heard at last, singing fearlessly from his expanded lungs, like a professional. Herein he differed from Englishmen, who always have a little feeling against music, and sing only from the throat, apologetically. He padded upstairs, and looked in at the open door of the reception-room without seeing her. Her heart leapt and her throat was dry when he turned away and passed, still singing, into the room opposite. It is alarming not to be seen.

He had left the door of this room open, and she could see into it, right across the landing. It was in a shocking mess. Food, bedclothes, patent-leather boots, dirty plates, and knives lay strewn over a large table and on the floor. But it was the mess that comes of life, not of desolation. It was preferable to the charnel-chamber in which she was standing now, and the light in it was soft and large, as from some gracious noble opening.

He stopped singing, and cried, 'Where is Perfetta?'

His back was turned, and he was lighting a cigar. He was not speaking to Miss Abbott. He could not even be expecting her. The vista of the landing and the two open doors made him both remote and significant, like an actor on the stage, intimate and unapproachable at the same time. She could no more call out to him than if he was Hamlet.

'You know!' he continued, 'but you will not tell me. Exactly like you.' He reclined on the table and blew a fat smoke-ring. 'And why won't you tell me the numbers? I have dreamt of a red hen—that is two hundred and five, and a friend unexpected—he means eighty-two. But I try for the Terno this week. So tell me another number.'

Miss Abbott did not know of the Tombola. His speech terrified her. She felt those subtle restrictions which come upon us in fatigue. Had she slept well she would have greeted him as soon as she saw him. Now it was impossible. He had got into another world.

She watched his smoke-ring. The air had carried it slowly away from him, and brought it out intact upon the landing.

'Two hundred and five—eighty-two. In any case I shall put them on Bari, not on Florence. I cannot tell you why; I have a feeling this week for Bari.' Again she tried to speak. But the ring mesmerised her. It had become vast and elliptical, and floated in at the reception-room door.

'Ah! you don't care if you get the profits. You won't even say "Thank you, Gino." Say it, or I'll drop hot, red-hot ashes on you. "Thank you, Gino—"'

The ring had extended its pale blue coils towards her. She lost self-control. It enveloped her. As if it was a breath from the pit, she screamed.

There he was, wanting to know what had frightened her, how she had got here, why she had never spoken. He made her sit down. He brought her wine, which she refused. She had not one word to say to him.

'What is it?' he repeated. 'What has frightened you?'

He, too, was frightened, and perspiration came starting through the tan. For it is a serious thing to have been watched. We all radiate something curiously intimate when we believe ourselves to be alone.

'Business—' she said at last.

'Business with me?'

'Most important business.' She was lying, white and limp, in the dusty chair.

'Before business you must get well; this is the best wine.'

She refused it feebly. He poured out a glass. She drank it. As she did so she became self-conscious. However important the business, it was not proper of her to have called on him, or to accept his hospitality.

'Perhaps you are engaged,' she said. 'And as I am not very well—'

'You are not well enough to go back. And I am not engaged.'

She looked nervously at the other room.

'Ah, now I understand,' he exclaimed. 'Now I see what frightened you. But why did you never speak?' And taking her into the room where he lived, he pointed to—the baby.

She had thought so much about this baby, of its welfare, its soul, its morals, its probable defects. But, like most unmarried people, she had only thought of it as a word—just as the healthy man only thinks of the word death, not of death itself. The real thing, lying asleep on a dirty rug, disconcerted her. It did not stand for a principle any longer. It was so much flesh and blood, so many inches and ounces of life—a glorious, unquestionable fact, which a man and another woman had given to the world. You could talk to it; in time it would answer you; in time it would not answer you unless it chose, but would secrete, within the compass of its body, thoughts and wonderful passions of its own. And this was the machine on which she and Mrs Herriton and Philip and Harriet had for the last month been exercising their various ideals—had determined that in time it should move this way or that way, should accomplish this and not that. It was to be Low Church, it was to be high-principled, it was to be tactful, gentlemanly, artistic—excellent things all. Yet now that she saw this baby, lying asleep on a dirty rug, she had a great disposition not to dictate one of them, and to exert no more influence than there may be in a kiss or in the vaguest of the heartfelt prayers.

But she had practised self-discipline, and her thoughts and actions were not yet to correspond. To recover her self-esteem she tried to imagine that she was in her district, and to behave accordingly.

'What a fine child, Signor Carella. And how nice of you to talk to it. Though I see that the ungrateful little fellow is asleep! Seven months? No, eight; of course eight. Still, he is a remarkably fine child for his age.'

Italian is a bad medium for condescension. The patronising words came out gracious and sincere, and he smiled with pleasure.

'You must not stand. Let us sit on the loggia, where it is cool. I am afraid the room is very untidy,' he added, with the air of a hostess who apologises for a stray thread on the drawing-room carpet. Miss Abbott picked her way to the chair. He sat near her, astride the parapet, with one foot in the loggia and the other dangling into the view. His face was in profile, and its beautiful contours drove artfully against the misty green of the opposing hills. 'Posing!' said Miss Abbott to herself. 'A born artist's model.'

'Mr Herriton called yesterday,' she began, 'but you were out.'

He started an elaborate and graceful explanation. He had gone for the day to Poggibonsi. Why had the Herritons not written to him, so that he could have received them properly? Poggibonsi would have done any day; not but what his business there was fairly important. What did she suppose that it was?

Naturally she was not greatly interested. She had not come from Sawston to guess why he had been to Poggibonsi. She answered politely that she had no idea, and returned to her mission.

'But guess!' he persisted, clapping the balustrade between his hands.

She suggested, with gentle sarcasm, that perhaps he had gone to Poggibonsi to find something to do.

He intimated that it was not as important as all that. Something to do—an almost hopeless quest! 'É manca questo!' He rubbed his thumb and forefinger together, to indicate that he had no money. Then he sighed, and blew another smoke-ring. Miss Abbott took heart and turned diplomatic.

'This house,' she said, 'is a large house.'

'Exactly,' was his gloomy reply. 'And when my poor wife died—' He got up, went in, and walked across the landing to the reception-room door, which he closed reverently. Then he shut the door of the living-room with his foot, returned briskly to his seat, and continued his sentence. 'When my poor wife died I thought of having my relatives to live here. My father wished to give up his practice at Empoli; my mother and sisters and two aunts were also willing. But it was impossible. They have their ways of doing things, and when I was younger I was content with them. But now I am a man. I have my own ways. Do you understand?'

'Yes, I do,' said Miss Abbott, thinking of her own dear father, whose tricks and habits, after twenty-five years spent in their company, were beginning to get on her nerves. She remembered, though, that she was not here to sympathise with Gino—at all events, not to show that she sympathised. She also reminded herself that he was not worthy of sympathy. 'It is a large house,' she repeated.

'Immense; and the taxes! But it will be better when— Ah! but you have never guessed why I went to Poggibonsi–why it was that I was out when he called.'

'I cannot guess, Signor Carella. I am here on business.'

'But try.'

'I cannot; I hardly know you.'

'But we are old friends,' he said, 'and your approval will be grateful to me. You gave it me once before. Will you give it now?'

'I have not come as a friend this time,' she answered stiffly. 'I am not likely, Signor Carella, to approve of anything you do.'

'Oh, Signorina!' He laughed, as if he found her piquante and amusing. 'Surely you approve of marriage?'

'Where there is love,' said Miss Abbott, looking at him hard. His face had altered in the last year, but not for the worse, which was baffling.

'Where there is love,' said he, politely echoing the English view. Then he smiled on her, expecting congratulations.

'Do I understand that you are proposing to marry again?'

He nodded.

'I forbid you, then!'

He looked puzzled, but took it for some foreign banter, and laughed.

'I forbid you!' repeated Miss Abbott, and all the indignation of her sex and her nationality went thrilling through the words.

'But why?' He jumped up frowning. His voice was squeaky and petulant, like that of a child who is suddenly forbidden a toy.

'You have ruined one woman; I forbid you to ruin another. It is not a year since Lilia died. You pretended to me the other day that you loved her. It is a lie. You wanted her money. Has this woman money too?'

'Why, yes!' he said irritably. 'A little.'

'And I suppose you will say that you love her.'

'I shall not say it. It will be untrue. Now my poor wife—' He stopped, seeing that the comparison would involve him in difficulties. And indeed he had often found Lilia as agreeable as anyone else.

Miss Abbott was furious at this final insult to her dead acquaintance. She was glad that after all she could be so angry with the boy. She glowed and throbbed; her tongue moved nimbly. At the finish, if the real business of the day had been completed, she could have swept majestically from the house. But the baby still remained, asleep on a dirty rug.

Gino was thoughtful, and stood scratching his head. He respected Miss Abbott. He wished that she would respect him. 'So you do not advise me?' he said dolefully. 'But why should it be a failure?'

Miss Abbott tried to remember that he was really a child still–a child with the strength and the passions of a disreputable man. 'How can it succeed,' she said solemnly, 'where there is no love?'

'But she does love me! I forgot to tell you that.'

'Indeed.'

'Passionately.' He laid his hand upon his own heart.

'Then God help her!'

He stamped impatiently. 'Whatever I say displeases you, Signorina. God help you, for you are most unfair. You say that I ill-treated my dear wife. It is not so. I have never ill-treated anyone. You complain that there is no love in this marriage. I prove that there is, and you become still more angry. What do you want? Do you suppose she will not be contented? Glad enough she is to get me, and she will do her duty well.'

'Her duty!' cried Miss Abbott, with all the bitterness of which she was capable.

'Why, of course. She knows why I am marrying her.'

'To succeed where Lilia failed! To be your housekeeper, your slave, your—' The words she would like to have said were too violent for her.

'To look after the baby, certainly,' said he.

'The baby—?' She had forgotten it.

'It is an English marriage,' he said proudly. 'I do not care about the money. I am having her for my son. Did you not understand that?'

'No,' said Miss Abbott, utterly bewildered. Then, for a moment, she saw light. 'It is not necessary, Signor Carella. Since you are tired of the baby—'

Ever after she remembered it to her credit that she saw her mistake at once. 'I don't mean that,' she added quickly.

'I know,' was his courteous response. 'Ah, in a foreign language (and how perfectly you speak Italian) one is certain to make slips.'

She looked at his face. It was apparently innocent of satire.

'You meant that we could not always be together yet, he and I. You are right. What is to be done? I cannot afford a nurse, and Perfetta is too rough. When he was ill I dare not let her touch him. When he has to be washed, which happens now and then, who does it?–I. I feed him, or settle what he shall have. I sleep with him and comfort him when he is unhappy in the night. No one talks, no one may sing to him but I. Do not be unfair this time; I like to do these things. But nevertheless' (his voice became pathetic) 'they take up a great deal of time, and are not all suitable for a young man.'

'Not at all suitable,' said Miss Abbott, and closed her eyes wearily. Each moment her difficulties were increasing. She wished that she was not so tired, so open to contradictory impressions. She longed for Harriet's burly obtuseness or for the soulless diplomacy of Mrs Herriton.

'A little more wine?' asked Gino kindly.

'Oh no, thank you! But marriage, Signor Carella, is a very serious step. Could you not manage more simply? Your relative, for example—'

'Empoli! I would as soon have him in England!'

'England, then—'

He laughed.

'He has a grandmother there, you know–Mrs Theobald.'

'He has a grandmother here. No, he is troublesome, but I must have him with me. I will not even have my father and mother too. For they would separate us,' he added.

'How?'

'They would separate our thoughts.'

She was silent. This cruel, vicious fellow knew of strange refinements. The horrible truth, that wicked people are capable of love, stood naked before her, and her moral being was abashed. It was her duty to rescue the baby, to save it from contagion, and she still meant to do her duty. But the comfortable sense of virtue left her. She was in the presence of something greater than right or wrong.

Forgetting that this was an interview, he had strolled back into the room, driven by the instinct she had aroused in him. 'Wake up!' he cried to his baby, as if it was some grown-up friend. Then he lifted his foot and trod lightly on its stomach.

Miss Abbott cried, 'Oh, take care!' She was unaccustomed to this method of wakening the young.

'He is not much longer than my boot, is he? Can you believe that in time his own boots will be as large? And that he also—'

'But ought you to treat him like that?'

He stood with one foot resting on the little body, suddenly musing, filled with the desire that his son should be like him, and should have sons like him, to people the earth. It is the strongest desire that can come to a man–if it comes to him at all–stronger even than love or the desire for personal immortality. All men vaunt it, and declare that it is theirs; but the hearts of most are set elsewhere. It is the exception who comprehends that physical and spiritual life may stream out of him for ever. Miss Abbott, for all her goodness, could not comprehend it, though such a thing is more within the comprehension of women. And when Gino pointed first to himself and then to his baby and said 'Father–son,' she still took it as a piece of nursery prattle, and smiled mechanically.

The child, the firstfruits, woke up and glared at her. Gino did not greet it, but continued the exposition of his policy.

'This woman will do exactly what I tell her. She is fond of children. She is clean; she has a pleasant voice. She is not beautiful; I cannot pretend that to you for a moment. But she is what I require.'

The baby gave a piercing yell.

'Oh, do take care!' begged Miss Abbott. 'You are squeezing it.'

'It is nothing. If he cries silently then you may be frightened. He thinks I am going to wash him, and he is quite right.'

'Wash him!' she cried. 'You? Here?' The homely piece of news seemed to shatter all her plans. She had spent a long half-hour in elaborate approaches, in high moral attacks; she had neither frightened her enemy nor made him angry, nor interfered with the least detail of his domestic life.

'I had gone to the Farmacia,' he continued, 'and was sitting there comfortably, when suddenly I remembered that Perfetta had heated water an hour ago–over there, look, covered with a cushion. You must excuse me. I can put it off no longer.'

'I have wasted your time,' she said feebly.

He walked sternly to the loggia and drew from it a large earthenware bowl. It was dirty inside; he dusted it with a tablecloth. Then he fetched the hot water, which was in a copper pot. He poured it out. He added cold. He felt in his pocket and brought out a piece of soap. Then he took up the baby, and, holding his cigar between his teeth, began to unwrap it. Miss Abbott turned to go.

'But why are you going? Excuse me if I wash him while we talk.'

'I have nothing more to say,' said Miss Abbott. All she could do now was to find Philip, confess her miserable defeat, and bid him go in her stead and prosper better. She cursed her feebleness: she longed to expose it, with apologies or tears.

'Oh, but stop a moment!' he cried. 'You have not seen him yet.'

'I have seen as much as I want, thank you.'

The last wrapping slid off. He held out to her in his two hands a little kicking image of bronze.

'Take him!'

She would not touch the child.

'I must go at once,' she cried; for the tears—the wrong tears—were hurrying to her eyes.

'Who would have believed his mother was blonde? For he is brown all over—brown every inch of him. Ah, but how beautiful he is! And he is mine; mine for ever. Even if he hates me he will be mine. He cannot help it; he is made out of me; I am his father.'

It was too late to go. She could not tell why, but it was too late. She turned away her head when Gino lifted his son to his lips. This was something too remote from the prettiness of the nursery. The man was majestic; he was a part of Nature; in no ordinary love scene could he ever be so great. For a wonderful physical tie binds the parents to the children; and—by some sad, strange irony—it does not bind us children to our parents. For if it did, if we could answer their love not with gratitude but with equal love, life would lose much of its pathos and much of its squalor, and we might be wonderfully happy. Gino passionately embracing, Miss Abbott reverently averting her eyes—both of them had parents whom they did not love so very much.

'May I help you to wash him?' she asked humbly.

He gave her his son without speaking, and they knelt side by side, tucking up their sleeves. The child had stopped crying, and his arms and legs were agitated by some overpowering joy. Miss Abbott had a woman's pleasure in cleaning anything—more especially when the thing was human. She understood little babies from long experience in a district, and Gino soon ceased to give her directions, and only gave her thanks.

'It is very kind of you,' he murmured, 'especially in your beautiful dress. He is nearly clean already. Why, I take the whole morning! There is so much more of a baby than one expects. And Perfetta washes him just as she washes clothes. Then he screams for hours. My wife is to have a light hand. Ah, how he kicks! Has he splashed you! I am very sorry.'

'I am ready for a soft towel now,' said Miss Abbott, who was strangely exalted by the service.

'Certainly! certainly!' He strode in a knowing way to a cupboard. But he

had no idea where the soft towel was. Generally he dabbed the baby on the
first dry thing he found.

'And if you had any powder.'

He struck his forehead despairingly. Apparently the stock of powder was
just exhausted.

She sacrificed her own clean handkerchief. He put a chair for her on the
loggia, which faced westward, and was still pleasant and cool. There she sat,
with twenty miles of view behind her, and he placed the dripping baby on
her knee. It shone now with health and beauty; it seemed to reflect light, like
a copper vessel. Just such a baby Bellini sets languid on his mother's lap, or
Signorelli flings wriggling on pavements of marble, or Lorenzo di Credi,
more reverent but less divine, lays carefully among flowers, with his head
upon a wisp of golden straw. For a time Gino contemplated them standing.
Then, to get a better view, he knelt by the side of the chair, with his hands
clasped before him.

So they were when Philip entered, and saw, to all intents and purposes,
the Virgin and Child, with Donor.

'Hallo!' he exclaimed; for he was glad to find things in such cheerful trim.

She did not greet him, but rose up unsteadily and handed the baby to his
father.

'No, do stop!' whispered Philip. 'I got your note. I'm not offended; you're
quite right. I really want you; I could never have done it alone.'

No words came from her, but she raised her hands to her mouth, like one
who is in sudden agony.

'Signorina, do stop a little—after all your kindness.'

She burst into tears.

'What is it?' said Philip kindly.

She tried to speak, and then went away, weeping bitterly.

The two men stared at each other. By a common impulse they ran on to the
loggia. They were just in time to see Miss Abbott disappear among the trees.

'What is it?' asked Philip again. There was no answer, and somehow he
did not want an answer. Some strange thing had happened which he could
not presume to understand. He would find out from Miss Abbott, if ever he
found out at all.

'Well, your business,' said Gino, after a puzzled sigh.

'Our business—Miss Abbott has told you of that.'

'No.'

'But surely—'

'She came for business. But she forgot about it; so did I.'

Perfetta, who had a genius for missing people, now returned, loudly
complaining of the size of Monteriano and the intricacies of its streets. Gino
told her to watch the baby. Then he offered Philip a cigar, and they
proceeded to the business.

Chapter Eight

'Mad!' screamed Harriet–'absolutely stark, staring, raving mad!'

Philip judged it better not to contradict her.

'What's she here for? Answer me that. What's she doing in Monteriano in August? Why isn't she in Normandy? Answer that. She won't. I can: she's come to thwart us; she's betrayed us–got hold of mother's plans. Oh, goodness, my head!'

He was unwise enough to reply, 'You mustn't accuse her of that. Though she is exasperating, she hasn't come here to betray us.'

'Then why has she come here? Answer me that.'

He made no answer. But fortunately his sister was too much agitated to wait for one. 'Bursting in on me–crying and looking a disgusting sight–and says she has been to see the Italian. Couldn't even talk properly; pretended she had changed her opinions. What are her opinions to us? I was very calm. I said: "Miss Abbott, I think there is a little misapprehension in this matter. My mother, Mrs Herriton—" Oh, goodness, my head! Of course you've failed–don't trouble to answer–I know you've failed. Where's the baby, pray? Of course you haven't got it. Dear sweet Caroline won't let you. Oh yes, and we're to go away at once and trouble the father no more. Those are her commands. Commands! COMMANDS!' And Harriet also burst into tears.

Philip governed his temper. His sister was annoying, but quite reasonable in her indignation. Moreover, Miss Abbott had behaved even worse than she supposed.

'I've not got the baby, Harriet, but at the same time I haven't exactly failed. I and Signor Carella are to have another interview this afternoon, at the Caffè Garibaldi. He is perfectly reasonable and pleasant. Should you be disposed to come with me, you would find him quite willing to discuss things. He is desperately in want of money, and has no prospect of getting any. I discovered that. At the same time, he has a certain affection for the child.' For Philip's insight, or perhaps his opportunities, had not been equal to Miss Abbott's.

Harriet would only sob, and accuse her brother of insulting her; how could a lady speak to such a horrible man? That, and nothing else, was enough to stamp Caroline. Oh, poor Lilia!

Philip drummed on the bedroom window-sill. He saw no escape from the deadlock. For though he spoke cheerfully about his second interview with Gino, he felt at the bottom of his heart that it would fail. Gino was too courteous: he would not break off negotiations by sharp denial; he loved this civil, half-humorous bargaining. And he loved fooling his opponent, and did it so nicely that his opponent did not mind being fooled.

'Miss Abbott has behaved extraordinarily,' he said at last; 'but at the same time—'

His sister would not hear him. She burst forth again on the madness, the interference, the intolerable duplicity of Caroline.

'Harriet, you must listen. My dear, you must stop crying. I have something quite important to say.'

'I shall not stop crying,' said she. But in time, finding that he would not speak to her, she did stop.

'Remember that Miss Abbott has done us no harm. She said nothing to him about the matter. He assumes that she is working with us: I gathered that.'

'Well, she isn't.'

'Yes; but if you're careful she may be. I interpret her behaviour thus: she went to see him, honestly intending to get the child away. In the note she left me she says so, and I don't believe she'd lie.'

'I do.'

'When she got there, there was some pretty domestic scene between him and the baby, and she has got swept off in a gush of sentimentalism. Before very long, if I know anything about psychology, there will be a reaction. She'll be swept back.'

'I don't understand your long words. Say plainly—'

'When she's swept back, she'll be invaluable. For she has made quite an impression on him. He thinks her so nice with the baby. You know, she washed it for him.'

'Disgusting!'

Harriet's ejaculations were more aggravating than the rest of her. But Philip was averse to losing his temper. The access of joy that had come to him yesterday in the theatre promised to be permanent. He was more anxious than heretofore to be charitable towards the world.

'If you want to carry off the baby, keep your peace with Miss Abbott. For if she chooses, she can help you better than I can.'

'There can be no peace between me and her,' said Harriet gloomily.

'Did you—'

'Oh, not all I wanted. She went away before I had finished speaking—just like those cowardly people!—into the church.'

'Into Santa Deodata's?'

'Yes; I'm sure she needs it. Anything more unchristian—'

In time Philip went to the church also, leaving his sister a little calmer and a little disposed to think over his advice. What had come over Miss Abbott? He had always thought her both stable and sincere. That conversation he had had with her last Christmas in the train to Charing Cross—that alone furnished him with a parallel. For the second time, Monteriano must have turned her head. He was not angry with her, for he was quite indifferent to the outcome of their expedition. He was only extremely interested.

It was now nearly midday, and the streets were clearing. But the intense heat had broken, and there was a pleasant suggestion of rain. The Piazza, with its three great attractions—the Palazzo Pubblico, the Collegiate Church, and the Caffè Garibaldi: the intellect, the soul, and the body—had never looked more charming. For a moment Philip stood in its centre, much inclined to be dreamy, and thinking how wonderful it must feel to belong to a city, however mean. He was here, however, as an emissary of civilisation and as a student of character, and, after a sigh, he entered Santa Deodata's to continue his mission.

There had been a festa two days before, and the church still smelt of incense and of garlic. The little son of the sacristan was sweeping the nave, more for amusement than for cleanliness, sending great clouds of dust over the frescoes and the scattered worshippers. The sacristan himself had propped a ladder in the centre of the Deluge—which fills one of the nave spandrels—and was freeing a column from its wealth of scarlet calico. Much scarlet calico also lay upon the floor—for the church can look as fine as any theatre—and the sacristan's little daughter was trying to fold it up. She was wearing a tinsel crown. The crown really belonged to St Augustine. But it had been cut too big: it fell down over his cheeks like a collar—you never saw anything so absurd. One of the canons had unhooked it just before the festa began, and had given it to the sacristan's daughter.

'Please,' cried Philip, 'is there an English lady here?'

The man's mouth was full of tin-tacks, but he nodded cheerfully towards a kneeling figure. In the midst of this confusion Miss Abbott was praying.

He was not much surprised: a spiritual breakdown was quite to be expected. For though he was growing more charitable towards mankind, he was still a little jaunty, and too apt to stake out beforehand the course that will be pursued by the wounded soul. It did surprise him, however, that she should greet him naturally, with none of the sour self-consciousness of a person who had just risen from her knees. This was indeed the spirit of Santa Deodata's, where a prayer to God is thought none the worse of because it comes next to a pleasant word to a neighbour. 'I am sure that I need it,' said she; and he, who had expected her to be ashamed, became confused, and knew not what to reply.

'I've nothing to tell you,' she continued. 'I have simply changed straight round. If I had planned the whole thing out, I could not have treated you worse. I can talk it over now; but please believe that I have been crying.'

'And please believe that I have not come to scold you,' said Philip. 'I know what has happened.'

'What?' asked Miss Abbott. Instinctively she led the way to the famous chapel, the fifth chapel on the right, wherein Giovanni da Empoli has painted the death and burial of the saint. Here they could sit out of the dust and the noise, and proceed with a discussion which promised to be important.

'What might have happened to me—he has made you believe that he loves the child.'

'Oh yes; he has. He will never give it up.'

'At present it is still unsettled.'

'It will never be settled.'

'Perhaps not. Well, as I said, I know what has happened, and I am not here to scold you. But I must ask you to withdraw from the thing for the present. Harriet is furious. But she will calm down when she realises that you have done us no harm, and will do none.'

'I can do no more,' she said. 'But I tell you plainly I have changed sides.'

'If you do no more, that is all we want. You promise not to prejudice our cause by speaking to Signor Carella?'

'Oh, certainly. I don't want to speak to him again; I shan't ever see him again.'

'Quite nice, wasn't he?'

'Quite.'

'Well, that's all I wanted to know. I'll go and tell Harriet of your promise, and I think things'll quiet down now.'

But he did not move, for it was an increasing pleasure to him to be near her, and her charm was at its strongest to-day. He thought less of psychology and feminine reaction. The gush of sentimentalism which had carried her away had only made her more alluring. He was content to observe her beauty and to profit by the tenderness and the wisdom that dwelt within her.

'Why aren't you angry with me?' she asked, after a pause.

'Because I understand you—all sides, I think—Harriet, Signor Carella, even my mother.'

'You do understand wonderfully. You are the only one of us who has a general view of the muddle.'

He smiled with pleasure. It was the first time she had ever praised him. His eyes rested agreeably on Santa Deodata, who was dying in full sanctity, upon her back. There was a window open behind her, revealing just such a view as he had seen that morning, and on her widowed mother's dresser there stood just such another copper pot. The saint looked neither at the view nor at the pot, and at her widowed mother still less. For lo! she had a vision: the head and shoulders of St Augustine were sliding like some miraculous enamel along the roughcast wall. It is a gentle saint who is content with half another saint to see her die. In her death, as in her life, Santa Deodata did not accomplish much.

'So what are you going to do?' said Miss Abbott.

Philip started, not so much at the words as at the sudden change in the voice. 'Do?' he echoed, rather dismayed. 'This afternoon I have another interview.'

'It will come to nothing. Well?'

'Then another. If that fails I shall wire home for instructions. I dare say we may fail altogether, but we shall fail honourably.'

She had often been decided. But now behind her decision there was a note of passion. She struck him not as different, but as more important, and he minded it very much when she said—

'That's not doing anything! You would be doing something if you kidnapped the baby, or if you went straight away. But that! To fail honourably! To come out of the thing as well as you can! Is that all you are after?'

'Why, yes,' he stammered. 'Since we talk openly, that is all I am after just now. What else is there? If I can persuade Signor Carella to give in, so much the better. If he won't, I must report the failure to my mother, and then go home. Why, Miss Abbott, you can't expect me to follow you through all these turns—'

'I don't! But I do expect you to settle what is right and to follow that. Do you want the child to stop with his father, who loves him and will bring him up badly, or do you want him to come to Sawston, where no one loves him, but where he will be brought up well? There is the question put dispassionately enough even for you. Settle it. Settle which side you'll fight on. But don't go talking about an "honourable failure," which means simply not thinking and not acting at all.'

'Because I understand the position of Signor Carella and of you, it's no reason that—'

'None at all. Fight as if you think us wrong. Oh, what's the use of your fairmindedness if you never decide for yourself? Anyone gets hold of you and makes you do what they want. And you see through them and laugh at them—and do it. It's not enough to see clearly; I'm muddle-headed and stupid, and not worth a quarter of you, but I have tried to do what seemed right at the time. And you—your brain and your insight are splendid. But when you see what's right you're too idle to do it. You told me once that we shall be judged by our intentions, not by our accomplishments. I thought it a grand remark. But we must intend to accomplish—not sit intending on a chair.'

'You are wonderful!' he said gravely.

'Oh, you appreciate me!' she burst out again. 'I wish you didn't. You appreciate us all—see good in all of us. And all the time you are dead—dead—dead. Look, why aren't you angry?' She came up to him, and then her mood suddenly changed, and she took hold of both his hands. 'You are so splendid, Mr Herriton, that I can't bear to see you wasted. I can't bear—she has not been good to you—your mother.'

'Miss Abbott, don't worry over me. Some people are born not to do things. I'm one of them; I never did anything at school or at the Bar. I came out to stop Lilia's marriage, and it was too late. I came out intending to get the baby, and I shall return an "honourable failure." I never expect anything to happen now, and so I am never disappointed. You would be surprised to know what my great events are. Going to the theatre yesterday, talking to you now—I don't suppose I shall ever meet anything greater. I seem fated to pass through the world without colliding with it or moving it—and I'm sure I can't tell you whether the fate's good or evil. I don't die—I don't fall in love. And if other people die or fall in love they always do it when I'm just not there. You are quite right; life to me is just a spectacle, which—thank God, and thank Italy, and thank you—is now more beautiful and heartening than it has ever been before.'

She said solemnly, 'I wish something would happen to you, my dear friend; I wish something would happen to you.'

'But why?' he asked, smiling. 'Prove to me why I don't do as I am.'

She also smiled, very gravely. She could not prove it. No argument existed. Their discourse, splendid as it had been, resulted in nothing, and their respective opinions and policies were exactly the same when they left the church as when they had entered it.

Harriet was rude at lunch. She called Miss Abbott a turncoat and a coward to her face. Miss Abbott resented neither epithet, feeling that one was justified and the other not unreasonable. She tried to avoid even the suspicion of satire in her replies. But Harriet was sure that she was satirical because she was so calm. She got more and more violent, and Philip at one time feared that she would come to blows.

'Look here!' he cried, with something of the old manner, 'it's too hot for this. We've been talking and interviewing each other all the morning, and I have another interview this afternoon. I do stipulate for silence. Let each lady retire to her bedroom with a book.'

'I retire to pack,' said Harriet. 'Please remind Signor Carella, Philip, that the baby is to be here by half-past eight this evening.'

'Oh, certainly, Harriet. I shall make a point of reminding him.'

'And order a carriage to take us to the evening train.'

'And please,' said Miss Abbott, 'would you order a carriage for me too?'

'You going?' he exclaimed.

'Of course,' she replied, suddenly flushing. 'Why not?'

'Why, of course you would be going. Two carriages, then. Two carriages for the evening train.' He looked at his sister hopelessly. 'Harriet, whatever are you up to? We shall never be ready.'

'Order my carriage for the evening train,' said Harriet, and departed.

'Well, I suppose I shall. And I shall also have my interview with Signor Carella.'

Miss Abbott gave a little sigh.

'But why should you mind? Do you suppose that I shall have the slightest influence over him?'

'No. But—I can't repeat all that I said in the church. You ought never to see him again. You ought to bundle Harriet into a carriage, not this evening, but now, and drive her straight away.'

'Perhaps I ought. But it isn't a very big "ought." Whatever Harriet and I do the issue is the same. Why, I can see the splendour of it—even the humour. Gino sitting up here on the mountain-top with his cub. We come and ask for it. He welcomes us. We ask for it again. He is equally pleasant. I'm agreeable to spend the whole week bargaining with him. But I know that at the end of it I shall descend empty-handed to the plains. It might be finer of me to make up my mind. But I'm not a fine character. And nothing hangs on it.'

'Perhaps I am extreme,' she said humbly. 'I've been trying to run you, just like your mother. I feel you ought to fight it out with Harriet. Every little trifle, for some reason, does seem incalculably important to-day, and when you say of a thing that "nothing hangs on it," it sounds like blasphemy. There's never any knowing—(how am I to put it?)—which of our actions, which of our idleness won't have things hanging on it for ever.'

He assented, but her remark had only an æsthetic value. He was not prepared to take it to his heart. All the afternoon he rested—worried, but not exactly despondent. The thing would jog out somehow. Probably Miss Abbott was right. The baby had better stop where it was loved. And that, probably, was what the fates had decreed. He felt little interest in the matter, and he was sure that he had no influence.

It was not surprising, therefore, that the interview at the Caffè Garibaldi came to nothing. Neither of them took it very seriously. And before long Gino had discovered how things lay, and was ragging his companion hopelessly. Philip tried to look offended, but in the end he had to laugh. 'Well, you are right,' he said. 'The affair *is* being managed by the ladies.'

'Ah, the ladies—the ladies!' cried the other, and then he roared like a millionaire for two cups of black coffee, and insisted on treating his friend, as a sign that their strife was over.

'Well, I have done my best,' said Philip, dipping a long slice of sugar into his cup, and watching the brown liquid ascend into it. 'I shall face my mother with a good conscience. Will you bear me witness that I've done my best?'

'My poor fellow, I will!' He laid a sympathetic hand on Philip's knee.

'And that I have—' The sugar was now impregnated with coffee, and he bent forward to swallow it. As he did so his eyes swept the opposite side of the Piazza, and he saw there, watching them, Harriet. 'Mia sorella!' he exclaimed. Gino, much amused, laid his hand upon the little table, and beat the marble humorously with his fists. Harriet turned away and began gloomily to inspect the Palazzo Pubblico.

'Poor Harriet!' said Philip, swallowing the sugar. 'One more wrench and it will all be over for her; we are leaving this evening.'

Gino was sorry for this. 'Then you will not be here this evening as you promised us. All three leaving?'

'All three,' said Philip, who had not revealed the secession of Miss Abbott; 'by the night train; at least, that is my sister's plan. So I'm afraid I shan't be here.'

They watched the departing figure of Harriet, and then entered upon the final civilities. They shook each other warmly by both hands. Philip was to come again next year, and to write beforehand. He was to be introduced to Gino's wife, for he was told of the marriage now. He was to be godfather to his next baby. As for Gino, he would remember some time that Philip liked vermouth. He begged him to give his love to Irma. Mrs Herriton—should he send her his sympathetic regards? No; perhaps that would hardly do.

So the two young men parted with a good deal of genuine affection. For the barrier of language is sometimes a blessed barrier, which only lets pass what is good. Or—to put the thing less cynically—we may be better in new clean words, which have never been tainted by our pettiness or vice. Philip, at all events, lived more graciously in Italian, the very phrases of which entice one to be happy and kind. It was horrible to think of the English of Harriet, whose every word would be as hard, as distinct, and as unfinished as a lump of coal.

Harriet, however, talked little. She had seen enough to know that her brother had failed again, and with unwonted dignity she accepted the situation. She did her packing, she wrote up her diary, she made a brown paper cover for the new Baedeker. Philip, finding her so amenable, tried to discuss their future plans. But she only said that they would sleep in Florence, and told him to telegraph for rooms. They had supper alone. Miss Abbott did not come down. The landlady told them that Signor Carella had called on Miss Abbott to say good-bye, but she, though in, had not been able to see him. She also told them that it had begun to rain. Harriet sighed, but indicated to her brother that he was not responsible.

The carriages came round at a quarter past eight. It was not raining much, but the night was extraordinarily dark, and one of the drivers wanted to go slowly to the station. Miss Abbott came down and said that she was ready, and would start at once.

'Yes, do,' said Philip, who was standing in the hall. 'Now that we have quarrelled we scarcely want to travel in procession all the way down the hill. Well, good-bye; it's all over at last; another scene in my pageant has shifted.'

'Good-bye; it's been a great pleasure to see you. I hope that won't shift, at all events.' She gripped his hand.

'You sound despondent,' he said, laughing. 'Don't forget that you return victorious.'

'I suppose I do,' she replied, more despondently than ever, and got into the carriage. He concluded that she was thinking of her reception at Sawston, whither her fame would doubtless precede her. Whatever would Mrs Herriton do? She could make things quite unpleasant when she thought it right. She might think it right to be silent, but then there was Harriet. Who would bridle Harriet's tongue? Between the two of them Miss Abbott was bound to have a bad time. Her reputation, both for consistency and for moral enthusiasm, would be lost for ever.

'It's hard luck on her,' he thought. 'She is a good person. I must do for her anything I can.' Their intimacy had been very rapid, but he too hoped that it would not shift. He believed that he understood her, and that she, by now, had seen the worst of him. What if after a long time—if after all—he flushed like a boy as he looked after her carriage.

He went into the dining-room to look for Harriet. Harriet was not to be found. Her bedroom, too, was empty. All that was left of her was the purple prayer-book which lay open on the bed. Philip took it up aimlessly, and saw—'Blessed be the Lord my God who teacheth my hands to war and my fingers to fight.' He put the book in his pocket, and began to brood over more profitable themes.

Santa Deodata gave out half-past eight. All the luggage was on, and still Harriet had not appeared. 'Depend upon it,' said the landlady, 'she has gone to Signor Carella's to say good-bye to her little nephew.' Philip did not think it likely. They shouted all over the house and still there was no Harriet. He began to be uneasy. He was helpless without Miss Abbott; her grave kind face had cheered him wonderfully, even when it looked displeased. Monteriano was sad without her; the rain was thickening; the scraps of

Donizetti floated tunelessly out of the wineshops, and of the great tower opposite he could only see the base, fresh papered with the advertisements of quacks.

A man came up the street with a note. Philip read, 'Start at once. Pick me up outside the gate. Pay the bearer. H.H.'

'Did the lady give you this note?' he cried.

The man was unintelligible.

'Speak up!' exclaimed Philip. 'Who gave it you—and where?'

Nothing but horrible sighings and bubblings came out of the man.

'Be patient with him,' said the driver, turning round on the box. 'It is the poor idiot.' And the landlady came out of the hotel and echoed 'The poor idiot. He cannot speak. He takes messages for us all.'

Philip then saw that the messenger was a ghastly creature, quite bald, with trickling eyes and grey twitching nose. In another country he would have been shut up; here he was accepted as a public institution, and part of Nature's scheme.

'Ugh!' shuddered the Englishman. 'Signora padrona, find out from him; this note is from my sister. What does it mean? Where did he see her?'

'It is no good,' said the landlady. 'He understands everything, but he can explain nothing.'

'He has visions of the saints,' said the man who drove the cab.

'But my sister—where has she gone? How has she met him?'

'She has gone for a walk,' asserted the landlady. It was a nasty evening, but she was beginning to understand the English. 'She has gone for a walk—perhaps to wish good-bye to her little nephew. Preferring to come back another way, she has sent you this note by the poor idiot and is waiting for you outside the Siena gate. Many of my guests do this.'

There was nothing to do but to obey the message. He shook hands with the landlady, gave the messenger a nickel piece, and drove away. After a dozen yards the carriage stopped. The poor idiot was running and whimpering behind.

'Go on,' cried Philip. 'I have paid him plenty.'

A horrible hand pushed three soldi into his lap. It was part of the idiot's malady only to receive what was just for his services. This was the change out of the nickel piece.

'Go on!' shouted Philip, and flung the money into the road. He was frightened at the episode; the whole of life had become unreal. It was a relief to be out of the Siena gate. They drew up for a moment on the terrace. But there was no sign of Harriet. The driver called to the Dogana men. But they had seen no English lady pass.

'What am I to do?' he cried; 'it is not like the lady to be late. We shall miss the train.'

'Let us drive slowly,' said the driver, 'and you shall call her by name as we go.'

So they started down into the night, Philip calling 'Harriet! Harriet! Harriet!' And there she was, waiting for them in the wet, at the first turn of the zigzag.

'Harriet, why don't you answer?'

'I heard you coming,' said she, and got quickly in. Not till then did he see that she carried a bundle.

'What's that?'

'Hush—'

'Whatever is that?'

'Hush—sleeping.'

Harriet had succeeded where Miss Abbott and Philip had failed. It was the baby.

She would not let him talk. The baby, she repeated, was asleep, and she put up an umbrella to shield it and her from the rain. He should hear all later, so he had to conjecture the course of the wonderful interview—an interview between the South Pole and the North. It was quite easy to conjecture: Gino crumpling up suddenly before the intense conviction of Harriet; being told, perhaps, to his face that he was a villain; yielding his only son perhaps for money, perhaps for nothing. 'Poor Gino,' he thought. 'He's no greater than I am, after all.'

Then he thought of Miss Abbott, whose carriage must be descending the darkness some mile or two below them, and his easy self-accusation failed. She, too, had conviction; he had felt its force; he would feel it again when she knew this day's sombre and unexpected close.

'You have been pretty secret,' he said; 'you might tell me a little now. What do we pay for him? All we've got?'

'Hush!' answered Harriet, and dandled the bundle laboriously, like some bony prophetess—Judith, or Deborah, or Jael. He had last seen the baby sprawling on the knees of Miss Abbott, shining and naked, with twenty miles of view behind him, and his father kneeling by his feet. And that remembrance, together with Harriet, and the darkness, and the poor idiot, and the silent rain, filled him with sorrow and with the expectation of sorrow to come.

Monteriano had long disappeared, and he could see nothing but the occasional wet stem of an olive, which their lamp illumined as they passed it. They travelled quickly, for this driver did not care how fast he went to the station, and would dash down each incline and scuttle perilously round the curves.

'Look here, Harriet,' he said at last, 'I feel bad; I want to see the baby.'

'Hush!'

'I don't mind if I do wake him up. I want to see him. I've as much right in him as you.'

Harriet gave in. But it was too dark for him to see the child's face. 'Wait a minute,' he whispered, and before she could stop him he had lit a match under the shelter of her umbrella. 'But he's awake!' he exclaimed. The match went out.

'Good ickle quiet boysey, then.'

Philip winced. 'His face, do you know, struck me as all wrong.'

'All wrong?'

'All puckered queerly.'

'Of course—with the shadows—you couldn't see him.'

'Well, hold him up again.' She did so. He lit another match. It went out quickly, but not before he had seen that the baby was crying.

'Nonsense,' said Harriet sharply. 'We should hear him if he cried.'

'No, he's crying hard; I thought so before, and I'm certain now.'

Harriet touched the child's face. It was bathed in tears. 'Oh, the night air, I suppose,' she said, 'or perhaps the wet of the rain.'

'I say, you haven't hurt it, or held it the wrong way, or anything; it is too uncanny—crying and no noise. Why didn't you get Perfetta to carry it to the hotel instead of muddling with the messenger? It's a marvel he understood about the note.'

'Oh, he understands.' And he could feel her shudder. 'He tried to carry the baby—'

'But why not Gino or Perfetta?'

'Philip, don't talk. Must I say it again? Don't talk. The baby wants to sleep.' She crooned harshly as they descended, and now and then she wiped up the tears which welled inexhaustibly from the little eyes. Philip looked away, winking at times himself. It was as if they were travelling with the whole world's sorrow, as if all the mystery, all the persistency of woe were gathered to a single fount. The roads were now coated with mud, and the carriage went more quietly but not less swiftly, sliding by long zigzags into the night. He knew the landmarks pretty well: here was the cross-road to Poggibonsi; and the last view of Monteriano, if they had light, would be from here. Soon they ought to come to that little wood where violets were so plentiful in spring. He wished the weather had not changed; it was not cold, but the air was extraordinarily damp. It could not be good for the child.

'I suppose he breathes, and all that sort of thing?' he said.

'Of course,' said Harriet, in an angry whisper. 'You've started him again. I'm certain he was asleep. I do wish you wouldn't talk; it makes me so nervous.'

'I'm nervous too. I wish he'd scream. It's too uncanny. Poor Gino! I'm terribly sorry for Gino.'

'Are you?'

'Because he's weak—like most of us. He doesn't know what he wants. He doesn't grip on to life. But I like that man, and I'm sorry for him.'

Naturally enough she made no answer.

'You despise him, Harriet, and you despise me. But you do us no good by it. We fools want some one to set us on our feet. Suppose a really decent woman had set up Gino—I believe Caroline Abbott might have done it—mightn't he have been another man?'

'Philip,' she interrupted, with an attempt at nonchalance, 'do you happen to have those matches handy? We might as well look at the baby again if you have.'

The first match blew out immediately. So did the second. He suggested that they should stop the carriage and borrow the lamp from the driver.

'Oh, I don't want all that bother. Try again.'

They entered the little wood as he tried to strike the third match. At last it caught. Harriet poised the umbrella rightly, and for a full quarter-minute they contemplated the face that trembled in the light of the trembling flame. Then there was a shout and a crash. They were lying in the mud in darkness. The carriage had overturned.

Philip was a good deal hurt. He sat up and rocked himself to and fro, holding his arm. He could just make out the outline of the carriage above him, and the outlines of the carriage cushions and of their luggage upon the grey road. The accident had taken place in the wood, where it was even darker than in the open.

'Are you all right?' he managed to say. Harriet was screaming, the horse was kicking, the driver was cursing some other man.

Harriet's screams became coherent. 'The baby—the baby—it slipped—it's gone from my arms! I stole it!'

'God help me!' said Philip. A cold circle came round his mouth, and he fainted.

When he recovered it was still the same confusion. The horse was kicking, the baby had not been found, and Harriet still screamed like a maniac, 'I stole it! I stole it! I stole it! It slipped out of my arms!'

'Keep still!' he commanded the driver. 'Let no one move. We may tread on it. Keep still.'

For a moment they all obeyed him. He began to crawl through the mud, touching first this, then that, grasping the cushions by mistake, listening for the faintest whisper that might guide him. He tried to light a match, holding the box in his teeth and striking at it with the uninjured hand. At last he succeeded, and the light fell upon the bundle which he was seeking.

It had rolled off the road into the wood a little way, and had fallen across a great rut. So tiny it was that had it fallen lengthways it would have disappeared, and he might never have found it.

'I stole it! I and the idiot—no one was there.' She burst out laughing.

He sat down and laid it on his knee. Then he tried to cleanse the face from the mud and the rain and the tears. His arm, he supposed, was broken, but he could still move it a little, and for the moment he forgot all pain. He was listening—not for a cry, but for the tick of a heart or the slightest tremor of breath.

'Where are you?' called a voice. It was Miss Abbott, against whose carriage they had collided. She had re-lit one of the lamps, and was picking her way towards him.

'Silence!' he called again, and again they obeyed. He shook the bundle; he breathed into it; he opened his coat and pressed it against him. Then he listened, and heard nothing but the rain and the panting horses, and Harriet, who was somewhere chuckling to herself in the dark.

Miss Abbott approached, and took it gently from him. The face was already chilly, but thanks to Philip it was no longer wet. Nor would it again be wetted by any tear.

Chapter Nine

The details of Harriet's crime were never known. In her illness she spoke more of the inlaid box that she had lent to Lilia—lent, not given—than of recent troubles. It was clear that she had gone prepared for an interview with Gino, and finding him out, she had yielded to a grotesque temptation. But how far this was the result of ill-temper, to what extent she had been fortified by her religion, when and how she had met the poor idiot—these questions were never answered, nor did they interest Philip greatly. Detection was certain: they would have been arrested by the police of Florence or Milan, or at the frontier. As it was, they had been stopped in a simpler manner a few miles out of the town.

As yet he could scarcely survey the thing. It was too great. Round the Italian baby who had died in the mud there centred deep passions and high hopes. People have been wicked or wrong in the matter; no one save himself had been trivial. Now the baby had gone, but there remained this vast apparatus of pride and pity and love. For the dead, who seem to take away so much, really take with them nothing that is ours. The passion they have aroused lives after them, easy to transmute or to transfer, but well-nigh impossible to destroy. And Philip knew that he was still voyaging on the same magnificent, perilous sea, with the sun or the clouds above him, and the tides below.

The course of the moment—that, at all events, was certain. He and no one else must take the news to Gino. It was easy to talk of Harriet's crime—easy also to blame the negligent Perfetta or Mrs Herriton at home. Every one had contributed—even Miss Abbott and Irma. If one chose, one might consider the catastrophe composite or the work of fate. But Philip did not so choose. It was his own fault, due to acknowledged weakness in his own character. Therefore he, and no one else, must take the news of it to Gino.

Nothing prevented him. Miss Abbott was engaged with Harriet, and people had sprung out of the darkness and were conducting them towards some cottage. Philip had only to get into the uninjured carriage and order the driver to return. He was back at Monteriano after a two hours' absence. Perfetta was in the house now, and greeted him cheerfully. Pain, physical and mental, had made him stupid. It was some time before he realised that she had never missed the child.

Gino was still out. The woman took him to the reception-room, just as she had taken Miss Abbott in the morning, and dusted a circle for him on one of the horse-hair chairs. But it was dark now, so she left the guest a little lamp.

'I will be as quick as I can,' she told him. 'But there are many streets in Monteriano; he is sometimes difficult to find. I could not find him this morning.'

'Go first to the Caffè Garibaldi,' said Philip, remembering that this was the hour appointed by his friends of yesterday.

He occupied the time he was left alone not in thinking—there was nothing to think about; he simply had to tell a few facts—but in trying to make a sling for his broken arm. The trouble was in the elbow-joint, and as long as he kept this motionless he could go on as usual. But inflammation was beginning, and the slightest jar gave him agony. The sling was not fitted before Gino leapt up the stairs, crying—

'So you are back! How glad I am! We are all waiting—'

Philip had seen too much to be nervous. In low, even tones, he told what had happened; and the other, also perfectly calm, heard him to the end. In the silence Perfetta called up that she had forgotten the baby's evening milk; she must fetch it. When she had gone Gino took up the lamp without a word, and they went into the other room.

'My sister is ill,' said Philip, 'and Miss Abbott is guiltless. I should be glad if you did not have to trouble them.'

Gino had stooped down by the way, and was feeling the place where his son had lain. Now and then he frowned a little and glanced at Philip.

'It is through me,' he continued. 'It happened because I was cowardly and idle. I have come to know what you will do.'

Gino had left the rug, and began to pat the table from the end, as if he was blind. The action was so uncanny that Philip was driven to intervene.

'Gently, man, gently; he is not here.'

He went up and touched him on the shoulder.

He twitched away, and began to pass his hands over things more rapidly—over the table, the chairs, the entire floor, the walls as high as he could reach them. Philip had not presumed to comfort him. But now the tension was too great—he tried.

'Break down, Gino; you must break down. Scream and curse and give in for a little; you must break down.'

There was no reply, and no cessation of the sweeping hands.

'It is time to be unhappy. Break down or you will be ill like my sister. You will go—'

The tour of the room was over. He had touched everything in it except Philip. Now he approached him. His face was that of a man who has lost his old reason for life and seeks a new one.

'Gino!'

He stopped for a moment; then he came nearer. Philip stood his ground.

'You are to do what you like with me, Gino. Your son is dead, Gino. He died in my arms, remember. It does not excuse me; but he did die in my arms.'

The left hand came forward, slowly this time. It hovered before Philip like an insect. Then it descended and gripped him by his broken elbow.

Philip struck out with all the strength of his other arm. Gino fell to the blow without a cry or a word.

'You brute!' exclaimed the Englishman. 'Kill me if you like! But just you leave my broken arm alone.'

Then he was seized with remorse, and knelt beside his adversary and tried to revive him. He managed to raise him up, and propped his body against his own. He passed his arm round him. Again he was filled with pity and tenderness. He awaited the revival without fear, sure that both of them were safe at last.

Gino recovered suddenly. His lips moved. For one blessed moment it seemed that he was going to speak. But he scrambled up in silence, remembering everything, and he made not towards Philip, but towards the lamp.

'Do what you like; but think first—'

The lamp was tossed across the room, out through the loggia. It broke against one of the trees below. Philip began to cry out in the dark.

Gino approached from behind and gave him a sharp pinch. Philip spun round with a yell. He had only been pinched on the back, but he knew what was in store for him. He struck out, exhorting the devil to fight him, to kill him, to do anything but this. Then he stumbled to the door. It was open. He lost his head and, instead of turning down the stairs, he ran across the landing into the room opposite. There he lay down on the floor between the stove and the skirting-board.

His senses grew sharper. He could hear Gino coming in on tiptoe. He even knew what was passing in his mind, how now he was at fault, now he was hopeful, now he was wondering whether after all the victim had not escaped down the stairs. There was a quick swoop above him, and then a low growl like a dog's. Gino had broken his finger-nails against the stove.

Physical pain is almost too terrible to bear. We can just bear it when it comes by accident or for our good—as it generally does in modern life—except at school. But when it is caused by the malignity of a man, full grown, fashioned like ourselves, all our control disappears. Philip's one thought was to get away from that room at whatever sacrifice of nobility or pride.

Gino was now at the farther end of the room, groping by the little tables. Suddenly the instinct came to him. He crawled quickly to where Philip lay and had him clean by the elbow.

The whole arm seemed red-hot, and the broken bone grated in the joint sending out shoots of the essence of pain. His other arm was pinioned against the wall, and Gino had trampled in behind the stove and was kneeling on his legs. For the space of a minute he yelled and yelled with all the force of his lungs. Then this solace was denied him. The other hand, moist and strong, began to close round his throat.

At first he was glad, for here, he thought, was death at last. But it was only a new torture; perhaps Gino inherited the skill of his ancestors—the childlike ruffians who flung each other from the towers. Just as the windpipe closed the hand fell off, and Philip was revived by the motion of his arm. And just as he was about to faint and gain at last one moment of oblivion, the motion stopped, and he would struggle instead against the pressure on this throat.

Vivid pictures were dancing through the pain—Lilia dying some months back in this very house, Miss Abbott bending over the baby, his mother at home, now reading evening prayers to the servants. He felt that he was growing weaker; his brain wandered; the agony did not seem so great. Not all Gino's care could indefinitely postpone the end. His yells and gurgles became mechanical—functions of the tortured flesh rather than true notes of indignation and despair. He was conscious of a horrid tumbling. Then his arm was pulled a little too roughly, and everything was quiet at last.

'But your son is dead, Gino. Your son is dead, dear Gino. Your son is dead.'

The room was full of light, and Miss Abbott had Gino by the shoulders, holding him down in a chair. She was exhausted with the struggle, and her arms were trembling.

'What is the good of another death? What is the good of more pain?'

He too began to tremble. Then he turned and looked curiously at Philip, whose face, covered with dust and foam, was visible by the stove. Miss Abbott allowed him to get up, though she still held him firmly. He gave a loud and curious cry—a cry of interrogation it might be called. Below there was the noise of Perfetta returning with the baby's milk.

'Go to him,' said Miss Abbott, indicating Philip. 'Pick him up. Treat him kindly.'

She released him, and he approached Philip slowly. His eyes were filling with trouble. He bent down, as if he would gently raise him up.

'Help! Help!' moaned Philip. His body had suffered too much from Gino. It could not bear to be touched by him.

Gino seemed to understand. He stopped, crouched above him. Miss Abbott herself came forward and lifted her friend in her arms.

'Oh, the foul devil!' he murmured. 'Kill him! Kill him for me.'

Miss Abbott laid him tenderly on the couch and wiped his face. Then she said gravely to them both, 'This thing stops here.'

'Latte! latte!' cried Perfetta, hilariously ascending the stairs.

'Remember,' she continued, 'there is to be no revenge. I will have no more intentional evil. We are not to fight with each other any more.'

'I shall never forgive him,' sighed Philip.

'Latte! latte freschìssimo! bianco come neve!' Perfetta came in with another lamp and a little jug.

Gino spoke for the first time. 'Put the milk on the table,' he said. 'It will not be wanted in the other room.' The peril was over at last. A great sob shook the whole body, another followed, and then he gave a piercing cry of woe, and stumbled towards Miss Abbott like a child and clung to her.

All through the day Miss Abbott had seemed to Philip like a goddess, and more than ever did she seem so now. Many people look younger and more intimate during great emotion. But some there are who look older, and remote, and he could not think that there was little difference in years, and none in composition, between her and the man whose head was laid upon her breast. Her eyes were open, full of infinite pity and full of majesty, as if they discerned the boundaries of sorrow, and saw unimaginable tracts beyond. Such eyes he had seen in great pictures but never in a mortal. Her hands were folded round the sufferer, stroking him lightly, for even a goddess can do no more than that. And it seemed fitting, too, that she should bend her head and touch his forehead with her lips.

Philip looked away, as he sometimes looked away from the great pictures where visible forms suddenly became inadequate for the things they have shown to us. He was happy; he was assured that there was greatness in the world. There came to him an earnest desire to be good through the example of this good woman. He would try henceforward to be worthy of the things she had revealed. Quietly, without hysterical prayers or banging of drums, he underwent conversion. He was saved.

'That milk,' said she, 'need not be wasted. Take it, Signor Carella, and persuade Mr Herriton to drink.'

Gino obeyed her, and carried the child's milk to Philip. And Philip obeyed also and drank.

'Is there any left?'

'A little,' answered Gino.

'Then finish it.' For she was determined to use such remnants as lie about the world.

'Will you not have some?'

'I do not care for milk; finish it all.'

'Philip, have you had enough milk?'

'Yes, thank you, Gino; finish it all.'

He drank the milk, and then, either by accident or in some spasm of pain, broke the jug to pieces. Perfetta exclaimed in bewilderment. 'It does not matter,' he told her. 'It does not matter. It will never be wanted any more.'

Chapter Ten

'He will have to marry her,' said Philip. 'I heard from him this morning, just as we left Milan. He finds he has gone too far to back out. It would be expensive. I don't know how much he minds—not as much as we suppose, I think. At all events there's not a word of blame in the letter. I don't believe he even feels angry. I never was so completely forgiven. Ever since you stopped him killing me, it has been a vision of perfect friendship. He nursed me, he lied for me at the inquest, and at the funeral, though he was crying, you would have thought it was my own son who had died. Certainly I was the only person he had to be kind to; he was so distressed not to make Harriet's acquaintance, and that he scarcely saw anything of you. In his letter he says so again.'

'Thank him, please, when you write,' said Miss Abbott, 'and give him my kindest regards.'

'Indeed I will.' He was surprised that she could slide away from the man so easily. For his own part, he was bound by ties of almost alarming intimacy. Gino had the southern knack of friendship. In the intervals of business he would pull out Philip's life, turn it inside out, remodel it, and advise him how to use it for the best. The sensation was pleasant, for he was a kind as well as a skilful operator. But Philip came away feeling that he had not a secret corner left. In that very letter Gino had again implored him, as a refuge from domestic difficulties, 'to marry Miss Abbott, even if her dowry is small.' And how Miss Abbott herself, after such tragic intercourse, could resume the conventions and send calm messages of esteem, was more than he could understand.

'When will you see him again?' she asked. They were standing together in the corridor of the train, slowly ascending out of Italy towards the San Gotthard tunnel.

'I hope next spring. Perhaps we shall paint Siena red for a day or two with some of the new wife's money. It was one of the arguments for marrying her.'

'He has no heart,' she said severely. 'He does not really mind about the child at all.'

'No; you're wrong. He does. He is unhappy, like the rest of us. But he doesn't try to keep up appearances as we do. He knows that the things that have made him happy once will probably make him happy again.'

'He said he would never be happy again.'

'In his passion. Not when he was calm. We English say it when we are calm—when we do not really believe it any longer. Gino is not ashamed of inconsistency. It is one of the many things I like him for.'

'Yes; I was wrong. That is so.'

'He's much more honest with himself than I am,' continued Philip, 'and he is honest without an effort and without pride. But you, Miss Abbott, what about you? Will you be in Italy next spring?'

'No.'

'I'm sorry. When will you come back, do you think?'

'I think never.'

'For whatever reason?' He stared at her as if she were some monstrosity.

'Because I understand the place. There is no need.'

'Understand Italy!' he exclaimed.

'Perfectly.'

'Well, I don't. And I don't understand you,' he murmured to himself, as he paced away from her up the corridor. By this time he loved her very much, and he could not bear to be puzzled. He had reached love by the spiritual path: her thoughts and her goodness and her nobility had moved him first, and now her whole body and all its gestures had become transfigured by them. The beauties that are called obvious—the beauties of her hair and her voice and her limbs—he had noticed these last; Gino, who never traversed any path at all, had commended them dispassionately to his friend.

Why was she so puzzling? He had known so much about her once—what she thought, how she felt, the reasons for her actions. And now he only knew that he loved her, and all the other knowledge seemed passing from him just as he needed it most. Why would she never come to Italy again? Why had she avoided himself and Gino ever since the evening that she had saved their lives? The train was nearly empty. Harriet slumbered in a compartment by herself. He must ask her these questions now, and he returned quickly to her down the corridor.

She greeted him with a question of her own. 'Are your plans decided?'

'Yes. I can't live at Sawston.'

'Have you told Mrs Herriton?'

'I wrote from Monteriano. I tried to explain things; but she will never understand me. Her view will be that the affair is settled—sadly settled since the baby is dead. Still it's over; our family circle need be vexed no more. She won't even be angry with you. You see, you have done us no harm in the long run. Unless, of course, you talk about Harriet and make a scandal. So that is my plan—London and work. What is yours?'

'Poor Harriet!' said Miss Abbott. 'As if I dare judge Harriet! Or anybody.' And without replying to Philip's question she left him to visit the other invalid.

Philip gazed after her mournfully, and then he looked mournfully out of the window at the decreasing streams. All the excitement was over—the inquest, Harriet's short illness, his own visit to the surgeon. He was convalescent, both in body and spirit, but convalescence brought no joy. In the looking-glass at the end of the corridor he saw his face haggard, and his shoulders pulled forward by the weight of the sling. Life was greater than he had supposed, but it was even less complete. He had seen the need for strenuous work and for righteousness. And now he saw what a very little way those things would go.

'Is Harriet going to be all right?' he asked. Miss Abbott had come back to him.

'She will soon be her old self,' was the reply. For Harriet, after a sharp paroxysm of illness and remorse, was quickly returning to her normal state. She had been 'thoroughly upset,' as she phrased it, but she soon ceased to realise that anything was wrong beyond the death of a poor little child. Already she spoke of 'this unlucky accident,' and 'the mysterious frustration of one's attempts to make things better.' Miss Abbott had seen that she was comfortable, and had given her a kind kiss. But she returned feeling that Harriet, like her mother, considered the affair as settled.

'I'm clear enough about Harriet's future, and about parts of my own. But I ask again, What about yours?'

'Sawston and work,' said Miss Abbott.

'No.'

'Why not?' she asked, smiling.

'You've seen too much. You've seen as much and done more than I have.'

'But it's so different. Of course I shall go to Sawston. You forget my father; and even if he wasn't there, I've a hundred ties: my district—I'm neglecting it shamefully—my evening classes, the St James'—'

'Silly nonsense!' he exploded, suddenly moved to have the whole thing out with her. 'You're too good—about a thousand times better than I am. You can't live in that hole; you must go among people who can hope to understand you. I mind for myself: I want to see you often—again and again.'

'Of course we shall meet whenever you come down; and I hope that it will mean often.'

'It's not enough; it'll only be in the old horrible way, each with a dozen relatives round us. No, Miss Abbott; it's not good enough.'

'We can write at all events.'

'You will write?' he cried, with a flush of pleasure. At times his hopes seemed so solid.

'I will indeed.'

'But I say it's not enough—you can't go back to the old life if you wanted to. Too much has happened.'

'I know that,' she said sadly.

'Not only pain and sorrow, but wonderful things: that tower in the sunlight—do you remember it, and all you said to me? The theatre, even. And the next day—in the church; and our times with Gino.'

'All the wonderful things are over,' she said. 'That is just where it is.'

'I don't believe it. At all events not for me. The most wonderful things may be to come—'

'The wonderful things are over,' she repeated, and looked at him so mournfully that he dare not contradict her. The train was crawling up the last ascent towards the Campanile of Airolo and the entrance of the tunnel.

'Miss Abbott,' he murmured, speaking quickly, as if their free intercourse might soon be ended, 'what is the matter with you? I thought I understood you, and I don't. All those two great first days at Monteriano I read you as clearly as you read me still. I saw why you had come, and why you changed sides, and afterwards I saw your wonderful courage and pity. And now you're frank with me one moment, as you used to be, and the next moment you shut me up. You see I owe too much to you—my life, and I don't know what besides. I won't stand it. You've gone too far to turn mysterious. I'll quote what you said to me: "Don't be mysterious; there isn't the time." I'll quote something else: "I and my life must be where I live." You can't live at Sawston.'

He had moved her at last. She whispered to herself hurriedly. 'It is tempting—' And those three words threw him into a tumult of joy. What was tempting to her? After all was the greatest of things possible? Perhaps, after long estrangement, after much tragedy, the South had brought them together in the end. That laughter in the theatre, those silver stars in the purple sky, even the violets of a departed spring, all had helped, and sorrow had helped also, and so had tenderness to others.

'It is tempting,' she repeated, 'not to be mysterious. I've wanted often to tell you, and then been afraid. I could never tell anyone else, certainly no woman, and I think you're the one man who might understand and not be disgusted.'

'Are you lonely?' he whispered. 'Is it anything like that?'

'Yes.' The train seemed to shake him towards her. He was resolved that though a dozen people were looking, he would yet take her in his arms. 'I'm terribly lonely, or I wouldn't speak. I think you must know already.' Their faces were crimson, as if the same thought was surging through them both.

'Perhaps I do.' He came close to her. 'Perhaps I could speak instead. But if you will say the word plainly you'll never be sorry; I will thank you for it all my life.'

She said plainly 'That I love him.' Then she broke down. Her body was shaken with sobs, and lest there should be any doubt she cried between the sobs for Gino! Gino! Gino!

He heard himself remark 'Rather! I love him too! When I can forget how he hurt me that evening. Though whenever we shake hands—' One of them must have moved a step or two, for when she spoke again she was already a little way apart.

'You've upset me.' She stifled something that was perilously near hysterics. 'I thought I was past all this. You're taking it wrongly. I'm in love with Gino—don't pass it off—I mean it crudely—you know what I mean. So laugh at me.'

'Laugh at love?' asked Philip.

'Yes. Pull it to pieces. Tell me I'm a fool or worse—that he's a cad. Say all you said when Lilia fell in love with him. That's the help I want. I dare tell you this because I like you—and because you're without passion; you look on life as a spectacle; you don't enter it; you only find it funny or beautiful. So I can trust you to cure me. Mr Herriton, isn't it funny?' She tried to laugh herself, but became frightened and had to stop. 'He's not a gentleman, nor a Christian, nor good in any way. He's never flattered me nor honoured me. But because he's handsome, that's been enough. The son of an Italian dentist, with a pretty face.' She repeated the phrase as if it was a charm against passion. 'Oh, Mr Herriton, isn't it funny!' Then, to his relief, she began to cry. 'I love him, and I'm not ashamed of it. I love him, and I'm going to Sawston, and if I mayn't speak about him to you sometimes, I shall die.'

In that terrible discovery Philip managed to think not of himself but of her. He did not lament. He did not even speak to her kindly, for he saw that she could not stand it. A flippant reply was what she asked and needed—something flippant and a little cynical. And indeed it was the only reply he could trust himself to make.

'Perhaps it is what the books call "a passing fancy"?'

She shook her head. Even this question was too pathetic. For as far as she knew anything about herself, she knew that her passions, once aroused, were sure. 'If I saw him often,' she said, 'I might remember what he is like. Or he might grow old. But I dare not risk it, so nothing can alter me now.'

'Well, if the fancy does pass, let me know.' After all, he could say what he wanted.

'Oh, you shall know quick enough.'

'But before you retire to Sawston—are you so mighty sure?'

'What of?' She had stopped crying. He was treating her exactly as she had hoped.

'That you and he—' He smiled bitterly at the thought of them together. Here was the cruel antique malice of the gods, such as they once sent forth against Pasiphae. Centuries of aspiration and culture—and the world could not escape it. 'I was going to say—whatever have you got in common?'

'Nothing except the times we have seen each other.' Again her face was crimson. He turned his own face away.

'Which—which times?'

'The time I thought you weak and heedless, and went instead of you to get the baby. That began it, as far as I know the beginning. Or it may have begun when you took us to the theatre, and I saw him mixed up with music and light. But I didn't understand till the morning. Then you opened the door—and I knew why I had been so happy. Afterwards, in the church, I prayed for us all; not for anything new, but that we might just be as we were—he with the child he loved, you and I and Harriet safe out of the place—and that I might never see him or speak to him again. I could have pulled through then—the thing was only coming near, like a wreath of smoke; it hadn't wrapped me round.'

'But through my fault,' said Philip solemnly, 'he is parted from the child he loves. And because my life was in danger you came and saw him and spoke to him again.' For the thing was even greater than she imagined. Nobody but himself would ever see round it now. And to see round it he was standing at an immense distance. He could even be glad that she had once held the beloved in her arms.

'Don't talk of "faults." You're my friend for ever, Mr Herriton, I think. Only don't be charitable and shift or take the blame. Get over supposing I'm refined. That's what puzzles you. Get over that.'

As she spoke she seemed to be transfigured, and to have indeed no part with refinement or unrefinement any longer. Out of this wreck there was revealed to him something indestructible—something which she, who had given it, could never take away.

'I say again, don't be charitable. If he had asked me, I might have given myself body and soul. That would have been the end of my rescue party. But all through he took me for a superior being—a goddess. I who was wor-shipping every inch of him, and every word he spoke. And that saved me.'

Philip's eyes were fixed on the Campanile of Airolo. But he saw instead the fair myth of Endymion. This woman was a goddess to the end. For her no love could be degrading; she stood outside all degradation. This episode, which she thought so sordid, and which was so tragic for him, remained supremely beautiful. To such a height was he lifted, that without regret he could now have told her that he was her worshipper too. But what was the use of telling her? For all the wonderful things had happened.

'Thank you,' was all that he permitted himself. 'Thank you for everything.'

She looked at him with great friendliness, for he had made her life endurable. At that moment the train entered the San Gotthard tunnel. They hurried back to the carriage to close the windows lest the smuts should get into Harriet's eyes.

THE END

_A_ ROOM WITH A VIEW

A ROOM WITH A VIEW

To H.O.M.

Chapter One

The Bertolini

'The Signora had no business to do it,' said Miss Bartlett, 'no business at all. She promised us south rooms with a view close together, instead of which here are north rooms, here are north rooms, looking into a courtyard, and a long way apart. Oh, Lucy!'

'And a Cockney, besides!' said Lucy, who had been further saddened by the Signora's unexpected accent. 'It might be London.' She looked at the two rows of English people who were sitting at the table; at the row of white bottles of water and red bottles of wine that ran between the English people; at the portraits of the late Queen and the late Poet Laureate that hung behind the English people, heavily framed; at the notice of the English church (Rev. Cuthbert Eager, M.A. Oxon), that was the only other decoration of the wall. 'Charlotte, don't you feel, too, that we might be in London? I can hardly believe that all kinds of other things are just outside. I suppose it is one's being so tired.'

'This meat has surely been used for soup,' said Miss Bartlett, laying down her fork.

'I wanted so to see the Arno. The rooms the Signora promised us in her letter would have looked over the Arno. The Signora had no business to do it at all. Oh, it is a shame!'

'Any nook does for me,' Miss Bartlett continued; 'but it does seem hard that you shouldn't have a view.'

Lucy felt that she had been selfish. 'Charlotte, you mustn't spoil me: of course, you must look over the Arno, too. I meant that. The first vacant room in the front—'

'You must have it,' said Miss Bartlett, part of whose travelling expenses were paid by Lucy's mother—a piece of generosity to which she made many a tactful allusion.

'No, no. You must have it.'

'I insist on it. Your mother would never forgive me, Lucy.'

'She would never forgive *me*.'

The ladies' voices grew animated, and—if the sad truth be owned—a little peevish. They were tired, and under the guise of unselfishness they wrangled. Some of their neighbours interchanged glances, and one of them—one of the ill-bred people whom one does meet abroad—leant forward over the table and actually intruded into their argument. He said:

'I have a view, I have a view.'

Miss Bartlett was startled. Generally at a pension people looked them over for a day or two before speaking, and often did not find out that they would 'do' till they had gone. She knew that the intruder was ill-bred, even before she glanced at him. He was an old man, of heavy build, with a fair, shaven face and large eyes. There was something childish in those eyes, though it was not the childishness of senility. What exactly it was Miss Bartlett did not stop to consider, for her glance passed on to his clothes. These did not attract her. He was probably trying to become acquainted with them before they got into the swim. So she assumed a dazed expression when he spoke to her, and then said: 'A view? Oh, a view! How delightful a view is!'

'This is my son,' said the old man; 'his name's George. He has a view, too.'

'Ah,' said Miss Bartlett, repressing Lucy, who was about to speak.

'What I mean,' he continued, 'is that you can have our rooms, and we'll have yours. We'll change.'

The better class of tourist was shocked at this, and sympathized with the new-comers. Miss Bartlett, in reply, opened her mouth as little as possible, and said:

'Thank you very much indeed: that is out of the question.'

'Why?' said the old man, with both fists on the table.

'Because it is quite out of the question, thank you.'

'You see, we don't like to take—' began Lucy.

Her cousin again repressed her.

'But why?' he persisted. 'Women like looking at a view; men don't.' And he thumped with his fists like a naughty child, and turned to his son, saying, 'George, persuade them!'

'It's so obvious they should have the rooms,' said the son. 'There's nothing else to say.'

He did not look at the ladies as he spoke, but his voice was perplexed and sorrowful. Lucy, too, was perplexed; but she saw that they were in for what is known as 'quite a scene,' and she had an odd feeling that whenever these ill-bred tourists spoke the contest widened and deepened till it dealt, not with rooms and views, but with—well, with something quite different, whose existence she had not realized before. Now the old man attacked Miss Bartlett almost violently: Why should she not change? What possible objection had she? They would clear out in half an hour.

Miss Bartlett, though skilled in the delicacies of conversation, was powerless in the presence of brutality. It was impossible to snub anyone so gross. Her face reddened with displeasure. She looked around as much as to say, 'Are you all like this?' And two little old ladies, who were sitting farther up the table, with shawls hanging over the backs of the chairs, looked back, clearly indicating 'We are not; we are genteel.'

'Eat your dinner, dear,' she said to Lucy, and began to toy again with the meat that she had once censured.

Lucy mumbled that those seemed very odd people opposite.

'Eat your dinner, dear. This pension is a failure. To-morrow we will make a change.'

Hardly had she announced this fell decision when she reversed it. The curtains at the end of the room parted, and revealed a clergyman, stout but attractive, who hurried forward to take his place at the table, cheerfully apologizing for his lateness. Lucy, who had not yet acquired decency, at once rose to her feet, exclaiming: 'Oh, oh! Why, it's Mr Beebe! Oh, how perfectly lovely! Oh, Charlotte, we must stop now, however bad the rooms are. Oh!'

Miss Bartlett said, with more restraint:

'How do you do, Mr Beebe? I expect that you have forgotten us: Miss Bartlett and Miss Honeychurch, who were at Tunbridge Wells when you helped the vicar of St Peter's that very cold Easter.'

The clergyman, who had the air of one on a holiday, did not remember the ladies quite as clearly as they remembered him. But he came forward pleasantly enough and accepted the chair into which he was beckoned by Lucy.

'I *am* so glad to see you,' said the girl, who was in a state of spiritual starvation, and would have been glad to see the waiter if her cousin had permitted it. 'Just fancy how small the world is. Summer Street, too, makes it so specially funny.'

'Miss Honeychurch lives in the parish of Summer Street,' said Miss Bartlett, filling up the gap, 'and she happened to tell me in the course of conversation that you have just accepted the living—'

'Yes, I heard from mother so last week. She didn't know that I knew you at Tunbridge Wells; but I wrote back at once, and I said: "Mr Beebe is—"'

'Quite right,' said the clergyman. 'I move into the Rectory at Summer Street next June. I am lucky to be appointed to such a charming neighbourhood.'

'Oh, how glad I am! The name of our house is Windy Corner.'

Mr Beebe bowed.

'There is mother and me generally, and my brother, though it's not often we get him to ch— The church is rather far off, I mean.'

'Lucy dearest, let Mr Beebe eat his dinner.'

'I am eating it, thank you, and enjoying it.'

He preferred to talk to Lucy, whose playing he remembered, rather than to Miss Bartlett, who probably remembered his sermons. He asked the girl whether she knew Florence well, and was informed at some length that she had never been there before. It is delightful to advise a new-comer, and he was first in the field.

'Don't neglect the country round,' his advice concluded. 'The first fine afternoon drive up to Fiesole, and round by Settignano, or something of that sort.'

'No!' cried a voice from the top of the table. 'Mr Beebe, you are wrong. The first fine afternoon your ladies must go to Prato.'

'That lady looks so clever,' whispered Miss Bartlett to her cousin. 'We are in luck.'

And, indeed, a perfect torrent of information burst on them. People told them what to see, when to see it, how to stop the electric trams, how to get rid of the beggars, how much to give for a vellum blotter, how much the place would grow upon them. The Pension Bertolini had decided, almost enthusiastically, that they would do. Whichever way they looked, kind ladies smiled and shouted at them. And above all rose the voice of the clever lady, crying: 'Prato! They must go to Prato. That place is too sweetly squalid for words. I love it; I revel in shaking off the trammels of respectability as you know.'

The young man named George glanced at the clever lady, and then returned moodily to his plate. Obviously he and his father did not do. Lucy, in the midst of her success, found time to wish they did. It gave her no extra pleasure that anyone should be left in the cold; and when she rose to go, she turned back and gave the two outsiders a nervous little bow.

The father did not see it; the son acknowledged it, not by another bow, but by raising his eyebrows and smiling; he seemed to be smiling across something.

She hastened after her cousin, who had already disappeared through the curtains—curtains which smote one in the face, and seemed heavy with more than cloth. Beyond them stood the unreliable Signora, bowing good-evening to her guests, and supported by 'Enery, her little boy, and Victorier, her daughter. It made a curious little scene, this attempt of the Cockney to convey the grace and geniality of the South. And even more curious was the drawing-room, which attempted to rival the solid comfort of a Bloomsbury boarding-house. Was this really Italy?

Miss Bartlett was already seated on a tightly stuffed arm-chair, which had the colour and the contours of a tomato. She was talking to Mr Beebe, and as she spoke, her long narrow head drove backwards and forwards, slowly, regularly, as though she were demolishing some invisible obstacle. 'We are most grateful to you,' she was saying. 'The first evening means so much. When you arrived we were in for a peculiarly *mauvais quart d'heure*.'

He expressed his regret.

'Do you, by any chance, know the name of an old man who sat opposite us at dinner?'

'Emerson.'

'Is he a friend of yours?'

'We are friendly—as one is in pensions.'

'Then I will say no more.'

He pressed her very slightly, and she said more.

'I am, as it were,' she concluded, 'the chaperon of my young cousin, Lucy, and it would be a serious thing if I put her under an obligation to people of whom we knew nothing. His manner was somewhat unfortunate. I hope I acted for the best.'

'You acted very naturally,' said he. He seemed thoughtful, and after a few moments added: 'All the same, I don't think much harm would have come of accepting.'

'No *harm*, of course. But we could not be under an obligation.'

'He is rather a peculiar man.' Again he hesitated, and then said gently: 'I think he would not take advantage of your acceptance, nor expect you to show gratitude. He has the merit–if it is one–of saying exactly what he means. He has rooms he does not value, and he thinks you would value them. He no more thought of putting you under an obligation than he thought of being polite. It is so difficult–at least, I find it difficult–to understand people who speak the truth.'

Lucy was pleased, and said: 'I was hoping that he was nice; I do so always hope that people will be nice.'

'I think he is; nice and tiresome. I differ from him on almost every point of any importance, and so, I expect–I may say I hope–you will differ. But his is a type one disagrees with rather than deplores. When he first came here he not unnaturally put people's backs up. He has no tact and no manners–I don't mean by that that he has bad manners–and he will not keep his opinions to himself. We nearly complained about him to our depressing Signora, but I am glad to say we thought better of it.'

'Am I to conclude,' said Miss Bartlett, 'that he is a Socialist?'

Mr Beebe accepted the convenient word, not without a slight twitching of the lips.

'And presumably he has brought up his son to be a Socialist, too?'

'I hardly know George, for he hasn't learnt to talk yet. He seems a nice creature, and I think he has brains. Of course, he has all his father's mannerisms, and it is quite possible that he, too, may be a Socialist.'

'Oh, you relieve me,' said Miss Bartlett. 'So you think I ought to have accepted their offer? You feel I have been narrow-minded and suspicious?'

'Not at all,' he answered; 'I never suggested that.'

'But ought I not to apologize, at all events, for my apparent rudeness?'

He replied, with some irritation, that it would be quite unnecessary, and got up from his seat to go to the smoking-room.

'Was I a bore?' said Miss Bartlett, as soon as he had disappeared. 'Why didn't you talk, Lucy? He prefers young people, I'm sure. I do hope I haven't monopolized him. I hoped you would have him all the evening, as well as all dinner-time.'

'He is nice,' exclaimed Lucy. 'Just what I remember. He seems to see good in every one. No one would take him for a clergyman.'

'My dear Lucia—'

'Well, you know what I mean. And you know how clergymen generally laugh; Mr Beebe laughs just like an ordinary man.'

'Funny girl! How you remind me of your mother. I wonder if she will approve of Mr Beebe.'

'I'm sure she will; and so will Freddy.'

'I think every one at Windy Corner will approve; it is the fashionable world. I am used to Tunbridge Wells, where we are all hopelessly behind the times.'

'Yes,' said Lucy despondently.

There was a haze of disapproval in the air, but whether the disapproval was of herself, or of Mr Beebe, or of the fashionable world at Windy Corner, or of the narrow world at Tunbridge Wells, she could not determine. She tried to locate it, but as usual she blundered. Miss Bartlett sedulously denied disapproving of anyone, and added: 'I am afraid you are finding me a very depressing companion.'

And the girl again thought: 'I must have been selfish or unkind; I must be more careful. It is so dreadful for Charlotte, being poor.'

Fortunately one of the little old ladies, who for some time had been smiling very benignly, now approached and asked if she might be allowed to sit where Mr Beebe had sat. Permission granted, she began to chatter gently about Italy, the plunge it had been to come there, the gratifying success of the plunge, the improvement in her sister's health, the necessity of closing the bedroom windows at night, and of thoroughly emptying the water-bottles in the morning. She handled her subjects agreeably, and they were, perhaps, more worthy of attention than the high discourse upon Guelfs and Ghibellines which was proceeding tempestuously at the other end of the room. It was a real catastrophe, not a mere episode, that evening of hers at Venice, when she had found in her bedroom something that is one worse than a flea, though one better than something else.

'But here you are as safe as in England; Signora Bertolini is so English.'

'Yet our rooms smell,' said poor Lucy. 'We dread going to bed.'

'Ah, then you look into the court.' She sighed. 'If only Mr Emerson was more tactful! We were so sorry for you at dinner.'

'I think he was meaning to be kind.'

'Undoubtedly he was,' said Miss Bartlett. 'Mr Beebe has just been scolding me for my suspicious nature. Of course, I was holding back on my cousin's account.'

'Of course,' said the little old lady; and they murmured that one could not be too careful with a young girl.

Lucy tried to look demure, but could not help feeling a great fool. No one was careful with her at home; or, at all events, she had not noticed it.

'About old Mr Emerson—I hardly know. No, he is not tactful; yet, have you ever noticed that there are people who do things which are most indelicate, and yet at the same time—beautiful?'

'Beautiful?' said Miss Bartlett, puzzled at the word. 'Are not beauty and delicacy the same?'

'So one would have thought,' said the other helplessly. 'But things are so difficult, I sometimes think.'

She proceeded no further into things, for Mr Beebe reappeared, looking extremely pleasant.

'Miss Bartlett,' he cried, 'it's all right about the rooms. I'm so glad. Mr Emerson was talking about it in the smoking-room, and, knowing what I did, I encouraged him to make the offer again. He has let me come and ask you. He would be so pleased.'

'Oh, Charlotte,' cried Lucy to her cousin, 'we must have the rooms now. The old man is just as nice and kind as he can be.'

Miss Bartlett was silent.

'I fear,' said Mr Beebe, after a pause, 'that I have been officious. I must apologize for my interference.'

Gravely displeased, he turned to go. Not till then did Miss Bartlett reply: 'My own wishes, dearest Lucy, are unimportant in comparison with yours. It would be hard indeed if I stopped you doing as you liked at Florence, when I am only here through your kindness. If you wish me to turn these gentlemen out of their rooms, I will do it. Would you then, Mr Beebe, kindly tell Mr Emerson that I accept his kind offer, and then conduct him to me, in order that I may thank him personally?'

She raised her voice as she spoke; it was heard all over the drawing-room, and silenced the Guelfs and the Ghibellines. The clergyman, inwardly cursing the female sex, bowed and departed with her message.

'Remember, Lucy, I alone am implicated in this. I do not wish the acceptance to come from you. Grant me that, at all events.'

Mr Beebe was back, saying rather nervously:

'Mr Emerson is engaged, but here is his son instead.'

The young man gazed down on the three ladies, who felt seated on the floor, so low were their chairs.

'My father,' he said, 'is in his bath, so you cannot thank him personally. But any message given by you to me will be given by me to him as soon as he comes out.'

Miss Bartlett was unequal to the bath. All her barbed civilities came forth wrong end first. Young Mr Emerson scored a notable triumph to the delight of Mr Beebe and to the secret delight of Lucy.

'Poor young man!' said Miss Bartlett, as soon as he had gone. 'How angry he is with his father about the rooms! It is all he can do to keep polite.'

'In half an hour or so your rooms will be ready,' said Mr Beebe. Then, looking rather thoughtfully at the two cousins, he retired to his own room, to write up his philosophic diary.

'Oh dear!' breathed the little old lady, and shuddered as if all the winds of heaven had entered the apartment. 'Gentlemen sometimes do not realize—' Her voice faded away, but Miss Bartlett seemed to understand, and a conversation developed, in which gentlemen who did not thoroughly realize played a principal part. Lucy, not realizing either, was reduced to literature. Taking up Baedeker's 'Handbook to Northern Italy,' she committed to memory the most important dates of Florentine History. For she was determined to enjoy herself on the morrow. Thus the half-hour crept profitably away, and at last Miss Bartlett rose with a sigh, and said:

'I think one might venture now. No, Lucy, do not stir. I will superintend the move.'

'How you do do everything,' said Lucy.

'Naturally, dear. It is my affair.'

'But I would like to help you.'

'No, dear.'

Charlotte's energy! And her unselfishness! She had been thus all her life, but really, on this Italian tour, she was surpassing herself. So Lucy felt, or strove to feel. And yet—there was a rebellious spirit in her which wondered whether the acceptance might not have been less delicate and more beautiful. At all events, she entered her own room without any feeling of joy.

'I want to explain,' said Miss Bartlett, 'why it is that I have taken the largest room. Naturally, of course, I should have given it to you; but I happen to know that it belongs to the young man, and I was sure your mother would not like it.'

Lucy was bewildered.

'If you are to accept a favour, it is more suitable you should be under an obligation to his father than to him. I am a woman of the world, in my small way, and I know where things lead to. However, Mr Beebe is a guarantee of a sort that they will not presume on this.'

'Mother wouldn't mind, I'm sure,' said Lucy, but again had the sense of larger and unsuspected issues.

Miss Bartlett only sighed, and enveloped her in a protecting embrace as she wished her good-night. It gave Lucy the sensation of a fog, and when she reached her own room she opened the window and breathed the clean night air, thinking of the kind old man who had enabled her to see the lights dancing in the Arno and the cypresses of San Miniato, and the foot-hills of the Apennines, black against the rising moon.

Miss Bartlett, in her room, fastened the window-shutters and locked the door, and then made a tour of the apartment to see where the cupboards led, and whether there were any oubliettes or secret entrances. It was then that she saw, pinned up over the wash-stand, a sheet of paper on which was scrawled an enormous note of interrogation. Nothing more.

'What does it mean?' she thought, and she examined it carefully by the light of a candle. Meaningless at first, it gradually became menacing, obnoxious, portentous with evil. She was seized with an impulse to destroy it, but fortunately remembered that she had no right to do so, since it must be the property of young Mr Emerson. So she unpinned it carefully, and put it between two pieces of blotting-paper to keep it clean for him. Then she completed her inspection of the room, sighed heavily according to her habit, and went to bed.

Chapter Two

In Santa Croce with no Baedeker

It was pleasant to wake up in Florence, to open the eyes upon a bright bare room, with a floor of red tiles which look clean though they are not; with a painted ceiling whereon pink griffins and blue amorini sport in a forest of yellow violins and bassoons. It was pleasant, too, to fling wide the windows, pinching the fingers in unfamiliar fastenings, to lean out into sunshine with beautiful hills and trees and marble churches opposite, and, close below, the Arno, gurgling against the embankment of the road.

Over the river men were at work with spades and sieves on the sandy foreshore, and on the river was a boat, also diligently employed for some mysterious end. An electric tram came rushing underneath the window. No one was inside it, except one tourist; but its platforms were overflowing with Italians, who preferred to stand. Children tried to hang on behind, and the conductor, with no malice, spat in their faces to make them let go. Then soldiers appeared–good-looking, under-sized men–wearing each a knap-sack covered with mangy fur, and a great-coat which had been cut for some larger soldier. Beside them walked officers, looking foolish and fierce, and before them went little boys, turning somersaults in time with the band. The tramcar became entangled in their ranks, and moved on painfully, like a caterpillar in a swarm of ants. One of the little boys fell down, and some white bullocks came out of an archway. Indeed, if it had not been for the good advice of an old man who was selling button-hooks, the road might never have got clear.

Over such trivialities as these many a valuable hour may slip away, and the traveller who has gone to Italy to study the tactile values of Giotto, or the corruption of the Papacy, may return remembering nothing but the blue sky and the men and women who live under it. So it was as well that Miss Bartlett should tap and come in, and having commented on Lucy's leaving the door unlocked, and on her leaning out of the window before she was fully dressed, should urge her to hasten herself, or the best of the day would be gone. By the time Lucy was ready her cousin had done her breakfast, and was listening to the clever lady among the crumbs.

A conversation then ensued, on not unfamiliar lines. Miss Bartlett was, after all, a wee bit tired, and thought they had better spend the morning settling in; unless Lucy would at all like to go out? Lucy would rather like to go out, as it was her first day in Florence, but, of course, she could go alone. Miss Bartlett could not allow this. Of course she would accompany Lucy everywhere. Oh, certainly not; Lucy would stop with her cousin. Oh no! that would never do! Oh yes!

At this point the clever lady broke in.

'If it is Mrs Grundy who is troubling you, I do assure you that you can neglect the good person. Being English, Miss Honeychurch will be perfectly safe. Italians understand. A dear friend of mine, Contessa Baroncelli, has two daughters, and when she cannot send a maid to school with them, she lets them go in sailor-hats instead. Every one takes them for English, you see, especially if their hair is strained tightly behind.'

Miss Bartlett was unconvinced by the safety of Contessa Baroncelli's daughters. She was determined to take Lucy herself, her head not being so very bad. The clever lady then said that she was going to spend a long morn-ing in Santa Croce, and if Lucy would come too, she would be delighted.

'I will take you by a dear dirty back way, Miss Honeychurch, and if you bring me luck, we shall have an adventure.'

Lucy said that this was most kind, and at once opened the Baedeker, to see where Santa Croce was.

'Tut, tut! Miss Lucy! I hope we shall soon emancipate you from Baedeker.

He does but touch the surface of things. As to the true Italy–he does not even dream of it. The true Italy is only to be found by patient observation.'

This sounded very interesting, and Lucy hurried over her breakfast, and started with her new friend in high spirits. Italy was coming at last. The Cockney Signora and her works had vanished like a bad dream.

Miss Lavish–for that was the clever lady's name–turned to the right along the sunny Lung' Arno. How delightfully warm! But a wind down the side streets that cut like a knife, didn't it? Ponte alle Grazie–particularly interesting, mentioned by Dante. San Miniato–beautiful as well as interesting; the crucifix that kissed a murderer–Miss Honeychurch would remember the story. The men on the river were fishing. (Untrue; but then, so is most information.) Then Miss Lavish darted under the archway of the white bullocks, and she stopped, and she cried:

'A smell! a true Florentine smell! Every city, let me teach you, has its own smell.'

'Is it a very nice smell?' said Lucy, who had inherited from her mother a distaste to dirt.

'One doesn't come to Italy for niceness,' was the retort; 'one comes for life. Buon giorno! Buon giorno!' bowing right and left. 'Look at that adorable wine-cart! How the driver stares at us, dear, simple soul!'

So Miss Lavish proceeded through the streets of the city of Florence, short, fidgety, and playful as a kitten, though without a kitten's grace. It was a treat for the girl to be with anyone so clever and so cheerful; and a blue military cloak, such as an Italian officer wears, only increased the sense of festivity.

'Buon giorno! Take the word of an old woman, Miss Lucy: you will never repent of a little civility to your inferiors. *That* is the true democracy. Though I am a real Radical as well. There, now you're shocked.'

'Indeed, I'm not!' exclaimed Lucy. 'We are Radicals, too, out and out. My father always voted for Mr Gladstone, until he was so dreadful about Ireland.'

'I see, I see. And now you have gone over to the enemy.'

'Oh, please—! If my father was alive, I am sure he would vote Radical again now that Ireland is all right. And as it is, the glass over our front-door was broken last election, and Freddy is sure it was the Tories; but mother says nonsense, a tramp.'

'Shameful! A manufacturing district, I suppose?'

'No–in the Surrey hills. About five miles from Dorking, looking over the Weald.'

Miss Lavish seemed interested, and slackened her trot.

'What a delightful part; I know it so well. It is full of the very nicest people. Do you know Sir Harry Otway–a Radical if ever there was?'

'Very well indeed.'

'And old Mrs Butterworth the philanthropist?'

'Why, she rents a field of us! How funny!'

Miss Lavish looked at the narrow ribbon of sky, and murmured:

'Oh, you have property in Surrey?'

'Hardly any,' said Lucy, fearful of being thought a snob. 'Only thirty acres—just the garden, all downhill, and some fields.'

Miss Lavish was not disgusted, and said it was just the size of her aunt's Suffolk estate. Italy receded. They tried to remember the last name of Lady Louisa someone, who had taken a house near Summer Street the other year, but she had not liked it, which was odd of her. And just as Miss Lavish had got the name she broke off and exclaimed:

'Bless us! Bless us and save us! We've lost the way.'

Certainly they had seemed a long time in reaching Santa Croce, the tower of which had been plainly visible from the landing window. But Miss Lavish had said so much about knowing her Florence by heart, that Lucy had followed her with no misgivings.

'Lost! lost! My dear Miss Lucy, during our political diatribes we have taken a wrong turning. How those horrid Conservatives would jeer at us! What are we to do? Two lone females in an unknown town. Now, this is what *I* call an adventure.'

Lucy, who wanted to see Santa Croce, suggested, as a possible solution, that they should ask the way there.

'Oh, but that is the word of a craven! And no, you are not, not, *not* to look at your Baedeker. Give it to me; I shan't let you carry it. We will simply drift.'

Accordingly they drifted through a series of those grey-brown streets, neither commodious nor picturesque, in which the eastern quarter of the city abounds. Lucy soon lost interest in the discontent of Lady Louisa, and became discontented herself. For one ravishing moment Italy appeared. She stood in the Square of the Annunziata and saw in the living terra-cotta those divine babies whom no cheap reproduction can ever stale. There they stood, with their shining limbs bursting from the garments of charity, and their strong white arms extended against circlets of heaven. Lucy thought she had never seen anything more beautiful; but Miss Lavish, with a shriek of dismay, dragged her forward, declaring that they were out of their path now by at least a mile.

The hour was approaching at which the continental breakfast begins, or rather ceases, to tell, and the ladies bought some hot chestnut paste out of a little shop, because it looked so typical. It tasted partly of the paper in which it was wrapped, partly of hair-oil, partly of the great unknown. But it gave them strength to drift into another Piazza, large and dusty, on the farther side of which rose a black-and-white façade of surpassing ugliness. Miss Lavish spoke to it dramatically. It was Santa Croce. The adventure was over.

'Stop a minute; let those two people go on, or I shall have to speak to them. I do detest conventional intercourse. Nasty! they are going into the church, too. Oh, the Britisher abroad!'

'We sat opposite them at dinner last night. They have given us their rooms. They were so very kind.'

'Look at their figures!' laughed Miss Lavish. 'They walk through my Italy like a pair of cows. It's very naughty of me, but I would like to set an examination paper at Dover, and turn back every tourist who couldn't pass it.'

'What would you ask us?'

Miss Lavish laid her hand pleasantly on Lucy's arm, as if to suggest that she, at all events, would get full marks. In this exalted mood they reached the steps of the great church, and were about to enter it when Miss Lavish stopped, squeaked, flung up her arms, and cried:

'There goes my local-colour box! I must have a word with him!'

And in a moment she was away over the Piazza, her military cloak flapping in the wind; nor did she slacken speed till she caught up an old man with white whiskers, and nipped him playfully upon the arm.

Lucy waited for nearly ten minutes. Then she began to get tired. The beggars worried her, the dust blew in her eyes, and she remembered that a young girl ought not to loiter in public places. She descended slowly into the Piazza with the intention of rejoining Miss Lavish, who was really almost too original. But at that moment Miss Lavish and her local-colour box moved also, and disappeared down a side street, both gesticulating largely.

Tears of indignation came to Lucy's eyes—partly because Miss Lavish had jilted her, partly because she had taken her Baedeker. How could she find her way home? How could she find her way about in Santa Croce? Her first morning was ruined, and she might never be in Florence again. A few minutes ago she had been all high spirits, talking as a woman of culture, and half-persuading herself that she was full of originality. Now she entered the church depressed and humiliated, not even able to remember whether it was built by the Franciscans or the Dominicans.

Of course, it must be a wonderful building. But how like a barn! And how very cold! Of course, it contained frescoes by Giotto, in the presence of whose tactile values she was capable of feeling what was proper. But who was to tell her which they were? She walked about disdainfully, unwilling to be enthusiastic over monuments of uncertain authorship or date. There was no one even to tell her which, of all the sepulchral slabs that paved the nave and transepts, was the one that was really beautiful, the one that had been most praised by Mr Ruskin.

Then the pernicious charm of Italy worked on her, and, instead of acquiring information, she began to be happy. She puzzled out the Italian notices—the notice that forbade people to introduce dogs into the church—the notice that prayed people, in the interests of health and out of respect to the sacred edifice in which they found themselves, not to spit. She watched the tourists; their noses were as red as their Baedekers, so cold was Santa Croce. She beheld the horrible fate that overtook three Papists—two he-babies and a she-baby—who began their career by sousing each other with the Holy Water, and then proceeded to the Machiavelli memorial, dripping, but hallowed. Advancing towards it very slowly and from immense distances, they touched the stone with their fingers, with their handkerchiefs, with their heads, and then retreated. What could this mean? They did it again and again. Then Lucy realized that they had mistaken Machiavelli for some saint, and by continual contact with his shrine were hoping to acquire virtue. Punishment followed quickly. The smallest he-baby stumbled over one of the sepulchral slabs so much admired by Mr Ruskin, and entangled his feet in the features of a recumbent bishop.

Protestant as she was, Lucy darted forward. She was too late. He fell heavily upon the prelate's upturned toes.

'Hateful bishop!' exclaimed the voice of Old Mr Emerson, who had darted forward also. 'Hard in life, hard in death. Go out into the sunshine, little boy, and kiss your hand to the sun, for that is where you ought to be. Intolerable bishop!'

The child screamed frantically at these words, and at these dreadful people who picked him up, dusted him, rubbed his bruises, and told him not to be superstitious.

'Look at him!' said Mr Emerson to Lucy. 'Here's a mess: a baby hurt, cold, and frightened! But what else can you expect from a church?'

The child's legs had become as melting wax. Each time that old Mr Emerson and Lucy set it erect it collapsed with a roar. Fortunately an Italian lady, who ought to have been saying her prayers, came to the rescue. By some mysterious virtue, which mothers alone possess, she stiffened the little boy's backbone and imparted strength to his knees. He stood. Still gibbering with agitation, he walked away.

'You are a clever woman,' said Mr Emerson. 'You have done more than all the relics in the world. I am not of your creed, but I do believe in those who make their fellow-creatures happy. There is no scheme of the universe—'

He paused for a phrase.

'Niente,' said the Italian lady, and returned to her prayers.

'I'm not sure she understands English,' suggested Lucy.

In her chastened mood she no longer despised the Emersons. She was determined to be gracious to them, beautiful rather than delicate, and, if possible, to erase Miss Bartlett's civility by some gracious reference to the pleasant rooms.

'That woman understands everything,' was Mr Emerson's reply. 'But what are you doing here? Are you doing the church? Are you through with the church?'

'No,' cried Lucy, remembering her grievance. 'I came here with Miss Lavish, who was to explain everything; and just by the door—it is too bad!—she simply ran away, and after waiting quite a time, I had to come in by myself.'

'Why shouldn't you?' said Mr Emerson.

'Yes, why shouldn't you come by yourself?' said the son, addressing the young lady for the first time.

'But Miss Lavish has even taken away Baedeker.'

'Baedeker?' said Mr Emerson. 'I'm glad it's *that* that you minded. It's worth minding, the loss of a Baedeker. *That's* worth minding.'

Lucy was puzzled. She was again conscious of some new idea, and was not sure whither it would lead her.

'If you've no Baedeker,' said the son, 'you'd better join us.'

Was this where the idea would lead? She took refuge in her dignity.

'Thank you very much, but I could not think of that. I hope you do not suppose that I came to join on to you. I really came to help with the child, and to thank you for so kindly giving us your rooms last night. I hope that you have not been put to any great inconvenience.'

'My dear,' said the old man gently, 'I think that you are repeating what you have heard older people say. You are pretending to be touchy; but you are not really. Stop being so tiresome, and tell me instead what part of the church you want to see. To take you to it will be a real pleasure.'

Now, this was abominably impertinent, and she ought to have been furious. But it is sometimes as difficult to lose one's temper as it is difficult at other times to keep it. Lucy could not get cross. Mr Emerson was an old man, and surely a girl might humour him. On the other hand, his son was a young man, and she felt that a girl ought to be offended with him, or at all events be offended before him. It was at him that she gazed before replying.

'I am not touchy, I hope. It is the Giottos that I want to see, if you will kindly tell me which they are.'

The son nodded. With a look of sombre satisfaction, he led the way to the Peruzzi Chapel. There was a hint of the teacher about him. She felt like a child in school who had answered a question rightly.

The chapel was already filled with an earnest congregation, and out of them rose the voice of a lecturer, directing them how to worship Giotto, not by tactile valuations, but by the standards of the spirit.

'Remember,' he was saying, 'the facts about this church of Santa Croce; how it was built by faith in the full fervour of medievalism, before any taint of the Renaissance had appeared. Observe how Giotto in these frescoes—now, unhappily, ruined by restoration—is untroubled by the snares of anatomy and perspective. Could anything be more majestic, more pathetic, beautiful, true? How little, we feel, avails knowledge and technical cleverness against a man who truly feels!'

'No!' exclaimed Mr Emerson, in much too loud a voice for church. 'Remember nothing of the sort! Built by faith indeed! That simply means the workmen weren't paid properly. And as for the frescoes, I see no truth in them. Look at that fat man in blue! He must weigh as much as I do, and he is shooting into the sky like an air-balloon.'

He was referring to the fresco of the Ascension of St John. Inside, the lecturer's voice faltered, as well it might. The audience shifted uneasily, and so did Lucy. She was sure that she ought not to be with these men; but they had cast a spell over her. They were so serious and so strange that she could not remember how to behave.

'Now, did this happen, or didn't it? Yes or no?'

George replied.

'It happened like this, if it happened at all. I would rather go up to heaven by myself than be pushed by cherubs; and if I got there I should like my friends to lean out of it, just as they do here.'

'You will never go up,' said his father. 'You and I, dear boy, will lie at peace in the earth that bore us, and our names will disappear as surely as our work survives.'

'Some of the people can only see the empty grave, not the saint, whoever he is, going up. It did happen like that, if it happened at all.'

'Pardon me,' said a frigid voice. 'The chapel is somewhat small for two parties. We will incommode you no longer.'

The lecturer was a clergyman, and his audience must be also his flock, for they held Prayer Books as well as guide-books in their hands. They filed out of the chapel in silence. Amongst them were the two little old ladies of the Pension Bertolini–Miss Teresa and Miss Catharine Alan.

'Stop!' cried Mr Emerson. 'There's plenty of room for us all. Stop!'

The procession disappeared without a word. Soon the lecturer could be heard in the next chapel, describing the life of St Francis.

'George, I do believe that clergyman is the Brixton curate.'

George went into the next chapel and returned, saying, 'Perhaps he is. I don't remember.'

'Then I had better speak to him and remind him who I am. It's that Mr Eager. Why did he go? Did we talk too loud? How vexatious! I shall go and say we are sorry. Hadn't I better? Then perhaps he will come back.'

'He will not come back,' said George.

But Mr Emerson, contrite and unhappy, hurried away to apologize to the Rev. Cuthbert Eager. Lucy, apparently absorbed in a lunette, could hear the lecture again interrupted, the anxious, aggressive voice of the old man, the curt, injured replies of his opponent. The son, who took every little contretemps as if it were a tragedy, was listening also.

'My father has that effect on nearly every one,' he informed her. 'He will try to be kind.'

'I hope we all try,' said she, smiling nervously.

'Because we think it improves our characters. But he is kind to people because he loves them; and they find him out, and are offended, or frightened.'

'How silly of them!' said Lucy, though in her heart she sympathized; 'I think that a kind action done tactfully—'

'Tact!'

He threw up his head in disdain. Apparently she had given the wrong answer. She watched the singular creature pace up and down the chapel. For a young man his face was rugged, and–until the shadows fell upon it–hard. Enshadowed, it sprang into tenderness. She saw him once again at Rome, on the ceiling of the Sistine Chapel, carrying a burden of acorns. Healthy and muscular, he yet gave her the feeling of greyness, of tragedy that might only find solution in the night. The feeling soon passed; it was unlike her to have entertained anything so subtle. Born of silence and of unknown emotion, it passed when Mr Emerson returned, and she could re-enter the world of rapid talk, which was alone familiar to her.

'Were you snubbed?' asked his son tranquilly.

'But we have spoilt the pleasure of I don't know how many people. They won't come back.'

'. . . full of innate sympathy . . . quickness to perceive good in others . . . vision of the brotherhood of man . . .' Scraps of the lecture on St Francis came floating round the partition wall.

'Don't let us spoil yours,' he continued to Lucy. 'Have you looked at those saints?'

'Yes,' said Lucy. 'They are lovely. Do you know which is the tombstone that is praised in Ruskin?'

He did not know, and suggested that they should try to guess it. George, rather to her relief, refused to move, and she and the old man wandered not unpleasantly about Santa Croce, which, though it is like a barn, has harvested many beautiful things inside its walls. There were also beggars to avoid, and guides to dodge round the pillars, and an old lady with her dog, and here and there was a priest modestly edging to his Mass through the groups of tourists. But Mr Emerson was only half-interested. He watched the lecturer, whose success he believed that he had impaired, and then he anxiously watched his son.

'Why will he look at that fresco?' he said uneasily. 'I saw nothing in it.'

'I like Giotto,' she replied. 'It is so wonderful what they say about his tactile values. Though I like things like the Della Robbia babies better.'

'So you ought. A baby is worth a dozen saints. And my baby's worth the whole of Paradise, and as far as I can see he lives in Hell.'

Lucy again felt that this did not do.

'In Hell,' he repeated. 'He's unhappy.'

'Oh dear!' said Lucy.

'How can he be unhappy when he is strong and alive? What more is one to give him? And think how he has been brought up—free from all the super-stition and ignorance that lead men to hate one another in the name of God. With such an education as that, I thought he was bound to grow up happy.'

She was no theologian, but she felt that here was a very foolish old man, as well as a very irreligious one. She also felt that her mother might not like her talking to that kind of person, and that Charlotte would object most strongly.

'What are we to do with him?' he asked. 'He comes out for his holiday to Italy, and behaves—like that; like the little child who ought to have been playing, and who hurt himself upon the tombstone. Eh? What did you say?'

Lucy had made no suggestion. Suddenly he said:

'Now don't be stupid over this. I don't require you to fall in love with my boy, but I do think you might try and understand him. You are nearer his age, and if you let yourself go I am sure you are sensible. You might help me. He has known so few women, and you have the time. You stop here several weeks, I suppose? But let yourself go. You are inclined to get muddled, if I may judge from last night. Let yourself go. Pull out from the depths those thoughts that you do not understand, and spread them out in the sunlight and know the meaning of them. By understanding George you may learn to understand yourself. It will be good for both of you.'

To this extraordinary speech Lucy found no answer.

'I only know what it is that's wrong with him; not why it is.'

'And what is it?' asked Lucy fearfully, expecting some harrowing tale.

'The old trouble; things won't fit.'

'What things?'

'The things of the universe. It is quite true. They don't.'

'Oh, Mr Emerson, whatever do you mean?'

In his ordinary voice, so that she scarcely realized he was quoting poetry, he said:

> 'From far, from eve and morning,
>   And yon twelve-winded sky,
> The stuff of life to knit me
>   Blew hither: here am I.

George and I both know this, but why does it distress him? We know that we come from the winds, and that we shall return to them; that all life is perhaps a knot, a tangle, a blemish in the eternal smoothness. But why should this make us unhappy? Let us rather love one another, and work and rejoice. I don't believe in this world sorrow.'

Miss Honeychurch assented.

'Then make my boy think like us. Make him realize that by the side of the everlasting Why there is a Yes—a transitory Yes if you like, but a Yes.'

Suddenly she laughed; surely one ought to laugh. A young man melancholy because the universe wouldn't fit, because life was a tangle or a wind, or a Yes, or something!

'I'm very sorry,' she cried. 'You'll think me unfeeling, but—but—' Then she became matronly. 'Oh, but your son wants employment. Has he no particular hobby? Why, I myself have worries, but I can generally forget them at the piano; and collecting stamps did no end of good for my brother. Perhaps Italy bores him; you ought to try the Alps or the Lakes.'

The old man's face saddened, and he touched her gently with his hand. This did not alarm her; she thought that her advice had impressed him, and that he was thanking her for it. Indeed, he no longer alarmed her at all; she regarded him as a kind thing, but quite silly. Her feelings were as inflated spiritually as they had been an hour ago æsthetically, before she lost Baedeker. The dear George, now striding towards them over the tombstones, seemed both pitiable and absurd. He approached, his face in the shadow. He said:

'Miss Bartlett.'

'Oh, good gracious me!' said Lucy, suddenly collapsing and again seeing the whole of life in a new perspective. 'Where? Where?'

'In the nave.'

'I see. Those gossiping little old Miss Alans must have—' She checked herself.

'Poor girl!' exploded old Mr Emerson. 'Poor girl!'

She could not let this pass, for it was just what she was feeling herself.

'Poor girl? I fail to understand the point of that remark. I think myself a very fortunate girl, I assure you. I'm thoroughly happy, and having a splendid time. Pray don't waste time mourning over *me*. There's enough sorrow in the world, isn't there, without trying to invent it. Good-bye. Thank you both so much for all your kindness. Ah yes! there does come my cousin. A delightful morning! Santa Croce is a wonderful church.'

She rejoined her cousin.

Chapter Three

Music, Violets, and the Letter S

It so happened that Lucy, who found daily life rather chaotic, entered a more solid world when she opened the piano. She was then no longer either deferential or patronizing; no longer either a rebel or a slave. The kingdom of music is not the kingdom of this world; it will accept those whom breeding and intellect and culture have alike rejected. The commonplace person begins to play, and shoots into the empyrean without effort, whilst we look up, marvelling how he has escaped us, and thinking how we could worship him and love him, would he but translate his visions into human words, and his experiences into human actions. Perhaps he cannot; certainly he does not, or does so very seldom. Lucy had done so never.

She was no dazzling *exécutante*; her runs were not at all like strings of pearls, and she struck no more right notes than was suitable for one of her age and situation. Nor was she the passionate young lady, who performs so tragically on a summer's evening with the window open. Passion was there, but it could not be easily labelled; it slipped between love and hatred and jealousy, and all the furniture of the pictorial style. And she was tragical only in the sense that she was great, for she loved to play on the side of Victory. Victory of what and over what—that is more than the words of daily life can tell us. But that some sonatas of Beethoven are written tragic no one can gainsay; yet they can triumph or despair as the player decides, and Lucy had decided that they should triumph.

A very wet afternoon at the Bertolini permitted her to do the thing she really liked, and after lunch she opened the little draped piano. A few people lingered round and praised her playing, but finding that she made no reply, dispersed to their rooms to write up their diaries or to sleep. She took no notice of Mr Emerson looking for his son, nor of Miss Bartlett looking for Miss Lavish, nor of Miss Lavish looking for her cigarette-case. Like every true performer, she was intoxicated by the mere feel of the notes: they were fingers caressing her own; and by touch, not by sound alone, did she come to her desire.

Mr Beebe, sitting unnoticed in the window, pondered over this illogical element in Miss Honeychurch, and recalled the occasion at Tunbridge Wells when he had discovered it. It was at one of those entertainments where the upper classes entertain the lower. The seats were filled with a respectful audience, and the ladies and gentlemen of the parish, under the auspices of their vicar, sang, or recited, or imitated the drawing of a champagne cork. Among the promised items was 'Miss Honeychurch. Piano. Beethoven,' and Mr Beebe was wondering whether it would be 'Adelaida,' or the march of 'The Ruins of Athens,' when his composure was disturbed by the opening bars of Opus III. He was in suspense all through the introduction, for not until the pace quickens does one know what the performer intends. With the roar of the opening theme he knew that things were going extraordinarily; in the chords that herald the conclusion he heard the hammer strokes of victory. He was glad that she only played the first movement, for he could have paid no attention to the winding intricacies of the measure of nine-sixteen. The audience clapped, no less respectful. It was Mr Beebe who started the stamping; it was all that one could do.

'Who is she?' he asked the vicar afterwards.

'Cousin of one of my parishioners. I do not consider her choice of a piece happy. Beethoven is so usually simple and direct in his appeal that it is sheer perversity to choose a thing like that, which, if anything, disturbs.'

'Introduce me.'

'She will be delighted. She and Miss Bartlett are full of the praises of your sermon.'

'My sermon?' cried Mr Beebe. 'Why ever did she listen to it?'

When he was introduced he understood why, for Miss Honeychurch, disjoined from her music-stool, was only a young lady with a quantity of dark hair and a very pretty, pale, undeveloped face. She loved going to concerts, she loved stopping with her cousin, she loved iced coffee and meringues. He did not doubt that she loved his sermon also. But before he left Tunbridge Wells he made a remark to the vicar, which he now made to Lucy herself when she closed the little piano and moved dreamily towards him.

'If Miss Honeychurch ever takes to live as she plays, it will be very exciting—both for us and for her.'

Lucy at once re-entered daily life.

'Oh, what a funny thing! Some one said just the same to mother, and she said she trusted I should never live a duet.'

'Doesn't Mrs Honeychurch like music?'

'She doesn't mind it. But she doesn't like one to get excited over anything; she thinks I am silly about it. She thinks—I can't make out. Once, you know, I said that I liked my own playing better than anyone's. She has never got over it. Of course, I didn't mean that I played well; I only meant—'

'Of course,' said he, wondering why she bothered to explain.

'Music—' said Lucy, as if attempting some generality. She could not complete it, and looked out absently upon Italy in the wet. The whole life of the South was disorganized, and the most graceful nation in Europe had turned into formless lumps of clothes. The street and the river were dirty yellow, the bridge was dirty grey, and the hills were dirty purple. Somewhere in their folds were concealed Miss Lavish, and Miss Bartlett, who had chosen this afternoon to visit the Torre del Gallo.

'What about music?' said Mr Beebe.

'Poor Charlotte will be sopped,' was Lucy's reply.

The expedition was typical of Miss Bartlett, who would return cold, tired, hungry, and angelic, with a ruined skirt, a pulpy Baedeker, and a tickling cough in her throat. On another day, when the whole world was singing and the air ran into the mouth like wine, she would refuse to stir from the drawing-room, saying that she was an old thing, and no fit companion for a hearty girl.

'Miss Lavish has led your cousin astray. She hopes to find the true Italy in the wet, I believe.'

'Miss Lavish is so original,' murmured Lucy. This was the stock remark, the supreme achievement of the Pension Bertolini in the way of definition. Miss Lavish was so original. Mr Beebe had his doubts, but they would have been put down to clerical narrowness. For that, and for other reasons, he held his peace.

'Is it true,' continued Lucy in awe-struck tones, 'that Miss Lavish is writing a book?'

'They do say so.'

'What is it about?'

'It will be a novel,' replied Mr Beebe, 'dealing with modern Italy. Let me refer you for an account to Miss Catharine Alan, who uses words herself more admirably than anyone I know.'

'I wish Miss Lavish would tell me herself. We started such friends. But I don't think she ought to have run away with Baedeker that morning in Santa Croce. Charlotte was most annoyed at finding me practically alone, and so I couldn't help being a little annoyed with Miss Lavish.'

'The two ladies, at all events, have made it up.'

He was interested in the sudden friendship between women so apparently dissimilar as Miss Bartlett and Miss Lavish. They were always in each other's company, with Lucy a slighted third. Miss Lavish he believed he understood, but Miss Bartlett might reveal unknown depths of strangeness, though not, perhaps, of meaning. Was Italy deflecting her from the path of prim chaperon, which he had assigned to her at Tunbridge Wells? All his life he had loved to study maiden ladies; they were his speciality, and his profession had provided him with ample opportunities for the work. Girls like Lucy were charming to look at, but Mr Beebe was, from rather profound reasons, somewhat chilly in his attitude towards the other sex, and preferred to be interested rather than enthralled.

Lucy, for the third time, said that poor Charlotte would be sopped. The Arno was rising in flood, washing away the traces of the little carts upon the foreshore. But in the south-west there had appeared a dull haze of yellow, which might mean better weather if it did not mean worse. She opened the window to inspect, and a cold blast entered the room, drawing a plaintive cry from Miss Catharine Alan, who entered at the same moment by the door.

'Oh, dear Miss Honeychurch, you will catch a chill! And Mr Beebe here besides. Who would suppose this is Italy? There is my sister actually nursing the hot-water can: no comforts or proper provisions.'

She sidled towards them and sat down, self-conscious as she always was on entering a room which contained one man, or a man and one woman.

'I could hear your beautiful playing, Miss Honeychurch, though I was in my room with the door shut. Doors shut; indeed, most necessary. No one has the least idea of privacy in this country. And one person catches it from another.'

Lucy answered suitably. Mr Beebe was not able to tell the ladies of his adventure at Modena, where the chambermaid burst in upon him in his bath, exclaiming cheerfully, 'Fa niente, sono vecchia.' He contented himself with saying: 'I quite agree with you, Miss Alan. The Italians are a most unpleasant people. They pry everywhere, they see everything, and they know what we want before we know it ourselves. We are at their mercy. They read our thoughts, they foretell our desires. From the cab-driver down to–to Giotto, they turn us inside out, and I resent it. Yet in their heart of hearts they are–how superficial! They have no conception of the intellectual life. How right is Signora Bertolini, who exclaimed to me the other day: "Ho, Mr Beebe, if you knew what I suffer over the children's edjucaishion! *Hi* won't 'ave my little Victorier taught by a hignorant Italian what can't explain nothink!"'

Miss Alan did not follow, but gathered that she was being mocked in an agreeable way. Her sister was a little disappointed in Mr Beebe, having expected better things from a clergyman whose head was bald and who wore a pair of russet whiskers. Indeed, who would have supposed that tolerance, sympathy, and a sense of humour would inhabit that militant form?

In the midst of her satisfaction she continued to sidle, and at last the cause was disclosed. From the chair beneath her she extracted a gun-metal cigarette case, on which were powdered in turquoise the initials 'E.L.'

'That belongs to Lavish,' said the clergyman. 'A good fellow, Lavish, but I wish she'd start a pipe.'

'Oh, Mr Beebe,' said Miss Alan, divided between awe and mirth. 'Indeed, though it is dreadful of her to smoke, it is not quite as dreadful as you suppose. She took to it, practically in despair, after her life's work was carried away in a landslip. Surely that makes it more excusable.'

'What was that?' asked Lucy.

Mr Beebe sat back complacently, and Miss Alan began as follows:

'It was a novel–and I am afraid, from what I can gather, not a very nice novel. It is so sad when people who have abilities misuse them, and I must say they nearly always do. Anyhow, she left it almost finished in the Grotto of the Calvary at the Capuccini Hotel at Amalfi while she went for a little ink. She said: "Can I have a little ink, please?" But you know what Italians are, and meanwhile the Grotto fell roaring on to the beach, and the saddest thing of all is that she cannot remember what she has written. The poor thing was very ill after it, and so got tempted into cigarettes. It is a great secret, but I am glad to say that she is writing another novel. She told Teresa and Miss Pole the other day that she had got up all the local colour–this novel is to be about modern Italy; the other was historical–but that she could not start till she had an idea. First she tried Perugia for an inspiration, then she came here–this must on no account get round. And so cheerful through it all! I cannot help thinking that there is something to admire in every one, even if you do not approve of them.'

Miss Alan was always thus being charitable against her better judgment.

A delicate pathos perfumed her disconnected remarks, giving them unexpected beauty, just as in the decaying autumn woods there sometimes rise odours reminiscent of spring. She felt she had made almost too many allowances, and apologized hurriedly for her toleration.

'All the same, she is a little too—I hardly like to say unwomanly, but she behaved most strangely when the Emersons arrived.'

Mr Beebe smiled as Miss Alan plunged into an anecdote which he knew she would be unable to finish in the presence of a gentleman.

'I don't know, Miss Honeychurch, if you have noticed that Miss Pole, the lady who has so much rather yellow hair, takes lemonade. That old Mr Emerson, who puts things very strangely—'

Her jaw dropped. She was silent. Mr Beebe, whose social resources were endless, went out to order some tea, and she continued to Lucy in a hasty whisper:

'Stomach. He warned Miss Pole of her stomach—acidity, he called it—and he may have meant to be kind. I must say I forgot myself and laughed; it was so sudden. As Teresa truly said, it was no laughing matter. But the point is that Miss Lavish was positively *attracted* by his mentioning S., and said that she liked plain speaking, and meeting different grades of thought. She thought they were commercial travellers—"drummers" was the word she used—and all through dinner she tried to prove that England, our great and beloved country, rests on nothing but commerce. Teresa was very much annoyed, and left the table before the cheese, saying as she did so: "There, Miss Lavish, is one who can confute you better than I," and pointed to that beautiful picture of Lord Tennyson. Then Miss Lavish said: "Tut! The early Victorians." Just imagine! "Tut! The early Victorians." My sister had gone, and I felt bound to speak. I said: "Miss Lavish, *I* am an early Victorian; at least, that is to say, I will hear no breath of censure against our dear Queen." It was horrible speaking. I reminded her how the Queen had been to Ireland when she did not want to go, and I must say she was dumbfounded, and made no reply. But, unluckily, Mr Emerson overheard this part, and called in his deep voice: "Quite so, quite so! I honour the woman for her Irish visit." The woman! I tell things so badly; but you see what a tangle we were in by this time, all on account of S. having been mentioned in the first place. But that was not all. After dinner Miss Lavish actually came up and said: "Miss Alan, I am going into the smoking-room to talk to those two nice men. Come, too." Needless to say, I refused such an unsuitable invitation, and she had the impertinence to tell me that it would broaden my ideas, and said that she had four brothers, all University men, except one who was in the army, who always made a point of talking to commercial travellers.'

'Let me finish the story,' said Mr Beebe, who had returned. 'Miss Lavish tried Miss Pole, myself, every one, and finally said: "I shall go alone." She went. At the end of five minutes she returned unobtrusively with a green baize board, and began playing patience.'

'Whatever happened?' cried Lucy.

'No one knows. No one will ever know. Miss Lavish will never dare to tell, and Mr Emerson does not think it worth telling.'

'Mr Beebe—old Mr Emerson, is he nice or not nice? I do so want to know.'

Mr Beebe laughed and suggested that she should settle the question for herself.

'No; but it is so difficult. Sometimes he is so silly, and then I do not mind him. Miss Alan, what do you think? Is he nice?'

The little old lady shook her head, and sighed disapprovingly. Mr Beebe, whom the conversation amused, stirred her up by saying:

'I consider that you are bound to class him as nice, Miss Alan, after that business of the violets.'

'Violets? Oh dear! Who told you about the violets? How do things get round? A pension is a sad place for gossips. No, I cannot forget how they behaved at Mr Eager's lecture at Santa Croce. Oh, poor Miss Honeychurch! It really was too bad! No, I have quite changed. I do *not* like the Emersons. They are *not* nice.'

Mr Beebe smiled nonchalantly. He had made a gentle effort to introduce the Emersons into Bertolini society, and the effort had failed. He was almost the only person who remained friendly to them. Miss Lavish, who represented intellect, was avowedly hostile, and now the Miss Alans, who stood for good breeding, were following her. Miss Bartlett, smarting under an obligation, would scarcely be civil. The case of Lucy was different. She had given him a hazy account of her adventures in Santa Croce, and he gathered that the two men had made a curious and possibly concerted attempt to annex her, to show her the world from their own strange standpoint, to interest her in their private sorrows and joys. This was impertinent; he did not wish their cause to be championed by a young girl: he would rather it should fail. After all, he knew nothing about them, and pension joys, pension sorrows, are flimsy things; whereas Lucy would be his parishioner.

Lucy, with one eye upon the weather, finally said that she thought the Emersons were nice; not that she saw anything of them now. Even their seats at dinner had been moved.

'But aren't they always waylaying you to go out with them, dear?' said the little lady inquisitively.

'Only once. Charlotte didn't like it, and said something—quite politely, of course.'

'Most right of her. They don't understand our ways. They must find their level.'

Mr Beebe rather felt that they had gone under. They had given up their attempt—if it was one—to conquer society, and now the father was almost as silent as the son. He wondered whether he would not plan a pleasant day for these folk before they left—some expedition, perhaps, with Lucy well chaperoned to be nice to them. It was one of Mr Beebe's chief pleasures to provide people with happy memories.

Evening approached while they chatted; the air became brighter; the colours on the trees and hills were purified, and the Arno lost its muddy solidity and began to twinkle. There were a few streaks of bluish-green among the clouds, a few patches of watery light upon the earth, and then the dripping façade of San Miniato shone brilliantly in the declining sun.

'Too late to go out,' said Miss Alan in a voice of relief. 'All the galleries are shut.'

'I think I shall go out,' said Lucy. 'I want to go round the town in the circular tram—on the platform by the driver.'

Her two companions looked grave. Mr Beebe, who felt responsible for her in the absence of Miss Bartlett, ventured to say:

'I wish we could. Unluckily I have letters. If you do want to go out alone, won't you be better on your feet?'

'Italians, dear, you know,' said Miss Alan.

'Perhaps I shall meet some one who reads me through and through!'

But they still looked disapproval, and she so far conceded to Mr Beebe as to say that she would only go for a little walk, and keep to the streets frequented by tourists.

'She oughtn't really to go at all,' said Mr Beebe, as they watched her from the window, 'and she knows it. I put it down to too much Beethoven.'

Chapter Four

Fourth Chapter

Mr Beebe was right. Lucy never knew her desires so clearly as after music. She had not really appreciated the clergyman's wit, nor the suggestive twitterings of Miss Alan. Conversation was tedious; she wanted something big, and she believed that it would have come to her on the wind-swept platform of an electric tram.

This she might not attempt. It was unladylike. Why? Why were most big things unladylike? Charlotte had once explained to her why. It was not that ladies were inferior to men; it was that they were different. Their mission was to inspire others to achievement rather than to achieve themselves. Indirectly, by means of tact and a spotless name, a lady could accomplish much. But if she rushed into the fray herself she would be first censured, then despised, and finally ignored. Poems had been written to illustrate this point.

There is much that is immortal in this medieval lady. The dragons have gone, and so have the knights, but still she lingers in our midst. She reigned in many an early Victorian castle, and was Queen of much early Victorian song. It is sweet to protect her in the intervals of business, sweet to pay her honour when she has cooked our dinner well. But alas! the creature grows degenerate. In her heart also there are springing up strange desires. She too is enamoured of heavy winds, and vast panoramas, and green expanses of the sea. She has marked the kingdom of this world, how full it is of wealth, and beauty, and war—a radiant crust, built around the central fires, spinning towards the receding heavens. Men, declaring that she inspires them to it, move joyfully over the surface, having the most delightful meetings with other men, happy, not because they are masculine, but because they are alive. Before the show breaks up she would like to drop the august title of the Eternal Woman, and go there as her transitory self.

Lucy does not stand for the medieval lady, who was rather an ideal to which she was bidden to lift her eyes when feeling serious. Nor has she any system of revolt. Here and there a restriction annoyed her particularly, and she would transgress it, and perhaps be sorry that she had done so. This afternoon she was peculiarly restive. She would really like to do something of which her well-wishers disapproved. As she might not go on the electric tram, she went to Alinari's shop.

There she bought a photograph of Botticelli's 'Birth of Venus.' Venus, being a pity, spoilt the picture, otherwise so charming, and Miss Bartlett had persuaded her to do without it. (A pity in art of course signified the nude.) Giorgione's 'Tempestà,' the 'Idolino,' some of the Sistine frescoes and the Apoxyomenos, were added to it. She felt a little calmer then, and bought Fra Angelico's 'Coronation,' Giotto's 'Ascension of St John,' some Della Robbia babies, and some Guido Reni Madonnas. For her taste was catholic, and she extended uncritical approval to every well-known name.

But though she spent nearly seven lire, the gates of liberty seemed still unopened. She was conscious of her discontent; it was new to her to be conscious of it. 'The world,' she thought, 'is certainly full of beautiful things, if only I could come across them.' It was not surprising that Mrs Honeychurch disapproved of music, declaring that it always left her daughter peevish, unpractical, and touchy.

'Nothing ever happens to me,' she reflected, as she entered the Piazza Signoria and looked nonchalantly at its marvels, now fairly familiar to her. The great square was in shadow; the sunshine had come too late to strike it. Neptune was already unsubstantial in the twilight, half god, half ghost, and his fountain plashed dreamily to the men and satyrs who idled together on its marge. The Loggia showed as the triple entrance of a cave, wherein dwelt many a deity, shadowy, but immortal, looking forth upon the arrivals and departures of mankind. It was the hour of unreality—the hour, that is, when unfamiliar things are real. An older person at such an hour and in such a place might think that sufficient was happening to him, and rest content. Lucy desired more.

She fixed her eyes wistfully on the tower of the palace, which rose out of the lower darkness like a pillar of roughened gold. It seemed no longer a tower, no longer supported by earth, but some unattainable treasure throbbing in the tranquil sky. Its brightness mesmerized her, still dancing before her eyes when she bent them to the ground and started towards home.

Then something did happen.

Two Italians by the Loggia had been bickering about a debt. 'Cinque lire,' they had cried, 'cinque lire!' They sparred at each other, and one of them was hit lightly upon the chest. He frowned; he bent towards Lucy with a look of interest, as if he had an important message for her. He opened his lips to deliver it, and a stream of red came out between them and trickled down his unshaven chin.

That was all. A crowd rose out of the dusk. It hid this extraordinary man from her, and bore him away to the fountain. Mr George Emerson happened to be a few paces away, looking at her across the spot where the man had been. How very odd! Across something. Even as she caught sight of him he grew dim; the palace itself grew dim, swayed above her, fell on to her softly, slowly, noiselessly, and the sky fell with it.

She thought: 'Oh, what have I done?'

'Oh, what have I done?' she murmured, and opened her eyes.

George Emerson still looked at her, but not across anything. She had complained of dullness, and lo! one man was stabbed, and another held her in his arms.

They were sitting on some steps in the Uffizi Arcade. He must have carried her. He rose when she spoke, and began to dust his knees. She repeated:

'Oh, what have I done?'

'You fainted.'

'I–I am very sorry.'

'How are you now?'

'Perfectly well–absolutely well.' And she began to nod and smile.

'Then let us come home. There's no point in our stopping.'

He held out his hand to pull her up. She pretended not to see it. The cries from the fountain–they had never ceased–rang emptily. The whole world seemed pale and void of its original meaning.

'How very kind you have been! I might have hurt myself falling. But now I am well. I can go alone, thank you.'

His hand was still extended.

'Oh, my photographs!' she exclaimed suddenly.

'What photographs?'

'I bought some photographs at Alinari's. I must have dropped them out there in the square.' She looked at him cautiously. 'Would you add to your kindness by fetching them?'

He added to his kindness. As soon as he had turned his back, Lucy arose with the cunning of a maniac and stole down the arcade towards the Arno.

'Miss Honeychurch!'

She stopped with her hand on her heart.

'You sit still; you aren't fit to go home alone.'

'Yes, I am, thank you so very much.'

'No, you aren't. You'd go openly if you were.'

'But I had rather—'

'Then I don't fetch your photographs.'

'I had rather be alone.'

He said imperiously: 'The man is dead–the man is probably dead; sit down till you are rested.' She was bewildered, and obeyed him. 'And don't move till I come back.'

In the distance she saw creatures with black hoods, such as appear in

dreams. The palace tower had lost the reflection of the declining day, and
joined itself to earth. How should she talk to Mr Emerson when he returned
from the shadowy square? Again the thought occurred to her, 'Oh, what
have I done?'—the thought that she, as well as the dying man, had crossed
some spiritual boundary.

He returned, and she talked of the murder. Oddly enough, it was an easy
topic. She spoke of the Italian character; she became almost garrulous over
the incident that had made her faint five minutes before. Being strong
physically, she soon overcame the horror of blood. She rose without his
assistance, and though wings seemed to flutter inside her, she walked firmly
enough towards the Arno. There a cabman signalled to them; they refused
him.

'And the murderer tried to kiss him, you say—how very odd Italians
are!—and gave himself up to the police! Mr Beebe was saying that Italians
know everything, but I think they are rather childish. When my cousin and I
were at the Pitti yesterday— What was that?'

He had thrown something into the stream.

'What did you throw in?'

'Things I didn't want,' he said crossly.

'Mr Emerson!'

'Well?'

'Where are the photographs?'

He was silent.

'I believe it was my photographs that you threw away.'

'I didn't know what to do with them,' he cried, and his voice was that of an
anxious boy. Her heart warmed towards him for the first time. 'They were
covered with blood. There! I'm glad I've told you; and all the time we were
making conversation I was wondering what to do with them.' He pointed
downstream. 'They've gone.' The river swirled under the bridge. 'I did
mind them so, and one is so foolish, it seemed better that they should go out
to the sea—I don't know; I may just mean that they frightened me.' Then the
boy verged into a man. 'For something tremendous has happened; I must
face it without getting muddled. It isn't exactly that a man has died.'

Something warned Lucy that she must stop him.

'It has happened,' he repeated, 'and I mean to find out what it is.'

'Mr Emerson—'

He turned towards her frowning, as if she had disturbed him in some
abstract quest.

'I want to ask you something before we go in.'

They were close to their pension. She stopped and leant her elbows
against the parapet of the embankment. He did likewise. There is at times a
magic in identity of position; it is one of the things that have suggested to us
eternal comradeship. She moved her elbows before saying:

'I have behaved ridiculously.'

He was following his own thoughts.

'I was never so much ashamed of myself in my life; I cannot think what
came over me.'

'I nearly fainted myself,' he said; but she felt that her attitude repelled him.

'Well, I owe you a thousand apologies.'

'Oh, all right.'

'And—this is the real point—you know how silly people are gossiping—ladies especially, I am afraid—you understand what I mean?'

'I'm afraid I don't.'

'I mean, would you not mention it to anyone, my foolish behaviour?'

'Your behaviour? Oh yes, all right—all right.'

'Thank you so much. And would you—'

She could not carry her request any further. The river was gushing below them, almost black in the advancing night. He had thrown her photographs into it, and then he had told her the reason. It struck her that it was hopeless to look for chivalry in such a man. He would do her no harm by idle gossip; he was trustworthy, intelligent, and even kind; he might even have a high opinion of her. But he lacked chivalry; his thoughts, like his behaviour, would not be modified by awe. It was useless to say to him, 'And would you—' and hope that he would complete the sentence for himself, averting his eyes from her nakedness like the knight in that beautiful picture. She had been in his arms, and he remembered it, just as he remembered the blood on the photographs that she had bought in Alinari's shop. It was not exactly that a man had died; something had happened to the living: they had come to a situation where character tells, and where Childhood enters upon the branching paths of Youth.

'Well, thank you so much,' she repeated. 'How quickly these accidents do happen, and then one returns to the old life!'

'I don't.'

Anxiety moved her to question him.

His answer was puzzling: 'I shall probably want to live.'

'But why, Mr Emerson? What do you mean?'

'I shall want to live, I say.'

Leaning her elbows on the parapet, she contemplated the River Arno, whose roar was suggesting some unexpected melody to her ears.

Chapter Five

Possibilities of a Pleasant Outing

It was a family saying that 'you never knew which way Charlotte Bartlett would turn.' She was perfectly pleasant and sensible over Lucy's adventure, found the abridged account of it quite adequate, and paid suitable tribute to the courtesy of Mr George Emerson. She and Miss Lavish had had an adventure also. They had been stopped at the Dazio coming back, and the young officials there, who seemed impudent and *désœuvré*, had tried to search their reticules for provisions. It might have been most unpleasant. Fortunately, Miss Lavish was a match for anyone.

For good or for evil, Lucy was left to face her problem alone. None of her friends had seen her, either in the Piazza or, later on, by the embankment. Mr Beebe, indeed, noticing her startled eyes at dinner-time, had again passed to himself the remark of 'Too much Beethoven.' But he only supposed that she was ready for an adventure, not that she had encountered it. This solitude oppressed her; she was accustomed to have her thoughts confirmed by others or, at all events, contradicted; it was too dreadful not to know whether she was thinking right or wrong.

At breakfast next morning she took decisive action. There were two plans between which she had to choose. Mr Beebe was walking up to the Torre del Gallo with the Emersons and some American ladies. Would Miss Bartlett and Miss Honeychurch join the party? Charlotte declined for herself; she had been there in the rain the previous afternoon. But she thought it an admirable idea for Lucy, who hated shopping, changing money, fetching letters, and other irksome duties—all of which Miss Bartlett must accomplish this morning, and could easily accomplish alone.

'No, Charlotte!' cried the girl, with real warmth. 'It's very kind of Mr Beebe, but I am certainly coming with you. I had much rather.'

'Very well, dear,' said Miss Bartlett, with a faint flush of pleasure that called forth a deep flush of shame on the cheeks of Lucy. How abominably she behaved to Charlotte, now as always! But now she should alter. All the morning she would be really nice to her.

She slipped her arm into her cousin's, and they started off along the Lung' Arno. The river was a lion that morning in strength, voice, and colour. Miss Bartlett insisted on leaning over the parapet to look at it. She then made her usual remark, which was:

'How I do wish Freddy and your mother could see this, too!'

Lucy fidgeted; it was tiresome of Charlotte to have stopped exactly where she did.

'Look, Lucia! Oh, you are watching for the Torre del Gallo party. I feared you would repent you of your choice.'

Serious as the choice had been, Lucy did not repent. Yesterday had been a muddle—queer and odd, the kind of thing one could not write down easily on paper—but she had a feeling that Charlotte and her shopping were preferable to George Emerson and the summit of the Torre del Gallo. Since she could not unravel the tangle, she must take care not to re-enter it. She could protest sincerely against Miss Bartlett's insinuations.

But though she had avoided the chief actor, the scenery unfortunately remained. Charlotte, with the complacency of fate, led her from the river to the Piazza Signoria. She could not have believed that stones, a Loggia, a fountain, a palace tower, would have such significance. For a moment she understood the nature of ghosts.

The exact site of the murder was occupied, not by a ghost, but by Miss

Lavish, who had the morning newspaper in her hand. She hailed them briskly. The dreadful catastrophe of the previous day had given her an idea which she thought would work up into a book.

'Oh, let me congratulate you!' said Miss Bartlett. 'After your despair of yesterday! What a fortunate thing!'

'Aha! Miss Honeychurch, come you here! I am in luck. Now, you are to tell me absolutely everything that you saw from the beginning.'

Lucy poked at the ground with her parasol.

'But perhaps you would rather not?'

'I'm sorry—if you could manage without it, I think I would rather not.'

The elder ladies exchanged glances, not of disapproval; it is suitable that a girl should feel deeply.

'It is I who am sorry,' said Miss Lavish. 'We literary hacks are shameless creatures. I believe there's no secret of the human heart into which we wouldn't pry.'

She marched cheerfully to the fountain and back, and did a few calculations in realism. Then she said that she had been in the Piazza since eight o'clock collecting material. A good deal of it was unsuitable, but of course one always had to adapt. The two men had quarrelled over a five-franc note. For the five-franc note she should substitute a young lady, which would raise the tone of the tragedy, and at the same time furnish an excellent plot.

'What is the heroine's name?' asked Miss Bartlett.

'Leonora,' said Miss Lavish; her own name was Eleanor.

'I do hope she's nice.'

That desideratum would not be omitted.

'And what is the plot?'

Love, murder, abduction, revenge, was the plot. Out it all came while the fountain plashed to the satyrs in the morning sun.

'I hope you will excuse me for boring on like this,' Miss Lavish concluded. 'It is so tempting to talk to really sympathetic people. Of course, this is the barest outline. There will be a deal of local colouring, descriptions of Florence and the neighbourhood, and I shall also introduce some humorous characters. And let me give you all fair warning: I intend to be unmerciful to the British tourist.'

'Oh, you wicked woman!' cried Miss Bartlett. 'I am sure you are thinking of the Emersons.'

Miss Lavish gave a Machiavellian smile.

'I confess that in Italy my sympathies are not with my own countrymen. It is the neglected Italians who attract me, and whose lives I am going to paint so far as I can. For I repeat and I insist, and I have always held most strongly, that a tragedy such as yesterday's is not the less tragic because it happened in humble life.'

There was a fitting silence when Miss Lavish had concluded. Then the cousins wished success to her labours, and walked slowly away across the square.

'She is my idea of a really clever woman,' said Miss Bartlett. 'That last remark struck me as so particularly true. It should be a most pathetic novel.'

Lucy assented. At present her great aim was not to get put into it. Her perceptions this morning were curiously keen, and she believed that Miss Lavish had her on trial for an *ingénue*.

'She is emancipated, but only in the very best sense of the word,' continued Miss Bartlett slowly. 'None but the superficial would be shocked at her. We had a long talk yesterday. She believes in justice and truth and human interest. She told me also that she has a high opinion of the destiny of woman—Mr Eager! Why, how nice! What a pleasant surprise!'

'Ah, not for me,' said the chaplain blandly, 'for I have been watching you and Miss Honeychurch for quite a little time.'

'We were chatting to Miss Lavish.'

His brow contracted.

'So I saw. Were you indeed? Andate via! sono occupato!' The last remark was made to a vendor of panoramic photographs who was approaching with a courteous smile. 'I am about to venture a suggestion. Would you and Miss Honeychurch be disposed to join me in a drive some day this week—a drive in the hills? We might go up by Fiesole and back by Settignano. There is a point on that road where we could get down and have an hour's ramble on the hill-side. The view thence of Florence is most beautiful—far better than the hackneyed view from Fiesole. It is the view that Alessio Baldovinetti is fond of introducing into his pictures. That man had a decided feeling for landscape. Decidedly. But who looks at it to-day? Ah, the world is too much with us.'

Miss Bartlett had not heard of Alessio Baldovinetti, but she knew that Mr Eager was no commonplace chaplain. He was a member of the residential colony who had made Florence their home. He knew the people who never walked about with Baedekers, who had learnt to take a siesta after lunch, who took drives the pension tourists had never heard of, and saw by private influence galleries which were closed to them. Living in delicate seclusion, some in furnished flats, others in Renaissance villas on Fiesole's slope, they read, wrote, studied, and exchanged ideas, thus attaining to that intimate knowledge, or rather perception, of Florence which is denied to all who carry in their pockets the coupons of Cook.

Therefore an invitation from the chaplain was something to be proud of. Between the two sections of his flock he was often the only link, and it was his avowed custom to select those of his migratory sheep who seemed worthy, and give them a few hours in the pastures of the permanent. Tea at a Renaissance villa? Nothing had been said about it yet. But if it did come to that—how Lucy would enjoy it!

A few days ago and Lucy would have felt the same. But the joys of life were grouping themselves anew. A drive in the hills with Mr Eager and Miss Bartlett—even if culminating in a residential tea-party—was no longer the greatest of them. She echoed the raptures of Charlotte somewhat faintly. Only when she heard that Mr Beebe was also coming did her thanks become more sincere.

'So we shall be a *partée carrée*,' said the chaplain. 'In these days of toil and tumult one has great needs of the country and its message of purity. Andate via! andate presto, presto! Ah, the town! Beautiful as it is, it is the town.'

They assented.

'This very square—so I am told—witnessed yesterday the most sordid of tragedies. To one who loves the Florence of Dante and Savonarola there is something portentous in such desecration—portentous and humiliating.'

'Humiliating indeed,' said Miss Bartlett. 'Miss Honeychurch happened to be passing through as it happened. She can hardly bear to speak of it.' She glanced at Lucy proudly.

'And how came we to have you here?' asked the chaplain paternally.

Miss Bartlett's recent liberalism oozed away at the question.

'Do not blame her, please, Mr Eager. The fault is mine: I left her unchaperoned.'

'So you were here alone, Miss Honeychurch?' His voice suggested sympathetic reproof, but at the same time indicated that a few harrowing details would not be unacceptable. His dark, handsome face drooped mournfully towards her to catch her reply.

'Practically.'

'One of our pension acquaintances kindly brought her home,' said Miss Bartlett, adroitly concealing the sex of the preserver.

'For her also it must have been a terrible experience. I trust that neither of you were at all—that it was not in your immediate proximity.'

Of the many things Lucy was noticing to-day, not the least remarkable was this: the ghoulish fashion in which respectable people will nibble after blood. George Emerson had kept the subject strangely pure.

'He died by the fountain, I believe,' was her reply.

'And you and your friend—'

'Were over at the Loggia.'

'That must have saved you much. You have not, of course, seen the disgraceful illustrations which the gutter Press— This man is a public nuisance; he knows that I am a resident perfectly well, and yet he goes on worrying me to buy his vulgar views.'

Surely the vendor of photographs was in league with Lucy—in the eternal league of Italy with youth. He had suddenly extended his book before Miss Bartlett and Mr Eager, binding their hands together by a long glossy ribbon of churches, pictures, and views.

'This is too much!' cried the chaplain, striking petulantly at one of Fra Angelico's angels. She tore. A shrill cry arose from the vendor. The book, it seemed, was more valuable than one would have supposed.

'Willingly would I purchase—' began Miss Bartlett.

'Ignore him,' said Mr Eager sharply, and they all walked rapidly away from the square.

But an Italian can never be ignored, least of all when he has a grievance. His mysterious persecution of Mr Eager became relentless; the air rang with his threats and lamentations. He appealed to Lucy; would not she intercede? He was poor—he sheltered a family—the tax on bread. He waited, he gibbered, he was recompensed, he was dissatisfied, he did not leave them until he had swept their minds clean of all thoughts, whether pleasant or unpleasant.

Shopping was the topic that now ensued. Under the chaplain's guidance they selected many hideous presents and mementoes—florid little picture-frames that seemed fashioned in gilded pastry; other little frames, more severe, that stood on little easels, and were carven out of oak; a blotting book of vellum; a Dante of the same material; cheap mosaic brooches, which the maids, next Christmas, would never tell from real; pins, pots, heraldic saucers, brown art-photographs; Eros and Psyche in alabaster; St Peter to match—all of which would have cost less in London.

This successful morning left no pleasant impressions on Lucy. She had been a little frightened, both by Miss Lavish and by Mr Eager, she knew not why. And as they frightened her, she had, strangely enough, ceased to respect them. She doubted that Miss Lavish was a great artist. She doubted that Mr Eager was as full of spirituality and culture as she had been led to suppose. They were tried by some new test, and they were found wanting. As for Charlotte—as for Charlotte she was exactly the same. It might be possible to be nice to her; it was impossible to love her.

'The son of a labourer; I happen to know if for a fact. A mechanic of some sort himself when he was young; then he took to writing for the Socialistic Press. I came across him at Brixton.'

They were talking about the Emersons.

'How wonderfully people rise in these days!' sighed Miss Bartlett, fingering a model of the Leaning Tower of Pisa.

'Generally,' replied Mr Eager, 'one has only sympathy with their success. The desire for education and for social advance—in these things there is something not wholly vile. There are some working men whom one would be very willing to see out here in Florence—little as they would make of it.'

'Is he a journalist now?' Miss Bartlett asked.

'He is not; he made an advantageous marriage.'

He uttered this remark with a voice full of meaning, and ended it with a sigh.

'Oh, so he has a wife.'

'Dead, Miss Bartlett, dead. I wonder—yes, I wonder how he has the effrontery to look me in the face, to dare to claim acquaintance with me. He was in my London parish long ago. The other day in Santa Croce, when he was with Miss Honeychurch, I snubbed him. Let him beware that he does not get more than a snub.'

'What?' cried Lucy, flushing.

'Exposure!' hissed Mr Eager.

He tried to change the subject; but in scoring a dramatic point he had interested his audience more than he had intended. Miss Bartlett was full of very natural curiosity. Lucy, though she wished never to see the Emersons again, was not disposed to condemn them on a single word.

'Do you mean,' she asked, 'that he is an irreligious man? We know that already.'

'Lucy dear—' said Miss Bartlett, gently reproving her cousin's penetration.

'I should be astonished if you knew all. The boy—an innocent child at the time—I will exclude. God knows what his education and his inherited qualities may have made him.'

'Perhaps,' said Miss Bartlett, 'it is something that we had better not hear.'

'To speak plainly,' said Mr Eager, 'it is. I will say no more.'

For the first time Lucy's rebellious thoughts swept out in words—for the first time in her life.

'You have said very little.'

'It was my intention to say very little,' was his frigid reply.

He gazed indignantly at the girl, who met him with equal indignation. She turned towards him from the shop counter; her breast heaved quickly. He observed her brow, and the sudden strength of her lips. It was intolerable that she should disbelieve him.

'Murder, if you want to know,' he cried angrily. 'That man murdered his wife!'

'How?' she retorted.

'To all intents and purposes he murdered her. That day in Santa Croce—did they say anything against me?'

'Not a word, Mr Eager—not a single word.'

'Oh, I thought they had been libelling me to you. But I suppose it is only their personal charms that make you defend them.'

'I'm not defending them,' said Lucy, losing her courage, and relapsing into the old chaotic methods. 'They're nothing to me.'

'How could you think she was defending them?' said Miss Bartlett, much discomfited by the unpleasant scene. The shopman was possibly listening.

'She will find it difficult. For that man has murdered his wife in the sight of God.'

The addition of God was striking. But the chaplain was really trying to qualify a rash remark. A silence followed which might have been impressive, but was merely awkward. Then Miss Bartlett hastily purchased the Leaning Tower, and led the way into the street.

'I must be going,' said he, shutting his eyes and taking out his watch.

Miss Bartlett thanked him for his kindness, and spoke with enthusiasm of the approaching drive.

'Drive? Oh, is our drive to come off?'

Lucy was recalled to her manners, and after a little exertion the complacency of Mr Eager was restored.

'Bother the drive!' exclaimed the girl, as soon as he had departed. 'It is just the drive we had arranged with Mr Beebe without any fuss at all. Why should he invite us in that absurd manner? We might as well invite him. We are each paying for ourselves.'

Miss Bartlett, who had intended to lament over the Emersons, was launched by this remark into unexpected thoughts.

'If that is so, dear—if the drive we and Mr Beebe are going with Mr Eager is really the same as the one we were going with Mr Beebe, then I foresee a sad kettle of fish.'

'How?'

'Because Mr Beebe has asked Eleanor Lavish to come, too.'

'That will mean another carriage.'

'Far worse. Mr Eager does not like Eleanor. She knows it herself. The truth must be told; she is too unconventional for him.'

They were now in the newspaper-room at the English bank. Lucy stood by the central table, heedless of 'Punch' and the 'Graphic,' trying to answer, or at all events to formulate the questions rioting in her brain. The well-known world had broken up, and there emerged Florence, a magic city where people thought and did the most extraordinary things. Murder, accusations of murder, a lady clinging to one man and being rude to another—were these the daily incidents of her streets? Was there more in her frank beauty than met the eye—the power, perhaps, to evoke passions, good and bad, and to bring them speedily to a fulfilment?

Happy Charlotte, who, though greatly troubled over things that did not matter, seemed oblivious to things that did; who could conjecture with admirable delicacy 'where things might lead to,' but apparently lost sight of the goal as she approached it! Now she was crouching in the corner trying to extract a circular note from a kind of linen nose-bag which hung in chaste concealment round her neck. She had been told that his was the only safe way to carry money in Italy; it must only be broached within the walls of the English bank. As she groped she murmured: 'Whether it is Mr Beebe who forgot to tell Mr Eager, or Mr Eager who forgot when he told us, or whether they have decided to leave Eleanor out altogether—which they could scarcely do—but in any case we must be prepared. It is you they really want; I am only asked for appearances. You shall go with the two gentlemen, and I and Eleanor will follow behind. A one-horse carriage would do for us. Yet how difficult it is!'

'It is indeed,' replied the girl, with a gravity that sounded sympathetic.

'What do you think about it?' asked Miss Bartlett, flushed from the struggle, and buttoning up her dress.

'I don't know what I think, nor what I want.'

'Oh dear, Lucy! I do hope Florence isn't boring you. Speak the word, and, as you know, I would take you to the ends of the earth to-morrow.'

'Thank you, Charlotte,' said Lucy, and pondered over the offer.

There were letters for her at the bureau—one from her brother, full of athletics and biology; one from her mother, delightful as only her mother's letters could be. She read in it of the crocuses which had been bought for yellow and were coming up puce, of the new parlour-maid, who had watered the ferns with essence of lemonade, of the semi-detached cottages which were ruining Summer Street, and breaking the heart of Sir Harry Otway. She recalled the free, pleasant life of her home, where she was allowed to do everything, and where nothing ever happened to her. The road up through the pine-woods, the clean drawing-room, the view over the Sussex Weald—all hung before her bright and distinct, but pathetic as the pictures in a gallery to which, after much experience, a traveller returns.

'And the news?' asked Miss Bartlett.

'Mrs Vyse and her son have gone to Rome,' said Lucy, giving the news that interested her least. 'Do you know the Vyses?'

'Oh, not that way back. We can never have too much of the dear Piazza Signoria.'

'They're nice people, the Vyses. So clever—my idea of what's really clever. Don't you long to be in Rome?'

'I die for it!'

The Piazza Signoria is too stony to be brilliant. It has no grass, no flowers, no frescoes, no glittering walls of marble or comforting patches of ruddy brick. By an odd chance—unless we believe in a presiding genius of places—the statues that relieve its severity suggest, not the innocence of childhood, nor the glorious bewilderment of youth, but the conscious achievements of maturity. Perseus and Judith, Hercules and Thusnelda, they have done or suffered something, and though they are immortal, immortality has come to them after experience, not before. Here, not only in the solitude of Nature, might a hero meet a goddess, or a heroine a god.

'Charlotte!' cried the girl suddenly. 'Here's an idea. What if we popped off to Rome to-morrow—straight—to the Vyses' hotel? For I do know what I want. I'm sick of Florence. Now, you said you'd go to the ends of the earth! Do! Do!'

Miss Bartlett, with equal vivacity, replied:

'Oh, you droll person! Pray, what would become of your drive in the hills?'

They passed together through the gaunt beauty of the square, laughing over the unpractical suggestion.

Chapter Six

*The Reverend Arthur Beebe, the Reverend Cuthbert Eager,
Mr Emerson, Mr George Emerson, Miss Eleanor Lavish,
Miss Charlotte Bartlett, and Miss Lucy Honeychurch,
Drive out in Carriages to see a View: Italians Drive them*

It was Phaethon who drove them to Fiesole that memorable day, a youth all irresponsibility and fire, recklessly urging his master's horses up the stony hill. Mr Beebe recognized him at once. Neither the Ages of Faith nor the Age of Doubt had touched him; he was Phaethon in Tuscany driving a cab. And it was Persephone whom he asked leave to pick up on the way, saying that she was his sister—Persephone, tall and slender and pale, returning with the spring to her mother's cottage, and still shading her eyes from the unaccustomed light. To her Mr Eager objected, saying that here was the thin edge of the wedge, and one must guard against imposition. But the ladies interceded, and when it had been made clear that it was a very great favour, the goddess was allowed to mount beside the god.

Phaethon at once slipped the left rein over her head, thus enabling himself to drive with his arm round her waist. She did not mind. Mr Eager, who sat with his back to the horses, saw nothing of the indecorous proceeding, and continued his conversation with Lucy. The other two occupants of the carriage were old Mr Emerson and Miss Lavish. For a dreadful thing had happened: Mr Beebe, without consulting Mr Eager, had doubled the size of the party. And though Miss Bartlett and Miss Lavish had planned all the morning how people were to sit, at the critical moment when the carriages came round they lost their heads, and Miss Lavish got in with Lucy, while Miss Bartlett, with George Emerson and Mr Beebe, followed on behind.

It was hard on the poor chaplain to have his *partie carrée* thus transformed. Tea at a Renaissance villa, if he had ever meditated it, was now impossible. Lucy and Miss Bartlett had a certain style about them, and Mr Beebe, though unreliable, was a man of parts. But a shoddy lady writer and a journalist who had murdered his wife in the sight of God—they should enter no villa at his introduction.

Lucy, elegantly dressed in white, sat erect and nervous amid these explosive ingredients, attentive to Mr Eager, repressive towards Miss Lavish, watchful of old Mr Emerson—hitherto fortunately asleep, thanks to a heavy lunch and the drowsy atmosphere of spring. She looked on the expedition as the work of Fate. But for it she would have avoided George Emerson successfully. In an open manner he had shown that he wished to continue their intimacy. She had refused, not because she disliked him, but because she did not know what had happened, and suspected that he did know. And this frightened her.

For the real event—whatever it was—had taken place, not in the Loggia, but by the river. To behave wildly at the sight of death is pardonable. But to discuss it afterwards, to pass from discussion into silence, and through silence into sympathy, that is an error, not of a startled emotion, but of the whole fabric. There was really something blameworthy (she thought) in their joint contemplation of the shadowy stream, in the common impulse which had turned them to the house without the passing of a look or word. This sense of wickedness had been slight at first. She had nearly joined the party to the Torre del Gallo. But each time that she avoided George it became more imperative that she should avoid him again. And now celestial irony, working through her cousin and two clergymen, did not suffer her to leave Florence till she had made this expedition with him through the hills.

Meanwhile Mr Eager held her in civil converse; their little tiff was over.

'So, Miss Honeychurch, you are travelling? As a student of art?'

'Oh dear me, no—oh no!'

'Perhaps as a student of human nature,' interposed Miss Lavish, 'like myself?'

'Oh no. I am here as a tourist.'

'Oh, indeed,' said Mr Eager. 'Are you indeed? If you will not think me rude, we residents sometimes pity you poor tourists not a little—handed about like a parcel of goods from Venice to Florence, from Florence to

Rome, living herded together in pensions or hotels, quite unconscious of anything that is outside Baedeker, their one anxiety to get "done" or "through" and go on somewhere else. The result is, they mix up towns, rivers, palaces in one inextricable whirl. You know the American girl in "Punch" who says: "Say, poppa, what did we see at Rome?" And the father replies: "Why, guess Rome was the place where we saw the yaller dog." There's travelling for you. Ha! ha! ha!'

'I quite agree,' said Miss Lavish, who had several times tried to interrupt his mordant wit. 'The narrowness and superficiality of the Anglo-Saxon tourist is nothing less than a menace.'

'Quite so. Now, the English colony at Florence, Miss Honeychurch—and it is of considerable size, though, of course, not all equally—a few are here for trade, for example. But the greater part are students. Lady Helen Laverstock is at present busy over Fra Angelico. I mention her name because we are passing her villa on the left. No, you can only see it if you stand—no, do not stand; you will fall. She is very proud of that thick hedge. Inside, perfect seclusion. One might have gone back six hundred years. Some critics believe that her garden was the scene of "The Decameron," which lends it an additional interest, does it not?'

'It does indeed!' cried Miss Lavish. 'Tell me, where do they place the scene of that wonderful seventh day?'

But Mr Eager proceeded to tell Miss Honeychurch that on the right lived Mr Someone Something, an American of the best type—so rare!—and that the Somebody Elses were farther down the hill. 'Doubtless you know her monographs in the series of "Mediæval Byways"? He is working at "Gemistus Pletho." Sometimes as I take tea in their beautiful grounds I hear, over the wall, the electric tram squealing up the new road with its load of hot, dusty, unintelligent tourists who are going to "do" Fiesole in an hour in order that they may say they have been there, and I think—I think—I think how little they think what lies so near them.'

During this speech the two figures on the box were sporting with each other disgracefully. Lucy had a spasm of envy. Granted that they wished to misbehave, it was pleasant for them to be able to do so. They were probably the only people enjoying the expedition. The carriage swept with agonizing jolts up through the Piazza of Fiesole and into the Settignano road.

'Piano! piano!' said Mr Eager, elegantly waving his hand over his head.

'Va bene, signore, va bene, va bene,' crooned the driver, and whipped his horses up again.

Now Mr Eager and Miss Lavish began to talk against each other on the subject of Alessio Baldovinetti. Was he a cause of the Renaissance, or was he one of its manifestations? The other carriage was left behind. As the pace increased to a gallop the large, slumbering form of Mr Emerson was thrown against the chaplain with the regularity of a machine.

'Piano! piano!' said he, with a martyred look at Lucy.

An extra lurch made him turn angrily in his seat. Phaethon, who for some time had been endeavouring to kiss Persephone, had just succeeded.

A little scene ensued, which, as Miss Bartlett said afterwards, was most unpleasant. The horses were stopped, the lovers were ordered to disentangle themselves, the boy was to lose his *pourboire*, the girl was immediately to get down.

'She is my sister,' said he, turning round on them with piteous eyes.

Mr Eager took the trouble to tell him that he was a liar. Phaethon hung down his head, not at the matter of the accusation, but at its manner. At this point Mr Emerson, whom the shock of stopping had awoken, declared that the lovers must on no account be separated, and patted them on the back to signify his approval. And Miss Lavish, though unwilling to ally with him, felt bound to support the cause of Bohemianism.

'Most certainly I would let them be,' she cried. 'But I dare say I shall receive scant support. I have always flown in the face of the conventions all my life. This is what *I* call an adventure.'

'We must not submit,' said Mr Eager. 'I knew he was trying it on. He is treating us as if we were a party of Cook's tourists.'

'Surely no!' said Miss Lavish, her ardour visibly decreasing.

The other carriage had drawn up behind, and sensible Mr Beebe called out that after this warning the couple would be sure to behave themselves properly.

'Leave them alone,' Mr Emerson begged the chaplain, of whom he stood in no awe. 'Do we find happiness so often that we should turn it off the box when it happens to sit there? To be driven by lovers— A king might envy us, and if we part them it's more like sacrilege than anything I know.'

Here the voice of Miss Bartlett was heard saying that a crowd had begun to collect.

Mr Eager, who suffered from an over-fluent tongue rather than a resolute will, was determined to make himself heard. He addressed the driver again. Italian in the mouth of Italians is a deep-voiced stream, with unexpected cataracts and boulders to preserve it from monotony. In Mr Eager's mouth it resembled nothing so much as an acid whistling fountain which played ever higher and higher, and quicker and quicker, and more and more shrilly, till abruptly it was turned off with a click.

'Signorina!' said the man to Lucy, when the display had ceased. Why should he appeal to Lucy?

'Signorina!' echoed Persephone in her glorious contralto. She pointed at the other carriage. Why?

For a moment the two girls looked at each other. Then Persephone got down from the box.

'Victory at last!' said Mr Eager, smiting his hands together as the carriages started again.

'It is not victory,' said Mr Emerson. 'It is defeat. You have parted two people who were happy.'

Mr Eager shut his eyes. He was obliged to sit next to Mr Emerson, but he would not speak to him. The old man was refreshed by sleep, and took up the matter warmly. He commanded Lucy to agree with him; he shouted for support to his son.

'We have tried to buy what cannot be bought with money. He has bargained to drive us, and he is doing it. We have no rights over his soul.'

Miss Lavish frowned. It is hard when a person you have classed as typically British speaks out of his character.

'He was not driving us well,' she said. 'He jolted us.'

'That I deny. It was as restful as sleeping. Aha! he is jolting us now. Can you wonder? He would like to throw us out, and most certainly he is justified. And if I were superstitious I'd be frightened of the girl, too. It doesn't do to injure young people. Have you ever heard of Lorenzo de Medici?'

Miss Lavish bristled.

'Most certainly I have. Do you refer to Lorenzo il Magnifico, or to Lorenzo, Duke of Urbino, or to Lorenzo surnamed Lorenzino on account of his diminutive stature?'

'The Lord knows. Possibly he does know, for I refer to Lorenzo the poet. He wrote a line—so I heard yesterday—which runs like this: "Don't go fighting against the Spring."'

Mr Eager could not resist the opportunity for erudition.

'Non fate guerra al Maggio,' he murmured. '"War not with the May" would render a correct meaning.'

'The point is, we have warred with it. Look.' He pointed to the Val d' Arno, which was visible far below them, through the budding trees. 'Fifty miles of spring, and we've come up to admire them. Do you suppose there's any difference between spring in nature and spring in man? But there we go, praising the one and condemning the other as improper, ashamed that the same laws work eternally through both.'

No one encouraged him to talk. Presently Mr Eager gave a signal for the carriages to stop, and marshalled the party for their ramble on the hill. A hollow like a great amphitheatre, full of terraced steps and misty olives, now lay between them and the heights of Fiesole, and the road, still following its curve, was about to sweep on to a promontory which stood out into the plain. It was this promontory, uncultivated, wet, covered with bushes and occasional trees, which had caught the fancy of Alessio Baldovinetti nearly five hundred years before. He had ascended it, that diligent and rather obscure master, possibly with an eye to business, possibly for the joy of ascending. Standing, there he had seen that view of the Val d' Arno and distant Florence, which he afterwards had introduced not very effectively into his work. But where exactly had he stood? That was the question which Mr Eager hoped to solve now. And Miss Lavish, whose nature was attracted by anything problematical, had become equally enthusiastic.

But it is not easy to carry the pictures of Alessio Baldovinetti in your head, even if you have remembered to look at them before starting. And the haze in the valley increased the difficulty of the quest. The party sprang about from tuft to tuft of grass, their anxiety to keep together being only equalled by their desire to go in different directions. Finally they split into groups. Lucy clung to Miss Bartlett and Miss Lavish; the Emersons returned to hold laborious converse with the drivers; while the two clergymen, who were expected to have topics in common, were left to each other.

The two elder ladies soon threw off the mask. In the audible whisper that was now so familiar to Lucy they began to discuss, not Alessio Baldovinetti, but the drive. Miss Bartlett had asked Mr George Emerson what his profession was, and he had answered 'the railway.' She was very sorry that she had asked him. She had no idea that it would be such a dreadful answer, or she would not have asked him. Mr Beebe had turned the conversation so cleverly, and she hoped that the young man was not very much hurt at her asking him.

'The railway!' gasped Miss Lavish. 'Oh, but I shall die! Of course it was the railway!' She could not control her mirth. 'He is the image of a porter—on, on the South-Eastern.'

'Eleanor, be quiet,' plucking at her vivacious companion. 'Hush! They'll hear—the Emersons—'

'I can't stop. Let me go my wicked way. A porter—'

'Eleanor!'

'I'm sure it's all right,' put in Lucy. 'The Emersons won't hear, and they wouldn't mind if they did.'

Miss Lavish did not seem pleased at this.

'Miss Honeychurch listening!' she said rather crossly. 'Pouf! wouf! You naughty girl! Go away!'

'Oh, Lucy, you ought to be with Mr Eager, I'm sure.'

'I can't find them now, and I don't want to either.'

'Mr Eager will be offended. It is your party.'

'Please, I'd rather stop here with you.'

'No, I agree,' said Miss Lavish. 'It's like a school feast; the boys have got separated from the girls. Miss Lucy, you are to go. We wish to converse on high topics unsuited for your ear.'

The girl was stubborn. As her time at Florence drew to its close she was only at ease amongst those to whom she felt indifferent. Such a one was Miss Lavish, and such for the moment was Charlotte. She wished she had not called attention to herself; they were both annoyed at her remark and seemed determined to get rid of her.

'How tired one gets,' said Miss Bartlett. 'Oh, I do wish Freddy and your mother could be here.'

Unselfishness with Miss Bartlett had entirely usurped the functions of enthusiasm. Lucy did not look at the view either. She would not enjoy anything till she was safe at Rome.

'Then sit you down,' said Miss Lavish. 'Observe my foresight.'

With many a smile she produced two of those mackintosh squares that protect the frame of the tourist from damp grass or cold marble steps. She sat on one; who was to sit on the other?

'Lucy; without a moment's doubt, Lucy. The ground will do for me. Really I have not had rheumatism for years. If I do feel it coming on I shall stand. Imagine your mother's feelings if I let you sit in the wet in your white linen.' She sat down heavily where the ground looked particularly moist. 'Here we are, all settled delightfully. Even if my dress is thinner it will not show so much, being brown. Sit down, dear; you are too unselfish; you don't assert yourself enough.' She cleared her throat. 'Now don't be alarmed; this isn't a cold. It's the tiniest cough, and I have had it three days. It's nothing to do with sitting here at all.'

There was only one way of treating the situation. At the end of five minutes Lucy departed in search of Mr Beebe and Mr Eager, vanquished by the makintosh square.

She addressed herself to the drivers, who were sprawling in the carriages, perfuming the cushions with cigars. The miscreant, a bony young man scorched black by the sun, rose to greet her with the courtesy of a host and the assurance of a relative.

'Dove?' said Lucy, after much anxious thought.

His face lit up. Of course he knew where. Not so far either. His arm swept three-fourths of the horizon. He should just think he did know where. He pressed his finger-tips to his forehead and then pushed them towards her, as if oozing with visible extract of knowledge.

More seemed necessary. What was the Italian for 'clergymen'?

'Dove buoni uomini?' said she at last.

Good? Scarcely the adjective for those noble beings! He showed her his cigar.

'Uno—piu—piccolo,' was her next remark, implying 'Has the cigar been given to you by Mr Beebe, the smaller of the two good men?'

She was correct as usual. He tied the horse to a tree, kicked it to make it stay quiet, dusted the carriage, arranged his hair, remoulded his hat, encouraged his moustache, and in rather less than a quarter of a minute was ready to conduct her. Italians are born knowing the way. It would seem that the whole earth lay before them, not as a map, but as a chessboard, whereon they continually behold the changing pieces as well as the squares. Anyone can find places, but the finding of people is a gift from God.

He only stopped once, to pick her some great blue violets. She thanked him with real pleasure. In the company of this common man the world was beautiful and direct. For the first time she felt the influence of spring. His arm swept the horizon gracefully; violets, like other things, existed in great profusion there; would she like to see them?

'Ma buoni uomini.'

He bowed. Certainly. Good men first, violets afterwards. They proceeded briskly through the undergrowth, which became thicker and thicker. They were nearing the edge of the promontory, and the view was stealing round them, but the brown network of the bushes shattered it into countless pieces. He was occupied in his cigar, and in holding back the pliant boughs. She was rejoicing in her escape from dullness. Not a step, not a twig, was unimportant to her.

'What is that?'

There was a voice in the wood, in the distance behind them. The voice of Mr Eager? He shrugged his shoulders. An Italian's ignorance is sometimes more remarkable than his knowledge. She could not make him understand that perhaps they had missed the clergymen. The view was forming at last; she could discern the river, the golden plain, other hills.

'Eccolo!' he exclaimed.

At the same moment the ground gave way, and with a cry she fell out of the wood. Light and beauty enveloped her. She had fallen on to a little open terrace, which was covered with violets from end to end.

'Courage!' cried her companion, now standing some six feet above. 'Courage and love.'

She did not answer. From her feet the ground sloped sharply into the view, and violets ran down in rivulets and streams and cataracts, irrigating the hill-side with blue, eddying round the tree stems, collecting into pools in the hollows, covering the grass with spots of azure foam. But never again were they in such profusion; this terrace was the well-head, the primal source whence beauty gushed out to water the earth.

Standing at its brink, like a swimmer who prepares, was the good man. But he was not the good man that she had expected, and he was alone.

George had turned at the sound of her arrival. For a moment he contemplated her, as one who had fallen out of heaven. He saw radiant joy in her face, he saw the flowers beat against her dress in blue waves. The bushes above them closed. He stepped quickly forward and kissed her.

Before she could speak, almost before she could feel, a voice called, 'Lucy! Lucy! Lucy!' The silence of life had been broken by Miss Bartlett, who stood brown against the view.

Chapter Seven

They Return

Some complicated game had been playing up and down the hill-side all the afternoon. What it was and exactly how the players had sided, Lucy was slow to discover. Mr Eager had met them with a questioning eye. Charlotte had repulsed him with much small talk. Mr Emerson, seeking his son, was told whereabouts to find him. Mr Beebe, who wore the heated aspect of a neutral, was bidden to collect the factions for the return home. There was a general sense of groping and bewilderment. Pan had been amongst them—not the great god Pan, who has been buried these two thousand years, but the little god Pan, who presides over social contretemps and unsuccessful picnics. Mr Beebe had lost every one, and had consumed in solitude the tea-basket which he had brought up as a pleasant surprise. Miss Lavish had lost Miss Bartlett. Lucy had lost Mr Eager. Mr Emerson had lost George. Miss Bartlett had lost a mackintosh square. Phaethon had lost the game.

That last fact was undeniable. He climbed on to the box shivering, with his collar up, prophesying the swift approach of bad weather.

'Let us go immediately,' he told them. 'The signorino will walk.'

'All the way? He will be hours,' said Mr Beebe.

'Apparently. I told him it was unwise.' He would look no one in the face; perhaps defeat was particularly mortifying for him. He alone had played skilfully, using the whole of his instinct, while the others had used scraps of their intelligence. He alone had divined what things were, and what he wished them to be. He alone had interpreted the message that Lucy had received five days before from the lips of a dying man. Persephone, who spends half her life in the grave—she could interpret it also. Not so these English. They gain knowledge slowly, and perhaps too late.

The thoughts of a cab-driver, however just, seldom affect the lives of his employers. He was the most competent of Miss Bartlett's opponents, but infinitely the least dangerous. Once back in the town, he and his insight and his knowledge would trouble English ladies no more. Of course, it was most unpleasant; she had seen his black head in the bushes; he might make a tavern story out of it. But after all, what have we to do with taverns? Real menace belongs to the drawing-room. It was of drawing-room people that Miss Bartlett thought as she journeyed downwards towards the fading sun. Lucy sat beside her; Mr Eager sat opposite, trying to catch her eye: he was vaguely suspicious. They spoke of Alessio Baldovinetti.

Rain and darkness came on together. The two ladies huddled together under an inadequate parasol. There was a lightning flash, and Miss Lavish, who was nervous, screamed from the carriage in front. At the next flash, Lucy screamed also. Mr Eager addressed her professionally.

'Courage, Miss Honeychurch, courage and faith, If I might say so, there is something almost blasphemous in this horror of the elements. Are we seriously to suppose that all these clouds, all this immense electrical display, is simply called into existence to extinguish you or me?'

'No—of course—'

'Even from the scientific standpoint the chances against our being struck are enormous. The steel knives, the only articles which might attract the current, are in the other carriage. And, in any case, we are infinitely safer than if we were walking. Courage—courage and faith.'

Under the rug, Lucy felt the kindly pressure of her cousin's hand. At times our need for a sympathetic gesture is so great that we care not what exactly it signifies or how much we may have to pay for it afterwards. Miss Bartlett, by this timely exercise of her muscles, gained more than she would have got in hours of preaching or cross-examination.

She renewed it when the two carriages stopped, half into Florence.

'Mr Eager!' called Mr Beebe. 'We want your assistance. Will you interpret for us?'

'George!' cried Mr Emerson. 'Ask your driver which way George went. The boy may lose his way. He may be killed.'

'Go, Mr Eager,' said Miss Bartlett. 'No, don't ask our driver; our driver is no help. Go and support poor Mr Beebe; he is nearly demented.'

'He may be killed!' cried the old man. 'He may be killed!'

'Typical behaviour,' said the chaplain, as he quitted the carriage. 'In the presence of reality that kind of person invariably breaks down.'

'What does he know?' whispered Lucy as soon as they were alone.

'Charlotte, how much does Mr Eager know?'

'Nothing, dearest; he knows nothing. But'–she pointed at the driver–'*he* knows everything. Dearest, had we better? Shall I?' She took out her purse. 'It is dreadful to be entangled with low-class people. He saw it all.' Tapping Phaethon's back with her guide-book, she said, 'Silenzio!' and offered him a franc.

'Va bene,' he replied, and accepted it. As well this ending to his day as any. But Lucy, a mortal maid, was disappointed in him.

There was an explosion up the road. The storm had struck the overhead wire of the tramline, and one of the great supports had fallen. If they had not stopped perhaps they might have been hurt. They chose to regard it as a miraculous preservation, and the floods of love and sincerity, which might fructify every hour of life, burst forth in tumult. They descended from the carriages; they embraced each other. It was as joyful to be forgiven past unworthinesses as to forgive them. For a moment they realized vast possibilities of good.

The older people recovered quickly. In the very height of their emotion they knew it to be unmanly or unladylike. Miss Lavish calculated that, even if they had continued, they would not have been caught in the accident. Mr Eager mumbled a temperate prayer. But the drivers, through miles of dark squalid road, poured out their souls to the dryads and the saints, and Lucy poured out hers to her cousin.

'Charlotte, dear Charlotte, kiss me. Kiss me again. Only you can understand me. You warned me to be careful. And I–I thought I was developing.'

'Do not cry, dearest. Take your time.'

'I have been obstinate and silly–worse than you know, far worse. Once by the river— Oh, but he isn't killed–he wouldn't be killed, would he!'

The thought disturbed her repentance. As a matter of fact, the storm was worst along the road; but she had been near danger, and so she thought it must be near to every one.

'I trust not. One would always pray against that.'

'He is really–I think he was taken by surprise, just as I was before. But this time I'm not to blame; I do want you to believe that. I simply slipped into those violets. No, I want to be really truthful. I am a little to blame. I had silly thoughts. The sky, you know, was gold, and the ground all blue, and for a moment he looked like some one in a book.'

'In a book?'

'Heroes–gods–the nonsense of schoolgirls.'

'And then?'

'But, Charlotte, you know what happened then.'

Miss Bartlett was silent. Indeed, she had little more to learn. With a certain amount of insight she drew her young cousin affectionately to her. All the way back Lucy's body was shaken by deep sighs, which nothing could repress.

'I want to be truthful,' she whispered. 'It is so hard to be absolutely truthful.'

'Don't be troubled, dearest. Wait till you are calmer. We will talk it over before bed-time in my room.'

So they re-entered the city with hands clasped. It was a shock to the girl to find how far emotion had ebbed in others. The storm had ceased, and Mr Emerson was easier about his son. Mr Beebe had regained good humour, and Mr Eager was already snubbing Miss Lavish. Charlotte alone she was sure of—Charlotte, whose exterior concealed so much insight and love.

The luxury of self-exposure kept her almost happy through the long evening. She thought not so much of what had happened as of how she should describe it. All her sensations, her spasms of courage, her moments of unreasonable joy, her mysterious discontent, should be carefully laid before her cousin. And together in divine confidence they would disentangle and interpret them all.

'At last,' thought she, ' I shall understand myself. I shan't again be troubled by things that come out of nothing, and mean I don't know what.'

Miss Alan asked her to play. She refused vehemently. Music seemed to her the employment of a child. She sat close to her cousin, who, with commendable patience, was listening to a long story about lost luggage. When it was over she capped it by a story of her own. Lucy became rather hysterical with the delay. In vain she tried to check, or at all events to accelerate, the tale. It was not till a late hour that Miss Bartlett had recovered her luggage and could say in her usual tone of gentle reproach: 'Well, dear, I at all events am ready for Bedfordshire. Come into my room, and I will give a good brush to your hair.'

With some solemnity the door was shut, and a cane chair placed for the girl. Then Miss Bartlett said:

'So what is to be done?'

She was unprepared for the question. It had not occurred to her that she would have to do anything. A detailed exhibition of her emotions was all that she had counted upon.

'What is to be done? A point, dearest, which you alone can settle.'

The rain was streaming down the black windows, and the great room felt damp and chilly. One candle burnt trembling on the chest of drawers close to Miss Bartlett's toque, which cast monstrous and fantastic shadows on the bolted door. A tram roared by in the dark, and Lucy felt unaccountably sad, though she had long since dried her eyes. She lifted them to the ceiling, where the griffins and bassoons were colourless and vague, the very ghosts of joy.

'It has been raining for nearly four hours,' she said at last.

Miss Bartlett ignored the remark.

'How do you propose to silence him?'

'The driver?'

'My dear girl, no; Mr George Emerson.'

Lucy began to pace up and down the room.

'I don't understand,' she said at last.

She understood very well, but she no longer wished to be absolutely truthful.

'How are you going to stop him talking about it?'

'I have a feeling that talk is a thing he will never do.'

'I, too, intend to judge him charitably. But unfortunately I have met the type before. They seldom keep their exploits to themselves.'

'Exploits?' cried Lucy, wincing under the horrible plural.

'My poor dear, did you suppose that this was his first? Come here and listen to me. I am only gathering it from his own remarks. Do you remember that day at lunch when he argued with Miss Alan that liking one person is an extra reason for liking another?'

'Yes,' said Lucy, whom at the time the argument had pleased.

'Well, I am no prude. There is no need to call him a wicked young man, but obviously he is thoroughly unrefined. Let us put it down to his deplorable antecedents and education, if you wish. But we are no further on with our question. What do you propose to do?'

An idea rushed across Lucy's brain, which, had she thought of it sooner and made it part of her, might have proved victorious.

'I propose to speak to him,' said she.

Miss Bartlett uttered a cry of genuine alarm.

'You see, Charlotte, your kindness—I shall never forget it. But—as you said—it is my affair. Mine and his.'

'And you are going to *implore* him, to *beg* him to keep silence?'

'Certainly not. There would be no difficulty. Whatever you ask him he answers, yes or no; then it is over. I have been frightened of him. But now I am not one little bit.'

'But we fear him for you, dear. You are so young and inexperienced, you have lived among such nice people, that you cannot realize what men can be—how they can take a brutal pleasure in insulting a woman whom her sex does not protect and rally round. This afternoon, for example, if I had not arrived, what would have happened?'

'I can't think,' said Lucy gravely.

Something in her voice made Miss Bartlett repeat her question, intoning it more vigorously.

'What would have happened if I hadn't arrived?'

'I can't think,' said Lucy again.

'When he insulted you, how would you have replied?'

'I hadn't time to think. You came.'

'Yes, but won't you tell me now what you would have done?'

'I should have—' She checked herself, and broke the sentence off. She went up to the dripping window and strained her eyes into the darkness. She could not think what she would have done.

'Come away from the window, dear,' said Miss Bartlett. 'You will be seen from the road.'

Lucy obeyed. She was in her cousin's power. She could not modulate out of the key of self-abasement in which she had started. Neither of them referred again to her suggestion that she should speak to George and settle the matter, whatever it was, with him.

Miss Bartlett became plaintive.

'Oh, for a real man! We are only two women, you and I. Mr Beebe is hopeless. There is Mr Eager, but you do not trust him. Oh, for your brother! He is young, but I know that his sister's insult would rouse in him a very lion. Thank God, chivalry is not yet dead. There are still left some men who can reverence woman.'

As she spoke, she pulled off her rings, of which she wore several, and ranged them upon the pin-cushion. Then she blew into her gloves and said:

'It will be a push to catch the morning train, but we must try.'

'What train?'

'The train to Rome.' She looked at her gloves critically.

The girl received the announcement as easily as it had been given.

'When does the train to Rome go?'

'At eight.'

'Signora Bertolini would be upset.'

'We must face that,' said Miss Bartlett, not liking to say that she had given notice already.

'She will make us pay for a whole week's pension.'

'I expect she will. However, we shall be much more comfortable at the Vyses' hotel. Isn't afternoon tea given there for nothing?'

'Yes, but they pay extra for wine.'

After this remark she remained motionless and silent. To her tired eyes Charlotte throbbed and swelled like a ghostly figure in a dream.

They began to sort their clothes for packing, for there was no time to lose, if they were to catch the train to Rome. Lucy, when admonished, began to move to and fro between the rooms, more conscious of the discomforts of packing by candle-light than of a subtler ill. Charlotte, who was practical without ability, knelt by the side of an empty trunk, vainly endeavouring to pave it with books of varying thickness and size. She gave two or three sighs, for the stooping posture hurt her back, and, for all her diplomacy, she felt that she was growing old. The girl heard her as she entered the room, and was seized with one of those emotional impulses to which she could never attribute a cause. She only felt that the candle would burn better, the packing go easier, the world be happier, if she could give and receive some human love. The impulse had come before to-day, but never so strongly. She knelt down by her cousin's side and took her in her arms.

Miss Bartlett returned the embrace with tenderness and warmth. But she was not a stupid woman, and she knew perfectly well that Lucy did not love her, but needed her to love. For it was in ominous tones that she said, after a long pause:

'Dearest Lucy, how will you ever forgive me?'

Lucy was on her guard at once, knowing by bitter experience what forgiving Miss Bartlett meant. Her emotion relaxed; she modified her embrace a little, and she said:

'Charlotte dear, what to you mean? As if I have anything to forgive!'

'You have a great deal, and I have a very great deal to forgive myself, too. I know well how much I vex you at every turn.'

'But no—'

Miss Bartlett assumed her favourite rôle, that of the prematurely aged martyr.

'Ah, but yes! I feel that our tour together is hardly the success I had hoped. I might have known it would not do. You want some one younger and stronger and more in sympathy with you. I am too uninteresting and old-fashioned—only fit to pack and unpack your things.'

'Please—'

'My only consolation was that you found people more to your taste, and were often able to leave me at home. I had my own poor ideas of what a lady ought to do, but I hope I did not inflict them on you more than was necessary. You had your own way about these rooms, at all events.'

'You mustn't say these things,' said Lucy softly.

She still clung to the hope that she and Charlotte loved each other, heart and soul. They continued to pack in silence.

'I have been a failure,' said Miss Bartlett, as she struggled with the straps of Lucy's trunk instead of strapping her own. 'Failed to make you happy; failed in my duty to your mother. She has been so generous to me; I shall never face her again after this disaster.'

'But mother will understand. It is not your fault, this trouble, and it isn't a disaster either.'

'It is my fault, it is a disaster. She will never forgive me, and rightly. For instance, what right had I to make friends with Miss Lavish?'

'Every right.'

'When I was here for your sake? If I have vexed you it is equally true that I have neglected you. Your mother will see this as clearly as I do, when you tell her.'

Lucy, from a cowardly wish to improve the situation, said:

'Why need mother hear of it?'

'But you tell her everything?'

'I suppose I do generally.'

'I dare not break your confidence. There is something sacred in it. Unless you feel that it is a thing you could not tell her.'

The girl would not be degraded to this.

'Naturally I should have told her. But in case she should blame you in any way, I promise I will not. I am very willing not to. I will never speak of it either to her or to anyone.'

Her promise brought the long-drawn interview to a sudden close. Miss Bartlett pecked her smartly on both cheeks, wished her good-night, and sent her to her own room.

For a moment the original trouble was in the background. George would seem to have behaved like a cad throughout; perhaps that was the view which one would take eventually. At present she neither acquitted nor condemned him; she did not pass judgment. At the moment when she was about to judge him her cousin's voice had intervened, and, ever since, it was Miss Bartlett who had dominated; Miss Bartlett who, even now, could be heard sighing into a crack in the partition wall; Miss Bartlett, who had really been neither pliable nor humble nor inconsistent. She had worked like a great artist; for a time—indeed, for years—she had been meaningless, but at the end there was presented to the girl the complete picture of a cheerless, loveless world in which the young rush to destruction until they learn better—a shame-faced world of precautions and barriers which may avert evil, but which do not seem to bring good, if we may judge from those who have used them most.

Lucy was suffering from the most grievous wrong which this world has yet discovered: diplomatic advantage had been taken of her sincerity, of her craving for sympathy and love. Such a wrong is not easily forgotten. Never again did she expose herself without due consideration and precaution against rebuff. And such a wrong may react disastrously upon the soul.

The door-bell rang, and she started to the shutters. Before she reached them she hesitated, turned, and blew out the candle. Thus it was that, though she saw some one standing in the wet below, he, though he looked up, did not see her.

To reach his room he had to go by hers. She was still dressed. It struck her that she might slip into the passage and just say that she would be gone before he was up, and that their extraordinary intercourse was over.

Whether she would have dared to do this was never proved. At the critical moment Miss Bartlett opened her own door, and her voice said:

'I wish one word with you in the drawing-room, Mr Emerson, please.'

Soon their footsteps returned, and Miss Bartlett said: 'Good night, Mr Emerson.'

His heavy, tired breathing was the only reply; the chaperon had done her work.

Lucy cried aloud: 'It isn't true. It can't all be true. I want not to be muddled. I want to grow older quickly.'

Miss Bartlett tapped on the wall.

'Go to bed at once, dear. You need all the rest you can get.'

In the morning they left for Rome.

BOOK TWO

Chapter Eight

Medieval

The drawing-room curtains at Windy Corner had been pulled to meet, for the carpet was new and deserved protection from the August sun. They were heavy curtains, reaching almost to the ground, and the light that filtered through them was subdued and varied. A poet—none was present—might have quoted, 'Life like a dome of many coloured glass,' or might have compared the curtains to sluice-gates, lowered against the intolerable tides of heaven. Without was poured a sea of radiance; within, the glory, though visible, was tempered to the capacities of man.

Two pleasant people sat in the room. One—a boy of nineteen—was studying a small manual of anatomy, and peering occasionally at a bone which lay upon the piano. From time to time he bounced in his chair and puffed, and groaned, for the day was hot and the print small, and the human frame fearfully made; and his mother, who was writing a letter, did continually read out to him what she had written. And continually did she rise from her seat and part the curtains so that a rivulet of light fell across the carpet, and make the remark that they were still there.

'Where aren't they?' said the boy, who was Freddy, Lucy's brother. 'I tell you I'm getting fairly sick.'

'For goodness' sake go out of my drawing-room, then!' cried Mrs Honeychurch, who hoped to cure her children of slang by taking it literally.

Freddy did not move or reply.

'I think things are coming to a head,' she observed, rather wanting her son's opinion on the situation if she could obtain it without undue supplication.

'Time they did.'

'I am glad that Cecil is asking her this once more.'

'It's his third go, isn't it?'

'Freddy, I do call the way you talk unkind.'

'I didn't mean to be unkind.' Then he added: 'But I do think Lucy might have got this off her chest in Italy. I don't know how girls manage things, but she can't have said "No" properly before, or she wouldn't have to say it again now. Over the whole thing—I can't explain—I do feel so uncomfortable.'

'Do you indeed, dear? How interesting!'

'I feel—never mind.'

He returned to his work.

'Just listen to what I have written to Mrs Vyse. I said: "Dear Mrs Vyse"—'

'Yes, mother, you told me. A jolly good letter.'

'I said: "Dear Mrs Vyse—Cecil has just asked my permission about it, and I should be delighted, if Lucy wishes it. But—"' She stopped reading. 'I was rather amused at Cecil asking my permission at all. He has always gone in for unconventionality, and parents nowhere, and so forth. When it comes to the point, he can't get on without me.'

'Nor me.'

'You?'

Freddy nodded.

'What do you mean?'

'He asked me for my permission also.'

She exclaimed: 'How very odd of him!'

'Why so?' asked the son and heir. 'Why shouldn't my permission be asked?'

'What do you know about Lucy or girls or anything? Whatever did you say?'

'I said to Cecil, "Take her or leave her; it's no business of mine!"'

'What a helpful answer!' But her own answer, though more normal in its wording, had been to the same effect.

'The bother is this,' began Freddy.

Then he took up his work again, too shy to say what the bother was. Mrs Honeychurch went back to the window.

'Freddy, you must come. There they still are!'

'I don't see you ought to go peeping like that.'

'Peeping like that! Can't I look out of my own window?'

But she returned to the writing-table, observing, as she passed her son, 'Still page 322?' Freddy snorted, and turned over two leaves. For a brief space they were silent. Close by, beyond the curtains, the gentle murmur of a long conversation had never ceased.

'The bother is this: I have put my foot in it with Cecil most awfully.' He gave a nervous gulp. 'Not content with "permission," which I did give—that is to say, I said, "I don't mind"—well, not content with that, he wanted to know whether I wasn't off my head with joy. He practically put it like this: Wasn't it a splendid thing for Lucy and for Windy Corner generally if he married her? And he would have an answer—he said it would strengthen his hand.'

'I hope you gave a careful answer, dear.'

'I answered "No,"' said the boy, grinding his teeth. 'There! Fly into a stew! I can't help it—I had to say it. I had to say no. He ought never to have asked me.'

'Ridiculous child!' cried his mother. 'You think you're so holy and truthful, but really it's only abominable conceit. Do you suppose that a man like Cecil would take the slightest notice of anything you say? I hope he boxed your ears. How dare you say no?'

'Oh, do keep quiet, mother! I had to say no when I couldn't say yes. I tried to laugh as if I didn't mean what I said, and, as Cecil laughed too, and went away, it may be all right. But I feel my foot's in it. Oh, do keep quiet, though, and let a man do some work.'

'No,' said Mrs Honeychurch, with the air of one who had considered the subject. 'I shall not keep quiet. You know all that has passed between them in Rome; you know why he is down here, and yet you deliberately insult him, and try to turn him out of my house.'

'Not a bit!' he pleaded. 'I only let out I didn't like him. I don't hate him, but I don't like him. What I mind is that he'll tell Lucy.'

He glanced at the curtains dismally.

'Well, *I* like him,' said Mrs Honeychurch. 'I know his mother; he's good, he's clever, he's rich, he's well connected— Oh, you needn't kick the piano! He's well connected— I'll say it again if you like: he's well connected.' She paused, as if rehearsing her eulogy, but her face remained dissatisfied. She added: 'And he has beautiful manners.'

'I liked him till just now. I suppose it's having him spoiling Lucy's first week at home; and it's also something that Mr Beebe said, not knowing.'

'Mr Beebe?' said his mother, trying to conceal her interest. 'I don't see how Mr Beebe comes in.'

'You know Mr Beebe's funny way, when you never quite know what he means. He said: "Mr Vyse is an ideal bachelor." I was very cute. I asked him what he meant. He said: "Oh, he's like me—better detached." I couldn't make him say any more, but it set me thinking. Since Cecil has come after Lucy he hasn't been so pleasant, at least—I can't explain.'

'You never can, dear. But I can. You are jealous of Cecil because he may stop Lucy knitting you silk ties.'

The explanation seemed plausible, and Freddy tried to accept it. But at the back of his brain there lurked a dim mistrust. Cecil praised one too much for being athletic. Was that it? Cecil made one talk in his way, instead of letting one talk in one's own way. This tired one. Was that it? And Cecil was the kind of fellow who would never wear another fellow's cap. Unaware of his own profundity, Freddy checked himself. He must be jealous, or he would not dislike a man for such foolish reasons.

'Will this do?' called his mother. '"Dear Mrs Vyse—Cecil has just asked my permission about it, and I should be delighted if Lucy wishes it." Then I put in at the top, "and I have told Lucy so." I must write the letter out again—"and I have told Lucy so. But Lucy seems very uncertain, and in these days young people must decide for themselves." I said that because I didn't want Mrs Vyse to think us old-fashioned. She goes in for lectures and improving her mind, and all the time a thick layer of flue under the beds, and the maids' dirty thumb-marks where you turn on the electric light. She keeps that flat abominably—'

'Suppose Lucy marries Cecil, would she live in a flat, or in the country?'

'Don't interrupt so foolishly. Where was I? Oh yes—"Young people must decide for themselves. I know that Lucy likes your son, because she tells me everything, and she wrote to me from Rome when he asked her first." No,

I'll cross that last bit out—it looks patronizing. I'll stop at "because she tells me everything." Or shall I cross that out, too?'

'Cross it out, too,' said Freddy.

Mrs Honeychurch left it in.

'Then the whole thing runs: "Dear Mrs Vyse—Cecil has just asked my permission about it, and I should be delighted if Lucy wishes it, and I have told Lucy so. But Lucy seems very uncertain, and in these days young people must decide for themselves. I know that Lucy likes your son, because she tells me everything. But I do not know—"'

'Look out!' cried Freddy.

The curtains parted.

Cecil's first movement was one of irritation. He couldn't bear the Honeychurch habit of sitting in the dark to save the furniture. Instinctively he gave the curtains a twitch, and sent them swinging down their poles. Light entered. There was revealed a terrace, such as is owned by many villas, with trees each side of it, and on it a little rustic seat, and two flower-beds. But it was transfigured by the view beyond, for Windy Corner was built on the range that overlooks the Sussex Weald. Lucy, who was in the little seat, seemed on the edge of a green magic carpet which hovered in the air above the tremulous world.

Cecil entered.

Appearing thus late in the story, Cecil must be at once described. He was medieval. Like a Gothic statue. Tall and refined, with shoulders that seemed braced square by an effort of the will, and a head that was tilted a little higher than the usual level of vision, he resembled those fastidious saints who guard the portals of a French cathedral. Well educated, well endowed, and not deficient physically, he remained in the grip of a certain devil whom the modern world knows as self-consciousness, and whom the medieval, with dimmer vision, worshipped as asceticism. A Gothic statue implies celibacy, just as a Greek statue implies fruition, and perhaps this was what Mr Beebe meant. And Freddy, who ignored history and art, perhaps meant the same when he failed to imagine Cecil wearing another fellow's cap.

Mrs Honeychurch left her letter on the writing-table and moved towards her young acquaintance.

'Oh, Cecil!' she exclaimed—'oh, Cecil, do tell me!'

'I promessi sposi,' said he.

They stared at him anxiously.

'She has accepted me,' he said, and the sound of the thing in English made him flush and smile with pleasure, and look more human.

'I am so glad,' said Mrs Honeychurch, while Freddy proffered a hand that was yellow with chemicals. They wished that they also knew Italian, for our phrases of approval and of amazement are so connected with little occasions that we fear to use them on great ones. We are obliged to become vaguely poetic, or to take refuge in Scriptural reminiscences.

'Welcome as one of the family!' said Mrs Honeychurch, waving her hand at the furniture. 'This is indeed a joyous day! I feel sure that you will make dear Lucy happy.'

'I hope so,' replied the young man, shifting his eyes to the ceiling.

'We mothers—' simpered Mrs Honeychurch, and then realized that she was affected, sentimental, bombastic—all the things she hated most. Why could she not be as Freddy, who stood stiff in the middle of the room, looking very cross and almost handsome?

'I say, Lucy!' called Cecil, for conversation seemed to flag.

Lucy rose from the seat. She moved across the lawn and smiled in at them, just as if she was going to ask them to play tennis. Then she saw her brother's face. Her lips parted, and she took him in her arms. He said, 'Steady on!'

'Not a kiss for me?' asked her mother.

Lucy kissed her also.

'Would you take them into the garden and tell Mrs Honeychurch all about it?' Cecil suggested. 'And I'd stop here and tell my mother.'

'We go with Lucy?' said Freddy, as if taking orders.

'Yes, you go with Lucy.'

They passed into the sunlight. Cecil watched them cross the terrace, and descend out of sight by the steps. They would descend—he knew their ways—past the shrubbery, and past the tennis-lawn and the dahlia-bed, until the reached the kitchen-garden, and there, in the presence of the potatoes and the peas, the great event would be discussed.

Smiling indulgently, he lit a cigarette, and rehearsed the events that had led to such a happy conclusion.

He had known Lucy for several years, but only as a commonplace girl who happened to be musical. He could still remember his depression that afternoon at Rome, when she and her terrible cousin fell on him out of the blue, and demanded to be taken to St Peter's. That day she had seemed a typical tourist—shrill, crude, and gaunt with travel. But Italy worked some marvel in her. It gave her light, and—which he held more precious—it gave her shadow. Soon he detected in her a wonderful reticence. She was like a woman of Leonardo da Vinci's, whom we love not so much for herself as for the things that she will not tell us. The things are assuredly not of this life; no woman of Leonardo's could have anything so vulgar as a 'story.' She did develop most wonderfully day by day.

So it happened that from patronizing civility he had slowly passed, if not to passion, at least to a profound uneasiness. Already at Rome he had hinted to her that they might be suitable for each other. It had touched him greatly that she had not broken away at the suggestion. Her refusal had been clear and gentle; after it—as the horrid phrase went—she had been exactly the same to him as before. Three months later, on the margin of Italy, among the flower-clad Alps, he had asked her again in bald, traditional language. She reminded him of a Leonardo more than ever; her sunburnt features were shadowed by fantastic rocks; at his words she had turned and stood between him and the light with immeasurable plains behind her. He walked home with her unashamed, feeling not at all like a rejected suitor. The things that really mattered were unshaken.

So now he had asked her once more, and, clear and gentle as ever, she had accepted him, giving no coy reasons for her delay, but simply saying that she loved him and would do her best to make him happy. His mother, too, would be pleased; she had counselled the step; he must write her a long account.

Glancing at his hand, in case any of Freddy's chemicals had come off on it, he moved to the writing-table. There he saw 'Dear Mrs Vyse,' followed by many erasures. He recoiled without reading any more, and after a little hesitation sat down elsewhere, and pencilled a note on his knee.

Then he lit another cigarette, which did not seem quite as divine as the first, and considered what might be done to make the Windy Corner drawing-room more distinctive. With that outlook it should have been a successful room, but the trail of Tottenham Court Road was upon it; he could almost visualize the motor-vans of Messrs Shoolbred and Messrs Maple arriving at the door and depositing this chair, those varnished book-cases, that writing-table. The table recalled Mrs Honeychurch's letter. He did not want to read that letter—his temptations never lay in that direction; but he worried about it none the less. It was his own fault that she was discussing him with his mother; he had wanted her support in his third attempt to win Lucy; he wanted to feel that others, no matter who they were, agreed with him, and so he had asked their permission. Mrs Honeychurch had been civil, but obtuse in essentials, while as for Freddy—

'He is only a boy,' he reflected. 'I represent all that he despises. Why should he want me for a brother-in-law?'

The Honeychurches were a worthy family, but he began to realize that Lucy was of another clay; and perhaps—he did not put it very definitely—he ought to introduce her into more congenial circles as soon as possible.

'Mr Beebe!' said the maid, and the new rector of Summer Street was shown in; he had at once started on friendly relations, owing to Lucy's praise of him in her letters from Florence.

Cecil greeted him rather critically.

'I've come for tea, Mr Vyse. Do you suppose that I shall get it?'

'I should say so. Food is the thing one does get here— Don't sit in that chair; young Honeychurch has left a bone in it.'

'Pfui!'

'I know,' said Cecil, 'I know. I can't think why Mrs Honeychurch allows it.'

For Cecil considered the bone and the Maple's furniture separately; he did not realize that, taken together, they kindled the room into the life that he desired.

'I've come for tea and for gossip. Isn't this news?'

'News? I don't understand you,' said Cecil. 'News?'

Mr Beebe, whose news was of a very different nature, prattled forward.

'I met Sir Harry Otway as I came up; I have every reason to hope that I am first in the field. He has bought Cissie and Albert from Mr Flack!'

'Has he indeed?' said Cecil, trying to recover himself. Into what a grotesque mistake had he fallen! Was it likely that a clergyman and a gentleman would refer to his engagement in a manner so flippant? But his stiffness remained, and, though he asked who Cissie and Albert might be, he still thought Mr Beebe rather a bounder.

'Unpardonable question! To have stopped a week at Windy Corner and not to have met Cissie and Albert, the semi-detached villas that have been run up opposite the church! I'll set Mrs Honeychurch after you.'

'I'm shockingly stupid over local affairs,' said the young man languidly. 'I can't even remember the difference between a Parish Council and a Local Government Board. Perhaps there is no difference, or perhaps those aren't the right names. I only go into the country to see my friends and to enjoy the scenery. It is very remiss of me. Italy and London are the only places where I don't feel to exist on sufferance.'

Mr Beebe, distressed at this heavy reception of Cissie and Albert, determined to shift the subject.

'Let me see, Mr Vyse—I forget—what is your profession?'

'I have no profession,' said Cecil. 'It is another example of my decadence. My attitude—quite an indefensible one—is that so long as I am no trouble to anyone I have a right to do as I like. I know I ought to be getting money out of people, or devoting myself to things I don't care a straw about, but somehow, I've not been able to begin.'

'You are very fortunate,' said Mr Beebe. 'It is a wonderful opportunity, the possession of leisure.'

His voice was rather parochial, but he did not quite see his way to answering naturally. He felt, as all who have regular occupation must feel, that others should have it also.

'I am glad that you approve. I daren't face the healthy person—for example, Freddy Honeychurch.'

'Oh, Freddy's a good sort, isn't he?'

'Admirable. The sort who has made England what she is.'

Cecil wondered at himself. Why, on this day of all others, was he so hopelessly contrary? He tried to get right by inquiring effusively after Mr Beebe's mother, an old lady for whom he had no particular regard. Then he flattered the clergyman, praised his liberal-mindedness, his enlightened attitude towards philosophy and science.

'Where are the others?' said Mr Beebe at last. 'I insist on extracting tea before evening service.'

'I suppose Anne never told them you were here. In this house one is so coached in the servants the day one arrives. The fault of Anne is that she begs your pardon when she hears you perfectly, and kicks the chair-legs with her feet. The faults of Mary—I forget the faults of Mary, but they are very grave. Shall we look in the garden?'

'I know the faults of Mary. She leaves the dust-pans standing on the stairs.'

'The fault of Euphemia is that she will not, simply will not, chop the suet sufficiently small.'

They both laughed, and things began to go better.

'The faults of Freddy—' Cecil continued.

'Ah, he has too many. No one but his mother can remember the faults of Freddy. Try the faults of Miss Honeychurch; they are not innumerable.'

'She has none,' said the young man, with grave sincerity.

'I quite agree. At present she has none.'

'At present?'

'I'm not cynical. I'm only thinking of my pet theory about Miss Honeychurch. Does it seem reasonable that she should play so wonderfully, and live so quietly? I suspect that one day she will be wonderful in both. The water-tight compartments in her will break down, and music and life will mingle. Then we shall have her heroically good, heroically bad—too heroic, perhaps, to be good or bad.'

Cecil found his companion interesting.

'And at present you think her not wonderful as far as life goes?'

'Well, I must say I've only seen her at Tunbridge Wells, where she was not wonderful, and at Florence. Since I came to Summer Street she has been away. You saw her, didn't you, at Rome and in the Alps. Oh, I forgot; of course, you knew her before. No, she wasn't wonderful in Florence either, but I kept on expecting that she would be.'

'In what way?'

Conversation had become agreeable to them, and they were pacing up and down the terrace.

'I could as easily tell you what tune she'll play next. There was simply the sense that she had found wings, and meant to use them. I can show you a beautiful picture in my Italian diary: Miss Honeychurch as a kite, Miss Bartlett holding the string. Picture number two: the string breaks.'

The sketch was in his diary, but it had been made afterwards, when he viewed things artistically. At the time he had given surreptitious tugs to the string himself.

'But the string never broke?'

'No. I mightn't have seen Miss Honeychurch rise, but I should certainly have heard Miss Bartlett fall.'

'It has broken now,' said the young man in low, vibrating tones.

Immediately he realized that of all the conceited, ludicrous, contemptible ways of announcing an engagement this was the worst. He cursed his love of metaphor; had he suggested that he was a star and that Lucy was soaring up to reach him?

'Broken? What do you mean?'

'I meant,' said Cecil stiffly, 'that she is going to marry me.'

The clergyman was conscious of some bitter disappointment which he could not keep out of his voice.

'I am sorry; I must apologize. I had no idea you were intimate with her, or I should never have talked in this flippant, superficial way. Mr Vyse, you ought to have stopped me.' And down the garden he saw Lucy herself; yes, he was disappointed.

Cecil, who naturally preferred congratulations to apologies, drew down his mouth at the corners. Was this the reception his action would get from the world? Of course, he despised the world as a whole; every thoughtful man should; it is almost a test of refinement. But he was sensitive to the successive particles of it which he encountered.

Occasionally he could be quite crude.

'I am sorry I have given you a shock,' he said dryly. 'I fear that Lucy's choice does not meet with your approval.'

'Not that. But you ought to have stopped me. I know Miss Honeychurch only a little as time goes. Perhaps I oughtn't to have discussed her so freely with anyone; certainly not with you.'

'You are conscious of having said something indiscreet?'

Mr Beebe pulled himself together. Really, Mr Vyse had the art of placing one in the most tiresome positions. He was driven to use the prerogatives of his profession.

'No, I have said nothing indiscreet. I foresaw at Florence that her quiet, uneventful childhood must end, and it has ended. I realized dimly enough that she might take some momentous step. She has taken it. She has learnt—you will let me talk freely, as I have begun freely—she has learnt what it is to love: the greatest lesson, some people will tell you, that our earthly life provides.' It was now time for him to wave his hat at the approaching trio. He did not omit to do so. 'She has learnt through you,' and if his voice was still clerical, it was now also sincere; 'let it be your care that her knowledge is profitable to her.'

'Grazie tante!' said Cecil, who did not like parsons.

'Have you heard?' shouted Mrs Honeychurch as she toiled up the sloping garden. 'Oh, Mr Beebe, have you heard the news?'

Freddy, now full of geniality, whistled the wedding march. Youth seldom criticizes the accomplished fact.

'Indeed I have!' he cried. He looked at Lucy. In her presence he could not act the parson any longer—at all events not without apology. 'Mrs Honeychurch, I'm going to do what I am always supposed to do, but generally I'm too shy. I want to invoke every kind of blessing on them, grave and gay, great and small. I want them all their lives to be supremely good and supremely happy as husband and wife, as father and mother. And now I want my tea.'

'You only asked for it just in time,' the lady retorted. 'How dare you be serious at Windy Corner?'

He took his tone from her. There was no more heavy beneficence, no more attempts to dignify the situation with poetry or the Scriptures. None of them dared or was able to be serious any more.

An engagement is so potent a thing that sooner or later it reduces all who speak of it to this state of cheerful awe. Away from it, in the solitude of their rooms, Mr Beebe, and even Freddy, might again be critical. But in its presence and in the presence of each other they were sincerely hilarious. It has a strange power, for it compels not only the lips, but the very heart. The chief parallel—to compare one great thing with another—is the power over us of a temple of some alien creed. Standing outside, we deride or oppose it, or at the most feel sentimental. Inside, though the saints and gods are not ours, we become true believers, in case any true believer should be present.

So it was that after the gropings and the misgivings of the afternoon they pulled themselves together and settled down to a very pleasant tea-party. If they were hypocrites they did not know it, and their hypocrisy had every chance of setting and of becoming true. Anne, putting down each plate as if it were a wedding present, stimulated them greatly. They could not lag behind that smile of hers which she gave them ere she kicked the drawing-room door. Mr Beebe chirruped. Freddy was at his wittiest, referring to Cecil as the 'Fiasco'–family honoured pun on fiancé. Mrs Honeychurch, amusing and portly, promised well as a mother-in-law. As for Lucy and Cecil, for whom the temple had been built, they also joined in the merry ritual, but waited, as earnest worshippers should, for the disclosure of some holier shrine of joy.

Chapter Nine

Lucy as a Work of Art

A few days after the engagement was announced Mrs Honeychurch made Lucy and her Fiasco come to a little garden-party in the neighbourhood, for naturally she wanted to show people that her daughter was marrying a presentable man.

Cecil was more than presentable; he looked distinguished, and it was very pleasant to see his slim figure keeping step with Lucy, and his long, fair face responding when Lucy spoke to him, People congratulated Mrs Honeychurch, which is, I believe, a social blunder, but it pleased her, and she introduced Cecil rather indiscriminately to some stuffy dowagers.

At tea a misfortune took place: a cup of coffee was upset over Lucy's figured silk, and though Lucy feigned indifference, her mother feigned nothing of the sort, but dragged her indoors to have the frock treated by a sympathetic maid. They were gone some time, and Cecil was left with the dowagers. When they returned he was not as pleasant as he had been.

'Do you go to much of this sort of thing?' he asked when they were driving home.

'Oh, now and then,' said Lucy, who had rather enjoyed herself.

'Is it typical of county society?'

'I suppose so. Mother, would it be?'

'Plenty of society,' said Mrs Honeychurch, who was trying to remember the hang of one of the dresses.

Seeing that her thoughts were elsewhere, Cecil bent towards Lucy and said:

'To me it seemed perfectly appalling, disastrous, portentous.'

'I am so sorry that you were stranded.'

'Not that, but the congratulations. It is so disgusting, the way an engagement is regarded as public property–a kind of waste place where every outsider may shoot his vulgar sentiment. All those old women smirking!'

'One has to go through it, I suppose. They won't notice us so much next time.'

'But my point is that their whole attitude is wrong. An engagement—horrid word in the first place—is a private matter, and should be treated as such.'

Yet the smirking old women, however wrong individually, were racially correct. The spirit of the generations had smiled through them, rejoicing in the engagement of Cecil and Lucy because it promised the continuance of life on earth. To Cecil and Lucy it promised something quite different—personal love. Hence Cecil's irritation and Lucy's belief that his irritation was just.

'How tiresome!' she said. 'Couldn't you have escaped to tennis?'

'I don't play tennis—at least, not in public. The neighbourhood is deprived of the romance of me being athletic. Such romance as I have is that of the Inglese Italianato.'

'Inglese Italianato?'

'E un diavolo incarnato! You know the proverb?'

She did not. Nor did it seem applicable to a young man who had spent a quiet winter in Rome with his mother. But Cecil, since his engagement, had taken to affect a cosmopolitan naughtiness which he was far from possessing.

'Well,' said he, 'I cannot help it if they do disapprove of me. There are certain irremovable barriers between myself and them, and I must accept them.'

'We all have our limitations, I suppose,' said wise Lucy.

'Sometimes they are forced on us, though,' said Cecil, who saw from her remark that she did not quite understand his position.

'How?'

'It makes a difference, doesn't it, whether we fence ourselves in, or whether we are fenced out by the barriers of others?'

She thought a moment, and agreed that it did make a difference.

'Difference?' cried Mrs Honeychurch, suddenly alert. 'I don't see any difference. Fences are fences, especially when they are in the same place.'

'We were speaking of motives,' said Cecil, on whom the interruption jarred.

'My dear Cecil, look here.' She spread out her knees and perched her card-case on her lap. 'This is me. That's Windy Corner. The rest of the pattern is the other people. Motives are all very well, but the fence comes here.'

'We weren't talking of real fences,' said Lucy, laughing.

'Oh, I see, dear—poetry.'

She leant placidly back. Cecil wondered why Lucy had been amused.

'I tell you who has no "fences," as you call them,' she said, 'and that's Mr Beebe.'

'A parson fenceless would mean a parson defenceless.'

Lucy was slow to follow what people said, but quick enough to detect what they meant. She missed Cecil's epigram, but grasped the feeling that prompted it.

'Don't you like Mr Beebe?' she asked thoughtfully.

'I never said so!' he cried. 'I consider him far above the average. I only denied—' And he swept off on the subject of fences again, and was brilliant.

'Now, a clergyman that I do hate,' said she, wanting to say something sympathetic, 'a clergyman that does have fences, and the most dreadful ones, is Mr Eager, the English chaplain at Florence. He was truly insincere—not merely the manner unfortunate. He was a snob, and so conceited, and he did say such unkind things.'

'What sort of things?'

'There was an old man at the Bertolini whom he said had murdered his wife.'

'Perhaps he had.'

'Why, no.'

'Why "no"?'

'He was such a nice old man, I'm sure.'

Cecil laughed at her feminine inconsequence.

'Well, I did try to sift the thing. Mr Eager would never come to the point. He prefers it vague—said the old man had "practically" murdered his wife—had murdered her in the sight of God.'

'Hush, dear!' said Mrs Honeychurch absently.

'But isn't it intolerable that a person whom we're told to imitate should go round spreading slander? It was, I believe, chiefly owing to him that the old man was dropped. People pretended he was vulgar, but he certainly wasn't that.'

'Poor old man! What was his name?'

'Harris,' said Lucy glibly.

'Let's hope that Mrs Harris there warn't no sich person,' said her mother. Cecil nodded intelligently.

'Isn't Mr Eager a parson of the cultured type?' he asked.

'I don't know. I hate him. I've heard him lecture on Giotto. I hate him. Nothing can hide a petty nature. I *hate* him!'

'My goodness gracious me, child!' said Mrs Honeychurch. 'You'll blow my head off! Whatever is there to shout over? I forbid you and Cecil to hate any more clergymen.'

He smiled. There was indeed something rather incongruous in Lucy's moral outburst over Mr Eager. It was as if one should see the Leonardo on the ceiling of the Sistine. He longed to hint to her that not here lay her vocation; that a woman's power and charm reside in mystery, not in muscular rant. But possibly rant is a sign of vitality: it mars the beautiful creature, but shows that she is alive. After a moment, he contemplated her flushed face and excited gestures with a certain approval. He forebore to repress the sources of youth.

Nature—simplest of topics, he thought—lay around them. He praised the pine-woods, the deep lakes of bracken, the crimson leaves that spotted the hurt-bushes, the serviceable beauty of the turnpike road. The outdoor world was not very familiar to him, and occasionally he went wrong in a question of fact. Mrs Honeychurch's mouth twitched when he spoke of the perpetual green of the larch.

'I count myself a lucky person,' he concluded. 'When I'm in London I feel I could never live out of it. When I'm in the country I feel the same about the country. After all, I do believe that birds and trees and the sky are the most wonderful things in life, and that the people who live amongst them must be the best. It's true that in nine cases out of ten they don't seem to notice anything. The country gentleman and the country labourer are each in their way the most depressing of companions. Yet they may have a tacit sympathy with the workings of Nature which is denied to us of the town. Do you feel that, Mrs Honeychurch?'

Mrs Honeychurch started and smiled. She had not been attending. Cecil, who was rather crushed on the front seat of the victoria, felt irritable, and determined not to say anything interesting again.

Lucy had not attended either. Her brow was wrinkled, and she still looked furiously cross—the result, he conluded, of too much moral gymnastics. It was sad to see her thus blind to the beauties of an August wood.

'"Come down, O maid, from yonder mountain height,"' he quoted, and touched her knee with his own.

She flushed again and said: 'What height?'

> 'Come down, O maid, from yonder mountain height,
> What pleasure lives in height (the shepherd sang),
> In height and in the splendour of the hills?

Let us take Mrs Honeychurch's advice and hate clergymen no more. What's this place?'

'Summer Street, of course,' said Lucy, and roused herself.

The woods had opened to leave space for a sloping triangular meadow. Pretty cottages lined it on two sides, and the upper and third side was occupied by a new stone church, expensively simple, with a charming shingled spire. Mr Beebe's house was near the church. In height it scarcely exceeded the cottages. Some great mansions were at hand, but they were hidden in the trees. The scene suggested a Swiss Alp rather than the shrine and centre of a leisured world, and was only marred by two ugly little villas—the villas that had competed with Cecil's engagement, having been acquired by Sir Harry Otway the very afternoon that Lucy had been acquired by him.

'Cissie' was the name of one of these villas, 'Albert' of the other. These titles were not only picked out in shaded Gothic on the garden gates, but appeared a second time on the porches, where they followed the semicircular curve of the entrance arch in block capitals. Albert was inhabited. His tortured garden was bright with geraniums and lobelias and polished shells. His little windows were chastely swathed in Nottingham lace. Cissie was to let. Three notice-boards, belonging to Dorking agents, lolled on her fence and announced the not surprising fact. Her paths were already weedy; her pocket-handkerchief of a lawn was yellow with dandelions.

'The place is ruined!' said the ladies mechanically. 'Summer Street will never be the same again.'

As the carriage passed, Cissie's door opened, and a gentleman came out of her.

'Stop!' cried Mrs Honeychurch, touching the coachman with her parasol. 'Here's Sir Harry. Now we shall know. Sir Harry, pull those things down at once!'

Sir Harry Otway—who need not be described—came to the carriage and said:

'Mrs Honeychurch, I meant to. I can't, I really can't turn out Miss Flack.'

'Am I not always right? She ought to have gone before the contract was signed. Does she still live rent free, as she did in her nephew's time?'

'But what can I do?' He lowered his voice. 'An old lady, so very vulgar, and almost bedridden.'

'Turn her out,' said Cecil bravely.

Sir Harry sighed, and looked at the villas mournfully. He had had full warning of Mr Flack's intentions, and might have bought the plot before building commenced; but he was apathetic and dilatory. He had known Summer Street for so many years that he could not imagine it being spoilt. Not till Mrs Flack had laid the foundation stone, and the apparition of red and cream brick began to rise, did he take alarm. He called on Mr Flack, the local builder—a most reasonable and respectful man—who agreed that tiles would have made a more artistic roof, but pointed out that slates were cheaper. He ventured to differ, however, about the Corinthian columns which were to cling like leeches to the frames of the bow-windows, saying that, for his part, he liked to relieve the façade by a bit of decoration. Sir Harry hinted that a column, if possible, should be structural as well as decorative. Mr Flack replied that all the columns had been ordered, adding, 'and all the capitals different—one with dragons in the foliage, another approaching to the Ionian style, another introducing Mrs Flack's initials—every one different.' For he had read his Ruskin. He built his villas according to his desire; and not till he had inserted an immovable aunt into one of them did Sir Harry buy.

This futile and unprofitable transaction filled the knight with sadness as he leant on Mrs Honeychurch's carriage. He had failed in his duties to the country-side, and the country-side was laughing at him as well. He had spent money, and yet Summer Street was spoilt as much as ever. All he could do now was to find a desirable tenant for Cissie—some one really desirable.

'The rent is absurdly low,' he told them, 'and perhaps I am an easy landlord. But it is such an awkward size. It is too large for the peasant class, and too small for anyone the least like ourselves.'

Cecil had been hesitating whether he should despise the villas or despise Sir Harry for despising them. The latter impulse seemed the more fruitful.

'You ought to find a tenant at once,' he said maliciously. 'It would be a perfect paradise for a bank clerk.'

'Exactly!' said Sir Harry excitedly. 'That is exactly what I fear, Mr Vyse. It will attract the wrong type of people. The train service has improved—a fatal improvement, to my mind. And what are five miles from a station in these days of bicycles?'

'Rather a strenuous clerk it would be,' said Lucy.

Cecil, who had his full share of medieval mischievousness, replied that the physique of the lower middle classes was improving at a most appalling rate. She saw that he was laughing at their harmless neighbour, and roused herself to stop him.

'Sir Harry!' she exclaimed, 'I have an idea. How would you like spinsters?'

'My dear Lucy, it would be splendid. Do you know any such?'

'Yes; I met them abroad.'

'Gentlewomen?' he asked tentatively.

'Yes, indeed, and at the present moment homeless. I heard from them last week. Miss Teresa and Miss Catharine Alan. I'm really not joking. They are quite the right people. Mr Beebe knows them, too. May I tell them to write to you?'

'Indeed you may!' he cried. 'Here we are with the difficulty solved already. How delightful it is! Extra facilities—please tell them they shall have extra facilities, for I shall have no agents' fees. Oh, the agents! The appalling people they have sent me! One woman, when I wrote—a tactful letter, you know—asking her to explain her social position to me, replied that she would pay the rent in advance. As if one cares about that! And several references I took up were most unsatisfactory—people swindlers, or not respectable. And oh, the deceit! I have seen a good deal of the seamy side this last week. The deceit of the most promising people! My dear Lucy, the deceit!'

She nodded.

'My advice,' put in Mrs Honeychurch, 'is to have nothing to do with Lucy and her decayed gentlewomen at all. I know the type. Preserve me from people who have seen better days, and bring heirlooms with them that make the house smell stuffy. It's a sad thing, but I'd far rather let to some one who is going up in the world than to some one who has come down.'

'I think I follow you,' said Sir Harry; 'but it is, as you say, a very sad thing.'

'The Miss Alans aren't that!' cried Lucy.

'Yes, they are!' said Cecil. 'I haven't met them, but I should say they were a highly unsuitable addition to the neighbourhood.'

'Don't listen to him, Sir Harry—he's tiresome.'

'It's I who am tiresome,' he replied. 'I oughtn't to come with my troubles to young people. But really I am so worried, and Lady Otway will only say that I cannot be too careful, which is quite true, but no real help.'

'Then may I write to my Miss Alans?'

'Please!' he cried.

But his eye wavered when Mrs Honeychurch exclaimed:

'Beware! They are certain to have canaries. Sir Harry, beware of canaries: they spit the seed out through the bars of the cages, and then the mice come. Beware of women altogether. Only let to a man.'

'Really—' he murmured gallantly, though he saw the wisdom of her remark.

'Men don't gossip over tea-cups. If they get drunk, there's an end of them—they lie down comfortably, and sleep it off. If they're vulgar, they somehow keep it to themselves. It doesn't spread so. Give me a man—of course, provided he's clean.'

Sir Harry blushed. Neither he nor Cecil enjoyed these open compliments to their sex. Even the exclusion of the dirty did not leave them much distinction. He suggested that Mrs Honeychurch, if she had time, should descend from the carriage and inspect Cissie for herself. She was delighted. Nature had intended her to be poor and to live in such a house. Domestic arrangements always attracted her, especially when they were on a small scale.

Cecil pulled Lucy back as she followed her mother.

'Mrs Honeychurch,' he said, 'what if we two walk home and leave you?'

'Certainly!' was her cordial reply.

Sir Harry likewise seemed almost too glad to get rid of them. He beamed at them knowingly, said, 'Aha! young people, young people, young people!' and then hastened to unlock the house.

'Hopeless vulgarian!' exclaimed Cecil, almost before they were out of earshot.

'Oh, Cecil!'

'I can't help it. It would be wrong not to loathe that man.'

'He isn't clever, but really he is nice.'

'No, Lucy; he stands for all that is bad in country life. In London he would keep his place. He would belong to a brainless club, and his wife would give brainless dinner-parties. But down here he acts the little god with his gentility, and his patronage, and his sham æsthetics, and every one—even your mother—is taken in.'

'All that you say is quite true,' said Lucy, though she felt discouraged. 'I wonder whether—whether it matters so very much.'

'It matters supremely. Sir Harry is the essence of that garden-party. Oh, goodness, how cross I feel! How I do hope he'll get some vulgar tenant in that villa—some woman so really vulgar that he'll notice it. *Gentlefolks!* Ugh! with his bald head and retreating chin! But let's forget him.'

This Lucy was glad enough to do. If Cecil disliked Sir Harry Otway and Mr Beebe, what guarantee was there that the people who really mattered to her would escape? For instance, Freddy. Freddy was neither clever, nor subtle, nor beautiful, and what prevented Cecil from saying, any minute, 'It would be wrong not to loathe Freddy'? And what would she reply? Further than Freddy she did not go, but he gave her anxiety enough. She could only assure herself that Cecil had known Freddy some time, and that they had always got on pleasantly, except, perhaps, during the last few days, which was an accident, perhaps.

'Which way shall we go?' she asked him.

Nature—simplest of topics, she thought—was around them. Summer Street lay deep in the woods, and she had stopped where a footpath diverged from the highroad.

'Are there two ways?'

'Perhaps the road is more sensible, as we're got up smart.'

'I'd rather go through the wood,' said Cecil, with that subdued irritation that she had noticed in him all the afternoon. 'Why is it, Lucy, that you always say the road? Do you know that you have never once been with me in the fields or the wood since we were engaged?'

'Haven't I? The wood, then,' said Lucy, startled at his queerness, but pretty sure that he would explain later; it was not his habit to leave her in doubt as to his meaning.

She led the way into the whispering pines, and sure enough he did explain before they had gone a dozen yards.

'I had got an idea–I dare say wrongly–that you feel more at home with me in a room.'

'A room?' she echoed, hopelessly bewildered.

'Yes. Or, at the most, in a garden, or on a road. Never in the real country like this.'

'Oh, Cecil, whatever do you mean? I have never felt anything of the sort. You talk as if I was a kind of poetess sort of person.'

'I don't know that you aren't. I connect you with a view–a certain type of view. Why shouldn't you connect me with a room?'

She reflected a moment, and then said, laughing:

'Do you know that you're right? I do. I must be a poetess after all. When I think of you it's always as in a room. How funny!'

To her surprise, he seemed annoyed.

'A drawing-room, pray? With no view?'

'Yes, with no view, I fancy. Why not?'

'I'd rather,' he said reproachfully, 'that you connected me with the open air.'

She said again, 'Oh, Cecil, whatever do you mean?'

As no explanation was forthcoming, she shook off the subject as too difficult for a girl, and led him farther into the wood, pausing every now and then at some particularly beautiful or familiar combination of the trees. She had known the wood between Summer Street and Windy Corner ever since she could walk alone; she had played at losing Freddy in it, when Freddy was a purple-faced baby; and though she had now been to Italy, it had lost none of its charm.

Presently they came to a little clearing among the pines–another tiny green alp, solitary this time, and holding in its bosom a shallow pool.

She exclaimed, 'The Sacred Lake!'

'Why do you call it that?'

'I can't remember why. I suppose it comes out of some book. It's only a puddle now, but you see that stream going through it? Well, a good deal of water comes down after heavy rains, and can't get away at once, and the pool becomes quite large and beautiful. Then Freddy used to bathe there. He is very fond of it.'

'And you?'

He meant, 'Are you fond of it?' But she answered dreamily, 'I bathed here, too, till I was found out. Then there was a row.'

At another time he might have been shocked, for he had depths of prudishness within him. But now, with his momentary cult of the fresh air, he was delighted at her admirable simplicity. He looked at her as she stood by the pool's edge. She was got up smart, as she phrased it, and she reminded him of some brilliant flower that has no leaves of its own, but blooms abruptly out of a world of green.

'Who found you out?'

'Charlotte,' she murmured. 'She was stopping with us. Charlotte –Charlotte.'

'Poor girl!'

She smiled gravely. A certain scheme, from which hitherto he had shrank, now appeared practical.

'Lucy!'

'Yes, I suppose we ought to be going,' was her reply.

'Lucy, I want to ask something of you that I have never asked before.'

At the serious note in his voice she stepped frankly and kindly towards him.

'What, Cecil?'

'Hitherto never–not even that day on the lawn when you agreed to marry me—'

He became self-conscious and kept glancing round to see if they were observed. His courage had gone.

'Yes?'

'Up to now I have never kissed you.'

She was as scarlet as if he had put the thing most indelicately.

'No–more you have,' she stammered.

'Then I ask you–may I now?'

'Of course you may, Cecil. You might before. I can't run at you, you know.'

At that supreme moment he was conscious of nothing but absurdities. Her reply was inadequate. She gave such a business-like lift to her veil. As he approached her he found time to wish that he could recoil. As he touched her, his gold pince-nez became dislodged and was flattened between them.

Such was the embrace. He considered, with truth, that it had been a failure. Passion should believe itself irresistible. It should forget civility and consideration and all the other curses of a refined nature. Above all, it should never ask for leave where there is a right of way. Why could he not do as any labourer or navvy–nay, as any young man behind the counter would have done? He recast the scene. Lucy was standing flower-like by the water; he rushed up and took her in his arms; she rebuked him, permitted him, and revered him ever after for his manliness. For he believed that woman revere men for their manliness.

They left the pool in silence, after this one salutation. He waited for her to make some remark which should show him her inmost thoughts. At last she spoke, and with fitting gravity.

'Emerson the name was, not Harris.'

'What name?'

'The old man's.'

'What old man?'

'That old man I told you about. The one Mr Eager was so unkind to.'

He could not know that this was the most intimate conversation they had ever had.

Chapter Ten

Cecil as a Humorist

The society out of which Cecil proposed to rescue Lucy was perhaps no very splendid affair, yet it was more splendid than her antecedents entitled her to. Her father, a prosperous local solicitor, had built Windy Corner as a speculation at the time the district was opening up, and, falling in love with his own creation, had ended by living there himself. Soon after his marriage, the social atmosphere began to alter. Other houses were built on the brow of that steep southern slope, and others, again, among the pine-trees behind, and northward on the chalk barrier of the downs. Most of these houses were larger than Windy Corner, and were filled by people who came, not from the district, but from London, and who mistook the Honeychurches for the remnants of an indigenous aristocracy. He was inclined to be frightened, but his wife accepted the situation without either pride or humility. 'I cannot think what people are doing,' she would say, 'but it is extremely fortunate for the children.' She called everywhere; her calls were returned with enthusiasm, and by the time people found out that she was not exactly of their *milieu*, they liked her, and it did not seem to matter. When Mr Honeychurch died, he had the satisfaction—which few honest solicitors despise—of leaving his family rooted in the best society obtainable.

The best obtainable. Certainly many of the immigrants were rather dull, and Lucy realized this more vividly since her return from Italy. Hitherto she had accepted their ideals without questioning—their kindly affluence, their inexplosive religion, their dislike of paper-bags, orange-peel, and broken bottles. A Radical out and out, she learnt to speak with horror of Suburbia. Life, so far as she troubled to conceive it, was a circle of rich, pleasant people, with identical interests and identical foes. In this circle one thought, married, and died. Outside, it were poverty and vulgarity, for ever trying to enter, just as the London fog tries to enter the pine-woods, pouring through the gaps in the northern hills. But in Italy, where anyone who chooses may warm himself in equality, as in the sun, this conception of life vanished. Her senses expanded; she felt that there was no one whom she might not get to like, that social barriers were irremovable, doubtless, but not particularly high. You jump over them just as you jump into a peasant's olive-yard in the Apennines, and he is glad to see you. She returned with new eyes.

So did Cecil; but Italy had quickened Cecil, not to tolerance, but to irritation. He saw that the local society was narrow, but, instead of saying. 'Does this very much matter?' he rebelled, and tried to substitute for it the society he called broad. He did not realize that Lucy had consecrated her environment by the thousand little civilities that create a tenderness in time, and that though her eyes saw its defects, her heart refused to despise it entirely. Nor did he realize a more important point—that if she was too great for this society, she was too great for all society, and had reached the stage where personal intercourse would alone satisfy her. A rebel she was, but not of the kind he understood—a rebel who desired, not a wider dwelling-room, but equality beside the man she loved. For Italy was offering her the most priceless of all possessions—her own soul.

Playing bumble-puppy with Minnie Beebe, niece to the rector, and aged thirteen—an ancient and most honourable game, which consists in striking tennis-balls high into the air, so that they fall over the net and immoderately bounce; some hit Mrs Honeychurch; others are lost. The sentence is confused, but the better illustrates Lucy's state of mind, for she was trying to talk to Mr Beebe at the same time.

'Oh, it has been such a nuisance—first he, then they—no one knowing what they wanted, and every one so tiresome.'

'But they really are coming now,' said Mr Beebe. 'I wrote to Miss Teresa a few days ago—she was wondering how often the butcher called, and my reply of once a month must have impressed her favourably. They are coming. I heard from them this morning.'

'I shall hate those Miss Alans!' Mrs Honeychurch cried. 'Just because they're old and silly one's expected to say, "How sweet!" I hate their "if"-ing and "but"-ing and "and"-ing. And poor Lucy—serve her right—worn to a shadow.'

Mr Beebe watched the shadow springing and shouting over the tennis-court. Cecil was absent—one did not play bumble-puppy when he was there.

'Well, if they are coming— No, Minnie, not Saturn.' Saturn was a tennis-ball whose skin was partially unsown. When in motion his orb was encircled by a ring. 'If they are coming, Sir Harry will let them move in before the twenty-ninth, and he will cross out the clause about whitewashing the ceilings, because it made them nervous, and put in the fair wear and tear one.—That doesn't count. I told you not Saturn.'

'Saturn's all right for bumble-puppy,' cried Freddy, joining them. 'Minnie, don't you listen to her.'

'Saturn doesn't bounce.'

'Saturn bounces enough.'

'No, he doesn't.'

'Well, he bounces better than the Beautiful White Devil.'

'Hush, dear,' said Mrs Honeychurch.

'But look at Lucy—complaining of Saturn, and all the time's got the Beautiful White Devil in her hand, ready to plug it in. That's right, Minnie, go for her—get her over the shins with the racquet—get her over the shins!'

Lucy fell; the Beautiful White Devil rolled from her hand.

Mr Beebe picked it up, and said: 'The name of this ball is Vittoria

Corombona, please.' But his correction passed unheeded.

Freddy possessed to a high degree the power of lashing little girls to fury, and in half a minute he had transformed Minnie from a well-mannered child into a howling wilderness. Up in the house Cecil heard them, and, though he was full of entertaining news, he did not come down to impart it, in case he got hurt. He was not a coward, and bore necessary pain as well as any man. But he hated the physical violence of the young. How right it was! Sure enough it ended in a cry.

'I wish the Miss Alans could see this,' observed Mr Beebe, just as Lucy, who was nursing the injured Minnie, was in turn lifted off her feet by her brother.

'Who are the Miss Alans?' Freddy panted.

'They have taken Cissie Villa.'

'That wasn't the name—'

Here his foot slipped, and they all fell most agreeably on to the grass. An interval elapses.

'Wasn't what name?' asked Lucy, with her brother's head in her lap.

'Alan wasn't. The name of the people Sir Harry's let to.'

'Nonsense, Freddy! You know nothing about it.'

'Nonsense yourself! I've this minute seen him. He said to me: "Ahem! Honeychurch"'–Freddy was an indifferent mimic–'"ahem! ahem! I have at last procured really dee-sire-rebel tenants." I said, "Hooray, old boy!" and slapped him on the back.'

'Exactly. The Miss Alans?'

'Rather not. More like Anderson.'

'Oh, good gracious, there isn't going to be another muddle!' Mrs Honeychurch exclaimed. 'Do you notice, Lucy, I'm always right? I *said* don't interfere with Cissie Villa. I'm always right. I'm quite uneasy at being always right so often.'

'It's only another muddle of Freddy's. Freddy doesn't even know the name of the people he pretends have taken it instead.'

'Yes, I do. I've got it. Emerson.'

'What name?'

'Emerson. I'll bet you anything you like.'

'What a weathercock Sir Harry is,' said Lucy quietly. 'I wish I had never bothered over it at all.'

Then she lay on her back and gazed at the cloudless sky. Mr Beebe, whose opinion of her rose daily, whispered to his niece that *that* was the proper way to behave if any little thing went wrong.

Meanwhile the name of the new tenants had diverted Mrs Honeychurch from the contemplation of her own abilities.

'Emerson, Freddy? Do you know what Emersons they are?'

'I don't know whether they're any Emersons,' retorted Freddy, who was democratic. Like his sister, and like most young people, he was naturally attracted by the idea of equality, and the undeniable fact that there are different kinds of Emersons annoyed him beyond due measure.

'I trust they are the right sort of person. All right, Lucy'–she was sitting up again–'I see you looking down your nose and thinking your mother's a snob. But there *is* a right sort and a wrong sort, and it's affectation to pretend there isn't.'

'Emerson's a common enough name,' Lucy remarked.

She was gazing sideways. Seated on a promontory herself, she could see the pine-clad promontories descending one beyond another into the Weald. The farther one descended the garden, the more glorious was this lateral view.

'I was merely going to remark, Freddy, that I trusted they were no relations of Emerson the philosopher, a most trying man. Pray, does that satisfy you?'

'Oh yes,' he grumbled. 'And you will be satisfied too, for they're friends of Cecil; so'–with elaborate irony–'you and the other county families will be able to call in perfect safety.'

'*Cecil?*' exclaimed Lucy.

'Don't be rude, dear,' said his mother placidly. 'Lucy, don't screech. It's a new bad habit you're getting into.'

'But has Cecil—'

'Friends of Cecil's,' he repeated, '"and so really dee-sire-rebel. Ahem! Honeychurch, I have just telegraphed to them."'

She got up from the grass.

It was hard on Lucy. Mr Beebe sympathized with her very much. While she believed that her snub about the Miss Alans came from Sir Harry Otway, she had borne it like a good girl. She might well 'screech' when she heard that it came partly from her lover. Mr Vyse was a tease–something worse than a tease: he took a malicious pleasure in thwarting people. The clergyman, knowing this, looked at Miss Honeychurch with more than his usual kindness.

When she exclaimed, 'But Cecil's Emersons–they can't possibly be the same ones–there is that—' he did not consider that the exclamation was strange, but saw in it an opportunity of diverting the conversation while she recovered her composure. He diverted it as follows:

'The Emersons who were at Florence, do you mean? No, I don't suppose it will prove to be them. It is probably a long cry from them to friends of Mr Vyse's. Oh, Mrs Honeychurch, the oddest people! The queerest people! For our part we liked them, didn't we?' He appealed to Lucy. 'There was a great scene over some violets. They picked violets and filled all the vases in the room of these very Miss Alans who have failed to come to Cissie Villa. Poor little ladies! So shocked and so pleased. It used to be one of Miss Catharine's great stories. "My dear sister loves flowers," it began. They found the whole room a mass of blue–vases and jugs–and the story ends with "So ungentlemanly and yet so beautiful. It is all very difficult." Yes, I always connect those Florentine Emersons with violets.'

'Fiasco's done you this time,' remarked Freddy, not seeing that his sister's face was very red. She could not recover herself. Mr Beebe saw it, and continued to divert the conversation.

'These particular Emersons consisted of a father and a son–the son a goodly, if not a good young man; not a fool, I fancy, but very immature—pessimism, et cetera. Our special joy was the father—such a sentimental darling, and people declared he had murdered his wife.'

In his normal state Mr Beebe would never have repeated such gossip, but he was trying to shelter Lucy in her little trouble. He repeated any rubbish that came into his head.

'Murdered his wife?' said Mrs Honeychurch. 'Lucy, don't desert us—go on playing bumble-puppy. Really, the Pension Bertolini must have been the oddest place. That's the second murderer I've heard of as being there. Whatever was Charlotte doing to stop? By the by, we really must ask Charlotte here some time.'

Mr Beebe could recall no second murderer. He suggested that his hostess was mistaken. At the hint of opposition she warmed. She was perfectly sure that there had been a second tourist of whom the same story had been told. The name escaped her. What was the name? Oh, what was the name? She clasped her knees for the name. Something in Thackeray. She struck her matronly forehead.

Lucy asked her brother whether Cecil was in.

'Oh, don't go!' he cried, and tried to catch her by the ankles.

'I must go,' she said gravely. 'Don't be silly. You always overdo it when you play.'

As she left them her mother's shout of 'Harris!' shivered the tranquil air, and reminded her that she had told a lie and had never put it right. Such a senseless lie, too, yet it shattered her nerves, and made her connect these Emersons, friends of Cecil's, with a pair of nondescript tourists. Hitherto truth had come to her naturally. She saw that for the future she must be more vigilant, and be—absolutely truthful? Well, at all events, she must not tell lies. She hurried up the garden, still flushed with shame. A word from Cecil would soothe her, she was sure.

'Cecil!'

'Hullo!' he called, and leant out of the smoking-room window. He seemed in high spirits. 'I was hoping you'd come. I heard you all bear-gardening, but there's better fun up here. I, even I, have won a great victory for the Comic Muse. George Meredith's right—the cause of Comedy and the cause of Truth are really the same; and I, even I, have found tenants for the distressful Cissie Villa. Don't be angry! Don't be angry! You'll forgive me when you hear it all.'

He looked very attractive when his face was bright, and he dispelled her ridiculous forebodings at once.

'I have heard,' she said. 'Freddy has told us. Naughty Cecil! I suppose I must forgive you. Just think of all the trouble I took for nothing! Certainly the Miss Alans are a little tiresome, and I'd rather have nice friends of yours. But you oughtn't to tease one so.'

'Friends of mine?' he laughed. 'But, Lucy, the whole joke is to come! Come here.' But she remained standing where she was. 'Do you know where I met these desirable tenants? In the National Gallery, when I was up to see my mother last week.'

'What an odd place to meet people!' she said nervously. 'I don't quite understand.'

'In the Umbrian Room. Absolute strangers. They were admiring Luca Signorelli—of course, quite stupidly. However, we got talking, and they refreshed me not a little. They had been to Italy.'

'But, Cecil—'

He proceeded hilariously.

'In the course of conversation they said that they wanted a country cottage—the father to live there, the son to run down for week-ends. I thought, "What a chance of scoring off Sir Harry!" and I took their address and a London reference, found they weren't actual blackguards—it was great sport—and wrote to him, making out—'

'Cecil! No, it's not fair. I've probably met them before—'

He bore her down.

'Perfectly fair. Anything is fair that punishes a snob. That old man will do the neighbourhood a world of good. Sir Harry is too disgusting with his "decayed gentlewomen." I meant to read him a lesson some time. No, Lucy, the classes ought to mix, and before long you'll agree with me. There ought to be intermarriage—all sorts of things. I believe in democracy—'

'No, you don't,' she snapped. 'You don't know what the word means.'

He stared at her, and felt again that she had failed to be Leonardesque. 'No, you don't?' Her face was inartistic—that of a peevish virago.

'It isn't fair, Cecil. I blame you—I blame you very much indeed. You had no business to undo my work about the Miss Alans, and make me look ridiculous. You call it scoring off Sir Harry, but do you realize that it is all at my expense? I consider it most disloyal of you.'

She left him.

'Temper!' he thought, raising his eyebrows.

No, it was worse than temper—snobbishness. As long as Lucy thought that his own smart friends were supplanting the Miss Alans, she had not minded. He perceived that these new tenants might be of value educationally. He would tolerate the father and draw out the son, who was silent. In the interests of the Comic Muse and of Truth, he would bring them to Windy Corner.

Chapter Eleven

In Mrs Vyse's well-appointed Flat

The Comic Muse, though able to look after her own interests, did not disdain the assistance of Mr Vyse. His idea of bringing the Emersons to Windy Corner struck her as decidedly good, and she carried through the negotiations without a hitch. Sir Harry Otway signed the agreement, met Mr Emerson, and was duly disillusioned. The Miss Alans were duly offended, and wrote a dignified letter to Lucy, whom they held responsible for the failure. Mr Beebe planned pleasant moments for the new-comers, and told Mrs Honeychurch that Freddy must call on them as soon as they arrived. Indeed, so ample was the Muse's equipment that she permitted Mr Harris, never a very robust criminal, to droop his head, to be forgotten, and to die.

Lucy—to descend from bright heaven to earth, whereon there are shadows because there are hills—Lucy was at first plunged into despair, but settled after a little thought that it did not matter in the very least. Now that she was engaged, the Emersons would scarcely insult her, and were welcome to come into the neighbourhood. And Cecil was welcome to bring whom he would into the neighbourhood. Therefore Cecil was welcome to bring the Emersons into the neighbourhood. But, as I say, this took a little thinking, and—so illogical are girls—the event remained rather greater and rather more dreadful than it should have done. She was glad that a visit to Mrs Vyse now fell due; the tenants moved into Cissie Villa while she was safe in the London flat.

'Cecil—Cecil darling,' she whispered the evening she arrived, and crept into his arms.

Cecil, too, became demonstrative. He saw that the needful fire had been kindled in Lucy. At last she longed for attention, as a woman should, and looked up to him because he was a man.

'So you do love me, little thing?' he murmured.

'Oh, Cecil, I do, I do! I don't know what I should do without you.'

Several days passed. Then she had a letter from Miss Bartlett.

A coolness had sprung up between the two cousins, and they had not corresponded since they parted in August. The coolness dated from what Charlotte would call 'the flight to Rome,' and in Rome it had increased amazingly. For the companion who is merely uncongenial in the medieval world becomes exasperating in the classical. Charlotte, unselfish in the Forum, would have tried a sweeter temper than Lucy's, and once, in the Baths of Caracalla, they had doubted whether they could continue their tour. Lucy had said she would join the Vyses—Mrs Vyse was an acquaintance of her mother, so there was no impropriety in the plan—and Miss Bartlett had replied that she was quite used to being abandoned suddenly. Finally nothing happened; but the coolness remained, and, for Lucy, was even increased when she opened the letter and read as follows. It had been forwarded from Windy Corner.

Tunbridge Wells
September

Dearest Lucia,

I have news of you at last! Miss Lavish has been bicycling in your parts, but was not sure whether a call would be welcome. Puncturing her tyre near Summer Street, and it being mended while she sat very woebegone in that pretty churchyard, she saw, to her astonishment, a door open opposite and the younger Emerson man come out. He said his father had just taken the house. He *said* he did not know that you lived in the neighbourhood (?). He never suggested giving Eleanor a cup of tea. Dear Lucy, I am much worried, and I advise you to make a clean breast of his past behaviour to your mother, Freddy and Mr Vyse, who will forbid him to enter the house, etc. That was a great misfortune, and I dare say you have told them already. Mr Vyse is so sensitive. I remember how I used to get on his nerves at Rome. I am very sorry about it all, and should not feel easy unless I warned you.

Believe me,

Your anxious and loving cousin,
Charlotte.

Lucy was much annoyed, and replied as follows:

Beauchamp Mansions, S.W.

Dear Charlotte,

Many thanks for your warning. When Mr Emerson forgot himself on the mountain, you made me promise not to tell mother, because you said she would blame you for not being always with me. I have kept that promise, and cannot possibly tell her now. I have said both to her and to Cecil that I met the Emersons at Florence, and that they are respectable people—which I *do* think—and the reason that he offered Miss Lavish no tea was probably that he had none himself. She should have tried at the Rectory. I cannot begin making a fuss at this stage. You must see that it would be too absurd. If the Emersons heard I had complained of them, they would think themselves of importance, which is exactly what they are not. I like the old father, and look forward to seeing him again. As for the son, I am sorry for *him* when we meet, rather than for myself. They are known to Cecil, who is very well, and spoke of you the other day. We expect to be married in January.

Miss Lavish cannot have told you much about me, for I am not at Windy Corner at all, but here. Please do not put 'Private' outside your envelope again. No one opens my letters.

Yours affectionately,
L. M. Honeychurch.

Secrecy has this disadvantage: we lose the sense of proportion; we cannot tell whether our secret is important or not. Were Lucy and her cousin closeted with a great thing which would destroy Cecil's life if he discovered it, or with a little thing which he would laugh at? Miss Bartlett suggested the former. Perhaps she was right. It had become a great thing now. Left to herself, Lucy would have told her mother and her lover ingenuously, and it would have remained a little thing. 'Emerson, not Harris': it was only that a few weeks ago. She tried to tell Cecil even now when they were laughing about some beautiful lady who had smitten his heart at school. But her body behaved so ridiculously that she stopped.

She and her secret stayed ten days longer in the deserted Metropolis visiting the scenes they were to know so well later on. It did her no harm, Cecil thought, to learn the framework of society, while society itself was absent on the golf-links or the moors. The weather was cool, and it did her no harm. In spite of the season, Mrs Vyse managed to scrape together a dinner-party consisting entirely of the grandchildren of famous people. The food was poor, but the talk had a witty weariness that impressed the girl. One was tired of everything, it seemed. One launched into enthusiasms only to collapse gracefully, and pick oneself up amid sympathetic laughter. In this atmosphere the Pension Bertolini and Windy Corner appeared equally crude, and Lucy saw that her London career would estrange her a little from all that she had loved in the past.

The grandchildren asked her to play the piano. She played Schumann. 'Now some Beethoven,' called Cecil, when the querulous beauty of the music had died. She shook her head and played Schumann again. The melody rose, unprofitably magical. It broke; it was resumed broken, not marching once from the cradle to the grave. The sadness of the incomplete—the sadness that is often Life, but should never be Art—throbbed in its disjected phrases, and made the nerves of the audience throb. Not thus had she played on the little draped piano at the Bertolini, and 'Too much Schumann' was not the remark that Mr Beebe had passed to himself when she returned.

When the guests were gone, and Lucy had gone to bed, Mrs Vyse paced up and down the drawing-room, discussing her little party with her son. Mrs Vyse was a nice woman, but her personality, like many another's, had been swamped by London, for it needs a strong head to live among many people. The too vast orb of her fate had crushed her; she had seen too many seasons, too many cities, too many men for her abilities, and even with Cecil she was mechanical, and behaved as if he was not one son, but, so to speak, a filial crowd.

'Make Lucy one of us,' she said, looking round intelligently at the end of each sentence, and straining her lips apart until she spoke again. 'Lucy is becoming wonderful—wonderful.'

'Her music always was wonderful.'

'Yes, but she is purging off the Honeychurch taint—most excellent Honeychurches, but you know what I mean. She is not always quoting servants, or asking one how the pudding is made.'

'Italy has done it.'

'Perhaps,' she murmured, thinking of the museum that represented Italy to her. 'It is just possible. Cecil, mind you marry her next January. She is one of us already.'

'But her music!' he exclaimed. 'The style of her! How she kept to Schumann when, like an idiot, I wanted Beethoven. Schumann was right for this evening. Schumann was the thing. Do you know, mother, I shall have our children educated just like Lucy. Bring them up among honest country folk for freshness, send them to Italy for subtlety, and then—not till then—let them come to London. I don't believe in these London educations—' He broke off, remembering that he had had one himself, and concluded, 'At all events, not for women.'

'Make her one of us,' repeated Mrs Vyse, and processed to bed.

As she was dozing off, a cry—the cry of nightmare—rang from Lucy's room. Lucy could ring for the maid if she liked, but Mrs Vyse thought it kind to go herself. She found the girl sitting upright with her hand on her cheek.

'I am so sorry, Mrs Vyse—it is these dreams.'

'Bad dreams?'

'Just dreams.'

The elder lady smiled and kissed her, saying very distinctly: 'You should have heard us talking about you, dear. He admires you more than ever. Dream of that.'

Lucy returned the kiss, still covering one cheek with her hand. Mrs Vyse recessed to bed. Cecil, whome the cry had not awoke, snored. Darkness enveloped the flat.

Chapter Twelve

Twelfth Chapter

It was a Saturday afternoon, gay and brilliant after abundant rains, and the spirit of youth dwelt in it, though the season was now autumn. All that was gracious triumphed. As the motor-cars passed through Summer Street they raised only a little dust, and their stench was soon dispersed by the wind and replaced by the scent of the wet birches or of the pines. Mr Beebe, at leisure for life's amenities, leant over his rectory gate. Freddy leant by him, smoking a pendant pipe.

'Suppose we go and hinder those new people opposite for a little.'

'M'm.'

'They might amuse you.'

Freddy, whom his fellow-creatures never amused, suggested that the new people might be feeling a bit busy, and so on, since they had only just moved in.

'I suggested we should hinder them,' said Mr Beebe. 'They are worth it.' Unlatching the gate, he sauntered over the triangular green to Cissie Villa. 'Hullo!' he called, shouting in at the open door, through which much squalor was visible.

A grave voice replied, 'Hullo!'

'I've brought some one to see you.'

'I'll be down in a minute.'

The passage was blocked by a wardrobe, which the removal men had failed to carry up the stairs. Mr Beebe edged round it with difficulty. The sitting-room itself was blocked with books.

'Are these people great readers?' Freddy whispered. 'Are they that sort?'

'I fancy they know how to read—a rare accomplishment. What have they got? Byron. Exactly. "A Shropshire Lad." Never heard of it. "The Way of all Flesh." Never heard of it. Gibbon. Hullo! dear George reads German. Um—um—Schopenhauer, Nietzsche, and so we go on. Well, I suppose your.

generation knows its own business, Honeychurch.'

'Mr Beebe, look at that,' said Freddy in awestruck tones.

On the cornice of the wardrobe the hand of an amateur had painted this inscription: 'Mistrust all enterprises that require new clothes.'

'I know. Isn't it jolly? I like that. I'm certain that's the old man's doing.'

'How very odd of him!'

'Surely you agree?'

But Freddy was his mother's son, and felt that one ought not to go spoiling the furniture.

'Pictures!' the clergyman continued, scrambling about the room. 'Giotto—they got that at Florence, I'll be bound.'

'The same as Lucy's got.'

'Oh, by the by, did Miss Honeychurch enjoy London?'

'She came back yesterday.'

'I suppose she had a good time?'

'Yes, very,' said Freddy, taking up a book. 'She and Cecil are thicker than ever.'

'That's good hearing.'

'I wish I wasn't such a fool, Mr Beebe.'

Mr Beebe ignored the remark.

'Lucy used to be nearly as stupid as I am, but it'll be very different now, mother thinks. She will read all kinds of books.'

'So will you.'

'Only medical books. Not books that you can talk about afterwards. Cecil is teaching Lucy Italian, and he says her playing is wonderful. There are all kinds of things in it that we have never noticed. Cecil says—'

'What on earth are those people doing upstairs? Emerson—we think we'll come another time.'

George ran downstairs and pushed them into the room without speaking.

'Let me introduce Mr Honeychurch, a neighbour.'

Then Freddy hurled one of the thunderbolts of youth. Perhaps he was shy, perhaps he was friendly, or perhaps he thought that George's face wanted washing. At all events, he greeted him with, 'How d'ye do? Come and have a bathe.'

'Oh, all right,' said George, impassive.

Mr Beebe was highly entertained.

'"How d'ye do? how d'ye do? Come and have a bathe,"' he chuckled. 'That's the best conversational opening I've ever heard. But I'm afraid it will only act between men. Can you picture a lady who has been introduced to another lady by a third lady opening civilities with "How do you do? Come and have a bathe"? And yet you will tell me that the sexes are equal.'

'I tell you that they shall be,' said Mr Emerson, who had been slowly descending the stairs. 'Good afternoon, Mr Beebe. I tell you they shall be comrades, and George thinks the same.'

'We are to raise ladies to our level?' the clergyman inquired.

'The Garden of Eden,' pursued Mr Emerson, still descending, 'which you place in the past, is really yet to come. We shall enter it when we no longer despise our bodies.'

Mr Beebe disclaimed placing the Garden of Eden anywhere.

'In this—not in other things—we men are ahead. We despise the body less than women do. But not until we are comrades shall we enter the garden.'

'I say, what about this bathe?' murmured Freddy, appalled at the mass of philosophy that was approaching him.

'I believed in a return to Nature once. But how can we return to Nature when we have never been with her? To-day, I believe that we must discover Nature. After many conquests we shall attain simplicity. It is our heritage.'

'Let me introduce Mr Honeychurch, whose sister you will remember at Florence.'

'How do you do? Very glad to see you, and that you are taking George for a bathe. Very glad to hear that your sister is going to marry. Marriage is a duty. I am sure that she will be happy, for we know Mr Vyse, too. He has been most kind. He met us by chance in the National Gallery, and arranged everything about this delightful house. Though I hope I have not vexed Sir Harry Otway. I have met so few Liberal landowners, and I was anxious to compare his attitude towards the game laws with the Conservative attitude. Ah, this wind! You do well to bathe. Yours is a glorious country, Honeychurch!'

'Not a bit!' mumbled Freddy. 'I must—that is to say, I have to—have the pleasure of calling on you later on, my mother says, I hope.'

'*Call*, my lad? Who taught us that drawing-room twaddle? Call on your grandmother! Listen to the wind among the pines! Yours is a glorious country.'

Mr Beebe came to the rescue.

'Mr Emerson, he will call, I shall call; you or your son will return our calls before ten days have elapsed. I trust that you have realized about the ten days' interval. It does not count that I helped you 'with the stair-eyes yesterday. It does not count that they are going to bathe this afternoon.'

'Yes, go and bathe, George. Why do you dawdle talking? Bring them back to tea. Bring back some milk, cakes, honey. The change will do you good. George has been working very hard at his office. I can't believe he's well.'

George bowed his head, dusty and sombre, exhaling the peculiar smell of one who has handled furniture.

'Do you really want this bathe?' Freddy asked him. 'It is only a pond, don't you know. I dare say you are used to something much better.'

'Yes—I have said "Yes" already.'

Mr Beebe felt bound to assist his young friend, and led the way out of the house into the pinewoods. How glorious it was! For a little time the voice of old Mr Emerson pursued them, dispensing good wishes and philosophy. It ceased, and they only heard the fair wind blowing the bracken and the trees.

Mr Beebe, who could be silent, but who could not bear silence, was compelled to chatter, since the expedition looked like a failure, and neither of his companions would utter a word. He spoke of Florence. George attended gravely, assenting or dissenting with slight but determined gestures that were as inexplicable as the motions of the tree-tops above their heads.

'And what a coincidence that you should meet Mr Vyse! Did you realize that you would find all the Pension Bertolini down here?'

'I did not. Miss Lavish told me.'

'When I was a young man I always meant to write a "History of Coincidence."'

No enthusiasm.

'Though, as a matter of fact, coincidences are much rare than we suppose. For example, it isn't pure coincidentality that you are here now, when one comes to reflect.'

To his relief, George began to talk.

'It is. I have reflected. It is Fate. Everything is Fate. We are flung together by Fate, drawn apart by Fate–flung together, drawn apart. The twelve winds blow us–we settle nothing—'

'You have not reflected at all,' rapped the clergyman. 'Let me give you a useful tip, Emerson: attribute nothing to Fate. Don't say, "I didn't do this," for you did it, ten to one. Now I'll cross-question you. Where did you first meet Miss Honeychurch and myself?'

'Italy.'

'And where did you meet Mr Vyse, who is going to marry Miss Honeychurch?'

'National Gallery.'

'Looking at Italian art. There you are, and yet you talk of coincidence and Fate! You naturally seek out things Italian, and so do we and our friends. This narrows the field immeasurably, and we meet again in it.'

'It is Fate that I am here,' persisted George. 'But you can call it Italy if it makes you less unhappy.'

Mr Beebe slid away from such heavy treatment of the subject. But he was infinitely tolerant of the young, and had no desire to snub George.

'And so for this and for other reasons my "History of Coincidence" is still to write.'

Silence.

Wishing to round off the episode, he added:

'We are all so glad that you have come.'

Silence.

'Here we are!' called Freddy.

'Oh, good!' exclaimed Mr Beebe, mopping his brow.

'In there's the pond. I wish it was bigger,' he added apologetically.

They climbed down a slippery bank of pine-needles. There lay the pond, set in its little alp of green–only a pond, but large enough to contain the human body, and pure enough to reflect the sky. On account of the rains, the waters had flooded the surrounding grass, which showed like a beautiful emerald path, tempting the feet towards the central pool.

'It's distinctly successful, as ponds go,' said Mr Beebe. 'No apologies are necessary for the pond.'

George sat down where the ground was dry, and drearily unlaced his boots.

'Aren't those masses of willow-herb splendid? I love willow-herb in seed. What's the name of this aromatic plant?'

No one knew, or seemed to care.

'These abrupt changes of vegetation–this little spongeous tract of water-plants, and on either side of it all the growths are tough or brittle–heather, bracken, hurts, pines. Very charming, very charming.'

'Mr Beebe, aren't you bathing?' called Freddy, as he stripped himself.

Mr Beebe thought he was not.

'Water's wonderful!' cried Freddy, prancing in.

'Water's water,' murmured George. Wetting his hair first–a sure sign of apathy–he followed Freddy into the divine, as indifferent as if he were a statue and the pond a pail of soapsuds. It was necessary to use his muscles. It was necessary to keep clean. Mr Beebe watched them, and watched the seeds of the willow-herb dance chorically above their heads.

'Apooshoo, apooshoo, apooshoo,' went Freddy, swimming for two strokes in either direction, and then becoming involved in reeds or mud.

'It is worth it?' asked the other, Michelangelesque on the flooded margin.

The bank broke away, and he fell into the pool before he had weighted the question properly.

'Hee–poof–I've swallowed a polly-wog. Mr Beebe, water's wonderful, water's simply ripping.'

'Water's not so bad,' said George, reappearing from his plunge, and sputtering at the sun.

'Water's wonderful. Mr Beebe, do.'

'Apooshoo, kouf.'

Mr Beebe, who was hot, and who always acquiesced where possible, looked around him. He could detect no parishioners except the pine-trees, rising up steeply on all sides, and gesturing to each other against the blue. How glorious it was! The world of motor-cars and Rural Deans receded illimitably. Water, sky, evergreens, a wind–these things not even the seasons can touch, and surely they lie beyond the intrusion of man?

'I may as well wash too'; and soon his garments made a third little pile on the sward, and he too asserted the wonder of the water.

It was ordinary water, nor was there very much of it, and, as Freddy said, it reminded one of swimming in a salad. The three gentlemen rotated in the pool breast high, after the fashion of the nymphs in Götterdämmerung. But either because the rains had given a freshness, or because the sun was shedding a most glorious heat, or because two of the gentlemen were young in years and the third young in the spirit–for some reason or other a change came over them, and they forgot Italy and Botany and Fate. They began to play. Mr Beebe and Freddy splashed each other. A little deferentially, they splashed George. He was quiet: they feared they had offended him. Then all the forces of youth burst out. He smiled, flung himself at them, splashed them, ducked them, kicked them, muddied them, and drove them out of the pool.

'Race you round it, then,' cried Freddy, and they raced in the sunshine, and George took a short cut and dirtied his shins, and had to bathe a second time. Then Mr Beebe consented to run—a memorable sight.

They ran to get dry, they bathed to get cool, they played at being Indians in the willow-herbs and in the bracken, they bathed to get clean. And all the time three little bundles lay discreetly on the sward, proclaiming:

'No. We are what matters. Without us shall no enterprise begin. To us shall all flesh turn in the end.'

'A try! A try!' yelled Freddy, snatching up George's bundle and placing it beside an imaginary goal-post.

'Socker rules,' George retorted, scattering Freddy's bundle with a kick.

'Goal!'

'Goal!'

'Pass!'

'Take care my watch!' cried Mr Beebe.

Clothes flew in all directions.

'Take care my hat! No, that's enough, Freddy. Dress now. No, I say!'

But the two young men were delirious. Away they twinkled into the trees, Freddy with a clerical waistcoat under his arm, George with a wideawake hat on his dripping hair.

'That'll do!' shouted Mr Beebe, remembering that after all he was in his own parish. Then his voice changed as if every pine-tree was a Rural Dean. 'Hi! Steady on! I see people coming, you fellows!'

Yells, and widening circles over the dappled earth.

'Hi! hi! *Ladies!*'

Neither George nor Freddy was truly refined. Still, they did not hear Mr Beebe's last warning or they would have avoided Mrs Honeychurch, Cecil, and Lucy, who were walking down to call on old Mrs Butterworth. Freddy dropped the waistcoat at their feet, and dashed into some bracken. George whooped in their faces, turned, and scudded away down the path to the pond, still clad in Mr Beebe's hat.

'Gracious alive!' cried Mrs Honeychurch. 'Whoever were those unfortunate people? Oh, dears, look away! And poor Mr Beebe, too! Whatever has happened?'

'Come this way immediately,' commanded Cecil, who always felt that he must lead women, though he knew not whither, and protect them, though he knew not against what. He led them now towards the bracken where Freddy sat concealed.

'Oh, poor Mr Beebe! Was that his waistcoat we left in the path? Cecil, Mr Beebe's waistcoat—'

'No business of ours,' said Cecil, glancing at Lucy, who was all parasol and evidently 'minded.'

'I fancy Mr Beebe jumped back into the pond.'

'This way, please, Mrs Honeychurch, this way.'

They followed him up the bank, attempting the tense yet nonchalant expression that is suitable for ladies on such occasions.

'Well, *I* can't help it,' said a voice close ahead, and Freddy reared a freckled face and a pair of snowy shoulders out of the fronds. 'I can't be trodden on, can I?'

'Good gracious me, dear; so it's you! What miserable management! Why not have a comfortable bath at home, with hot and cold laid on?'

'Look here, mother: a fellow must wash, and a fellow's got to dry, and if another fellow—'

'Dear, no doubt you're right as usual, but you are in no position to argue. Come, Lucy,' They turned. 'Oh, look–don't look! Oh, poor Mr Beebe! How unfortunate again—'

For Mr Beebe was just crawling out of the pond, on whose surface garments of an intimate nature did float; while George, the world-weary George, shouted to Freddy that he had hooked a fish.

'And me, I've swallowed one, answered he of the bracken. 'I've swallowed a polly-wog. It wriggleth in my tummy. I shall die–Emerson, you beast, you've got on my bags.'

'Hush, dears,' said Mrs Honeychurch, who found it impossible to remain shocked. 'And do be sure you dry yourselves thoroughly first. All these colds come of not drying thoroughly.'

'Mother, do come away,' said Lucy. 'Oh, for goodness' sake, do come.'

'Hullo!' cried George, so that again the ladies stopped.

He regarded himself as dressed. Barefoot, bare-chested, radiant and personable against the shadowy woods, he called:

'Hullo, Miss Honeychurch! Hullo!'

'Bow, Lucy; better bow. Whoever is it? I shall bow.'

Miss Honeychurch bowed.

That evening and all that night the water ran away. On the morrow the pool had shrunk to its old size and lost its glory. It had been a call to the blood and to the relaxed will, a passing benediction whose influence did not pass, a holiness, a spell, a momentary chalice for youth.

Chapter Thirteen

How Miss Bartlett's Boiler was so Tiresome

How often had Lucy rehearsed this bow, this interview! But she had always rehearsed them indoors, and with certain accessories, which surely we have a right to assume. Who could foretell that she and George would meet in the rout of a civilization, amidst an army of coats and collars and boots that lay wounded over the sunlit earth? She had imagined a young Mr Emerson, who might be shy or morbid or indifferent or furtively impudent. She was prepared for all of these. But she had never imagined one who would be happy and greet her with the shout of the morning star.

Indoors herself, partaking of tea with old Mrs Butterworth, she reflected that it is impossible to foretell the future with any degree of accuracy, that it is impossible to rehearse life. A fault in the scenery, a face in the audience, an irruption of the audience on to the stage, and all our carefully planned gestures mean nothing, or mean too much. 'I will bow,' she had thought. 'I will not shake hands with him. That will be just the proper thing.' She had bowed—but to whom? To gods, to heroes, to the nonsense of schoolgirls! She had bowed across the rubbish that cumbers the world.

So ran her thoughts, while her faculties were busy with Cecil. It was another of those dreadful engagement calls. Mrs Butterworth had wanted to see him, and he did not want to be seen. He did not want to hear about hydrangeas, why they change their colour at the seaside. He did not want to join the C.O.S. When cross he was always elaborate, and made long, clever answers where 'Yes' or 'No' would have done. Lucy soothed him and tinkered at the conversation in a way that promised well for their married peace. No one is perfect, and surely it is wiser to discover the imperfections before wedlock. Miss Bartlett, in deed, though not in word, had taught the girl that this our life contains nothing satisfactory. Lucy, though she disliked the teacher, regarded the teaching as profound, and applied it to her lover.

'Lucy,' said her mother, when they got home, 'is anything the matter with Cecil?'

The question was ominous: up till now Mrs Honeychurch had behaved with charity and restraint.

'No, I don't think so, mother; Cecil's all right.'

'Perhaps he's tired.'

Lucy compromised: perhaps Cecil was a little tired.

'Because otherwise'—she pulled out her bonnet-pins with gathering displeasure—'because otherwise I cannot account for him.'

'I do think Mrs Butterworth is rather tiresome, if you mean that.'

'Cecil has told you to think so. You were devoted to her as a little girl, and nothing will describe her goodness to you through the typhoid fever. No—it is just the same thing everywhere.'

'Let me just put your bonnet away, may I?'

'Surely he could answer her civilly for one half-hour?'

'Cecil has a very high standard for people,' faltered Lucy, seeing trouble ahead. 'It's part of his ideals—it is really that that makes him sometimes seem—'

'Oh, rubbish! If high ideals make a young man rude, the sooner he gets rid of them the better,' said Mrs Honeychurch, handing her the bonnet.

'Now mother! I've seen you cross with Mrs Butterworth yourself!'

'Not in that way. At times I could wring her neck. But not in that way. No. It is the same with Cecil all over.'

'By the by—I never told you. I had a letter from Charlotte while I was away in London.'

This attempt to divert the conversation was too puerile, and Mrs Honeychurch resented it.

'Since Cecil came back from London, nothing appears to please him. Whenever I speak he winces;—I see him, Lucy; it is useless to contradict me. No doubt I am neither artistic nor literary nor intellectual nor musical, but I cannot help the drawing-room furniture: your father bought it and we must put up with it, will Cecil kindly remember.'

'I–I see what you mean, and certainly Cecil oughtn't to. But he does not mean to be uncivil–he once explained–it is the *things* that upset him–he is easily upset by ugly things–he is not uncivil to *people*.'

'Is it a thing or a person when Freddy sings?'

'You can't expect a really musical person to enjoy comic songs as we do.'

'Then why didn't he leave the room? Why sit wriggling and sneering and spoiling every one's pleasure?'

'We mustn't be unjust to people,' faltered Lucy. Something had enfeebled her, and the case for Cecil, which she had mastered so perfectly in London, would not come forth in an effective form. The two civilizations had clashed–Cecil had hinted that they might–and she was dazzled and bewildered, as though the radiance that lies behind all civilization had blinded her eyes. Good taste and bad taste were only catch-words, garments of diverse cut; and music itself dissolved to a whisper through pine-trees, where the song is not distinguishable from the comic song.

She remained in much embarrassment, while Mrs Honeychurch changed her frock for dinner; and every now and then she said a word, and made things no better. There was no concealing the fact–Cecil had meant to be supercilious, and he had succeeded. And Lucy–she knew not why–wished that the trouble could have come at any other time.

'Go and dress, dear; you'll be late.'

'All right, mother—'

'Don't say "All right" and stop. Go.'

She obeyed, but loitered disconsolately at the landing window. It faced north, so there was little view, and now view of the sky. Now, as in the winter, the pine-trees hung close to her eyes. One connected the landing window with depression. No definite problem menaced her, but she sighed to herself, 'Oh dear, what shall I do, what shall I do?' It seemed to her that every one else was behaving very badly. And she ought not to have mentioned Miss Bartlett's letter. She must be more careful: her mother was rather inquisitive, and might have asked what it was about. Oh dear, what should she do?–and then Freddy came bounding upstairs, and joined the ranks of the ill-behaved.

'I say, those are topping people.'

'My dear baby, how tiresome you've been! You had no business to take them bathing in the Sacred Lake: it's much too public. It was all right for you, but most awkward for every one else. Do be more careful. You forget the place is growing half suburban.'

'I say, is anything on to-morrow week?'

'Not that I know of.'

'Then I want to ask the Emersons up to Sunday tennis.'

'Oh, I wouldn't do that, Freddy, I wouldn't do that with all this muddle.'

'What's wrong with the court? They won't mind a bump or two, and I've ordered new balls.'

'I meant *it's* better not. I really mean it.'

He seized her by the elbows and humorously danced her up and down the passage. She pretended not to mind, but she could have screamed with temper. Cecil glanced at them as he proceeded to his toilet and they impeded Mary with her brood of hot-water cans. Then Mrs Honeychurch opened her door and said: 'Lucy, what a noise you're making! I have something to say to you. Did you say you had had a letter from Charlotte?' and Freddy ran away.

'Yes. I really can't stop. I must dress too.'

'How's Charlotte?'

'All right.'

'Lucy!'

The unfortunate girl returned.

'You've a bad habit of hurrying away in the middle of one's sentences. Did Charlotte mention her boiler?'

'Her *what*?'

'Don't you remember that her boiler was to be had out in October, and her bath cistern cleaned out, and all kinds of terrible to-doing?'

'I can't remember all Charlotte's worries,' said Lucy bitterly. 'I shall have enough of my own, now that you are not pleased with Cecil.'

Mrs Honeychurch might have flamed out. She did not. She said: 'Come here, old lady—thank you for putting away my bonnet—kiss me.' And, though nothing is perfect, Lucy felt for the moment that her mother and Windy Corner and the Weald in the declining sun were perfect.

So the grittiness went out of life. It generally did at Windy Corner. At the last minute, when the social machine was clogged hopelessly, one member or other of the family poured in a drop of oil. Cecil despised their methods—perhaps rightly. At all events, they were not his own.

Dinner was at half-past seven. Freddy gabbled a grace, and they drew up their heavy chairs and fell to. Fortunately, the men were hungry. Nothing untoward occurred until the pudding. Then Freddy said:

'Lucy, what's Emerson like?'

'I saw him in Florence,' said Lucy, hoping that this would pass for a reply.

'Is he the clever sort, or is he a decent chap?'

'Ask Cecil; it is Cecil who brought him here.'

'He is the clever sort, like myself,' said Cecil.

Freddy looked at him doubtfully.

'How well did you know them at the Bertolini?' asked Mrs Honeychurch.

'Oh, very slightly. I mean, Charlotte knew them even less than I did.'

'Oh, that reminds me—you never told me what Charlotte said in her letter.'

'One thing and another,' said Lucy, wondering whether she would get through the meal without a lie. 'Among other things, that an awful friend of hers had been bicycling through Summer Street, wondered if she'd come up and see us, and mercifully didn't.'

'Lucy, I do call the way you talk unkind.'

'She was a novelist,' said Lucy craftily. The remark was a happy one, for nothing roused Mrs Honeychurch so much as literature in the hands of females. She would abandon every topic to inveigh against those women who (instead of minding their houses and their children) seek notoriety by print. Her attitude was: 'If books must be written, let them be written by men'; and she developed it at great length, while Cecil yawned and Freddy played at "This year, next year, now, never," with his plumstones, and Lucy artfully fed the flames of her mother's wrath. But soon the conflagration died down, and the ghosts began to gather in the darkness. There were too many ghosts about. The original ghost—that touch of lips on her cheek—had surely been laid long ago; it could be nothing to her that a man had kissed her on a mountain once. But it had begotten a spectral family—Mr Harris, Miss Bartlett's letter, Mr Beebe's memories of violets—and one or other of these was bound to haunt her before Cecil's very eyes. It was Miss Bartlett who returned now, and with appalling vividness.

'I have been thinking, Lucy, of that letter of Charlotte's. How is she?'

'I tore the thing up.'

'Didn't she say how she was? How does she sound? Cheerful?'

'Oh yes, I suppose so—no—not very cheerful, I suppose.'

'Then, depend upon it, it *is* the boiler. I know myself how water preys upon one's mind. I would rather anything else—even a misfortune with the Meat.'

Cecil laid his hand over his eyes.

'So would I,' asserted Freddy, backing his mother up—backing up the spirit of her remark rather than its substance.

'And I have been thinking,' she added rather nervously, 'surely we could squeeze Charlotte in here next week, and give her a nice holiday while the plumbers at Tunbridge Wells finish. I have not seen poor Charlotte for so long.'

It was more than her nerves could stand. And yet she could not protest violently after her mother's goodness to her upstairs.

'Mother, no!' she pleaded. 'It's impossible. We can't have Charlotte on the top of the other things; we're squeezed to death as it is. Freddy's got a friend coming Tuesday, there's Cecil, and you've promised to take in Minnie Beebe because of the diphtheria scare. It simply can't be done.'

'Nonsense! It can.'

'If Minnie sleeps in the bath. Not otherwise.'

'Minnie can sleep with you.'

'I won't have her.'

'Then, if you're so selfish, Mr Floyd must share a room with Freddy.'

'Miss Bartlett, Miss Bartlett, Miss Bartlett,' moaned Cecil, again laying his hand over his eyes.

'It's impossible,' repeated Lucy. 'I don't want to make difficulties, but it really isn't fair on the maids to fill up the house so.'

Alas!

'The truth is, dear, you don't like Charlotte.'

'No, I don't. And no more does Cecil. She gets on our nerves. You haven't seen her lately, and don't realize how tiresome she can be, though so good. So please, mother, don't worry us this last summer; but spoil us by not asking her to come.'

'Hear, hear!' said Cecil.

Mrs Honeychurch, with more gravity than usual, and with more feeling than she usually permitted herself replied: 'This isn't very kind of you two. You have each other and all these woods to walk in, so full of beautiful things; and poor Charlotte has only the water turned off and plumbers. You are young, dears, and however clever young people are, and however many books they read, they will never guess what it feels like to grow old.'

Cecil crumbled his bread.

'I must say Cousin Charlotte was very kind to me that year I called on my bike,' put in Freddy. 'She thanked me for coming till I felt like such a fool, and fussed round no end to get an egg boiled for my tea just right.'

'I know, dear. She is kind to every one, and yet Lucy makes this difficulty when we try to give her some little return.'

But Lucy hardened her heart. It was no good being kind to Miss Bartlett. She had tried herself too often and too recently. One might lay up treasure in heaven by the attempt, but one enriched neither Miss Bartlett nor anyone else upon earth. She was reduced to saying: 'I can't help it, mother. I don't like Charlotte. I admit it's horrid of me.'

'From your own account, you told her as much.'

'Well, she would leave Florence so stupidly. She flurried—'

The ghosts were returning; they filled Italy, they were even usurping the places she had known as a child. The Sacred Lake would never be the same again, and, on Sunday week, something would even happen to Windy Corner. How would she fight against ghosts? For a moment the visible world faded away, and memories and emotions alone seemed real.

'I suppose Miss Bartlett must come, since she boils eggs so well,' said Cecil, who was in rather a happier frame of mind, thanks to the admirable cooking.

'I didn't mean the egg was *well* boiled,' corrected Freddy, 'because in point of fact she forgot to take it off, and as a matter of fact I don't care for eggs. I only meant how jolly kind she seemed.'

Cecil frowned again. Oh, these Honeychurches! Eggs, boilers, hydrangeas, maids—of such were their lives compact. 'May me and Lucy get down from our chairs?' he asked, with scarcely veiled insolence. 'We don't want no dessert.'

Chapter Fourteen

How Lucy Faced the External Situation Bravely

Of course Miss Bartlett accepted. And, equally of course, she felt sure that she would prove a nuisance, and begged to be given an inferior spare room—something with no view, anything. Her love to Lucy. And, equally of course, George Emerson could come to tennis on the Sunday week.

Lucy faced the situation bravely, though, like most of us, she only faced the situation that encompassed her. She never gazed inwards. If at times strange images rose from the depths, she put them down to nerves. When Cecil brought the Emersons to Summer Street, it had upset her nerves. Charlotte would burnish up past foolishness, and this might upset her nerves. She was nervous at night. When she talked to George—they met again almost immediately at the Rectory—his voice moved her deeply, and she wished to remain near him. How dreadful if she really wished to remain near him! Of course, the wish was due to nerves, which love to play such perverse tricks upon us. Once she had suffered from 'things that came out of nothing and meant she didn't know what.' Now Cecil had explained psychology to her one wet afternoon, and all the troubles of youth in an unknown world could be dismissed.

It is obvious enough for the reader to conclude, 'She loves young Emerson.' A reader in Lucy's place would not find it obvious. Life is easy to chronicle, but bewildering to practise, and we welcome 'nerves' or any other shibboleth that will cloak our personal desire. She loved Cecil; George made her nervous; will the reader explain to her that the phrases should have been reversed?

But the external situation—she will face that bravely.

The meeting at the Rectory had passed off well enough. Standing between Mr Beebe and Cecil, she had made a few temperate allusions to Italy, and George had replied. She was anxious to show that she was not shy, and was glad that he did not seem shy either.

'A nice fellow,' said Mr Beebe afterwards. 'He will work off his crudities in time. I rather mistrust young men who slip into life gracefully.'

Lucy said, 'He seems in better spirits. He laughs more.'

'Yes,' replied the clergyman. 'He is waking up.

That was all. But, as the week wore on, more of her defences fell, and she entertained an image that had physical beauty.

In spite of the clearest directions, Miss Bartlett contrived to bungle her arrival. She was due at the South-Eastern station at Dorking, whither Mrs Honeychurch drove to meet her. She arrived at the London and Brighton station, and had to hire a cab up. No one was at home except Freddy and his friend, who had to stop their tennis and to entertain her for a solid hour. Cecil and Lucy turned up at four o'clock, and these, with little Minnie Beebe, made a somewhat lugubrious sextette upon the upper lawn for tea.

'I shall never forgive myself,' said Miss Bartlett, who kept on rising from her seat, and had to be begged by the united company to remain. 'I have upset everything. Bursting in on young people! But I insist on paying for my cab up. Grant me that, at any rate.'

'Our visitors never do such a dreadful thing,' said Lucy, while her brother, in whose memory the boiled egg had already grown unsubstantial, exclaimed in irritable tones: 'Just what I've been trying to convince Cousin Charlotte of, Lucy, for the last half-hour.'

'I do not feel myself an ordinary visitor,' said Miss Bartlett, and looked at her frayed gloves.

'All right, if you'd really rather. Five shillings, and I gave a bob to the driver.'

Miss Bartlett looked in her purse. Only sovereigns and pennies. Could anyone give her change? Freddy had half a quid and his friend had four half-crowns. Miss Bartlett accepted their moneys and then said: 'But who am I to give the sovereign to?'

'Let's leave it all till mother comes back,' suggested Lucy.

'No, dear; your mother may take quite a long drive now that she is not hampered with me. We all have our little foibles, and mine is the promptly settling of accounts.'

Here Freddy's friend, Mr Floyd, made the one remark of his that need be quoted: he offered to toss Freddy for Miss Bartlett's quid. A solution seemed in sight, and even Cecil, who had been ostentatiously drinking his tea at the view, felt the eternal attraction of Chance, and turned round.

But this did not do, either.

'Please—please—I know I am a sad spoil-sport, but it would make me wretched. I should practically be robbing the one who lost.'

'Freddy owes me fifteen shillings,' interposed Cecil. 'So it will work out right if you give the pound to me.'

'Fifteen shillings,' said Miss Bartlett dubiously. 'How is that, Mr Vyse?'

'Because, don't you see, Freddy paid your cab. Give me the pound, and we shall avoid this deplorable gambling.'

Miss Bartlett, who was poor at figures, became bewildered and rendered up the sovereign, amidst the suppressed gurgles of the other youths. For a moment Cecil was happy. He was playing at nonsense among his peers. Then he glanced at Lucy, in whose face petty anxieties had marred the smiles. In January he would rescue his Leonardo from this stupefying twaddle.

'But I don't see that!' exclaimed Minnie Beebe, who had narrowly watched the iniquitous transaction. 'I don't see why Mr Vyse is to have the quid.'

'Because of the fifteen shillings and the five,' they said solemnly. 'Fifteen shillings and five shillings make one pound, you see.'

'But I don't see—'

They tried to stifle her with cake.

'No, thank you. I'm done. I don't see why— Freddy, don't poke me. Miss Honeychurch, your brother's hurting me. Ow! What about Mr Floyd's ten shillings? Ow! No, I don't see and I never shall see why Miss What's-her-name shouldn't pay that bob for the driver.'

'I had forgotten the driver,' said Miss Bartlett, reddening. 'Thank you, dear, for reminding me. A shilling was it? Can anyone give me change for half a crown?'

'I'll get it,' said the young hostess, rising with decision. 'Cecil, give me that sovereign. No—give me up that sovereign. I'll get Euphemia to change it, and we'll start the whole thing again from the beginning.'

'Lucy—Lucy—what a nuisance I am!' protested Miss Bartlett, and
followed her across the lawn. Lucy tripped ahead, simulating hilarity. When
they were out of earshot, Miss Bartlett stopped her wails and said quite
briskly: 'Have you told him about him yet?'

'No, I haven't,' replied Lucy, and then could have bitten her tongue for
understanding so quickly what her cousin meant. 'Let me see—a sovereign's
worth of silver.'

She escaped into the kitchen. Miss Bartlett's sudden transitions were too
uncanny. It sometimes seemed as if she planned every word she spoke or
caused to be spoken; as if all this worry about cabs and change had been a
ruse to surprise the soul.

'No, I haven't told Cecil or anyone,' she remarked, when she returned. 'I
promised you I shouldn't. Here is your money—all shillings, except two
half-crowns. Would you count it? You can settle your debt nicely now.'

Miss Bartlett was in the drawing-room, gazing at the photograph of St
John ascending, who had been framed.

'How dreadful!' she murmured, 'how more than dreadful, if Mr Vyse
should come to hear of it from some other source.'

'Oh no, Charlotte,' said the girl, entering the battle, 'George Emerson is
all right, and what other source is there?'

Miss Bartlett considered. 'For instance, the driver. I saw him looking
through the bushes at you. I remember he had a violet between his teeth.'

Lucy shuddered a little. 'We shall get the silly affair on our nerves if we
aren't careful. How could a Florentine cab-driver ever get hold of Cecil?'

'We must think of every possibility.'

'Oh, it's all right.'

'Or perhaps old Mr Emerson knows. In fact, he is certain to know.'

'I don't care if he does. I was grateful to you for your letter, but even if the
news does get round, I think I can trust Cecil to laugh at it.'

'To contradict it?'

'No, to laugh at it.' But she knew in her heart that she could not trust him,
for he desired her untouched.

'Very well, dear, you know best. Perhaps gentlemen are different to what
they were when I was young. Ladies are certainly different.'

'Now, Charlotte!' She struck at her playfully. 'You kind, anxious thing!
What *would* you have me do? First you say, "Don't tell"; and then you say,
"Tell." Which is it to be? Quick!'

Miss Bartlett sighed. 'I am no match for you in conversation, dearest. I
blush when I think how I interfered at Florence, and you so well able to look
after yourself, and so much cleverer in all ways than I am. You will never
forgive me.'

'Shall we go out, then? They will smash all the china if we don't.'

For the air rang with the shrieks of Minnie, who was being scalped with a
teaspoon.

'Dear, one moment—we may not have this chance for a chat again. Have
you seen the young one yet?'

'Yes, I have.'

'What happened?'

'We met at the Rectory.'

'What line is he taking up?'

'No line. He talked about Italy, like any other person. It is really all right. What advantage would he get from being a cad, to put it bluntly? I do wish I could make you see it my way. He really won't be any nuisance, Charlotte.'

'Once a cad, always a cad. That is my poor opinion.'

Lucy paused. 'Cecil said one day—and I thought it so profound—that there are two kinds of cads—the conscious and the subconscious.' She paused again, to be sure of doing justice to Cecil's profundity. Through the window she saw Cecil himself, turning over the pages of a novel. It was a new one from Smith's library. Her mother must have returned from the station.

'Once a cad, always a cad,' droned Miss Bartlett.

'What I mean by subconscious is that Mr Emerson lost his head. I fell into all those violets, and he was silly and surprised. I don't think we ought to blame him very much. It makes such a difference when you see a person with beautiful things behind him unexpectedly. It really does; it makes an enormous difference, and he lost his head: he doesn't admire me, or any of that nonsense, one straw. Freddy rather likes him, and has asked him up here on Sunday, so you can judge for yourself. He has improved: he doesn't always look as if he is going to burst into tears. He is a clerk in the General Manager's office at one of the big railways—not a porter! and runs down to his father for week-ends. Papa was to do with journalism, but is rheumatic and has retired. There! Now for the garden.' She took hold of her guest by the arm. 'Suppose we don't talk about this silly Italian business any more. We want you to have a nice restful visit at Windy Corner, with no worriting.'

Lucy thought this rather a good speech. The reader may have detected an unfortunate slip in it. Whether Miss Bartlett detected the slip one cannot say, for it is impossible to penetrate into the minds of elderly people. She might have spoken further, but they were interrupted by the entrance of her hostess. Explanations took place, and in the midst of them Lucy escaped, the images throbbing a little more vividly in her brain.

Chapter Fifteen

The Disaster Within

The Sunday after Miss Bartlett's arrival was a glorious day, like most of the days of that year. In the Weald, autumn approached, breaking up the green monotony of summer, touching the parks with the grey bloom of mist, the beech-trees with russet, the oak-trees with gold. Up on the heights, battalions of black pines witnessed the change, themselves unchangeable.

Either country was spanned by a cloudless sky, and in either arose the tinkle of church bells.

The garden of Windy Corner was deserted except for a red book, which lay sunning itself upon the gravel path. From the house came incoherent sounds, as of females preparing for worship. 'The men say they won't go'–'Well, I don't blame them'–'Minnie says, need she go?'–'Tell her, no nonsense'–'Anne! Mary! Hook me behind!'–'Dearest Lucia, may I trespass upon you for a pin?' For Miss Bartlett had announced that she at all events was one for church.

The sun rose higher on its journey, guided, not by Phaethon, but by Apollo, competent, unswerving, divine. Its rays fell on the ladies whenever they advanced towards the bedroom windows; on Mr Beebe down at Summer Street as he smiled over a letter from Miss Catharine Alan; on George Emerson cleaning his father's boots; and lastly, to complete the catalogue of memorable things, on the red book mentioned above. The ladies move, Mr Beebe moves, George moves, and movement may engender shadow. But this book lies motionless, to be caressed all the morning by the sun and to raise its covers slightly, as though acknowledging the caress.

Presently Lucy steps out of the drawing-room window. Her new cerise dress has been a failure, and makes her look tawdry and wan. At her throat is a garnet brooch, on her finger a ring set with rubies–an engagement ring. Her eyes are bent to the Weald. She frowns a little–not in anger, but as a brave child frowns when he is trying not to cry. In all that expanse no human eye is looking at her, and she may frown unrebuked and measure the spaces that yet survive between Apollo and the western hills.

'Lucy! Lucy! What's that book? Who's been taking a book out of the shelf and leaving it about to spoil?'

'It's only the library book that Cecil's been reading.'

'But pick it up, and don't stand idling there like a flamingo.'

Lucy picked up the book and glanced at the title listlessly, 'Under a Loggia.' She no longer read novels herself, devoting all her spare time to solid literature in the hope of catching Cecil up. It was dreadful how little she knew, and even when she thought she knew a thing, like the Italian painters, she found she had forgotten it. Only this morning she had confused Francesco Francia with Piero della Francesca, and Cecil had said, 'What! you aren't forgetting your Italy already?' And this too had lent anxiety to her eyes when she saluted the dear view and the dear garden in the foreground, and above them, scarce conceivable elsewhere, the dear sun.

'Lucy–have you a sixpence for Minnie and a shilling for yourself?'

She hastened in to her mother, who was rapidly working herself into a Sunday fluster.

'It's a special collection–I forget what for. I do beg, no vulgar clinking in the plate with halfpennies; see that Minnie has a nice bright sixpence. Where is the child? Minnie! That book's all warped' (Gracious, how plain you look!) Put it under the Atlas to press. Minnie!'

'Oh, Mrs Honeychurch—' from the upper regions.

'Minnie, don't be late. Here comes the horse'–it was always the horse, never the carriage. 'Where's Charlotte? Run up and hurry her. Why is she so long? She had nothing to do. She never brings anything but blouses. Poor Charlotte—How I do detest blouses! Minnie!'

Paganism is infectious—more infectious than diphtheria or piety—and the Rector's niece was taken to church protesting. As usual, she didn't see why. Why shouldn't she sit in the sun with the young men? The young men, who had now appeared, mocked her with ungenerous words. Mrs Honeychurch defended orthodoxy, and in the midst of the confusion Miss Bartlett, dressed in the very height of the fashion, came strolling down the stairs.

'Dear Marian, I am very sorry, but I have no small change—nothing but sovereigns and half-crowns. Could anyone give me—'

'Yes, easily. Jump in. Gracious me, how smart you look. What a lovely frock! You put us all to shame.'

'If I did not wear my best rags and tatters now, when should I wear them?' said Miss Bartlett reproachfully. She got into the victoria and placed herself with her back to the horse. The necessary uproar ensued, and then they drove off.

'Goodbye! Be good!' called out Cecil.

Lucy bit her lip, for the tone was sneering. On the subject of 'church and so on' they had had rather an unsatisfactory conversation. He had said that people ought to overhaul themselves, and she did not want to overhaul herself: she did not know how it was done. Honest orthodoxy Cecil respected, but he always assumed that honesty is the result of a spiritual crisis: he could not imagine it as a natural birthright, that might grow heavenward like the flowers. All that he said on this subject pained her, though he exuded tolerance from every pore; somehow the Emersons were different.

She saw the Emersons after church. There was a line of carriages down the road, and the Honeychurch vehicle happened to be opposite Cissie Villa. To save time, they walked over the green to it, and found father and son smoking in the garden.

'Introduce me,' said her mother. 'Unless the young man considers that he knows me already.'

He probably did; but Lucy ignored the Sacred Lake and introduced them formally. Old Mr. Emerson claimed her with much warmth, and said how glad he was that she was going to be married. She said yes, she was glad too; and then, as Miss Bartlett and Minnie were lingering behind with Mr Beebe, she turned the conversation to a less disturbing topic, and asked him how he liked his new house.

'Very much,' he replied, but there was a note of offence in his voice: she had never known him offended before. He added: 'We find, though, that the Miss Alans were coming, and that we have turned them out. Women mind such a thing. I am very much upset about it.'

'I believe that there was some misunderstanding,' said Mrs Honeychurch uneasily.

'Our landlord was told that we should be a different type of person,' said George, who seemed disposed to carry the matter further. 'He thought we should be artistic. He is disappointed.'

'And I wonder whether we ought to write to the Miss Alans and offer to give it up. What do you think?' He appealed to Lucy.

'Oh, stop now you have come,' said Lucy lightly. She must avoid censuring Cecil. For it was on Cecil that the little episode turned, though his name was never mentioned.

'So George says. He says that the Miss Alans must go to the wall. Yet it does seem so unkind.'

'There is only a certain amount of kindness in the world,' said George, watching the sunlight flash on the panels of the passing carriages.

'Yes!' exclaimed Mrs Honeychurch. 'That's exactly what I say. Why all this twiddling and twaddling over two Miss Alans?'

'There is a certain amount of kindness, just as there is a certain amount of light,' he continued in measured tones. 'We cast a shadow on something wherever we stand, and it is no good moving from place to place to save things; because the shadow always follows. Choose a place where you won't do harm—yes, choose a place where you won't do very much harm, and stand in it for all you are worth, facing the sunshine.'

'Oh, Mr Emerson, I see you're clever!'

'Eh—?'

'I see you're going to be clever. I hope you didn't go behaving like that to poor Freddy.'

George's eyes laughed, and Lucy suspected that he and her mother would get on rather well.

'No, I didn't,' he said. 'He behaved that way to me. It is his philosophy. Only he starts life with it; and I have tried the Note of Interrogation first.'

'What *do* you mean? No, never mind what you mean. Don't explain. He looks forward to seeing you this afternoon. Do you play tennis? Do you mind tennis on Sunday—?'

'George mind tennis on Sunday! George, after his education, distinguish between Sunday—'

'Very well, George doesn't mind tennis on Sunday. No more do I. That's settled. Mr Emerson, if you could come with your son we should be so pleased.'

He thanked her, but the walk sounded rather far: he could only potter about in these days.

She turned to George: 'And then he wants to give up his house to the Miss Alans.'

'I know,' said George, and put his arm round his father's neck. The kindness that Mr Beebe and Lucy had always known to exist in him came out suddenly, like sunlight touching a vast landscape—a touch of the morning sun? She remembered that in all his perversities he had never spoken against affection.

Miss Bartlett approached.

'You know our cousin, Miss Bartlett,' said Mrs Honeychurch pleasantly. 'You met her with my daughter in Florence.'

'Yes, indeed!' said the old man, and made as if he would come out of the

garden to greet the lady. Miss Bartlett promptly got into the victoria. Thus
entrenched, she emitted a formal bow. It was the Pension Bertolini again,
the dining-table with the decanters of water and wine. It was the old, old
battle of the room with the view.

George did not respond to the bow. Like any boy, he blushed and was
ashamed: he knew that the chaperon remembered. He said: 'I–I'll come up
to tennis if I can manage it,' and went into the house. Perhaps anything that
he did would have pleased Lucy, but his awkwardness went straight to her
heart: men were not gods after all, but as human and as clumsy as girls; even
men might suffer from unexplained desires, and need help. To one of her
upbringing, and of her destination, the weakness of men was a truth
unfamiliar, but she had surmised it at Florence, when George threw her
photographs into the River Arno.

'George, don't go,' cried his father, who thought it a great treat for people
if his son would talk to them. 'George has been in such good spirits to-day,
and I am sure he will end by coming up this afternoon.'

Lucy caught her cousin's eye. Something in its mute appeal made her
reckless. 'Yes,' she said, raising her voice, 'I do hope he will.' Then she went
to the carriage and murmured, 'The old man hasn't been told; I knew it was
all right.' Mrs Honeychurch followed her, and they drove away.

Satisfactory that Mr Emerson had not been told of the Florence escapade;
yet Lucy's spirits should not have leapt up as if she had sighted the ramparts
of heaven. Satisfactory; yet surely she greeted it with disproportionate joy.
All the way home the horses' hoofs sang a tune to her: 'He has not told, he
has not told.' Her brain expanded the melody: 'He has not told his father–to
whom he tells all things. It was not an exploit. He did not laugh at me when I
had gone.' She raised her hand to her cheek. 'He does not love me. No. How
terrible if he did! But he has not told. He will not tell.'

She longed to shout the words: 'It is all right. It's a secret between us two
for ever. Cecil will never hear.' She was even glad that Miss Bartlett had
made her promise secrecy, that last dark evening at Florence, when they had
knelt packing in his room. The secret, big or little, was guarded. Only three
English people knew of it in the world.

Thus she interpreted her joy. She greeted Cecil with unusual radiance,
because she felt so safe. As he helped her out of the carriage, she said:

'The Emersons have been so nice. George Emerson has improved
enormously.'

'Oh, how are my protégés?' asked Cecil, who took no real interest in them,
and had long since forgotten his resolution to bring them to Windy Corner
for educational purposes.

'Protégés!' she exclaimed with some warmth.

For the only relationship which Cecil conceived was feudal: that of
protector and protected. He had no glimpse of the comradeship after which
the girl's soul yearned.

'You shall see for youself how your protégés are. George Emerson is
coming up this afternoon. He is a most interesting man to talk to. Only
don't—' She nearly said, 'Don't protect him.' But the bell was ringing for

lunch, and, as often happened, Cecil had paid no great attention to her remarks. Charm, not argument, was to be her forte.

Lunch was a cheerful meal. Generally Lucy was depressed at meals. Some one had to be soothed—either Cecil or Miss Bartlett or a Being not visible to the mortal eye—a Being who whispered to her soul: 'It will not last, this cheerfulness. In January you must go to London to entertain the grandchildren of celebrated men.' But to-day she felt she had received a guarantee. Her mother would always sit there, her brother here. The sun, though it had moved a little since the morning, would never be hidden behind the western hills. After luncheon they asked her to play. She had seen Gluck's 'Armide' that year, and played from memory the music of the enchanted garden—the music to which Renaud approaches, beneath the light of an eternal dawn, the music that never gains, never wanes, but ripples for ever like the tideless seas of fairyland. Such music is not for the piano, and her audience began to get restive, and Cecil, sharing the discontent, called out: 'Now play us the other garden—the one in "Parsifal."'

She closed the instrument.

'Not very dutiful,' said her mother's voice.

Fearing that she had offended Cecil, she turned quickly round. There George was. He had crept in without interrupting her.

'Oh, I had no idea?' she exclaimed, getting very red; and then, without a word of greeting, she reopened the piano. Cecil should have the 'Parsifal,' and anything else that he liked.

'Our performer has changed her mind,' said Miss Bartlett, perhaps implying, 'she will play the music to Mr Emerson. Lucy did not know what to do, nor even what she wanted to do. She played a few bars of the Flower Maidens' song very badly, and then she stopped.

'I vote tennis,' said Freddy, disgusted at the scrappy entertainment.

'Yes, so do I.' Once more she closed the unfortunate piano. 'I vote you have a men's four.'

'All right.'

'Not for me, thank you,' said Cecil. 'I will not spoil the set.' He never realized that it may be an act of kindness in a bad player to make up a fourth.

'Oh, come along, Cecil. I'm bad, Floyd's rotten, and so I dare say's Emerson.'

George corrected him: 'I am not bad.'

One looked down one's nose at this. 'Then certainly I won't play,' said Cecil, while Miss Bartlett, under the impression that she was snubbing George, added: 'I agree with you, Mr Vyse. You had much better not play. Much better not.'

Minnie, rushing in where Cecil feared to tread, announced that she would play. 'I shall miss every ball anyway, so what does it matter?' But Sunday intervened and stamped heavily upon the kind suggestion.

'Then it will have to be Lucy,' said Mrs Honeychurch; 'you must fall back on Lucy. There is no other way out of it. Lucy, go and change your frock.'

Lucy's Sabbath was generally of this amphibious nature. She kept it without hypocrisy in the morning, and broke it without reluctance in the afternoon. As she changed her frock, she wondered whether Cecil was sneering at her: really she must overhaul herself and settle everything up before she married him.

Mr Floyd was her partner. She liked music, but how much better tennis seemed. How much better to run about in comfortable clothes than to sit at the piano and feel girt under the arms. Once more music appeared to her the employment of a child. George served, and surprised her by his anxiety to win. She remembered how he had sighed among the tombs at Santa Croce because things wouldn't fit; how after the death of that obscure Italian he had leant over the parapet by the Arno and said to her: 'I shall want to live, I tell you.' He wanted to live now, to win at tennis, to stand for all he was worth in the sun—in the sun which had begun to decline and was shining in her eyes; and he did win.

Ah, how beautiful the Weald looked! The hills stood out above its radiance, as Fiesole stands above the Tuscan Plain, and the South Downs, if one chose, were the mountains of Carrara. She might be forgetting her Italy, but she was noticing more things in her England. One could play a new game with the view, and try to find in its innumerable folds some town or village that would do for Florence. Ah, how beautiful the Weald looked!

But now Cecil claimed her. He chanced to be in a lucid critical mood, and would not sympathize with exaltation. He had been rather a nuisance all through the tennis, for the novel that he was reading was so bad that he was obliged to read it aloud to others. He would stroll round the precincts of the court and call out: 'I say, listen to this, Lucy. Three split infinitives.' 'Dreadful!' said Lucy, and missed her stroke. When they had finished their set, he still went on reading; there was some murder scene, and really every one must listen to it. Freddy and Mr Floyd were obliged to hunt for a lost ball in the laurels, but the other two acquiesced.

'The scene is laid in Florence.'

'What fun, Cecil! Read away. Come, Mr Emerson, sit down after all your energy.' She had 'forgiven' George, as she put it, and she made a point of being pleasant to him.

He jumped over the net and sat down at her feet, asking: 'You—and are you tired?'

'Of course I'm not!'

'Do you mind being beaten?'

She was going to answer 'No,' when it struck her that she did mind, so she answered 'Yes.' She added merrily, 'I don't see *you're* such a splendid player, though. The light was behind you, and it was in my eyes.'

'I never said I was.'

'Why, you did!'

'You didn't attend.'

'You said—oh, don't go in for accuracy at this house. We all exaggerate, and we get very angry with people who don't.'

'The scene is laid in Florence,' repeated Cecil, with an upward note.

Lucy recollected herself.

'"Sunset. Leonora was speeding—"'

Lucy interrupted. 'Leonora? Is Leonora the heroine? Who's the book by?'

'Joseph Emery Prank. "Sunset. Leonora was speeding across the square. Pray the saints she might not arrive too late. Sunset—the sunset of Italy. Under Orcagna's Loggia—the Loggia de' Lanzi, as we sometimes call it now—"'

Lucy burst into laughter. '"Joseph Emery Prank" indeed! Why, it's Miss Lavish! It's Miss Lavish's novel, and she's publishing it under somebody else's name.'

'Who may Miss Lavish be?'

'Oh, a dreadful person—Mr Emerson, you remember Miss Lavish?' Excited by her pleasant afternoon, she clapped her hands.

George looked up. 'Of course I do. I saw her the day I arrived at Summer Street. It was she who told me that you lived here.'

'Weren't you pleased?' She meant—'to see Miss Lavish,' but when he bent down to the grass without replying, it struck her that she could mean something else. She watched his head, which was almost resting against her knee, and she thought that the ears were reddening. 'No wonder the novel's bad,' she added. 'I never liked Miss Lavish. But I suppose one ought to read it as one's met her.'

'All modern books are bad,' said Cecil, who was annoyed at her inattention, and vented his annoyance on literature. 'Every one writes for money in these days.'

'Oh, Cecil—!'

'It is so. I will inflict Joseph Emery Prank on you no longer.'

Cecil, this afternoon, seemed such a twittering sparrow. The ups and downs in his voice were noticeable, but they did not affect her. She had dwelt amongst melody and movement, and her nerves refused to answer to the clang of his. Leaving him to be annoyed, she gazed at the black head again. She did not want to stroke it, but she saw herself wanting to stroke it: the sensation was curious.

'How do you like this view of ours, Mr Emerson?'

'I never notice much difference in views.'

'What do you mean?'

'Because they are all alike. Because all that matters in them is distance and air.'

'H'm!' said Cecil, uncertain whether the remark was striking or not.

'My father'—he looked up at her (and he was a little flushed)—'says that there is only one perfect view—the view of the sky straight over our heads, and that all these views on earth are but bungled copies of it.'

'I expect your father has been reading Dante,' said Cecil, fingering the novel, which alone permitted him to lead the conversation.

'He told us another day that views are really crowds – crowds of trees and houses and hills—and are bound to resemble each other, like human crowds—and that the power they have over us is something supernatural, for the same reason.'

Lucy's lips parted.

'For a crowd is more than the people who make it up. Something gets added to it—no one knows how—just as something has got added to those hills.'

He pointed with his racquet to the South Downs.

'What a splendid idea!' she murmured. 'I shall enjoy hearing your father talk again. I'm so sorry he's not so well.'

'No, he isn't well.'

'There's an absurd account of a view in this book,' said Cecil.

'Also that men fall into two classes—those who forget views and those who remember them, even in small rooms.'

'Mr Emerson, have you any brothers or sisters?'

'None. Why?'

'You spoke of "us."'

'My mother, I was meaning.'

Cecil closed the novel with a bang.

'Oh, Cecil—how you make me jump!'

'I will inflict Joseph Emery Prank on you no longer.'

'I can just remember us all three going into the country for the day and seeing as far as Hindhead. It is the first thing that I remember.'

Cecil got up: the man was ill-bred—he hadn't put on his coat after tennis—he didn't do. He would have strolled away if Lucy had not stopped him.

'Cecil, do read the thing about the view.'

'Not while Mr Emerson is here to entertain us.'

'No—read away. I think nothing's funnier than to hear silly things read out loud. If Mr Emerson thinks us frivolous he can go.'

This struck Cecil as subtle, and pleased him. It put their visitor in the position of a prig. Somewhat mollified, he sat down again.

'Mr Emerson, go and find tennis balls.' She opened the book. Cecil must have his reading and anything else that he liked. But her attention wandered to George's mother, who—according to Mr Eager—had been murdered in the sight of God and – according to her son—had seen as far as Hindhead.

'Am I really to go?' asked George.

'No, of course, not really,' she answered.

'Chapter two,' said Cecil, yawning. 'Find me chapter two, if it isn't bothering you.'

Chapter two was found, and she glanced at its opening sentences.

She thought she had gone mad.

'Here—hand me the book.'

She heard her voice saying: 'It isn't worth reading—it's too silly to read—I never saw such rubbish – it oughtn't to be allowed to be printed.'

He took the book from her.

'"Leonora,"' he read, '"sat pensive and alone. Before her lay the rich champaign of Tuscany, dotted over with many a smiling village. The season was spring."'

Miss Lavish knew, somehow, and had printed the past in draggled prose, for Cecil to read and for George to hear.

'"A golden haze,"' he read. He read: '"Afar off the towers of Florence, while the bank on which she sat was carpeted with violets. All unobserved, Antonio stole up behind her—'''

Lest Cecil should see her face she turned to George, and she saw his face.

He read: '''There came from his lips no wordy protestation such as formal lovers use. No eloquence was his, nor did he suffer from the lack of it. He simply enfolded her in his manly arms.'''

There was a silence.

'This isn't the passage I wanted,' he informed them. 'There is another much funnier, further on.' He turned over the leaves.

'Should we go in to tea?' said Lucy, whose voice remained steady.

She led the way up the garden, Cecil following her, George last. She thought a disaster was averted. But when they entered the shrubbery it came. The book, as if it had not worked mischief enough, had been forgotten, and Cecil must go back for it; and George, who loved passionately, must blunder against her in the narrow path.

'No—' she gasped, and, for the second time, was kissed by him.

As if no more was possible, he slipped back; Cecil rejoined her; they reached the upper lawn alone.

Chapter Sixteen

Lying to George

But Lucy had developed since the spring. That is to say, she was now better able to stifle the emotions of which the conventions and the world disapprove. Though the danger was greater, she was not shaken by deep sobs. She said to Cecil, 'I am not coming in to tea—tell mother—I must write some letters,' and went up to her room. There she prepared for action. Love felt and returned, love which our bodies exact and our hearts have transfigured, love which is the most real thing that we shall ever meet, reappeared now as the world's enemy, and she must stifle it.

She sent for Miss Bartlett.

The contest lay not between love and duty. Perhaps there never is such a contest. It lay between the real and the pretended, and Lucy's first aim was to defeat herself. As her brain clouded over, as the memory of the views grew dim and the words of the book died away, she returned to her old shibboleth of nerves. She 'conquered her breakdown'. Tampering with the truth, she forgot that the truth had ever been. Remembering that she was engaged to Cecil, she compelled herself to confused remembrances of George; he was nothing to her: he never had been anything: he had behaved abominably; she had never encouraged him. The armour of falsehood is subtly wrought out of darkness, and hides a man not only from others, but from his own soul. In a few moments Lucy was equipped for battle.

'Something too awful has happened,' she began, as soon as her cousin arrived. 'Do you know anything about Miss Lavish's novel?'

Miss Bartlett looked surprised, and said that she had not read the book, nor known that it was published; Eleanor was a reticent woman at heart.

'There is a scene in it. The hero and heroine make love. Do you know about that?'

'Dear—?'

'Do you know about it, please?' she repeated. 'They are on a hill-side, and Florence is in the distance.'

'My good Lucia, I am all at sea. I know nothing about it whatever.'

'There are violets. I cannot believe it is a coincidence. Charlotte, Charlotte, how *could* you have told her? I have thought before speaking: it *must* be you.'

'Told her what?' she asked, with growing agitation.

'About that dreadful afternoon in February.'

Miss Bartlett was genuinely moved. 'Oh, Lucy, dearest girl—she hasn't put that in her book?'

Lucy nodded.

'Not so that one could recognize it?'

'Yes.'

'Then never–never–never more shall Eleanor Lavish be friend of mine.'

'So you did tell?'

'I did just happen–when I had tea with her at Rome–in the course of conversation—'

'But, Charlotte–what about the promise you gave me when we were packing? Why did you tell Miss Lavish, when you wouldn't even let me tell mother?'

'I will never forgive Eleanor. She has betrayed my confidence.'

'Why did you tell her, though? This is a most serious thing.'

Why does anyone tell anything? The question is eternal, and it was not surprising that Miss Bartlett should only sigh faintly in response. She had done wrong–she admitted it; she only hoped that she had not done harm; she had told Eleanor in the strictest confidence.

Lucy stamped with irritation.

'Cecil happened to read out the passage aloud to me and to Mr Emerson; it upset Mr Emerson, and he insulted me again. Behind Cecil's back. Ugh! Is it possible that men are such brutes? Behind Cecil's back as we were walking up the garden.'

Miss Bartlett burst into self-accusations and regrets.

'What is to be done now? Can you tell me?'

'Oh, Lucy–I shall never forgive myself, never to my dying day. Fancy if your prospects—'

'I know,' said Lucy, wincing at the word. 'I see now why you wanted me to tell Cecil, and what you meant by "some other source". You knew that you had told Miss Lavish, and that she was not reliable.'

It was Miss Bartlett's turn to wince.

'However,' said the girl, despising her cousin's shiftiness, 'what's done's done. You have put me in a most awkward position. How am I to get out of it?'

Miss Bartlett could not think. The days of her energy were over. She was a visitor, not a chaperon, and a discredited visitor at that. She stood with clasped hands while the girl worked herself into the necessary rage.

'He must—that man must have such a setting down that he won't forget. And who's to give it him? I can't tell mother now—owing to you. Nor Cecil, Charlotte, owing to you. I am caught up every way. I think I shall go mad. I have no one to help me. That's why I've sent for you. What's wanted is a man with a whip.'

Miss Bartlett agreed: one wanted a man with a whip.

'Yes—but it's no good agreeing. What's to be *done*? We women go maundering on. What *does* a girl do when she comes across a cad?'

'I always said he was a cad, dear. Give me credit for that, at all events. From the very first moment—when he said his father was having a bath.'

'Oh, bother the credit and who's been right or wrong! We've both made a muddle of it. George Emerson is still down the garden there, and is he to be left unpunished, or isn't he? I want to know.'

Miss Bartlett was absolutely helpless. Her own exposure had unnerved her, and thoughts were colliding painfully in her brain. She moved feebly to the window, and tried to detect the cad's white flannels among the laurels.

'You were ready enough at the Bertolini when you rushed me off to Rome. Can't you speak again to him now?'

'Willingly would I move heaven and earth—'

'I want something more definite,' said Lucy contemptuously. 'Will you speak to him? It is the least you can do, surely, considering it all happened because you broke your word.'

'Never again shall Eleanor Lavish be friend of mine.'

Really, Charlotte was outdoing herself.

'Yes or no, please: yes or no.'

'It is the kind of thing that only a gentleman can settle.'

George Emerson was coming up the garden with a tennis ball in his hand.

'Very well,' said Lucy, with an angry gesture. 'No one will help me. I will speak to him myself.' And immediately she realized that this was what her cousin had intended all along.

'Hullo, Emerson!' called Freddy from below. 'Found the lost ball? Good man! Want any tea?' And there was an irruption from the house on to the terrace.

'Oh, Lucy, but that is brave of you! I admire you—'

They had gathered round George, who beckoned, she felt, over the rubbish, the sloppy thoughts, the furtive yearnings that were beginning to cumber her soul. Her anger faded at the sight of him. Ah! the Emersons were fine people in their way. She had to subdue a rush in her blood before saying:

'Freddy has taken him into the dining-room. The others are going down the garden. Come. Let us get this over quickly. Come. I want you in the room, of course.'

'Lucy, do you mind doing it?'

'How can you ask such a ridiculous question?'

'Poor Lucy—' She stretched out her hand. 'I seem to bring nothing but misfortune wherever I go.' Lucy nodded. She remembered their last evening at Florence–the packing, the candle, the shadow of Miss Bartlett's toque on the door. She was not to be trapped by pathos a second time. Eluding her cousin's caress, she led the way downstairs.

'Try the jam,' Freddy was saying. 'The jam's jolly good.'

George, looking big and dishevelled, was pacing up and down the dining-room. As she entered he stopped, and said:

'No–nothing to eat.'

'You go down to the others,' said Lucy; 'Charlotte and I will give Mr Emerson all he wants. Where's mother?'

'She's started on her Sunday writing. She's in the drawing-room.'

'That's all right. You go away.'

He went off singing.

Lucy sat down at the table. Miss Bartlett, who was thoroughly frightened, took up a book and pretended to read.

She would not be drawn into an elaborate speech. She just said: 'I can't have it, Mr Emerson. I cannot even talk to you. Go out of this house, and never come into it again as long as I live here'–flushing as she spoke and pointing to the door. 'I hate a row. Go, please.'

'What—'

'No discussion.'

'But I can't—'

She shook her head. 'Go, please. I do not want to call in Mr Vyse.'

'You don't mean,' he said, absolutely ignoring Miss Bartlett–'you don't mean that you are going to marry that man?'

The line was unexpected.

She shrugged her shoulders, as if his vulgarity wearied her. 'You are merely ridiculous,' she said quietly.

Then his words rose gravely over hers: 'You cannot live with Vyse. He's only for an acquaintance. He is for society and cultivated talk. He should know no one intimately, least of all a woman.'

It was a new light on Cecil's character.

'Have you ever talked to Vyse without feeling tired?'

'I can scarcely discuss—'

'No, but have you ever? He is the sort who are all right so long as they keep to things–books, pictures–but kill when they come to people. That's why I'll speak out through all this muddle even now. It's shocking enough to lose you in any case, but generally a man must deny himself joy, and I would have held back if your Cecil had been a different person. I would never have let myself go. But I saw him first in the National Gallery, when he winced because my father mispronounced the names of great painters. Then he brings us here, and we find it is to play some silly trick on a kind neighbour. That is the man all over–playing tricks on people, on the most sacred form of life that he can find. Next, I meet you together, and find him protecting and

teaching you and your mother to be shocked, when it was for *you* to settle
whether you were shocked or no. Cecil all over again. He daren't let a woman
decide. He's the type who's kept Europe back for a thousand years. Every
moment of his life he's forming you, telling you what's charming or amusing
or ladylike, telling you what a man thinks womanly; and you, you of all
women, listen to his voice instead of your own. So it was at the Rectory,
when I met you both again; so it has been the whole of this afternoon.
Therefore—not "therefore I kissed you," because the book made me do that,
and I wish to goodness I had more self-control. I'm not ashamed. I don't
apologize. But it has frightened you, and you may not have noticed that I
love you. Or would you have told me to go, and dealt with a tremendous
thing so lightly? But therefore—therefore I settled to fight him.'

Lucy thought of a very good remark.

'You say Mr Vyse wants me to listen to him, Mr Emerson. Pardon me for
suggesting that you have caught the habit.'

And he took the shoddy reproof and touched it into immortality. He said:

'Yes, I have,' and sank down as if suddenly weary. 'I'm the same kind of
brute at bottom. This desire to govern a woman—it lies very deep, and men
and women must fight it together before they shall enter the garden. But I do
love you—surely in a better way than he does.' He thought. 'Yes—really in a
better way. I want you to have your own thoughts even when I hold you in
my arms.' He stretched them towards her. 'Lucy, be quick—there's no time
for us to talk now—come to me as you came in the spring, and afterwards I
will be gentle and explain. I have cared for you since that man died. I cannot
live without you. "No, good," I thought: "she is marrying some one else";
but I meet you again when all the world is glorious water and sun. As you
came through the wood I saw that nothing else mattered. I called. I wanted
to live and have my chance of joy.'

'And Mr Vyse?' said Lucy, who kept commendably calm. 'Does he not
matter? That I love Cecil and shall be his wife shortly? A detail of no
importance, I suppose?'

But he stretched his arms over the table towards her.

'May I ask what you intend to gain by this exhibition?'

He said: 'It is our last chance. I shall do all that I can.' And as if he had
done all else, he turned to Miss Bartlett, who sat like some portent against
the skies of evening. 'You wouldn't stop us this second time if you
understood,' he said. 'I have been into the dark, and I am going back into it,
unless you will try to understand.'

Her long, narrow head drove backwards and forwards, as though
demolishing some invisible obstacle. She did not answer.

'It is being young,' he said quietly, picking up his racquet from the floor
and preparing to go. 'It is being certain that Lucy cares for me really. It is
that love and youth matter intellectually.'

In silence the two women watched him. His last remark, they knew, was
nonsense, but was he going after it or not? Would not he, the cad, the
charlatan, attempt a more dramatic finish? No. He was apparently content.
He left them, carefully closing the front door; and when they looked through

the hall window, they saw him go up the drive and begin to climb the slopes of withered fern behind the house. Their tongues were loosed, and they burst into stealthy rejoicings.

'Oh, Lucia–come back here–oh, what an awful man!'

Lucy had no reaction–at least, not yet. 'Well, he amuses me,' she said. 'Either I'm mad, or else he is, and I'm inclined to think it's the latter. One more fuss through with you, Charlotte. Many thanks. I think, though, that this is the last. My admirer will hardly trouble me again.'

And Miss Bartlett, too, essayed the roguish:

'Well, it isn't every one who could boast such a conquest, dearest, is it? Oh, one oughtn't to laugh, really. It might have been very serious. But you were so sensible and brave–so unlike the girls of my day.'

'Let's go down to them.'

But, once in the open air, she paused. Some emotion–pity, terror, love, but the emotion was strong–seized her, and she was aware of autumn. Summer was ending, and the evening brought her odours of decay, the more pathetic because they were reminiscent of spring. That something or other mattered intellectually? A leaf, violently agitated, danced past her, while other leaves lay motionless. That the earth was hastening to re-enter darkness, and the shadows of those trees to creep over Windy Corner?

'Hullo, Lucy! There's still light enough for another set, if you two'll hurry.'

'Mr Emerson has had to go.'

'What a nuisance! That spoils the four. I say. Cecil, do play, do, there's a good chap. It's Floyd's last day. Do play tennis with us, just this once.'

Cecil's voice came: 'My dear Freddy, I am no athlete. As you well remarked this very morning, "There are some chaps who are no good for anything but books"; I plead guilty to being such a chap, and will not inflict myself on you.'

The scales fell from Lucy's eyes. How had she stood Cecil for a moment? He was absolutely intolerable, and the same evening she broke her engagement off.

Chapter Seventeen

Lying to Cecil

He was bewildered. He had nothing to say. He was not even angry, but stood, with a glass of whisky between his hands, trying to think what had led her to such a conclusion.

She had chosen the moment before bed, when, in accordance with their bourgeois habit, she always dispensed drinks to the men. Freddy and Mr Floyd were sure to retire with their glasses, while Cecil invariably lingered, sipping at his while she locked up the sideboard.

'I am very sorry about it,' she said; 'I have carefully thought things over. We are too different. I must ask you to release me, and try to forget that there ever was such a foolish girl.'

It was a suitable speech, but she was more angry than sorry, and her voice showed it.

'Different—how—how—'

'I haven't had a really good education, for one thing,' she continued, still on her knees by the sideboard. 'My Italian trip came too late, and I am forgetting all that I learnt there. I shall never be able to talk to your friends, or behave as a wife of yours should.'

'I don't understand you. You aren't like yourself. You're tired, Lucy.'

'Tired!' she retorted, kindling at once. 'That is exactly like you. You always think women don't mean what they say.'

'Well, you sound tired, as if something has worried you.'

'What if I do? It doesn't prevent me from realizing the truth. I can't marry you, and you will thank me for saying so some day.'

'You had that bad headache yesterday— All right'—for she had exclaimed indignantly—'I see it's much more than headaches. But give me a moment's time.' He closed his eyes. 'You must excuse me if I say stupid things, but my brain has gone to pieces. Part of it lives three minutes back, when I was sure that you loved me, and the other part—I find it difficult—I am likely to say the wrong thing.'

It struck her that he was not behaving so badly, and her irritation increased. She again desired a struggle, not a discussion. To bring on the crisis, she said:

'There are days when one sees clearly, and this is one of them. Things must come to a breaking-point some time, and it happens to be to-day. If you want to know, quite a little thing decided me to speak to you—when you wouldn't play tennis with Freddy.'

'I never do play tennis,' said Cecil, painfully bewildered; 'I never could play. I don't understand a word you say.'

'You can play well enough to make up a four. I thought it abominably selfish of you.'

'No, I can't—well, never mind the tennis. Why couldn't you—couldn't you have warned me if you felt anything wrong? You talked of our wedding at lunch—at least, you let me talk.'

'I knew you wouldn't understand,' said Lucy quite crossly. 'I might have known there would have been these dreadful explanations. Of course, it isn't the tennis—that was only the last straw to all I have been feeling for weeks. Surely it was better not to speak till I felt certain.' She developed this position. 'Often before I have wondered if I was fitted for your wife—for instance, in London; and are you fitted to be my husband? I don't think so. You don't like Freddy, nor my mother. There was always a lot against our engagement, Cecil, but all our relations seemed pleased, and we met so often, and it was no good mentioning it until—well, until all things came to a point. They have to-day. I see clearly. I must speak. That's all.'

'I cannot think you were right,' said Cecil gently. 'I cannot tell why, but though all that you say sounds true, I feel that you are not treating me fairly. It's all too horrible.'

'What's the good of a scene?'

'No good. But surely I have a right to hear a little more.'

He put down his glass and opened the window. From where she knelt, jangling her keys, she could see a slit of darkness, and, peering into it, as if it would tell him that 'little more,' his long, thoughtful face.

'Don't open the window; and you'd better draw the curtain, too; Freddy or anyone might be outside.' He obeyed. 'I really think we had better to go bed, if you don't mind. I shall only say things that will make me unhappy afterwards. As you say, it is all too horrible, and it is no good talking.'

But to Cecil, now that he was about to lose her, she seemed each moment more desirable. He looked at her, instead of through her, for the first time since they were engaged. From a Leonardo she had become a living woman, with mysteries and forces of her own, with qualities that even eluded art. His brain recovered from the shock, and in a burst of genuine devotion, he cried: 'But I love you, and I did think you loved me!'

'I did not,' she said. 'I thought I did at first. I am sorry, and ought to have refused you this last time, too.'

He began to walk up and down the room, and she grew more and more vexed at his dignified behaviour. She had counted on his being petty. It would have made things easier for her. By a cruel irony she was drawing out all that was finest in his disposition.

'You don't love me, evidently. I dare say you are right not to. But it would hurt a little less if I knew why.'

'Because'–a phrase came to her, and she accepted it–'you're the sort who can't know anyone intimately.'

A horrified look came into his eyes.

'I don't mean exactly that. But you will question me, though I beg you not to, and I must say something. It is that, more or less. When we were only acquaintances, you let me be myself, but now you're always protecting me.' Her voice swelled. 'I won't be protected. I will choose for myself what is ladylike and right. To shield me is an insult. Can't I be trusted to face the truth but I must get it second-hand through you? A woman's place! You despise my mother–I know you do–because she's conventional and bothers over puddings; but, oh goodness!'–she rose to her feet–'conventional, Cecil, you're that, for you may understand beautiful things, but you don't know how to use them; and you wrap yourself up in art and books and music, and would try to wrap up me. I won't be stifled, not by the most glorious music, for people are more glorious, and you hide them from me. That's why I break off my engagement. You were all right as long as you kept to things, but when you came to people—' She stopped.

There was a pause. Then Cecil said with great emotion:

'It is true.'

'True on the whole,' she corrected, full of some vague shame.

'True, every word. It is a revelation. It is–I.'

'Anyhow, those are my reasons for not being your wife.'

He repeated: '"The sort that can know no one intimately." It is true. I fell
to pieces the very first day we were engaged. I behaved like a cad to Beebe
and to your brother. You are even greater than I thought.' She withdrew a
step. 'I'm not going to worry you. You are far too good to me. I shall never
forget your insight; and, dear, I only blame you for this: you might have
warned me in the early stages, before you felt you wouldn't marry me, and so
have given me a chance to improve. I have never known you till this evening.
I have just used you as a peg for my silly notions of what a woman should be.
But this evening you are a different person: new thoughts—even a new
voice—'

'What do you mean by a new voice?' she asked, seized with incontrollable
anger.

'I mean that a new person seems speaking through you,' said he.

Then she lost her balance. She cried: 'If you think I am in love with some
one else, you are very much mistaken.'

'Of course I don't think that. You are not that kind, Lucy.'

'Oh yes, you do think it. It's your old idea, the idea that has kept Europe
back—I mean the idea that women are always thinking of men. If a girl breaks
off her engagement, every one says: "Oh, she had some one else in her mind;
she hopes to get some one else." It's disgusting, brutal! As if a girl can't
break it off for the sake of freedom.'

He answered reverently: 'I may have said that in the past. I shall never say
it again. You have taught me better.'

She began to redden, and pretended to examine the windows again.

'Of course, there is no question of "some one else" in this, no "jilting" or
any such nauseous stupidity. I beg your pardon most humbly if my words
suggested that there was. I only meant that there was a force in you that I
hadn't known of up till now.'

'All right, Cecil, that will do. Don't apologize to me. It was my mistake.'

'It is a question between ideals, yours and mine—pure abstract ideals, and
yours are the nobler. I was bound up in the old vicious notions, and all the
time you were splendid and new.' His voice broke. 'I must actually thank
you for what you have done—for showing me what I really am. Solemnly, I
thank you for showing me a true woman. Will you shake hands?'

'Of course I will,' said Lucy, twisting up her other hand in the curtains.
'Good night, Cecil. Good-bye. That's all right. I'm sorry about it. Thank
you very much for your gentleness.'

'Let me light your candle, shall I?'

They went into the hall.

'Thank you. Good night again. God bless you, Lucy!'

'Good-bye, Cecil.'

She watched him steal upstairs, while the shadows from the banisters
passed over her face like the beat of wings. On the landing he paused, strong
in his renunciation, and gave her a look of memorable beauty. For all his
culture, Cecil was an ascetic at heart, and nothing in his love became him like
the leaving of it.

She could never marry. In the tumult of her soul, that stood firm. Cecil believed in her; she must some day believe in herself. She must be one of the women whom she had praised so eloquently, who care for liberty and not for men; she must forget that George loved her, that George had been thinking through her and gained her this honourable release, that George had gone away into—what was it?—the darkness.

She put out the lamp.

It did not do to think, nor, for the matter of that, to feel. She gave up trying to understand herself, and joined the vast armies of the benighted, who follow neither the heart nor the brain, and march to their destiny by catch-words. The armies are full of pleasant and pious folk. But they have yielded to the only enemy that matters—the enemy within. They have sinned against passion and truth, and vain will be their strife after virtue. As the years pass, they are censured. Their pleasantry and their piety show cracks, their wit becomes cynicism, their unselfishness hypocrisy; they feel and produce discomfort wherever they go. They have sinned against Eros and against Pallas Athene, and not by any heavenly intervention, but by the ordinary course of nature, those allied deities will be avenged.

Lucy entered this army when she pretended to George that she did not love him, and pretended to Cecil that she loved no one. The night received her, as it had received Miss Bartlett thirty years before.

Chapter Eighteen

Lying to Mr Beebe, Mrs Honeychurch, Freddy, and the Servants

Windy Corner lay, not on the summit of the ridge, but a few hundred feet down the southern slope, at the springing of one of the great buttresses that supported the hill. On either side of it was a shallow ravine, filled with ferns and pine-trees, and down the ravine on the left ran the highway into the Weald.

Whenever Mr Beebe crossed the ridge and caught sight of these noble dispositions of the earth, and, poised in the middle of them, Windy Corner—he laughed. The situation was so glorious, the house so commonplace, not to say impertinent. The late Mr Honeychurch had affected the cube, because it gave him the most accommodation for his money, and the only addition made by his widow had been a small turret, shaped like a rhinoceros' horn, where she could sit in wet weather and watch the carts going up and down the road. So impertinent—and yet the house 'did,' for it was the home of people who loved their surroundings honestly. Other houses in the neighbourhood had been built by expensive architects, over others their inmates had fidgeted sedulously, yet all these suggested the accidental, the temporary; while Windy Corner seemed as inevitable as an ugliness of Nature's own creation. One might laugh at the house, but one never shuddered.

Mr Beebe was bicycling over this Monday afternoon with a little piece of gossip. He had heard from the Miss Alans. These admirable ladies, since they could not go to Cissie Villa, had changed their plans. They were going to Greece instead.

'Since Florence did my poor sister so much good,' wrote Miss Catherine, 'we do not see why we should not try Athens this winter. Of course, Athens is a plunge, and the doctor has ordered her special digestive bread; but, after all, we can take that with us, and it is only getting first into a steamer and then into a train. But is there an English Church?' And the letter went on to say: 'I do not expect we shall go any farther than Athens, but if you knew of a really comfortable pension at Constantinople, we should be so grateful.'

Lucy would enjoy this letter, and the smile with which Mr Beebe greeted Windy Corner was partly for her. She would see the fun of it, and some of its beauty, for she must see some beauty. Though she was hopeless about pictures, and though she dressed so unevenly—oh, that cerise frock yesterday at church!—she must see some beauty in life, or she could not play the piano as she did. He had a theory that musicians are incredibly complex, and know far less than other artists what they want and what they are; that they puzzle themselves as well as their friends; that their psychology is a modern development, and has not yet been understood. This theory, had he known it, had possibly just been illustrated by facts. Ignorant of the events of yesterday, he was only riding over to get some tea, to see his niece, and to observe whether Miss Honeychurch saw anything beautiful in the desire of two old ladies to visit Athens.

A carriage was drawn up outside Windy Corner, and just as he caught sight of the house it started, bowled up the drive, and stopped abruptly when it reached the main road. Therefore it must be the horse, who always expected people to walk up the hill in case they tired him. The door opened obediently, and two men emerged, whom Mr Beebe recognized as Cecil and Freddy. They were an odd couple to go driving; but he saw a trunk beside the coachman's legs. Cecil, who wore a bowler, must be going away, while Freddy—(a cap)—was seeing him to the station. They walked rapidly, taking the short cuts, and reached the summit while the carriage was still pursuing the windings of the road.

They shook hands with the clergyman, but did not speak.

'So you're off for a minute, Mr Vyse?' he asked.

Cecil said 'Yes,' while Freddy edged away.

'I was coming to show you this delightful letter from those friends of Miss Honeychurch's.' He quoted from it. 'Isn't it wonderful? Isn't it romance? Most certainly they will go to Constantinople. They are taken in a snare that cannot fail. They will end by going round the world.'

Cecil listened civilly, and said he was sure that Lucy would be amused and interested.

'Isn't Romance capricious! I never notice it in you young people; you do nothing but play lawn tennis, and say that Romance is dead, while the Miss Alans are struggling with all the weapons of propriety against the terrible thing. "A really comfortable pension at Constantinople!" So they call it out of decency, but in their hearts they want a pension with magic windows opening on the foam of perilous seas in fairylands forlorn! No ordinary view will content the Miss Alans. They want the Pension Keats.'

'I'm awfully sorry to interrupt, Mr Beebe,' said Freddy, 'but have you any matches?'

'I have,' said Cecil, and it did not escape Mr Beebe's notice that he spoke to the boy more kindly.

'You have never met these Miss Alans, have you, Mr Vyse?'

'Never.'

'Then you don't see the wonder of this Greek visit. I haven't been to Greece myself, and don't mean to go, and I can't imagine any of my friends going. It is altogether too big for our little lot. Don't you think so? Italy is just about as much as we can manage. Italy is heroic, but Greece is godlike or devilish—I am not sure which, and in either case absolutely out of our suburban focus. All right, Freddy—I am not being clever, upon my word I am not—I took the idea from another fellow; and give me those matches when you've done with them.' He lit a cigarette, and went on talking to the two young men. 'I was saying, if our poor little Cockney lives must have a background, let it be Italian. Big enough in all conscience. The ceiling of the Sistine Chapel for me. There the contrast is just as much as I can realize. But not the Parthenon, not the frieze of Phidias at any price; and here comes the victoria.'

'You're quite right,' said Cecil. 'Greece is not for our little lot'; and he got in. Freddy followed, nodding to the clergyman, whom he trusted not to be pulling one's leg, really. And before they had gone a dozen yards he jumped out, and came running back for Vyse's match-box, which had not been returned. As he took it, he said: 'I am so glad you only talked about books. Cecil's hard hit. Lucy won't marry him. If you'd gone on about her, as you did about them, he might have broken down.'

'But when—'

'Late last night. I must go.'

'Perhaps they won't want me down there.'

'No—go on. Good-bye.'

'Thank goodness!' exclaimed Mr Beebe to himself, and struck the saddle of his bicycle approvingly. 'It was the one foolish thing she ever did. Oh, what a glorious riddance!' And, after a little thought, he negotiated the slope into Windy Corner, light of heart. The house was again as it ought to be—cut off for ever from Cecil's pretentious world.

He would find Miss Minnie down the garden.

In the drawing-room Lucy was tinkling at a Mozart Sonata. He hesitated a moment, but went down the garden as requested. There he found a mournful company. It was a blustering day, and the wind had taken and broken the dahlias. Mrs Honeychurch, who looked cross, was tying them up, while Miss Bartlett, unsuitably dressed, impeded her with offers of assistance. At a little distance stood Minnie and the 'garden-child,' a minute importation, each holding either end of a long piece of bass.

'Oh, how do you do, Mr Beebe? Gracious, what a mess everything is! Look at my scarlet pompoms, and the wind blowing your skirts about, and the ground so hard that not a prop will stick in, and then the carriage having to go out, when I had counted on having Powell, who—give every one their due—does tie up dahlias properly.'

Evidently Mrs Honeychurch was shattered.

'How do you do?' said Miss Bartlett, with a meaning glance, as though conveying that more than dahlias had been broken off by the autumn gales.

'Here, Lennie, the bass,' cried Mrs Honeychurch. The garden-child, who did not know what bass was, stood rooted to the path with horror. Minnie slipped to her uncle and whispered that every one was very disagreeable to-day, and that it was not her fault if dahlia-strings would tear longways instead of across.

'Come for a walk with me,' he told her. 'You have worried them as much as they can stand. Mrs Honeychurch, I only called in aimlessly. I shall take her up to tea at the Beehive Tavern, if I may.'

'Oh, must you? Yes, do.—Not the scissors, thank you, Charlotte, when both my hands are full already—I'm perfectly certain that the orange cactus will go before I can get to it.'

Mr Beebe, who was an adept at relieving situations, invited Miss Bartlett to accompany them to this mild festivity.

'Yes, Charlotte, I don't want you—do go; there's nothing to stop about for, either in the house or out of it.'

Miss Bartlett said that her duty lay in the dahlia-bed, but when she had exasperated every one, except Minnie, by a refusal, she turned round and exasperated Minnie by an acceptance. As they walked up the garden, the orange cactus fell, and Mr Beebe's last vision was of the garden-child clasping it like a lover, his dark head buried in a wealth of blossom.

'It is terrible, this havoc among the flowers,' he remarked.

'It is always terrible when the promise of months is destroyed in a moment,' enunciated Miss Bartlett.

'Perhaps we ought to send Miss Honeychurch down to her mother. Or will she come with us?'

'I think we had better leave Lucy to herself, and to her own pursuits.'

'They're angry with Miss Honeychurch, because she was late for breakfast,' whispered Minnie, 'and Mr Floyd has gone, and Mr Vyse has gone, and Freddy won't play with me. In fact, Uncle Arthur, the house is not *at all* what it was yesterday.'

'Don't be a prig,' said her Uncle Arthur. 'Go and put on your boots.'

He stepped into the drawing-room, where Lucy was still attentively pursuing the Sonatas of Mozart. She stopped when he entered.

'How do you do? Miss Bartlett and Minnie are coming with me to tea at the Beehive. Would you come too?'

'I don't think I will, thank you.'

'No, I didn't suppose you would care to much.'

Lucy turned to the piano and struck a few chords.

'How delicate those Sonatas are!' said Mr Beebe, though, at the bottom of his heart, he thought them silly little things.

Lucy passed into Schumann.

'Miss Honeychurch!'

'Yes.'

'I met them on the hill. Your brother told me.'

'Oh, did he?' She sounded annoyed. Mr Beebe felt hurt, for he had thought that she would like him to be told.

'I needn't say that it will go no further.'

'Mother, Charlotte, Cecil, Freddy, you,' said Lucy, playing a note for each person who knew, and then playing a sixth note.

'If you'll let me say so, I am very glad, and I am certain that you have done the right thing.'

'So I hoped other people would think, but they don't seem to.'

'I could see that Miss Bartlett thought it unwise.'

'So does mother. Mother minds dreadfully.'

'I am very sorry for that,' said Mr Beebe with feeling.

Mrs Honeychurch, who hated all changes, did mind, but not nearly as much as her daughter pretended, and only for the minute. It was really a ruse of Lucy's to justify her despondency–a ruse of which she was not herself conscious, for she was marching in the armies of darkness.

'And Freddy minds.'

'Still Freddy never hit it off with Vyse much, did he? I gathered that he disliked the engagement, and felt it might separate him from you.'

'Boys are so odd.'

Minnie could be heard arguing with Miss Bartlett through the floor. Tea at the Beehive appparently involved a complete change of apparel. Mr Beebe saw that Lucy–very properly–did not wish to discuss her action, so after a sincere expression of sympathy, he said, 'I have had an absurd letter from Miss Alan. That was really what brought me over. I thought it might amuse you all.'

'How delightful!' said Lucy, in a dull voice.

For the sake of something do do, he began to read her the letter. After a few words her eyes grew alert, and soon she interrupted him with–'Going abroad? When do they start?'

'Next week, I gather.'

'Did Freddy say whether he was driving straight back?'

'No, he didn't.'

'Because I do hope he won't go gossiping.'

So she did want to talk about her broken engagement. Always complaisant, he put the letter away. But she at once exclaimed in a high voice, 'Oh, do tell me more about the Miss Alans! How perfectly splendid of them to go abroad!'

'I want them to start from Venice, and go in a cargo steamer down the Illyrian coast!'

She laughed heartily. 'Oh, delightful! I wish they'd take me.'

'Has Italy filled you with the fever of travel? Perhaps George Emerson is right. He says that "Italy is only an euphuism for Fate."'

'Oh, not Italy, but Constantinople. I have always longed to go to Constantinople. Constantinople is practically Asia, isn't it?'

Mr Beebe reminded her that Constantinople was still unlikely, and that the Miss Alans only aimed at Athens, 'with Delphi, perhaps, if the roads are safe.' But this made no difference to her enthusiasm. She had always longed to go to Greece even more, it seemed. He saw, to his surprise, that she was apparently serious.

'I didn't realize that you and the Miss Alans were still such friends, after Cissie Villa.'

'Oh, that's nothing; I assure you Cissie Villa's nothing to me; I would give anything to go with them.'

'Would your mother spare you again so soon? You have scarcely been home three months.'

'She *must* spare me!' cried Lucy, in growing excitement. 'I simply *must* go away. I have to.' She ran her fingers hysterically through her hair. 'Don't you see that I *have* to go away? I didn't realize at the time—and of course I want to see Constantinople so particularly.'

'You mean that since you have broken off your engagement you feel—'

'Yes, yes. I knew you would understand.'

Mr Beebe did not quite understand. Why could not Miss Honeychurch repose in the bosom of her family? Cecil had evidently taken up the dignified line, and was not going to annoy her. Then it struck him that her family itself might be annoying. He hinted this to her, and she accepted the hint eagerly.

'Yes, of course; to go to Constantinople until they are used to the idea and everything has calmed down.'

'I am afraid it has been a bothersome business,' he said gently.

'No, not at all. Cecil was very kind indeed; only—I had better tell you the whole truth, since you have heard a little—it was that he is so masterful. I found that he wouldn't let me go my own way. He would improve me in places where I can't be improved. Cecil won't let a woman decide for herself—in fact, he daren't. What nonsense I do talk! but that is the kind of thing.'

'It is what I gathered from my own observation of Mr Vyse; it is what I gather from all that I have known of you. I do sympathize and agree most profoundly. I agree so much that you must let me make one little criticism: Is it worth while rushing off to Greece?'

'But I must go somewhere!' she cried. 'I have been worrying all the morning, and here comes the very thing.' She struck her knees with clenched fists, and repeated: 'I must! And the time I shall have with mother, and all the money she spent on me last spring. You all think much too highly of me. I wish you weren't so kind.' At this moment Miss Bartlett entered, and her nervousness increased. 'I must get away, ever so far. I must know my own mind and where I want to go.'

'Come along; tea, tea, tea,' said Mr Beebe, and hustled his guests out of the front door. He hustled them so quickly that he forgot his hat. When he returned for it he heard, to his relief and surprise, the tinkling of a Mozart Sonata.

'She is playing again,' he said to Miss Bartlett.

'Lucy can always play,' was the acid reply.

'One is very thankful that she has such a resource. She is evidently much worried, as, of course, she ought to be. I know all about it. The marriage was so near that it must have been a hard struggle before she could wind herself up to speak.'

Miss Bartlett gave a kind of wriggle, and he prepared for a discussion. He had never fathomed Miss Bartlett. As he had put it to himself at Florence, 'she might yet reveal depths of strangeness, if not of meaning.' But she was so unsympathetic that she must be reliable. He assumed that much, and he had no hesitation in discussing Lucy with her. Minnie was fortunately collecting ferns.

She opened the discussion with: 'We had much better let the matter drop.'

'I wonder.'

'It is of the highest importance that there should be no gossip in Summer Street. It would be *death* to gossip about Mr Vyse's dismissal at the present moment.'

Mr Beebe raised his eyebrows. Death is a strong word–surely too strong. There was no question of tragedy. He said: 'Of course, Miss Honeychurch will make the fact public in her own way, and when she chooses. Freddy only told me because he knew she would not mind.'

'I know,' said Miss Bartlett civilly. 'Yet Freddy ought not to have told even you. One cannot be too careful.'

'Quite so.'

'I do implore absolute secrecy. A chance word to a chattering friend, and—'

'Exactly.' He was used to these nervous old maids and to the exaggerated importance that they attach to words. A rector lives in a web of petty secrets, and confidences, and warnings, and the wiser he is the less he will regard them. He will change the subject, as did Mr Beebe, saying cheerfully: 'Have you heard from any Bertolini people lately? I believe you keep up with Miss Lavish. It is odd how we of that pension, who seemed such a fortuitous collection, have been working into one another's lives. Two, three, four, six of us–no, eight; I had forgotten the Emersons–have kept more or less in touch. We must really give the Signora a testimonial.'

And, Miss Bartlett not favouring the scheme, they walked up the hill in a silence which was only broken by the rector naming some fern. On the summit they paused. They sky had grown wilder since he stood there last hour, giving to the land a tragic greatness that is rare in Surrey. Grey clouds were charging across tissues of white, which stretched and shredded and tore slowly, until through their final layers there gleamed a hint of the disappearing blue. Summer was retreating. The wind roared, the trees groaned, yet the noise seemed insufficient for those vast operations in heaven. The weather was breaking up, breaking, broken, and it is a sense of the fit rather than of the supernatural that equips such crises with the salvos of angelic artillery. Mr Beebe's eyes rested on Windy Corner, where Lucy sat, practising Mozart. No smile came to his lips, and, changing the subject again, he said: 'We shan't have rain, but we shall have darkness, so let us hurry on. The darkness last night was appalling.'

They reached the Beehive Tavern at about five o'clock. That amiable hostelry possesses a verandah, in which the young and the unwise do dearly love to sit, while guests of more mature years seek a pleasant sanded room, and have tea at a table comfortably. Mr Beebe saw that Miss Bartlett would be cold if she sat out, and that Minnie would be dull if she sat in, so he proposed a division of forces. They would hand the child her food through the window. Thus he was incidentally enabled to discuss the fortunes of Lucy.

'I have been thinking, Miss Bartlett,' he said, 'and, unless you very much object, I would like to reopen that discussion.' She bowed. 'Nothing about the past. I know little and care less about that; I am absolutely certain that it is to your cousin's credit. She has acted loftily and rightly, and it is like her gentle modesty to say that we think too highly of her. But the future. Seriously, what do you think of this Greek plan?' He pulled out the letter again. 'I don't know whether you overheard, but she wants to join the Miss Alans in their mad career. It's all—I can't explain—it's wrong.'

Miss Bartlett read the letter in silence, laid it down, seemed to hesitate, and then read it again.

'I can't see the point of it myself.'

To his astonishment, she replied: 'There I cannot agree with you. In it I spy Lucy's salvation.'

'Really. Now, why?'

'She wanted to leave Windy Corner.'

'I know—but it seems so odd, so unlike her, so—I was going to say—selfish.'

'It is natural, surely—after such painful scenes—that she should desire a change.'

Here, apparently, was one of those points that the male intellect misses. Mr Beebe exclaimed: 'So she says herself, and since another lady agrees with her, I must own that I am partially convinced. Perhaps she must have a change. I have no sisters or—and I don't understand these things. But why need she go as far as Greece?'

'You may well ask that,' replied Miss Bartlett, who was evidently interested, and had almost dropped her evasive manner. 'Why Greece? (What is it, Minnie dear—jam?) Why not Tunbridge Wells? Oh, Mr Beebe! I had a long and most unsatisfactory interview with dear Lucy this morning. I cannot help her. I will say no more. Perhaps I have already said too much. I am not to talk—a point on which she is almost bitter. I am not to talk. I wanted her to spend six months with me at Tunbridge Wells, and she refused.'

Mr Beebe poked at a crumb with his knife.

'But my feelings are of no importance. I know too well that I get on Lucy's nerves. Our tour was a failure. She wanted to leave Florence, and when we got to Rome she did not want to be in Rome, and all the time I felt that I was spending her mother's money—'

'Let us keep to the future, though,' interrupted Mr Beebe. 'I want your advice.'

'Very well,' said Charlotte, with a choky abruptness that was new to him, though familiar to Lucy. 'I for one will help her to go to Greece. Will you?'

Mr Beebe considered.

'It is absolutely necessary,' she continued, lowering her veil and whispered through it with a passion, an intensity, that surprised him. 'I know–I *know*.' The darkness was coming on, and he felt that this odd woman really did know. 'She must not stop here a moment, and we must keep quiet till she goes. I trust that the servants know nothing. Afterwards–but I may have said too much already. Only, Lucy and I are helpless against Mrs Honeychurch alone. If you help, we may succeed. Otherwise—'

'Otherwise—?'

'Otherwise,' she repeated, as if the word held finality.

'Yes, I will help her,' said the clergyman, setting his jaw firm. 'Come, let us go back now, and settle the whole thing up.'

Miss Bartlett burst into florid gratitude. The tavern sign–a beehive trimmed evenly with bees–creaked in the wind outside as she thanked him. Mr Beebe did not quite understand the situation; but then, he did not desire to understand it, nor to jump to the conclusion of "another man" that would have attracted a grosser mind. He only felt that Miss Bartlett knew of some vague influence from which the girl desired to be delivered, and which might well be clothed in the fleshly form. Its very vagueness spurred him into knight-errantry. His belief in celibacy, so reticent, so carefully concealed beneath his tolerance and culture, now came to the surface and expanded like some delicate flower. "They that marry do well, but they that refrain do better." So ran his belief, and he never heard that an engagement was broken off but with a slight feeling of pleasure. In the case of Lucy, the feeling was intensified through dislike of Cecil; and he was willing to go further–to place her out of danger until she could confirm her resolution of virginity. The feeling was very subtle and quite undogmatic, and he never imparted it to any other of the characters in this entanglement. Yet it existed, and it alone explains his action subsequently, and his influence on the action of others. The compact that he made with Miss Bartlett in the tavern was to help not only Lucy, but religion also.

They hurried home through a world of black and grey. He conversed on indifferent topics: the Emersons' need of a housekeeper; servants; Italian servants; novels about Italy; novels with a purpose; could literature influence life? Windy Corner glimmered. In the garden, Mrs Honeychurch, now helped by Freddy, still wrestled with the lives of her flowers.

'It gets too dark,' she said hopelessly. 'This comes of putting off. We might have known the weather would break up soon; and now Lucy wants to go to Greece. I don't know what the world's coming to.'

'Mrs Honeychurch,' he said, 'go to Greece she must. Come up to the house and let's talk it over. Do you, in the first place, mind her breaking with Vyse?'

'Mr Beebe, I'm thankful—simply thankful.'

'So am I,' said Freddy.

'Good. Now come up to the house.'

They conferred in the dining-room for half and hour.

Lucy would never have carried the Greek scheme alone. It was expensive and dramatic—both qualities that her mother loathed. Nor would Charlotte have succeeded. The honours of the day rested with Mr Beebe. By his tact and common sense, and by his influence as a clergyman—for a clergyman who was not a fool influenced Mrs Honeychurch greatly—he bent her to their purpose.

'I don't see why Greece is necessary,' she said; 'but as you do, I suppose it is all right. It must be something I can't understand. Lucy! Let's tell her. Lucy!'

'She is playing the piano,' Mr Beebe said. He opened the door, and heard the words of a song:

> *Look not thou on beauty's charming.*

'I didn't know that Miss Honeychurch sang, too.'

> *Sit thou still when kings are arming,*
> *Taste not when the wine-cup glistens—*

'It's a song that Cecil gave her. How odd girls are!'

'What's that?' called Lucy, stopping short.

'All right, dear,' said Mrs Honeychurch kindly. She went into the drawing-room, and Mr Beebe heard her kiss Lucy and say: 'I am sorry I was so cross about Greece, but it came on the top of the dahlias.'

Rather a hard voice said: 'Thank you, mother; that doesn't matter a bit.'

'And you are right, too—Greece will be all right; you can go if the Miss Alans will have you.'

'Oh, splendid! Oh, thank you!'

Mr Beebe followed. Lucy still sat at the piano with her hands over the keys. She was glad, but he had expected greater gladness. Her mother bent over her. Freddy, to whom she had been singing, reclined on the floor with his head against her, and an unlit pipe between his lips. Oddly enough, the group was beautiful. Mr Beebe, who loved the art of the past, was reminded of a favourite theme, the *Santa Conversazione*, in which people who care for one another are painted chatting together about noble things—a theme neither sensual nor sensational, and therefore ignored by the art of to-day. Why should Lucy want either to marry or to travel when she had such friends at home?

> *Taste not when the wine-cup glistens,*
> *Speak not when the people listens.*

she continued.

'Here's Mr Beebe.'

'Mr Beebe knows my rude ways.'

'It's a beautiful song and a wise one,' said he. 'Go on.'

'It isn't very good,' she said listlessly. 'I forget why—harmony or something.'

'I suspected it was unscholarly. It's so beautiful.'

'The tune's right enough,' said Freddy, 'but the words are rotten. Why throw up the sponge?'

'How stupidly you talk!' said his sister. The *Santa Conversazione* was broken up. After all, there was no reason that Lucy should talk about Greece or thank him for persuading her mother, so he said good-bye.

Freddy lit his bicycle-lamp for him in the porch, and with his usual felicity of phrase, said: 'This has been a day and a half.'

> *Stop thine ear against the singer—*

'Wait a minute; she is finishing.'

> *From the red gold keep thy finger;*
> *Vacant heart and hand and eye*
> *Easy live and quiet die.*

'I love weather like this,' said Freddy.

Mr Beebe passed into it.

The two main facts were clear. She had behaved splendidly, and he had helped her. He could not expect to master the details of so big a change in a girl's life. If here and there he was dissatisfied or puzzled, he must acquiesce: she was choosing the better part.

> *Vacant heart and hand and eye—*

Perhaps the song stated 'the better part' rather too strongly. He half fancied that the soaring accompaniment—which he did not lose in the shout of the gale—really agreed with Freddy, and was gently criticizing the words that it adorned:

> *Vacant heart and hand and eye*
> *Easy live and quiet die.*

However. For the fourth time Windy Corner lay poised below him—now as a beacon in the roaring tides of darkness.

Chapter Nineteen

Lying to Mr Emerson

The Miss Alans were found in their beloved temperance hotel near Bloomsbury—a clean, airless establishment much patronized by provincial England. They always perched there before crossing the great seas, and for a week or two would fidget gently over clothes, guide-books, mackintosh squares, digestive bread, and other Continental necessaries. That there are shops abroad, even in Athens, never occurred to them, for they regarded travel as a species of warfare, only to be undertaken by those who have been fully armed at the Haymarket Stores. Miss Honeychurch, they trusted, would take care to equip herself duly. Quinine could now be obtained in tabloids; paper soap was a great help towards freshening up one's face in the train. Lucy promised, a little depressed.

'But, of course, you know all about these things, and you have Mr Vyse to help you. A gentleman is such a stand-by.'

Mrs Honeychurch, who had come up to town with her daughter, began to drum nervously upon her cardcase.

'We think it so good of Mr Vyse to spare you,' Miss Catharine continued. 'It is not every young man who would be so unselfish. But perhaps he will come out and join you later on.'

'Or does his work keep him in London?' said Miss Teresa, the more acute and less kindly of the two sisters.

'However, we shall see him when he sees you off. I do so long to see him.'

'No one will see Lucy off,' interposed Mrs Honeychurch. 'She doesn't like it.'

'No, I hate seeings-off,' said Lucy.

'Really? How funny! I should have thought that in this case—'

'Oh, Mrs Honeychurch, you aren't going? It is such a pleasure to have met you!'

They escaped, and Lucy said with relief: 'That's all right. We just got through that time.'

But her mother was annoyed. 'I shall be told, dear, that I am unsympathetic. But I cannot see why you didn't tell your friends about Cecil and be done with it. There all the time we had to sit fencing, and almost telling lies, and be seen through, too, I dare say, which is most unpleasant.'

Lucy had plenty to say in reply. She described the Miss Alans' character: they were such gossips, and if one told them, the news would be everywhere in no time.

'But why shouldn't it be everywhere in no time?'

'Because I settled with Cecil not to announce it until I left England. I shall tell them then. It's much pleasanter. How wet it is! Let's turn in here.'

'Here' was the British Museum. Mrs Honeychurch refused. If they must take shelter, let it be in a shop. Lucy felt contemptuous, for she was on the tack of caring for Greek sculpture, and had already borrowed a mythological dictionary from Mr Beebe to get up the names of the goddesses and gods.

'Oh, well, let it be a shop, then. Let's go to Mudie's. I'll buy a guide-book.'

'You know, Lucy, you and Charlotte and Mr Beebe all tell me I'm so stupid, so I suppose I am, but I shall never understand this hole-and-corner work. You've got rid of Cecil—well and good, and I'm thankful he's gone, though I did feel angry for the minute. But why not announce it? Why this hushing up and tip-toeing?'

'It's only for a few days.'

'But why at all?'

Lucy was silent. She was drifting away from her mother. It was quite easy to say, 'Because George Emerson has been bothering me, and if he hears I've given up Cecil may begin again'—quite easy, and it had the incidental advantage of being true. But she could not say it. She disliked confidences, for they might lead to self-knowledge and to that king of terrors—Light. Ever since that last evening at Florence she had deemed it unwise to reveal her soul.

Mrs Honeychurch, too, was silent. She was thinking, 'My daughter won't answer me; she would rather be with those inquisitive old maids than with Freddy and me. Any rag, tag and bobtail apparently does if she can leave her home.' And as in her case thoughts never remained unspoken long, she burst out with: 'You're tired of Windy Corner.'

This was perfectly true. Lucy had hoped to return to Windy Corner when she escaped from Cecil, but she discovered that her home existed no longer. It might exist for Freddy, who still lived and thought straight, but not for one who had deliberately warped the brain. She did not acknowledge that her brain was warped, for the brain itself must assist in that acknowledgment, and she was disordering the very instruments of life. She only felt, 'I do not love George; I broke off my engagement because I did not love George; I must go to Greece because I do not love George; it is more important that I should look up gods in the dictionary than that I should help my mother; every one else is behaving very badly.' She only felt irritable and petulant, and anxious to do what she was not expected to do, and in this spirit she proceeded with the conversation.

'Oh, mother, what rubbish you talk! Of course I'm not tired of Windy Corner.'

'Then why not say so at once, instead of considering half an hour first?'

She laughed faintly, 'Half a *minute* would be nearer.'

'Perhaps you would like to stay away from your home altogether?'

'Hush, mother! People will hear you'; for they had entered Mudie's. She bought Baedeker, and then continued: 'Of course I want to live at home; but as we are talking about it, I may as well say that I shall want to be away in the future more than I have been. You see, I come into my money next year.'

Tears came into her mother's eyes.

Driven by nameless bewilderment, by what is in older people termed 'eccentricity,' Lucy determined to make this point clear. 'I've seen the world so little—I felt so out of things in Italy. I have seen so little of life; one ought to come up to London more—not a cheap ticket like to-day, but to stop. I might even share a flat for a little with some other girl.'

'And mess with typewriters and latch-keys,' exploded Mrs Honeychurch. 'And agitate and scream, and be carried off kicking by the police. And call it a Mission—when no one wants you! And call it Duty—when it means that you can't stand your own home! And call it Work—when thousands of men are starving with the competition as it is! And then to prepare yourself, find two doddering old ladies, and go abroad with them.'

'I want more independence,' said Lucy lamely; she knew that she wanted something, and independence is a useful cry: we can always say that we have not got it. She tried to remember her emotions in Florence: those had been sincere and passionate, and had suggested beauty rather than short skirts and latch-keys. But independence was certainly her cue.

'Very well. Take your independence and be gone. Rush up and down and round the world, and come back as thin as a lath with the bad food. Despise the house that your father built and the garden that he planted, and our dear view—and then share a flat with another girl.'

Lucy screwed up her mouth and said: 'Perhaps I spoke hastily.'

'Oh, goodness!' her mother flashed. 'How you do remind me of Charlotte Bartlett!'

'*Charlotte?*' flashed Lucy in her turn, pierced at last by a vivid pain.

'More every moment.'

'I don't know what you mean, mother; Charlotte and I are not the very least alike.'

'Well, I see the likeness. The same eternal worrying, the same taking back of words. You and Charlotte trying to divide two apples among three people last night might be sisters.'

'What rubbish! And if you dislike Charlotte so, it's rather a pity you asked her to stop. I warned you about her; I begged you, implored you not to, but of course I was not listened to.'

'There you go.'

'I beg your pardon?'

'Charlotte again, my dear; that's all; her very words.'

Lucy clenched her teeth. 'My point is that you oughtn't to have asked Charlotte to stop. I wish you would keep to the point.' And the conversation dies off into a wrangle.

She and her mother shopped in silence, spoke little in the train, little again in the carriage, which met them at Dorking Station. It had poured all day, and as they ascended through the deep Surrey lanes showers of water fell from the overhanging beech-trees and rattled on the hood. Lucy complained that the hood was stuffy. Leaning forward, she looked out into the steaming dusk, and watched the carriage-lamp pass like a search-light over mud and leaves, and reveal nothing beautiful. 'The crush when Charlotte gets in will be abominable,' she remarked. For they were to pick up Miss Bartlett at Summer Street, where she had been dropped as the carriage went down, to pay a call on Mr. Beebe's old mother. 'We shall have to sit three a side, because the trees drop, and yet it isn't raining. Oh for a little air!' Then she listened to the horse's hoofs–'He has not told–he has not told.' That melody was blurred by the soft road. *'Can't* we have the hood down?' she demanded, and her mother, with sudden tenderness, said: 'Very well, old lady, stop the horse.' And the horse was stopped, and Lucy and Powell wrestled with the hood, and squirted water down Mrs Honeychurch's neck. But now that the hood was down, she did see something that she would have missed– there were no lights in the windows of Cissie Villa, and round the garden gate she fancied she saw a padlock.

'Is that house to let again, Powell?' she called.

'Yes, miss,' he replied.

'Have they gone?'

'It is too far out of town for the young gentleman, and his father's rheumatism has come on, so he can't stop on alone, so they are trying to let furnished,' was the answer.

'They have gone, then?'

'Yes, miss, they have gone.'

Lucy sank back. The carriage stopped at the Rectory. She got out to call for Miss Bartlett. So the Emersons had gone, and all this bother about Greece had been unnecessary. Waste! That word seemed to sum up the whole of life. Wasted plans, wasted money, wasted love, and she had wounded her mother. Was it possible that she had muddled things away? Quite possible. Other people had. When the maid opened the door, she was unable to speak, and stared stupidly into the hall.

Miss Bartlett at once came forward, and after a long preamble asked a great favour: might she go to church? Mr Beebe and his mother had already gone, but she had refused to start until she obtained her hostess's full sanction, for it would mean keeping the horse waiting a good ten minutes more.

'Certainly,' said the hostess wearily. 'I forgot it was Friday. Let's all go. Powell can go round to the stables.'

'Lucy dearest—'

'No church for me, thank you.'

A sigh, and they departed. The church was invisible, but up in the darkness to the left there was a hint of colour. This was a stained window, through which some feeble light was shining, and when the door opened Lucy heard Mr Beebe's voice running through the litany to a minute congregation. Even their church, built upon the slope of the hill so artfully, with its beautiful raised transept and its spire of silvery shingle–even their church had lost its charm; and the thing one never talked about– religion–was fading like all the other things.

She followed the maid into the Rectory.

Would she object to sitting in Mr Beebe's study? There was only that one fire.

She would not object.

Some one was there already, for Lucy heard the words 'A lady to wait, sir.'
Old Mr Emerson was sitting by the fire, with his foot upon a gout-stool.
'Oh, Miss Honeychurch, that you should come!' he quavered; and Lucy
saw an alteration in him since last Sunday.

Not a word would come to her lips. George she had faced, and could have
faced again, but she had forgotten how to treat his father.

'Miss Honeychurch, dear, we are so sorry! George is so sorry! He thought
he had a right to try. I cannot blame my boy, and yet I wish he had told me
first. He ought not to have tried. I knew nothing about it at all.'

If only she could remember how to behave!

He held up his hand. 'But you must not scold him.'

Lucy turned her back, and began to look at Mr Beebe's books.

'I taught him,' he quavered, 'to trust in love. I said: "When love comes,
that is reality." I said: "Passion does not blind. No. Passion is sanity, and the
woman you love, she is the only person you will ever really understand."' He
sighed: 'True, everlastingly true, though my day is over, and though there is
the result. Poor boy! He is so sorry! He said he knew it was madness when
you brought your cousin in; that whatever you felt you did not mean.
Yet'—his voice gathered strength; he spoke out to make certain—'Miss
Honeychurch, do you remember Italy?'

Lucy selected a book—a volume of Old Testament commentaries.
Holding it up to her eyes, she said: 'I have no wish to discuss Italy or any
subject connected with your son.'

'But you do remember it?'

'He has misbehaved himself from the first.'

'I only was told that he loved you last Sunday. I never could judge
behaviour. I—I—suppose he has.'

Feeling a little steadier, she put the book back and turned round to him.
His face was drooping and swollen, but his eyes, though they were sunken
deep, gleamed with a child's courage.

'Why, he has behaved abominably,' she said. 'I am glad he is sorry. Do
you know what he did?'

'Not "abominably,"' was the gentle correction. 'He only tried when he
should not have tried. You have all you want, Miss Honeychurch: you are
going to marry the man you love. Do not go out of George's life saying he is
abominable.'

'No, of course,' said Lucy, ashamed at the reference to Cecil.
'"Abominable" is much too strong. I am sorry I used it about your son. I
think I will go to church, after all. My mother and my cousin have gone. I
shall not be so very late—'

'Especially as he has gone under,' he said quietly.

'What was that?'

'Gone under naturally.' He beat his palms together in silence; his head fell
on his chest.

'I don't understand.'

'As his mother did.'

'But, Mr Emerson—*Mr Emerson*—what are you talking about?'

'When I wouldn't have George baptized,' said he.

Lucy was frightened.

'And she agreed that baptism was nothing, but he caught that fever when he was twelve, and she turned round. She thought it a judgment.' He shuddered. 'Oh, horrible, when we had given up that sort of thing and broken away from her parents. Oh, horrible—worst of all—worse than death, when you have made a little clearing in the wilderness, planted your little garden, let in your sunlight, and then the weeds creep in again! A judgment! And our boy had typhoid because no clergyman had dropped water on him in church! Is it possible, Miss Honeychurch? Shall we slip back into the darkness for ever?'

'I don't know,' gasped Lucy. 'I don't understand this sort of thing. I was not meant to understand it.'

'But Mr Eager—he came when I was out, and acted according to his principles. I don't blame him or anyone . . . but by the time George was well she was ill. He made her think about sin, and she went under thinking about it.'

It was thus that Mr Emerson had murdered his wife in the sight of God.

'Oh, how terrible!' said Lucy, forgetting her own affairs at last.

'He was not baptized,' said the old man. 'I did hold firm.' And he looked with unwavering eyes at the rows of books, as if—at what cost!—he had won a victory over them. 'My boy shall go back to the earth untouched.'

She asked whether young Mr Emerson was ill.

'Oh—last Sunday.' He started into the present. 'George last Sunday—no, not ill: just gone under. He is never ill. But he is his mother's son. Her eyes were his, and she had that forehead that I think so beautiful, and he will not think it worth while to live. It was always touch and go. He will live; but he will not think it worth while to live. He will never think anything worth while. You remember that church at Florence?'

Lucy did remember, and how she had suggested that George should collect postage-stamps.

'After you left Florence—horrible. Then we take the house here, and he goes bathing with your brother, and became better. You saw him bathing?'

'I am so sorry, but it is no good discussing this affair. I am really deeply sorry about it.'

'Then there came something about a novel. I didn't follow it all; I had to hear so much, and he minded telling me; he finds me too old. Ah, well, one must have failures. George comes down to-morrow, and takes me up to his London rooms. He can't bear to be about here, and I must be where he is.'

'Mr Emerson,' cried the girl, 'don't leave—at least, not on my account. I am going to Greece. Don't leave your comfortable house.'

It was the first time her voice had been kind, and he smiled. 'How good every one is! And look at Mr Beebe housing me—came over this morning and heard I was going! Here I am so comfortable with a fire.'

'Yes, but you won't go back to London. It's absurd.'

'I must be with George; I must make him care to live, and down here he can't. He says the thought of seeing you and of hearing about you— I am not justifying him: I am only saying what has happened.'

'Oh, Mr Emerson'—she took hold of his hand—'you mustn't. I've been bother enough to the world by now. I can't have you moving out of your house when you like it, and perhaps losing money through it—all on my account. You must stop! I am just going to Greece.'

'All the way to Greece?'

Her manner altered.

'To Greece?'

'So you must stop. You won't talk about this business, I know. I can trust you both.'

'Certainly you can. We either have you in our lives, or leave you to the life that you have chosen.'

'I shouldn't want—'

'I suppose Mr. Vyse is very angry with George? No, it was wrong of George to try. We have pushed our beliefs too far. I fancy that we deserve sorrow.'

She looked at the books again—black, brown, and that acrid, theological blue. They surrounded the visitors on every side; they were piled on the tables, they pressed against the very ceiling. To Lucy—who could not see that Mr Emerson was profoundly religious, and differed from Mr Beebe chiefly by his acknowledgment of passion—it seemed dreadful that the old man should crawl into such a sanctum, when he was unhappy, and be dependent on the bounty of a clergyman.

More certain than ever that she was tired, he offered her his chair.

'No, please sit still. I think I will sit in the carriage.'

'Miss Honeychurch, you do sound tired.'

'Not a bit,' said Lucy, with trembling lips.

'But you are, and there's a look of George about you. And what were you saying about going abroad?'

She was silent.

'Greece'—and she saw that he was thinking the word over—'Greece'; but you were to be married this year, I thought.'

'Not till January, it wasn't,' said Lucy, clasping her hands. Would she tell an actual lie when it came to the point?

'I suppose that Mr. Vyse is going with you. I hope—it isn't because George spoke that you are both going?'

'No.'

'I hope that you will enjoy Greece with Mr Vyse.'

'Thank you.'

At that moment Mr Beebe came back from church. His cassock was covered with rain. 'That's all right,' he said kindly. 'I counted on you two keeping each other company. It's pouring again. The entire congregation, which consists of your cousin, your mother, and my mother, stands waiting in the church till the carriage fetches it. Did Powell go round?'

'I think so; I'll see.'

'No—of course, I'll see. How are the Miss Alans?'

'Very well, thank you.'

'Did you tell Mr Emerson about Greece?'

'I–I did.'

'Don't you think it very plucky of her, Mr Emerson, to undertake the two Miss Alans? Now, Miss Honeychurch, go back–keep warm. I think three is such a courageous number to go travelling.' And he hurried off to the stables.

'He is not going,' she said hoarsely. 'I made a slip. Mr Vyse does stop behind in England.' Somehow it was impossible to cheat this old man. To George, to Cecil, she would have lied again; but he seemed so near the end of things, so dignified in his approach to the gulf, of which he gave one account, and the books that surrounded him another, so mild to the rough paths that he had traversed, that the true chivalry–not the worn-out chivalry of sex, but the true chivalry that all the young may show to all the old–awoke in her, and, at whatever risk, she told him that Cecil was not her companion to Greece. And she spoke so seriously that the risk became a certainty and he, lifting his eyes, said: 'You are leaving him? You are leaving the man you love?'

'I–I had to.'

'Why, Miss Honeychurch, why?'

Terror came over her, and she lied again. She made the long, convincing speech that she had made to Mr Beebe, and intended to make to the world when she announced that her engagement was no more. He heard her in silence, and then said: 'My dear, I am worried about you. It seems to me'–dreamily; she was not alarmed–'that you are in a muddle.'

She shook her head.

'Take an old man's word: there's nothing worse than a muddle in all the world. It is easy to face Death and Fate, and the things that sound so dreadful. It is on my muddles that I look back with horror–on the things that I might have avoided. We can help one another but little. I used to think I could teach young people the whole of life, but I know better now, and all my teaching of George has come down to this: beware of muddle. Do you remember in that church, when you pretended to be annoyed with me and weren't? Do you remember before, when you refused the room with the view? Those were muddles–little, but ominous–and I am fearing that you are in one now.' She was silent. 'Do trust me, Miss Honeychurch. Though life is very glorious, it is difficult.' She was still silent. '"Life", wrote a friend of mine, "is a public performance on the violin, in which you must learn the instrument as you go along." I think he puts it well. Man has to pick up the use of his functions as he goes along–especially the function of Love.' Then he burst out excitedly: 'That's it; that's what I mean. You love George!' And after his long preamble, the three words burst against Lucy like waves from the open sea.

'But you do,' he went on, not waiting for contradiction. 'You love the boy body and soul, plainly, directly, as he loves you, and no other word expresses it. You won't marry the other man for his sake.'

'How dare you!' gasped Lucy, with the roaring of waters in her ears. 'Oh, how like a man!—I mean, to suppose that a woman is always thinking about a man.'

'But you are.'

She summoned physical disgust.

'You're shocked, but I mean to shock you. It's the only hope at times. I can reach you no other way. You must marry, or your life will be wasted. You have gone too far to retreat. I have no time for the tenderness, and the comradeship, and the poetry, and the things that really matter, and *for which* you marry. I know that, with George, you will find them, and that you love him. Then be his wife. He is already part of you. Though you fly to Greece, and never see him again, or forget his very name, George will work in your thoughts till you die. It isn't possible to love and to part. You will wish that it was. You can transmute love, ignore it, muddle it, but you can never pull it out of you. I know by experience that the poets are right: love is eternal.'

Lucy began to cry with anger, and though her anger passed away soon, her tears remained.

'I only wish poets would say this, too: that love is of the body; not the body, but of the body. Ah! the misery that would be saved if we confessed that! Ah for a little directness to liberate the soul! Your soul, dear Lucy! I hate the word now, because of all the cant with which superstition has wrapped it round. But we have souls. I cannot say how they came nor whither they go, but we have them, and I see you ruining yours. I cannot bear it. It is again the darkness creeping in; it is hell.' Then he checked himself. 'What nonsense I have talked—how abstract and remote! And I have made you cry! Dear girl, forgive my prosiness; marry my boy. When I think what life is, and how seldom love is answered by love— Marry him; it is one of the moments for which the world was made.'

She could not understand him: the words were indeed remote. Yet as he spoke the darkness was withdrawn, veil after veil, and she saw to the bottom of her soul.

'Then, Lucy—'

'You've frightened me,' she moaned. 'Cecil—Mr Beebe—the ticket's bought—everything.' She fell sobbing into the chair. 'I'm caught in the tangle. I must suffer and grow old away from him. I cannot break the whole of life for his sake. They trusted me.'

A carriage drew up at the front door.

'Give George my love—once only. Tell him "muddle."' Then she arranged her veil, while the tears poured over her cheeks inside.

'Lucy—'

'No—they are in the hall—oh, please not, Mr Emerson—they trust me—'

'But why should they, when you have deceived them?'

Mr Beebe opened the door, saying: 'Here's my mother.'

'You're not worthy of their trust.'

'What's that?' said Mr Beebe sharply.

'I was saying, why should you trust her when she deceived you?'

'One minute, mother.' He came in and shut the door.

'I don't follow you, Mr Emerson. To whom do you refer? Trust whom?'

'I mean, she has pretended to you that she did not love George. They have loved one another all along.'

Mr Beebe looked at the sobbing girl. He was very quiet, and his white face, with its ruddy whiskers, seemed suddenly inhuman. A long black column, he stood and awaited her reply.

'I shall never marry him,' quavered Lucy.

A look of contempt came over him, and he said, 'Why not?'

'Mr Beebe–I have misled you–I have misled myself—'

'Oh, rubbish, Miss Honeychurch!'

'It is not rubbish!' said the old man hotly. 'It's the part of people that you don't understand.'

Mr Beebe laid his hand on his shoulder pleasantly.

'Lucy! Lucy!' called voices from the carriage.

'Mr Beebe, could you help me?'

He looked amazed at the request, and said in a low, stern voice: 'I am more grieved than I can possibly express. It is lamentable, lamentable–incredible.'

'What's wrong with the boy?' fired up the other again.

'Nothing, Mr Emerson, except that he no longer interests me. Marry George, Miss Honeychurch. He will do admirably.'

He walked out and left them. They heard him guiding his mother upstairs.

'Lucy!' the voices called.

She turned to Mr Emerson in despair. But his face revived her. It was the face of a saint who understood.

'Now it is all dark. Now Beauty and Passion seem never to have existed. I know. But remember the mountains over Florence and the view. Ah, dear, if I were George, and gave you one kiss, it would make you brave. You have to go cold into a battle that needs warmth, out into the muddle that you have made yourself; and your mother and all your friends will despise you, oh my darling, and rightly, if it is ever right to despise. George still dark, all the tussle and the misery without a word from him. Am I justified?' Into his own eyes tears came. 'Yes, for we fight for more than Love or Pleasure: there is Truth. Truth counts, Truth does count.'

'You kiss me,' said the girl. 'You kiss me. I will try.'

He gave her a sense of deities reconciled, a feeling that, in gaining the man she loved, she would gain something for the whole world. Throughout the squalor of her homeward drive–she spoke at once–his salutation remained. He had robbed the body of its taint, the world's taunts of their sting; he had shown her the holiness of direct desire. She 'never exactly understood,' she would say in after years, 'how he managed to strengthen her. It was as if he had made her see the whole of everything at once.'

Chapter Twenty

The End of the Middle Ages

The Miss Alans did go to Greece, but they went by themselves. They alone of this little company will double Malea and plough the waters of the Saronic gulf. They alone will visit Athens and Delphi, and either shrine of intellectual song—that upon the Acropolis, encircled by blue seas; that under Parnassus, where the eagles build and the bronze charioteer drives undismayed towards infinity. Trembling, anxious, cumbered with much digestive bread, they did proceed to Constantinople, they did go round the world. The rest of us must be contented with a fair, but a less arduous, goal. Italiam petimus: we return to the Pension Bertolini.

George said it was his old room.

'No, it isn't,' said Lucy; 'because it is the room I had, and I had your father's room. I forget why; Charlotte made me, for some reason.'

He knelt on the tiled floor, and laid his face in her lap.

'George, you baby, get up.'

'Why shouldn't I be a baby?' murmured George.

Unable to answer this question, she put down his sock, which she was trying to mend, and gazed out through the window. It was evening and again the spring.

'Oh, bother Charlotte,' she said thoughtfully. 'What can such people be made of?'

'Same stuff as parsons are made of.'

'Nonsense!'

'Quite right. It is nonsense.'

'Now you get up off the cold floor, or you'll be starting rheumatism next, and you stop laughing and being so silly.'

'Why shouldn't I laugh?' he asked, pinning her with his elbows, and advancing his face to hers. 'What's there to cry at? Kiss me here.' He indicated the spot where a kiss would be welcome.

He was a boy, after all. When it came to the point, it was she who remembered the past, she into whose soul the iron had entered, she who knew whose this room had been last year. It endeared him to her strangely that he should be sometimes wrong.

'Any letters?' he asked.

'Just a line from Freddy.'

'Now kiss me here; then here.'

Then, threatened again with rheumatism, he strolled to the window, opened it (as the English will), and leant out. There was the parapet, there the river, there to the left the beginnings of the hills. The cab-driver, who at once saluted him with the hiss of a serpent, might be that very Phaethon who had set this happiness in motion twelve months ago. A passion of gratitude–all feelings grow to passions in the South–came over the husband, and he blessed the people and the things who had taken so much trouble about a young fool. He had helped himself, it is true, but how stupidly! All the fighting that mattered had been done by others–by Italy, by his father, by his wife.

'Lucy, you come and look at the cypresses; and the church, whatever its name is, still shows.'

'San Miniato. I'll just finish your sock.'

'Signorino, domani faremo uno giro,' called the cabman, with engaging certainty.

George told him that he was mistaken; they had no money to throw away on driving.

And the people who had not meant to help–the Miss Lavishes, the Cecils, the Miss Bartletts! Ever prone to magnify Fate, George counted up the forces that had swept him into this contentment.

'Anything good in Freddy's letter?'

'Not yet.'

His own content was absolute, but hers held bitterness: the Honeychurches had not forgiven them; they were disgusted at her past hypocrisy; she had alienated Windy Corner, perhaps for ever.

'What does he say?'

'Silly boy! He thinks he's being dignified. He knew we should go off in the spring–he has known it for six months–that if mother wouldn't give her consent we should take the thing into our own hands. They had fair warning, and now he calls it an elopement. Ridiculous boy—'

'Signorino, domani faremo uno giro—'

'But it will all come right in the end. He has to build us both up from the beginning again. I wish, though, that Cecil had not turned so cynical about women. He has, for the second time, quite altered. Why will men have theories about women? I haven't any about men. I wish, too, that Mr Beebe—'

'You may well wish that.'

'He will never forgive us–I mean, he will never be interested in us again. I wish that he did not influence them so much at Windy Corner. I wish he hadn't— But if we act the truth, the people who really love us are sure to come back to us in the long-run.'

'Perhaps.' Then he said more gently: 'Well, I acted the truth–the only thing I did do–and you came back to me. So possibly you know.' He turned back into the room. 'Nonsense with that sock.' He carried her to the window, so that she, too, saw all the view. They sank upon their knees invisible from the road, they hoped, and began to whisper one another's names. Ah! it was worth while; it was the great joy that they had expected, and countless little joys of which they had never dreamt. They were silent.

'Signorino, domani faremo—'

'Oh, bother that man!'

But Lucy remembered the vendor of photographs and said, 'No, don't be rude to him.' Then, with a catching of her breath, she murmured: 'Mr Eager and Charlotte, dreadful frozen Charlotte! How cruel she would be to a man like that!'

'Look at the lights going over the bridge.'

'But this room reminds me of Charlotte. How horrible to grow old in Charlotte's way! To think that evening at the Rectory that she shouldn't have heard your father was in the house. For she would have stopped me going in, and he was the only person alive who could have made me see sense. You couldn't have made me. When I am very happy'—she kissed him—'I remember on how little it all hangs. If Charlotte had only known, she would have stopped me going in, and I should have gone to silly Greece, and become different for ever.'

'But she did know,' said George; 'she did see my father, surely. He said so.'

'Oh no, she didn't see him. She was upstairs with old Mrs Beebe, don't you remember, and then went straight to the church. She said so.'

George was obstinate again. 'My father,' said he, 'saw her, and I prefer his word. He was dozing by the study fire, and he opened his eyes, and there was Miss Bartlett. A few minutes before you came in. She was turning to go as he woke up. He didn't speak to her.'

Then they spoke of other things—the desultory talk of those who have been fighting to reach one another, and whose reward is to rest quietly in each other's arms. It was long ere they returned to Miss Bartlett, but when they did her behaviour seemed more interesting. George, who disliked any darkness, said: 'It's clear that she knew. Then, why did she risk the meeting? She knew he was there, and yet she went to church.'

They tried to piece the thing together.

As they talked, an incredible solution came into Lucy's mind. She rejected it, and said: 'How like Charlotte to undo her work by a feeble muddle at the last moment.' But something in the dying evening, in the roar of the river, in their very embrace, warned them that her words fell short of life, and George whispered: 'Or did she mean it?'

'Mean what?'

'Signorino, domani faremo uno giro—'

Lucy bent forward and said with gentleness: 'Lascia, prego, lascia. Siamo sposati.'

'Scusi tanto, signora,' he replied, in tones as gentle, and whipped up his horse.

'Buona sera—e grazie.'

'Niente.'

The cabman drove away singing.

'Mean what, George?'

He whispered: 'Is it this? Is this possible? I'll put a marvel to you. That your cousin has always hoped. That from the very first moment we met, she hoped, far down in her mind, that we should be like this—of course, very far down. That she fought us on the surface, and yet she hoped. I can't explain her any other way. Can you? Look how she kept me alive in you all the summer; how she gave you no peace; how month after month she became more eccentric and unreliable. The sight of us haunted her – or she couldn't have described us as she did to her friend. There are details – it burnt. I read the book afterwards. She is not frozen, Lucy, she is not withered up all through. She tore us apart twice, but in the Rectory that evening she was given one more chance to make us happy. We can never make friends with her or thank her. But I do believe that, far down in her heart, far below all speech and behaviour, she is glad.'

'It is impossible,' murmured Lucy, and then, remembering the experiences of her own heart, she said: 'No – it is just possible.'

Youth enwrapped them; the song of Phaethon announced passion requited, love attained. But they were conscious of a love more mysterious than this. The song died away; they heard the river, bearing down the snows of winter into the Mediterranean.

THE END

HOWARDS END

'Only connect . . .'

Chapter One

One may as well begin with Helen's letters to her sister.

Howards End
Tuesday

Dearest Meg,

It isn't going to be what we expected. It is old and little, and altogether delightful—red brick. We can scarcely pack in as it is, and the dear knows what will happen when Paul (younger son) arrives to-morrow. From hall you go right or left into dining-room or drawing-room. Hall itself is practically a room. You open another door in it, and there are the stairs going up in a sort of tunnel to the first-floor. Three bedrooms in a row there, and three attics in a row above. That isn't all the house really, but it's all that one notices—nine windows as you look up from the front garden.

Then there's a very big wych-elm—to the left as you look up—leaning a little over the house, and standing on the boundary between the garden and meadow. I quite love that tree already. Also ordinary elms, oaks—no nastier than ordinary oaks—pear-trees, apple-trees, and a vine. No silver birches, though. However, I must get on to my host and hostess. I only wanted to show that it isn't the least what we expected. Why did we settle that their house would be all gables and wiggles, and their garden all gamboge-coloured paths? I believe simply because we associate them with expensive hotels—Mrs Wilcox trailing in beautiful dresses down long corridors, Mr Wilcox bullying porters, etc. We females are that unjust.

I shall be back Saturday; will let you know train later. They are as angry as I am that you did not come too; really Tibby is too tiresome, he starts a new mortal disease every month. How could he have got hay fever in London? and even if he could, it seems hard that you should give up a visit to hear a schoolboy sneeze. Tell him that Charles Wilcox (the son who is here) has hay fever too, but he's brave, and gets quite cross when we inquire after it. Men like the Wilcoxes would do Tibby a power of good. But you won't agree, and I'd better change the subject.

This long letter is because I'm writing before breakfast. Oh, the beautiful vine leaves! The house is covered with a vine. I looked out earlier, and Mrs Wilcox was already in the garden. She evidently loves it. No wonder she sometimes looks tired. She was watching the large red poppies come out. Then she walked off the lawn to the meadow, whose corner to the right I can just see. Trail, trail, went her long dress over the sopping grass, and she came back with her hands full of the hay that was cut yesterday – I suppose for rabbits or something, as she kept on smelling it. The air here is delicious. Later on I heard the noise of croquet balls, and looked out again, and it was Charles Wilcox practising; they are keen on all games. Presently he started sneezing and had to stop. Then I hear more clicketing, and it is Mr Wilcox practising, and then, 'a-tissue, a-tissue': he has to stop too. Then Evie comes out, and does some calisthenic exercises on a machine that is tacked on to a greengage-tree – they put everything to use – and then she says 'a-tissue,' and in she goes. And finally Mrs Wilcox reappears, trail, trail, still smelling hay and looking at the flowers. I inflict all this on you because once you said that life is sometimes life and sometimes only a drama, and one must learn to distinguish tother from which, and up to now I have always put that down as 'Meg's clever nonsense.' But this morning, it really does seem not life but a play, and it did amuse me enormously to watch the W's. Now Mrs Wilcox has come in.

I am going to wear [omission]. Last night Mrs Wilcox wore an [omission], and Evie [omission]. So it isn't exactly a go-as-you-please place, and if you shut your eyes it still seems the wiggly hotel that we expected. Not if you open them. The dog-roses are too sweet. There is a great hedge of them over the lawn – magnificently tall, so that they fall down in garlands, and nice and thin at the bottom, so that you can see ducks through it and a cow. These belong to the farm, which is the only house near us. There goes the breakfast gong. Much love. Modified love to Tibby. Love to Aunt Juley; how good of her to come and keep you company, but what a bore. Burn this. Will write again Thursday.

Helen

Howards End
Friday

Dearest Meg,

I am having a glorious time. I like them all. Mrs Wilcox, if quieter than in Germany, is sweeter than ever, and I never saw anything like her steady unselfishness, and the best of it is that the others do not take advantage of her. They are the very happiest, jolliest family that you can imagine. I do really feel that we are making friends. The fun of it is that they think me a noodle, and say so – at least, Mr Wilcox does – and when that happens, and one doesn't mind, it's a pretty sure test, isn't it? He says the most horrid things about women's suffrage so nicely, and when I said I believed in equality he just folded his arms and gave me such a setting down as I've never heard. Meg, shall we ever learn to talk less? I never felt so ashamed of myself in my life. I couldn't point to a time when men had been equal, nor even to a time when the wish to be equal had made them happier in other ways. I couldn't say a word. I had just picked up the notion that equality is good from some book – probably from poetry, or you. Anyhow, it's been knocked into pieces, and, like all people who are really strong, Mr Wilcox did it without hurting me. On the other hand, I laugh at them for catching hay fever. We live like fighting-cocks, and Charles takes us out every day in the motor–a tomb with trees in it, a hermit's house, a wonderful road that was made by the Kings of Mercia–tennis–a cricket match–bridge–and at night we squeeze up in this lovely house. The whole clan's here now–it's like a rabbit warren. Evie is a dear. They want me to stop over Sunday–I suppose it won't matter if I do. Marvellous weather and the views marvellous–views westward to the high ground. Thank you for your letter. Burn this.

Your affectionate

Helen

Howards End

Sunday

Dearest dearest Meg,

I do not know what you will say: Paul and I are in love–the younger son who only came here Wednesday.

Chapter Two

Margaret glanced at her sister's note and pushed it over the breakfast-table to her aunt. There was a moment's hush, and then the flood-gates opened.

'I can tell you nothing, Aunt Juley. I know no more than you do. We met–we only met the father and mother abroad last spring. I know so little that I didn't even know their son's name. It's all so—' She waved her hand and laughed a little.

'In that case it is far too sudden.'

'Who knows, Aunt Juley, who knows?'

'But, Margaret dear, I mean, we mustn't be unpractical now that we've come to facts. It is too sudden, surely.'

'Who knows!'

'But Margaret dear—'

'I'll go for her other letters,' said Margaret. 'No, I won't, I'll finish my breakfast. In fact, I haven't them. We met the Wilcoxes on an awful expedition that we made from Heidelberg to Speyer. Helen and I had got it into our heads that there was a grand old cathedral at Speyer–the Archbishop of Speyer was one of the seven electors–you know–"Speyer, Maintz, and Köln." Those three sees once commanded the Rhine Valley and got it the name of Priest Street.'

'I still feel quite uneasy about this business, Margaret.'

'The train crossed by a bridge of boats, and at first sight it looked quite fine. But oh, in five minutes we had seen the whole thing. The cathedral had been ruined, absolutely ruined, by restoration; not an inch left of the original structure. We wasted a whole day, and came across the Wilcoxes as we were eating our sandwiches in the public gardens. They too, poor things, had been taken in–they were actually stopping at Speyer–and they rather liked Helen insisting that they must fly with us to Heidelberg. As a matter of fact, they did come on next day. We all took some drives together. They knew us well enough to ask Helen to come and see them–at least, I was asked too, but Tibby's illness prevented me, so last Monday she went alone. That's all. You know as much as I do now. It's a young man out the unknown. She was to have come back Saturday, but put off till Monday, perhaps on account of–I don't know.'

She broke off, and listened to the sounds of a London morning. Their house was in Wickham Place, and fairly quiet, for a lofty promontory of buildings separated it from the main thoroughfare. One had the sense of a backwater, or rather of an estuary, whose waters flowed in from the invisible sea, and ebbed into a profound silence while the waves without were still beating. Though the promontory consisted of flats–expensive, with cavernous entrance halls, full of concierges and palms–it fulfilled its purpose, and gained for the older houses opposite a certain measure of peace. These, too, would be swept away in time, and another promontory would arise upon their site, as humanity piled itself higher and higher on the precious soil of London.

Mrs Munt had her own method of interpreting her nieces. She decided that Margaret was a little hysterical, and was trying to gain time by a torrent of talk. Feeling very diplomatic, she lamented the fate of Speyer, and declared that never, never should she be so misguided as to visit it, and added of her own accord that the principles of restoration were ill understood in Germany. 'The Germans,' she said, 'are too thorough, and this is all very well sometimes, but at other times it does not do.'

'Exactly,' said Margaret; 'Germans are too thorough.' And her eyes began to shine.

'Of course I regard you Schlegels as English,' said Mrs Munt hastily–'English to the backbone.'

Margaret leaned forward and stroked her hand.

'And that reminds me–Helen's letter—'

'Oh yes, Aunt Juley, I am thinking all right about Helen's letter. I know–I must go down and see her. I am thinking about her all right. I am meaning to go down.'

'But go with some plan,' said Mrs Munt, admitting into her kindly voice a note of exasperation. 'Margaret, if I may interfere, don't be taken by surprise. What do you think of the Wilcoxes? Are they our sort? Are they likely people? Could they appreciate Helen, who is to my mind a very special sort of person? Do they care about Literature and Art? That is most important when you come to think of it. Literature and Art. Most important. How old would the son be? She says "younger son." Would he be in a position to marry? Is he likely to make Helen happy? Did you gather—'

'I gathered nothing.'

They began to talk at once.

'Then in that case—'

'In that case I can make no plans, don't you see.'

'On the contrary—'

'I hate plans. I hate lines of action. Helen isn't a baby.'

'Then in that case, my dear, why go down?'

Margaret was silent. If her aunt could not see why she must go down, she was not going to tell her. She was not going to say 'I love my dear sister; I must be near her at this crisis of her life.' The affections are more reticent than the passions, and their expression more subtle. If she herself should ever fall in love with a man, she, like Helen, would proclaim it from the house-tops, but as she only loved a sister she used the voiceless language of sympathy.

'I consider you odd girls,' continued Mrs Munt, 'and very wonderful girls, and in many ways far older than your years. But—you won't be offended?—frankly, I feel you are not up to this business. It requires an older person. Dear, I have nothing to call me back to Swanage.' She spread out her plump arms. 'I am all at your disposal. Let me go down to this house whose name I forget instead of you.'

'Aunt Juley'—she jumped up and kissed her—'I must, must go to Howards End myself. You don't exactly understand, though I can never thank you properly for offering.'

'I do understand,' retorted Mrs Munt, with immense confidence. 'I go down in no spirit of interference, but to make inquiries. Inquiries are necessary. Now, I am going to be rude. You would say the wrong thing; to a certainty you would. In your anxiety for Helen's happiness you would offend the whole of these Wilcoxes by asking one of your impetuous questions—not that one minds offending them.'

'I shall ask no questions. I have it in Helen's writing that she and a man are in love. There is no question to ask as long as she keeps to that. All the rest isn't worth a straw. A long engagement if you like, but inquiries, questions, plans, lines of action—no, Aunt Juley, no.'

Away she hurried, not beautiful, not supremely brilliant, but filled with something that took the place of both qualities—something best described as a profound vivacity, a continual and sincere response to all that she encountered in her path through life.

'If Helen had written the same to me about a shop-assistant or a penniless clerk—'

'Dear Margaret, do come into the library and shut the door. Your good maids are dusting the banisters.'

'—or if she had wanted to marry the man who calls for Carter Paterson, I should have said the same.' Then, with one of those turns that convinced her aunt that she was not mad really, and convinced observers of another type that she was not a barren theorist, she added: 'Though in the case of Carter Paterson I should want it to be a very long engagement indeed, I must say.'

'I should think so,' said Mrs Munt; 'and, indeed, I can scarcely follow you. Now, just imagine if you said anything of that sort to the Wilcoxes. I understand it, but most good people would think you mad. Imagine how disconcerting for Helen! What is wanted is a person who will go slowly, slowly in this business, and see how things are and where they are likely to lead to.'

Margaret was down on this.

'But you implied just now that the engagement must be broken off.'

'I think probably it must; but slowly.'

'Can you break an engagement off slowly?' Her eyes lit up. 'What's an engagement made of, do you suppose? I think it's made of some hard stuff, that may snap, but can't break. It is different to the other ties of life. They stretch or bend. They admit of degree. They're different.'

'Exactly so. But won't you let me just run down to Howards House, and save you all the discomfort? I will really not interfere, but I do so thoroughly understand the kind of thing you Schlegels want that one quiet look round will be enough for me.'

Margaret again thanked her, again kissed her, and then ran upstairs to see her brother.

He was not so well.

The hay fever had worried him a good deal all night. His head ached, his eyes were wet, his mucous membrane, he informed her, in a most unsatisfactory condition. The only thing that made life worth living was the thought of Walter Savage Landor, from whose 'Imaginary Conversations' she had promised to read at frequent intervals during the day.

It was rather difficult. Something must be done about Helen. She must be assured that it is not a criminal offence to love at first sight. A telegram to this effect would be cold and cryptic, a personal visit seemed each moment more impossible. Now the doctor arrived, and said that Tibby was quite bad. Might it really be best to accept Aunt Juley's kind offer, and to send her down to Howards End with a note?

Certainly Margaret was impulsive. She did swing rapidly from one decision to another. Running downstairs into the library, she cried: 'Yes, I have changed my mind; I do wish that you would go.'

There was a train from King's Cross at eleven. At half-past ten Tibby, with rare self-effacement, fell asleep, and Margaret was able to drive her aunt to the station.

'You will remember, Aunt Juley, not to be drawn into discussing the engagement. Give my letter to Helen, and say whatever you feel yourself, but do keep clear of the relatives. We have scarcely got their names straight yet, and, besides, that sort of thing is so uncivilized and wrong.'

'So uncivilized?' queried Mrs Munt, fearing that she was losing the point of some brilliant remark.

'Oh, I used an affected word. I only meant would you please only talk the thing over with Helen.'

'Only with Helen.'

'Because—' But it was no moment to expound the personal nature of love. Even Margaret shrank from it, and contented herself with stroking her good aunt's hand, and with meditating, half sensibly and half poetically, on the journey that was about to begin from King's Cross.

Like many others who have lived long in a great capital, she had strong feelings about the various railway termini. They are our gates to the glorious and the unknown. Through them we pass out into adventure and sunshine, to them, alas! we return. In Paddington all Cornwall is latent and the remoter west; down the inclines of Liverpool Street lie fenlands and the illimitable Broads; Scotland is through the pylons of Euston; Wessex behind the poised chaos of Waterloo. Italians realize this, as is natural; those of them who are so unfortunate as to serve as waiters in Berlin call the Anhalt Bahnhof the Stazione d'Italia, because by it they must return to their homes. And he is a chilly Londoner who does not endow his stations with some personality, and extend to them, however shyly, the emotions of fear and love.

To Margaret—I hope that it will not set the reader against her—the station of King's Cross had always suggested Infinity. Its very situation—withdrawn a little behind the facile splendours of St Pancras—implied a comment on the materialism of life. Those two great arches, colourless, indifferent, shouldering between them an unlovely clock, were fit portals for some eternal adventure, whose issue might be prosperous, but would certainly not be expressed in the ordinary language of prosperity. If you think this ridiculous, remember that it is not Margaret who is telling you about it; and let me hasten to add that they were in plenty of time for the train; that Mrs Munt secured a comfortable seat, facing the engine, but not too near it; and that Margaret, on her return to Wickham Place, was confronted with the following telegram

'ALL OVER. WISH I HAD NEVER WRITTEN. TELL NO ONE.—HELEN.'

But Aunt Juley was gone—gone irrevocably, and no power on earth could stop her.

Chapter Three

Most complacently did Mrs Munt rehearse her mission. Her nieces were independent young women, and it was not often that she was able to help them. Emily's daughters had never been quite like other girls. They had been left motherless when Tibby was born, when Helen was five and Margaret herself but thirteen. It was before the passing of the Deceased Wife's Sister Bill, so Mrs Munt could without impropriety offer to go and keep house at Wickham Place. But her brother-in-law, who was peculiar and a German, had referred the question to Margaret, who with the crudity of youth had answered, 'No, they could manage much better alone.' Five years later Mr Schlegel had died too, and Mrs Munt had repeated her offer. Margaret, crude no longer, had been grateful and extremely nice, but the substance of her answer had been the same. 'I must not interfere a third time,' thought Mrs Munt. However, of course she did. She learnt, to her horror, that Margaret, now of age, was taking her money out of the old safe investments and putting it into Foreign Things, which always smash. Silence would have been criminal. Her own fortune was invested in Home Rails, and most ardently did she beg her niece to imitate her. 'Then we should be together, dear.' Margaret, out of politeness, invested a few hundreds in the Nottingham and Derby Railway, and though the Foreign Things did admirably and the Nottingham and Derby declined with the steady dignity of which only Home Rails are capable, Mrs Munt never ceased to rejoice, and to say, 'I did manage that, at all events. When the smash comes poor Margaret will have a nest-egg to fall back upon.' This year Helen came of age, and exactly the same thing happened in Helen's case; she also would shift her money out of Consols, but she, too, almost without being pressed, consecrated a fraction of it to the Nottingham and Derby Railway. So far so good, but in social matters their aunt had accomplished nothing. Sooner or later the girls would enter on the process known as throwing themselves away, and if they had delayed hitherto, it was only that they might throw themselves more vehemently in the future. They saw too many people at Wickham Place—unshaven musicians, an actress even, German cousins (one knows what foreigners are), acquaintances picked up at Continental hotels (one knows what they are too). It was interesting, and down at Swanage no one appreciated culture more than Mrs Munt; but it was dangerous, and disaster was bound to come. How right she was, and how lucky to be on the spot when the disaster came!

The train sped northward, under innumerable tunnels. It was only an hour's journey, but Mrs Munt had to raise and lower the window again and again. She passed through the South Welwyn Tunnel, saw light for a moment, and entered the North Welwyn Tunnel, of tragic fame. She traversed the immense viaduct, whose arches span untroubled meadows and the dreamy flow of Tewin Water. She skirted the parks of politicians. At times the Great North Road accompanied her, more suggestive of infinity than any railway, awakening, after a nap of a hundred years, to such life as is conferred by the stench of motor-cars, and to such culture as is implied by the advertisements of antibilious pills. To history, to tragedy, to the past, to the future, Mrs Munt remained equally indifferent; hers but to concentrate on the end of her journey, and to rescue poor Helen from this dreadful mess.

The station for Howards End was at Hilton, one of the large villages that are strung so frequently along the North Road, and that owe their size to the traffic of coaching and pre-coaching days. Being near London, it had not shared in the rural decay, and its long High Street had budded out right and left into residential estates. For about a mile a series of tiled and slated houses passed before Mrs Munt's inattentive eyes, a series broken at one point by six Danish tumuli that stood shoulder to shoulder along the highroad, tombs of soldiers. Beyond these tumuli habitations thickened, and the train came to a standstill in a tangle that was almost a town.

The station, like the scenery, like Helen's letters, struck an indeterminate
note. Into which country will it lead, England or Suburbia? It was new, it
had island platforms and a subway, and the superficial comfort exacted by
business men. But it held hints of local life, personal intercourse, as even
Mrs Munt was to discover.

'I want a house,' she confided to the ticket boy. 'Its name is Howards
Lodge. Do you know where it is?'

'Mr Wilcox!' the boy called.

A young man in front of them turned round.

'She's wanting Howards End.'

There was nothing for it but to go forward, though Mrs Munt was too
much agitated even to stare at the stranger. But remembering that there were
two brothers, she had the sense to say to him, 'Excuse me asking, but are you
the younger Mr Wilcox or the elder?'

'The younger. Can I do anything for you?'

'Oh, well'—she controlled herself with difficulty. 'Really. Are you? I—'
She moved away from the ticket boy and lowered her voice. 'I am Miss
Schlegel's aunt. I ought to introduce myself, oughtn't I? My name is Mrs
Munt.'

She was conscious that he raised his cap and said quite coolly, 'Oh, rather;
Miss Schlegel is stopping with us. Did you want to see her?'

'Possibly—'

'I'll call you a cab. No; wait a mo.' He thought. 'Our motor's here. I'll run
you up in it.'

'That is very kind—'

'Not at all, if you'll just wait till they bring out a parcel from the office.
This way.'

'My niece is not with you by any chance?'

'No; I came over with my father. He has gone on north in your train.
You'll see Miss Schlegel at lunch. You're coming up to lunch, I hope?'

'I should like to come *up*,' said Mrs Munt, not committing herself to
nourishment until she had studied Helen's lover a little more. He seemed a
gentleman, but had so rattled her round that her powers of observation were
numbed. She glanced at him stealthily. To a feminine eye there was nothing
amiss in the sharp depressions at the corners of his mouth, nor in the rather
box-like construction of his forehead. He was dark, clean-shaven, and
seemed accustomed to command.

'In front or behind? Which do you prefer? It may be windy in front.'

'In front if I may; then we can talk.'

'But excuse me one moment—I can't think what they're doing with that
parcel.' He strode into the booking-office, and called with a new voice: 'Hi!
hi, you there! Are you going to keep me waiting all day? Parcel for Wilcox,
Howards End. Just look sharp!' Emerging, he said in quieter tones: 'This
station's abominably organized; if I had my way, the whole lot of 'em should
get the sack. May I help you in?'

'This is very good of you,' said Mrs Munt, as she settled herself into a
luxurious cavern of red leather, and suffered her person to be padded with

rugs and shawls. She was more civil than she had intended, but really this young man was very kind. Moreover, she was a little afraid of him: his self-possession was extraordinary. 'Very good indeed,' she repeated, adding: 'It is just what I should have wished.'

'Very good of you to say so,' he replied, with a slight look of surprise, which, like most slight looks, escaped Mrs Munt's attention. 'I was just tooling my father over to catch the down train.'

'You see, we heard from Helen this morning.'

Young Wilcox was pouring in petrol, starting his engine, and performing other actions with which this story has no concern. The great car began to rock, and the form of Mrs Munt, trying to explain things, sprang agreeably up and down among the red cushions. 'The mater will be very glad to see you,' he mumbled. 'Hi! I say. Parcel. Parcel for Howards End. Bring it out. Hi!'

A bearded porter emerged with the parcel in one hand and an entry book in the other. With the gathering whir of the motor these ejaculations mingled: 'Sign, must I? Why the —— should I sign after all this bother? Not even got a pencil on you? Remember next time I report you to the station-master. My time's of value, though yours mayn't be. Here'–here being a tip.

'Extremely sorry, Mrs Munt.'

'Not at all, Mr Wilcox.'

'And do you object to going through the village? It is rather a longer spin, but I have one or two commissions.'

'I should love going through the village. Naturally I am very anxious to talk things over with you.'

As she said this she felt ashamed, for she was disobeying Margaret's instructions. Only disobeying them in the letter, surely. Margaret had only warned her against discussing the incident with outsiders. Surely it was not 'uncivilized or wrong' to discuss it with the young man himself, since chance had thrown them together.

A reticent fellow, he made no reply. Mounting by her side, he put on gloves and spectacles, and off they drove, the bearded porter–life is a mysterious business–looking after them with admiration.

The wind was in their faces down the station road, blowing the dust into Mrs Munt's eyes. But as soon as they turned into the Great North Road she opened fire. 'You can well imagine,' she said, 'that the news was a great shock to us.'

'What news?'

'Mr Wilcox,' she said frankly, 'Margaret has told me everything–everything. I have seen Helen's letter.'

He could not look her in the face, as his eyes were fixed on his work; he was travelling as quickly as he dared down the High Street. But he inclined his head in her direction, and said, 'I beg your pardon; I didn't catch.'

'About Helen. Helen, of course. Helen is a very exceptional person–I am sure you will let me say this, feeling towards her as you do–indeed, all the Schlegels are exceptional. I come in no spirit of interference, but it was a great shock.'

They drew up opposite a draper's. Without replying, he turned round in his seat, and contemplated the cloud of dust that they had raised in their passage through the village. It was settling again, but not all into the road from which he had taken it. Some of it had percolated through the open windows, some had whitened the roses and gooseberries of the wayside gardens, while a certain proportion had entered the lungs of the villagers. 'I wonder when they'll learn wisdom and tar the roads,' was his comment. Then a man ran out of the draper's with a roll of oilcloth, and off they went again.

'Margaret could not come herself, on account of poor Tibby, so I am here to represent her and to have a good talk.'

'I'm sorry to be so dense,' said the young man, again drawing up outside a shop. 'But I still haven't quite understood.'

'Helen, Mr Wilcox—my niece and you.'

He pushed up his goggles and gazed at her, absolutely bewildered. Horror smote her to the heart, for even she began to suspect that they were at cross-purposes, and that she had commenced her mission by some hideous blunder.

'Miss Schlegel and myself?' he asked, compressing his lips.

'I trust there has been no misunderstanding,' quavered Mrs Munt. 'Her letter certainly read that way.'

'What way?'

'That you and she—' She paused, then drooped her eyelids.

'I think I catch your meaning,' he said stickily. 'What an extraordinary mistake!'

'Then you didn't the least—' she stammered, getting blood-red in the face, and wishing she had never been born.

'Scarcely, as I am already engaged to another lady.' There was a moment's silence, and then he caught his breath and exploded with, 'Oh, good God! Don't tell me it's some silliness of Paul's.'

'But you are Paul.'

'I'm not.'

'Then why did you say so at the station?'

'I said nothing of the sort.'

'I beg your pardon, you did.'

'I beg your pardon, I did not. My name is Charles.'

'Younger' may mean son as opposed to father, or second brother as opposed to first. There is much to be said for either view, and later on they said it. But they had other questions before them now.

'Do you mean to tell me that Paul—'

But she did not like his voice. He sounded as if he was talking to a porter, and, certain that he had deceived her at the station, she too grew angry.

'Do you mean to tell me that Paul and your niece—'

Mrs Munt—such is human nature—determined that she would champion the lovers. She was not going to be bullied by a severe young man. 'Yes, they care for one another very much indeed,' she said. 'I dare say they will tell you about it by-and-by. We heard this morning.'

And Charles clenched his fist and cried, 'The idiot, the idiot, the little fool!'

Mrs Munt tried to divest herself of her rugs. 'If that is your attitude, Mr Wilcox, I prefer to walk.'

'I beg you will do no such thing. I take you up this moment to the house. Let me tell you the thing's impossible, and must be stopped.'

Mrs Munt did not often lose her temper, and when she did it was only to protect those whom she loved. On this occasion she blazed out. 'I quite agree, sir. The thing is impossible, and I will come up and stop it. My niece is a very exceptional person, and I am not inclined to sit still while she throws herself away on those who will not appreciate her.'

Charles worked his jaws.

'Considering she has only known your brother since Wednesday, and only met your father and mother at a stray hotel—'

'Could you possibly lower your voice? The shopman will overhear.'

'Esprit de classe'—if one may coin the phrase—was strong in Mrs Munt. She sat quivering while a member of the lower orders deposited a metal funnel, a saucepan, and a garden squirt beside the roll of oilcloth.

'Right behind?'

'Yes, sir.' And the lower orders vanished in a cloud of dust.

'I warn you: Paul hasn't a penny, it's useless.'

'No need to warn us, Mr Wilcox, I assure you. The warning is all the other way. My niece has been very foolish, and I shall give her a good scolding and take her back to London with me.'

'He has to make his way out in Nigeria. He couldn't think of marrying for years, and when he does it must be a woman who can stand the climate, and is in other ways— Why hasn't he told us? Of course he's ashamed. He knows he's been a fool. And so he has—a damned fool.'

She grew furious.

'Whereas Miss Schlegel has lost no time in publishing the news.'

'If I were a man, Mr Wilcox, for the last remark I'd box your ears. You're not fit to clean my niece's boots, to sit in the same room with her, and you dare—you actually dare— I decline to argue with such a person.'

'All I know is, she's spread the thing and he hasn't, and my father's away and I—'

'And all that I know is—'

'Might I finish my sentence, please?'

'No.'

Charles clenched his teeth and sent the motor swerving all over the lane. She screamed.

So they played the game of Capping Families, a round of which is always played when love would unite two members of our race. But they played it with unusual vigour, stating in so many words that Schlegels were better than Wilcoxes, Wilcoxes better than Schlegels. They flung decency aside. The man was young, the woman deeply stirred; in both a vein of coarseness was latent. Their quarrel was no more surprising than are most quarrels—inevitable at the time, incredible afterwards. But it was more than usually futile. A few minutes, and they were enlightened. The motor drew up at Howards End, and Helen, looking very pale, ran out to meet her aunt.

'Aunt Juley, I have just had a telegram from Margaret; I–I meant to stop your coming. It isn't–it's over.'

The climax was too much for Mrs Munt. She burst into tears.

'Aunt Juley dear, don't. Don't let them know I've been so silly. It wasn't anything. Do bear up for my sake.'

'Paul,' cried Charles Wilcox, pulling his gloves off.

'Don't let them know. They are never to know.'

'Oh, my darling Helen—'

'Paul! Paul!'

A very young man came out of the house.

'Paul, is there any truth in this?'

'I didn't–I don't—'

'Yes or no, man; plain question, plain answer. Did or didn't Miss Schlegel—'

'Charles dear,' said a voice from the garden. 'Charles, dear Charles, one doesn't ask plain questions. There aren't such things.'

They were all silent. It was Mrs Wilcox.

She approached just as Helen's letter had described her, trailing noiselessly over the lawn, and there was actually a wisp of hay in her hands. She seemed to belong not to the young people and their motor, but to the house, and to the tree that overshadowed it. One knew that she worshipped the past, and that the instinctive wisdom the past can alone bestow had descended upon her–that wisdom to which we give the clumsy name of aristocracy. High born she might not be. But assuredly she cared about her ancestors, and let them help her. When she saw Charles angry, Paul frightened, and Mrs Munt in tears, she heard her ancestors say, 'Separate those human beings who will hurt each other most. The rest can wait.' So she did not ask questions. Still less did she pretend that nothing had happened, as a competent society hostess would have done. She said, 'Miss Schlegel, would you take your aunt up to your room or to my room, whichever you think best. Paul, do find Evie, and tell her lunch for six, but I'm not sure whether we shall all be downstairs for it.' And when they had obeyed her, she turned to her elder son, who still stood in the throbbing, stinking car, and smiled at him with tenderness, and without saying a word, turned away from him towards her flowers.

'Mother,' he called, 'are you aware that Paul has been playing the fool again?'

'It is all right, dear. They have broken off the engagement.'

'Engagement—!'

'They do not love any longer, if you prefer it put that way,' said Mrs Wilcox, stooping down to smell a rose.

Chapter Four

Helen and her aunt returned to Wickham Place in a state of collapse, and for a little time Margaret had three invalids on her hands. Mrs Munt soon recovered. She possessed to a remarkable degree the power of distorting the past, and before many days were over she had forgotten the part played by her own imprudence in the catastrophe. Even at the crisis she had cried, 'Thank goodness, poor Margaret is saved this!' which during the journey to London evolved into, 'It had to be gone through by someone,' which in its turn ripened into the permanent form of 'The one time I really did help Emily's girls was over the Wilcox business.' But Helen was a more serious patient. New ideas had burst upon her like a thunder clap, and by them and by their reverberations she had been stunned.

The truth was that she had fallen in love, not with an individual, but with a family.

Before Paul arrived she had, as it were, been tuned up into his key. The energy of the Wilcoxes had fascinated her, had created new images of beauty in her responsive mind. To be all day with them in the open air, to sleep at night under their roof, had seemed the supreme joy of life, and had led to that abandonment of personality that is a possible prelude to love. She had liked giving in to Mr Wilcox, or Evie, or Charles; she had liked being told that her notions of life were sheltered or academic; that Equality was nonsense, Votes for Women nonsense, Socialism nonsense, Art and Literature, except when conducive to strengthening the character, nonsense. One by one the Schlegel fetiches had been overthrown, and, though professing to defend them, she had rejoiced. When Mr Wilcox said that one sound man of business did more good to the world than a dozen of your social reformers, she had swallowed the curious assertion without a gasp, and had leant back luxuriously among the cushions of his motor-car. When Charles said, 'Why be so polite to servants? they don't understand it,' she had not given the Schlegel retort of, 'If they don't understand it, I do.' No; she had vowed to be less polite to servants in the future. 'I am swathed in cant,' she thought, 'and it is good for me to be stripped of it.' And all that she thought or did or breathed was a quiet preparation for Paul. Paul was inevitable. Charles was taken up with another girl, Mr Wilcox was so old, Evie so young, Mrs Wilcox so different. Round the absent brother she began to throw the halo of Romance, to irradiate him with all the splendour of those happy days, to feel that in him she should draw nearest to the robust ideal. He and she were about the same age, Evie said. Most people thought

Paul handsomer than his brother. He was certainly a better shot, though not
so good at golf. And when Paul appeared, flushed with the triumph of
getting through an examination, and ready to flirt with any pretty girl, Helen
met him halfway, or more than halfway, and turned towards him on the
Sunday evening.

He had been talking of his approaching exile in Nigeria, and he should
have continued to talk of it, and allowed their guest to recover. But the heave
of her bosom flattered him. Passion was possible, and he became passionate.
Deep down in him something whispered, 'This girl would let you kiss her;
you might not have such a chance again.'

That was 'how it happened,' or, rather, how Helen described it to her
sister, using words even more unsympathetic than my own. But the poetry
of that kiss, the wonder of it, the magic that there was in life for hours after
it—who can describe that? It is so easy for an Englishman to sneer at these
chance collisions of human beings. To the insular cynic and the insular
moralist they offer an equal opportunity. It is so easy to talk of 'passing
emotion,' and to forget how vivid the emotion was ere it passed. Our impulse
to sneer, to forget, is at root a good one. We recognize that emotion is not
enough, and that men and women are personalities capable of sustained
relations, not mere opportunities for an electrical discharge. Yet we rate the
impulse too highly. We do not admit that by collisions of this trivial sort the
doors of heaven may be shaken open. To Helen, at all events, her life was to
bring nothing more intense than the embrace of this boy who played no part
in it. He had drawn her out of the house, where there was danger of surprise
and light; he had led her by a path he knew, until they stood under the
column of the vast wych-elm. A man in the darkness, he had whispered 'I
love you' when she was desiring love. In time his slender personality faded,
the scene that he had evoked endured. In all the variable years that followed
she never saw the like of it again.

'I understand,' said Margaret—'at least, I understand as much as ever is
understood of these things. Tell me now what happened on the Monday
morning.'

'It was over at once.'

'How, Helen?'

'I was still happy while I dressed, but as I came downstairs I got nervous,
and when I went into the dining-room I knew it was no good. There was
Evie—I can't explain—managing the tea-urn, and Mr Wilcox reading the
"Times."'

'Was Paul there?'

'Yes; and Charles was talking to him about Stocks and Shares, and he
looked frightened.'

By slight indications the sisters could convey much to each other.
Margaret saw horror latent in the scene, and Helen's next remark did not
surprise her.

'Somehow, when that kind of man looks frightened it is too awful. It is all
right for us to be frightened, or for men of another sort—father, for instance;
but for men like that! When I saw all the others so placid, and Paul mad with

terror in case I said the wrong thing, I felt for a moment that the whole
Wilcox family was a fraud, just a wall of newspapers and motor-cars and
golf-clubs, and that if it fell I should find nothing behind it but panic and
emptiness.'

'I don't think that. The Wilcoxes struck me as being genuine people,
particularly the wife.'

'No, I don't really think that. But Paul was so broad-shouldered; all kinds
of extraordinary things made it worse, and I knew that it would never
do—never. I said to him after breakfast, when the others were practising
strokes, "We rather lost our heads," and he looked better at once, though
frightfully ashamed. He began a speech about having no money to marry on,
but it hurt him to make it, and I stopped him. Then he said, "I must beg
your pardon over this, Miss Schlegel; I can't think what came over me last
night." And I said, "Nor what over me; never mind." And then we
parted—at least, until I remembered that I had written straight off to tell you
the night before, and that frightened him again. I asked him to send a
telegram for me, for he knew you would be coming or something; and he
tried to get hold of the motor, but Charles and Mr Wilcox wanted it to go to
the station; and Charles offered to send the telegram for me, and then I had
to say that the telegram was of no consequence, for Paul said Charles might
read it, and though I wrote it out several times, he always said people would
suspect something. He took it himself at last, pretending that he must walk
down to get cartridges, and, what with one thing and the other, it was not
handed in at the Post Office until too late. It was the most terrible morning.
Paul disliked me more and more, and Evie talked cricket averages till I
nearly screamed. I cannot think how I stood her all the other days. At last
Charles and his father started for the station, and then came your telegram
warning me that Aunt Juley was coming by that train, and Paul—oh, rather
horrible—said that I had muddled it. But Mrs Wilcox knew.'

'Knew what?'

'Everything; though we neither of us told her a word, and had known all
along, I think.'

'Oh, she must have overheard you.'

'I suppose so, but it seemed wonderful. When Charles and Aunt Juley
drove up, calling each other names, Mrs Wilcox stepped in from the garden
and made everything less terrible. Ugh! but it has been a disgusting
business. To think that—' She sighed.

'To think that because you and a young man meet for a moment, there
must be all these telegrams and anger,' supplied Margaret.

Helen nodded.

'I've often thought about it, Helen. It's one of the most interesting things
in the world. The truth is that there is a great outer life that you and I
have never touched—a life in which telegrams and anger count. Personal
relations, that we think supreme, are not supreme there. There love means
marriage settlements, death, death duties. So far I'm clear. But here my
difficulty. This outer life, though obviously horrid, often seems the real
one—there's grit in it. It does breed character. Do personal relations lead

to sloppiness in the end?'

'Oh, Meg, that's what I felt, only not so clearly, when the Wilcoxes were so competent, and seemed to have their hands on all the ropes.'

'Don't you feel it now?'

'I remember Paul at breakfast,' said Helen quietly. 'I shall never forget him. He had nothing to fall back upon. I know that personal relations are the real life, for ever and ever.'

'Amen!'

So the Wilcox episode fell into the background, leaving behind it memories of sweetness and horror that mingled, and the sisters pursued the life that Helen had commended. They talked to each other and to other people, they filled the tall thin house at Wickham Place with those whom they liked or could befriend. They even attended public meetings. In their own fashion they cared deeply about politics, though not as politicians would have us care; they desired that public life should mirror whatever is good in the life within. Temperance, tolerance, and sexual equality were intelligible cries to them; whereas they did not follow our Forward Policy in Thibet with the keen attention that it merits, and would at times dismiss the whole British Empire with a puzzled, if reverent, sigh. Not out of them are the shows of history erected: the world would be a grey, bloodless place were it entirely composed of Miss Schlegels. But the world being what it is, perhaps they shine out in it like stars.

A word on their origin. They were not 'English to the backbone,' as their aunt had piously asserted. But, on the other hand, they were not 'Germans of the dreadful sort.' Their father had belonged to a type that was more prominent in Germany fifty years ago than now. He was not the aggressive German, so dear to the English journalist, nor the domestic German, so dear to the English wit. If one classed him at all it would be as the countryman of Hegel and Kant, as the idealist, inclined to be dreamy, whose Imperialism was the Imperialism of the air. Not that his life had been inactive. He had fought like blazes against Denmark, Austria, France. But he had fought without visualizing the results of victory. A hint of the truth broke on him after Sedan, when he saw the dyed moustaches of Napoleon going grey; another when he entered Paris, and saw the smashed windows of the Tuileries. Peace came—it was all very immense, one had turned into an Empire—but he knew that some quality had vanished for which not all Alsace-Lorraine could compensate him. Germany a commercial Power, Germany a naval Power, Germany with colonies here and a Forward Policy there, and legitimate aspirations in the other place, might appeal to others, and be fitly served by them; for his own part, he abstained from the fruits of victory, and naturalized himself in England. The more earnest members of his family never forgave him, and knew that his children, though scarcely English of the dreadful sort, would never be German to the backbone. He had obtained work in one of our provincial Universities, and there married Poor Emily (or Die Engländerin as the case may be), and as she had money, they proceeded to London, and came to know a good many people. But his gaze was always fixed beyond the sea. It was his hope that the clouds of materialism obscuring the Fatherland would part in time, and the mild intellectual light re-emerge. 'Do you imply that we Germans are stupid, Uncle Ernst?' exclaimed a haughty and magnificent nephew. Uncle Ernst replied, 'To my mind. You use the intellect, but you no longer care about it. That I call stupidity.' As the haughty nephew did not follow, he continued, 'You only care about the things that you can use, and therefore arrange them in the following order: Money, supremely useful; intellect, rather useful; imagination, of no use at all. No'–for the other had protested–'your Pan-Germanism is no more imaginative than is our Imperialism over here. It is the vice of a vulgar mind to be thrilled by bigness, to think that a thousand square miles are a thousand times more wonderful than one square mile, and that a million square miles are almost the same as heaven. That is not imagination. No, it kills it. When their poets over here try to celebrate bigness they are dead at once, and naturally. Your poets too are dying, your philosophers, your musicians, to whom Europe has listened for two hundred years. Gone. Gone with the little courts that nurtured them–gone with Esterhaz and Weimar. What? What's that? Your Universities? Oh yes, you have learned men, who collect more facts than do the learned men of England. They collect facts, and facts, and empires of facts. But which of them will rekindle the light within?'

To all this Margaret listened, sitting on the haughty nephew's knee.

It was a unique education for the little girls. The haughty nephew would be at Wickham Place one day, bringing with him an even haughtier wife, both convinced that Germany was appointed by God to govern the world. Aunt Juley would come the next day, convinced that Great Britain had been appointed to the same post by the same authority. Were both these loud-voiced parties right? On one occasion they had met, and Margaret with clasped hands had implored them to argue the subject out in her presence. Whereat they blushed, and began to talk about the weather. 'Papa,' she cried–she was a most offensive child–'why will they not discuss this most clear question?' Her father, surveying the parties grimly, replied that he did not know. Putting her head on one side, Margaret then remarked, 'To me one of two things is very clear; either God does not know his own mind about England and Germany, or else these do not know the mind of God.' A hateful little girl, but at thirteen she had grasped a dilemma that most people travel through life without perceiving. Her brain darted up and down; it grew pliant and strong. Her conclusion was, that any human being lies nearer to the unseen than any organization, and from this she never varied.

Helen advanced along the same lines, though with a more irresponsible tread. In character she resembled her sister, but she was pretty, and so apt to have a more amusing time. People gathered round her more readily, especially when they were new acquaintances, and she did enjoy a little homage very much. When their father died and they ruled alone at Wickham Place, she often absorbed the whole of the company, while Margaret–both were tremendous talkers–fell flat. Neither sister bothered about this. Helen never apologized afterwards, Margaret did not feel the slightest rancour. But looks have their influence upon character. The sisters were alike as little girls, but at the time of the Wilcox episode their methods were beginning to diverge; the younger was rather apt to entice people, and, in enticing them, to be herself enticed; the elder went straight ahead, and accepted an occasional failure as part of the game.

Little need be premised about Tibby. He was now an intelligent man of sixteen, but dyspeptic and difficile.

Chapter Five

It will be generally admitted that Beethoven's Fifth Symphony is the most sublime noise that has ever penetrated into the ear of man. All sorts and conditions are satisfied by it. Whether you are like Mrs Munt, and tap surreptitiously when the tunes come—of course, not so as to disturb the others—or like Helen, who can see heroes and shipwrecks in the music's flood; or like Margaret, who can only see the music; or like Tibby, who is profoundly versed in counterpoint, and holds the full score open on his knee; or like their cousin, Fräulein Mosebach, who remembers all the time that Beethoven is 'echt Deutsch'; or like Fräulein Mosebach's young man, who can remember nothing but Fräulein Mosebach: in any case, the passion of your life becomes more vivid, and you are bound to admit that such a noise is cheap at two shillings. It is cheap, even if you hear it in the Queen's Hall, dreariest music-room in London, though not as dreary as the Free Trade Hall, Manchester; and even if you sit on the extreme left of that hall, so that the brass bumps at you before the rest of the orchestra arrives, it is still cheap.

'Who is Margaret talking to?' said Mrs Munt, at the conclusion of the first movement. She was again in London on a visit to Wickham Place.

Helen looked down the long line of their party, and said that she did not know.

'Would it be some young man or other whom she takes an interest in?'

'I expect so,' Helen replied. Music enwrapped her, and she could not enter into the distinction that divides young men whom one takes an interest in from young men whom one knows.

'You girls are so wonderful in always having— Oh dear! one mustn't talk.'

For the Andante had begun—very beautiful, but bearing a family likeness to all the other beautiful Andantes that Beethoven had written, and, to Helen's mind, rather disconnecting the heroes and shipwrecks of the first movement from the heroes and goblins of the third. She heard the tune through once, and then her attention wandered, and she gazed at the audience, or the organ, or the architecture. Much did she censure the attenuated Cupids who encircle the ceiling of the Queen's Hall, inclining each to each with vapid gesture, and clad in sallow pantaloons, on which the October sunlight struck. 'How awful to marry a man like those Cupids!'

thought Helen. Here Beethoven started decorating his tune, so she heard him through once more, and then she smiled at her cousin Frieda. But Frieda, listening to Classical Music, could not respond. Herr Liesecke, too, looked as if wild horses could not make him inattentive; there were lines across his forehead, his lips were parted, his pince-nez at right angles to his nose, and he had laid a thick, white hand on either knee. And next to her was Aunt Juley, so British, and wanting to tap. How interesting that row of people was! What diverse influences had gone to the making! Here Beethoven, after humming and hawing with great sweetness, said 'Heigho,' and the Andante came to an end. Applause, and a round of 'wunderschön-ing' and 'pract' volleying from the German contingent. Margaret started talking to her new young man; Helen said to her aunt: 'Now comes the wonderful movement: first of all the goblins, and then a trio of elephants dancing;' and Tibby implored the company generally to look out for the transitional passage on the drum.

'On the what, dear?'

'On the *drum*, Aunt Juley.'

'No; look out for the part where you think you have done with the goblins and they come back,' breathed Helen, as the music started with a goblin walking quietly over the universe, from end to end. Others followed him. They were not aggressive creatures; it was that that made them so terrible to Helen. They merely observed in passing that there was no such thing as splendour or heroism in the world. After the interlude of elephants dancing, they returned and made the observation for the second time. Helen could not contradict them, for, once at all events, she had felt the same, and had seen the reliable walls of youth collapse. Panic and emptiness! Panic and emptiness! The goblins were right.

Her brother raised his finger: it was the transitional passage on the drum.

For, as if things were going too far, Beethoven took hold of the goblins and made them do what he wanted. He appeared in person. He gave them a little push, and they began to walk in major key instead of in a minor, and then—he blew with his mouth and they were scattered! Gusts of splendour, gods and demi-gods contending with vast swords, colour and fragrance broadcast on the field of battle, magnificent victory, magnificent death! Oh, it all burst before the girl, and she even stretched out her gloved hands as if it was tangible. Any fate was titanic; any contest desirable; conqueror and conquered would alike be applauded by the angels of the utmost stars.

And the goblins—they had not really been there at all? They were only the phantoms of cowardice and unbelief? One healthy human impulse would dispel them? Men like the Wilcoxes, or President Roosevelt, would say yes. Beethoven knew better. The goblins really had been there. They might return—and they did. It was as if the splendour of life might boil over and waste to steam and froth. In its dissolution one heard the terrible, ominous note, and a goblin, with increased malignity, walked quietly over the universe from end to end. Panic and emptiness! Panic and emptiness! Even the flaming ramparts of the world might fall.

Beethoven chose to make all right in the end. He built the ramparts up. He blew with his mouth for the second time, and again the goblins were scattered. He brought back the gusts of splendour, the heroism, the youth, the magnificence of life and of death, and, amid vast roarings of a superhuman joy, he led his Fifth Symphony to its conclusion. But the goblins were there. They could return. He had said so bravely, and that is why one can trust Beethoven when he says other things.

Helen pushed her way out during the applause. She desired to be alone. The music had summed up to her all that had happened or could happen in her career. She read it as a tangible statement, which could never be superseded. The notes meant this and that to her, and they could have no other meaning, and life could have no other meaning. She pushed right out of the building, and walked slowly down the outside staircase, breathing the autumnal air, and then she strolled home.

'Margaret,' called Mrs Munt, 'is Helen all right?'

'Oh yes.'

'She is always going away in the middle of a programme,' said Tibby.

'The music had evidently moved her deeply,' said Fräulein Mosebach.

'Excuse me,' said Margaret's young man, who had for some time been preparing a sentence, 'but that lady has, quite inadvertently, taken my umbrella.'

'Oh, good gracious me!—I am so sorry. Tibby, run after Helen.'

'I shall miss the Four Serious Songs if I do.'

'Tibby love, you must go.'

'It isn't of any consequence,' said the young man, in truth a little uneasy about his umbrella.

'But of course it is. Tibby! Tibby!'

Tibby rose to his feet, and wilfully caught his person on the backs of the chairs. By the time he had tipped up the seat and had found his hat, and had deposited his full score in safety, it was 'too late' to go after Helen. The Four Serious Songs had begun, and one could not move during their performance.

'My sister is so careless,' whispered Margaret.

'Not at all,' replied the young man; but his voice was dead and cold.

'If you would give me your address—'

'Oh, not at all, not at all;' and he wrapped his greatcoat over his knees.

Then the Four Serious Songs rang shallow in Margaret's ears. Brahms, for all his grumbling and grizzling, had never guessed what it felt like to be suspected of stealing an umbrella. For this fool of a young man thought that she and Helen and Tibby had been playing the confidence trick on him, and that if he gave his address they would break into his rooms some midnight or other and steal his walking-stick too. Most ladies would have laughed, but Margaret really minded, for it gave her a glimpse into squalor. To trust people is a luxury in which only the wealthy can indulge; the poor cannot afford it. As soon as Brahms had grunted himself out, she gave him her card and said, 'That is where we live; if you preferred, you could call for the umbrella after the concert, but I didn't like to trouble you when it has all been our fault.'

His face brightened a little when he saw that Wickham Place was W. It was sad to see him corroded with suspicion, and yet not daring to be impolite, in case these well-dressed people were honest after all. She took it as a good sign that he said to her, 'It's a fine programme this afternoon, is it not?' for this was the remark with which he had originally opened, before the umbrella intervened.

'The Beethoven's fine,' said Margaret, who was not a female of the encouraging type. 'I don't like the Brahms, though, nor the Mendelssohn that came first—and ugh! I don't like this Elgar that's coming.'

'What, what?' called Herr Liesecke, overhearing. 'The "Pomp and Circumstance" will not be fine?'

'Oh, Margaret, you tiresome girl!' cried her aunt. 'Here have I been persuading Herr Liesecke to stop for "Pomp and Circumstance," and you are undoing all my work. I am so anxious for him to hear what *we* are doing in music. Oh, you mustn't run down our English composers, Margaret.'

'For my part, I have heard the composition at Stettin,' said Fräulein Mosebach. 'On two occasions. It is dramatic, a little.'

'Frieda, you despise English music. You know you do. And English art. And English literature, except Shakespeare and he's a German. Very well, Frieda, you may go.'

The lovers laughed and glanced at each other. Moved by a common impulse, they rose to their feet and fled from 'Pomp and Circumstance.'

'We have this call to pay in Finsbury Circus, it is true,' said Herr Liesecke, as he edged past her and reached the gangway just as the music started.

'Margaret—' loudly whispered by Aunt Juley. 'Margaret, Margaret! Fräulein Mosebach has left her beautiful little bag behind her on the seat.'

Sure enough, there was Frieda's reticule, containing her address book, her pocket dictionary, her map of London, and her money.

'Oh, what a bother—what a family we are! Fr-frieda!'

'Hush!' said all those who thought the music fine.

'But it's the number they want in Finsbury Circus—'

'Might I—couldn't I—' said the suspicious young man, and got very red.

'Oh, I would be so grateful.'

He took the bag—money clinking inside it—and slipped up the gangway with it. He was just in time to catch them at the swing-door, and he received a pretty smile from the German girl and a fine bow from her cavalier. He returned to his seat upsides with the world. The trust that they had reposed in him was trivial, but he felt that it cancelled his mistrust for them, and that probably he would not be 'had' over his umbrella. This young man had been 'had' in the past—badly, perhaps overwhelmingly—and now most of his energies went in defending himself against the unknown. But this afternoon—perhaps on account of music—he perceived that one must slack off occasionally, or what is the good of being alive? Wickham Place, W., though a risk, was as safe as most things, and he would risk it.

So when the concert was over and Margaret said, 'We live quite near; I am going there now. Could you walk round with me, and we'll find your umbrella?' he said, 'Thank you,' peaceably, and followed her out of the

Queen's Hall. She wished that he was not so anxious to hand a lady downstairs, or to carry a lady's programme for her–his class was near enough her own for its manners to vex her. But she found him interesting on the whole–everyone interested the Schlegels on the whole at that time–and while her lips talked culture, her heart was planning to invite him to tea.

'How tired one gets after music!' she began.

'Do you find the atmosphere of Queen's Hall oppressive?'

'Yes, horribly.'

'But surely the atmosphere of Covent Garden is even more oppressive.'

'Do you go there much?'

'When my work permits, I attend the gallery for the Royal Opera.'

Helen would have exclaimed, 'So do I. I love the gallery,' and thus have endeared herself to the young man. Helen could do these things. But Margaret had an almost morbid horror of 'drawing people out,' of 'making things go.' She had been to the gallery at Covent Garden, but she did not 'attend' it, preferring the more expensive seats; still less did she love it. So she made no reply.

'This year I have been three times–to "Faust," "Tosca," and—' Was it 'Tannhouser' or 'Tannhoyser'? Better not risk the word.

Margaret disliked 'Tosca' and 'Faust.' And so, for one reason and another, they walked on in silence, chaperoned by the voice of Mrs Munt, who was getting into difficulties with her nephew.

'I do in a *way* remember the passage, Tibby, but when every instrument is so beautiful, it is difficult to pick out one thing rather than another. I am sure that you and Helen take me to the very nicest concerts. Not a dull note from beginning to end. I only wish that our German friends would have stayed till it finished.'

'But surely you haven't forgotten the drum steadily beating on the low C, Aunt Juley?' came Tibby's voice. 'No one could. It's unmistakable.'

'A specially loud part?' hazarded Mrs Munt. 'Of course I do not go in for being musical,' she added, the shot failing. 'I only care for music–a very different thing. But still I will say this for myself–I do know when I like a thing and when I don't. Some people are the same about pictures. They can go into a picture gallery–Miss Conder can–and say straight off what they feel, all round the wall. I never could do that. But music is so different to pictures, to my mind. When it comes to music I am as safe as houses, and I assure you, Tibby, I am by no means pleased by everything. There was a thing–something about a faun in French–which Helen went into ecstasies over, but I thought it most tinkling and superficial, and said so, and I held to my opinion too.'

'Do you agree?' asked Margaret. 'Do you think music is so different to pictures?'

'I–I should have thought so, kind of,' he said.

'So should I. Now, my sister declares they're just the same. We have great arguments over it. She says I'm dense; I say she's sloppy.' Getting under way, she cried: 'Now, doesn't it seem absurd to you? What *is* the good of the Arts if they're interchangeable? What *is* the good of the ear if it tells you the same as the eye? Helen's one aim is to translate tunes into the language of painting, and pictures into the language of music. It's very ingenious, and she says several pretty things in the process, but what's gained, I'd like to know? Oh, it's all rubbish, radically false. If Monet's really Debussy, and Debussy's really Monet, neither gentleman is worth his salt—that's my opinion.'

Evidently these sisters quarrelled.

'Now, this very symphony that we've just been having—she won't let it alone. She labels it with meanings from start to finish; turns it into literature. I wonder if the day will ever return when music will be treated as music. Yet I don't know. There's my brother—behind us. He treats music as music, and oh, my goodness! He makes me angrier than anyone, simply furious. With him I daren't even argue.'

An unhappy family, if talented.

'But, of course, the real villain is Wagner. He had done more than any man in the nineteenth century towards the muddling of the arts. I do feel that music is in a very serious state just now, though extraordinarily interesting. Every now and then in history there do come these terrible geniuses, like Wagner, who stir up all the wells of thought at once. For a moment it's splendid. Such a splash as never was. But afterwards—such a lot of mud; and the wells—as it were, they communicate with each other too easily now, and not one of them will run quite clear. That's what Wagner's done.'

Her speeches fluttered away from the young man like birds. If only he could talk like this, he would have caught the world. Oh to acquire culture! Oh, to pronounce foreign names correctly! Oh, to be well informed, discoursing at ease on every subject that a lady started! But it would take one years. With an hour at lunch and a few shattered hours in the evening, how was it possible to catch up with leisured women, who had been reading steadily from childhood? His brain might be full of names, he might have even heard of Monet and Debussy; the trouble was that he could not string them together into a sentence, he could not make them 'tell,' he could not quite forget about his stolen umbrella. Yes, the umbrella was the real trouble. Behind Monet and Debussy the umbrella persisted, with the steady beat of a drum. 'I suppose my umbrella will be all right,' he was thinking. 'I don't really mind about it. I will think about music instead. I suppose my umbrella will be all right.' Earlier in the afternoon he had worried about seats. Ought he to have paid as much as two shillings? Earlier still he had wondered, 'Shall I try to do without a programme?' There had always been something to worry him ever since he could remember, always something that distracted him in the pursuit of beauty. For he did pursue beauty, and, therefore, Margaret's speeches did flutter away from him like birds.

Margaret talked ahead, occasionally saying, 'Don't you think so? don't you feel the same?' And once she stopped, and said, 'Oh, do interrupt me!' which terrified him. She did not attract him, though she filled him with awe. Her figure was meagre, her face seemed all teeth and eyes, her references to her sister and brother were uncharitable. For all her cleverness and culture, she was probably one of those soulless, atheistical women who have been so shown up by Miss Corelli. It was surprising (and alarming) that she should suddenly say, 'I do hope that you'll come in and have some tea.'

'I do hope that you'll come in and have some tea. We should be so glad. I have dragged you so far out of your way.'

They had arrived at Wickham Place. The sun had set, and the backwater, in deep shadow, was filling with a gentle haze. To the right the fantastic sky-line of the flats towered black against the hues of evening; to the left of the older houses raised a square-cut, irregular parapet against the grey. Margaret fumbled for her latchkey. Of course she had forgotten it. So, grasping her umbrella by its ferrule, she leant over the area and tapped at the dining-room window.

'Helen! Let us in!'

'All right,' said a voice.

'You've been taking this gentleman's umbrella.'

'Taken a what?' said Helen, opening the door. 'Oh, what's that? Do come in! How do you do?'

'Helen, you must not be so ramshackly. You took this gentleman's umbrella away from Queen's Hall, and he has had the trouble of coming round for it.'

'Oh, I am so sorry!' cried Helen, all her hair flying. She had pulled off her hat as soon as she returned, and had flung herself into the big dining-room chair. 'I do nothing but steal umbrellas. I am so very sorry! Do come in and choose one. Is yours a hooky or a nobbly? Mine's a nobbly—at least, I *think* it is.'

The light was turned on, and they began to search the hall, Helen, who had abruptly parted with the Fifth Symphony, commenting with shrill little cries.

'Don't you talk, Meg! You stole an old gentleman's silk top-hat. Yes, she did, Aunt Juley. It is a positive fact. She thought it was a muff. Oh, heavens! I've knocked the In and Out card down. Where's Frieda? Tibby, why don't you ever— No, I can't remember what I was going to say. That wasn't it, but do tell the maids to hurry tea up. What about this umbrella?' She opened it. 'No, it's all gone along the seams. It's an appalling umbrella. It must be mine.'

But it was not.

He took it from her, murmured a few words of thanks, and then fled, with the lilting step of the clerk.

'But if you will stop—' cried Margaret. 'Now, Helen, how stupid you've been!'

'Whatever have I done?'

'Don't you see that you've frightened him away? I meant him to stop to tea. You oughtn't to talk about stealing or holes in an umbrella. I saw his nice eyes getting so miserable. No, it's not a bit of good now.' For Helen had darted out into the street, shouting. 'Oh, do stop!'

'I dare say it is all for the best,' opined Mrs Munt. 'We know nothing about the young man, Margaret, and your drawing-room is full of very tempting little things.'

But Helen cried: 'Aunt Juley, how can you! You make me more and more ashamed. I'd rather he *had* been a thief and taken all the apostle spoons than that I— Well, I must shut the front-door, I suppose. One more failure for Helen.'

'Yes, I think the apostle spoons could have gone as rent,' said Margaret. Seeing that her aunt did not understand, she added: 'You remember "rent"? It was one of father's words—Rent to the ideal, to his own faith in human nature. You remember how he would trust strangers, and if they fooled him he would say, "It's better to be fooled than to be suspicious"—that the confidence trick is the work of man, but the want-of-confidence-trick is the work of the devil.'

'I remember something of the sort now,' said Mrs Munt, rather tartly, for she longed to add, 'It was lucky that your father married a wife with money.' But this was unkind, and she contended herself with, 'Why, he might have stolen the little Ricketts picture as well.'

'Better that he had,' said Helen stoutly.

'No, I agree with Aunt Juley,' said Margaret. 'I'd rather mistrust people than lose my little Ricketts. There are limits.'

Their brother, finding the incident commonplace, had stolen upstairs to see whether there were scones for tea. He warmed the teapot—almost too deftly—rejected the Orange Pekoe that the parlour-maid had provided, poured in five spoonfuls of a superior blend, filled up with really boiling water, and now called to the ladies to be quick or they would lose the aroma.

'All right, Auntie Tibby,' called Helen, while Margaret, thoughtful again, said: 'In a way, I wish we had a real boy in the house—the kind of boy who cares for men. It would make entertaining so much easier.'

'So do I,' said her sister. 'Tibby only cares for cultured females singing Brahms.' And when they joined him she said rather sharply: 'Why didn't you make that young man welcome, Tibby? You must do the host a little, you know. You ought to have taken his hat and coaxed him into stopping, instead of letting him be swamped by screaming women.'

Tibby sighed, and drew a long strand of hair over his forehead.

'Oh, it's no good looking superior. I mean what I say.'

'Leave Tibby alone!' said Margaret, who could not bear her brother to be scolded.

'Here's the house a regular hen-coop!' grumbled Helen.

'Oh, my dear!' protested Mrs Munt. 'How can you say such dreadful things! The number of men you get here has always astonished me. If there is any danger it's the other way round.'

'Yes, but it's the wrong sort of men, Helen means.'

'No, I don't,' corrected Helen. 'We get the right sort of man, but the wrong side of him, and I say that's Tibby's fault. There ought to be a something about the house—an—I don't know what.'

'A touch of the W.'s, perhaps?'

Helen put out her tongue.

'Who are the W.'s?' asked Tibby.

'The W.'s are things I and Meg and Aunt Juley know about and you don't, so there!'

'I suppose that ours is a female house,' said Margaret, 'and one must just accept it. No, Aunt Juley, I don't mean that this house is full of women. I am trying to say something much more clever. I mean that it was irrevocably feminine, even in father's time. Now I'm sure you understand! Well, I'll give you another example. It'll shock you, but I don't care. Suppose Queen Victoria gave a dinner-party, and that the guests had been Leighton, Millais, Swinburne, Rossetti, Meredith, Fitzgerald, etc. Do you suppose that the atmosphere of that dinner would have been artistic? Heavens, no! The very chairs on which they sat would have seen to that. So with our house–it must be feminine, and all we can do is to see that it isn't effeminate. Just as another house that I can mention, but won't, sounded irrevocably masculine, and all its inmates can do is to see that it isn't brutal.'

'That house being the W.'s house, I presume,' said Tibby.

'You're not going to be told about the W.'s, my child,' Helen cried, 'so don't you think it. And on the other hand, I don't the least mind if you find out, so don't you think you've done anything clever, in either case. Give me a cigarette.'

'You do what you can for the house,' said Margaret. 'The drawing-room reeks of smoke.'

'If you smoked too, the house might suddenly turn masculine. Atmosphere is probably a question of touch and go. Even at Queen Victoria's dinner-party–if something had been just a little different– perhaps if she'd worn a clinging Liberty tea-gown instead of a magenta satin—'

'With an Indian shawl over her shoulders—'

'Fastened at the bosom with a Cairngorm-pin—'

Bursts of disloyal laughter–you must remember that they are half German–greeted these suggestions, and Margaret said pensively, 'How inconceivable it would be if the Royal Family cared about Art.' And the conversation drifted away and away, and Helen's cigarette turned to a spot in the darkness, and the great flats opposite were sown with lighted windows, which vanished and were relit again, and vanished incessantly. Beyond them the thoroughfare roared gently–a tide that could never be quiet, while in the east, invisible behind the smokes of Wapping, the moon was rising.

'That reminds me, Margaret. We might have taken that young man into the dining-room, at all events. Only the majolica plate–and that is so firmly set in the wall. I am really distressed that he had no tea.'

For that little incident had impressed the three women more than might be supposed. It remained as a goblin footfall, as a hint that all is not for the best in the best of all possible worlds, and that beneath these superstructures of wealth and art there wanders an ill-fed boy, who has recovered his umbrella indeed, but who has left no address behind him, and no name.

Chapter Six

We are not concerned with the very poor. They are unthinkable, and only to be approached by the statistician or the poet. This story deals with gentlefolk, or with those who are obliged to pretend that they are gentlefolk.

The boy, Leonard Bast, stood at the extreme verge of gentility. He was not in the abyss, but he could see it, and at times people whom he knew had dropped in, and counted no more. He knew that he was poor, and would admit it: he would have died sooner than confess any inferiority to the rich. This may be splendid of him. But he was inferior to most rich people, there is not the least doubt of it. He was not as courteous as the average rich man, nor as intelligent, nor as healthy, nor as lovable. His mind and his body had been alike underfed, because he was poor, and because he was modern they were always craving better food. Had he lived some centuries ago, in the brightly coloured civilizations of the past, he would have had a definite status, his rank and his income would have corresponded. But in his day the angel of Democracy had arisen, enshadowing the classes with leathern wings, and proclaiming, 'All men are equal–all men, that is to say, who possess umbrellas,' and so he was obliged to assert gentility, lest he slipped into the abyss where nothing counts, and the statements of Democracy are inaudible.

As he walked away from Wickham Place, his first care was to prove that he was as good as the Miss Schlegels. Obscurely wounded in his pride, he tried to wound them in return. They were probably not ladies. Would real ladies have asked him to tea? They were certainly ill-natured and cold. At each step his feeling of superiority increased. Would a real lady have talked about stealing an umbrella? Perhaps they were thieves after all, and if he had gone into the house they would have clapped a chloroformed handkerchief over his face. He walked on complacently as far as the Houses of Parliament. There an empty stomach asserted itself, and told him that he was a fool.

'Evening, Mr Bast.'

'Evening, Mr Dealtry.'

'Nice evening.'

'Evening.'

Mr Dealtry, a fellow clerk, passed on, and Leonard stood wondering whether he would take the tram as far as a penny would take him, or whether he would walk. He decided to walk–it is no good giving in, and he had spent money enough at Queen's Hall–and he walked over Westminster Bridge, in front of St Thomas's Hospital and through the immense tunnel that passes under the South-Western main line at Vauxhall. In the tunnel he paused and listened to the roar of the trains. A sharp pain darted through his head, and he was conscious of the exact form of his eye sockets. He pushed on for another mile, and did not slacken speed until he stood at the entrance of a road called Camelia Road, which was at present his home.

Here he stopped again, and glanced suspiciously to right and left, like a rabbit that is going to bolt into its hole. A block of flats, constructed with extreme cheapness, towered on either hand. Farther down the road two more blocks were being built, and beyond these an old house was being demolished to accommodate another pair. It was the kind of scene that may be observed all over London, whatever the locality—bricks and mortar rising and falling with the restlessness of the water in a fountain, as the city receives more and more men upon her soil. Camelia Road would soon stand out like a fortress, and command, for a little, an extensive view. Only for a little. Plans were out for the erection of flats in Magnolia Road also. And again a few years, and all the flats in either road might be pulled down, and new buildings, a vastness at present unimaginable, might arise where they had fallen.

'Evening, Mr Bast.'

'Evening, Mr Cunningham.

'Very serious thing this decline of the birth-rate in Manchester.'

'I beg your pardon?'

'Very serious thing this decline of the birth-rate in Manchester,' repeated Mr Cunningham, tapping the Sunday paper, in which the calamity in question had just been announced to him.

'Ah, yes,' said Leonard, who was not going to let on that he had not bought a Sunday paper.

'If this kind of thing goes on the population of England will be stationary in 1960.'

'You don't say so.'

'I call it a very serious thing, eh?'

'Good-evening, Mr Cunningham.'

'Good-evening, Mr Bast.'

Then Leonard entered Block B of the flats, and turned, not upstairs, but down, into what is known to house agents as a semi-basement, and to other men as a cellar. He opened the door, and cried 'Hullo!' with the pseudo-geniality of the Cockney. There was no reply. 'Hullo!' he repeated. The sitting-room was empty, though the electric light had been left burning. A look of relief came over his face, and he flung himself into the armchair.

The sitting-room contained, besides the armchair, two other chairs, a piano, a three-legged table, and a cosy corner. Of the walls, one was occupied by a window, the other by a draped mantelshelf bristling with Cupids. Opposite the window was the door, and beside the door a bookcase, while over the piano there extended one of the masterpieces of Maud Goodman. It was an amorous and not unpleasant little hole when the curtains were drawn, and the lights turned on, and the gas-stove unlit. But it struck that shallow makeshift note that is so often heard in the modern dwelling-place. It had been too easily gained, and could be relinquished too easily.

As Leonard was kicking off his boots he jarred the three-legged table, and a photograph frame, honourably poised upon it, slid sideways, fell off into the fireplace, and smashed. He swore in a colourless sort of way, and picked the photograph up. It represented a young lady called Jacky, and had been taken at the time when young ladies called Jacky were often photographed with their mouths open. Teeth of dazzling whiteness extended along either of Jacky's jaws, and positively weighed her head sideways, so large were they and so numerous. Take my word for it, that smile was simply stunning, and it is only you and I who will be fastidious, and complain that true joy begins in the eyes, and that the eyes of Jacky did not accord with her smile, but were anxious and hungry.

Leonard tried to pull out the fragments of glass, and cut his fingers and swore again. A drop of blood fell on the frame, another followed, spilling over on to the exposed photograph. He swore more vigorously, and dashed into the kitchen, where he bathed his hands. The kitchen was the same size as the sitting-room: through it was a bedroom. This completed his home. He was renting the flat furnished: of all the objects that encumbered it none were his own except the photograph frame, the Cupids, and the books.

'Damn, damn, damnation!' he murmured, together with such other words as he had learnt from older men. Then he raised his hand to his forehead and said, 'Oh, damn it all—' which meant something different. He pulled himself together. He drank a little tea, black and silent, that still survived upon an upper shelf. He swallowed some dusty crumbs of a cake. Then he went back to the sitting-room, settled himself anew, and began to read a volume of Ruskin.

'Seven miles to the north of Venice—'

How perfectly the famous chapter opens! How supreme its command of admonition and of poetry! The rich man is speaking to us from his gondola.

'Seven miles to the north of Venice the banks of sand which nearer the city rise little above low-water mark attain by degrees a higher level, and knit themselves at last into fields of salt morass, raised here and there into shapeless mounds, and intercepted by narrow creeks of sea.'

Leonard was trying to form his style on Ruskin: he understood him to be the greatest master of English Prose. He read forward steadily, occasionally making a few notes.

'Let us consider a little each of these characters in succession, and first (for of the shafts enough has been said already), what is very peculiar to this church—its luminousness.'

Was there anything to be learnt from this fine sentence? Could he adapt it to the needs of daily life? Could he introduce it, with modifications, when he next wrote a letter to his brother, the lay-reader? For example—

'Let us consider a little each of these characters in succession, and first (for of the absence of ventilation enough has been said already), what is very peculiar to this flat—its obscurity.'

Something told him that the modifications would not do; and that something, had he known it, was the spirit of English Prose. 'My flat is dark as well as stuffy.' Those were the words for him.

And the voice in the gondola rolled on, piping melodiously of Effort and Self-Sacrifice, full of high purpose, full of beauty, full even of sympathy and the love of men, yet somehow eluding all that was actual and insistent in Leonard's life. For it was the voice of one who had never been dirty or hungry, and had not guessed successfully what dirt and hunger are.

Leonard listened to it with reverence. He felt that he was being done good to, and that if he kept on with Ruskin, and the Queen's Hall Concerts, and some pictures by Watts, he would one day push his head out of the grey waters and see the universe. He believed in sudden conversion, a belief which may be right, but which is peculiarly attractive to a half-baked mind. It is the basis of much popular religion: in the domain of business it dominates the Stock Exchange, and becomes that 'bit of luck' by which all successes and failures are explained. 'If only I had a bit of luck, the whole thing would come straight. . . . He's got a most magnificent place down at Streatham and a 20 h.p. Fiat, but then, mind you, he's had luck. . . . I'm sorry the wife's so late, but she never has any luck over catching trains.' Leonard was superior to these people; he did believe in effort and in a steady preparation for the change that he desired. But of a heritage that may expand gradually, he had no conception: he hoped to come to Culture suddenly, much as the Revivalist hopes to come to Jesus. Those Miss Schlegels had come to it; they had done the trick; their hands were upon the ropes, once and for all. And meanwhile, his flat was dark, as well as stuffy.

Presently there was a noise on the staircase. He shut up Margaret's card in the pages of Ruskin, and opened the door. A woman entered, of whom it is simplest to say that she was not respectable. Her appearance was awesome. She seemed all strings and bell-pulls—ribbons, chains, bead necklaces that clinked and caught—and a boa of azure feathers hung round her neck, with the ends uneven. Her throat was bare, wound with a double row of pearls, her arms were bare to the elbows, and might again be detected at the shoulder, through cheap lace. Her hat, which was flowery, resembled those punnets covered with flannel, which we sowed with mustard and cress in our childhood, and which germinated here yes, and there no. She wore it on the back of her head. As for her hair, or rather hairs, they are too complicated to describe, but one system went down her back, lying in a thick pad there, while another, created for a lighter destiny, rippled around her forehead. The face—the face does not signify. It was the face of the photograph, but older, and the teeth were not so numerous as the photographer had suggested, and certainly not so white. Yes, Jacky was past her prime, whatever that prime may have been. She was descending quicker than most women into the colourless years, and the look in her eyes confessed it.

'What ho!' said Leonard, greeting the apparition with much spirit, and helping it off with its boa.

Jacky, in husky tones, replied. 'What ho?'

'Been out?' he asked. The question sounds superfluous, but it cannot have been really, for the lady answered, 'No,' adding, 'Oh, I am so tired.'

'You tired?'

'Eh?'

'I'm tired,' said he, hanging the boa up.

'Oh, Len, I am so tired.'

'I've been to that classical concert I told you about,' said Leonard.

'What's that?'

'I came back as soon as it was over.'

'Anyone been round to our place?' asked Jacky.

'Not that I've seen. I met Mr Cunningham outside, and we passed a few remarks.'

'What, not Mr Cunningham?'

'Yes.'

'Oh, you mean Mr Cunningham.'

'Yes. Mr Cunningham.'

'I've been out to tea at a lady friend's.'

Her secret being at last given to the world, and the name of the lady-friend being even adumbrated, Jacky made no further experiments in the difficult and tiring art of conversation. She never had been a great talker. Even in her photographic days she had relied upon her smile and her figure to attract, and now that she was—

> *On the shelf,*
> *On the shelf,*
> *Boys, boys, I'm on the shelf,*

she was not likely to find her tongue. Occasional bursts of song (of which the above is an example) still issued from her lips, but the spoken word was rare.

She sat down on Leonard's knee, and began to fondle him. She was now a massive woman of thirty-three, and her weight hurt him, but he could not very well say anything. Then she said, 'Is that a book you're reading?' and he said, 'That's a book,' and drew it from her unreluctant grasp. Margaret's card fell out of it. It fell face downwards, and he murmured, 'Book-marker.'

'Len—'

'What is it?' he asked, a little wearily, for she only had one topic of conversation when she sat upon his knee.

'You do love me?'

'Jacky, you know that I do. How can you ask such questions?'

'But you do love me, Len, don't you?'

'Of course I do.'

A pause. The other remark was still due.

'Len—'

'Well? What is it?'

'Len, you will make it all right?'

'I can't have you ask me that again,' said the boy, flaring up into a sudden passion. 'I've promised to marry you when I'm of age, and that's enough. My word's my word. I've promised to marry you as soon as ever I'm twenty-one, and I can't keep on being worried. I've worries enough. It isn't likely I'd throw you over, let alone my word, when I've spent all this money. Besides, I'm an Englishman, and I never go back on my word. Jacky, do be reasonable. Of course I'll marry you. Only do stop badgering me.

'When's your birthday, Len?'

'I've told you again and again, the eleventh of November next. Now get off my knee a bit; someone must get supper, I suppose.'

Jacky went through to the bedroom, and began to see to her hat. This meant blowing at it with short sharp puffs. Leonard tidied up the sitting-room, and began to prepare their evening meal. He put a penny into the slot of the gas-meter, and soon the flat was reeking with metallic fumes. Somehow he could not recover his temper, and all the time he was cooking he continued to complain bitterly.

'It really is too bad when a fellow isn't trusted. It makes one feel so wild, when I've pretended to the people here that you're my wife—all right, all right, you *shall* be my wife—and I've bought you the ring to wear, and I've taken this flat furnished, and it's far more than I can afford, and yet you aren't content, and I've also not told the truth when I've written home.' He lowered his voice. 'He'd stop it.' In a tone of horror, that was a little luxurious, he repeated: 'My brother'd stop it I'm going against the whole world, Jacky.

'That's what I am, Jacky. I don't take any heed of what anyone says. I just go straight forward, I do. That's always been my way. I'm not one of your weak knock-kneed chaps. If a woman's in trouble, I don't leave her in the lurch. That's not my street. No, thank you.

'I'll tell you another thing too. I care a good deal about improving myself by means of Literature and Art, and so getting a wider outlook. For instance, when you came in I was reading Ruskin's "Stones of Venice." I don't say this to boast, but just to show you the kind of man I am. I can tell you, I enjoyed that classical concert this afternoon.'

To all his moods Jacky remained equally indifferent. When supper was ready—and not before—she emerged from the bedroom, saying: 'But you do love me, don't you?'

They began with a soup square, which Leonard had just dissolved in some hot water. It was followed by the tongue—a freckled cylinder of meat, with a little jelly at the top, and a great deal of yellow fat at the bottom—ending with another square dissolved in water (jelly: pineapple), which Leonard had prepared earlier in the day. Jacky ate contentedly enough, occasionally looking at her man with those anxious eyes, to which nothing else in her appearance corresponded, and which yet seemed to mirror her soul. And Leonard managed to convince his stomach that it was having a nourishing meal.

After supper they smoked cigarettes and exchanged a few statements. She observed that her 'likeness' had been broken. He found occasion to remark, for the second time, that he had come straight back home after the concert at Queen's Hall. Presently she sat upon his knee. The inhabitants of Camelia Road tramped to and fro outside the window, just on a level with their heads, and the family in the flat on the ground-floor began to sing, 'Hark, my soul, it is the Lord.'

'That tune fairly gives me the hump,' said Leonard.

Jacky followed this, and said that, for her part, she thought it a lovely tune.

'No; I'll play you something lovely. Get up, dear, for a minute.'

He went to the piano and jingled out a little Grieg. He played badly and vulgarly, but the performance was not without its effect, for Jacky said she thought she'd be going to bed. As she receded, a new set of interests possessed the boy, and he began to think of what had been said about music by that odd Miss Schlegel—the one that twisted her face about so when she spoke. Then the thoughts grew sad and envious. There was the girl named Helen, who had pinched his umbrella, and the German girl who had smiled at him pleasantly, and Herr someone, and Aunt someone, and the brother—all, all with their hands on the ropes. They had all passed up that narrow, rich staircase at Wickham Place, to some ample room, whither he could never follow them, not if he read for ten hours a day. Oh, it was no good, this continual aspiration. Some are born cultured; the rest had better go in for whatever comes easy. To see life steadily and to see it whole was not for the likes of him.

From the darkness beyond the kitchen a voice called, 'Len?'

'You in bed?' he asked, his forehead twitching.

'M'm.'

'All right.'

Presently she called him again.

'I must clean my boots ready for the morning,' he answered.

Presently she called him again.

'I rather want to get this chapter done.'

'What?'

He closed his ears against her.

'What's that?'

'All right, Jacky, nothing; I'm reading a book.'

'What?'

'What?' he answered, catching her degraded deafness.

Presently she called him again.

Ruskin had visited Torcello by this time, and was ordering his gondoliers to take him to Murano. It occurred to him, as he glided over the whispering lagoons, that the power of Nature could not be shortened by the folly, nor her beauty altogether saddened by the misery, of such as Leonard.

Chapter Seven

'Oh, Margaret,' cried her aunt next morning, 'such a most unfortunate thing has happened. I could not get you alone.'

The most unfortunate thing was not very serious. One of the flats in the ornate block opposite had been taken furnished by the Wilcox family, 'coming up, no doubt, in the hope of getting into London society.' That Mrs

Munt should be the first to discover the misfortune was not remarkable, for she was so interested in the flats, that she watched their every mutation with unwearying care. In theory she despised them—they took away that old-world look—they cut off the sun—flats house a flashy type of person. But if the truth had been known, she found her visits to Wickham Place twice as amusing since Wickham Mansions had arisen, and would in a couple of days learn more about them than her nieces in a couple of months, or her nephew in a couple of years. She would stroll across and make friends with the porters, and inquire what the rents were, exclaiming for example: 'What! a hundred and twenty for a basement? You'll never get it!' And they would answer: 'One can but try, madam.' The passenger lifts, the provision lifts, the arrangement for coals (a great temptation for a dishonest porter), were all familiar matters to her, and perhaps a relief from the politico-economical-æsthetic atmosphere that reigned at the Schlegels'.

Margaret received the information calmly, and did not agree that it would throw a cloud over poor Helen's life.

'Oh, but Helen isn't a girl with no interests,' she explained. 'She has plenty of other things and other people to think about. She made a false start with the Wilcoxes, and she'll be as willing as we are to have nothing more to do with them.'

'For a clever girl, dear, how very oddly you do talk. Helen'll *have* to have something more to do with them, now that they're all opposite. She may meet that Paul in the street. She cannot very well not bow.'

'Of course she must bow. But look here; let's do the flowers. I was going to say, the will to be interested in him has died, and what else matters? I look on that disastrous episode (over which you were so kind) as the killing of a nerve in Helen. It's dead, and she'll never be troubled with it again. The only things that matter are the things that interest one. Bowing, even calling and leaving cards, even a dinner-party—we can do all those things to the Wilcoxes, if they find it agreeable; but the other thing, the one important thing—never again. Don't you see?'

Mrs. Munt did not see, and indeed Margaret was making a most questionable statement—that any emotion, any interest once vividly aroused, can wholly die.

'I also have the honour to inform you that the Wilcoxes are bored with us. I didn't tell you at the time—it might have made you angry, and you had enough to worry you—but I wrote a letter to Mrs W., and apologized for the trouble that Helen had given them. She didn't answer it.'

'How very rude!'

'I wonder. Or was it sensible?'

'No, Margaret, most rude.'

'In either case one can class it as reassuring.'

Mrs Munt sighed. She was going back to Swanage on the morrow, just as her nieces were wanting her most. Other regrets crowded upon her: for instance, how magnificently she would have cut Charles if she had met him face to face. She had already seen him, giving an order to the porter—and very common he looked in a tall hat. But unfortunately his back was turned to her, and though she had cut his back, she could not regard this as a telling snub.

'But you will be careful, won't you?' she exhorted.

'Oh, certainly. Fiendishly careful.'

'And Helen must be careful, too.'

'Careful over what?' cried Helen, at that moment coming into the room with her cousin.

'Nothing,' said Margaret, seized with a momentary awkwardness.

'Careful over what, Aunt Juley?'

Mrs Munt assumed a cryptic air. 'It is only that a certain family, whom we know by name but do not mention, as you said yourself last night after the concert, have taken the flat opposite from the Mathesons—where the plants are in the balcony.'

Helen began some laughing reply, and then disconcerted them all by blushing. Mrs Munt was so disconcerted that she exclaimed, 'What, Helen, you don't mind them coming, do you?' and deepened the blush to crimson.

'Of course I don't mind,' said Helen a little crossly. 'It is that you and Meg are both so absurdly grave about it, when there's nothing to be grave about at all.'

'I'm not grave,' protested Margaret, a little cross in her turn.

'Well, you look grave; doesn't she, Frieda?'

'I don't feel grave, that's all I can say; you're going quite on the wrong tack.'

'No, she does not feel grave,' echoed Mrs Munt. 'I can bear witness to that. She disagrees—'

'Hark!' interrupted Fräulein Mosebach. 'I hear Bruno entering the hall.'

For Herr Liesecke was due at Wickham Place to call for the two younger girls. He was not entering the hall—in fact, he did not enter it for quite five minutes. But Frieda detected a delicate situation, and said that she and Helen had much better wait for Bruno down below, and leave Margaret and Mrs Munt to finish arranging the flowers. Helen acquiesced. But, as if to prove that the situation was not delicate really, she stopped in the doorway and said:

'Did you say the Mathesons' flat, Aunt Juley? How wonderful you are! *I* never knew that the woman who laced too tightly's name was Matheson.'

'Come, Helen,' said her cousin.

'Go, Helen,' said her aunt; and continued to Margaret almost in the same breath: 'Helen cannot deceive me. She does mind.'

'Oh, hush!' breathed Margaret. 'Frieda'll hear you, and she can be so tiresome.'

'She minds,' persisted Mrs Munt, moving thoughtfully about the room, and pulling the dead chrysanthemums out of the vases. 'I knew she'd mind—and I'm sure a girl ought to! Such an experience! Such awful coarse-grained people! I know more about them than you do, which you forget, and if Charles had taken you that motor drive—well, you'd have reached the house a perfect wreck. Oh, Margaret, you don't know what you are in for. They're all bottled up against the drawing-room window. There's Mrs

Wilcox—I've seen her. There's Paul. There's Evie, who is a minx. There's Charles—I saw him to start with. And who would an elderly man with a moustache and a copper-coloured face be?'

'Mr Wilcox, possibly.'

'I knew it. And there's Mr Wilcox.'

'It's a shame to call his face copper colour,' complained Margaret. 'He has a remarkably good complexion for a man of his age.'

Mrs Munt, triumphant elsewhere, could afford to concede Mr Wilcox his complexion. She passed on from it to the plan of campaign that her nieces should pursue in the future. Margaret tried to stop her.

'Helen did not take the news quite as I expected, but the Wilcox nerve is dead in her really, so there's no need for plans.'

'It's as well to be prepared.'

'No—it's as well not to be prepared.'

'Why?'

'Because—'

Her thought drew being from the obscure borderland. She could not explain in so many words, but she felt that those who prepare for all the emergencies of life beforehand may equip themselves at the expense of joy. It is necessary to prepare for an examination, or a dinner-party, or a possible fall in the price of stock: those who attempt human relations must adopt another method, or fail. 'Because I'd sooner risk it,' was her lame conclusion.

'But imagine the evenings,' exclaimed her aunt, pointing to the Mansions with the spout of the watering-can. 'Turn the electric light on here and there, and it's almost the same room. One evening they may forget to draw their blinds down, and you'll see them; and the next, you yours, and they'll see you. Impossible to sit out on the balconies. Impossible to water the plants, or even speak. Imagine going out of the front-door, and they come out opposite at the same moment. And yet you tell me that plans are unnecessary, and you'd rather risk it.'

'I hope to risk things all my life.'

'Oh, Margaret, most dangerous.'

'But after all,' she continued with a smile, 'there's never any great risk as long as you have money.'

'Oh, shame! What a shocking speech!'

'Money pads the edges of things,' said Miss Schlegel. 'God help those who have none.'

'But this is something quite new!' said Mrs Munt, who collected new ideas as a squirrel collects nuts, and was especially attracted by those that are portable.

'New for me; sensible people have acknowledged it for years. You and I and the Wilcoxes stand upon money as upon islands. It is so firm beneath our feet that we forget its very existence. It's only when we see someone near us tottering that we realize all that an independent income means. Last night, when we were talking up here round the fire, I began to think that the very soul of the world is economic, and that the lowest abyss is not the absence of love, but the absence of coin.'

'I call that rather cynical.'

'So do I. But Helen and I, we ought to remember, when we are tempted to criticize others, that we are standing on these islands, and that most of the others are down below the surface of the sea. The poor cannot always reach those whom they want to love, and they can hardly ever escape from those whom they love no longer. We rich can. Imagine the tragedy last June if Helen and Paul Wilcox had been poor people, and couldn't invoke railways and motor-cars to part them.'

'That's more like Socialism,' said Mrs Munt suspiciously.

'Call it what you like. I call it going through life with one's hand spread open on the table. I'm tired of these rich people who pretend to be poor, and think it shows a nice mind to ignore the piles of money that keep their feet above the waves. I stand each year upon six hundred pounds, and Helen upon the same, and Tibby will stand upon eight, and as fast as our pounds crumble away into the sea they are renewed–from the sea, yes, from the sea. And all our thoughts are the thoughts of six-hundred-pounders, and all our speeches; and because we don't want to steal umbrellas ourselves, we forget that below the sea people do want to steal them, and do steal them sometimes, and that what's a joke up here is down there reality—'

'There they go–there goes Fräulein Mosebach. Really, for a German she does dress charmingly. Oh—!'

'What is it?'

'Helen was looking up at the Wilcoxes' flat.'

'Why shouldn't she?'

'I beg your pardon, I interrupted you. What was it you were saying about reality?'

'I had worked round to myself, as usual,' answered Margaret in tones that were suddenly preoccupied.

'Do tell me this, at all events. Are you for the rich or for the poor?'

'Too difficult. Ask me another. Am I for poverty or for riches? For riches. Hurrah for riches!'

'For riches!' echoed Mrs Munt, having, as it were, at last secured her nut.

'Yes. For riches. Money for ever!'

'So am I, and so, I am afraid, are most of my acquaintances at Swanage, but I am surprised that you agree with us.'

'Thank you so much, Aunt Juley. While I have talked theories, you have done the flowers.'

'Not at all, dear. I wish you would let me help you in more important things.'

'Well, would you be very kind? Would you come round with me to the registry office? There's a housemaid who won't say yes but doesn't say no.'

On their way thither they too looked up at the Wilcoxes' flat. Evie was in the balcony, 'staring most rudely,' according to Mrs Munt. Oh yes, it was a nuisance, there was no doubt of it. Helen was proof against a passing encounter, but— Margaret began to lose confidence. Might it reawake the dying nerve if the family were living close against her eyes? And Frieda

Mosebach was stopping with them for another fortnight, and Frieda was sharp, abominably sharp, and quite capable of remarking, 'You love one of the young gentlemen opposite, yes?' The remark would be untrue, but of the kind which, if started often enough, may become true; just as the remark, 'England and Germany are bound to fight,' renders war a little more likely each time that it is made, and is therefore made the more readily by the gutter press of either nation. Have the private emotions also their gutter press? Margaret thought so, and feared that good Aunt Juley and Frieda were typical specimens of it. They might, by continual chatter, lead Helen into a repetition of the desires of June. Into a repetition—they could not do more; they could not lead her into lasting love. They were—she saw it clearly—Journalism; her father, with all his defects and wrong-headedness, had been Literature, and had he lived, he would have persuaded his daughter rightly.

The registry office was holding its morning reception. A string of carriages filled the street. Miss Schlegel waited her turn, and finally had to be content with an insidious 'temporary,' being rejected by genuine housemaids on the ground of her numerous stairs. Her failure depressed her, and though she forgot the failure, the depression remained. On her way home she again glanced up at the Wilcoxes' flat, and took the rather matronly step of speaking about the matter to Helen.

'Helen, you must tell me whether this thing worries you.'

'If what?' said Helen, who was washing her hands for lunch.

'The W.s' coming.'

'No, of course not.'

'Really?'

'Really.' Then she admitted that she was a little worried on Mrs Wilcox's account; she implied that Mrs Wilcox might reach backward into deep feelings, and be pained by things that never touched the other members of that clan. 'I shan't mind if Paul points at our house and says, "There lives the girl who tried to catch me." But she might.'

'If even that worries you, we could arrange something. There's no reason we should be near people who displease us or whom we displease, thanks to our money. We might even go away for a little.'

'Well, I am going away. Frieda's just asked me to Stettin, and I shan't be back till after the New Year. Will that do? Or must I fly the country altogether? Really, Meg, what has come over you to make such a fuss?'

'Oh, I'm getting an old maid, I suppose. I thought I minded nothing, but really I—I should be bored if you fell in love with the same man twice and'—she cleared her throat—'you did go red, you know, when Aunt Juley attacked you this morning. I shouldn't have referred to it otherwise.'

But Helen's laugh rang true, as she raised a soapy hand to heaven and swore that never, nowhere and nohow, would she again fall in love with any of the Wilcox family, down to its remotest collaterals.

Chapter Eight

The friendship between Margaret and Mrs Wilcox, which was to develop so quickly and with such strange results, may perhaps have had its beginnings at Speyer, in the spring. Perhaps the elder lady, as she gazed at the vulgar, ruddy cathedral, and listened to the talk of Helen and her husband, may have detected in the other and less charming of the sisters a deeper sympathy, a sounder judgment. She was capable of detecting such things. Perhaps it was she who had desired the Miss Schlegels to be invited to Howards End, and Margaret whose presence she had particularly desired. All this is speculation: Mrs Wilcox has left few clear indications behind her. It is certain that she came to call at Wickham Place a fortnight later, the very day that Helen was going with her cousin to Stettin.

'Helen!' cried Fräulein Mosebach in awestruck tones (she was now in her cousin's confidence)–'his mother has forgiven you!' And then, remembering that in England the new-comer ought not to call before she is called upon, she changed her tone from awe to disapproval, and opined that Mrs Wilcox was 'keine Dame.'

'Bother the whole family!' snapped Margaret. 'Helen, stop giggling and pirouetting, and go and finish your packing. Why can't the woman leave us alone?'

'I don't know what I shall do with Meg,' Helen retorted, collapsing upon the stairs. She's got Wilcox and Box upon the brain. Meg, Meg, I don't love the young gentleman; I don't love the young genterman, Meg, Meg. Can a body speak plainer?'

'Most certainly her love has died.' asserted Fräulein Mosebach.

'Most certainly it has, Frieda, but that will not prevent me from being bored with the Wilcoxes if I return the call.'

Then Helen simulated tears, and Fräulein Mosebach, who thought her extremely amusing, did the same. 'Oh, boo hoo! boo hoo hoo! Meg's going to return the call, and I can't. 'Cos why? 'Cos I'm going to German-eye.'

'If you are going to Germany, go and pack; if you aren't, go and call on the Wilcoxes instead of me.'

'But, Meg, Meg, I don't love the young gentleman; I don't love the young– O lud, who's that coming down the stairs? I vow 'tis my brother. O crimini!'

A male–even such a male as Tibby–was enough to stop the foolery. The barrier of sex, though decreasing among the civilized, is still high, and higher on the side of women. Helen could tell her sister all, and her cousin much about Paul; she told her brother nothing. It was not prudishness, for she now spoke of 'the Wilcox ideal' with laughter, and even with a growing brutality. Nor was it precaution, for Tibby seldom repeated any news that did not concern himself. It was rather the feeling that she betrayed a secret into the camp of men, and that, however trivial it was on this side of the barrier, it would become important on that. So she stopped, or rather began to fool on other subjects, until her long-suffering relatives drove her upstairs. Fräulein Mosebach followed her, but lingered to say heavily over the banisters to Margaret, 'It is all right—she does not love the young man—he has not been worthy of her.'

'Yes, I know; thanks very much.'

'I thought I did right to tell you.'

'Ever so many thanks.'

'What's that?' asked Tibby. No one told him, and he proceeded into the dining-room, to eat Elvas plums.

That evening Margaret took decisive action. The house was very quiet, and the fog—we are in November now—pressed against the windows like an excluded ghost. Frieda and Helen and all their luggages had gone. Tibby, who was not feeling well, lay stretched on a sofa by the fire. Margaret sat by him, thinking. Her mind darted from impulse to impulse, and finally marshalled them all in review. The practical person, who knows what he wants at once, and generally knows nothing else, will excuse her of indecision. But this was the way her mind worked. And when she did act, no one could accuse her of indecision then. She hit out as lustily as if she had not considered the matter at all. The letter that she wrote Mrs Wilcox glowed with the native hue of resolution. The pale cast of thought was with her a breath rather than a tarnish, a breath that leaves the colours all the more vivid when it has been wiped away.

> Dear Mrs Wilcox,
>   I have to write something discourteous. It would be better if we did not meet. Both my sister and my aunt have given displeasure to your family, and, in my sister's case, the grounds for displeasure might recur. As far as I know, she no longer occupies her thoughts with your son. But it would not be fair, either to her or to you, if they met, and it is therefore right that our acquaintance, which began so pleasantly, should end.
>   I fear that you will not agree with this; indeed, I know that you will not, since you have been good enough to call on us. It is only an instinct on my part, and no doubt the instinct is wrong. My sister would, undoubtedly, say that it is wrong. I write without her knowledge, and I hope that you will not associate her with my discourtesy.
>
>   Believe me,
>   Yours truly,
>   M. J. Schlegel.

Margaret sent this letter round by the post. Next morning she received the following reply by hand:

> Dear Miss Schlegel,
>   You should not have written me such a letter. I called to tell you that Paul has gone abroad.
>
>   Ruth Wilcox.

Margaret's cheeks burnt. She could not finish her breakfast. She was on fire with shame. Helen had told her that the youth was leaving England, but other things had seemed more important, and she had forgotten. All her absurd anxieties fell to the ground, and in their place arose the certainty that she had been rude to Mrs Wilcox. Rudeness affected Margaret like a bitter taste in the mouth. It poisoned life. At times it is necessary, but woe to those who employ it without due need. She flung on a hat and shawl, just like a poor woman, and plunged into the fog, which still continued. Her lips were compressed, the letter remained in her hand, and in this state she crossed the street, entered the marble vestibule of the flats, eluded the concierges, and ran up the stairs till she reached the second-floor.

She sent in her name, and to her surprise was shown straight into Mrs Wilcox's bedroom.

'Oh, Mrs Wilcox, I have made the baddest blunder. I am more, more ashamed and sorry than I can say.'

Mrs Wilcox bowed gravely. She was offended, and did not pretend to the contrary. She was sitting up in bed, writing letters on an invalid table that spanned her knees. A breakfast tray was on another table beside her. The light of the fire, the light from the window, and the light of a candle-lamp, which threw a quivering halo round her hands, combined to create a strange atmosphere of dissolution.

'I knew he was going to India in November, but I forgot.'

'He sailed on the 17th for Nigeria, in Africa.'

'I knew—I know. I have been too absurd all through. I am very much ashamed.'

Mrs Wilcox did not answer.

'I am more sorry than I can say, and I hope that you will forgive me.'

'It doesn't matter, Miss Schlegel. It is good of you to have come round so promptly.'

'It does matter,' cried Margaret. 'I have been rude to you; and my sister is not even at home, so there was not even that excuse.'

'Indeed?'

'She has just gone to Germany.'

'She gone as well,' murmured the other. 'Yes, certainly, it is quite safe—safe, absolutely, now.'

'You've been worrying too!' exclaimed Margaret, getting more and more excited, and taking a chair without invitation. 'How perfectly extraordinary! I can see that you have. You felt as I do; Helen mustn't meet him again.'

'I did think it best.'

'Now why?'

'That's a most difficult question,' said Mrs Wilcox, smiling, and a little losing her expression of annoyance. 'I think you put it best in your letter—it was an instinct, which may be wrong.'

'It wasn't that your son still—'

'Oh no; he often—my Paul is very young, you see.'

'Then what was it?'

She repeated: 'An instinct which may be wrong.'

'In other words, they belong to types that can fall in love, but couldn't live together. That's dreadfully probable. I'm afraid that in nine cases out of ten Nature pulls one way and human nature another.'

'These are indeed "other words,"' said Mrs Wilcox. 'I had nothing so coherent in my head. I was merely alarmed when I knew that my boy cared for your sister.'

'Ah, I have always been wanting to ask you. How *did* you know? Helen was so surprised when our aunt drove up, and you stepped forward and arranged things. Did Paul tell you?'

'There is nothing to be gained by discussing that,' said Mrs Wilcox after a moment's pause.

'Mrs Wilcox, were you very angry with us last June? I wrote you a letter and you didn't answer it.'

'I was certainly against taking Mrs Matheson's flat. I knew it was opposite your house.'

'But it's all right now?'

'I think so.'

'You only think? You aren't sure? I do love these little muddles tidied up?'

'Oh yes, I'm sure,' said Mrs Wilcox, moving with uneasiness beneath the clothes. 'I always sound uncertain over things. It is my way of speaking.'

'That's all right, and I'm sure too.'

Here the maid came in to remove the breakfast-tray. They were interrupted, and when they resumed conversation it was on more normal lines.

'I must say good-bye now—you will be getting up.'

'No—please stop a little longer—I am taking a day in bed. Now and then I do.'

'I thought of you as one of the early risers.'

'At Howards End—yes; there is nothing to get up for in London.'

'Nothing to get up for?' cried the scandalized Margaret. 'When there are all the autumn exhibitions, and Ysaye playing in the afternoon! Not to mention people.'

'The truth is, I am a little tired. First came the wedding, and then Paul went off, and, instead of resting yesterday, I paid a round of calls.'

'A wedding?'

'Yes; Charles, my elder son, is married.'

'Indeed!'

'We took the flat chiefly on that account, and also that Paul could get his African outfit. The flat belongs to a cousin of my husband's, and she most kindly offered it to us. So before the day came we were able to make the acquaintance of Dolly's people, which we had not yet done.'

Margaret asked who Dolly's people were.

'Fussell. The father is in the Indian army—retired; the brother is in the army. The mother is dead.'

So perhaps these were the 'chinless sunburnt men' whom Helen had espied one afternoon through the window. Margaret felt mildly interested in the fortunes of the Wilcox family. She had acquired the habit on Helen's account, and it still clung to her. She asked for more information about Miss Dolly Fussell that was, and was given it in even, unemotional tones. Mrs Wilcox's voice, though sweet and compelling, had little range of expression. It suggested that pictures, concerts, and people are all of small and equal value. Only once had it quickened—when speaking of Howards End.

'Charles and Albert Fussell have known one another some time. They belong to the same club, and are both devoted to golf. Dolly plays golf too, though I believe not so well, and they first met in a mixed foursome. We all like her, and are very much pleased. They were married on the 11th, a few days before Paul sailed. Charles was very anxious to have his brother as best man, so he made a great point of having it on the 11th. The Fussells would have preferred it after Christmas, but they were very nice about it. There is Dolly's photograph—in that double frame.'

'Are you quite certain that I'm not interrupting, Mrs Wilcox?'

'Yes, quite.'

'Then I will stay. I'm enjoying this.'

Dolly's photograph was now examined. It was signed 'For dear Mims,' which Mrs Wilcox interpreted as 'the name she and Charles had settled that she should call me.' Dolly looked silly, and had one of those triangular faces that so often prove attractive to a robust man. She was very pretty. From her Margaret passed to Charles, whose features prevailed opposite. She speculated on the forces that had drawn the two together till God parted them. She found time to hope that they would be happy.

'They have gone to Naples for their honeymoon.'

'Lucky people!'

'I can hardly imagine Charles in Italy.'

'Doesn't he care for travelling?'

'He likes travel, but he does see through foreigners so. What he enjoys most is a motor tour in England, and I think that would have carried the day if the weather had not been so abominable. His father gave him a car of his own for a wedding present, which for the present is being stored at Howards End.'

'I suppose you have a garage there?'

'Yes. My husband built a little one only last month, to the west of the house, not far from the wych-elm, in what used to be the paddock for the pony.'

The last words had an indescribable ring about them.

'Where's the pony gone?' asked Margaret after a pause.

'The pony? Oh, dead, ever so long ago.'

'The wych-elm I remember. Helen spoke of it as a very splendid tree.'

'It is the finest wych-elm in Hertfordshire. Did your sister tell you about the teeth?'

'No.'

'Oh, it might interest you. There are pigs' teeth stuck into the trunk, about four feet from the ground. The country people put them in long ago, and they think that if they chew a piece of the bark, it will cure the toothache. The teeth are almost grown over now, and no one comes to the tree.'

'I should. I love folklore and all festering superstitions.'

'Do you think that the tree really did cure toothache, if one believed in it?'

'Of course it did. It would cure anything—once.'

'Certainly I remember cases—you see I lived at Howards End long, long before Mr Wilcox knew it. I was born there.'

The conversation again shifted. At the time it seemed little more than aimless chatter. She was interested when her hostess explained that Howards End was her own property. She was bored when too minute an account was given of the Fussell family, of the anxieties of Charles concerning Naples, of the movements of Mr Wilcox and Evie, who were motoring in Yorkshire. Margaret could not bear being bored. She grew inattentive, played with the photograph frame, dropped it, smashed Dolly's glass, apologized, was pardoned, cut her finger thereon, was pitied, and finally said she must be going—there was all the housekeeping to do, and she had to interview Tibby's riding-master.

Then the curious note was struck again.

'Good-bye, Miss Schlegel, good-bye. Thank you for coming. You have cheered me up.'

'I'm so glad!'

'I—I wonder whether you ever think about yourself?'

'I think of nothing else,' said Margaret, blushing, but letting her hand remain in that of the invalid.

'I wonder. I wondered at Heidelberg.'

'*I'm* sure!'

'I almost think—'

'Yes?' asked Margaret, for there was a long pause—a pause that was somehow akin to the flicker of the fire, the quiver of the reading-lamp upon their hands, the white blur from the window; a pause of shifting and eternal shadows.

'I almost think you forget you're a girl.'

Margaret was startled and a little annoyed. 'I'm twenty-nine,' she remarked. 'That's not so wildly girlish.'

Mrs Wilcox smiled.

'What makes you say that? Do you mean that I have been gauche and rude?'

A shake of the head. 'I only meant that I am fifty-one, and that to me, both of you— Read it all in some book or other; I cannot put things clearly.'

'Oh, I've got it—inexperience. I'm no better than Helen, you mean, and yet I presume to advise her.'

'Yes. You have got it. Inexperience is the word.'

'Inexperience,' repeated Margaret, in serious yet buoyant tones. 'Of course, I have everything to learn—absolutely everything—just as much as Helen. Life's very difficult and full of surprises. At all events, I've got as far as that. To be humble and kind, to go straight ahead, to love people rather than pity them, to remember the submerged—well, one can't do all these things at once, worse luck, because they're so contradictory. It's then that proportion comes in—to live by proportion. Don't *begin* with proportion. Only prigs do that. Let proportion come in as a last resource, when the better things have failed, and a deadlock— Gracious me, I've started preaching!'

'Indeed, you put the difficulties of life splendidly,' said Mrs Wilcox, withdrawing her hand into the deeper shadows. 'It is just what I should have liked to say about them myself.'

Chapter Nine

Mrs Wilcox cannot be accused of giving Margaret much information about life. And Margaret, on the other hand, has made a fair show of modesty, and has pretended to an inexperience that she certainly did not feel. She had kept house for over ten years; she had entertained, almost with distinction; she had brought up a charming sister, and was bringing up a brother. Surely, if experience is attainable, she had attained it.

Yet the little luncheon-party that she gave in Mrs Wilcox's honour was not a success. The new friend did not blend with the 'one or two delightful people' who had been asked to meet her, and the atmosphere was one of polite bewilderment. Her tastes were simple, her knowledge of culture slight, and she was not interested in the New English Art Club, nor in the dividing-line between Journalism and Literature, which was started as a conversational hare. The delightful people darted after it with cries of joy, Margaret leading them, and not till the meal was half over did they realize that the principal guest had taken no part in the chase. There was no common topic. Mrs Wilcox, whose life had been spent in the service of husband and sons, had little to say to strangers who had never shared it, and whose age was half her own. Clever talk alarmed her, and withered her delicate imaginings; it was the social counterpart of a motor-car, all jerks, and she was a wisp of hay, a flower. Twice she deplored the weather, twice criticized the train service on the Great Northern Railway. They vigorously assented, and rushed on, and when she inquired whether there was any news of Helen, her hostess was too much occupied in placing Rothenstein to answer. The question was repeated: 'I hope that your sister is safe in Germany by now.' Margaret checked herself and said 'Yes, thank you; I heard on Tuesday.' But the demon of vociferation was in her, and the next moment she was off again.

'Only on Tuesday, for they live right away at Stettin. Did you ever know anyone living at Stettin?'

'Never,' said Mrs Wilcox gravely, while her neighbour, a young man low down in the Education Office, began to discuss what people who lived at Stettin ought to look like. Was there such a thing as Stettininity? Margaret swept on.

'People at Stettin drop things into boats out of overhanging warehouses. At least, our cousins do, but aren't particularly rich. The town isn't interesting, except for a clock that rolls its eyes, and the view of the Oder,

which truly is something special. Oh, Mrs Wilcox, you would love the Oder!
The river, or rather rivers—there seem to be dozens of them—are intense
blue, and the plain they run through an intensest green.'

'Indeed! That sounds like a most beautiful view, Miss Schlegel.'

'So I say, but Helen, who will muddle things, says no, it's like music. The
course of the Oder is to be like music. It's obliged to remind her of a
symphonic poem. The part by the landing-stage is in B minor, if I remember
rightly, but lower down things get extremely mixed. There is a slodgy theme
in several keys at once, meaning mud-banks, and another for the navigable
canal, and the exit into the Baltic is in C sharp major, pianissimo.'

'What do the overhanging warehouses make of that?' asked the man,
laughing.

'They make a great deal of it,' replied Margaret, unexpectedly rushing off
on a new track. 'I think it's affectation to compare the Oder to music, and so
do you, but the overhanging warehouses of Stettin take beauty seriously,
which we don't, and the average Englishman doesn't, and despises all who
do. Now don't say "Germans have no taste," or I shall scream. They
haven't. But—but—such a tremendous but!—they take poetry seriously.
They do take poetry seriously.'

'Is anything gained by that?'

'Yes, yes. The German is always on the lookout for beauty. He may miss it
through stupidity, or misinterpret it, but he is always asking beauty to enter
his life, and I believe that in the end it will come. At Heidelberg I met a fat
veterinary surgeon whose voice broke with sobs as he repeated some
mawkish poetry. So easy for me to laugh—I, who never repeat poetry, good
or bad, and cannot remember one fragment of verse to thrill myself with. My
blood boils—well, I'm half German, so put it down to patriotism—when I
listen to the tasteful contempt of the average islander for things Teutonic,
whether they're Böcklin or my veterinary surgeon. "Oh, Böcklin," they say;
"he strains after beauty, he peoples Nature with gods too consciously." Of
course Böcklin strains, because he wants something—beauty and all the
other intangible gifts that are floating about the world. So his landscapes
don't come off, and Leader's do.'

'I am not sure that I agree. Do you?' said he, turning to Mrs Wilcox.

She replied: 'I think Miss Schlegel puts everything splendidly'; and a chill
fell on the conversation.

'Oh, Mrs Wilcox, say something nicer than that. It's such a snub to be told
you put things splendidly.'

'I do not mean it as a snub. Your last speech interested me so much.
Generally people do not seem quite to like Germany. I have long wanted to
hear what is said on the other side.'

'The other side? Then you do disagree. Oh, good! Give us your side.'

'I have no side. But my husband'—her voice softened, the chill
increased—'has very little faith in the Continent, and our children have all
taken after him.'

'On what grounds? Do they feel that the Continent is in bad form?'

Mrs Wilcox had no idea; she paid little attention to grounds. She was not intellectual, nor even alert, and it was odd that, all the same, she should give the idea of greatness. Margaret, zig-zagging with her friends over Thought and Art, was conscious of a personality that transcended their own and dwarfed their activities. There was no bitterness in Mrs Wilcox; there was not even criticism; she was lovable, and no ungracious or uncharitable word had passed her lips. Yet she and daily life were out of focus: one or the other must show blurred. And at lunch she seemed more out of focus than usual, and nearer the line that divides daily life from a life that may be of greater importance.

'You will admit, though, that the Continent—it seems silly to speak of "the Continent," but really it is all more like itself than any part of it is like England. England is unique. Do have another jelly first. I was going to say that the Continent, for good or for evil, is interested in ideas. Its Literature and Art have what one might call the kink of the unseen about them, and this persists even through decadence and affectation. There is more liberty of action in England, but for liberty of thought go to bureaucratic Prussia. People will there discuss with humility vital questions that we here think ourselves too good to touch with tongs.

'I do not want to go to Prussia,' said Mrs Wilcox—'not even to see that interesting view that you were describing. And for discussing with humility I am too old. We never discuss anything at Howards End.'

'Then you ought to!' said Margaret. 'Discussion keeps a house alive. It cannot stand by bricks and mortar alone.'

'It cannot stand without them,' said Mrs Wilcox, unexpectedly catching on to the thought, and rousing, for the first and last time, a faint hope in the breasts of the delightful people. 'It cannot stand without them, and I sometimes think— But I cannot expect your generation to agree, for even my daughter disagrees with me here.'

'Never mind us or her. Do say!'

'I sometimes think that it is wiser to leave action and discussion to men.'

There was a little silence.

'One admits that the arguments against the suffrage *are* extraordinarily strong,' said a girl opposite, leaning forward and crumbling her bread.

'Are they? I never follow any arguments. I am only too thankful not to have a vote myself.'

'We didn't mean the vote, though, did we?' supplied Margaret. 'Aren't we differing on something much wider, Mrs Wilcox? Whether women are to remain what they have been since the dawn of history; or whether, since men have moved forward so far, they too may move forward a little now. I say they may. I would even admit a biological change.'

'I don't know, I don't know.'

'I must be getting back to my overhanging warehouse,' said the man. 'They've turned disgracefully strict.'

Mrs Wilcox also rose.

'Oh, but come upstairs for a little. Miss Quested plays. Do you like MacDowell? Do you mind him only having two noises? If you must really go, I'll see you out. Won't you even have coffee?'

They left the dining-room, closing the door behind them, and as Mrs Wilcox buttoned up her jacket, she said: 'What an interesting life you all lead in London!'

'No, we don't,' said Margaret, with a sudden revulsion. 'We lead the lives of gibbering monkeys. Mrs Wilcox—really—— We have something quiet and stable at the bottom. We really have. All my friends have. Don't pretend you enjoyed lunch, for you loathed it, but forgive me by coming again, alone, or by asking me to you.'

'I am used to young people,' said Mrs Wilcox, and with each word she spoke the outlines of known things grew dim. 'I hear a great deal of chatter at home, for we, like you, entertain a great deal. With us it is more sport and politics, but—I enjoyed my lunch very much, Miss Schlegel, dear, and am not pretending, and only wish I could have joined in more. For one thing, I'm not particularly well just to-day. For another, you younger people move so quickly that it dazes me. Charles is the same, Dolly the same. But we are all in the same boat, old and young. I never forget that.'

They were silent for a moment. Then, with a newborn emotion, they shook hands. The conversation ceased suddenly when Margaret re-entered the dining-room: her friends had been talking over her new friend, and had dismissed her as uninteresting.

Chapter Ten

Several days passed.

Was Mrs Wilcox one of the unsatisfactory people—there are many of them—who dangle intimacy and then withdraw it? They evoke our interests and affections, and keep the life of the spirit dawdling round them. Then they withdraw. When physical passion is involved, there is a definite name for such behaviour—flirting—and if carried far enough it is punishable by law. But no law—not public opinion even—punishes those who coquette with friendship, though the dull ache that they inflict, the sense of misdirected effort and exhaustion, may be as intolerable. Was she one of these?

Margaret feared so at first, for, with a Londoner's impatience, she wanted everything to be settled up immediately. She mistrusted the periods of quiet that are essential to true growth. Desiring to book Mrs Wilcox as a friend, she pressed on the ceremony, pencil, as it were, in hand, pressing the more because the rest of the family were away, and the opportunity seemed favourable. But the elder woman would not be hurried. She refused to fit in with the Wickham Place set, or to reopen discussion of Helen and Paul, whom Margaret would have utilized as a short-cut. She took her time, or perhaps let time take her, and when the crisis did come all was ready.

The crisis opened with a message: would Miss Schlegel come shopping? Christmas was nearing, and Mrs Wilcox felt behind-hand with the presents.

She had taken some more days in bed, and must make up for lost time. Margaret accepted, and at eleven o'clock one cheerless morning they started out in a brougham.

'First of all,' began Margaret, 'we must make a list and tick off the people's names. My aunt always does, and this fog may thicken up any moment. Have you any ideas?'

'I thought we would go to Harrod's or the Haymarket Stores,' said Mrs Wilcox rather hopelessly. 'Everything is sure to be there. I am not a good shopper. The din is so confusing, and your aunt is quite right—one ought to make a list. Take my note-book, then, and write your own name at the top of the page.'

'Oh, hooray!' said Margaret, writing it. 'How very kind of you to start with me!' But she did not want to receive anything expensive. Their acquaintance was singular rather than intimate, and she divined that the Wilcox clan would resent any expenditure on outsiders; the more compact families do. She did not want to be thought a second Helen, who would snatch presents since she could not snatch young men, nor to be exposed, like a second Aunt Juley, to the insults of Charles. A certain austerity of demeanour was best, and she added: 'I don't really want a Yuletide gift, though. In fact, I'd rather not.'

'Why?'

'Because I've odd ideas about Christmas. Because I have all that money can buy. I want more people, but no more things.'

'I should like to give you something worth your acquaintance, Miss Schlegel, in memory of your kindness to me during my lonely fortnight. It has so happened that I have been left alone, and you have stopped me from brooding. I am too apt to brood.'

'If that is so,' said Margaret, 'if I have happened to be of use to you, which I didn't know, you cannot pay me back with anything tangible.'

'I suppose not, but one would like to. Perhaps I shall think of something as we go about.'

Her name remained at the head of the list, but nothing was written opposite it. They drove from shop to shop. The air was white, and when they alighted it tasted like cold pennies. At times they passed through a clot of grey. Mrs Wilcox's vitality was low that morning, and it was Margaret who decided on a horse for this little girl, a golliwog for that, for the rector's wife a copper warming-tray. 'We always give the servants money.' 'Yes, do you, yes, much easier,' replied Margaret, but felt the grotesque impact of the unseen upon the seen, and saw issuing from a forgotten manger at Bethlehem this torrent of coins and toys. Vulgarity reigned. Public-houses, besides their usual exhortation against temperance reform, invited men to 'Join our Christmas goose club'—one bottle of gin, etc., or two, according to subscription. A poster of a woman in tights heralded the Christmas pantomime, and little red devils, who had come in again that year, were prevalent upon the Christmas-cards. Margaret was no morbid idealist. She did not wish this spate of business and self-advertisement checked. It was only the occasion of it that struck her with amazement annually. How many of these vacillating shoppers and tired shop-assistants realized that it was a divine event that drew them together? She realized it, though standing outside in the matter. She was not a Christian in the accepted sense; she did not believe that God had ever worked among us as a young artisan. These people, or most of them, believed it, and if pressed, would affirm it in words. But the visible signs of their belief were Regent Street or Drury Lane, a little mud displaced, a little money spent, a little food cooked, eaten, and forgotten. Inadequate. But in public who shall express the unseen adequately? It is private life that holds out the mirror to infinity; personal intercourse, and that alone, that ever hints at a personality beyond our daily vision.

'No, I do like Christmas on the whole,' she announced. 'In its clumsy way, it does approach Peace and Goodwill. But oh, it is clumsier every year.'

'Is it? I am only used to country Christmases.'

'We are usually in London, and play the game with vigour—carols at the Abbey, clumsy midday meal, clumsy dinner for the maids, followed by Christmas-tree and dancing of poor children, with songs from Helen. The drawing-room does very well for that. We put the tree in the powder-closet, and draw a curtain when the candles are lighted, and with the looking-glass behind it looks quite pretty. I wish we might have a powder-closet in our next house. Of course, the tree has to be very small, and the presents don't hang on it. No; the presents reside in a sort of rocky landscape made of crumpled brown paper.'

'You spoke of your "next house," Miss Schlegel. Then are you leaving Wickham Place?'

'Yes, in two or three years, when the lease expires. We must.'

'Have you been there long?'

'All our lives.'

'You will be very sorry to leave it.'

'I suppose so. We scarcely realize it yet. My father— She broke off, for they had reached the stationery department of the Haymarket Stores, and Mrs Wilcox wanted to order some private greeting cards.

'If possible, something distinctive,' she sighed. At the counter she found a friend, bent on the same errand, and conversed with her insipidly, wasting much time. 'My husband and our daughter are motoring.' 'Bertha too? Oh, fancy, what a coincidence!' Margaret, though not practical, could shine in such company as this. While they talked, she went through a volume of specimen cards, and submitted one for Mrs Wilcox's inspection. Mrs Wilcox was delighted—so original, words so sweet; she would order a hundred like that, and could never be sufficiently grateful. Then, just as the assistant was booking the order, she said: 'Do you know, I'll wait. On second thoughts, I'll wait. There's plenty of time still, isn't there, and I shall be able to get Evie's opinion.'

They returned to the carriage by devious paths; when they were in, she said, 'But couldn't you get it renewed?'

'I beg your pardon?' asked Margaret.

'The lease, I mean.'

'Oh, the lease! Have you been thinking of that all the time? How very kind of you!'

'Surely something could be done.'

'No; values have risen too enormously. They mean to pull down Wickham Place, and build flats like yours.'

'But how horrible!'

'Landlords are horrible.'

Then she said vehemently: 'It is monstrous, Miss Schlegel; it isn't right. I had no idea that this was hanging over you. I do pity you from the bottom of my heart. To be parted from your house, your father's house–it oughtn't to be allowed. It is worse than dying. I would rather die than— Oh, poor girls! Can what they call civilization be right, if people mayn't die in the room where they were born? My dear, I am so sorry—'

Margaret did not know what to say. Mrs Wilcox had been overtired by the shopping, and was inclined to hysteria.

'Howards End was nearly pulled down once. It would have killed me.'

'Howards End must be a very different house to ours. We are fond of ours, but there is nothing distinctive about it. As you saw, it is an ordinary London house. We shall easily find another.'

'So you think.'

'Again my lack of experience, I suppose!' said Margaret, easing away from the subject. 'I can't say anything when you take up that line, Mrs Wilcox. I wish I could see myself as you see me–foreshortened into a backfisch. Quite the ingénue. Very charming–wonderfully well read for my age, but incapable—'

Mrs Wilcox would not be deterred. 'Come down with me to Howards End now,' she said, more vehemently than ever. 'I want you to see it. You have never seen it. I want to hear what you say about it, for you do put things so wonderfully.'

Margaret glanced at the pitiless air and then at the tired face of her companion. 'Later on I should love it,' she continued, 'but it's hardly the weather for such an expedition, and we ought to start when we're fresh. Isn't the house shut up, too?'

She received no answer. Mrs Wilcox appeared to be annoyed.

'Might I come some other day?'

Mrs Wilcox bent forward and tapped the glass. 'Back to Wickham Place, please!' was her order to the coachman. Margaret had been snubbed.

'A thousand thanks, Miss Schlegel, for all your help.'

'Not at all.'

'It is such a comfort to get the presents off my mind–the Christmas-cards especially. I do admire your choice.'

It was her turn to receive no answer. In her turn Margaret became annoyed.

'My husband and Evie will be back the day after to-morrow. That is why I dragged you out shopping to-day. I stayed in town chiefly to shop, but got through nothing, and now he writes that they must cut their tour short, the weather is so bad, and the police-traps have been so bad–nearly as bad as in

Surrey. Ours is such a careful chauffeur, and my husband feels it particularly hard that they should be treated like road-hogs.'

'Why?'

'Well, naturally he—he isn't a road-hog.'

'He was exceeding the speed-limit, I conclude. He must expect to suffer with the lower animals.'

Mrs Wilcox was silenced. In growing discomfort they drove homewards. The city seemed Satanic, the narrower streets oppressing like the galleries of a mine. No harm was done by the fog to trade, for it lay high, and the lighted windows of the shops were thronged with customers. It was rather a darkening of the spirit which fell back upon itself, to find a more grievous darkness within. Margaret nearly spoke a dozen times, but something throttled her. She felt petty and awkward, and her meditations on Christmas grew more cynical. Peace? It may bring other gifts, but is there a single Londoner to whom Christmas is peaceful? The craving for excitement and for elaboration has ruined that blessing. Goodwill? Had she seen any example of it in the hordes of purchasers? Or in herself? She had failed to respond to this investigation merely because it was a little queer and imaginative—she, whose birthright it was to nourish imagination! Better to have accepted, to have tired themselves a little by the journey, than coldly to reply, 'Might I come some other day?' Her cynicism left her. There would be no other day. This shadowy woman would never ask her again.

They parted at the Mansions. Mrs Wilcox went in after due civilities, and Margaret watched the tall, lonely figure sweep up the hall to the lift. As the glass doors closed on it she had the sense of an imprisonment. The beautiful head disappeared first, still buried in the muff; the long trailing skirt followed. A woman of undefinable rarity was going up heavenward, like a specimen in a bottle. And into what a heaven—a vault as of hell, sooty black, from which soots descended!

At lunch her brother, seeing her inclined for silence, insisted on talking. Tibby was not ill-natured, but from babyhood something drove him to do the unwelcome and the unexpected. Now he gave her a long account of the day-school that he sometimes patronized. The account was interesting, and she had often pressed him for it before, but she could not attend now, for her mind was focussed on the invisible. She discerned that Mrs Wilcox, though a loving wife and mother, had only one passion in life—her house—and that the moment was solemn when she invited a friend to share this passion with her. To answer 'another day' was to answer as a fool. 'Another day' will do for brick and mortar, but not for the Holy of Holies into which Howards End had been transfigured. Her own curiosity was slight. She had heard more than enough about it in the summer. The nine windows, the vine, and the wych-elm had no pleasant connections for her, and she would have preferred to spend the afternoon at a concert. But imagination triumphed. While her brother held forth she determined to go, at whatever cost, and to compel Mrs Wilcox to go, too. When lunch was over she stepped over to the flats.

Mrs Wilcox had just gone away for the night.

Margaret said that it was of no consequence, hurried downstairs, and took a hansom to King's Cross. She was convinced that the escapade was important, though it would have puzzled her to say why. There was question of imprisonment and escape, and though she did not know the time of the train, she strained her eyes for St Pancras' clock.

Then the clock of King's Cross swung into sight, a second moon in that infernal sky, and her cab drew up at the station. There was a train for Hilton in five minutes. She took a ticket, asking in her agitation for a single. As she did so, a grave and happy voice saluted her and thanked her.

'I will come if I still may,' said Margaret, laughing nervously.

'You are coming to sleep, dear, too. It is in the morning that my house is most beautiful. You are coming to stop. I cannot show you my meadow properly except at sunrise. These fogs'–she pointed at the station roof–'never spread far. I dare say they are sitting in the sun in Hertfordshire, and you will never repent joining them.'

'I shall never repent joining you.'

'It is the same.'

They began the walk up the long platform. Far at its end stood the train, breasting the darkness without. They never reached it. Before imagination could triumph, there were cries of 'Mother! mother!' and a heavy-browed girl darted out of the cloak-room and seized Mrs Wilcox by the arm.

'Evie!' she gasped–'Evie, my pet—'

The girl called, 'Father! I say! look who's here.'

'Evie, dearest girl, why aren't you in Yorkshire?'

'No–motor smash–changed plans–father's coming.'

'Why, Ruth!' cried Mr Wilcox, joining them. 'What in the name of all that's wonderful are you doing here, Ruth?'

Mrs Wilcox had recovered herself.

'Oh, Henry dear!–here's a lovely surprise–but let me introduce–but I think you know Miss Schlegel.'

'Oh yes,' he replied, not greatly interested. 'But how's yourself, Ruth?'

'Fit as a fiddle,' she answered gaily.

'So are we, and so was our car, which ran A1 as far as Ripon, but there a wretched horse and cart which a fool of a driver—'

'Miss Schlegel, our little outing must be for another day.'

'I was saying that this fool of a driver, as the policeman himself admits—'

'Another day, Mrs Wilcox. Of course.'

'—But as we've insured against third party risks, it won't so much matter—'

'—Cart and car being practically at right angles—'

The voice of the happy family rose high. Margaret was left alone. No one wanted her. Mrs Wilcox walked out of King's Cross between her husband and her daughter, listening to both of them.

Chapter Eleven

The funeral was over. The carriages had rolled away through the soft mud,
and only the poor remained. They approached to the newly-dug shaft and
looked their last at the coffin, now almost hidden beneath the spadefuls of
clay. It was their moment. Most of them were women from the dead
woman's district, to whom black garments had been served out by Mr
Wilcox's orders. Pure curiosity had brought others. They thrilled with the
excitement of a death, and of a rapid death, and stood in groups or moved
between the graves, like drops of ink. The son of one of them, a wood-cutter,
was perched high above their heads, pollarding one of the churchyard elms.
From where he sat he could see the village of Hilton, strung upon the North
Road, with its accreting suburbs; the sunset beyond, scarlet and orange,
winking at him beneath brows of grey; the church; the plantations; and
behind him an unspoilt country of fields and farms. But he, too, was rolling
the event luxuriously in his mouth. He tried to tell his mother down below
all that he had felt when he saw the coffin approaching: how he could not
leave his work, and yet did not like to go on with it; how he had almost
slipped out of the tree, he was so upset; the rooks had cawed, and no
wonder—it was as if rooks knew too. His mother claimed the prophetic
power herself—she had seen a strange look about Mrs Wilcox for some time.
London had done the mischief, said others. She had been a kind lady; her
grandmother had been kind, too—a plainer person, but very kind. Ah, the
old sort was dying out! Mr Wilcox, he was a kind gentleman. They advanced
to the topic again and again, dully, but with exaltation. The funeral of a rich
person was to them what the funeral of Alcestis or Ophelia is to the educated.
It was Art; though remote from life, it enhanced life's values, and they
witnessed it avidly.

The grave-diggers, who had kept up an undercurrent of disapproval—
they disliked Charles; it was not a moment to speak of such things, but they
did not like Charles Wilcox—the grave-diggers finished their work and piled
up the wreaths and crosses above it. The sun set over Hilton: the grey brows
of the evening flushed a little, and were cleft with one scarlet frown.
Chattering sadly to each other, the mourners passed through the lych-gate
and traversed the chestnut avenues that led down to the village. The young
wood-cutter stayed a little longer, poised above the silence and swaying
rhythmically. At last the bough fell beneath his saw. With a grunt, he
descended, his thoughts dwelling no longer on death, but on love, for he was
mating. He stopped as he passed the new grave; a sheaf of tawny chrysan-

themums had caught his eye. 'They didn't ought to have coloured flowers at buryings,' he reflected. Trudging on a few steps, he stopped again, looked furtively at the dusk, turned back, wrenched a chrysanthemum from the sheaf, and hid it in his pocket.

After him came silence absolute. The cottage that abutted on the churchyard was empty, and no other house stood near. Hour after hour the scene of the interment remained without an eye to witness it. Clouds drifted over it from the west; or the church may have been a ship, high-prowed, steering with all its company towards infinity. Towards morning the air grew colder, the sky clearer, the surface of the earth hard and sparkling above the prostrate dead. The wood-cutter, returning after a night of joy, reflected: 'They lilies, they chrysants; it's a pity I didn't take them all.'

Up at Howards End they were attempting breakfast. Charles and Evie sat in the dining-room, with Mrs Charles. Their father, who could not bear to see a face, breakfasted upstairs. He suffered acutely. Pain came over him in spasms, as if it was physical, and even while he was about to eat, his eyes would fill with tears, and he would lay down the morsel untasted.

He remembered his wife's even goodness during thirty years. Not anything in detail—not courtship or early raptures—but just the unvarying virtue, that seemed to him a woman's noblest quality. So many women are capricious, breaking into odd flaws of passion or frivolity. Not so his wife. Year after year, summer and winter, as bride and mother, she had been the same, he had always trusted her. Her tenderness! Her innocence! The wonderful innocence that was hers by the gift of God. Ruth knew no more of worldly wickedness and wisdom than did the flowers in her garden, or the grass in her field. Her idea of business—'Henry, why do people who have enough money try to get more money?' Her idea of politics—'I am sure that if the mothers of various nations could meet, there would be no more wars.' Her idea of religion—ah, this had been a cloud, but a cloud that passed. She came of Quaker stock, and he and his family, formerly Dissenters, were now members of the Church of England. The rector's sermons had at first repelled her, and she had expressed a desire for 'a more inward light,' adding, 'not so much for myself as for baby' (Charles). Inward light must have been granted, for he heard no complaints in later years. They brought up their three children without dispute. They had never disputed.

She lay under the earth now. She had gone, and as if to make her going the more bitter, had gone with a touch of mystery that was all unlike her. 'Why didn't you tell me you knew of it?' he had moaned, and her faint voice had answered: 'I didn't want to, Henry—I might have been wrong—and everyone hates illnesses.' He had been told of the horror by a strange doctor, whom she had consulted during his absence from town. Was this altogether just? Without fully explaining, she had died. It was a fault on her part, and – tears rushed into his eyes—what a little fault! It was the only time she had deceived him in those thirty years.

He rose to his feet and looked out of the window, for Evie had come in with the letters, and he could meet no one's eye. Ah yes—she had been a good woman—she had been steady. He chose the word deliberately. To him steadiness included all praise.

He himself, gazing at the wintry garden, is in appearance a steady man. His face was not as square as his son's, and, indeed, the chin, though firm enough in outline, retreated a little, and the lips, ambiguous, were curtained by a moustache. But there was no external hint of weakness. The eyes, if capable of kindness and good-fellowship, if ruddy for the moment with tears, were the eyes of one who could not be driven. The forehead, too, was like Charles's. High and straight, brown and polished, merging abruptly into temples and skull, it had the effect of a bastion that protected his head from the world. At times it had the effect of a blank wall. He had dwelt behind it, intact and happy, for fifty years.

'The post's come, father,' said Evie awkwardly.

'Thanks. Put it down.'

'Has the breakfast been all right?'

'Yes, thanks.'

The girl glanced at him and at it with constraint. She did not know what to do.

'Charles says do you want the "Times"?'

'No, I'll read it later.'

'Ring if you want anything, father, won't you?'

'I've all I want.'

Having sorted the letters from the circulars, she went back to the dining-room.

'Father's eaten nothing,' she announced, sitting down with wrinkled brows behind the tea-urn.

Charles did not answer, but after a moment he ran quickly upstairs, opened the door, and said: 'Look here, father, you must eat, you know;' and having paused for a reply that did not come, stole down again. 'He's going to read his letters first, I think,' he said evasively; 'I dare say he will go on with his breakfast afterwards.' Then he took up the 'Times,' and for some time there was no sound except the clink of cup against saucer and of knife on plate.

Poor Mrs Charles sat between her silent companions, terrified at the course of events, and a little bored. She was a rubbishy little creature, and she knew it. A telegram had dragged her from Naples to the death-bed of a woman whom she had scarcely known. A word from her husband had plunged her into mourning. She desired to mourn inwardly as well, but she wished that Mrs Wilcox, since fated to die, could have died before the marriage, for then less would have been expected of her. Crumbling her toast, and too nervous to ask for the butter, she remained almost motionless, thankful only for this, that her father-in-law was having his breakfast upstairs.

At last Charles spoke. 'They had no business to be pollarding those elms yesterday,' he said to his sister.

'No indeed.'

'I must make a note of that,' he continued. 'I am surprised that the rector allowed it.'

'Perhaps it may not be the rector's affair.'

'Whose else could it be?'

'The lord of the manor.'

'Impossible.'

'Butter, Dolly?'

'Thank you, Evie dear. Charles—'

'Yes, dear?'

'I didn't know one could pollard elms. I thought one only pollarded willows.'

'Oh no, one can pollard elms.'

'Then why oughtn't the elms in the churchyard to be pollarded?' Charles frowned a little, and turned again to his sister.

'Another point. I must speak to Chalkeley.'

'Yes, rather; you must complain to Chalkeley.'

'It's no good him saying he is not responsible for those men. He is responsible.'

'Yes, rather.'

Brother and sister were not callous. They spoke thus, partly because they desired to keep Chalkeley up to the mark—a healthy desire in its way—partly because they avoided the personal note in life. All Wilcoxes did. It did not seem to them of supreme importance. Or it may be as Helen supposed: they realized its importance, but were afraid of it. Panic and emptiness, could one glance behind. They were not callous, and they left the breakfast-table with aching hearts. Their mother never had come in to breakfast. It was in the other rooms, and especially in the garden, that they felt her loss most. As Charles went out to the garage, he was reminded at every step of the woman who had loved him and whom he could never replace. What battles he had fought against her gentle conservatism! How she had disliked improvements, yet how loyally she had accepted them when made! He and his father—what trouble they had had to get this very garage! With what difficulty had they persuaded her to yield them the paddock for it—the paddock that she loved more dearly than the garden itself! The vine—she had got her way about the vine. It still encumbered the south wall with its unproductive branches. And so with Evie, as she stood talking to the cook. Though she could take up her mother's work inside the house, just as the man could take it up without, she felt that something unique had fallen out of her life. Their grief, though less poignant than their father's, grew from deeper roots, for a wife may be replaced; a mother never.

Charles would go back to the office. There was little to do at Howards End. The contents of his mother's will had been long known to them. There were no legacies, no annuities, none of the posthumous bustle with which some of the dead prolong their activities. Trusting her husband, she had left him everything without reserve. She was quite a poor woman—the house had been all her dowry, and the house would come to Charles in time. Her watercolours Mr Wilcox intended to reserve for Paul, while Evie would take the jewellery and lace. How easily she slipped out of life! Charles thought the habit laudable, though he did not intend to adopt it himself, whereas

Margaret would have seen in it an almost culpable indifference to earthly fame. Cynicism—not the superficial cynicism that snarls and sneers, but the cynicism that can go with courtesy and tenderness—that was the note of Mrs Wilcox's will. She wanted not to vex people. That accomplished, the earth might freeze over her for ever.

No, there was nothing for Charles to wait for. He could not go on with his honeymoon, so he would go up to London and work—he felt too miserable hanging about. He and Dolly would have the furnished flat while his father rested quietly in the country with Evie. He could also keep an eye on his own little house, which was being painted and decorated for him in one of the Surrey suburbs, and in which he hoped to instal himself soon after Christmas. Yes, he would go up after lunch in his new motor, and the town servants, who had come down for the funeral, would go up by train.

He found his father's chauffeur in the garage, said 'Morning' without looking at the man's face, and, bending over the car, continued: 'Hullo! my new car's been driven!'

'Has it, sir?'

'Yes,' said Charles, getting rather red; 'and whoever's driven it hasn't cleaned it properly, for there's mud on the axle. Take it off.'

The man went for the cloths without a word. He was a chauffeur as ugly as sin—not that this did him disservice with Charles, who thought charm in a man rather rot, and had soon got rid of the little Italian beast with whom they had started.

'Charles—' His bride was tripping after him over the hoar-frost, a dainty black column, her little face and elaborate mourning hat forming the capital thereof.

'One minute, I'm busy. Well, Crane, who's been driving it, do you suppose?'

'Don't know, I'm sure, sir. No one's driven it since I've been back, but, of course, there's the fortnight I've been away with the other car in Yorkshire.'

The mud came off easily.

'Charles, your father's down. Something's happened. He wants you in the house at once. Oh, Charles!'

'Wait, dear, wait a minute. Who had the key of the garage while you were away, Crane?'

'The gardener, sir.'

'Do you mean to tell me that old Penny can drive a motor?'

'No, sir; no one's had the motor out, sir.'

'Then how do you account for the mud on the axle?'

'I can't, of course, say for the time I've been in Yorkshire. No more mud now, sir.'

Charles was vexed. The man was treating him as a fool, and if his heart had not been so heavy he would have reported him to his father. But it was not a morning for complaints. Ordering the motor to be round after lunch, he joined his wife, who had all the while been pouring out some incoherent story about a letter and a Miss Schlegel.

'Now, Dolly, I can attend to you. Miss Schlegel? What does she want?'

When people wrote a letter Charles always asked what they wanted. Want was to him the only cause of action. And the question in this case was correct, for his wife replied, 'She wants Howards End.'

'Howards End? Now, Crane, just don't forget to put on the Stepney wheel.'

'No, sir.'

'Now, mind you don't forget, for I— Come, little woman.' When they were out of the chauffeur's sight he put his arm round her waist and pressed her against him. All his affection and half his attention–it was what he granted her throughout their happy married life.

'But you haven't listened, Charles—'

'What's wrong?'

'I keep on telling you–Howards End. Miss Schlegel's got it.'

'Got what?' said Charles, unclasping her. 'What the dickens are you talking about?'

'Now, Charles, you promised not to say those naughty—'

'Look here, I'm in no mood for foolery. It's no morning for it either.'

'I tell you–I keep on telling you–Miss Schlegel–she's got it–your mother's left it to her–and you've all got to move out!'

'*Howards End?*'

'*Howards End!*' she screamed, mimicking him, and as she did so Evie came dashing out of the shrubbery.

'Dolly, go back at once! My father's much annoyed with you. Charles'–she hit herself wildly–'come in at once to father. He's had a letter that's too awful.'

Charles began to run, but checked himself, and stepped heavily across the gravel path. There the house was–the nine windows, the unprolific vine. He exclaimed, 'Schlegels again!' and as if to complete chaos, Dolly said, 'Oh no, the matron of the nursing home has written instead of her.'

'Come in, all three of you!' cried his father, no longer inert. 'Dolly, why have you disobeyed me?'

'Oh, Mr Wilcox—'

'I told you not to go out to the garage. I've heard you all shouting in the garden. I won't have it. Come in.'

He stood in the porch, transformed, letters in his hand.

'Into the dining-room, every one of you. We can't discuss private matters in the middle of all the servants. Here, Charles, here; read these. See what you make.'

Charles took two letters, and read them as he followed the procession. The first was a covering note from the matron. Mrs Wilcox had desired her, when the funeral should be over to forward the enclosed. The enclosed–it was from his mother herself. She had written: 'To my husband: I should like Miss Schlegel (Margaret) to have Howards End.'

'I suppose we're going to have a talk about this?' he remarked, ominously calm.

'Certainly. I was coming out to you when Dolly—'

'Well, let's sit down.'

'Come, Evie, don't waste time, sit down.'

In silence they drew up to the breakfast-table. The events of yesterday—indeed, of this morning—suddenly receded into a past so remote that they seemed scarcely to have lived in it. Heavy breathings were heard. They were calming themselves. Charles, to steady them further, read the enclosure out loud: 'A note in my mother's handwriting, in an envelope addressed to my father, sealed. Inside: "I should like Miss Schlegel (Margaret) to have Howards End." No date, no signature. Forwarded through the matron of that nursing home. Now, the question is—'

Dolly interrupted him. 'But I say that note isn't legal. Houses ought to be done by a lawyer, Charles, surely.'

Her husband worked his jaw severely. Little lumps appeared in front of either ear—a sympton that she had not yet learnt to respect, and she asked whether she might see the note. Charles looked at his father for permission, who said abstractedly, 'Give it her.' She seized it, and at once exclaimed: 'Why, it's only in pencil! I said so. Pencil never counts.'

'We know that it is not legally binding, Dolly,' said Mr Wilcox, speaking from out of his fortress. 'We are aware of that. Legally, I should be justified in tearing it up and throwing it into the fire. Of course, my dear, we consider you as one of the family, but it will be better if you do not interfere with what you do not understand.'

Charles, vexed both with his father and his wife, then repeated: 'The question is—' He had cleared a space of the breakfast-table from plates and knives, so that he could draw patterns on the tablecloth. 'The question is whether Miss Schlegel, during the fortnight we were all away, whether she unduly—' He stopped.

'I don't think that,' said his father, whose nature was nobler than his son's.

'Don't think what?'

'That she would have—that it is a case of undue influence. No, to my mind the question is the—the invalid's condition at the time she wrote.'

'My dear father, consult an expert if you like, but I don't admit it is my mother's writing.'

'Why, you just said it was!' cried Dolly.

'Never mind if I did,' he blazed out; 'and hold your tongue.'

The poor little wife coloured at this, and, drawing her handkerchief from her pocket, shed a few tears. No one noticed her. Evie was scowling like an angry boy. The two men were gradually assuming the manner of the committee-room. They were both at their best when serving on committees. They did not make the mistake of handling human affairs in the bulk, but disposed of them item by item, sharply. Caligraphy was the item before them now, and on it they turned their well-trained brains. Charles, after a little demur, accepted the writing as genuine, and they passed on to the next point. It is the best—perhaps the only—way of dodging emotion. They were the average human article, and had they considered the note as a whole it would have driven them miserable or mad. Considered item by item, the emotional content was minimized, and all went forward smoothly. The clock ticked, the coals blazed higher, and contended with the white radiance that poured in through the windows. Unnoticed, the sun occupied his sky, and the shadows of the tree stems, extraordinarily solid, fell like trenches of purple across the frosted lawn. It was a glorious winter morning. Evie's fox terrier, who had passed for white, was only a dirty grey dog now, so intense was the purity that surrounded him. He was discredited, but thĕ blackbirds that he was chasing glowed with Arabian darkness, for all the conventional colouring of life had been altered. Inside, the clock struck ten with a rich and confident note. Other clocks confirmed it, and the discussion moved towards its close.

To follow it is unnecessary. It is rather a moment when the commentator should step forward. Ought the Wilcoxes to have offered their home to Margaret? I think not. The appeal was too flimsy. It was not legal; it had been written in illness, and under the spell of a sudden friendship; it was contrary to the dead woman's intentions in the past, contrary to her very nature, so far as that nature was understood by them. To them Howards End was a house: they could not know that to her it had been a spirit, for which she sought a spiritual heir. And—pushing one step farther in these mists—may they not have decided even better than they supposed? Is it credible that the possessions of the spirit can be bequeathed at all? Has the soul offspring? A wych-elm tree, a vine, a wisp of hay with dew on it—can passion for such things be transmitted where there is no bond of blood? No; the Wilcoxes are not to be blamed. The problem is too terrific, and they could not even perceive a problem. No; it is natural and fitting that after due debate they should tear the note up and throw it on to their dining-room fire. The practical moralist may acquit them absolutely. He who strives to look deeper may acquit them—almost. For one hard fact remains. They did neglect a personal appeal. The woman who had died did say to them, 'Do this,' and they answered, 'We will not.'

The incident made a most painful impression on them. Grief mounted into the brain and worked there disquietingly. Yesterday they had lamented: 'She was a dear mother, a true wife: in our absence she neglected her health and died.' To-day they thought: 'She was not as true, as dear, as we supposed.' The desire for a more inward light had found expression at last, the unseen had impacted on the seen, and all that they could say was 'Treachery.' Mrs Wilcox had been treacherous to the family, to the laws of property, to her own written word. How did she expect Howards End to be conveyed to Miss Schlegel? Was her husband, to whom it legally belonged, to make it over to her as a free gift? Was the said Miss Schlegel to have a life interest in it, or to own it absolutely? Was there to be no compensation for the garage and other improvements that they had made under the assumption that all would be theirs some day? Treacherous! treacherous and absurd! When we think the dead both treacherous and absurd, we have gone far towards reconciling ourselves to their departure. That note, scribbled in pencil, sent through the matron, was unbusinesslike as well as cruel, and decreased at once the value of the woman who had written it.

'Ah, well!' said Mr Wilcox, rising from the table. 'I shouldn't have thought it possible.'

'Mother couldn't have meant it,' said Evie, still frowning.

'No, my girl, of course not.'

'Mother believed so in ancestors too—it isn't like her to leave anything to an outsider, who'd never appreciate.'

'The whole thing is unlike her,' he announced. 'If Miss Schlegel had been poor, if she had wanted a house, I could understand it a little. But she has a house of her own. Why should she want another? She wouldn't have any use for Howards End.'

'That time may prove,' murmured Charles.

'How?' asked his sister.

'Presumably she knows—mother will have told her. She got twice or three times into the nursing home. Presumably she is awaiting developments.'

'What a horrid woman!' And Dolly, who had recovered, cried, 'Why, she may be coming down to turn us out now!'

Charles put her right. 'I wish she would,' he said ominously. 'I could then deal with her.'

'So could I,' echoed his father, who was feeling rather in the cold. Charles had been kind in undertaking the funeral arrangements and in telling him to eat his breakfast, but the boy as he grew up was a little dictatorial, and assumed the post of chairman too readily. 'I could deal with her, if she comes, but she won't come. You're all a bit hard on Miss Schlegel.'

'That Paul business was pretty scandalous, though.'

'I want no more of the Paul business, Charles, as I said at the time, and besides, it is quite apart from this business. Margaret Schlegel has been officious and tiresome during this terrible week, and we have all suffered under her, but upon my soul she's honest. She's *not* in collusion with the matron. I'm absolutely certain of it. Nor was she with the doctor, I'm equally certain of that. She did not hide anything from us, for up to that very afternoon she was as ignorant as we are. She, like ourselves, was a dupe—' He stopped for a moment. 'You see, Charles, in her terrible pain your poor mother put us all in false positions. Paul would not have left England, you would not have gone to Italy, nor Evie and I into Yorkshire, if only we had known. Well, Miss Schlegel's position has been equally false. Take all in all, she has not come out of it badly.'

Evie said: 'But those chrysanthemums—'

'Or coming down to the funeral at all—' echoed Dolly.

'Why shouldn't she come down? She had the right to, and she stood far back among the Hilton women. The flowers—certainly we should not have sent such flowers, but they may have seemed the right thing to her, Evie, and for all you know they may be the custom in Germany.'

'Oh, I forget she isn't really English,' cried Evie. 'That would explain a lot.'

'She's a cosmopolitan,' said Charles, looking at his watch. 'I admit I'm rather down on cosmopolitans. My fault, doubtless. I cannot stand them, and a German cosmopolitan is the limit. I think that's about all, isn't it? I want to run down and see Chalkeley. A bicycle will do. And, by the way, I wish you'd speak to Crane some time. I'm certain he's had my new car out.'

'Has he done it any harm?'

'No.'

'In that case I shall let it pass. It's not worth while having a row.'

Charles and his father sometimes disagreed. But they always parted with an increased regard for one another, and each desired no doughtier comrade when it was necessary to voyage for a little past the emotions. So the sailors of Ulysses voyaged past the Sirens, having first stopped one another's ears with wool.

Chapter Twelve

Charles need not have been anxious. Miss Schlegel had never heard of his mother's strange request. She was to hear of it in after years, when she had built up her life differently, and it was to fit into position as the headstone of the corner. Her mind was bent on other questions now, and by her also it would have been rejected as the fantasy of an invalid.

She was parting from these Wilcoxes for the second time. Paul and his mother, ripple and great wave, had flowed into her life and ebbed out of it for ever. The ripple had left no traces behind: the wave had strewn at her feet fragments torn from the unknown. A curious seeker, she stood for a while at the verge of the sea that tells so little, but tells a little, and watched the outgoing of this last tremendous tide. Her friend had vanished in agony, but not, she believed, in degradation. Her withdrawal had hinted at other things besides disease and pain. Some leave our life with tears, others with an insane frigidity; Mrs Wilcox had taken the middle course, which only rarer natures can pursue. She had kept proportion. She had told a little of her grim secret to her friends, but not too much; she had shut up her heart—almost, but not entirely. It is thus, if there is any rule, that we ought to die—neither as victim nor as fanatic, but as the seafarer who can greet with an equal eye the deep that he is entering, and the shore that he must leave.

The last word—whatever it would be—had certainly not been said in Hilton churchyard. She had not died there. A funeral is not death, any more than baptism is birth or marriage union. All three are the clumsy devices, coming now too late, now too early, by which Society would register the quick motions of man. In Margaret's eyes Mrs Wilcox had escaped registration. She had gone out of life vividly, her own way, and no dust was so truly dust as the contents of that heavy coffin, lowered with ceremonial until it rested on the dust of the earth, no flowers so utterly wasted as the chrysanthemums that the frost must have withered before morning. Margaret had once said she 'loved superstition.' It was not true. Few women had tried more earnestly to pierce the accretions in which body and soul are enwrapped. The death of Mrs Wilcox had helped her in her work. She saw a little more clearly than hitherto what a human being is, and to what he may aspire. Truer relationships gleamed. Perhaps the last word would be hope—hope even on this side of the grave.

Meanwhile, she could take an interest in the survivors. In spite of her Christmas duties, in spite of her brother, the Wilcoxes continued to play a considerable part in her thoughts. She had seen so much of them in the final week. They were not 'her sort,' they were often suspicious and stupid, and deficient where she excelled; but collision with them stimulated her, and she felt an interest that verged into liking, even for Charles. She desired to protect them, and often felt that they could protect her, excelling where she was deficient. Once past the rocks of emotion, they knew so well what to do, whom to send for; their hands were on all the ropes, they had grit as well as grittiness, and she valued grit enormously. They led a life that she could not attain to—the outer life of 'telegrams and anger,' which had detonated when Helen and Paul had touched in June, and had detonated again the other week. To Margaret this life was to remain a real force. She could not despise it, as Helen and Tibby affected to do. It fostered such virtues as neatness, decision, and obedience, virtues of the second rank, no doubt, but they have formed our civilization. They form character, too; Margaret could not doubt it: they keep the soul from becoming sloppy. How dare Schlegels despise Wilcoxes, when it takes all sorts to make a world?

'Don't brood too much,' she wrote to Helen, 'on the superiority of the unseen to the seen. It's true, but to brood on it is medieval. Our business is not to contrast the two, but to reconcile them.'

Helen replied that she had no intention of brooding on such a dull subject. What did her sister take her for? The weather was magnificent. She and the Mosebachs had gone tobogganing on the only hill that Pomerania boasted. It was fun, but over-crowded, for the rest of Pomerania had gone there too. Helen loved the country, and her letter glowed with physical exercise and poetry. She spoke of the scenery, quiet, yet august; of the snow-clad fields, with their scampering herds of deer; of the river and its quaint entrance into the Baltic Sea; of the Oderberge, only three hundred feet high, from which one slid all too quickly back into the Pomeranian plains, and yet these Oderberge were real mountains, with pine-forests, streams, and views complete. 'It isn't size that counts so much as the way things are arranged.' In another paragraph she referred to Mrs Wilcox sympathetically, but the news had not bitten into her. She had not realized the accessories of death, which are in a sense more memorable than death itself. The atmosphere of precautions and recriminations, and in the midst a human body growing more vivid because it was in pain; the end of that body in Hilton churchyard; the survival of something that suggested hope, vivid in its turn against life's workaday cheerfulness;—all these were lost to Helen, who only felt that a pleasant lady could now be pleasant no longer. She returned to Wickham Place full of her own affairs—she had had another proposal—and Margaret, after a moment's hesitation, was content that this should be so.

The proposal had not been a serious matter. It was the work of Fräulein Mosebach, who had conceived the large and patriotic notion of winning back her cousins to the Fatherland by matrimony. England had played Paul

Wilcox, and lost; Germany played Herr Förstmeister someone–Helen could not remember his name. Herr Förstmeister lived in a wood, and, standing on the summit of the Oderberge, he had pointed out his house to Helen, or rather, had pointed out the wedge of pines in which it lay. She had exclaimed, 'Oh, how lovely! That's the place for me!' and in the evening Frieda appeared in her bedroom. 'I have a message, dear Helen,' etc., and so she had, but had been very nice when Helen laughed; quite understood–a forest too solitary and damp–quite agreed, but Herr Förstmeister believed he had assurance to the contrary. Germany had lost, but with good-humour; holding the manhood of the world, she felt bound to win. 'And there will even be someone for Tibby,' concluded Helen. 'There now, Tibby, think of that; Frieda is saving up a little girl for you, in pig-tails and white worsted stockings, but the feet of the stockings are pink, as if the little girl had trodden in strawberries. I've talked too much. My head aches. Now you talk.'

Tibby consented to talk. He too was full of his own affairs, for he had just been up to try for a scholarship at Oxford. The men were down, and the candidates had been housed in various colleges, and had dined in hall. Tibby was sensitive to beauty, the experience was new, and he gave a description of his visit that was almost glowing. The august and mellow University, soaked with the richness of the western counties that it has served for a thousand years, appealed at once to the boy's taste: it was the kind of thing he could understand, and he understood it all the better because it was empty. Oxford is–Oxford: not a mere receptacle for youth, like Cambridge. Perhaps it wants its inmates to love it rather than to love one another: such at all events was to be its effect on Tibby. His sisters sent him there that he might make friends, for they knew that his education had been cranky, and had severed him from other boys and men. He made no friends. His Oxford remained Oxford empty, and he took into life with him, not the memory of a radiance, but the memory of a colour scheme.

It pleased Margaret to hear her brother and sister talking. They did not get on overwell as a rule. For a few moments she listened to them, feeling elderly and benign. Then something occurred to her, and she interrupted:

'Helen, I told you about poor Mrs Wilcox; that sad business?'

'Yes.'

'I have had a correspondence with her son. He was winding up the estate, and wrote to ask me whether his mother had wanted me to have anything. I thought it good of him, considering I knew her for so little. I said that she had once spoken of giving me a Christmas present, but we both forgot about it afterwards.'

'I hope Charles took the hint.'

'Yes–that is to say, her husband wrote later on, and thanked me for being a little kind to her, and actually gave me her silver vinaigrette. Don't you think that is extraordinarily generous? It has made me like him very much. He hopes that this will not be the end of our acquaintance, but that you and I will go and stop with Evie some time in the future. I like Mr Wilcox. He is taking up his work–rubber–it is a big business. I gather he is launching out rather. Charles is in it, too. Charles is married—a pretty little creature, but she doesn't seem wise. They took on the flat, but now they have gone off to a house of their own.'

Helen, after a decent pause, continued her account of Stettin. How quickly a situation changes! In June she had been in a crisis; even in November she could blush and be unnatural; now it was January, and the whole affair lay forgotten. Looking back on the past six months, Margaret realized the chaotic nature of our daily life, and its difference from the orderly sequence that has been fabricated by historians. Actual life is full of false clues and sign-posts that lead nowhere. With infinite effort we nerve ourselves for a crisis that never comes. The most successful career must show a waste of strength that might have removed mountains, and the most unsuccessful is not that of the man who is taken unprepared, but of him who has prepared and is never taken. On a tragedy of that kind our national morality is duly silent. It assumes that preparation against danger is in itself a good, and that men, like nations, are the better for staggering through life fully armed. The tragedy of preparedness has scarcely been handled, save by the Greeks. Life is indeed dangerous, but not in the way morality would have us believe. It is indeed unmanageable, but the essence of it is not a battle. It is unmanageable because it is a romance, and its essence is romantic beauty.

Margaret hoped that for the future she would be less cautious, not more cautious, than she had been in the past.

Chapter Thirteen

Over two years passed, and the Schlegel household continued to lead its life of cultured but not ignoble ease, still swimming gracefully on the grey tides of London. Concerts and plays swept past them, money had been spent and renewed, reputations won and lost, and the city herself, emblematic of their lives, rose and fell in a continual flux, while her shallows washed more widely against the hills of Surrey and over the fields of Hertfordshire. This famous building had arisen, that was doomed. To-day Whitehall had been transformed: it would be the turn of Regent Street to-morrow. And month by month the roads smelt more strongly of petrol, and were more difficult to cross, and human beings heard each other speak with greater difficulty, breathed less of the air, and saw less of the sky. Nature withdrew: the leaves were falling by midsummer; the sun shone through dirt with an admired obscurity.

To speak against London is no longer fashionable. The Earth as an artistic cult has had its day, and the literature of the near future will probably ignore the country and seek inspiration from the town. One can understand the reaction. Of Pan and the elemental forces, the public has heard a little too much–they seem Victorian, while London is Georgian–and those who care for the earth with sincerity may wait long ere the pendulum swings back to her again. Certainly London fascinates. One visualizes it as a tract of quivering grey, intelligent without purpose, and excitable without love; as a spirit that has altered before it can be chronicled; as a heart that certainly beats, but with no pulsation of humanity. It lies beyond everything: Nature, with all her cruelty, comes nearer to us than do these crowds of men. A friend explains himself: the earth is explicable–from her we came, and we must return to her. But who can explain Westminster Bridge Road or Liverpool Street in the morning–the city inhaling–or the same thoroughfares in the evening–the city exhaling her exhausted air? We reach in desperation beyond the fog, beyond the very stars, the voids of the universe are ransacked to justify the monster, and stamped with a human face. London is religion's opportunity–not the decorous religion of theologians, but anthropomorphic, crude. Yes, the continuous flow would be tolerable if a man of our own sort–not anyone pompous or tearful–were caring for us up in the sky.

The Londoner seldom understands his city until it sweeps him, too, away from his moorings, and Margaret's eyes were not opened until the lease of Wickham Place expired. She had always known that it must expire, but the knowledge only became vivid about nine months before the event. Then the house was suddenly ringed with pathos. It had seen so much happiness. Why had it to be swept away? In the streets of the city she noted for the first time the architecture of hurry, and heard the language of hurry on the mouths of its inhabitants–clipped words, formless sentences, potted expressions of approval or disgust. Month by month things were stepping livelier, but to what goal? The population still rose, but what was the quality of the men born? The particular millionaire who owned the freehold of Wickham Place, and desired to erect Babylonian flats upon it–what right had he to stir so large a portion of the quivering jelly? He was not a fool–she had heard him expose Socialism–but true insight began just where his intelligence ended, and one gathered that this was the case with most millionaires. What right had such men— But Margaret checked herself. That way lies madness. Thank goodness she, too, had some money, and could purchase a new home.

Tibby, now in his second year at Oxford, was down for the Easter vacation, and Margaret took the opportunity of having a serious talk with him. Did he at all know where he wanted to live? Tibby didn't know that he did know. Did he at all know what he wanted to do? He was equally uncertain, but when pressed remarked that he should prefer to be quite free of any profession. Margaret was not shocked, but went on sewing for a few minutes before she replied:

'I was thinking of Mr Vyse. He never strikes me as particularly happy.'

'Ye-es,' said Tibby, and then held his mouth open in a curious quiver, as if he, too, had thought of Mr Vyse, had seen round, through, over, and beyond Mr Vyse, had weighed Mr Vyse, grouped him, and finally dismissed him as having no possible bearing on the subject under discussion. That bleat of

Tibby's infuriated Helen. But Helen was now down in the dining-room preparing a speech about political economy. At times her voice could be heard declaiming through the floor.

'But Mr Vyse is rather a wretched, weedy man, don't you think? Then there's Guy. That was a pitiful business. Besides'—shifting to the general—'everyone is the better for some regular work.'

Groans.

'I shall stick to it,' she continued, smiling. 'I am not saying it to educate you; it is what I really think. I believe that in the last century men have developed the desire for work, and they must not starve it. It's a new desire. It goes with a great deal that's bad, but in itself it's good, and I hope that for women, too, "not to work" will soon become as shocking as "not to be married" was a hundred years ago.'

'I have no experience of this profound desire to which you allude,' enunciated Tibby.

'Then we'll leave the subject till you do. I'm not going to rattle you round. Take your time. Only do think over the lives of the men you like most, and see how they've arranged them.'

'I like Guy and Mr Vyse most,' said Tibby faintly, and leant so far back in his chair that he extended in a horizontal line from knees to throat.

'And don't think I'm not serious because I don't use the traditional arguments—making money, a sphere awaiting you, and so on—all of which are, for various reasons, cant.' She sewed on. 'I'm only your sister. I haven't any authority over you, and I don't want to have any. Just to put before you what I think the truth. You see'—she shook off the pince-nez to which she had recently taken—'in a few years we shall be the same age practically, and I shall want you to help me. Men are so much nicer than women.'

'Labouring under such a delusion, why do you not marry?'

'I sometimes jolly well think I would if I got the chance.'

'Has no body arst you?'

'Only ninnies.'

'Do people ask Helen?'

'Plentifully.'

'Tell me about them.'

'No.'

'Tell me about your ninnies, then.'

'They were men who had nothing better to do,' said his sister, feeling that she was entitled to score this point. 'So take warning: you must work, or else you must pretend to work, which is what I do. Work, work, work if you'd save your soul and your body. It is honestly a necessity, dear boy. Look at the Wilcoxes, look at Mr Pembroke. With all their defects of temper and understanding, such men give me more pleasure than many who are better equipped, and I think it is because they have worked regularly and honestly.'

'Spare me the Wilcoxes,' he moaned.

'I shall not. They are the right sort.'

'Oh, goodness me, Meg!' he protested, suddenly sitting up, alert and angry. Tibby, for all his defects, had a genuine personality.

'Well, they're as near the right sort as you can imagine.'

'No, no—oh, no!'

'I was thinking of the younger son, whom I once classed as a ninny, but who came back so ill from Nigeria. He's gone out there again, Evie Wilcox tells me—out to his duty.'

'Duty' always elicited a groan.

'He doesn't want the money, it is work he wants, though it is beastly work—dull country, dishonest natives, an eternal fidget over fresh water and food. A nation who can produce men of that sort may well be proud. No wonder England has become an Empire.'

'*Empire!*'

'I can't bother over results,' said Margaret, a little sadly. 'They are too difficult for me. I can only look at the men. An Empire bores me, so far, but I can appreciate the heroism that builds it up. London bores me, but what thousands of splendid people are labouring to make London—'

'What it is,' he sneered.

'What it is, worse luck. I want activity without civilization. How paradoxical! Yet I expect that is what we shall find in heaven.'

'And I,' said Tibby, 'want civilization without activity, which, I expect, is what we shall find in the other place.'

'You needn't go as far as the other place, Tibbikins, if you want that. You can find it at Oxford.'

'Stupid—'

'If I'm stupid, get me back to the house-hunting. I'll even live in Oxford if you like—North Oxford. I'll live anywhere except Bournemouth, Torquay, and Cheltenham. Oh yes, or Ilfracombe and Swanage and Tunbridge Wells and Surbiton and Bedford. There on no account.'

'London, then.'

'I agree, but Helen rather wants to get away from London. However, there's no reason we shouldn't have a house in the country and also a flat in town, provided we all stick together and contribute. Though of course— Oh, how one does maunder on, and to think, to think of the people who are really poor. How do they live? Not to move about the world would kill me.'

As she spoke, the door was flung open, and Helen burst in in a state of extreme excitement.

'Oh, my dears, what do you think? You'll never guess. A woman's been here asking me for her husband. Her *what?*' (Helen was fond of supplying her own surprise.) 'Yes, for her husband, and it really is so.'

'Not anything to do with Bracknell?' cried Margaret, who had lately taken on an unemployed of that name to clean the knives and boots.

'I offered Bracknell, and he was rejected. So was Tibby. (Cheer up, Tibby!) It's no one we know. I said, "Hunt, my good woman; have a good look round, hunt under the tables, poke up the chimney, shake out the antimacassars. Husband? husband?' Oh, and she so magnificently dressed and tinkling like a chandelier.'

'Now, Helen, what did happen really?'

'What I say. I was, as it were, orating my speech. Annie opens the door like a fool, and shows a female straight in on me, with my mouth open. Then we began—very civilly. "I want my husband, what I have reason to believe is here." No—how unjust one is. She said "whom," not "what." She got it perfectly. So I said, "Name, please?" and she said, "Lan, Miss," and there we were.'

'Lan?'

'Lan or Len. We were not nice about our vowels. Lanoline.'

'But what an extraordinary—'

'I said, "My good Mrs Lanoline, we have some grave misunderstanding here. Beautiful as I am, my modesty is even more remarkable than my beauty, and never, never has Mr Lanoline rested his eyes on mine.'

'I hope you were pleased,' said Tibby.

'Of course,' Helen squeaked. 'A perfectly delightful experience. Oh, Mrs Lanoline's a dear—she asked for a husband as if he was an umbrella. She mislaid him Saturday afternoon—and for a long time suffered no inconvenience. But all night, and all this morning her apprehensions grew. Breakfast didn't seem the same—no, no more did lunch, and so she strolled up to 2, Wickham Place as being the most likely place for the missing article.'

'But how on earth—'

'Don't begin how on earthing. "I know what I know," she kept repeating, not uncivilly, but with extreme gloom. In vain I asked her what she did know. Some knew what others knew, and others didn't, and if they didn't, then others again had better be careful. Oh dear, she was incompetent! She had a face like a silkworm, and the dining-room reeks of orris-root. We chatted pleasantly a little about husbands, and I wondered where hers was too, and advised her to go to the police. She thanked me. We agreed that Mr Lanoline's a notty, notty man, and hasn't no business to go on the lardy-da. But I think she suspected me up to the last. Bags I writing to Aunt Juley about this. Now, Meg, remember—bags I.'

'Bag it by all means,' murmured Margaret, putting down her work. 'I'm not sure that this is so funny, Helen. It means some horrible volcano smoking somewhere, doesn't it?'

'I don't think so—she doesn't really mind. The admirable creature isn't capable of tragedy.'

'Her husband may be, though,' said Margaret, moving to the window.

'Oh no, not likely. No one capable of tragedy could have married Mrs Lanoline.'

'Was she pretty?'

'Her figure may have been good once.'

The flats, their only outlook, hung like an ornate curtain between Margaret and the welter of London. Her thoughts turned sadly to house-hunting. Wickham Place had been so safe. She feared, fantastically, that her own little flock might be moving into turmoil and squalor, into nearer contact with such episodes as these.

'Tibby and I have again been wondering where we'll live next September,' she said at last.

'Tibby had better first wonder what he'll do,' retorted Helen; and that topic was resumed, but with acrimony. Then tea came, and after tea Helen went on preparing her speech, and Margaret prepared one, too, for they were going out to a discussion society on the morrow. But her thoughts were poisoned. Mrs Lanoline had risen out of the abyss, like a faint smell, a goblin footfall, telling of a life where love and hatred had both decayed.

Chapter Fourteen

The mystery, like so many mysteries, was explained. Next day, just as they were dressed to go out to dinner, a Mr Bast called. He was a clerk in the employment of the Porphyrion Fire Insurance Company. Thus much from his card. He had come 'about the lady yesterday.' Thus much from Annie, who had shown him into the dining-room.

'Cheers, children!' cried Helen. 'It's Mrs Lanoline.'

Tibby was interested. The three hurried downstairs, to find, not the gay dog they expected, but a young man, colourless, toneless, who had already the mournful eyes above a drooping moustache that are so common in London, and that haunt some streets of the city like accusing presences. One guessed him as the third generation, grandson to the shepherd or ploughboy whom civilization had sucked into the town; as one of the thousands who have lost the life of the body and failed to reach the life of the spirit. Hints of robustness survived in him, more than a hint of primitive good looks, and Margaret, noting the spine that might have been straight, and the chest that might have broadened, wondered whether it paid to give up the glory of the animal for a tail coat and a couple of ideas. Culture had worked in her own case, but during the last few weeks she had doubted whether it humanized the majority, so wide and so widening is the gulf that stretches between the natural and the philosophic man, so many the good chaps who are wrecked in trying to cross it. She knew this type very well–the vague aspirations, the mental dishonesty, the familiarity with the outsides of books. She knew the tones in which he would address her. She was only unprepared for an example of her own visiting-card.

'You wouldn't remember giving me this, Miss Schlegel?' said he, uneasily familiar.

'No; I can't say I do.'

'Well, that was how it happened, you see.'

'Where did we meet, Mr Bast? For the minute I don't remember.'

'It was a concert at the Queen's Hall. I think you will recollect,' he added pretentiously, 'when I tell you that it included a performance of the Fifth Symphony of Beethoven.'

'We hear the Fifth practically every time it's done, so I'm not sure–do you remember, Helen?'

'Was it the time the sandy cat walked round the balustrade?'

He thought not.

'Then I don't remember. That's the only Beethoven I ever remember specially.'

'And you, if I may say so, took away my umbrella, inadvertently of course.'

'Likely enough,' Helen laughed, 'for I steal umbrellas even oftener than I hear Beethoven. Did you get it back?'

'Yes, thank you, Miss Schlegel.'

'The mistake arose out of my card, did it?' interposed Margaret.

'Yes, the mistake arose—it was a mistake.'

'The lady who called here yesterday thought that you were calling too, and that she could find you?' she continued, pushing him forward, for, though he had promised an explanation, he seemed unable to give one.

'That's so, calling too—a mistake.'

'Then why—?' began Helen, but Margaret laid a hand on her arm.

'I said to my wife,' he continued more rapidly—'I said to Mrs Bast, "I have to pay a call on some friends," and Mrs Bast said to me, "Do go." While I was gone, however, she wanted me on important business, and thought I had come here, owing to the card, and so came after me, and I beg to tender my apologies, and hers as well, for any inconvenience we may have inadvertently caused you.'

'No inconvenience,' said Helen; 'but I still don't understand.'

An air of evasion characterized Mr Bast. He explained again, but was obviously lying, and Helen didn't see why he should get off. She had the cruelty of youth. Neglecting her sister's pressure, she said, 'I still don't understand. When did you say you paid this call?'

'Call? What call?' said he, staring as if her question had been a foolish one, a favourite device of those in mid-stream.

'This afternoon call.'

'In the afternoon, of course!' he replied, and looked at Tibby to see how the repartee went. But Tibby, himself a repartee, was unsympathetic, and said, 'Saturday afternoon or Sunday afternoon?'

'S—Saturday.'

'Really!' said Helen; 'and you were still calling on Sunday, when your wife came here. A long visit.'

'I don't call that fair,' said Mr Bast, going scarlet and handsome. There was fight in his eyes. 'I know what you mean, and it isn't so.'

'Oh, don't let us mind,' said Margaret, distressed again by odours from the abyss.

'It was something else,' he asserted, his elaborate manner breaking down. 'I was somewhere else to what you think, so there!'

'It was good of you to come and explain,' she said. 'The rest is naturally no concern of ours.'

'Yes, but I want—I wanted—have you ever read "The Ordeal of Richard Feverel"?'

Margaret nodded.

'It's a beautiful book. I wanted to get back to the Earth, don't you see, like

Richard does in the end. Or have you ever read Stevenson's "Prince Otto"?'

Helen and Tibby groaned gently.

'That's another beautiful book. You get back to the Earth in that. I wanted—' He mouthed affectedly. Then through the mists of his culture came a hard fact, hard as a pebble. 'I walked all the Saturday night,' said Leonard. 'I walked.' A thrill of approval ran through the sisters. But culture closed in again. He asked whether they had ever read E. V. Lucas's 'Open Road.'

Said Helen, 'No doubt it's another beautiful book, but I'd rather hear about your road.'

'Oh, I walked.'

'How far?'

'I don't know, nor for how long. It got too dark to see my watch.'

'Were you walking alone, may I ask?'

'Yes,' he said, straightening himself; 'but we'd been talking it over at the office. There's been a lot of talk at the office lately about these things. The fellows there said one steers by the Pole Star, and I looked it up in the celestial atlas, but once out of doors everything gets so mixed—'

'Don't talk to me about the Pole Star,' interrupted Helen, who was becoming interested. 'I know its little ways. It goes round and round, and you go round after it.'

'Well, I lost it entirely. First of all the street lamps, then the trees, and towards morning it got cloudy.'

Tibby, who preferred his comedy undiluted, slipped from the room. He knew that this fellow would never attain to poetry, and did not want to hear him trying. Margaret and Helen remained. Their brother influenced them more than they knew: in his absence they were stirred to enthusiasm more easily.

'Where did you start from?' cried Margaret. 'Do tell us more.'

'I took the Underground to Wimbledon. As I came out of the office I said to myself, "I must have a walk once in a way. If I don't take this walk now, I shall never take it." I had a bit of dinner at Wimbledon, and then—'

'But not good country there, is it?'

'It was gas-lamps for hours. Still, I had all the night, and being out was the great thing. I did get into woods, too, presently.'

'Yes, go on,' said Helen.

'You've no idea how difficult uneven ground is when it's dark.'

'Did you actually go off the roads?'

'Oh yes. I always meant to go off the roads, but the worst of it is that it's more difficult to find one's way.'

'Mr Bast, you're a born adventurer,' laughed Margaret. 'No professional athlete would have attempted what you've done. It's a wonder your walk didn't end in a broken neck. Whatever did your wife say?'

'Professional athletes never move without lanterns and compasses,' said Helen. 'Besides, they can't walk. It tires them. Go on.'

'I felt like R. L. S. You probably remember how in "Virginibus—"'

'Yes, but the wood. This 'ere wood. How did you get out of it?'

'I managed one wood, and found a road the other side which went a good bit uphill. I rather fancy it was those North Downs, for the road went off into grass, and I got into another wood. That was awful, with gorse bushes. I did wish I'd never come, but suddenly it got light—just while I seemed going under one tree. Then I found a road down to a station, and took the first train I could back to London.'

'But was the dawn wonderful?' asked Helen.

With unforgettable sincerity he replied, 'No.' The word flew again like a pebble from the sling. Down toppled all that had seemed ignoble or literary in his talk, down toppled tiresome R. L. S. and the 'love of the earth' and his silk top-hat. In the presence of these women Leonard had arrived, and he spoke with a flow, an exultation, that he had seldom known.

'The dawn was only grey, it was nothing to mention—'

'Just a grey evening turned upside down. I know.'

'—and I was too tired to lift up my head to look at it, and so cold too. I'm glad I did it, and yet at the time it bored me more than I can say. And besides—you can believe me or not as you choose—I was very hungry. That dinner at Wimbledon—I meant it to last me all night like other dinners. I never thought that walking would make such a difference. Why, when you're walking you want, as it were, a breakfast and luncheon and tea during the night as well, and I'd nothing but a packet of Woodbines. Lord, I did feel bad! Looking back, it wasn't what you may call enjoyment. It was more a case of sticking to it. I did stick. I—I was determined. Oh, hang it all! what's the good—I mean, the good of living in a room for ever? There one goes on day after day, same old game, same up and down to town, until you forget there is any other game. You ought to see once in a way what's going on outside, if it's only nothing particular after all.'

'I should just think you ought,' said Helen, sitting on the edge of the table.

The sound of a lady's voice recalled him from sincerity, and he said: 'Curious it should all come about from reading something of Richard Jefferies.'

'Excuse me, Mr Bast, but you're wrong there. It didn't. It came from something far greater.'

But she could not stop him. Borrow was imminent after Jefferies—Borrow, Thoreau, and sorrow. R. L. S. brought up the rear, and the outburst ended in a swamp of books. No disrespect to these great names. The fault is ours, not theirs. They mean us to use them for sign-posts, and are not to blame if, in our weakness, we mistake the sign-post for the destination. And Leonard had reached the destination. He had visited the county of Surrey when darkness covered its amenities, and its cosy villas had re-entered ancient night. Every twelve hours this miracle happens, but he had troubled to go and see for himself. Within his cramped little mind dwelt something that was greater than Jefferies' books—the spirit that led Jefferies to write them; and his dawn, though revealing nothing but monotones, was part of the eternal sunrise that shows George Borrow Stonehenge.

'Then you don't think I was foolish?' he asked, becoming again the naïve and sweet-tempered boy for whom Nature had intended him.

'Heavens, no!' replied Margaret.

'Heaven help us if we do!' replied Helen.

'I'm very glad you say that. Now, my wife would never understand—not if I explained for days.'

'No, it wasn't foolish!' cried Helen, her eyes aflame. 'You've pushed back the boundaries; I think it splendid of you.'

'You've not been content to dream as we have—'

'Though we have walked, too—'

'I must show you a picture upstairs—'

Here the door-bell rang. The hansom had come to take them to their evening party.

'Oh, bother, not to say dash—I had forgotten we were dining out; but do, do, come round again and have a talk.'

'Yes, you must—do,' echoed Margaret.

Leonard, with extreme sentiment, replied: 'No, I shall not. It's better like this.'

'Why better?' asked Margaret.

'No, it is better not to risk a second interview. I shall always look back on this talk with you as one of the finest things in my life. Really. I mean this. We can never repeat. It has done me real good, and there we had better leave it.'

'That's rather a sad view of life, surely.'

'Things so often get spoiled.'

'I know,' flashed Helen, 'but people don't.'

He could not understand this. He continued in a vein which mingled true imagination and false. What he said wasn't wrong, but it wasn't right, and a false note jarred. One little twist, they felt, and the instrument might be in tune. One little strain, and it might be silent for ever. He thanked the ladies very much, but he would not call again. There was a moment's awkwardness, and then Helen said: 'Go, then; perhaps you know best; but never forget you're better than Jefferies.' And he went. Their hansom caught him up at the corner, passed with a waving of hands, and vanished with its accomplished load into the evening.

London was beginning to illuminate herself against the night. Electric lights sizzled and jagged in the main thoroughfares, gas-lamps in the side streets glimmered a canary gold or green. The sky was a crimson battlefield of spring, but London was not afraid. Her smoke mitigated the splendour, and the clouds down Oxford Street were a delicately painted ceiling, which adorned while it did not distract. She has never known the clear-cut armies of the purer air. Leonard hurried through her tinted wonders, very much part of the picture. His was a grey life, and to brighten it he had ruled off a few corners for romance. The Miss Schlegels—or, to speak more accurately, his interview with them—were to fill such a corner, nor was it by any means the first time that he had talked intimately to strangers. The habit was analogous to a debauch, an outlet, though the worst of outlets, for instincts that would not be denied. Terrifying him, it would beat down his suspicions and prudence until he was confiding secrets to people whom he had scarcely seen. It brought him many fears and some pleasant memories. Perhaps the keenest happiness he had ever known was during a railway journey to Cambridge, where a decent-mannered undergraduate had spoken to him. They had got into conversation, and gradually Leonard flung reticence aside, told some of his domestic troubles, and hinted at the rest. The undergraduate, supposing they could start a friendship, asked him to 'coffee after hall,' which he accepted, but afterwards grew shy, and took care not to stir from the commercial hotel where he lodged. He did not want Romance to collide with the Porphyrion, still less with Jacky, and people with fuller, happier lives are slow to understand this. To the Schlegels, as to the undergraduate, he was an interesting creature, of whom they wanted to see more. But they to him were denizens of Romance, who must keep to the corner he had assigned them, pictures that must not walk out of their frames.

His behaviour over Margaret's visiting-card had been typical. His had scarcely been a tragic marriage. Where there is no money and no inclination to violence tragedy cannot be generated. He could not leave his wife, and he did not want to hit her. Petulance and squalor was enough. Here 'that card' had come in. Leonard, though furtive, was untidy, and left it lying about. Jacky found it, and then began, 'What's that card, eh?' 'Yes, don't you wish you knew what that card was?' 'Len, who's Miss Schlegel?' etc. Months passed, and the card, now as a joke, now as a grievance, was handed about, getting dirtier and dirtier. It followed them when they moved from Camelia Road to Tulse Hill. It was submitted to third parties. A few inches of pasteboard, it became the battlefield on which the souls of Leonard and his wife contended. Why did he not say, 'A lady took my umbrella, another gave me this that I might call for my umbrella'? Because Jacky would have disbelieved him? Partly, but chiefly because he was sentimental. No affection gathered round the card, but it symbolized the life of culture, that Jacky should never spoil. At night he would say to himself, 'Well, at all events, she doesn't know about that card. Yah! done her there.'

Poor Jacky! she was not a bad sort, and had a great deal to bear. She drew her own conclusion—she was only capable of drawing one conclusion—and in the fulness of time she acted upon it. All the Friday Leonard had refused to speak to her, and had spent the evening observing the stars. On the Saturday he went up, as usual, to town, but he came not back Saturday night, nor Sunday morning, nor Sunday afternoon. The inconvenience grew intolerable, and though she was now of a retiring habit, and shy of women, she went up to Wickham Place. Leonard returned in her absence. The card, the fatal card, was gone from the pages of Ruskin, and he guessed what had happened.

'Well?' he had exclaimed, greeting her with peals of laughter. 'I know where you've been, but you don't know where I've been.'

Jacky sighed, said, 'Len, I do think you might explain,' and resumed domesticity.

Explanations were difficult at this stage, and Leonard was too silly—or it is tempting to write, too sound a chap to attempt them. His reticence was not

entirely the shoddy article that a business life promotes, the reticence that
pretends that nothing is something, and hides behind the 'Daily Telegraph.'
The adventurer, also, is reticent, and it is an adventure for a clerk to walk for
a few hours in darkness. You may laugh at him, you who have slept nights
out on the veldt, with your rifle beside you and all the atmosphere of
adventure pat. And you also may laugh who think adventures silly. But do
not be surprised if Leonard is shy whenever he meets you, and if the
Schlegels rather than Jacky hear about the dawn.

That the Schlegels had not thought him foolish became a permanent joy.
He was at his best when he thought of them. It buoyed him as he journeyed
home beneath fading heavens. Somehow the barriers of wealth had fallen,
and there had been—he could not phrase it—a general assertion of the wonder
of the world. 'My conviction,' says the mystic, 'gains infinitely the moment
another soul will believe in it,' and they had agreed that there was something
beyond life's daily grey. He took off his top-hat and smoothed it
thoughtfully. He had hitherto supposed the unknown to be books,
literature, clever conversation, culture. One raised oneself by study, and got
upsides with the world. But in that quick interchange a new light dawned.
Was that 'something' walking in the dark among the suburban hills?

He discovered that he was going bareheaded down Regent Street. London
came back with a rush. Few were about at this hour, but all whom he passed
looked at him with a hostility that was the more impressive because it was
unconscious. He put his hat on. It was too big; his head disappeared like a
pudding into a basin, the ears bending outwards at the touch of the curly
brim. He wore it a little backwards, and its effect was greatly to elongate the
face and to bring out the distance between the eyes and the moustache. Thus
equipped, he escaped criticism. No one felt uneasy as he titupped along the
pavements, the heart of a man ticking fast in his chest.

Chapter Fifteen

The sisters went out to dinner full of their adventure, and when they were
both full of the same subject, there were few dinner-parties that could stand
up against them. This particular one, which was all ladies, had more kick in
it than most, but succumbed after a struggle. Helen at one part of the table,
Margaret at the other, would talk of Mr Bast and of no one else, and
somewhere about the entrée their monologues collided, fell ruining, and
became common property. Nor was this all. The dinner-party was really an
informal discussion club; there was a paper after it, read amid coffee-cups
and laughter in the drawing-room, but dealing more or less thoughtfully
with some topic of general interest. After the paper came a debate, and in this
debate Mr Bast also figured, appearing now as a bright spot in civilization,
now as a dark spot, according to the temperament of the speaker. The

subject of the paper had been, 'How ought I to dispose of my money?' the reader professing to be a millionaire on the point of death, inclined to bequeath her fortune for the foundation of local art galleries, but open to conviction from other sources. The various parts had been assigned beforehand, and some of the speeches were amusing. The hostess assumed the ungrateful rôle of 'the millionaire's eldest son,' and implored her expiring parent not to dislocate Society by allowing such vast sums to pass out of the family. Money was the fruit of self-denial, and the second generation had a right to profit by the self-denial of the first. What right had 'Mr Bast' to profit? The National Gallery was good enough for the likes of him. After property had had its say—a saying that is necessarily ungracious—the various philanthropists stepped forward. Something must be done for 'Mr Bast'; his conditions must be improved without impairing his independence; he must have a free library, or free tennis-courts; his rent must be paid in such a way that he did not know it was being paid; it must be made worth his while to join the Territorials; he must be forcibly parted from his uninspiring wife, the money going to her as compensation; he must be assigned a Twin Star, some member of the leisured classes who would watch over him ceaselessly (groans from Helen); he must be given food but no clothes, clothes but no food, a third-return ticket to Venice, without either food or clothes when he arrived there. In short, he might be given anything and everything so long as it was not the money itself.

And here Margaret interrupted.

'Order, order, Miss Schlegel!' said the reader of the paper. 'You are here, I understand, to advise me in the interest of the Society for the Preservation of Places of Historic Interest or Natural Beauty. I cannot have you speaking out of your rôle. It makes my poor head go round, and I think you forget that I am very ill.'

'Your head won't go round if only you'll listen to my argument,' said Margaret. 'Why not give him the money itself? You're supposed to have about thirty thousand a year.'

'Have I? I thought I had a million.'

'Wasn't a million your capital? Dear me! we ought to have settled that. Still, it doesn't matter. Whatever you've got, I order you to give as many poor men as you can three hundred a year each.'

'But that would be pauperizing them,' said an earnest girl, who liked the Schlegels, but thought them a little unspiritual at times.

'Not if you gave them so much. A big windfall would not pauperize a man. It is these little driblets, distributed among too many, that do the harm. Money's educational. It's far more educational than the things it buys.' There was a protest. 'In a sense,' added Margaret, but the protest continued. 'Well, isn't the most civilized thing going, the man who has learnt to wear his income properly?'

'Exactly what your Mr Basts won't do.'

'Give them a chance. Give them money. Don't dole them out poetry-books and railway-tickets like babies. Give them the wherewithal to buy these things. When your Socialism comes it may be different, and we may think in terms of commodities instead of cash. Till it comes give people cash, for it is the warp of civilization, whatever the woof may be. The imagination ought to play upon money and realize it vividly, for it's the—the second most important thing in the world. It is so slurred over and hushed up, there is so little clear thinking—oh, political economy, of course, but so few of us think clearly about our own private incomes, and admit that independent thoughts are in nine cases out of ten the result of independent means. Money: give Mr Bast money, and don't bother about his ideals. He'll pick up those for himself.'

She leant back while the more earnest members of the club began to misconstrue her. The female mind, though cruelly practical in daily life, cannot bear to hear ideals belittled in conversation, and Miss Schlegel was asked however she could say such dreadful things, and what it would profit Mr Bast if he gained the whole world and lost his own soul. She answered, 'Nothing, but he would not gain his soul until he had gained a little of the world.' Then they said, 'No, they did not believe it,' and she admitted that an overworked clerk may save his soul in the superterrestrial sense, where the effort will be taken for the deed, but she denied that he will ever explore the spiritual resources of this world, will ever know the rarer joys of the body, or attain to clear and passionate intercourse with his fellows. Others had attacked the fabric of Society—Property, Interest, etc.; she only fixed her eyes on a few human beings, to see how, under present conditions, they could be made happier. Doing good to humanity was useless: the many-coloured efforts thereto spreading over the vast area like films and resulting in an universal grey. To do good to one, or, as in this case, to a few, was the utmost she dare hope for.

Between the idealists, and the political economists, Margaret had a bad time. Disagreeing elsewhere, they agreed in disowning her, and in keeping the administration of the millionaire's money in their own hands. The earnest girl brought forward a scheme of 'personal supervision and mutual help,' the effect of which was to alter poor people until they became exactly like people who were not so poor. The hostess pertinently remarked that she, as eldest son, might surely rank among the millionaire's legatees. Margaret weakly admitted the claim, and another claim was at once set up by Helen, who declared that she had been the millionaire's housemaid for over forty years, overfed and underpaid; was nothing to be done for her, so corpulent and poor? The millionaire then read out her last will and testament, in which she left the whole of her fortune to the Chancellor of the Exchequer. Then she died. The serious parts of the discussion had been of higher merit than the playful—in a men's debate is the reverse more general?—but the meeting broke up hilariously enough, and a dozen happy ladies dispersed to their homes.

Helen and Margaret walked the earnest girl as far as Battersea Bridge Station, arguing copiously all the way. When she had gone they were conscious of an alleviation, and of the great beauty of the evening. They turned back towards Oakley Street. The lamps and the plane-trees, following the line of the embankment, struck a note of dignity that is rare in

English cities. The seats, almost deserted, were here and there occupied by gentlefolk in evening dress, who had strolled out from the houses behind to enjoy fresh air and the whisper of the rising tide. There is something continental about Chelsea Embankment. It is an open space used rightly, a blessing more frequent in Germany than here. As Margaret and Helen sat down, the city behind them seemed to be a vast theatre, an opera-house in which some endless trilogy was performing, and they themselves a pair of satisfied subscribers, who did not mind losing a little of the second act.

'Cold?'

'No.'

'Tired?'

'Doesn't matter.'

The earnest girl's train rumbled away over the bridge.

'I say, Helen—'

'Well?'

'Are we really going to follow up Mr Bast?'

'I don't know.'

'I think we won't.'

'As you like.'

'It's no good, I think, unless you really mean to know people. The discussion brought that home to me. We got on well enough with him in a spirit of excitement, but think of rational intercourse. We mustn't play at friendship. No, it's no good.'

'There's Mrs Lanoline, too,' Helen yawned. 'So dull.'

'Just so, and possibly worse than dull.'

'I should like to know how he got hold of your card.'

'But he said—something about a concert and an umbrella—'

'Then did the card see the wife—'

'Helen, come to bed.'

'No, just a little longer, it is so beautiful. Tell me; oh yes; did you say money is the warp of the world?'

'Yes.'

'Then what's the woof?'

'Very much what one chooses,' said Margaret. 'It's something that isn't money—one can't say more.'

'Walking at night?'

'Probably.'

'For Tibby, Oxford?'

'It seems so.'

'For you?'

'Now that we have to leave Wickham Place, I begin to think it's that. For Mrs Wilcox it was certainly Howards End.'

One's own name will carry immense distances. Mr Wilcox, who was sitting with friends many seats away, heard his, rose to his feet, and strolled along towards the speakers.

'It is sad to suppose that places may ever be more important than people,' continued Margaret.

'Why, Meg? They're so much nicer generally. I'd rather think of that forester's house in Pomerania than of the fat Herr Förstmeister who lived in it.'

'I believe we shall come to care about people less and less, Helen. The more people one knows the easier it becomes to replace them. It's one of the curses of London. I quite expect to end my life caring most for a place.'

Here Mr Wilcox reached them. It was several weeks since they had met.

'How do you do?' he cried. 'I thought I recognized your voices. Whatever are you both doing down here?'

His tones were protective. He implied that one ought not to sit out on Chelsea Embankment without a male escort. Helen resented this, but Margaret accepted it as part of the good man's equipment.

'What an age it is since I've seen you, Mr Wilcox. I met Evie in the Tube, though, lately. I hope you have good news of your son.'

'Paul?' said Mr Wilcox, extinguishing his cigarette, and sitting down between them. 'Oh, Paul's all right. We had a line from Madeira. He'll be at work again by now.'

'Ugh—' said Helen, shuddering from complex causes.

'I beg your pardon?'

'Isn't the climate of Nigeria too horrible?'

'Someone's got to go,' he said simply. 'England will never keep her trade overseas unless she is prepared to make sacrifices. Unless we get firm in West Africa, Ger— untold complications my follow. Now tell me all your news.'

'Oh, we've had a splendid evening,' cried Helen, who always woke up at the advent of a visitor. 'We belong to a kind of club that reads papers, Margaret and I–all women, but there is a discussion after. This evening it was on how one ought to leave one's money–whether to one's family, or to the poor, and if so how–oh, most interesting.'

The man of business smiled. Since his wife's death he had almost doubled his income. He was an important figure at last, a reassuring name on company prospectuses, and life had treated him very well. The world seemed in his grasp as he listened to the River Thames, which still flowed inland from the sea. So wonderful to the girls, it held no mysteries for him. He had helped to shorten its long tidal trough by taking shares in the lock at Teddington, and if he and other capitalists thought good, some day it could be shortened again. With a good dinner inside him and an amiable but academic woman on either flank, he felt that his hands were on all the ropes of life, and that what he did not know could not be worth knowing.

'Sounds a most original entertainment!' he exclaimed, and laughed in his pleasant way. 'I wish Evie would go to that sort of thing. But she hasn't the time. She's taken to breed Aberdeen terriers–jolly little dogs.'

'I expect we'd better be doing the same, really.'

'We pretend we're improving ourselves, you see,' said Helen a little sharply, for the Wilcox glamour is not of the kind that returns, and she had bitter memories of the days when a speech such as he had just made would have impressed her favourably. 'We suppose it a good thing to waste an evening once a fortnight over a debate, but, as my sister says, it may be better to breed dogs.'

'Not at all. I don't agree with your sister. There's nothing like a debate to teach one quickness. I often wish I had gone in for them when I was a youngster. It would have helped me no end.'

'Quickness—?'

'Yes. Quickness in argument. Time after time I've missed scoring a point because the other man has had the gift of the gab and I haven't. Oh, I believe in these discussions.'

The patronizing tone, thought Margaret, came well enough from a man who was old enough to be their father. She had always maintained that Mr Wilcox had a charm. In times of sorrow or emotion his inadequacy had pained her, but it was pleasant to listen to him now, and to watch his thick brown moustache and high forehead confronting the stars. But Helen was nettled. The aim of *their* debates she implied was Truth.

'Oh yes, it doesn't much matter what subject you take,' said he.

Margaret laughed and said, 'But this is going to be far better than the debate itself.' Helen recovered herself and laughed too. 'No, I won't go on,' she declared. 'I'll just put our special case to Mr Wilcox.'

'About Mr Bast? Yes, do. He'll be more lenient to a special case.'

'But, Mr Wilcox, do first light another cigarette. It's this. We've just come across a young fellow, who's evidently very poor, and who seems interest—'

'What's his profession?'

'Clerk.'

'What in?'

'Do you remember, Margaret?'

'Porphyrion Fire Insurance Company.'

'Oh yes; the nice people who gave Aunt Juley a new hearth-rug. He seems interesting, in some ways very, and one wishes one could help him. He is married to a wife whom he doesn't seem to care for much. He likes books, and what one may roughly call adventure, and if he had a chance— But he is so poor. He lives a life where all the money is apt to go on nonsense and clothes. One is so afraid that circumstances will be too strong for him and that he will sink. Well, he got mixed up in our debate. He wasn't the subject of it, but it seemed to bear on his point. Suppose a millionaire died, and desired to leave money to help such a man. How should he be helped? Should he be given three hundred pounds a year direct, which was Margaret's plan? Most of them thought this would pauperize him. Should he and those like him be given free libraries? I said "No!" He doesn't want more books to read, but to read books rightly. My suggestion was he should be given something every year towards a summer holiday, but then there is his wife, and they said she would have to go too. Nothing seemed quite right! Now what do you think? Imagine that you were a millionaire, and wanted to help the poor. What would you do?'

Mr Wilcox, whose fortune was not so very far below the standard indicated, laughed exuberantly. 'My dear Miss Schlegel, I will not rush in where your sex has been unable to tread. I will not add another plan to the numerous excellent ones that have been already suggested. My only contribution is this: let your young friend clear out of the Porphyrion Fire Insurance Company with all possible speed.'

'Why?' said Margaret.

He lowered his voice. 'This is between friends. It'll be in the Receiver's hands before Christmas. It'll smash,' he added, thinking that she had not understood.

'Dear me, Helen, listen to that. And he'll have to get another place!'

'*Will* have? Let him leave the ship before it sinks. Let him get one now.'

'Rather than wait, to make sure?'

'Decidedly.'

'Why's that?'

Again the Olympian laugh, and the lowered voice. 'Naturally the man who's in a situation when he applies stands a better chance, is in a stronger position, than the man who isn't. It looks as if he's worth something. I know by myself–(this is letting you into the State secrets)–it affects an employer greatly. Human nature, I'm afraid.'

'I hadn't thought of that,' murmured Margaret, while Helen said, 'Our human nature appears to be the other way round. We employ people because they're unemployed. The boot man, for instance.'

'And how does he clean the boots?'

'Not well,' confessed Margaret.

'There you are!'

'Then do you really advise us to tell this youth—?'

'I advise nothing,' he interrupted, glancing up and down the Embankment, in case his indiscretion had been overhead. 'I oughtn't to have spoken–but I happen to know, being more or less behind the scenes. The Porphyrion's a bad, bad concern— Now, don't say I said so. It's outside the Tariff Ring.'

'Certainly I won't say. In fact, I don't know what that means.'

'I thought an insurance company never smashed,' was Helen's contribution. 'Don't the others always run in and save them?'

'You're thinking of reinsurance,' said Mr Wilcox mildly. 'It is exactly there that the Porphyrion is weak. It has tried to undercut, has been badly hit by a long series of small fires, and it hasn't been able to reinsure. I'm afraid that public companies don't save one another for love.'

'"Human nature," I suppose,' quoted Helen, and he laughed and agreed that it was. When Margaret said that she supposed that clerks, like everyone else, found it extremely difficult to get situations in these days, he replied, 'Yes, extremely,' and rose to rejoin his friends. He knew by his own office–seldom a vacant post, and hundreds of applicants for it; at present no vacant post.

'And how's Howards End looking?' said Margaret, wishing to change the subject before they parted. Mr Wilcox was a little apt to think one wanted to get something out of him.

'It's let.'

'Really. And you wandering homeless in long-haired Chelsea? How strange are the ways of Fate!'

'No; it's let unfurnished. We've moved.'

'Why, I thought of you both as anchored there for ever. Evie never told me.'

'I dare say when you met Evie the thing wasn't settled. We only moved a week ago. Paul has rather a feeling for the old place, and we held on for him to have his holiday there; but, really, it is impossibly small. Endless drawbacks. I forget whether you've been up to it?'

'As far as the house, never.'

'Well, Howards End is one of those converted farms. They don't really do, spend what you will on them. We messed away with a garage all among the wych-elm roots, and last year we enclosed a bit of the meadow and attempted a rockery. Evie got rather keen on Alpine plants. But it didn't do—no, it didn't do. You remember, or your sister will remember, the farm with those abominable guinea-fowls, and the hedge that the old woman never would cut properly, so that it all went thin at the bottom. And, inside the house, the beams—and the staircase through a door—picturesque enough, but not a place to live in.' He glanced over the parapet cheerfully. 'Full tide. And the position wasn't right either. The neighbourhood's getting suburban. Either be in London or out of it, I say; so we've taken a house in Ducie Street, close to Sloane Street, and a place right down in Shropshire—Oniton Grange. Ever heard of Oniton? Do come and see us—right away from everywhere, up towards Wales.'

'What a change!' said Margaret. But the change was in her own voice, which had become most sad. 'I can't imagine Howards End or Hilton without you.'

'Hilton isn't without us,' he replied. 'Charles is there still.'

'Still?' said Margaret, who had not kept up with the Charles'. 'But I thought he was still at Epsom. They were furnishing that Christmas—one Christmas. How everything alters! I used to admire Mrs Charles from our windows very often. Wasn't it Epsom?'

'Yes, but they moved eighteen months ago. Charles, the good chap'—his voice dropped—'thought I should be lonely. I didn't want him to move, but he would, and took a house at the other end of Hilton, down by the Six Hills. He had a motor, too. There they all are, a very jolly party—he and she and the two grandchildren.'

'I manage other people's affairs so much better than they manage them themselves,' said Margaret as they shook hands. 'When you moved out of Howards End, I should have moved Mr Charles Wilcox into it. I should have kept so remarkable a place in the family.'

'So it is,' he replied. 'I haven't sold it, and don't mean to.'

'No; but none of you are there.'

'Oh, we've got a splendid tenant—Hamar Bryce, an invalid. If Charles ever wanted it—but he won't. Dolly is so dependent on modern conveniences. No, we have all decided against Howards End. We like it in a way, but now we feel that it is neither one thing nor the other. One must have one thing or the other.'

'And some people are lucky enough to have both. You're doing yourself proud, Mr Wilcox. My congratulations.'

'And mine,' said Helen.

'Do remind Evie to come and see us—two, Wickham Place. We shan't be there very long, either.'

'You, too, on the move?'

'Next September,' Margaret sighed.

'Everyone moving! Good-bye.'

The tide had begun to ebb. Margaret leant over the parapet and watched it sadly. Mr Wilcox had forgotten his wife, Helen her lover; she herself was probably forgetting. Everyone moving. Is it worth while attempting the past when there is this continual flux even in the hearts of men?

Helen roused her by saying: 'What a prosperous vulgarian Mr Wilcox has grown! I have very little use for him in these days. However, he did tell us about the Porphyrion. Let us write to Mr Bast as soon as ever we get home, and tell him to clear out of it at once.'

'Do; yes, that's worth doing. Let us.'

'Let's ask him to tea.'

Chapter Sixteen

Leonard accepted the invitation to tea next Saturday. But he was right; the visit proved a conspicuous failure.

'Sugar?' said Margaret.

'Cake?' said Helen. 'The big cake or the little deadlies? I'm afraid you thought my letter rather odd, but we'll explain—we aren't cold, really—nor affected, really. We're over-expressive: that's all.'

As a lady's lap-dog Leonard did not excel. He was not an Italian, still less a Frenchman, in whose blood there runs the very spirit of persiflage and of gracious repartee. His wit was the Cockney's; it opened no doors into imagination, and Helen was drawn up short by 'The more a lady has to say, the better,' administered waggishly.

'Oh yes,' she said.

'Ladies brighten—'

'Yes, I know. The darlings are regular sunbeams. Let me give you a plate.'

'How do you like your work?' interposed Margaret.

He, too, was drawn up short. He would not have these women prying into his work. They were Romance, and so was the room to which he had at last penetrated, with the queer sketches of people bathing upon its walls, and so were the very tea-cups, with their delicate borders of wild strawberries. But he would not let Romance interfere with his life. There is the devil to pay then.

'Oh, well enough,' he answered.

'Your company is the Porphyrion, isn't it?'

'Yes, that's so'—becoming rather offended. 'It's funny how things get round.'

'Why funny?' asked Helen, who did not follow the workings of his mind. 'It was written as large as life on your card, and considering we wrote to you there, and that you replied on the stamped paper—'

'Would you call the Porphyrion one of the big Insurance Companies?' pursued Margaret.

'It depends what you call big.'

'I mean by big, a solid, well-established concern, that offers a reasonably good career to its employés.'

' I couldn't say—some would tell you one thing and others another,' said the employé uneasily. 'For my own part'—he shook his head—'I only believe half I hear. Not that even; it's safer. Those clever ones come to the worse grief, I've often noticed. Ah, you can't be too careful.'

He drank, and wiped his moustache, which was going to be one of those moustaches that always droop into tea-cups—more bother than they're worth, surely, and not fashionable either.

'I quite agree, and that's why I was curious to know: is it a solid, well-established concern?'

Leonard had no idea. He understood his own corner of the machine, but nothing beyond it. He desired to confess neither knowledge nor ignorance, and under these circumstances, another motion of the head seemed safest. To him, as to the British public, the Porphyrion was the Porphyrion of the advertisement—a giant, in the classical style, but draped sufficiently, who held in one hand a burning torch, and pointed with the other to St Paul's and Windsor Castle. A large sum of money was inscribed below, and you drew your own conclusions. This giant caused Leonard to do arithmetic and write letters, to explain the regulations to new clients, and re-explain them to old ones. A giant was of an impulsive morality—one knew that much. He would pay for Mrs Munt's hearth-rug with ostentatious haste, a large claim he would repudiate quietly, and fight court by court. But his true fighting weight, his antecedents, his amours with other members of the commercial Pantheon—all these were as uncertain to ordinary mortals as were the escapades of Zeus. While the gods are powerful, we learn little about them. It is only in the days of their decadence that a strong light beats into heaven.

'We were told the Porphyrion's no go,' blurted Helen. 'We wanted to tell you; that's why we wrote.'

'A friend of ours did think that it is insufficiently reinsured,' said Margaret.

Now Leonard had his clue. He must praise the Porphyrion. 'You can tell your friend,' he said, 'that he's quite wrong.'

'Oh, good!'

The young man coloured a little. In his circle to be wrong was fatal. The Miss Schlegels did not mind being wrong. They were genuinely glad that they had been misinformed. To them nothing was fatal but evil.

'Wrong, so to speak,' he added.

'How "so to speak"?'

'I mean I wouldn't say he's right altogether.'

But this was a blunder. 'Then he is right partly,' said the elder woman, quick as lightening.

Leonard replied that everyone was right partly, if it came to that.

'Mr Bast, I don't understand business, and I dare say my questions are stupid, but can you tell me what makes a concern "right" or "wrong"?'

Leonard sat back with a sigh.

'Our friend, who is also a business man, was so positive. He said before Christmas—'

'And advised you to clear out of it,' concluded Helen. 'But I don't see why he should know better than you do.'

Leonard rubbed his hands. He was tempted to say that he knew nothing about the thing at all. But a commercial training was too strong for him. Nor could he say it was a bad thing, for this would be giving it away; not yet that it was good, for this would be giving it away equally. He attempted to suggest that it was something between the two, with vast possibilities in either direction, but broke down under the gaze of four sincere eyes. And yet he scarcely distinguished between the two sisters. One was more beautiful and more lively, but 'the Miss Schlegels' still remained a composite Indian god, whose waving arms and contradictory speeches were the product of a single mind.

'One can but see,' he remarked, adding, 'as Ibsen says, "things happen."' He was itching to talk about books and make the most of his romantic hour. Minute after minute slipped away, while the ladies, with imperfect skill, discussed the subject of reinsurance or praised their anonymous friend. Leonard grew annoyed–perhaps rightly. He made vague remarks about not being one of those who minded their affairs being talked over by others, but they did not take the hint. Men might have shown more tact. Women, however tactful elsewhere, are heavy-handed here. They cannot see why we should shroud our incomes and our prospects in a veil. 'How much exactly have you, and how much do you expect to have next June?' And these were women with a theory, who held that reticence about money matters is absurd, and that life would be truer if each would state the exact size of the golden island upon which he stands, the exact stretch of warp over which he throws the woof that is not money. How can we do justice to the pattern otherwise?

And the precious minutes slipped away, and Jacky and squalor came nearer. At last he could bear it no longer, and broke in, reciting the names of books feverishly. There was a moment of piercing joy when Margaret said, 'So *you* like Carlyle,' and then the door opened, and 'Mr Wilcox, Miss Wilcox' entered, preceded by two prancing puppies.

'Oh, the dears! Oh, Evie, how too impossibly sweet!' screamed Helen, falling on her hands and knees.

'We brought the little fellows round,' said Mr Wilcox.

'I bred 'em myself.'

'Oh, really! Mr Bast, come and play with puppies.'

'I've got to be going now,' said Leonard sourly.

'But play with puppies a little first.'

'This is Ahab, that's Jezebel,' said Evie, who was one of those who name animals after the less successful characters of Old Testament history.

'I've got to be going.'

Helen was too much occupied with puppies to notice him.

'Mr Wilcox, Mr Ba— Must you be really? Good-bye!'

'Come again,' said Helen from the floor.

Then Leonard's gorge arose. Why should he come again? What was the good of it? He said roundly: 'No, I shan't; I knew it would be a failure.'

Most people would have let him go. 'A little mistake. We tried knowing another class—impossible.' But the Schlegels had never played with life. They had attempted friendship, and they would take the consequences. Helen retorted, 'I call that a very rude remark. What do you want to turn on me like that for?' and suddenly the drawing-room re-echoed to a vulgar row.

'You ask me why I turn on you?'

'Yes.'

'What do you want to have me here for?'

'To help you, you silly boy!' cried Helen. 'And don't shout.'

'*I* don't want your patronage. *I* don't want your tea. I was quite happy. What do you want to unsettle me for?' He turned to Mr Wilcox. 'I put it to this gentleman. I ask you, sir, am I to have my brain picked?'

Mr Wilcox turned to Margaret with the air of humorous strength that he could so well command. 'Are we intruding, Miss Schlegel? Can we be of any use, or shall we go?'

But Margaret ignored him.

'I'm connected with a leading insurance company, sir. I receive what I take to be an invitation from these—ladies' (he drawled the word). 'I come, and it's to have my brain picked. I ask you, is it fair?'

'Highly unfair,' said Mr Wilcox, drawing a gasp from Evie, who knew that her father was becoming dangerous.

'There, you hear that? Most unfair, the gentleman says. There! Not content with'—pointing at Margaret—'you can't deny it.' His voice rose: he was falling into the rhythm of a scene with Jacky. 'But as soon as I'm useful it's a very different thing. "Oh yes, send for him. Cross-question him. Pick his brains." Oh yes. Now, take me on the whole, I'm a quiet fellow: I'm law-abiding, I don't wish any unpleasantness; but I—I—'

'You,' said Margaret—'you—you—'

Laughter from Evie, as at a repartee.

'You are the man who tried to walk by the Pole star.'

More laughter.

'You saw the sunrise.'

Laughter.

'You tried to get away from the fogs that are stifling us all—away past books and houses to the truth. You were looking for a real home.'

'I fail to see the connection,' said Leonard, hot with stupid anger.

'So do I.' There was a pause. 'You were that last Sunday—you are this today. Mr Bast! I and my sister have talked you over. We wanted to help you; we also supposed you might help us. We did not have you here out of charity—which bores us—but because we hoped there would be a connection between last Sunday and other days. What is the good of your stars and trees, your sunrise and the wind, if they do not enter into our daily lives? They have never entered into mine, but into yours, we thought— Haven't we all to struggle against life's daily greyness, against pettiness, against mechanical cheerfulness, against suspicion? I struggle by remembering my friends; others I have known by remembering some place—some beloved place or tree—we thought you one of these.'

'Of course, if there's been any misunderstanding,' mumbled Leonard, 'all I can do is to go. But I beg to state—' He paused. Ahab and Jezebel danced at his boots and made him look ridiculous. 'You were picking my brain for official information—I can prove it—I—' He blew his nose and left them.

'Can I help you now?' said Mr Wilcox, turning to Margaret. 'May I have one quiet word with him in the hall?'

'Helen, go after him—do anything—*anything*—to make the noodle understand.'

Helen hesitated.

'But really—' said their visitor. 'Ought she to?'

At once she went.

He resumed. 'I would have chimed in, but I felt that you could polish him off for yourselves—I didn't interfere. You were splendid, Miss Schlegel—absolutely splendid. You can take my word for it, but there are very few women who could have managed him.'

'Oh yes,' said Margaret distractedly.

'Bowling him over with those long sentences was what fetched me,' cried Evie.

'Yes, indeed,' chuckled her father; 'all that part about "mechanical cheerfulness"—oh, fine!'

'I'm very sorry,' said Margaret, collecting herself. 'He's a nice creature really. I cannot think what set him off. It has been most unpleasant for you.'

'Oh, *I* didn't mind.' Then he changed his mood. He asked if he might speak as an old friend, and, permission given, said: 'Oughtn't you really to be more careful?'

Margaret laughed, though her thoughts still strayed after Helen. 'Do you realize that it's all your fault?' she said. 'You're responsible.'

'I?'

'This is the young man whom we were to warn against the Porphyrion. We warn him, and—look!'

Mr Wilcox was annoyed. 'I hardly consider that a fair deduction,' he said.

'Obviously unfair,' said Margaret. 'I was only thinking how tangled things are. It's our fault mostly—neither yours nor his.'

'Not his?'

'No.'

'Miss Schlegel, you are too kind.'

'Yes, indeed,' nodded Evie, a little contemptuously.

'You behave much too well to people, and then they impose on you. I know the world and that type of man, and as soon as I entered the room I saw you had not been treating him properly. You must keep that type at a distance. Otherwise they forget themselves. Sad, but true. They aren't our sort, and one must face the fact.'

'Ye-es.'

'Do admit that we should never have had the outburst if he was a gentleman.'

'I admit it willingly,' said Margaret, who was pacing up and down the room. 'A gentleman would have kept his suspicions to himself.'

Mr Wilcox watched her with a vague uneasiness.

'What did he suspect you of?'

'Of wanting to make money out of him.'

'Intolerable brute! But how were you to benefit?'

'Exactly. How indeed! Just horrible, corroding suspicion. One touch of thought or of goodwill would have brushed it away. Just the senseless fear that does make men intolerable brutes.'

'I come back to my original point. You ought to be more careful, Miss Schlegel. Your servants ought to have orders not to let such people in.'

She turned to him frankly. 'Let me explain exactly why we like this man, and want to see him again.'

'That's your clever way of talking. I shall never believe you like him.'

'I do. Firstly, because he cares for physical adventure, just as you do. Yes, you go motoring and shooting; he would like to go camping out. Secondly, he cares for something special *in* adventure. It is quickest to call that special something poetry—'

'Oh, he's one of that writer sort.'

'No—oh no! I mean he may be, but it would be loathsome stuff. His brain is filled with the husks of books, culture—horrible; we want him to wash out his brain and go to the real thing. We want to show him how he may get upsides with life. As I said, either friends or the country, some'—she hesitated—'either some very dear person or some very dear place seems necessary to relieve life's daily grey, and to show that it is grey. If possible, one should have both.'

Some of her words ran past Mr Wilcox. He let them run past. Others he caught and criticized with admirable lucidity.

'Your mistake is this, and it is a very common mistake. This young bounder has a life of his own. What right have you to conclude it is an unsuccessful life, or, as you call it, "grey"?'

'Because—'

'One minute. You know nothing about him. He probably has his own joys and interests—wife, children, snug little home. That's where we practical fellows'—he smiled—'are more tolerant than you intellectuals. We live and let live, and assume that things are jogging on fairly well elsewhere, and that the ordinary plain man may be trusted to look after his own affairs. I quite grant—I look at the faces of the clerks in my own office, and observe them to be dull, but I don't know what's going on beneath. So, by the way, with

London. I have heard you rail against London, Miss Schlegel, and it seems a funny thing to say but I was very angry with you. What do you know about London? You only see civilization from the outside. I don't say in your case, but in too many cases that attitude leads to morbidity, discontent, and Socialism.'

She admitted the strength of his position, though it undermined imagination. As he spoke, some outposts of poetry and perhaps of sympathy fell ruining, and she retreated to what she called her 'second line'—to the special facts of the case.

'His wife is an old bore,' she said simply. 'He never came home last Saturday night because he wanted to be alone, and she thought he was with us.'

'With *you*?'

'Yes.' Evie tittered. 'He hasn't got the cosy home that you assumed. He needs outside interests.

'Naughty young man!' cried the girl.

'Naughty?' said Margaret, who hated naughtiness more than sin. 'When you're married, Miss Wilcox, won't you want outside interests?'

'He has apparently got them,' put in Mr Wilcox slyly.

'Yes, indeed, father.'

'He was tramping in Surrey, if you mean that,' said Margaret, pacing away rather crossly.

'Oh, I dare say!'

'Miss Wilcox, he was!'

'M-m-m-m!' from Mr Wilcox, who thought the episode amusing, if risqué. With most ladies he would not have discussed it, but he was trading on Margaret's reputation as an emancipated woman.

'He said so, and about such a thing he wouldn't lie.'

They both began to laugh.

'That's where I differ from you. Men lie about their positions and prospects, but not about a thing of that sort.'

He shook his head. 'Miss Schlegel, excuse me, but I know the type.'

'I said before—he isn't a type. He cares about adventures rightly. He's certain that our smug existence isn't all. He's vulgar and hysterical and bookish, but don't think that sums him up. There's manhood in him as well. Yes, that's what I'm trying to say. He's a real man.'

As she spoke their eyes met, and it was as if Mr Wilcox's defences fell. She saw back to the real man in him. Unwittingly she had touched his emotions. A woman and two men—they had formed the magic triangle of sex, and the male was thrilled to jealousy, in case the female was attracted by another male. Love, say the ascetics, reveals our shameful kinship with the beasts. Be it so: one can bear that; jealousy is the real shame. It is jealousy, not love, that connects us with the farmyard intolerably, and calls up visions of two angry cocks and a complacent hen. Margaret crushed complacency down because she was civilized. Mr Wilcox, uncivilized, continued to feel anger long after he had rebuilt his defences, and was again presenting a bastion to the world.

'Miss Schlegel, you're a pair of dear creatures, but you really *must* be careful in this uncharitable world. What does your brother say?'

'I forget.'

'Surely he has some opinion?'

'He laughs, if I remember correctly.'

'He's very clever, isn't he?' said Evie, who had met and detested Tibby at Oxford.

'Yes, pretty well—but I wonder what Helen's doing.'

'She is very young to undertake this sort of thing,' said Mr Wilcox.

Margaret went out into the landing. She heard no sound, and Mr Bast's topper was missing from the hall.

'Helen!' she called.

'Yes!' replied a voice from the library.

'You in there?'

'Yes—he's gone some time.'

Margaret went to her. 'Why, you're all alone,' she said.

'Yes—it's all right, Meg. Poor, poor creature—'

'Come back to the Wilcoxes and tell me later—Mr W. much concerned, and slightly titillated.'

'Oh, I've no patience with him. I hate him. Poor dear Mr Bast! he wanted to talk literature, and we would talk business. Such a muddle of a man, and yet so worth pulling through. I like him extraordinarily.'

'Well done,' said Margaret, kissing her, 'but come into the drawing-room now, and don't talk about him to the Wilcoxes. Make light of the whole thing.'

Helen came and behaved with a cheerfulness that reassured their visitor—this hen at all events was fancy-free.

'He's gone with my blessing,' she cried, 'and now for puppies.'

As they drove away, Mr Wilcox said to his daughter:

'I am really concerned at the way those girls go on. They are as clever as you make 'em, but unpractical—God bless me! One of these days they'll go too far. Girls like that oughtn't to live alone in London. Until they marry, they ought to have someone to look after them. We must look in more often—we're better than no one. You like them, don't you, Evie?'

Evie replied: 'Helen's right enough, but I can't stand the toothy one. And I shouldn't have called either of them girls.'

Evie had grown up handsome. Dark-eyed, with the glow of youth under sunburn, built firmly and firm-lipped, she was the best the Wilcoxes could do in the way of feminine beauty. For the present, puppies and her father were the only things she loved, but the net of matrimony was being prepared for her, and a few days later she was attracted to a Mr Percy Cahill, an uncle of Mrs Charles', and he was attracted to her.

Chapter Seventeen

The Age of Property holds bitter moments even for a proprietor. When a move is imminent, furniture becomes ridiculous, and Margaret now lay awake at nights wondering where, where on earth they and all their belongings would be deposited in September next. Chairs, tables, pictures, books, that had rumbled down to them through the generations, must rumble forward again like a slide of rubbish to which she longed to give the final push, and send toppling into the sea. But there were all their father's books—they never read them, but they were their father's and must be kept. There was the marble-topped cheffonier—their mother had set store by it, they could not remember why. Round every knob and cushion in the house sentiment gathered, a sentiment that was at times personal, but more often a faint piety to the dead, a prolongation of rites that might have ended at the grave.

It was absurd, if you came to think of it; Helen and Tibby came to think of it: Margaret was too busy with the house-agents. The feudal ownership of land did bring dignity, whereas the modern ownership of movables is reducing us again to a nomadic horde. We are reverting to the civilization of luggage, and historians of the future will note how the middle classes accreted possessions without taking root in the earth, and may find in this the secret of their imaginative poverty. The Schlegels were certainly the poorer for the loss of Wickham Place. It had helped to balance their lives, and almost to counsel them. Nor is their ground-landlord spiritually the richer. He has built flats on its site, his motor-cars grow swifter, his exposures of Socialism more trenchant. But he has spilt the precious distillation of the years, and no chemistry of his can give it back to society again.

Margaret grew depressed; she was anxious to settle on a house before they left town to pay their annual visit to Mrs Munt. She enjoyed this visit, and wanted to have her mind at ease for it. Swanage, though dull, was stable, and this year she longed more than usual for its fresh air and for the magnificent downs that guard it on the north. But London thwarted her; in its atmosphere she could not concentrate. London only stimulates, it cannot sustain; and Margaret, hurrying over its surface for a house without knowing what sort of a house she wanted, was paying for many a thrilling sensation in the past. She could not even break loose from culture, and her time was wasted by concerts which it would be a sin to miss, and invitations which it would never do to refuse. At last she grew desperate; she resolved that she would go nowhere and be at home to no one until she found a house, and broke the resolution in half an hour.

Once she had humorously lamented that she had never been to Simpson's restaurant in the Strand. Now a note arrived from Miss Wilcox, asking her to lunch there. Mr Cahill was coming, and the three would have such a jolly chat, and perhaps end up at the Hippodrome. Margaret had no strong regard for Evie, and no desire to meet her fiancé, and she was surprised that Helen, who had been far funnier about Simpson's, had not been asked instead. But the invitation touched her by its intimate tone. She must know Evie Wilcox better than she supposed, and declaring that she 'simply must,' she accepted.

But when she saw Evie at the entrance of the restaurant, staring fiercely at nothing after the fashion of athletic women, her heart failed her anew. Miss Wilcox had changed perceptibly since her engagement. Her voice was gruffer, her manner more downright, and she was inclined to patronize the more foolish virgin. Margaret was silly enough to be pained at this. Depressed at her isolation, she saw not only houses and furniture, but the vessel of life itself slipping past her, with people like Evie and Mr Cahill on board.

There are moments when virtue and wisdom fail us, and one of them came to her at Simpson's in the Strand. As she trod the staircase, narrow, but carpeted thickly, as she entered the eating-room, where saddles of mutton were being trundled up to expectant clergymen, she had a strong, if erroneous, conviction of her own futility, and wished she had never come out of her backwater, where nothing happened except art and literature, and where no one ever got married or succeeded in remaining engaged. Then came a little surprise. 'Father might be of the party—yes, father was.' With a smile of pleasure she moved forward to greet him, and her feeling of loneliness vanished.

'I thought I'd get round if I could,' said he. 'Evie told me of her little plan, so I just slipped in and secured a table. Always secure a table first. Evie, don't pretend you want to sit by your old father, because you don't. Miss Schlegel, come in my side, out of pity. My goodness, but you look tired! Been worrying round after your young clerks?'

'No, after houses,' said Margaret, edging past him into the box. 'I'm hungry, not tired; I want to eat heaps.'

'That's good. What'll you have?'

'Fish pie,' said she, with a glance at the menu.

'Fish pie! Fancy coming for fish pie to Simpson's. It's not a bit the thing to go for here.'

'Go for something for me, then,' said Margaret, pulling off her gloves. Her spirits were rising, and his reference to Leonard Bast had warmed her curiously.

'Saddle of mutton,' said he after profound reflection; 'and cider to drink. That's the type of thing. I like this place, for a joke, once in a way. It is so thoroughly Old English. Don't you agree?'

'Yes,' said Margaret, who didn't. The order was given, the joint rolled up, and the carver, under Mr Wilcox's direction, cut the meat where it was succulent, and piled their plates high. Mr Cahill insisted on sirloin, but admitted that he had made a mistake later on. He and Evie soon fell into a conversation of the 'No I didn't; yes, you did' type–conversation which, though fascinating to those who are engaged in it, neither desires nor deserves the attention of others.

'It's a golden rule to tip the carver. Tip everywhere's my motto.'

'Perhaps it does make life more human.'

'Then the fellows know one again. Especially in the East, if you tip, they remember you from year's end to year's end.'

'Have you been in the East?'

'Oh, Greece and the Levant. I used to go out for sport and business to Cyprus; some military society of a sort there. A few piastres, properly distributed, help to keep one's memory green. But you, of course, think this shockingly cynical. How's your discussion society getting on? Any new Utopias lately?'

'No, I'm house-hunting, Mr Wilcox, as I've already told you once. Do you know of any houses?'

'Afraid I don't.'

'Well, what's the point of being practical if you can't find two distressed females a house? We merely want a small house with large rooms, and plenty of them.'

'Evie, I like that! Miss Schlegel expects me to turn house agent for her!'

'What's that, father!'

'I want a new home in September, and someone must find it. I can't.'

'Percy, do you know of anything?'

'I can't say I do,' said Mr Cahill.

'How like you! You're never any good.'

'Never any good. Just listen to her! Never any good. Oh, come!'

'Well, you aren't. Miss Schlegel, is he?'

The torrent of their love, having splashed these drops at Margaret, swept away on its habitual course. She sympathized with it now, for a little comfort had restored her geniality. Speech and silence pleased her equally, and while Mr Wilcox made some preliminary inquiries about cheese, her eyes surveyed the restaurant, and admired its well-calculated tributes to the solidity of our past. Though no more Old English than the works of Kipling, it had selected its reminiscences so adroitly that her criticism was lulled, and the guests whom it was nourishing for imperial purposes bore the outer semblance of Parson Adams or Tom Jones. Scraps of their talk jarred oddly on the ear. 'Right you are! I'll cable out to Uganda this evening,' came from the table behind. 'Their Emperor wants war; well, let him have it,' was the opinion of a clergyman. She smiled at such incongruities. 'Next time,' she said to Mr Wilcox, 'you shall come to lunch with me at Mr Eustace Miles's.'

'With pleasure.'

'No, you'd hate it,' she said, pushing her glass towards him for some more cider. 'It's all proteids and body buildings, and people come up to you and beg your pardon, but you have such a beautiful aura.'

'A what?'

'Never heard of an aura? Oh, happy, happy man! I scrub at mine for hours. Nor of an astral plane?'

He had heard of astral planes, and censured them.

'Just so. Luckily it was Helen's aura, not mine, and she had to chaperone it and do the politeness. I just sat with my handkerchief in my mouth till the man went.'

'Funny experiences seem to come to you two girls. No one's ever asked me about my—what d'ye call it? Perhaps I've not got one.'

'You're bound to have one, but it may be such a terrible colour that no one dares mention it.'

'Tell me, though, Miss Schlegel, do you really believe in the supernatural and all that?'

'Too difficult a question.'

'Why's that? Gruyère or Stilton?'

'Gruyère, please.'

'Better have Stilton.'

'Stilton. Because, though I don't believe in auras, and think Theosophy's only a halfway-house—'

'—Yet there may be something in it all the same,' he concluded, with a frown.

'Not even that. It may be halfway in the wrong direction. I can't explain. I don't believe in all these fads, and yet I don't like saying that I don't believe in them.'

He seemed unsatisfied, and said: 'So you wouldn't give me your word that you *don't* hold with astral bodies and all the rest of it?'

'I could,' said Margaret, surprised that the point was of any importance to him. 'Indeed, I will. When I talked about scrubbing my aura, I was only trying to be funny. But why do you want this settled?'

'I don't know.'

'Now, Mr Wilcox, you do know.'

'Yes, I am,' 'No, you're not,' burst from the lovers opposite. Margaret was silent for a moment, and then changed the subject.

'How's your house?'

'Much the same as when you honoured it last week.'

'I don't mean Ducie Street. Howards End, of course.'

'Why "of course"?'

'Can't you turn out your tenant and let it to us? We're nearly demented.'

'Let me think. I wish I could help you. But I thought you wanted to be in town. One bit of advice: fix your district, then fix your price, and then don't budge. That's how I got both Ducie Street and Oniton. I said to myself, 'I mean to be exactly here,' and I was, and Oniton's a place in a thousand.'

'But I do budge. Gentlemen seem to mesmerize houses—cow them with an eye, and up they come, trembling. Ladies can't. It's the houses that are mesmerizing me. I've no control over the saucy things. Houses are alive. No?'

'I'm out of my depth,' he said, and added: 'Didn't you talk rather like that to your office boy?'

'Did I – I mean I did, more or less. I talk the same way to everyone – or try to.'

'Yes, I know. And how much do you suppose that he understood of it?'

'That's his lookout. I don't believe in suiting my conversation to my company. One can doubtless hit upon some medium of exchange that seems to do well enough, but it's no more like the real thing than money is like food. There's no nourishment in it. You pass it to the lower classes, and they pass it back to you, and this you call 'social intercourse' or 'mutual endeavour,' when it's mutual priggishness if it's anything. Our friends at Chelsea don't see this. They say one ought to be at all costs intelligible, and sacrifice—'

'Lower classes,' interrupted Mr Wilcox, as it were thrusting his hand into her speech. 'Well, you do admit that there are rich and poor. That's something.'

Margaret could not reply. Was he incredibly stupid, or did he understand her better than she understood herself?

'You do admit that, if wealth was divided up equally, in a few years there would be rich and poor again just the same. The hard-working man would come to the top, the wastrel sink to the bottom.'

'Everyone admits that.'

'Your Socialists don't.'

'My Socialists do. Yours mayn't; but I strongly suspect yours of being not Socialists, but ninepins, which you have constructed for your own amusement. I can't imagine any living creature who would bowl over quite so easily.'

He would have resented this had she not been a woman. But women may say anything – it was one of his holiest beliefs – and he only retorted, with a gay smile: 'I don't care. You've made two damaging admissions, and I'm heartily with you in both.'

In time they finished lunch, and Margaret, who had excused herself from the Hippodrome, took her leave. Evie had scarcely addressed her, and she suspected that the entertainment had been planned by the father. He and she were advancing out of their respective families towards a more intimate acquaintance. It had begun long ago. She had been his wife's friend, and, as such, he had given her that silver vinaigrette as a memento. It was pretty of him to have given that vinaigrette, and he had always preferred her to Helen – unlike most men. But the advance had been astonishing lately. They had done more in a week than in two years, and were really beginning to know each other.

She did not forget his promise to sample Eustace Miles, and asked him as soon as she could secure Tibby as his chaperon. He came, and partook of body-building dishes with humility.

Next morning the Schlegels left for Swanage. They had not succeeded in finding a new home.

Chapter Eighteen

As they were seated at Aunt Juley's breakfast-table at The Bays, parrying her excessive hospitality and enjoying the view of the bay, a letter came for Margaret and threw her into perturbation. It was from Mr Wilcox. It announced an 'important change' in his plans. Owing to Evie's marriage, he had decided to give up his house in Ducie Street, and was willing to let it on a yearly tenancy. It was a businesslike letter, and stated frankly what he would do for them and what he would not do. Also the rent. If they approved, Margaret was to come up *at once*—the words were underlined, as is necessary when dealing with women—and to go over the house with him. If they disapproved, a wire would oblige, as he should put it into the hands of an agent.

The letter perturbed, because she was not sure what it meant. If he liked her, if he had manœuvred to get her to Simpson's, might this be a manœuvre to get her to London, and result in an offer of marriage? She put it to herself as indelicately as possible, in the hope that her brain would cry, 'Rubbish, you're a self-conscious fool!' But her brain only tingled a little and was silent, and for a time she sat gazing at the mincing waves, and wondering whether the news would seem strange to the others.

As soon as she began speaking, the sound of her own voice reassured her. There could be nothing in it. The replies also were typical, and in the burr of conversation her fears vanished.

'You needn't go though—' began her hostess.

'I needn't, but hadn't I better? It's really getting rather serious. We let chance after chance slip, and the end of it is we shall be bundled out bag and baggage into the street. We don't know what we *want*, that's the mischief with us—'

'No, we have no real ties,' said Helen, helping herself to toast.

'Shan't I go up to town to-day, take the house if it's the least possible, and then come down by the afternoon train to-morrow, and start enjoying myself. I shall be no fun to myself or to others until this business is off my mind.'

'But you won't do anything rash, Margaret?'

'There's nothing rash to do.'

'Who *are* the Wilcoxes?' said Tibby, a question that sounds silly, but was really extremely subtle, as his aunt found to her cost when she tried to answer it. 'I don't *manage* the Wilcoxes; I don't see where they come *in*.'

'No more do I,' agreed Helen. 'It's funny that we just don't lose sight of them. Out of all our hotel acquaintances, Mr Wilcox is the only one who has stuck. It is now over three years, and we have drifted away from far more interesting people in that time.'

'Interesting people don't get one houses.'

'Meg, if you start in your honest-English vein, I shall throw the treacle at you.'

'It's a better vein than the cosmopolitan,' said Margaret, getting up. 'Now, children, which is it to be? You know the Ducie Street house. Shall I say yes or shall I say no? Tibby love—which? I'm specially anxious to pin you both.'

'It all depends what meaning you attach to the word "possi—"'

'It depends on nothing of the sort. Say "yes."'

'Say "no."'

Then Margaret spoke rather seriously. 'I think,' she said, 'that our race is degenerating. We cannot settle even this little thing; what will it be like when we have to settle a big one?'

'It will be as easy as eating,' returned Helen.

'I was thinking of father. How could he settle to leave Germany as he did, when he had fought for it as a young man, and all his feelings and friends were Prussian? How could he break loose with Patriotism and begin aiming at something else? It would have killed me. When he was nearly forty he could change countries and ideals—and we, at our age, can't change houses. It's humiliating.'

'Your father may have been able to change countries,' said Mrs Munt with asperity, 'and that may or may not be a good thing. But he could change houses no better than you can, in fact, much worse. Never shall I forget what poor Emily suffered in the move from Manchester.'

'I knew it,' cried Helen. 'I told you so. It is the little things one bungles at. The big, real ones are nothing when they come.'

'Bungle, my dear! You are too little to recollect—in fact, you weren't there. But the furniture was actually in the vans and on the move before the lease for Wickham Place was signed, and Emily took train with baby—who was Margaret then—and the smaller luggage for London, without so much as knowing where her new home would be. Getting away from that house may be hard, but it is nothing to the misery that we all went through getting you into it.'

Helen, with her mouth full, cried:

'And that's the man who beat the Austrians, and the Danes, and the French, and who beat the Germans that were inside himself. And we're like him.'

'Speak for yourself,' said Tibby. 'Remember that I am cosmopolitan, please.'

'Helen may be right.'

'Of course she's right,' said Helen.

Helen might be right, but she did not go up to London. Margaret did that. An interrupted holiday is the worst of the minor worries, and one may be pardoned for feeling morbid when a business letter snatches one away from the sea and friends. She could not believe that her father had ever felt the same. Her eyes had been troubling her lately, so that she could not read in the train, and it bored her to look at the landscape, which she had seen but yesterday. At Southampton she 'waved' to Frieda: Frieda was on her way down to join them at Swanage, and Mrs Munt had calculated that their trains would cross. But Frieda was looking the other way, and Margaret travelled on to town feeling solitary and old-maidish. How like an old maid to fancy that Mr Wilcox was courting her! She had once visited a spinster–poor, silly, and unattractive–whose mania it was that every man who approached her fell in love. How Margaret's heart had bled for the deluded thing! How she had lectured, reasoned, and in despair acquiesced! 'I may have been deceived by the curate, my dear, but the young fellow who brings the midday post really is fond of me, and has, as a matter fact—' It had always seemed to her the most hideous corner of old age, yet she might be driven into it herself by the mere pressure of virginity.

Mr Wilcox met her at Waterloo himself. She felt certain that he was not the same as usual; for one thing, he took offence at everything she said.

'This is awfully kind of you,' she began, 'but I'm afraid it's not going to do. The house has not been built that suits the Schlegel family.'

'What! Have you come up determined not to deal?'

'Not exactly.'

'Not exactly? In that case let's be starting.'

She lingered to admire the motor, which was new, and a fairer creature than the vermilion giant that had borne Aunt Juley to her doom three years before.

'Presumably it's very beautiful,' she said. 'How do you like it, Crane?'

'Come, let's be starting,' repeated her host. 'How on earth did you know that my chauffeur was called Crane?'

'Why, I know Crane: I've been for a drive with Evie once. I know that you've got a parlourmaid called Milton. I know all sorts of things.'

'Evie!' he echoed in injured tones. 'You won't see her. She's gone out with Cahill. It's no fun, I can tell you, being left so much alone. I've got my work all day–indeed, a great deal too much of it–but when I come home in the evening, I tell you, I can't stand the house.'

'In my absurd way, I'm lonely too,' Margaret replied. 'It's heart-breaking to leave one's old home. I scarcely remember anything before Wickham Place, and Helen and Tibby were born there. Helen says—'

'You, too, feel lonely?'

'Horribly. Hullo, Parliament's back!'

Mr Wilcox glanced at Parliament contemptuously. The more important ropes of life lay elsewhere. 'Yes, they are talking again,' said he. 'But you were going to say—'

'Only some rubbish about furniture. Helen says it alone endures while men and houses perish, and that in the end the world will be a desert of chairs and sofas–just imagine it!–rolling through infinity with no one to sit upon them.'

'Your sister always likes her little joke.'

'She says "Yes," my brother says "No," to Ducie Street. It's no fun helping us, Mr Wilcox, I assure you.'

'You are not as unpractical as you pretend. I shall never believe it.'

Margaret laughed. But she was—quite as unpractical. She could not concentrate on details. Parliament, the Thames, the irresponsive chauffeur, would flash into the field of house-hunting, and all demand some comment or response. It is impossible to see modern life steadily and see it whole, and she had chosen to see it whole. Mr Wilcox saw steadily. He never bothered over the mysterious or the private. The Thames might run inland from the sea, the chauffeur might conceal all passion and philosophy beneath his unhealthy skin. They knew their own business, and he knew his.

Yet she liked being with him. He was not a rebuke, but a stimulus, and banished morbidity. Some twenty years her senior, he preserved a gift that she supposed herself to have already lost – not youth's creative power, but its self-confidence and optimism. He was so sure that it was a very pleasant world. His complexion was robust, his hair had receded but not thinned, the thick moustache and the eyes that Helen had compared to brandy-balls had an agreeable menace in them, whether they were turned towards the slums or towards the stars. Some day—in the millennium—there may be no need for his type. At present, homage is due to it from those who think themselves superior, and who possibly are.

'At all events you responded to my telegram promptly,' he remarked.

'Oh, even I know a good thing when I see it.'

'I'm glad you don't despise the goods of this world.'

'Heavens, no! Only idiots and prigs do that.'

'I am glad, very glad,' he repeated, suddenly softening and turning to her, as if the remark had pleased him. 'There is so much cant talked in would-be intellectual circles. I am glad you don't share it. Self-denial is all very well as a means of strengthening the character. But I can't stand those people who run down comforts. They have usually some axe to grind. Can you?'

'Comforts are of two kinds,' said Margaret, who was keeping herself in hand—'those we can share with others, like fire, weather, or music; and those we can't—food, for instance. It depends.'

'I mean reasonable comforts, of course. I shouldn't like to think that you—' He bent nearer; the sentence died unfinished. Margaret's head turned very stupid, and the inside of it seemed to revolve like the beacon in a lighthouse. He did not kiss her, for the hour was half-past twelve, and the car was passing by the stables of Buckingham Palace. But the atmosphere was so charged with emotion that people only seemed to exist on her account, and she was surprised that Crane did not realize this, and turn round. Idiot though she might be, surely Mr Wilcox was more – how should one put it? – more psychological than usual. Always a good judge of character for business purposes, he seemed this afternoon to enlarge his field, and to note qualities outside neatness, obedience, and decision.

'I want to go over the whole house,' she announced when they arrived. 'As soon as I get back to Swanage, which will be to-morrow afternoon, I'll talk it over once more with Helen and Tibby, and wire you "yes" or "no."'

'Right. The dining-room.' And they began their survey.

The dining-room was big, but over-furnished. Chelsea would have moaned aloud. Mr Wilcox had eschewed those decorative schemes that wince, and relent, and refrain, and achieve beauty by sacrificing comfort and pluck. After so much self-colour and self-denial, Margaret viewed with relief the sumptuous dado, the frieze, the gilded wall-paper, amid whose foliage parrots sang. It would never do with her own furniture, but those heavy chairs, that immense sideboard loaded with presentation plate, stood up against its pressure like men. The room suggested men, and Margaret, keen to derive the modern capitalist from the warriors and hunters of the past, saw it as an ancient guest-hall, where the lord sat at meat among his thanes. Even the Bible–the Dutch Bible that Charles had brought back from the Boer War–fell into position. Such a room admitted loot.

'Now the entrance-hall.'

The entrance-hall was paved.

'Here we fellows smoke.'

We fellows smoked in chairs of maroon leather. It was as if a motor-car had spawned. 'Oh, jolly!' said Margaret, sinking into one of them.

'You do like it?' he said, fixing his eyes on her upturned face, and surely betraying an almost intimate note. 'It's all rubbish not making oneself comfortable. Isn't it?'

'Ye-es. Semi-rubbish. Are those Cruikshanks?'

'Gillrays. Shall we go on upstairs?'

'Does all this furniture come from Howards End?'

'The Howards End furniture has all gone to Oniton.'

'Does— However, I'm concerned with the house, not the furniture. How big is this smoking-room?'

'Thirty by fifteen. No, wait a minute. Fifteen and a half.'

'Ah, well. Mr Wilcox, aren't you ever amused at the solemnity with which we middle classes approach the subject of houses?'

They proceeded to the drawing-room. Chelsea managed better here. It was sallow and ineffective. One could visualize the ladies withdrawing to it, while their lords discussed life's realities below, to the accompaniment of cigars. Had Mrs Wilcox's drawing-room looked thus at Howards End? Just as this thought entered Margaret's brain, Mr Wilcox did ask her to be his wife, and the knowledge that she had been right so overcame her that she nearly fainted.

But the proposal was not to rank among the world's great love scenes.

'Miss Schlegel'–his voice was firm–'I have had you up on false pretences. I want to speak about a much more serious matter than a house.'

Margaret almost answered: 'I know—'

'Could you be induced to share my–is it probable—'

'Oh, Mr Wilcox!' she interrupted, holding the piano and averting her eyes. 'I see, I see. I will write to you afterwards if I may.'

He began to stammer. 'Miss Schlegel–Margaret–you don't understand.'

'Oh yes! Indeed, yes!' said Margaret.

'I am asking you to be my wife.'

So deep already was her sympathy, that when he said, 'I am asking you to be my wife,' she made herself give a little start. She must show surprise if he expected it. An immense joy came over her. It was indescribable. It had nothing to do with humanity, and most resembled the all-pervading happiness of fine weather. Fine weather is due to the sun, but Margaret could think of no central radiance here. She stood in his drawing-room happy, and longing to give happiness. On leaving him she realized that the central radiance had been love.

'You aren't offended, Miss Schlegel?'

'How could I be offended?'

There was a moment's pause. He was anxious to get rid of her, and she knew it. She had too much intuition to look at him as he struggled for possessions that money cannot buy. He desired comradeship and affection, but he feared them, and she, who had taught herself only to desire, and could have clothed the struggle with beauty, held back, and hesitated with him.

'Good-bye,' she continued. 'You will have a letter from me—I am going back to Swanage to-morrow.'

'Thank you.'

'Good-bye, and it's you I thank.'

'I may order the motor round, mayn't I?'

'That would be most kind.'

'I wish I had written instead. Ought I to have written?'

'Not at all.'

'There's just one question—'

She shook her head. He looked a little bewildered, and they parted.

They parted without shaking hands: she had kept the interview, for his sake, in tints of the quietest grey. Yet she thrilled with happiness ere she reached her own house. Others had loved her in the past, if one may apply to their brief desires so grave a word, but those others had been 'ninnies'—young men who had nothing to do, old men who could find nobody better. And she had often 'loved,' too, but only so far as the facts of sex demanded: mere yearnings for the masculine, to be dismissed for what they were worth, with a smile. Never before had her personality been touched. She was not young or very rich, and it amazed her that a man of any standing should take her seriously. As she sat trying to do accounts in her empty house, amidst beautiful pictures and noble books, waves of emotion broke, as if a tide of passion was flowing through the night air. She shook her head, tried to concentrate her attention, and failed. In vain did she repeat: 'But I've been through this sort of thing before.' She had never been through it; the big machinery, as opposed to the little, had been set in motion, and the idea that Mr Wilcox loved, obsessed her before she came to love him in return.

She would come to no decision yet. 'Oh, sir, this is so sudden'—that prudish phrase exactly expressed her when her time came. Premonitions are not preparation. She must examine more closely her own nature and his; she must talk it over judicially with Helen. It has been a strange love-scene—the central radiance unacknowledged from first to last. She, in his place, would have said 'Ich liebe dich,' but perhaps it was not his habit to open the heart. He might have done it if she had pressed him—as a matter of duty, perhaps; England expects every man to open his heart once; but the effort would have jarred him, and never, if she could avoid it, should he lose those defences that he had chosen to raise against the world. He must never be bothered with emotional talk, or with a display of sympathy. He was an elderly man now, and it would be futile and impudent to correct him.

Mrs Wilcox strayed in and out, ever a welcome ghost; surveying the scene, thought Margaret, without one hint of bitterness.

Chapter Nineteen

If one wanted to show a foreigner England, perhaps the wisest course would be to take him to the final section of the Purbeck Hills, and stand him on their summit, a few miles to the east of Corfe. Then system after system of our island would roll together under his feet. Beneath him is the valley of the Frome, and all the wild lands that come tossing down from Dorchester, black and gold, to mirror their gorse in the expanses of Poole. The valley of the Stour is beyond, unaccountable stream, dirty at Blandford, pure at Wimborne—the Stour, sliding out of fat fields, to marry the Avon beneath the tower of Christchurch. The valley of the Avon—invisible, but far to the north the trained eye may see Clearbury Ring that guards it, and the imagination may leap beyond that on to Salisbury Plain itself, and beyond the Plain to all the glorious downs of Central England. Nor is Suburbia absent. Bournemouth's ignoble coast cowers to the right, heralding the pine-trees that mean, for all their beauty, red houses, and the Stock Exchange, and extend to the gates of London itself. So tremendous is the City's trail! But the cliffs of Freshwater it shall never touch, and the island will guard the Island's purity till the end of time. Seen from the west, the Wight is beautiful beyond all laws of beauty. It is as if a fragment of England floated forward to greet the foreigner—chalk of our chalk, turf of our turf, epitome of what will follow. And behind the fragment lies Southampton, hostess to the nations, and Portsmouth, a latent fire, and all around it, with double and treble collision of tides, swirls the sea. How many villages appear in this view! How many castles! How many churches, vanished or triumphant! How many ships, railways, and roads! What incredible variety of men working beneath that lucent sky to what final end! The reason fails, like a wave on the Swanage beach; the imagination swells, spreads, and deepens, until it becomes geographic and encircles England.

So Frieda Mosebach, now Frau Architect Liesecke, and mother to her husband's baby, was brought up to these heights to be impressed, and, after a prolonged gaze, she said that the hills were more swelling here than in Pomerania, which was true, but did not seem to Mrs Munt apposite. Poole

Harbour was dry, which led her to praise the absence of muddy foreshore at
Friedrich Wilhelms Bad, Rügen, where beech-trees hang over the tideless
Baltic, and cows may contemplate the brine. Rather unhealthy Mrs Munt
thought his would be, water being safer when it moved about.

'And your English lakes–Vindermere, Grasmere–are they, then,
unhealthy?'

'No, Frau Liesecke; but that is because they are fresh water, and different.
Salt water ought to have tides, and go up and down a great deal, or else it
smells. Look, for instance, at an aquarium.'

'An aquarium! Oh, *Meesis* Munt, you mean to tell me that fresh
aquariums stink less than salt? Why, when Victor, my brother-in-law,
collected many tadpoles—'

'You are not to say "stink,"' interrupted Helen; 'at least, you may say it,
but you must pretend you are being funny while you say it.'

'Then "smell." And the mud of your Pool down there–does it not smell,
or may I say "stink, ha, ha"?'

'There always has been mud in Poole Harbour,' said Mrs Munt, with a
slight frown. 'The rivers bring it down, and a most valuable oyster-fishery
depends upon it.'

'Yes, that is so,' conceded Frieda; and another international incident was
closed.

'"Bournemouth is,"' resumed their hostess, quoting a local rhyme to
which she was much attached–'"Bournemouth is, Poole was, and Swanage
is to be the most important town of all and biggest of the three." Now, Frau
Liesecke, I have shown you Bournemouth, and I have shown you Poole, so
let us walk backward a little, and look down again at Swanage.'

'Aunt Juley, wouldn't that be Meg's train?'

A tiny puff of smoke had been circling the harbour, and now was bearing
southwards towards them over the black and the gold.

'Oh, dearest Margaret, I do hope she won't be overtired.'

'Oh, I do wonder–I do wonder whether she's taken the house.'

'I hope she hasn't been hasty.'

'So do I–oh, *so* do I.'

'Will it be as beautiful as Wickham Place?' Frieda asked.

'I should think it would. Trust Mr Wilcox for doing himself proud. All
those Ducie Street houses are beautiful in their modern way, and I can't
think why he doesn't keep on with it. But it's really for Evie that he went
there, and now that Evie's going to be married—'

'Ah?'

'You've never seen Miss Wilcox, Frieda. How absurdly matrimonial you
are!'

'But sister to that Paul?'

'Yes.'

'And to that Charles,' said Mrs Munt with feeling. 'Oh, Helen, Helen,
what a time that was!'

Helen laughed. 'Meg and I haven't got such tender hearts. If there's a
chance of a cheap house, we go for it.'

'Now look, Frau Liesecke, at my niece's train. You see, it is coming towards us—coming, coming; and, when it gets to Corfe, it will actually go *through* the downs, on which we are standing, so that, if we walk over, as I suggested, and look down on Swanage, we shall see it coming on the other side. Shall we?'

Frieda assented, and in a few minutes they had crossed the ridge and exchanged the greater view for the lesser. Rather a dull valley lay below, backed by the slope of the coastward downs. They were looking across the Isle of Purbeck and on to Swanage, soon to be the most important town of all, and ugliest of the three. Margaret's train reappeared as promised, and was greeted with approval by her aunt. It came to a standstill in the middle distance, and there it had been planned that Tibby should meet her, and drive her, and a tea-basket, up to join them.

'You see,' continued Helen to her cousin, 'the Wilcoxes collect houses as your Victor collects tadpoles. They have, one, Ducie Street; two, Howards End, where my great rumpus was; three, a country seat in Shropshire; four, Charles has a house in Hilton; and five, another near Epsom; and six, Evie will have a house when she marries, and probably a pied-à-terre in the country—which makes seven. Oh yes, and Paul a hut in Africa makes eight. I wish we could get Howards End. That was something like a dear little house! Didn't you think so, Aunt Juley?'

'I had too much to do, dear, to look at it,' said Mrs Munt, with a gracious dignity. 'I had everything to settle and explain, and Charles Wilcox to keep in his place besides. It isn't likely I should remember much. I just remember having lunch in your bedroom.'

'Yes, so do I. But, oh dear, dear, how dead it all seems! And in the autumn there began that anti-Pauline movement—you, and Frieda, and Meg, and Mrs Wilcox, all obsessed with the idea that I might yet marry Paul.'

'You yet may,' said Frieda despondently.

Helen shook her head. 'The Great Wilcox Peril will never return. If I'm certain of anything it's of that.'

'One is certain of nothing but the truth of one's own emotions.'

The remark fell damply on the conversation. But Helen slipped her arm round her cousin, somehow liking her the better for making it. It was not an original remark, nor had Frieda appropriated it passionately, for she had a patriotic rather than a philosophic mind. Yet it betrayed that interest in the universal which the average Teuton possesses and the average Englishman does not. It was, however illogically, the good, the beautiful, the true, as opposed to the respectable, the pretty, the adequate. It was a landscape of Böcklin's beside a landscape of Leader's, strident and ill-considered, but quivering into supernatural life. It sharpened idealism, stirred the soul. It may have been a bad preparation for what followed.

'Look!' cried Aunt Juley, hurrying away from generalities over the narrow summit of the down. 'Stand where I stand, and you will see the pony-cart coming. I see the pony-cart coming.'

They stood and saw the pony-cart coming. Margaret and Tibby were presently seen coming in it. Leaving the outskirts of Swanage, it drove for a little through the budding lanes, and then began the ascent.

'Have you got the house?' they shouted, long before she could possibly hear.

Helen ran down to meet her. The highroad passed over a saddle, and a track went thence at right angles along the ridge of the down.

'Have you got the house?'

Margaret shook her head.

'Oh, what a nuisance! So we're as we were?'

'Not exactly.'

She got out, looking tired.

'Some mystery,' said Tibby. 'We are to be enlightened presently.'

Margaret came close up to her and whispered that she had had a proposal of marriage from Mr Wilcox.

Helen was amused. She opened the gate on to the downs so that her brother might lead the pony through. 'It's just like a widower,' she remarked. 'They've cheek enough for anything, and invariably select one of their first wife's friends.'

Margaret's face flashed despair.

'That type—' She broke off with a cry. 'Meg, not anything wrong with you?'

'Wait one minute,' said Margaret, whispering always.

'But you've never conceivably–you've never—' She pulled herself together. 'Tibby, hurry up through; I can't hold this gate indefinitely. Aunt Juley! I say, Aunt Juley, make the tea, will you, and Frieda; we've got to talk houses, and 'll come on afterwards.' And then, turning her face to her sister's, she burst into tears.

Margaret was stupefied. She heard herself saying, 'Oh, really—' She felt herself touched with a hand that trembled.

'Don't,' sobbed Helen, 'don't, don't, Meg, don't!' She seemed incapable of saying any other word. Margaret, trembling herself, led her forward up the road, till they strayed through another gate on to the down.

'Don't, don't do such a thing! I tell you not to–don't! I know–don't!'

'What do you know?'

'Panic and emptiness,' sobbed Helen. 'Don't!'

Then Margaret thought, 'Helen is a little selfish. I have never behaved like this when there has seemed a chance of her marrying.' She said: 'But we would still see each other very often, and you—'

'It's not a thing like that,' sobbed Helen. And she broke right away and wandered distractedly upwards, stretching her hands towards the view and crying.

'What's happened to you?' called Margaret, following through the wind that gathers at sundown on the northern slopes of hills. 'But it's stupid!' And suddenly stupidity seized her, and the immense landscape was blurred. But Helen turned back.

'Meg—'

'I don't know what's happened to either of us,' said Margaret, wiping her eyes. 'We must both have gone mad.' Then Helen wiped hers, and they even laughed a little.

'Look here, sit down.'

'All right; I'll sit down if you'll sit down.'

'There. (One kiss.) Now, whatever, whatever is the matter?'

'I do mean what I said. Don't; it wouldn't do.'

'Oh, Helen, stop saying "don't"! It's ignorant. It's as if your head wasn't out of the slime. "Don't" is probably what Mrs Bast says all the day to Mr Bast.'

Helen was silent.

'Well?'

'Tell me about it first, and meanwhile perhaps I'll have got my head out of the slime.'

'That's better. Well, where shall I begin? When I arrived at Waterloo—no, I'll go back before that, because I'm anxious you should know everything from the first. The "first" was about ten days ago. It was the day Mr Bast came to tea and lost his temper. I was defending him, and Mr Wilcox became jealous about me, however slightly. I thought it was the involuntary thing, which men can't help any more than we can. You know—at least, I know in my own case—when a man has said to me, "So-and-so's a pretty girl," I am seized with a momentary sourness against So-and-so, and long to tweak her ear. It's a tiresome feeling, but not an important one, and one easily manages it. But it wasn't only this in Mr Wilcox's case, I gather now.'

'Then you love him?'

Margaret considered. 'It is wonderful knowing that a real man cares for you,' she said. 'The mere fact of that grows more tremendous. Remember, I've known and liked him steadily for nearly three years.'

'But loved him?'

Margaret peered into her past. It is pleasant to analyze feelings while they are still only feelings, and unembodied in the social fabric. With her arm round Helen, and her eyes shifting over the view, as if this county or that could reveal the secret of her own heart, she meditated honestly, and said, 'No.'

'But you will?'

'Yes,' said Margaret, 'of that I'm pretty sure. Indeed, I began the moment he spoke to me.'

'And have settled to marry him?'

'I had, but am wanting a long talk about it now. What *is* it against him, Helen? You must try and say.'

Helen, in her turn, looked outwards. 'It is ever since Paul,' she said finally.

'But what has Mr Wilcox to do with Paul?'

'But he was there, they were all there that morning when I came down to breakfast, and saw that Paul was frightened—the man who loved me frightened and all his paraphernalia fallen, so that I knew it was impossible, because personal relations are the important thing for ever and ever, and not this outer life of telegrams and anger.'

She poured the sentence forth in one breath, but her sister understood it, because it touched on thoughts that were familiar between them.

'That's foolish. In the first place, I disagree about the outer life. Well, we've often argued that. The real point is that there is the widest gulf

between my love-making and yours. Yours was romance; mine will be prose.
I'm not running it down–a very good kind of prose, but well considered,
well thought out. For instance, I know all Mr Wilcox's faults. He's afraid of
emotion. He cares too much about success, too little about the past. His
sympathy lacks poetry, and so isn't sympathy really. I'd even say'–she
looked at the shining lagoons–'that, spiritually, he's not as honest as I am.
Doesn't that satisfy you?'

'No, it doesn't,' said Helen. 'It makes me feel worse and worse. You must
be mad.'

Margaret made a movement of irritation.

'I don't intend him, or any man or any woman, to be all my life–good
heavens, no! There are heaps of things in me that he doesn't, and shall never,
understand.'

Thus she spoke before the wedding ceremony and the physical union,
before the astonishing glass shade had fallen that interposes between
married couples and the world. She was to keep her independence more than
do most women as yet. Marriage was to alter her fortunes rather than her
character, and she was not far wrong in boasting that she understood her
future husband. Yet he did alter her character–a little. There was an
unforeseen surprise, a cessation of the winds and odours of life, a social
pressure that would have her think conjugally.

'So with him,' she continued. 'There are heaps of things in him–more
especially things that he does–that will always be hidden from me. He has all
those public qualities which you so despise and enable all this—' She waved
her hand at the landscape, which confirmed anything. 'If Wilcoxes hadn't
worked and died in England for thousands of years, you and I couldn't sit
here without having our throats cut. There would be no trains, no ships to
carry us literary people about in, no fields even. Just savagery. No–perhaps
not even that. Without their spirit life might never have moved out of
protoplasm. More and more do I refuse to draw my income and sneer at
those who guarantee it. There are times when it seems to me—'

'And to me, and to all women. So one kissed Paul.'

'That's brutal,' said Margaret. 'Mine is an absolutely different case. I've
thought things out.'

'It makes no difference thinking things out. They come to the same.'

'Rubbish!'

There was a long silence, during which the tide returned into Poole
Harbour. 'One would lose something,' murmured Helen, apparently to
herself. The water crept over the mud-flats towards the gorse and the
blackened heather. Branksea Island lost its immense foreshores, and became
a sombre episode of trees. Frome was forced inward towards Dorchester,
Stour against Wimborne, Avon towards Salisbury, and over the immense
displacement the sun presided, leading it to triumph ere he sank to rest.
England was alive, throbbing through all her estuaries, crying for joy
through the mouths of all her gulls, and the north wind, with contrary
motion, blew stronger against her rising seas. What did it mean? For what
end are her fair complexities, her changes of soil, her sinuous coast? Does she

belong to those who have moulded her and made her feared by other lands, or to those who have added nothing to her power, but have somehow seen her, seen the whole island at once, lying as a jewel in a silver sea, sailing as a ship of souls, with all the brave world's fleet accompanying her towards eternity?

Chapter Twenty

Margaret had often wondered at the disturbance that takes place in the world's waters, when Love, who seems so tiny a pebble, slips in. Whom does Love concern beyond the beloved and the lover? Yet his impact deluges a hundred shores. No doubt the disturbance is really the spirit of the generations, welcoming the new generation, and chafing against the ultimate Fate, who holds all the seas in the palm of her hand. But Love cannot understand this. He cannot comprehend another's infinity; he is conscious only of his own—flying sunbeam, falling rose, pebble that asks for one quiet plunge below the fretting interplay of space and time. He knows that he will survive at the end of things, and be gathered by Fate as a jewel from the slime, and be handed with admiration round the assembly of the gods. 'Men did produce this,' they will say, and, saying, they will give men immortality. But meanwhile—what agitations meanwhile! The foundations of Property and Propriety are laid bare, twin rocks; Family Pride flounders to the surface, puffing and blowing, and refusing to be comforted; Theology, vaguely ascetic, gets up a nasty ground swell. Then the lawyers are aroused—cold brood—and creep out of their holes. They do what they can; they tidy up Property and Propriety, reassure Theology and Family Pride. Half-guineas are poured on the troubled waters, the lawyers creep back, and, if all has gone well, Love joins one man and woman together in Matrimony.

Margaret had expected the disturbance, and was not irritated by it. For a sensitive woman she had steady nerves, and could bear with the incongruous and the grotesque; and, besides, there was nothing excessive about her love-affair. Good-humour was the dominant note of her relations with Mr Wilcox, or, as I must now call him, Henry. Henry did not encourage romance, and she was no girl to fidget for it. An acquaintance had become a lover, might become a husband, but would retain all that she had noted in the acquaintance; and love must confirm an old relation rather than reveal a new one.

In this spirit she promised to marry him.

He was in Swanage on the morrow, bearing the engagement-ring. They greeted one another with a hearty cordiality that impressed Aunt Juley. Henry dined at The Bays, but had engaged a bedroom in the principal hotel: he was one of those men who know the principal hotel by instinct. After dinner he asked Margaret if she wouldn't care for a turn on the Parade. She accepted, and could not repress a little tremor; it would be her first real love scene. But as she put on her hat she burst out laughing. Love was so unlike the article served up in books: the joy, though genuine, was different; the mystery an unexpected mystery. For one thing, Mr Wilcox still seemed a stranger.'

For a time they talked about the ring; then she said:

'Do you remember the Embankment at Chelsea? It can't be ten days ago.'

'Yes,' he said, laughing. 'And you and your sister were head and ears deep in some Quixotic scheme. Ah well!'

'I little thought then, certainly. Did you?'

'I don't know about that; I shouldn't like to say.'

'Why, was it earlier?' she cried. 'Did you think of me this way earlier! How extraordinarily interesting, Henry! Tell me.'

But Henry had no intention of telling. Perhaps he could not have told, for his mental states became obscure as soon as he had passed through them. He misliked the very word 'interesting,' connoting it with wasted energy and even with morbidity. Hard facts were enough for him.

'I didn't think of it,' she pursued. 'No; when you spoke to me in the drawing-room, that was practically the first. It was all so different from what it's supposed to be. On the stage or in books, a proposal is—how shall I put it?—a full-blown affair, a kind of bouquet; it loses its literal meaning. But in life a proposal really is a proposal—'

'By the way—'

'—a suggestion, a seed,' she concluded; and the thought flew away into darkness.

'I was thinking, if you didn't mind, that we ought to spend this evening in a business talk; there will be so much to settle.'

'I think so too. Tell me, in the first place, how did you get on with Tibby?'

'With your brother?'

'Yes, during cigarettes.'

'Oh, very well.'

'I am so glad,' she answered, a little surprised. 'What did you talk about? Me, presumably.'

'About Greece too.'

'Greece was a very good card, Henry. Tibby's only a boy still, and one has to pick and choose subjects a little. Well done.'

'I was telling him I have shares in a currant-farm near Calamata.'

'What a delightful thing to have shares in! Can't we go there for our honeymoon?'

'What to do?'

'To eat the currants. And isn't there marvellous scenery?'

'Moderately, but it's not the kind of place one could possibly go to with a lady.'

'Why not?'

'No hotels.'

'Some ladies do without hotels. Are you aware that Helen and I have walked alone over the Apennines, with our luggage on our backs?'

'I wasn't aware, and, if I can manage it, you will never do such a thing again.'

She said more gravely: 'You haven't found time for a talk with Helen yet, I suppose?'

'No.'

'Do, before you go. I am so anxious you two should be friends.'

'Your sister and I have always hit it off,' he said negligently. 'But we're drifting away from our business. Let me begin at the beginning. You know that Evie is going to marry Percy Cahill.'

'Dolly's uncle.'

'Exactly. The girl's madly in love with him. A very good sort of fellow, but he demands—and rightly—a suitable provision with her. And in the second place, you will naturally understand, there is Charles. Before leaving town, I wrote Charles a very careful letter. You see, he has an increasing family and increasing expenses, and the I. and W.A. is nothing particular just now, though capable of development.'

'Poor fellow!' murmured Margaret, looking out to sea, and not understanding.

'Charles being the elder son, some day Charles will have Howards End; but I am anxious, in my own happiness, not to be unjust to others.'

'Of course not,' she began, and then gave a little cry. 'You mean money. How stupid I am! Of course not!'

Oddly enough, he winced a little at the word. 'Yes. Money, since you put it so frankly. I am determined to be just to all—just to you, just to them. I am determined that my children shall have no case against me.'

'Be generous to them,' she said sharply. 'Bother justice!'

'I am determined—and have already written to Charles to that effect—'

'But how much have you got?'

'What?'

'How much have you a year? I've six hundred.'

'My income?'

'Yes. We must begin with how much you have, before we can settle how much you can give Charles. Justice, and even generosity, depend on that.'

'I must say you're a downright young woman,' he observed, patting her arm and laughing a little. 'What a question to spring on a fellow!'

'Don't you know your income? Or don't you want to tell it me?'

'I—'

'That's all right'—now she patted him—'don't tell me. I don't want to know. I can do the sum just as well by proportion. Divide your income into ten parts. How many parts would you give to Evie, how many to Charles, how many to Paul?'

'The fact is, my dear, I hadn't any intention of bothering you with details. I only wanted to let you know that—well, that something must be done for the others, and you've understood me perfectly, so let's pass on to the next point.'

'Yes, we've settled that,' said Margaret, undisturbed by his strategic blunderings. 'Go ahead; give away all you can, bearing in mind I've a clear six hundred. What a mercy it is to have all this money about one!'

'We've none too much, I assure you; you're marrying a poor man.'

'Helen wouldn't agree with me here,' she continued. 'Helen daren't slang the rich, being rich herself, but she would like to. There's an odd notion, that I haven't yet got hold of, running about at the back of her brain, that poverty is somehow "real." She dislikes all organization, and probably confuses wealth with the technique of wealth. Sovereigns in a stocking wouldn't bother her; cheques do. Helen is too relentless. One can't deal in her high-handed manner with the world.'

'There's this other point, and then I must go back to my hotel and write some letters. What's to be done now about the house in Ducie Street?'

'Keep it on—at least, it depends. When do you want to marry me?'

She raised her voice, as too often, and some youths, who were also taking the evening air, overheard her. 'Getting a bit hot, eh?' said one. Mr Wilcox turned on them, and said sharply, 'I say!' There was silence. 'Take care I don't report you to the police.' They moved away quietly enough, but were only biding their time, and the rest of the conversation was punctuated by peals of ungovernable laughter.

Lowering his voice and infusing a hint of reproof into it, he said: 'Evie will probably be married in September. We could scarcely think of anything before then.'

'The earlier the nicer, Henry. Females are not supposed to say such things, but the earlier the nicer.'

'How about September for us too?' he asked, rather dryly.

'Right. Shall we go into Ducie Street ourselves in September? Or shall we try to bounce Helen and Tibby into it? That's rather an idea. They are so unbusinesslike, we could make them do anything by judicious management. Look here—yes. We'll do that. And we ourselves could live at Howards End or Shropshire.'

He blew out his cheeks. 'Heavens! how you women do fly round! My head's in a whirl. Point by point, Margaret. Howards End's impossible. I let it to Hamar Bryce on a three years' agreement last March. Don't you remember? Oniton. Well, that is much, much too far away to rely on entirely. You will be able to be down there entertaining a certain amount, but we must have a house within easy reach of Town. Only Ducie Street has huge drawbacks. There's a mews behind.'

Margaret could not help laughing. It was the first she had heard of the mews behind Ducie Street. When she was a possible tenant it had suppressed itself, not consciously, but automatically. The breezy Wilcox manner, though genuine, lacked the clearness of vision that is imperative for truth. When Henry lived in Ducie Street he remembered the mews; when he tried to let he forgot it; and if anyone had remarked that the mews must be either there or not, he would have felt annoyed, and afterwards have found some opportunity of stigmatizing the speaker as academic. So does my grocer stigmatize me when I complain of the quality of his sultanas, and he answers in one breath that they are the best sultanas, and how can I expect the best sultanas at that price? It is a flaw inherent in the business mind, and Margaret may do well to be tender to it, considering all that the business mind has done for England.

'Yes, in summer especially, the mews is a serious nuisance. The smoking-room, too, is an abominable little den. The house opposite has been taken by operatic people. Ducie Street's going down, it's my private opinion.'

'How sad! It's only a few years since they built those pretty houses.'

'Shows things are moving. Good for trade.'

'I hate this continual flux in London. It is an epitome of us at our worst—eternal formlessness; all the qualities, good, bad, and indifferent, streaming away—streaming, streaming for ever. That's why I dread it so. I mistrust rivers, even in scenery. Now, the sea—'

'High tide, yes.'

'Hoy toid'—from the promenading youths.

'And these are the men to whom we give the vote,' observed Mr Wilcox, omitting to add that they were also the men to whom he gave work as clerks—work that scarcely encouraged them to grow into other men. 'However, they have their own lives and interests. Let's get on.'

He turned as he spoke, and prepared to see her back to The Bays. The business was over. His hotel was in the opposite direction, and if he accompanied her his letters would be late for the post. She implored him not to come, but he was obdurate.

'A nice beginning, if your aunt saw you slip in alone!'

'But I always do go about alone. Considering I've walked over the Apennines, it's common sense. You will make me so angry. I don't the least take it as a compliment.'

He laughed, and lit a cigar. 'It isn't meant as a compliment, my dear. I just won't have you going about in the dark. Such people about too! It's dangerous.'

'Can't I look after myself? I do wish—'

'Come along, Margaret; no wheedling.'

A younger woman might have resented his masterly ways, but Margaret had too firm a grip of life to make a fuss. She was, in her own way, as masterly. If he was a fortress she was a mountain peak, whom all might tread, but whom the snows made nightly virginal. Disdaining the heroic outfit, excitable in her methods, garrulous, episodical, shrill, she misled her lover much as she had misled her aunt. He mistook her fertility for weakness. He supposed her 'as clever as they make 'em,' but no more, not realizing that she was penetrating to the depths of his soul, and approving of what she found there.

And if insight were sufficient, if the inner life were the whole of life, their happiness had been assured.

They walked ahead briskly. The parade and the road after it were well lighted, but it was darker in Aunt Juley's garden. As they were going up by the side-paths, through some rhododendrons, Mr Wilcox, who was in front, said 'Margaret' rather huskily, turned, dropped his cigar, and took her in his arms.

She was startled, and nearly screamed, but recovered herself at once, and kissed with genuine love the lips that were pressed against her own. It was their first kiss, and when it was over he saw her safely to the door and rang the bell for her, but disappeared into the night before the maid answered it. On looking back, the incident displeased her. It was so isolated. Nothing in their previous conversation had heralded it, and, worse still, no tenderness had ensued. If a man cannot lead up to passion he can at all events lead down from it, and she had hoped, after her complaisance, for some interchange of gentle words. But he had hurried away as if ashamed, and for an instant she was reminded of Helen and Paul.

Chapter Twenty-one

Charles had just been scolding his Dolly. She deserved the scolding, and had bent before it, but her head, though bloody, was unsubdued, and her chirrupings began to mingle with his retreating thunder.

'You've woken the baby. I knew you would. (Rum-ti-foo, Rackety-tackety-Tompkin!) I'm not responsible for what Uncle Percy does, nor for anybody else or anything, so there!'

'Who asked him while I was away! Who asked my sister down to meet him! Who sent them out in the motor day after day?'

'Charles, that reminds me of some poem.'

'Does it indeed? We shall all be dancing to a very different music presently. Miss Schlegel has fairly got us on toast.'

'I could simply scratch that woman's eyes out, and to say it's my fault is most unfair.'

'It's your fault, and five months ago you admitted it.'

'I didn't.'

'You did.'

'Tootle, tootle, playing on the pootle!' exclaimed Dolly, suddenly devoting herself to the child.

'It's all very well to turn the conversation, but father would never have dreamt of marrying as long as Evie was there to make him comfortable. But you must needs start match-making. Besides, Cahill's too old.'

'Of course, if you're going to be rude to Uncle Percy—'

'Miss Schlegel always meant to get hold of Howards End, and, thanks to you, she's got it.'

'I call the way you twist things round and make them hang together most unfair. You couldn't have been nastier if you'd caught me flirting. Could he, diddums?'

'We're in a bad hole, and must make the best of it. I shall answer the pater's letter civilly. He's evidently anxious to do the decent thing. But I do not intend to forget these Schlegels in a hurry. As long as they're on their best behaviour–Dolly, are you listening?–we'll behave, too. But if I find them giving themselves airs, or monopolizing my father, or at all ill-treating him, or worrying him with their artistic beastliness, I intend to put my foot down, yes, firmly. Taking my mother's place! Heaven knows what poor old Paul will say when the news reaches him.'

The interlude closes. It has taken place in Charles's garden at Hilton. He and Dolly are sitting in deck-chairs, and their motor is regarding them placidly from its garage across the lawn. A short-frocked edition of Charles also regards them placidly; a perambulator edition is squeaking; a third edition is expected shortly. Nature is turning out Wilcoxes in this peaceful abode, so that they may inherit the earth.

Chapter Twenty-two

Margaret greeted her lord with peculiar tenderness on the morrow. Mature as he was, she might yet be able to help him to the building of the rainbow bridge that should connect the prose in us with the passion. Without it we are meaningless fragments, half monks, half beasts, unconnected arches that have never joined into a man. With it love is born, and alights on the highest curve, glowing against the grey, sober against the fire. Happy the man who sees from either aspect the glory of these outspread wings. The roads of his soul lie clear, and he and his friends shall find easy-going.

It was hard-going in the roads of Mr Wilcox's soul. From boyhood he had neglected them. 'I am not a fellow who bothers about my own inside.' Outwardly he was cheerful, reliable, and brave; but within, all had reverted to chaos, ruled, so far as it was ruled at all, by an incomplete asceticism. Whether as boy, husband, or widower, he had always the sneaking belief that bodily passion is bad, a belief that is desirable only when held passionately. Religion had confirmed him. The words that were read aloud on Sunday to him and to other respectable men were the words that had once kindled the souls of St Catharine and St Francis into a white-hot hatred of the carnal. He could not be as the saints and love the Infinite with a seraphic ardour, but he could be a little ashamed of loving a wife. 'Amabat, amare timebat.' And it was here that Margaret hoped to help him.

It did not seem so difficult. She need trouble him with no gift of her own. She would only point out the salvation that was latent in his own soul, and in the soul of every man. Only connect! That was the whole of her sermon. Only connect the prose and the passion, and both will be exalted, and human love will be seen at its height. Live in fragments no longer. Only connect, and the beast and the monk, robbed of the isolation that is life to either, will die.

Nor was the message difficult to give. It need not take the form of a good 'talking.' By quiet indications the bridge would be built and span their lives with beauty.

But she failed. For there was one quality in Henry for which she was never prepared, however much she reminded herself of it: his obtuseness. He simply did not notice things, and there was no more to be said. He never noticed that Helen and Frieda were hostile, or that Tibby was not interested in currant plantations; he never noticed the lights and shades that exist in the greyest conversation, the finger-posts, the milestones, the collisions, the illimitable views. Once–on another occasion–she scolded him about it. He was puzzled, but replied with a laugh: 'My motto is Concentrate. I've no intention of frittering away my strength on that sort of thing.' 'It isn't frittering away the strength,' she protested. 'It's enlarging the space in which you may be strong.' He answered: 'You're a clever little woman, but my motto's Concentrate.' And this morning he concentrated with a vengeance.

They met in the rhododendrons of yesterday. In the daylight the bushes were inconsiderable and the path was bright in the morning sun. She was with Helen, who had been ominously quiet since the affair was settled. 'Here we all are!' she cried, and took him by one hand, retaining her sister's in the other.

'Here we are. Good-morning, Helen.'

Helen replied, 'Good-morning, Mr Wilcox.'

'Henry, she has had such a nice letter from the queer, cross boy. Do you remember him? He had a sad moustache, but the back of his head was young.'

'I have had a letter too. Not a nice one–I want to talk it over with you:' for Leonard Bast was nothing to him now that she had given him her word; the triangle of sex was broken for ever.

'Thanks to your hint, he's clearing out of the Porphyrion.'

'Not a bad business that Porphyrion,' he said absently, as he took his own letter out of his pocket.

'Not a *bad*—' she exclaimed, dropping his hand. 'Surely, on Chelsea Embankment—'

'Here's our hostess. Good-morning, Mrs Must. Fine rhododendrons. Good-morning, Frau Liesecke; we manage to grow flowers in England, don't we?'

'Not a *bad* business?'

'No. My letter's about Howards End. Bryce has been ordered abroad, and wants to sublet it. I am far from sure that I shall give him permission. There was no clause in the agreement. In my opinion, subletting is a mistake. If he can find me another tenant, whom I consider suitable, I may cancel the agreement. Morning, Schlegel. Don't you think that's better than subletting?'

Helen had dropped her hand now, and he had steered her past the whole party to the seaward side of the house. Beneath them was the bourgeois little bay, which must have yearned all through the centuries for just such a watering-place as Swanage to be built on its margin. The waves were colourless, and the Bournemouth steamer gave a further touch of insipidity, drawn up against the pier and hooting wildly for excursionists.

'When there is a sublet I find that damage—'

'Do excuse me, but about the Porphyrion. I don't feel easy—might I just bother you, Henry?'

Her manner was so serious that he stopped, and asked her a little sharply what she wanted.

'You said on Chelsea Embankment, surely, that it was a bad concern, so we advised this clerk to clear out. He writes this morning that he's taken our advice, and now you say it's not a bad concern.'

'A clerk who clears out of any concern, good or bad, without securing a berth somewhere else first, is a fool, and I've no pity for him.'

'He has not done that. He's going into a bank in Camden Town, he says. The salary's much lower, but he hopes to manage—a branch of Dempster's Bank. Is that all right?'

'Dempster! My goodness me, yes.'

'More than that the Porphyrion?'

'Yes, yes, yes; safe as houses—safer.'

'Very many thanks. I'm sorry—if you sublet—?'

'If he sublets, I shan't have the same control. In theory there should be no more damage done at Howards End; in practice there will be. Things may be done for which no money can compensate. For instance, I shouldn't want that fine wych-elm spoilt. It hangs— Margaret, we must go and see the old place some time. It's pretty in its way. We'll motor down and have lunch with Charles.'

'I should enjoy that,' said Margaret bravely.

'What about next Wednesday?'

'Wednesday? No, I couldn't well do that. Aunt Juley expects us to stop here another week at least.'

'But you can give that up now.'

'Er—no,' said Margaret, after a moment's thought.

'Oh, that'll be all right. I'll speak to her.'

'This visit is a high solemnity. My aunt counts on it year after year. She turns the house upside down for us; she invites our special friends—she scarcely knows Frieda, and we can't leave her on her hands. I missed one day, and she would be so hurt if I didn't stay the full ten.'

'But I'll say a word to her. Don't you bother.'

'Henry, I won't go. Don't bully me.'

'You want to see the house, though?'

'Very much—I've heard so much about it, one way or the other. Aren't there pigs' teeth in the wych-elm?'

'*Pig's teeth?*'

'And you chew the bark for toothache.'

'What a rum notion! Of course not!'

'Perhaps I have confused it with some other tree. There are still a great number of sacred trees in England, it seems.'

But he left her to intercept Mrs Munt, whose voice could be heard in the distance: to be intercepted himself by Helen.

'Oh, Mr Wilcox, about the Porphyrion—' she began, and went scarlet all over her face.

'It's all right,' called Margaret, catching them up. 'Dempster's Bank's better.'

'But I think you told us the Porphyrion was bad, and would smash before Christmas.'

'Did I? It was still outside the Tariff Ring, and had to take rotten policies. Lately it came in—safe as houses now.'

'In other words, Mr Bast need never have left it.'

'No, the fellow needn't.'

'—and needn't have started life elsewhere at a greatly reduced salary.'

'He only says "reduced,"' corrected Margaret, seeing trouble ahead.

'With a man so poor, every reduction must be great. I consider it a deplorable misfortune.'

Mr Wilcox, intent on his business with Mrs Munt, was going steadily on, but the last remark made him say: 'What? What's that? Do you mean that I'm responsible?'

'You're ridiculous, Helen.'

'You seem to think—' He looked at his watch. 'Let me explain the point to you. It is like this. You seem to assume, when a business concern is conducting a delicate negotiation, it ought to keep the public informed stage by stage. The Porphyrion, according to you, was bound to say, "I am trying all I can to get into the Tariff Ring. I am not sure that I shall succeed, but it is the only thing that will save me from insolvency, and I am trying." My dear Helen—'

'Is that your point? A man who had little money has less—that's mine.'

'I am grieved for your clerk. But it is all in the day's work. It's part of the battle of life.'

'A man who had little money,' she repeated, 'has less, owing to us. Under these circumstances I do not consider "the battle of life" a happy expression.'

'Oh come, come!' he protested pleasantly. 'You're not to blame. No one's to blame.'

'Is no one to blame for anything?'

'I wouldn't say that, but you're taking it far too seriously. Who is this fellow?'

'We have told you about the fellow twice already,' said Helen. 'You have even met the fellow. He is very poor and his wife is an extravagant imbecile. He is capable of better things. We—we, the upper classes—thought we would help him from the height of our superior knowledge—and here's the result!'

He raised his finger. 'Now, a word of advice.'

'I require no more advice.'

'A word of advice. Don't take up that sentimental attitude over the poor. See that she doesn't, Margaret. The poor are poor, and one's sorry for them, but there it is. As civilization moves forward, the shoe is bound to pinch in places, and it's absurd to pretend that anyone is responsible personally. Neither you, nor I, nor my informant, nor the man who informed him, nor the directors of the Porphyrion, are to blame for this clerk's loss of salary.

It's just the shoe pinching—no one can help it; and it might easily have been worse.'

Helen quivered with indignation.

'By all means subscribe to charities—subscribe to them largely—but don't get carried away by absurd schemes of Social Reform. I see a good deal behind the scenes, and you can take it from me that there is no Social Question—except for a few journalists who try to get a living out of the phrase. There are just rich and poor, as there always have been and always will be. Point me out a time when men have been equal—'

'I didn't say—'

'Point me out a time when desire for equality has made them happier. No, no. You can't. There always have been rich and poor. I'm no fatalist. Heaven forbid! But our civilization is moulded by great impersonal forces' (his voice grew complacent; it always did when he eliminated the personal), 'and there always will be rich and poor. You can't deny it' (and now it was a respectful voice)—'and you can't deny that, in spite of all, the tendency of civilization has on the whole been upward.'

'Owing to God, I suppose,' flashed Helen.

He stared at her.

'You grab the dollars. God does the rest.'

It was no good instructing the girl if she was going to talk about God in that neurotic modern way. Fraternal to the last, he left her for the quieter company of Mrs Munt. He thought, 'She rather reminds me of Dolly.'

Helen looked out at the sea.

'Don't ever discuss political economy with Henry,' advised her sister. 'It'll only end in a cry.'

'But he must be one of those men who have reconciled science with religion,' said Helen slowly. 'I don't like those men. They are scientific themselves, and talk of the survival of the fittest, and cut down the salaries of their clerks, and stunt the independence of all who may menace their comfort, but yet they believe that somehow good—it is always that sloppy "somehow"—will be the outcome, and that in some mystical way the Mr Basts of the future will benefit because the Mr Basts of to-day are in pain.'

'He is such a man in theory. But oh, Helen, in theory!'

'But oh, Meg, what a theory!'

'Why should you put things so bitterly, dearie?'

'Because I'm an old maid,' said Helen, biting her lip. 'I can't think why I go on like this myself.' She shook off her sister's hand and went into the house. Margaret, distressed at the day's beginning, followed the Bournemouth steamer with her eyes. She saw that Helen's nerves were exasperated by the unlucky Bast business beyond the bounds of politeness. There might at any minute be a real explosion, which even Henry would notice. Henry must be removed.

'Margaret!' her aunt called. 'Magsy! It isn't true, surely, what Mr Wilcox says, that you want to go away early next week?'

'Not "want,"' was Margaret's prompt reply; 'but there is so much to be settled, and I do want to see the Charles'.'

'But going away without taking the Weymouth trip, or even the Lulworth?' said Mrs Munt, coming nearer. 'Without going once more up Nine Barrows Down?'

'I'm afraid so.'

Mr Wilcox rejoined her with, 'Good! I did the breaking of the ice.'

A wave of tenderness came over her. She put a hand on either shoulder, and looked deeply into the black, bright eyes. What was behind their competent stare? She knew, but was not disquieted.

Chapter Twenty-three

Margaret had no intention of letting things slide, and the evening before she left Swanage she gave her sister a thorough scolding. She censured her, not for disapproving of the engagement, but for throwing over her disapproval a veil of mystery. Helen was equally frank. 'Yes,' she said, with the air of one looking inwards, 'there is a mystery. I can't help it. It's not my fault. It's the way life has been made.' Helen in those days was over-interested in the subconscious self. She exaggerated the Punch and Judy aspect of life, and spoke of mankind as puppets, whom an invisible showman twitches into love and war. Margaret pointed out that if she dwelt on this she, too, would eliminate the personal. Helen was silent for a minute, and then burst into a queer speech, which cleared the air. 'Go on and marry him. I think you're splendid; and if anyone can pull it off, you will.' Margaret denied that there was anything to 'pull off,' but she continued: 'Yes, there is, and I wasn't up to it with Paul. I can only do what's easy. I can only entice and be enticed. I can't, and won't, attempt difficult relations. If I marry, it will either be a man who's strong enough to boss me or whom I'm strong enough to boss. So I shan't ever marry, for there aren't such men. And Heaven help anyone whom I do marry, for I shall certainly run away from him before you can say "Jack Robinson." There! Because I'm uneducated. But you, you're different; you're a heroine.'

'Oh, Helen! Am I? Will it be as dreadful for poor Henry as all that?'

'You mean to keep proportion, and that's heroic, it's Greek, and I don't see why it shouldn't succeed with you. Go on and fight with him and help him. Don't ask *me* for help, or even for sympathy. Henceforward I'm going my own way. I mean to be thorough, because thoroughness is easy. I mean to dislike your husband, and to tell him so. I mean to make no concessions to Tibby. If Tibby wants to live with me, he must lump me. I mean to love *you* more than ever. Yes, I do. You and I have built up something real, because it is purely spiritual. There's no veil of mystery over us. Unreality and mystery begin as soon as one touches the body. The popular view is, as usual, exactly the wrong one. Our bothers are over tangible things—money, husbands, house-hunting. But Heaven will work of itself.'

Margaret was grateful for this expression of affection, and answered, 'Perhaps.' All vistas close in the unseen–no one doubts it–but Helen closed them rather too quickly for her taste. At every turn of speech one was confronted with reality and the absolute. Perhaps Margaret grew too old for metaphysics, perhaps Henry was weaning her from them, but she felt that there was something a little unbalanced in the mind that so readily shreds the visible. The business man who assumes that this life is everything, and the mystic who asserts that it is nothing, fail, on this side and on that, to hit the truth. 'Yes, I see, dear; it's about halfway between,' Aunt Juley had hazarded in earlier years. No; truth, being alive, was not halfway between anything. It was only to be found by continuous excursions into either realm, and though proportion is the final secret, to espouse it at the outset is to insure sterility.

Helen, agreeing here, disagreeing there, would have talked till midnight, but Margaret, with her packing to do, focussed the conversation on Henry. She might abuse Henry behind his back, but please would she always be civil to him in company? 'I definitely dislike him, but I'll do what I can,' promised Helen. 'Do what you can with my friends in return.'

This conversation made Margaret easier. Their inner life was so safe that they could bargain over externals in a way that would have been incredible to Aunt Juley, and impossible for Tibby or Charles. There are moments when the inner life actually 'pays,' when years of self-scrutiny, conducted for no ulterior motive, are suddenly of practical use. Such moments are still rare in the West; that they come at all promises a fairer future. Margaret, though unable to understand her sister, was assured against estrangement, and returned to London with a more peaceful mind.

The following morning, at eleven o'clock, she presented herself at the offices of the Imperial and West African Rubber Company. She was glad to go there, for Henry had implied his business rather than described it, and the formlessness and vagueness that one associates with Africa itself had hitherto brooded over the main sources of his wealth. Not that a visit to the office cleared things up. There was just the ordinary surface scum of ledgers and polished counters and brass bars that began and stopped for no possible reason, of electric-light globes blossoming in triplets, of little rabbit-hutches faced with glass or wire, of little rabbits. And even when she penetrated to the inner depths, she found only the ordinary table and Turkey carpet, and though the map over the fireplace did depict a helping of West Africa, it was a very ordinary map. Another map hung opposite, on which the whole continent appeared, looking like a whale marked out for a blubber, and by its side was a door, shut, but Henry's voice came through it, dictating a 'strong' letter. She might have been at the Porphyrion, or Dempster's Bank, or her own wine-merchant's. Everything seems just alike in these days. But perhaps she was seeing the Imperial side of the company rather than its West African, the Imperialism always had been one of her difficulties.

'One minute!' called Mr Wilcox on receiving her name. He touched a bell, the effect of which was to produce Charles.

Charles had written his father an adequate letter–more adequate than

Evie's, through which a girlish indignation throbbed. And he greeted his future stepmother with propriety.

'I hope that my wife—how do you do?—will give you a decent lunch,' was his opening. 'I left instructions, but we live in a rough-and-ready way. She expects you back to tea, too, after you have had a look at Howards End. I wonder what you'll think of the place. I wouldn't touch it with tongs myself. Do sit down! It's a measly little place.'

'I shall enjoy seeing it,' said Margaret, feeling, for the first time, shy.

'You'll see it at its worst, for Bryce decamped abroad last Monday without even arranging for a charwoman to clear up after him. I never saw such a disgraceful mess. It's unbelievable. He wasn't in the house a month.'

'I've more than a little bone to pick with Bryce,' called Henry from the inner chamber.

'Why did he go so suddenly?'

'Invalid type; couldn't sleep.'

'Poor fellow!'

'Poor fiddlesticks!' said Mr Wilcox, joining them. 'He had the impudence to put up notice-boards without as much as saying with your leave or by your leave. Charles flung them down.'

'Yes, I flung them down,' said Charles modestly.

'I've sent a telegram after him, and a pretty sharp one, too. He, and he in person, is responsible for the upkeep of that house for the next three years.'

'The keys are at the farm; we wouldn't have the keys.'

'Quite right.'

'Dolly would have taken them, but I was in, fortunately.'

'What's Mr Bryce like?' asked Margaret.

But nobody cared. Mr Bryce was the tenant, who had no right to sublet; to have defined him further was a waste of time. On his misdeeds they descanted profusely, until the girl who had been typing the strong letter came out with it. Mr Wilcox added his signature. 'Now we'll be off,' said he.

A motor-drive, a form of felicity detested by Margaret, awaited her. Charles saw them in, civil to the last, and in a moment the offices of the Imperial and West African Rubber Company faded away. But it was not an impressive drive. Perhaps the weather was to blame, being grey and banked high with weary clouds. Perhaps Hertfordshire is scarcely intended for motorists. Did not a gentleman once motor so quickly through Westmoreland that he missed it? and if Westmoreland can be missed, it will fare ill with a county whose delicate structure particularly needs the attentive eye. Hertfordshire is England at its quietest, with little emphasis of river and hill; it is England meditative. If Drayton were with us again to write a new edition of his incomparable poem, he would sing the nymphs of Hertfordshire as indeterminate of feature, with hair obfuscated by the London smoke. Their eyes would be sad, and averted from their fate towards the Northern flats, their leader not Isis or Sabrina, but the slowly flowing Lea. No glory of raiment would be theirs, no urgency of dance; but they would be real nymphs.

The chauffeur could not travel as quickly as he had hoped, for the Great

North Road was full of Easter traffic. But we went quite quick enough for Margaret, a poor-spirited creature, who had chickens and children on the brain.

'They're all right,' said Mr Wilcox. 'They'll learn—like the swallows and the telegraph-wires.'

'Yes, but, while they're learning—'

'The motor's come to stay,' he answered. 'One must get about. There's a pretty church—oh, you aren't sharp enough. Well, look, out, if the road worries you—right outward at the scenery.'

She looked at the scenery. It heaved and merged like porridge. Presently it congealed. They had arrived.

Charles's house on the left; on the right the swelling forms of the Six Hills. Their appearance in such a neighbourhood surprised her. They interrupted the stream of residences that was thickening up towards Hilton. Beyond them she saw meadows and a wood, and beneath them she settled that soldiers of the best kind lay buried. She hated war and liked soldiers—it was one of her amiable inconsistencies.

But here was Dolly, dressed up to the nines, standing at the door to greet them, and here were the first drops of the rain. They ran in gaily and, after a long wait in the drawing-room, sat down to the rough-and-ready lunch, every dish in which concealed or exuded cream. Mr Bryce was the chief topic of conversation. Dolly described his visit with the key, while her father-in-law gave satisfaction by chaffing her and contradicting all she said. It was evidently the custom to laugh at Dolly. He chaffed Margaret, too, and Margaret, roused from a grave meditation, was pleased, and chaffed him back. Dolly seemed surprised, and eyed her curiously. After lunch the two children came down. Margaret disliked babies, but hit it off better with the two-year-old, and sent Dolly into fits of laughter by talking sense to him. 'Kiss then now, and come away,' said Mr Wilcox. She came, but refused to kiss them: it was such hard luck on the little things, she said, and though Dolly proffered Chorly-worly and Porgly-woggles in turn, she was obdurate.

By this time it was raining steadily. The car came round with the hood up, and again she lost all sense of space. In a few minutes they stopped, and Crane opened the door of the car.

'What's happened?' asked Margaret.

'What do you suppose?' said Henry.

A little porch was close up against her face.

'Are we there already?'

'We are.'

'Well, I never! In years ago it seemed so far away.'

Smiling, but somehow disillusioned, she jumped out, and her impetus carried her to the front-door. She was about to open it, when Henry said: 'That's no good; it's locked. Who's got the key?'

As he had himself forgotten to call for the key at the farm, no one replied. He also wanted to know who had left the front gate open, since a cow had strayed in from the road, and was spoiling the croquet lawn. Then he said rather crossly: 'Margaret, you wait in the dry. I'll go down for the key. It isn't a hundred yards.'

'Mayn't I come too?'

'No; I shall be back before I'm gone.'

Then the car turned away, and it was as if a curtain had risen. For the second time that day she saw the appearance of the earth.

There were the greengage-trees that Helen had once described, there the tennis lawn, there the hedge that would be glorious with dog-roses in June, but the vision now was of black and palest green. Down by the dell-hole more vivid colours were awakening, and Lent lilies stood sentinel on its margin, or advanced in battalions over the grass. Tulips were a tray of jewels. She could not see the wych-elm tree, but a branch of the celebrated vine, studded with velvet knobs, had covered the porch. She was struck by the fertility of the soil; she had seldom been in a garden where the flowers looked so well, and even the weeds she was idly plucking out of the porch were intensely green. Why had poor Mr Bryce fled from all this beauty? For she had already decided that the place was beautiful.

'Naughty cow! Go away!' cried Margaret to the cow, but without indignation.

Harder came the rain, pouring out of a windless sky, and spattering up from the notice-boards of the house-agents, which lay in a row on the lawn where Charles had hurled them. She must have interviewed Charles in another world–where one did have interviews. How Helen would revel in such a notion! Charles dead, all people dead, nothing alive but houses and gardens. The obvious dead, the intangible alive, and–no connection at all between them! Margaret smiled. Would that her own fancies were as clear-cut! Would that she could deal as high-handedly with the world! Smiling and sighing, she laid her hand upon the door. It opened. The house was not locked up at all.

She hesitated. Ought she to wait for Henry? He felt strongly about property, and might prefer to show her over himself. On the other hand, he had told her to keep in the dry, and the porch was beginning to drip. So she went in, and the draught from inside slammed the door behind.

Desolation greeted her. Dirty finger-prints were on the hall-windows, flue and rubbish on its unwashed boards. The civilization of luggage had been here for a month, and then decamped. Dining-room and drawing-room–right and left–were guessed only by their wall-papers. They were just rooms where one could shelter from the rain. Across the ceiling of each ran a great beam. The dining-room and hall revealed theirs openly, but the drawing-room's was match-boarded–because the facts of life must be concealed from ladies? Drawing-room, dining-room, and hall–how petty the names sounded! Here were simply three rooms where children could play and friends shelter from the rain. Yes, and they were beautiful.

Then she opened one of the doors opposite–there were two–and exchanged wall-papers for whitewash. It was the servants' part, though she scarcely realized that: just rooms again, where friends might shelter. The garden at the back was full of flowering cherries and plums. Farther on were hints of the meadow and a black cliff of pines. Yes, the meadow was beautiful.

Penned in by the desolate weather, she recaptured the sense of space which the motor had tried to rob from her. She remembered again that ten square miles are not ten times as wonderful as one square mile, that a thousand square miles are not practically the same as heaven. The phantom of bigness, which London encourages, was laid for ever when she paced from the hall at Howards End to its kitchen and heard the rains run this way and that where the watershed of the roof divided them.

Now Helen came to her mind, scrutinizing half Wessex from the ridge of the Purbeck Downs, and saying: 'You will have to lose something.' She was not so sure. For instance, she would double her kingdom by opening the door that concealed the stairs.

Now she thought of the map of Africa; of empires; of her father; of the two supreme nations, streams of whose life warmed her blood, but, mingling, had cooled her brain. She paced back into the hall, and as she did so the house reverberated.

'Is that you, Henry?' she called.

There was no answer, but the house reverberated again.

'Henry, have you got in?'

But it was the heart of the house beating, faintly at first, then loudly, martially. It dominated the rain.

It is the starved imagination, not the well-nourished, that is afraid. Margaret flung open the doors to the stairs. A noise as of drums seemed to deafen her. A woman, an old woman, was descending, with figure erect, with face impassive, with lips that parted and said dryly:

'Oh! Well, I took you for Ruth Wilcox.'

Margaret stammered: 'I— Mrs Wilcox–I?'

'In fancy, of course–in fancy. You had her way of walking. Good-day.' And the old woman passed out into the rain.

Chapter Twenty-four

'It gave her quite a turn,' said Mr Wilcox, when retailing the incident to Dolly at tea-time. 'None of you girls have any nerves, really. Of course, a word from me put it all right, but silly old Miss Avery–she frightened you, didn't she, Margaret? There you stood clutching a bunch of weeds. She might have said something, instead of coming down the stairs with that alarming bonnet on. I passed her as I came in. Enough to make the car shy. I believe Miss Avery goes in for being a character; some old maids do.' He lit a cigarette. 'It is their last resource. Heaven knows what she was doing in the place; but that's Bryce's business, not mine.'

'I wasn't as foolish as you suggest,' said Margaret. 'She only startled me, for the house had been silent so long.'

'Did you take her for a spook?' asked Dolly, for whom 'spooks' and 'going to church' summarized the unseen.

'Not exactly.'

'She really did frighten you,' said Henry, who was far from discouraging timidity in females. 'Poor Margaret! And very naturally. Uneducated classes are so stupid.'

'Is Miss Avery uneducated classes?' Margaret asked, and found herself looking at the decoration scheme of Dolly's drawing-room.

'She's just one of the crew at the farm. People like that always assume things. She assumed you'd know who she was. She left all the Howards End keys in the front lobby, and assumed that you'd seen them as you came in, that you'd lock up the house when you'd gone, and would bring them down to her. And there was her niece hunting for them down at the farm. Lack of education makes people very casual. Hilton was full of woman like Miss Avery once.'

'I shouldn't have disliked it, perhaps.'

'Or Miss Avery giving me a wedding present,' said Dolly.

Which was illogical but interesting. Through Dolly, Margaret was destined to learn a good deal.

'But Charles said I must try not to mind, because she had known his grandmother.'

'As usual, you've got the story wrong, my good Dorothea.'

'I meant great-grandmother—the one who left Mrs Wilcox the house. Weren't both of them and Miss Avery friends when Howards End, too, was a farm?'

Her father-in-law blew out a shaft of smoke. His attitude to his dead wife was curious. He would allude to her, and hear her discussed, but never mentioned her by name. Nor was he interested in the dim, bucolic past. Dolly was—for the following reason.

'Then hadn't Mrs Wilcox a brother—or was it an uncle? Anyhow, he popped the question, and Miss Avery, she said "No." Just imagine, if she'd said "Yes," she would have been Charles's aunt. (Oh, I say, that's rather good! "Charlie's Aunt"! I must chaff him about that this evening.) And the man went out and was killed. Yes, I'm certain I've got it right now. Tom Howard—he was the last of them.'

'I believe so,' said Mr Wilcox negligently.

'I say! Howards End—Howards Ended!' cried Dolly. 'I'm rather on the spot this evening, eh?'

'I wish you'd ask whether Crane's ended.'

'Oh, Mr Wilcox, how *can* you?'

'Because, if he has had enough tea, we ought to go.—Dolly's a good little woman,' he continued, 'but a little of her goes a long way. I couldn't live near her if you paid me.'

Margaret smiled. Though presenting a firm front to outsiders, no Wilcox could live near, or near the possessions of, any other Wilcox. They had the colonial spirit, and were always making for some spot where the white man might carry his burden unobserved. Of course, Howards End was impossible, so long as the younger couple were established in Hilton. His objections to the house were plain as daylight now.

Crane had had enough tea, and was sent to the garage, where their car had been trickling muddy water over Charles's. The downpour had surely penetrated the Six Hills by now, bringing news of our restless civilization. 'Curious mounds,' said Henry, 'but in with you now; another time.' He had to be up in London by seven–if possible, by six-thirty. Once more she lost the sense of space; once more trees, houses, people, animals, hills, merged and heaved into one dirtiness, and she was at Wickham Place.

Her evening was pleasant. The sense of flux which had haunted her all the year disappeared for a time. She forgot the luggage and the motor-cars, and the hurrying men who know so much and connect so little. She recaptured the sense of space, which is the basis of all earthly beauty, and, starting from Howards End, she attempted to realize England. She failed–visions do not come when we try, though they may come through trying. But an unexpected love of the island awoke in her, connecting on this side with the joys of the flesh, on that with the inconceivable. Helen and her father had known this love, poor Leonard Bast was groping after it, but it had been hidden from Margaret till this afternoon. It had certainly come through the house and old Miss Avery. Through them: the notion of 'through' persisted; her mind trembled towards a conclusion which only the unwise have put into words. Then, veering back into warmth, it dwelt on ruddy bricks, flowering plum-trees, and all the tangible joys of spring.

Henry, after allaying her agitation, had taken her over his property, and had explained to her the use and dimensions of the various rooms. He had sketched the history of the little estate. 'It is so unlucky,' ran the monologue, 'that money wasn't put into it about fifty years ago. Then it had four–five–times the land–thirty acres at least. One could have made something out of it then–a small park, or at all events shrubberies, and rebuilt the house farther away from the road. What's the good of taking it in hand now? Nothing but the meadow left, and even that was heavily mortgaged when I first had to do with things–yes, and the house too. Oh, it was no joke.' She saw two women as he spoke, one old, the other young, watching their inheritance melt away. She saw them greet him as a deliverer. 'Mismanagement did it–besides, the days for small farms are over. It doesn't pay–except with intensive cultivation. Small holdings, back to the land–ah! philanthropic bunkum. Take it as a rule that nothing pays on a small scale. Most of the land you see (they were standing at an upper window, the only one which faced west) belongs to the people at the Park–they made their pile over copper–good chaps. Avery's Farm, Sishe's–what they call the Common, where you see that ruined oak–one after the other fell in, and so did this, as near as is no matter.' But Henry had saved it; without fine feelings or deep insight, but he had saved it, and she loved him for the deed. 'When I had more control I did what I could: sold off the two and a half animals, and the mangy pony, and the superannuated tools; pulled down the outhouses; drained; thinned out I don't know how many guelder-roses and elder-trees; and inside the house I turned the old kitchen into a hall, and made a kitchen behind where the dairy was. Garage and so on came later. But one could still tell it's been an old farm. And yet it isn't the place that would fetch one of your artistic crew.' No, it wasn't; and if he did not quite understand it, the artistic crew would still less: it was English, and the wych-elm that she saw from the window was an English tree. No report had prepared her for its peculiar glory. It was neither warrior, nor lover, nor god; in none of these rôles do the English excel. It was a comrade, bending over the house, strength and adventure in its roots, but in its utmost fingers tenderness, and the girth, that a dozen men could not have spanned, became in the end evanescent, till pale bud clusters seemed to float in the air. It was a comrade. House and tree transcended any similes of sex. Margaret thought of them now, and was to think of them through many a windy night and London day, but to compare either to man, to woman, always dwarfed the vision. Yet they kept within limits of the human. Their message was not of eternity, but of hope on this side of the grave. As she stood in the one, gazing at the other, truer relationship had gleamed.

Another touch, and the account of her day is finished. They entered the garden for a minute, and to Mr Wilcox's surprise she was right. Teeth, pigs' teeth, could be seen in the bark of the wych-elm tree—just the white tips of them showing. 'Extraordinary!' he cried. 'Who told you?'

'I heard of it one winter in London,' was her answer, for she, too, avoided mentioning Mrs Wilcox by name.

Chapter Twenty-five

Evie heard of her father's engagement when she was in for a tennis tournament, and her play went simply to pot. That she should marry and leave him had seemed natural enough; that he, left alone, should do the same was deceitful; and now Charles and Dolly said that it was all her fault. 'But I never dreamt of such a thing,' she grumbled. 'Dad took me to call now and then, and made me ask her to Simpson's. Well, I'm altogether off dad.' It was also an insult to their mother's memory; there they were agreed, and Evie had the idea of returning Mrs Wilcox's lace and jewellery 'as a protest.' Against what it would protest she was not clear; but being only eighteen, the idea of renunciation appealed to her, the more as she did not care for jewellery or lace. Dolly then suggested that she and Uncle Percy should pretend to break off their engagement, and then perhaps Mr Wilcox would quarrel with Miss Schlegel, and break off his; or Paul might be cabled for. But at this point Charles told them not to talk nonsense. So Evie settled to marry as soon as possible; it was no good hanging about with these Schlegels eyeing her. The date of her wedding was consequently put forward from September to August, and in the intoxication of presents she recovered much of her good-humour.

Margaret found that she was expected to figure at this function, and to figure largely; it would be such an opportunity, said Henry, for her to get to know his set. Sir James Bidder would be there, and all the Cahills and the Fussells, and his sister-in-law, Mrs Warrington Wilcox, had fortunately got back from her tour round the world. Henry she loved, but his set promised to be another matter. He had not the knack of surrounding himself with nice people—indeed, for a man of ability and virtue his choice had been singularly unfortunate; he had no guiding principle beyond a certain preference for mediocrity; he was content to settle one of the greatest things in life haphazard, and so, while his investments went right, his friends generally went wrong. She would be told, 'Oh, So-and-so's a good sort—a thundering good sort,' and find, on meeting him, that he was a brute or a bore. If Henry had shown real affection, she would have understood, for affection explains everything. But he seemed without sentiment. The 'thundering good sort' might at any moment become 'a fellow for whom I never did have much use, and have less now,' and be shaken off cheerily into oblivion. Margaret had done the same as a schoolgirl. Now she never forgot anyone for whom she had once cared; she connected, though the connection might be bitter, and she hoped that some day Henry would do the same.

Evie was not to be married from Ducie Street. She had a fancy for something rural, and, besides, no one would be in London then, so she left her boxes for a few weeks at Oniton Grange, and her banns were duly published in the parish church, and for a couple of days the little town, dreaming between the ruddy hills, was roused by the clang of our civilization, and drew up by the roadside to let the motors pass. Oniton had been a discovery of Mr Wilcox's—a discovery of which he was not altogether proud. It was up towards the Welsh border, and so difficult of access that he had concluded it must be something special. A ruined castle stood in the grounds. But having got there, what was one to do? The shooting was bad, the fishing indifferent, and women-folk reported the scenery as nothing much. The place turned out to be in the wrong part of Shropshire, damn it, and though he never damned his own property aloud, he was only waiting to get it off his hands, and then to let fly. Evie's marriage was its last appearance in public. As soon as a tenant was found, it became a house for which he never had had much use, and had less now, and, like Howards End, faded into Limbo.

But on Margaret Oniton was destined to make a lasting impression. She regarded it as her future home, and was anxious to start straight with the clergy, etc., and, if possible, to see something of the local life. It was a market-town—as tiny a one as England possesses—and had for ages served that lonely valley, and guarded our marches against the Kelt. In spite of the occasion, in spite of the numbling hilarity that greeted her as soon as she got into the reserved saloon at Paddington, her senses were awake and watching, and though Oniton was to prove one of her innumerable false starts, she never forgot it, nor the things that happened there.

The London party only numbered eight—the Fussells, father and son, two Anglo-Indian ladies named Mrs Plynlimmon and Lady Edser, Mrs

Warrington Wilcox and her daughter, and, lastly, the little girl, very smart
and quiet, who figures at so many weddings, and who kept a watchful eye on
Margaret, the bride-elect. Dolly was absent—a domestic event detained her
at Hilton; Paul had cabled a humorous message; Charles was to meet them
with a trio of motors at Shrewsbury. Helen had refused her invitation;
Tibby had never answered his. The management was excellent, as was to be
expected with anything that Henry undertook; one was conscious of his
sensible and generous brain in the background. They were his guests as soon
as they reached the train; a special label for their luggage; a courier; a special
lunch; they had only to look pleasant and, where possible, pretty. Margaret
thought with dismay of her own nuptials—presumably under the
management of Tibby. 'Mr Theobald Schlegel and Miss Helen Schlegel
request the pleasure of Mrs Plynlimmon's company on the occasion of the
marriage of their sister Margaret.' The formula was incredible, but it must
soon be printed and sent, and though Wickham Place need not compete with
Oniton, it must feed its guests properly, and provide them with sufficient
chairs. Her wedding would either be ramshackly or bourgeois—she hoped
the latter. Such an affair as the present, staged with a deftness that was
almost beautiful, lay beyond her powers and those of her friends.

The low rich purr of a Great Western express is not the worst background
for conversation, and the journey passed pleasantly enough. Nothing could
have exceeded the kindness of the two men. They raised windows for some
ladies, and lowered them for others, they rang the bell for the servant, they
identified the colleges as the train slipped past Oxford, they caught books or
bag-purses in the act of tumbling on to the floor. Yet there was nothing
finicking about their politeness: it had the Public School touch, and, though
sedulous, was virile. More battles than Waterloo have been won on our
playing-fields, and Margaret bowed to a charm of which she did not wholly
approve, and said nothing when the Oxford colleges were identified
wrongly. 'Male and female created He them'; the journey to Shrewsbury
confirmed this questionable statement, and the long glass saloon, that
moved so easily and felt so comfortable, became a forcing-house for the idea
of sex.

At Shrewsbury came fresh air. Margaret was all for sightseeing, and while
the others were finishing their tea at the Raven, she annexed a motor and
hurried over the astonishing city. Her chauffeur was not the faithful Crane,
but an Italian, who dearly loved making her late. Charles, watch in hand,
though with a level brow, was standing in front of the hotel when they
returned. It was perfectly all right, he told her; she was by no means the last.
And then he dived into the coffee-room, and she heard him say, 'For God's
sake, hurry the women up; we shall never be off,' and Albert Fussell reply,
'Not I; I've done my share,' and Colonel Fussell opine that the ladies were
getting themselves up to kill. Presently Myra (Mrs Warrington's daughter)
appeared, and as she was his cousin, Charles blew her up a little: she had
been changing her smart travelling hat for a smart motor hat. Then Mrs
Warrington herself, leading the quiet child; the two Anglo-Indian ladies
were always last. Maids, courier, heavy luggage, had already gone on by a

branch-line to a station nearer Oniton, but there were five hat-boxes and four dressing-bags to be packed, and five dust-cloaks to be put on, and to be put off at the last moment, because Charles declared them not necessary. The men presided over everything with unfailing good-humour. By half-past five the party was ready, and went out of Shrewsbury by the Welsh Bridge.

Shropshire had not the reticence of Hertfordshire. Though robbed of half its magic by swift movement, it still conveyed the sense of hills. They were nearing the buttresses that force the Severn eastward and make it an English stream, and the sun, sinking over the Sentinels of Wales, was straight in their eyes. Having picked up another guest, they turned southward, avoiding the greater mountains, but conscious of an occasional summit, rounded and mild, whose colouring differed in quality from that of the lower earth, and whose contours altered more slowly. Quiet mysteries were in progress behind those tossing horizons: the West, as ever, was retreating with some secret which may not be worth the discovery, but which no practical man will ever discover.

They spoke of Tariff Reform.

Mrs Warrington was just back from the Colonies. Like many other critics of Empire, her mouth had been stopped with food, and she could only exclaim at the hospitality with which she had been received and warn the Mother Country against trifling with young Titans. 'They threaten to cut the painter,' she cried, 'and where shall we be then? Miss Schlegel, you'll undertake to keep Henry sound about Tariff Reform? It is our last hope.'

Margaret playfully confessed herself on the other side, and they began to quote from their respective hand-books while the motor carried them deep into the hills. Curious these were rather than impressive, for their outlines lacked beauty, and the pink fields on their summits suggested the handkerchiefs of a giant spread out to dry. An occasional outcrop of rock, an occasional wood, an occasional 'forest,' treeless and brown, all hinted at wildness to follow, but the main colour was an agricultural green. The air grew cooler; they had surmounted the last gradient, and Oniton lay below them with its church, its radiating houses, its castle, its river-girt peninsula. Close to the castle was a grey mansion, unintellectual but kindly, stretching with its grounds across the peninsula's neck—the sort of mansion that was built all over England in the beginning of the last century, while architecture was still an expression of the national character. That was the Grange, remarked Albert, over his shoulder, and then he jammed the break on, and the motor slowed down and stopped. 'I'm sorry,' said he, turning round. 'Do you mind getting out—by the door on the right. Steady on.'

'What's happened?' asked Mrs Warrington.

Then the car behind them drew up, and the voice of Charles was heard saying: 'Get out the women at once.' There was a concourse of males, and Margaret and her companions were hustled out and received into the second car. What had happened? As it started off again, the door of a cottage opened, and a girl screamed wildly at them.

'What is it?' the ladies cried.

Charles drove them a hundred yards without speaking. Then he said: 'It's all right. Your car just touched a dog.'

'But stop!' cried Margaret, horrified.

'It didn't hurt him.'

'Didn't really hurt him?' asked Myra.

'No.'

'Do *please* stop!' said Margaret, leaning forward. She was standing up in the car, the other occupants holding her knees to steady her. 'I want to go back, please.'

Charles took no notice.

'We've left Mr Fussell behind,' said another: 'and Angelo, and Crane.'

'Yes, but no woman.'

'I expect a little of'—Mrs Warrington scratched her palm—'will be more to the point than one of us!'

'The insurance company see to that,' remarked Charles, 'and Albert will do the talking.'

'I want to go back, though, I say!' repeated Margaret, getting angry.

Charles took no notice. The motor, loaded with refugees, continued to travel very slowly down the hill. 'The men are there,' chorused the others. 'Men will see to it.'

'The men *can't* see to it. Oh, this is ridiculous! Charles, I ask you to stop.'

'Stopping's no good,' drawled Charles.

'Isn't it?' said Margaret, and jumped straight out of the car.

She fell on her knees, cut her gloves, shook her hat over her ear. Cries of alarm followed her. 'You've hurt yourself,' exclaimed Charles, jumping after her.

'Of course I've hurt myself!' she retorted.

'May I ask what—'

'There's nothing to ask,' said Margaret.

'Your hand's bleeding.'

'I know.'

'I'm in for a frightful row from the pater.'

'You should have thought of that sooner, Charles.'

Charles had never been in such a position before. It was a woman in revolt who was hobbling away from him, and the sight was too strange to leave any room for anger. He recovered himself when the others caught them up: their sort he understood. He commanded them to go back.

Albert Fussell was seen walking towards them.

'It's all right!' he called. 'It wasn't a dog, it was a cat.'

'There!' exclaimed Charles triumphantly. 'It's only a rotten cat.'

'Got room in your car for a little un? I cut as soon as I saw it wasn't a dog; the chauffeurs are tackling the girl.' But Margaret walked forward steadily. Why should the chauffeurs tackle the girl? Ladies sheltering behind men, men sheltering behind servants—the whole system's wrong, and she must challenge it.

'Miss Schlegel! 'Pon my word, you've hurt your hand.'

'I'm just going to see,' said Margaret. 'Don't you wait Mr Fussell.'

The second motor came round the corner. 'It is all right madam,' said Crane in his turn. He had taken to call her madam.

'What's all right? The cat?'

'Yes, madam. The girl will receive compensation for it.'

'She was a very ruda girla,' said Angelo from the third motor thoughtfully.

'Wouldn't you have been rude?'

The Italian spread out his hands, implying that he had not thought of rudeness, but would produce it if it pleased her. The situation became absurd. The gentlemen were again buzzing round Miss Schlegel with offers of assistance, and Lady Edser began to bind up her hand. She yielded, apologizing slightly, and was led back to the car, and soon the landscape resumed its motion, the lonely cottage disappeared, the castle swelled on its cushion of turf, and they had arrived. No doubt she had disgraced herself. But she felt their whole journey from London had been unreal. They had no part with the earth and its emotions. They were dust, and a stink, and cosmopolitan chatter, and the girl whose cat had been killed had lived more deeply than they.

'Oh, Henry,' she exclaimed, 'I have been so naughty,' for she had decided to take up this line. 'We ran over a cat. Charles told me not to jump out, but I would, and look!' She held out her bandaged hand. 'Your poor Meg went such a flop.'

Mr Wilcox looked bewildered. In evening dress, he was standing to welcome his guests in the hall.

'Thinking it was a dog,' added Mrs Warrington.

'Ah, a dog's a companion!' said Colonel Fussell. 'A dog'll remember you.'

'Have you hurt yourself, Margaret?'

'Not to speak about; and it's my left hand.'

'Well, hurry up and change.'

She obeyed, as did the others. Mr Wilcox then turned to his son.

'Now, Charles, what's happened?'

Charles was absolutely honest. He described what he believed to have happened. Albert had flattened out a cat, and Miss Schlegel had lost her nerve, as any woman might. She had been got safely into the other car, but when it was in motion had leapt out again, in spite of all that they could say. After walking a little on the road, she had calmed down and had said that she was sorry. His father accepted this explanation, and neither knew that Margaret had artfully prepared the way for it. It fitted in too well with their view of feminine nature. In the smoking-room, after dinner, the Colonel put forward the view that Miss Schlegel had jumped it out of devilry. Well he remembered as a young man, in the harbour of Gibraltar once, how a girl–a handsome girl, too–had jumped overboard for a bet. He could see her now, and all the lads overboard after her. But Charles and Mr Wilcox agreed it was much more probably ˌnerves in Miss Schlegel's case. Charles was depressed. That woman had a tongue. She would bring worse disgrace on his father before she had done with them. He strolled out on to the castle mound to think the matter over. The evening was exquisite. On three sides of him a little river whispered, full of messages from the west; above his head the ruins made patterns against the sky. He carefully reviewed their dealings with this family, until he fitted Helen, and Margaret, and Aunt Juley into an orderly conspiracy. Paternity had made him suspicious. He had two children to look after, and more coming, and day by day they seemed less likely to grow up rich men. 'It is all very well,' he reflected, 'the pater saying that he will be just to all, but one can't be just indefinitely. Money isn't elastic. What's to happen if Evie has a family? And, come to that, so may the pater. There'll not be enough to go round, for there's none coming in, either through Dolly or Percy. It's damnable!' He looked enviously at the Grange, whose windows poured light and laughter. First and last, this wedding would cost a pretty penny. Two ladies were strolling up and down the garden terrace, and as the syllables 'Imperialism' were wafted to his ears, he guessed that one of them was his aunt. She might have helped him, if she too had not had a family to provide for. 'Everyone for himself,' he repeated—a maxim which had cheered him in the past, but which rang grimly enough among the ruins of Oniton. He lacked his father's ability in business, and so had an ever higher regard for money; unless he could inherit plenty, he feared to leave his children poor.

As he sat thinking, one of the ladies left the terrace and walked into the meadow; he recognized her as Margaret by the white bandage that gleamed on her arm, and put out his cigar, lest the gleam should betray him. She climbed up the mound in zigzags, and at times stooped down, as if she was stroking the turf. It sounds absolutely incredible, but for a moment Charles thought that she was in love with him, and had come out to tempt him. Charles believed in temptresses, who are indeed the strong man's necessary complement, and having no sense of humour, he could not purge himself of the thought by a smile. Margaret, who was engaged to his father, and his sister's wedding-guest, kept on her way without noticing him, and he admitted that he had wronged her on this point. But what was she doing? Why was she stumbling about amongst the rubble and catching her dress in brambles and burrs? As she edged round the keep, she must have got to windward and smelt his cigar-smoke, for she exclaimed, 'Hullo! Who's that?'

Charles made no answer.

'Saxon or Kelt?' she continued, laughing in the darkness. 'But it doesn't matter. Whichever you are, you will have to listen to me. I love this place. I love Shropshire. I hate London. I am glad that this will be my home. Ah, dear'—she was now moving back towards the house—'what a comfort to have arrived!'

'That woman means mischief,' thought Charles, and compressed his lips. In a few minutes he followed her indoors, as the ground was getting damp. Mists were rising from the river, and presently it became invisible, though it whispered more loudly. There had been a heavy downpour in the Welsh hills.

Chapter Twenty-six

Next morning a fine mist covered the peninsula. The weather promised well, and the outline of the castle mound grew clearer each moment that Margaret watched it. Presently she saw the keep, and the sun painted the rubble gold, and charged the white sky with blue. The shadow of the house gathered itself together, and fell over the garden. A cat looked up at her window and mewed. Lastly the river appeared, still holding the mists between its banks and its overhanging alders, and only visible as far as a hill, which cut off its upper reaches.

Margaret was fascinated by Oniton. She had said that she loved it, but it was rather its romantic tension that held her. The rounded Druids of whom she had caught glimpses in her drive, the rivers hurrying down from them to England, the carelessly modelled masses of the lower hills, thrilled her with poetry. The house was insignificant, but the prospect from it would be an eternal joy, and she thought of all the friends she would have to stop in it, and of the conversion of Henry himself to a rural life. Society, too, promised favourably. The rector of the parish had dined with them last night, and she found that he was a friend of her father's, and so knew what to find in her. She liked him. He would introduce her to the town. While, on her other side, Sir James Bidder sat, repeating that she only had to give the word, and he would whip up the county families for twenty miles round. Whether Sir James, who was Garden Seeds, had promised what he could perform, she doubted, but so long as Henry mistook them for the county families when they did call, she was content.

Charles and Albert Fussell now crossed the lawn. They were going for a morning dip, and a servant followed them with their bathing-dresses. She had meant to take a stroll herself before breakfast, but saw that the day was still sacred to men, and amused herself by watching their contretemps. In the first place the key of the bathing-shed could not be found. Charles stood by the riverside with folded hands, tragical, while the servant shouted, and was misunderstood by another servant in the garden. Then came a difficulty about a spring-board, and soon three people were running backwards and forwards over the meadow, with orders and counter orders and recriminations and apologies. If Margaret wanted to jump from a motor-car, she jumped; if Tibby thought paddling would benefit his ankles, he paddled; if a clerk desired adventure, he took a walk in the dark. But these athletes seemed paralyzed. They could not bathe without their appliances, though the morning sun was calling and the last mists were rising from the dimpling stream. Had they found the life of the body after all? Could not the men whom they despised as milksops beat them, even on their own ground?

She thought of the bathing arrangements as they should be in her day—no worrying of servants, no appliances, beyond good sense. Her reflections were disturbed by the quiet child, who had come out to speak to the cat, but was now watching her watch the men. She called, 'Good-morning, dear,' a little sharply. Her voice spread consternation. Charles looked round, and though completely attired in indigo blue, vanished into the shed, and was seen no more.

'Miss Wilcox is up—' the child whispered, and then became unintelligible.

'What's that?'

It sounded like, '—cut-yoke—sack-back—'

'I can't hear.'

'—On the bed—tissue-paper—'

Gathering that the wedding-dress was on view, and that a visit would be seemly, she went to Evie's room. All was hilarity here. Evie, in a petticoat, was dancing with one of the Anglo-Indian ladies, while the other was adoring yards of white satin. They screamed, they laughed, they sang, and the dog barked.

Margaret screamed a little too, but without conviction. She could not feel that a wedding was so funny. Perhaps something was missing in her equipment.

Evie gasped: 'Dolly is a rotter not to be here! Oh, we would rag just then!' Then Margaret went down to breakfast.

Henry was already installed; he ate slowly and spoke little, and was, in Margaret's eyes, the only member of their party who dodged emotion successfully. She could not suppose him indifferent either to the loss of his daughter or to the presence of his future wife. Yet he dwelt intact, only issuing orders occasionally—orders that promoted the comfort of his guests. He inquired after her hand; he set her to pour out the coffee and Mrs Warrington to pour out the tea. When Evie came down there was a moment's awkwardness, and both ladies rose to vacate their places. 'Burton,' called Henry, 'serve tea and coffee from the sideboard!' It wasn't genuine tact, but it was tact, of a sort—the sort that is as useful as the genuine, and saves even more situations at Board meetings. Henry treated a marriage like a funeral, item by item, never raising his eyes to the whole, and 'Death, where is they sting? Love, where is thy victory?' one would exclaim at the close.

After breakfast she claimed a few words with him. It was always best to approach him formally. She asked for the interview, because he was going on to shoot grouse to-morrow, and she was returning to Helen in town.

'Certainly, dear,' said he. 'Of course, I have the time. What do you want?'

'Nothing.'

'I was afraid something had gone wrong.'

'No; I have nothing to say, but you may talk.'

Glancing at his watch, he talked of the nasty curve at the lych-gate. She heard him with interest. Her surface could always respond to his without contempt, though all her deeper being might be yearning to help him. She had abandoned any plan of action. Love is the best, and the more she let herself love him, the more chance was there that he would set his soul in order. Such a moment as this, when they sat under fair weather by the walks of their future home, was so sweet to her that its sweetness would surely pierce to him. Each lift of his eyes, each parting of the thatched lip from the clean-shaven, must prelude the tenderness that kills the Monk and the Beast at a single blow. Disappointed a hundred times, she still hoped. She loved him with too clear a vision to fear his cloudiness. Whether he droned trivialities, as to-day, or sprang kisses on her in the twilight, she could pardon him, she could respond.

'If there is this nasty curve,' she suggested, 'couldn't we walk to the church? Not, of course, you and Evie; but the rest of us might very well go on first, and that would mean fewer carriages.'

'One can't have ladies walking through the Market Square. The Fussells wouldn't like it; they were awfully particular at Charles's wedding. My—she—one of our party was anxious to walk, and certainly the church was just round the corner, and I shouldn't have minded; but the Colonel made a great point of it.'

'You men shouldn't be so chivalrous,' said Margaret thoughtfully.

'Why not?'

She knew why not, but said that she did not know. He then announced that, unless she had anything special to say, he must visit the wine-cellar, and they went off together in search of Burton. Though clumsy and a little inconvenient, Oniton was a genuine country-house. They clattered down flagged passages, looking into room after room, and scaring unknown maids from the performance of obscure duties. The wedding-breakfast must be in readiness when they come back from church, and tea would be served in the garden. The sight of so many agitated and serious people made Margaret smile, but she reflected that they were paid to be serious, and enjoyed being agitated. Here were the lower wheels of the machine that was tossing Evie up into nuptial glory. A little boy blocked their way with pig-pails. His mind could not grasp their greatness, and he said: 'By your leave; let me pass, please.' Henry asked him where Burton was. But the servants were so new that they did not know one another's names. In the still-room sat the band, who had stipulated for champagne as part of their fee, and who were already drinking beer. Scents of Araby came from the kitchen, mingled with cries. Margaret knew what had happened there, for it happened at Wickham Place. One of the wedding dishes had boiled over, and the cook was throwing cedar-shavings to hide the smell. At last they came upon the butler. Henry gave him the keys, and handed Margaret down the cellar-stairs. Two doors were unlocked. She, who kept all her wine at the bottom of the linen-cupboard, was astonished at the sight. 'We shall never get through it!' she cried, and the two men were suddenly drawn into brotherhood, and exchanged smiles. She felt as if she had again jumped out of the car while it was moving.

Certainly Oniton would take some digesting. It would be no small business to remain herself, and yet to assimilate such an establishment. She must remain herself, for his sake as well as her own, since a shadowy wife degrades the husband whom she accompanies; and she must assimilate for reasons of common honesty, since she had no right to marry a man and make him uncomfortable. Her only ally was the power of Home. The loss of Wickham Place had taught her more than its possession. Howards End had repeated the lesson. She was determined to create new sanctities among these hills.

After visiting the wine-cellar, she dressed, and then came the wedding, which seemed a small affair when compared with the preparations for it. Everything went like one o'clock. Mr Cahill materialized out of space, and was waiting for his bride at the church door. No one dropped the ring or mispronounced the responses, or trod on Evie's train, or cried. In a few minutes the clergymen performed their duty, the register was signed, and they were back in their carriages, negotiating the dangerous curve by the lych-gate. Margaret was convinced that they had not been married at all, and that the Norman church had been intent all the time on other business.

There were more documents to sign at the house, and the breakfast to eat, and then a few more people dropped in for the garden party. There had been a great many refusals, and after all it was not a very big affair—not as big as Margaret's would be. She noted the dishes and the strips of red carpet, that outwardly she might give Henry what was proper. But inwardly she hoped for something better than this blend of Sunday church and fox-hunting. If only someone had been upset! But this wedding had gone off so particularly well—'quite like a Durbar' in the opinion of Lady Edser, and she thoroughly agreed with her.

So the wasted day lumbered forward, the bride and bridegroom drove off, yelling with laughter, and for the second time the sun retreated towards the hills of Wales. Henry, who was more tired than he owned, came up to her in the castle meadow, and, in tones of unusual softness, said that he was pleased. Everything had gone off so well. She felt that he was praising her, too, and blushed; certainly she had done all she could with his intractable friends, and had made a special point of kow-towing to the men. They were breaking camp this evening: only the Warringtons and quiet child would stay the night, and the others were already moving towards the house to finish their packing. 'I think it did go off well,' she agreed. 'Since I had to jump out of the motor, I'm thankful I lighted on my left hand. I am so very glad about it, Henry dear; I only hope that the guests at ours may be half as comfortable. You must all remember that we have no practical person among us, except my aunt, and she is not used to entertainments on a large scale.'

'I know,' he said gravely. 'Under the circumstances, it would be better to put everything into the hands of Harrod's or Whiteley's, or even to go to some hotel.'

'You desire a hotel?'

'Yes, because—well, I mustn't interfere with you. No doubt you want to be married from your old home.'

'My old home's falling into pieces, Henry. I only want my new. Isn't it a perfect evening—'

'The Alexandrina isn't bad—'

'The Alexandrina,' she echoed, more occupied with the threads of smoke that were issuing from their chimneys, and ruling the sunlit slopes with parallels of grey.

'It's off Curzon Street.'

'Is it? Let's be married from off Curzon Street.'

Then she turned westward, to gaze at the swirling gold. Just where the river rounded the hill the sun caught it. Fairyland must lie above the bend, and its precious liquid was pouring towards them past Charles's bathing-shed. She gazed so long that her eyes were dazzled, and when they moved back to the house, she could not recognize the faces of people who were coming out of it. A parlour-maid was preceding them.

'Who are those people?' she asked.

'They're callers!' exclaimed Henry. 'It's too late for callers.'

'Perhaps they're town people who want to see the wedding presents.'

'I'm not at home yet to townees.'

'Well, hide among the ruins, and if I can stop them, I will.'

He thanked her.

Margaret went forward, smiling socially. She supposed that these were unpunctual guests, who would have to be content with vicarious civility, since Evie and Charles were gone, Henry tired, and the others in their rooms. She assumed the airs of a hostess; not for long. For one of the group was Helen—Helen in her oldest clothes, and dominated by that tense, wounding excitement that had made her a terror in their nursery days.

'What is it?' she called. 'Oh, what's wrong? Is Tibby ill?'

Helen spoke to her two companions, who fell back. Then she bore forward furiously.

'They're starving!' she shouted. 'I found them starving!'

'Who? Why have you come?'

'The Basts.'

'Oh, Helen!' moaned Margaret. 'Whatever have you done now?'

'He has lost his place. He has been turned out of his bank. Yes, he's done for. We upper classes have ruined him, and I suppose you'll tell me it's the battle of life. Starving. His wife is ill. Starving. She fainted in the train.'

'Helen, are you mad?'

'Perhaps. Yes. If you like, I'm mad. But I've brought them. I'll stand injustice no longer. I'll show up the wretchedness that lies under this luxury, this talk of impersonal forces, this cant about God doing what we're too slack to do ourselves.'

'Have you actually brought two starving people from London to Shropshire, Helen?'

Helen was checked. She had not thought of this, and her hysteria abated. 'There was a restaurant car on the train,' she said.

'Don't be absurd. They aren't starving, and you know it. Now, begin from the beginning. I won't have such theatrical nonsense. How dare you! Yes,

how dare you!' she repeated, as anger filled her, 'bursting in to Evie's
wedding in this heartless way. My goodness! but you've a perverted notion
of philanthropy. Look'—she indicated the house—'servants, people out of
the windows. They think it's some vulgar scandal, and I must explain, "Oh
no, it's only my sister screaming, and only two hangers-on of ours, whom
she has brought here for no conceivable reason."'

'Kindly take back that word "hangers-on,"' said Helen, ominously calm.

'Very well,' conceded Margaret, who for all her wrath was determined to
avoid a real quarrel. 'I, too, am sorry about them, but it beats me why you've
brought them here, or why you're here yourself.'

'It's our last chance of seeing Mr Wilcox.'

Margaret moved towards the house at this. She was determined not to
worry Henry.

'He's going to Scotland. I know he is. I insist on seeing him.'

'Yes, to-morrow.'

'I knew it was our last chance.'

'How do you do, Mr Bast?' said Margaret, trying to control her voice.
'This is an odd business. What view do you take of it?'

'There is Mrs Bast, too,' prompted Helen.

Jacky also shook hands. She, like her husband, was shy, and, furthermore,
ill, and, furthermore, so bestially stupid that she could not grasp what was
happening. She only knew that the lady had swept down like a whirlwind
last night, had paid the rent, redeemed the furniture, provided them with a
dinner and a breakfast, and ordered them to meet her at Paddington next
morning. Leonard had feebly protested, and when the morning came, had
suggested that they shouldn't go. But she, half mesmerized, had obeyed.
The lady had told them to, and they must, and their bed-sitting-room had
accordingly changed into Paddington, and Paddington into a railway
carriage, that shook, and grew hot, and grew cold, and vanished entirely, and
reappeared amid torrents of expensive scent. 'You have fainted,' said the
lady in an awe-struck voice. 'Perhaps the air will do you good.' And perhaps
it had, for here she was, feeling rather better among a lot of flowers.

'I'm sure I don't want to intrude,' begun Leonard, in answer to
Margaret's question. 'But you have been so kind to me in the past in warning
me about the Porphyrion that I wondered—why, I wondered whether—'

'Whether we could get him back into the Porphyrion again,' supplied
Helen. 'Meg, this has been a cheerful business. A bright evening's work that
was on Chelsea Embankment.'

Margaret shook her head and returned to Mr Bast.

'I don't understand. You left the Porphyrion because we suggested it was
a bad concern, didn't you?'

'That's right.'

'And went into a bank instead?'

'I told you all that,' said Helen; 'and they reduced their staff after he had
been in a month, and now he's penniless, and I consider that we and our
informant are directly to blame.'

'I hate all this,' Leonard muttered.

'I hope you do, Mr Bast. But it's no good mincing matters. You have done yourself no good by coming here. If you intend to confront Mr Wilcox, and to call him to account for a chance remark, you will make a very great mistake.'

'I brought them. I did it all,' cried Helen.

'I can only advise you to go at once. My sister has put you in a false position, and it is kindest to tell you so. It's too late to get to town, but you'll find a comfortable hotel in Oniton, where Mrs Bast can rest, and I hope you'll be my guests there.'

'That isn't what I want, Miss Schlegel,' said Leonard. 'You're very kind, and do doubt it's a false position, but you make me miserable. I seem no good at all.'

'It's work he wants,' interpreted Helen. 'Can't you see?'

Then he said: 'Jacky, let's go. We're more bother than we're worth. We're costing these ladies pounds and pounds already to get work for us, and they never will. There's nothing we're good enough to do.'

'We would like to find you work,' said Margaret rather conventionally. 'We want to–I, like my sister. You're only down in your luck. Go to the hotel, have a good night's rest, and some day you shall pay me back the bill, if you prefer it.'

But Leonard was near the abyss, and at such moments men see clearly. 'You don't know what you're talking about,' he said. 'I shall never get work now. If rich people fail at one profession, they can try another. Not I. I had my groove, and I've got out of it. I could do one particular branch of insurance in one particular office well enough to command a salary, but that's all. Poetry's nothing, Miss Schlegel. One's thoughts about this and that are nothing. Your money, too, is nothing, if you'll understand me. I mean if a man over twenty once loses his own particular job, it's all over with him. I have seen it happen to others. Their friends gave them money for a little, but in the end they fall over the edge. It's no good. It's the whole world pulling. There always will be rich and poor.'

He ceased. 'Won't you have something to eat?' said Margaret. 'I don't know what to do. It isn't my house, and though Mr Wilcox would have been glad to see you at any other time–as I say, I don't know what to do, but I undertake to do what I can for you. Helen, offer them something. Do try a sandwich, Mrs Bast.'

They moved to a long table behind which a servant was still standing. Iced cakes, sandwiches innumerable, coffee, claret-cup, champagne, remained almost intact: their overfed guests could do no more. Leonard refused. Jacky thought she could manage a little. Margaret left them whispering together, and had a few more words with Helen.

She said: 'Helen, I like Mr Bast. I agree that he's worth helping. I agree that we are directly responsible.'

'No, indirectly. Via Mr Wilcox.'

'Let me tell you once and for all that if you take up that attitude, I'll do nothing. No doubt you're right logically, and are entitled to say a great many scathing things about Henry. Only, I won't have it. So choose.'

Helen looked at the sunset.

'If you promise to take them quietly to the George, I will speak to Henry about them—in my own way, mind; there is to be none of this absurd screaming about justice. I have no use for justice. If it was only a question of money, we could do it ourselves. But he wants work, and that we can't give him, but possibly Henry can.'

'It's his duty to,' grumbled Helen.

'Nor am I concerned with duty. I'm concerned with the characters of various people whom we know, and how, things being as they are, things may be made a little better. Mr Wilcox hates being asked favours: all business men do. But I am going to ask him, at the risk of a rebuff, because I want to make things a little better.'

'Very well. I promise. You take it very calmly.'

'Take them off to the George, then, and I'll try. Poor creatures! but they look tired.' As they parted, she added: 'I haven't nearly done with you, though, Helen. You have been most self-indulgent. I can't get over it. You have less restraint rather than more as you grow older. Think it over and alter yourself, or we shan't have happy lives.'

She rejoined Henry. Fortunately he had been sitting down: these physical matters were important. 'Was it townees?' he asked, greeting her with a pleasant smile.

'You'll never believe me,' said Margaret, sitting down beside him. 'It's all right now, but it was my sister.'

'Helen here?' he cried, preparing to rise. 'But she refused the invitation. I thought she despised weddings.'

'Don't get up. She has not come to the wedding. I've bundled her off to the George.'

Inherently hospitable, he protested.

'No; she has two of her protégés with her, and must keep with them.'

'Let 'em all come.'

'My dear Henry, did you see them?'

'I did catch sight of a brown bunch of a woman, certainly.'

'The brown bunch was Helen, but did you catch sight of a sea-green and salmon bunch?'

'What! are they out beanfeasting?'

'No; business. They wanted to see me, and later on I want to talk to you about them.'

She was ashamed of her own diplomacy. In dealing with a Wilcox, how tempting it was to lapse from comradeship, and to give him the kind of woman that he desired! Henry took the hint at once, and said: 'Why later on? Tell me now. No time like the present.'

'Shall I?'

'If it isn't a long story.'

'Oh, not five minutes; but there's a sting at the end of it, for I want you to find the man some work in your office.'

'What are his qualifications?'

'I don't know. He's a clerk.'

'How old?'

'Twenty-five, perhaps.'

'What's his name?'

'Bast,' said Margaret, and was about to remind him that they had met at Wickham Place, but stopped herself. It had not been a successful meeting.

'Where was he before?'

'Dempster's Bank.'

'Why did he leave?' he asked, still remembering nothing.

'They reduced their staff.'

'All right; I'll see him.'

It was the reward of her tact and devotion through the day. Now she understood why some women prefer influence to rights. Mrs Plynlimmon, when condemning suffragettes, had said: 'The woman who can't influence her husband to vote the way she wants ought to be ashamed of herself.' Margaret had winced, but she was influencing Henry now, and though pleased at her little victory, she knew that she had won it by the methods of the harem.

'I should be glad if you took him,' she said, 'but I don't know whether he's qualified.'

'I'll do what I can. But, Margaret, this mustn't be taken as a precedent.'

'No, of course—of course—'

'I can't fit in your protégés every day. Business would suffer.'

'I can promise you he's the last. He—he's rather a special case.'

'Protégés always are.'

She let it stand at that. He rose with a little extra touch of complacency, and held out his hand to help her up. How wide the gulf between Henry as he was and Henry as Helen thought he ought to be! And she herself—hovering as usual between the two, now accepting men as they are, now yearning with her sister for Truth. Love and Truth—their warfare seems eternal. Perhaps the whole visible world rests on it, and if they were one, life itself, like the spirits when Prospero was reconciled to his brother, might vanish into air, into thin air.

'Your protégé has made us late,' said he. 'The Fussells will just be starting.'

On the whole she sided with men as they are. Henry would save the Basts as he had saved Howards End, while Helen and her friends were discussing the ethics of salvation. His was a slap-dash method, but the world has been built slap-dash, and the beauty of mountain and river and sunset may be but the varnish with which the unskilled artificer hides his joins. Oniton, like herself, was imperfect. Its apple-trees were stunted, its castle ruinous. It, too, had suffered in the border warfare between the Anglo-Saxon and the Kelt, between things as they are and as they ought to be. Once more the west was retreating, once again the orderly stars were dotting the eastern sky. There is certainly no rest for us on the earth. But there is happiness, and as Margaret descended the mound on her lover's arm, she felt that she was having her share.

To her annoyance, Mrs Bast was still in the garden; the husband and

Helen had left her there to finish her meal while they went to engage rooms. Margaret found this woman repellent. She had felt, when shaking her hand, an overpowering shame. She remembered the motive of her call at Wickham Place, and smelt again odours from the abyss—odours the more disturbing because they were involuntary. For there was no malice in Jacky. There she sat, a piece of cake in one hand, an empty champagne glass in the other, doing no harm to anybody.

'She's overtired,' Margaret whispered.

'She's something else,' said Henry. 'This won't do. I can't have her in my garden in this state.'

'Is she—' Margaret hesitated to add 'drunk.' Now that she was going to marry him, he had grown particular. He discountenanced risqué conversations now.

Henry went up to the woman. She raised her face, which gleamed in the twilight like a puff-ball.

'Madam, you will be more comfortable at the hotel,' he said sharply.

Jacky replied: 'If it isn't Hen!'

'Ne crois pas que le mari lui ressemble,' apologized Margaret. 'Il est tout à fait différent.'

'Henry!' she repeated, quite distinctly.

Mr Wilcox was much annoyed. 'I can't congratulate you on your protégés,' he remarked.

'Hen, don't go. You do love me, dear, don't you?'

'Bless us, what a person!' sighed Margaret, gathering up her skirts.

Jacky pointed with her cake. 'You're a nice boy, you are.' She yawned. 'There now, I love you.'

'Henry, I am awfully sorry.'

'And pray why?' he asked, and looked at her so sternly that she feared he was ill. He seemed more scandalized than the facts demanded.

'To have brought this down on you.'

'Pray don't apologize.'

The voice continued.

'Why does she call you "Hen"?' said Margaret innocently. 'Has she ever seen you before?'

'Seen Hen before!' said Jacky. 'Who hasn't seen Hen? He's serving you like me, my dear. These boys! You wait—Still we love 'em.'

'Are you now satisfied?' Henry asked.

Margaret began to grow frightened. 'I don't know what it is all about,' she said. 'Let's come in.'

But he thought she was acting. He thought he was trapped. He saw his whole life crumbling. 'Don't you indeed?' he said bitingly. 'I do. Allow me to congratulate you on the success of your plan.'

'This is Helen's plan, not mine.'

'I now understand your interest in the Basts. Very well thought out. I am amused at your caution, Margaret. You are quite right—it was necessary. I am a man, and have lived a man's past. I have the honour to release you from your engagement.'

Still she could not understand. She knew of life's seamy side as a theory; she could not grasp it as a fact. More words from Jacky were necessary—words unequivocal, undenied.

'So that—' burst from her, and she went indoors. She stopped herself from saying more.

'So what?' asked Colonel Fussell, who was getting ready to start in the hall.

'We were saying—Henry and I were just having the fiercest argument, my point being—' Seizing his fur coat from a footman, she offered to help him on. He protested, and there was a playful little scene.

'No, let me do that,' said Henry, following.

'Thanks so much! You see—he has forgiven me!'

The Colonel said gallantly: 'I don't expect there's much to forgive.'

He got into the car. The ladies followed him after an interval. Maids, courier, and heavier luggage had been sent on earlier by the branch-line. Still chattering, still thanking their host and patronizing their future hostess, the guests were borne away.

Then Margaret continued: 'So that woman has been your mistress?'

'You put it with your usual delicacy,' he replied.

'When please?'

'Why?'

'When, please?'

'Ten years ago.'

She left him without a word. For it was not her tragedy: it was Mrs Wilcox's.

Chapter Twenty-seven

Helen began to wonder why she had spent a matter of eight pounds in making some people ill and others angry. Now that the wave of excitement was ebbing, and had left her, Mr Bast, and Mrs Bast stranded for the night in a Shropshire hotel, she asked herself what forces had made the wave flow. At all events, no harm was done. Margaret would play the game properly now, and though Helen disapproved of her sister's methods, she knew that the Basts would benefit by them in the long run.

'Mr Wilcox is so illogical,' she explained to Leonard, who had put his wife to bed, and was sitting with her in the empty coffee room. 'If we told him it was his duty to take you on, he might refuse to do it. The fact is, he isn't properly educated. I don't want to set you against him, but you'll find him a trial.'

'I can never thank you sufficiently, Miss Schlegel,' was all that Leonard felt equal to.

'I believe in personal responsibility. Don't you? And in personal everything. I hate—I suppose I oughtn't to say that—but the Wilcoxes are on the wrong tack surely. Or perhaps it isn't their fault. Perhaps the little thing that says "I" is missing out of the middle of their heads, and then it's a waste of time to blame them. There's a nightmare of a theory that says a special race is being born which will rule the rest of us in the future just because it lacks the little thing that says "I." Had you heard that?'

'I get no time for reading.'

'Had you thought it, then? That there are two kinds of people—our kind, who live straight from the middle of their heads, and the other kind who can't, because their heads have no middle? They can't say "I." They *aren't* in fact, and so they're supermen. Pierpont Morgan has never said "I" in his life.'

Leonard roused himself. If his benefactress wanted intellectual conversation, she must have it. She was more important than his ruined past. 'I never got on to Nietzsche,' he said. 'But I always understood that those supermen were rather what you may call egoists.'

'Oh no, that's wrong,' replied Helen. 'No superman ever said "I want," because "I want" must lead to the question, "Who am I?" and so to Pity and to Justice. He only says "want." "Want Europe," if he's Napoleon; "want wives," if he's Bluebeard; "want Botticelli," if he's Pierpont Morgan. Never the "I"; and if you could pierce through him, you'd find panic and emptiness in the middle.'

Leonard was silent for a moment. Then he said: 'May I take it, Miss Schlegel, that you and I are both the sort that say "I"?'

'Of course.'

'And your sister too?'

'Of course,' repeated Helen, a little sharply. She was annoyed with Margaret, but did not want her discussed. 'All presentable people say "I."'

'But Mr Wilcox—he is not perhaps—'

'I don't know that it's any good discussing Mr Wilcox either.'

'Quite so, quite so,' he agreed. Helen asked herself why she had snubbed him. Once or twice during the day she had encouraged him to criticize, and then had pulled him up short. Was she afraid of him presuming? If so, it was disgusting of her.

But he was thinking the snub quite natural. Everything she did was natural, and incapable of causing offence. While the Miss Schlegels were together he had felt them scarcely human—a sort of admonitory whirligig. But a Miss Schlegel alone was different. She was in Helen's case unmarried, in Margaret's about to be married, in neither case an echo of her sister. A light had fallen at last into this rich upper world, and he saw that it was full of men and women, some of whom were more friendly to him than others. Helen had become 'his' Miss Schlegel, who scolded him and corresponded with him, and had swept down yesterday with grateful vehemence. Margaret, though not unkind, was severe and remote. He would not presume to help her, for instance. He had never liked her, and began to think that his original impression was true, and that her sister did not like her either. Helen was certainly lonely. She, who gave away so much, was receiving too little. Leonard was pleased to think that he could spare her vexation by holding his tongue and concealing what he knew about Mr Wilcox. Jacky had announced her discovery when he fetched her from the lawn. After the first shock, he did not mind for himself. By now he had no illusions about his wife, and this was only one new stain on the face of a love that had never been pure. To keep perfection perfect, that should be his ideal, if the future gave him time to have ideals. Helen, and Margaret for Helen's sake, must not know.

Helen disconcerted him by turning the conversation to his wife. 'Mrs Bast—does she ever say "I"?' she asked, half mischievously, and then, 'Is she very tired?'

'It's better she stops in her room,' said Leonard.

'Shall I sit up with her?'

'No, thank you; she does not need company.'

'Mr Bast, what kind of woman is your wife?'

Leonard blushed up to his eyes.

'You ought to know my ways by now. Does that question offend you?'

'No, oh no, Miss Schlegel, no.'

'Because I love honesty. Don't pretend your marriage has been a happy one. You and she can have nothing in common.'

He did not deny it, but said shyly: 'I suppose that's pretty obvious; but Jacky never meant to do anybody any harm. When things went wrong, or I heard things, I used to think it was her fault, but, looking back, it's more mine. I needn't have married her, but as I have I must stick to her and keep her.'

'How long have you been married?'

'Nearly three years.'

'What did your people say?'

'They will not have anything to do with us. They had a sort of family council when they heard I was married, and cut us off altogether.'

Helen began to pace up and down the room. 'My good boy, what a mess!' she said gently. 'Who are your people?'

He could answer this. His parents, who were dead, had been in trade; his sisters had married commercial travellers; his brother was a lay-reader.

'And your grandparents?'

Leonard told her a secret that he had held shameful up to now. 'They were just nothing at all,' he said—'agricultural labourers and that sort.'

'So! From which part?'

'Lincolnshire mostly, but my mother's father—he, oddly enough, came from these parts round here.'

'From this very Shropshire. Yes, that is odd. My mother's people were Lancashire. But why do your brother and your sisters object to Mrs Bast?'

'Oh, I don't know.'

'Excuse me, you do know. I am not a baby. I can bear anything you tell me, and the more you tell the more I shall be able to help. Have they heard anything against her?'

He was silent.

'I think I have guessed now,' said Helen very gravely.

'I don't think so, Miss Schlegel; I hope not.'

'We must be honest, even over these things. I have guessed. I am frightfully, dreadfully sorry, but it does not make the least difference to me. I shall feel just the same to both of you. I blame, not your wife for these things, but men.'

Leonard left it at that—so long as she did not guess the man. She stood at the window and slowly pulled up the blinds. The hotel looked over a dark square. The mists had begun. When she turned back to him her eyes were shining.

'Don't you worry,' he pleaded. 'I can't bear that. We shall be all right if I get work. If I could only get work—something regular to do. Then it wouldn't be so bad again. I don't trouble after books as I used. I can imagine that with regular work we should settle down again. It stops one thinking.'

'Settle down to what?'

'Oh, just settle down.'

'And that's to be life!' said Helen, with a catch in her throat. 'How can you, with all the beautiful things to see and do—with music—with walking at night—'

'Walking is well enough when a man's in work,' he answered. 'Oh, I did talk a lot of nonsense once, but there's nothing like a bailiff in the house to drive it out of you. When I saw him fingering my Ruskins and Stevensons, I seemed to see life straight real, and it isn't a pretty sight. My books are back again, thanks to you, but they'll never be the same to me again, and I shan't ever again think night in the woods is wonderful.'

'Why not?' asked Helen, throwing up the window.

'Because I see one must have money.'

'Well, you're wrong.'

'I wish I was wrong, but—the clergyman—he has money of his own, or else he's paid; the poet or the musician—just the same; the tramp—he's no different. The tramp goes to the workhouse in the end, and is paid for with other people's money. Miss Schlegel, the real thing's money, and all the rest is a dream.'

'You're still wrong. You've forgotten Death.'

Leonard could not understand.

'If we lived for ever, what you say would be true. But we have to die, we have to leave life presently. Injustice and greed would be the real thing if we lived for ever. As it is, we must hold to other things, because Death is coming. I love Death—not morbidly, but because He explains. He shows me the emptiness of Money. Death and Money are the eternal foes. Not Death and Life. Never mind what lies behind Death, Mr Bast, but be sure that the poet and the musician and the tramp will be happier in it than the man who has never learnt to say, "I am I."'

'I wonder.'

'We are all in a mist—I know, but I can help you this far—men like the Wilcoxes are deeper in the mist than any. Sane, sound Englishmen! building up empires, levelling all the world into what they call common sense. But mention Death to them and they're offended, because Death's really Imperial, and He cries out against them for ever.'

'I am as afraid of Death as anyone.'

'But not of the idea of Death.'

'But what is the difference?'

'Infinite difference,' said Helen, more gravely than before.

Leonard looked at her wondering, and had the sense of great things sweeping out of the shrouded night. But he could not receive them, because his heart was still full of little things. As the lost umbrella had spoilt the concert at Queen's Hall, so the lost situation was obscuring the diviner harmonies now. Death, Life and Materialism were fine words, but would Mr Wilcox take him on as a clerk? Talk as one would, Mr Wilcox was king of this world, the superman, with his own morality, whose head remained in the clouds.

'I must be stupid,' he said apologetically.

While to Helen the paradox became clearer and clearer. 'Death destroys a man: the idea of Death saves him.' Behind the coffins and the skeletons that stay the vulgar mind lies something so immense that all that is great in us responds to it. Men of the world may recoil from the charnel-house that they will one day enter, but Love knows better. Death is his foe, but his peer, and in their age-long struggle the thews of Love have been strengthened, and his vision cleared, until there is no one who can stand against him.

'So never give in,' continued the girl, and restated again and again the vague yet convincing plea that the Invisible lodges against the Visible. Her excitement grew as she tried to cut the rope that fastened Leonard to the earth. Woven of bitter experience, it resisted her. Presently the waitress entered and gave her a letter from Margaret. Another note, addressed to Leonard, was inside. They read them, listening to the murmurings of the river.

Chapter Twenty-eight

For many hours Margaret did nothing; then she controlled herself, and wrote some letters. She was too bruised to speak to Henry; she could pity him, and even determine to marry him, but as yet all lay too deep in her heart for speech. On the surface the sense of his degradation was too strong. She could not command voice or look, and the gentle words that she forced out through her pen seemed to proceed from some other person.

'My dearest boy,' she began, 'this is not to part us. It is everything or nothing, and I mean it to be nothing. It happened long before we ever met, and even if it had happened since, I should be writing the same, I hope. I do understand.'

But she crossed out 'I do understand'; it struck a false note. Henry could not bear to be understood. She also crossed out, 'It is everything or nothing.' Henry would resent so strong a grasp of the situation. She must not comment; comment is unfeminine.

'I think that'll about do,' she thought.

Then the sense of his degradation choked her. Was he worth all this bother? To have yielded to a woman of that sort was everything, yes, it was, and she could not be his wife. She tried to translate his temptation into her own language, and her brain reeled. Men must be different, even to want to yield to such a temptation. Her belief in comradeship was stifled, and she saw life as from that glass saloon on the Great Western, which sheltered male and female alike from the fresh air. Are the sexes really races, each with its own code of morality, and their mutual love a mere device of Nature to keep things going? Strip human intercourse of the proprieties, and is it reduced to this? Her judgment told her no. She knew that out of Nature's device we have built a magic that will win us immortality. Far more mysterious than the call of sex to sex is the tenderness that we throw into that call; far wider is the gulf between us and the farmyard than between the farmyard and the garbage that nourishes it. We are evolving, in ways that Science cannot measure, to ends that Theology dares not contemplate. 'Men did produce one jewel,' the gods will say, and, saying, will give us immortality. Margaret knew all this, but for the moment she could not feel it, and transformed the marriage of Evie and Mr Cahill into a carnival of fools, and her own marriage—too miserable to think of that, she tore up the letter, and then wrote another:

> Dear Mr Bast,
> I have spoken to Mr Wilcox about you, as I promised, and am sorry to say that he has no vacancy for you.
>
> > Yours truly,
> > M. J. Schlegel.

She enclosed this in a note to Helen, over which she took less trouble than she might have done; but her head was aching, and she could not stop to pick her words:

> Dear Helen,
> Give him this. The Basts are no good. Henry found the woman drunk on the lawn. I am having a room got ready for you here, and will you please come round at once on getting this? The Basts are not at all the type we should trouble about. I may go round to them myself in the morning, and do anything that is fair.
>
> > M.

In writing this, Margaret felt that she was being practical. Something might be arranged for the Basts later on, but they must be silenced for the moment. She hoped to avoid a conversation between the woman and Helen. She rang the bell for a servant, but no one answered it; Mr Wilcox and the Warringtons were gone to bed, and the kitchen was abandoned to Saturnalia. Consequently she went over to the George herself. She did not enter the hotel, for discussion would have been perilous, and, saying that the letter was important, she gave it to the waitress. As she recrossed the square she saw Helen and Mr Bast looking out of the window of the coffee-room, and feared she was already too late. Her task was not yet over; she ought to tell Henry what she had done.

This came easily, for she saw him in the hall. The night wind had been rattling the pictures against the wall, and the noise had disturbed him.

'Who's there?' he called, quite the householder.

Margaret walked in and past him.

'I have asked Helen to sleep,' she said. 'She is best here; so don't lock the front-door.'

'I thought someone had got in,' said Henry.

'At the same time I told the man that we could do nothing for him. I don't know about later, but now the Basts must clearly go.'

'Did you say that your sister is sleeping here, after all?'

'Probably.'

'Is she to be shown up to your room?'

'I have naturally nothing to say to her; I am going to bed. Will you tell the servants about Helen? Could someone go to carry her bag?'

He tapped a little gong, which had been bought to summon the servants.

'You must make more noise than that if you want them to hear.'

Henry opened a door, and down the corridor came shouts of laughter. 'Far too much screaming there,' he said, and strode towards it. Margaret went upstairs, uncertain whether to be glad that they had met, or sorry. They had behaved as if nothing had happened, and her deepest instincts told her that this was wrong. For his own sake, some explanation was due.

And yet – what could an explanation tell her? A date, a place, a few details, which she could imagine all too clearly. Now that the first shock was over, she saw that there was every reason to premise a Mrs Bast. Henry's inner life had long laid open to her – his intellectual confusion, his obtuseness to personal influence, his strong but furtive passions. Should she refuse him because his outer life corresponded? Perhaps. Perhaps, if the dishonour had been done to her, but it was done long before her day. She struggled against the feeling. She told herself that Mrs Wilcox's wrong was her own. But she was not a barren theorist. As she undressed, her anger, her regard for the dead, her desire for a scene, all grew weak. Henry must have it as he liked, for she loved him and some day she would use her love to make him a better man.

Pity was at the bottom of her actions all through this crisis. Pity, if one may generalize, is at the bottom of woman. When men like us, it is for our better qualities, and however tender their liking, we dare not be unworthy of it, or they will quietly let us go. But unworthiness stimulates woman. It brings out her deeper nature, for good or for evil.

Here was the core of the question. Henry must be forgiven, and made better by love; nothing else mattered. Mrs Wilcox, that unquiet yet kindly ghost, must be left to her own wrong. To her everything was in proportion now, and she, too, would pity the man who was blundering up and down their lives. Had Mrs Wilcox known of his trespass? An interesting question, but Margaret fell asleep, tethered by affection, and lulled by the murmurs of the river that descended all the night from Wales. She felt herself at one with her future home, colouring it and coloured by it, and awoke to see, for the second time, Oniton Castle conquering the morning mists.

Chapter Twenty-nine

'Henry dear—' was her greeting.

He had finished his breakfast, and was beginning the 'Times.' His sister-in-law was packing. She knelt by him and took the paper from him, feeling that it was unusually heavy and thick. Then, putting her face where it had been, she looked up in his eyes.

'Henry dear, look at me. No, I won't have you shirking. Look at me. There. That's all.'

'You're referring to last evening,' he said huskily. 'I have released you from your engagement. I could find excuses, but I won't. No, I won't. A thousand times no. I'm a bad lot, and must be left at that.'

Expelled from his old fortress, Mr Wilcox was building a new one. He could no longer appear respectable to her, so he defended himself instead in a lurid past. It was not true repentance.

'Leave it where you will, boy. It's not going to trouble us: I know what I'm talking about, and it will make no difference.'

'No difference?' he inquired. 'No difference, when you find that I am not the fellow you thought?' He was annoyed with Miss Schlegel here. He would have preferred her to be prostrated by the blow, or even to rage. Against the tide of his sin flowed the feeling that she was not altogether womanly. Her eyes gazed too straight; they had read books that are suitable for men only. And though he had dreaded a scene, and though she had determined against one, there was a scene, all the same. It was somehow imperative.

'I am unworthy of you,' he began. 'Had I been worthy, I should not have released you from your engagement. I know what I am talking about. I can't bear to talk of such things. We had better leave it.'

She kissed his hand. He jerked it from her, and, rising to his feet, went on: 'You, with your sheltered life, and refined pursuits, and friends, and books, you and your sister, and women like you—I say, how can you guess the temptations that lie round a man?'

'It is difficult for us,' said Margaret; 'but if we are worth marrying, we do guess.'

'Cut off from decent society and family ties, what do you suppose happens to thousands of young fellows overseas? Isolated. No one near. I know by bitter experience, and yet you say it makes "no difference."'

'Not to me.'

He laughed bitterly. Margaret went to the sideboard and helped herself to one of the breakfast dishes. Being the last down, she turned out the spirit-lamp that kept them warm. She was tender, but grave. She knew that Henry was not so much confessing his soul as pointing out the gulf between the male soul and the female, and she did not desire to hear him on this point.

'Did Helen come?' she asked.

He shook his head.

'But that won't do at all, at all! We don't want her gossiping with Mrs Bast.'

'Good God! no!' he exclaimed, suddenly natural. Then he caught himself up. 'Let them gossip. My game's up, though I thank you for your unselfishness—little as my thanks are worth.'

'Didn't she send me a message or anything?'

'I heard of none.'

'Would you ring the bell, please?'

'What to do?'

'Why, to inquire.'

He swaggered up to it tragically, and sounded a peal. Margaret poured herself out some coffee. The butler came, and said that Miss Schlegel had slept at the George, so far as he had heard. Should he go round to the George?

'I'll go, thank you,' said Margaret, and dismissed him.

'It is no good,' said Henry. 'Those things leak out; you cannot stop a story once it has started. I have known cases of other men—I despised them once, I thought that *I'm* different, *I* shall never be tempted. Oh, Margaret—' He came and sat down near her, improvising emotion. She could not bear to listen to him. 'We fellows all come to grief once in our time. Will you believe that? There are moments when the strongest man— "Let him who standeth, take heed lest he fall." That's true, isn't it? If you knew all, you would excuse me. I was far from good influences—far even from England. I was very, very lonely, and longed for a woman's voice. That's enough. I have told you too much already for you to forgive me now.'

'Yes, that's enough, dear.'

'I have'—he lowered his voice—'I have been through hell.'

Gravely she considered this claim. Had he? Had he suffered tortures of remorse, or had it been, 'There! that's over. Now for respectable life again'? The latter, if she read him rightly. A man who has been through hell does not boast of his virility. He is humble and hides it, if, indeed, it still exists. Only in legend does the sinner come forth penitent, but terrible, to conquer pure woman by his resistless power. Henry was anxious to be terrible, but had not got it in him. He was a good average Englishman, who had slipped. The really culpable point—his faithlessness to Mrs Wilcox—never seemed to strike him. She longed to mention Mrs Wilcox.

And bit by bit the story was told her. It was a very simple story. Ten years ago was the time, a garrison town in Cyprus the place. Now and then he asked her whether she could possibly forgive him, and she answered, 'I have already forgiven you, Henry.' She chose her words carefully, and so saved him from panic. She played the girl, until he could rebuild his fortress and hide his soul from the world. When the butler came to clear away, Henry was in a very different mood—asked the fellow what he was in such a hurry for, complained of the noise last night in the servants' hall. Margaret looked intently at the butler. He, as a handsome young man, was faintly attractive to her as a woman—an attraction so faint as scarcely to be perceptible, yet the skies would have fallen if she had mentioned it to Henry.

On her return from the George the building operations were complete, and the old Henry fronted her, competent, cynical, and kind. He had made a clean breast, had been forgiven, and the great thing now was to forget his failure, and to send it the way of other unsuccessful investments. Jacky rejoined Howards End and Ducie Street, and the vermilion motor-car, and the Argentine Hard Dollars, and all the things and people for whom he had never had much use, and had less now. Their memory hampered him. He could scarcely attend to Margaret, who brought back disquieting news from the George. Helen and her clients had gone.

'Well, let them go—the man and his wife, I mean, for the more we see of your sister the better.'

'But they have gone separately—Helen very early, the Basts just before I arrived. They have left no message. They have answered neither of my notes. I don't like to think what it all means.'

'What did you say in the notes?'

'I told you last night.'

'Oh—ah—yes! Dear, would you like one turn in the garden?'

Margaret took his arm. The beautiful weather soothed her. But the wheels of Evie's wedding were still at work, tossing the guests outwards as deftly as they had drawn them in, and she could not be with him long. It had been arranged that they should motor to Shrewsbury, whence he would go north, and she back to London with the Warringtons. For a fraction of time she was happy. Then her brain recommenced.

'I am afraid there has been gossiping of some kind at the George. Helen would not have left unless she had heard something. I mismanaged that. It is wretched. I ought to have parted her from that woman at once.'

'Margaret!' he exclaimed, loosing her arm impressively.

'Yes—yes, Henry?'

'I am far from a saint—in fact, the reverse—but you have taken me, for better or worse. Bygones must be bygones. You have promised to forgive me. Margaret, a promise is a promise. Never mention that woman again.'

'Except for some practical reason—never.'

'Practical! You practical!'

'Yes, I'm practical,' she murmured, stooping over the mowing-machine and playing with the grass which trickled through her fingers like sand.

He had silenced her, but her fears made him uneasy. Not for the first time, he was threatened with blackmail. He was rich and supposed to be moral; the Basts knew that he was not, and might find it profitable to hint as much.

'At all events, you mustn't worry,' he said. 'This is a man's business.' He thought intently. 'On no account mention it to anybody.'

Margaret flushed at advice so elementary, but he was really paving the way for a lie. If necessary he would deny that he had ever known Mrs Bast, and prosecute her for libel. Perhaps he never had known her. Here was Margaret, who behaved as if he had not. There the house. Round them were half a dozen gardeners, clearing up after his daughter's wedding. All was so solid and spruce, that the past flew up out of sight like a spring-blind, leaving only the last five minutes unrolled.

Glancing at these, he saw that the car would be round during the next five, and plunged into action. Gongs were tapped, orders issued, Margaret was sent to dress, and the housemaid to sweep up the long trickle of grass that she had left across the hall. As is Man to the Universe, so was the mind of Mr Wilcox to the minds of some men—a concentrated light upon a tiny spot, a little Ten Minutes moving self-contained through its appointed years. No Pagan he, who lives for the Now, and may be wiser than all philosophers. He lived for the five minutes that have past, and the five to come; he had the business mind.

How did he stand now, as his motor slipped out of Oniton and breasted the great round hills? Margaret had heard a certain rumour, but was all right. She had forgiven him, God bless her, and he felt the manlier for it. Charles and Evie had not heard it, and never must hear. No more must Paul. Over his children he felt great tenderness, which he did not try to track to a cause: Mrs Wilcox was too far back in his life. He did not connect her with the sudden aching love that he felt for Evie. Poor little Evie! he trusted that Cahill would make her a decent husband.

And Margaret? How did she stand?

She had several minor worries. Clearly her sister had heard something. She dreaded meeting her in town. And she was anxious about Leonard, for whom they certainly were responsible. Nor ought Mrs Bast to starve. But the main situation had not altered. She still loved Henry. His actions, not his disposition, had disappointed her, and she could bear that. And she loved her future home. Standing up in the car, just where she had leapt from it two days before, she gazed back with deep emotion upon Oniton. Beside the Grange and the Castle keep, she could now pick out the church and the black-and-white gables of the George. There was the bridge, and the river nibbling its green peninsula. She could even see the bathing-shed, but while she was looking for Charles's new spring-board, the forehead of the hill rose up and hid the whole scene.

She never saw it again. Day and night the river flows down into England, day after day the sun retreats into the Welsh mountains, and the tower chimes, 'See the Conquering Hero.' But the Wilcoxes have no part in the place, nor in any place. It is not their names that recur in the parish register. It is not their ghosts that sigh among the alders at evening. They have swept into the valley and swept out of it, leaving a little dust and a little money behind.

Chapter Thirty

Tibby was now approaching his last year at Oxford. He had moved out of college, and was contemplating the Universe, or such portions of it as concerned him, for his comfortable lodgings in Long Wall. He was not concerned with much. When a young man is untroubled by passions and sincerely indifferent to public opinion, his outlook is necessarily limited. Tibby neither wished to strengthen the position of the rich nor to improve that of the poor, and so was well content to watch the elms nodding behind the mildly embattled parapets of Magdalen. There are worse lives. Though selfish, he was never cruel; though affected in manner, he never posed. Like Margaret, he disdained the heroic equipment, and it was only after many visits that men discovered Schlegel to possess a character and a brain. He had done well in Mods, much to the surprise of those who attended lectures and took proper exercise, and was now glancing disdainfully at Chinese in case he should some day consent to qualify as a Student Interpreter. To him thus employed Helen entered. A telegram had preceded her.

He noticed, in a distant way, that his sister had altered. As a rule he found her too pronounced, and had never come across this look of appeal, pathetic yet dignified—the look of a sailor who has lost everything at sea.

'I have come from Oniton,' she began. 'There has been a great deal of trouble there.'

'Who's for lunch?' said Tibby, picking up the claret, which was warming in the hearth. Helen sat down submissively at the table. 'Why such an early start?' he asked.

'Sunrise or something—when I could get away.'

'So I surmise. Why?'

'I don't know what's to be done, Tibby. I am very much upset at a piece of news that concerns Meg, and do not want to face her, and I am not going back to Wickham Place. I stopped here to tell you this.'

The landlady came in with the cutlets. Tibby put a marker in the leaves of his Chinese Grammar and helped them. Oxford – the Oxford of the vacation—dreamed and rustled outside, and indoors the little fire was coated with grey where the sunshine touched it. Helen continued her odd story.

'Give Meg my love and say that I want to be alone. I mean to go to Munich or else Bonn.'

'Such a message is easily given,' said her brother.

'As regards Wickham Place and my share of the furniture, you and she are to do exactly as you like. My own feeling is that everything may just as well be sold. What does one want with dusty economic books, which have made the world no better, or with mother's hideous cheffoniers? I have also another commission for you. I want you to deliver a letter.' She got up. 'I haven't written it yet. Why shouldn't I post it, though?' She sat down again. 'My head is rather wretched. I hope that none of your friends are likely to come in.'

Tibby locked the door. His friends often found it in this condition. Then he asked whether anything had gone wrong at Evie's wedding.

'Not there,' said Helen, and burst into tears.

He had known her hysterical—it was one of her aspects with which he had no concern—and yet these tears touched him as something unusual. They were nearer the things that did concern him, such as music. He laid down his knife and looked at her curiously. Then, as she continued to sob, he went on with his lunch.

The time came for the second course, and she was still crying. Apple Charlotte was to follow, which spoils by waiting. 'Do you mind Mrs Martlett coming in?' he asked, 'or shall I take it from her at the door?'

'Could I bathe my eyes, Tibby?'

He took her to his bedroom, and introduced the pudding in her absence. Having helped himself, he put it down to warm in the hearth. His hand stretched towards the Grammar, and soon he was turning over the pages, raising his eyebrows scornfully, perhaps at human nature, perhaps at Chinese. To him thus employed Helen returned. She had pulled herself together, but the grave appeal had not vanished from her eyes.

'Now for the explanation,' she said. 'Why didn't I begin with it? I have found out something about Mr Wilcox. He has behaved very wrongly indeed, and ruined two people's lives. It all came on me very suddenly last night; I am very much upset, and I do not know what to do. Mrs Bast—'

'Oh, those people!'

Helen seemed silenced.

'Shall I lock the door again?'

'No thanks, Tibbikins. You're being very good to me. I want to tell you the story before I go abroad. You must do exactly what you like—treat it as part of the furniture. Meg cannot have heard it yet, I think. But I cannot face her and tell her that the man she is going to marry has misconducted himself. I don't even know whether she ought to be told. Knowing as she does that I dislike him, she will suspect me, and think that I want to ruin her match. I simply don't know what to make of such a thing. I trust your judgment. What would you do?'

'I gather he has had a mistress,' said Tibby.

Helen flushed with shame and anger. 'And ruined two people's lives. And goes about saying that personal actions count for nothing, and there always will be rich and poor. He met her when he was trying to get rich out in Cyprus—I don't wish to make him worse than he is, and no doubt she was ready enough to meet him. But there it is. They met. He goes his way and she goes hers. What do you suppose is the end of such women?'

He conceded that it was a bad business.

'They end in two ways: Either they sink till the lunatic asylums and the workhouses are full of them, and cause Mr Wilcox to write letters to the papers complaining of our national degeneracy, or else they entrap a boy into marriage before it is too late. She—I can't blame her.'

'But this isn't all,' she continued after a long pause, during which the landlady served them with coffee. 'I come now to the business that took us to Oniton. We went all three. Acting on Mr Wilcox's advice, the man throws up a secure situation and takes an insecure one, from which he is dismissed. There are certain excuses, but in the main Mr Wilcox is to blame, as Meg herself admitted. It is only common justice that he should employ the man himself. But he meets the woman, and, like the cur that he is, he refuses, and tries to get rid of them. He makes Meg write. Two notes came from her late that evening—one for me, one for Leonard, dismissing him with barely a reason. I couldn't understand. Then it comes out that Mrs Bast had spoken to Mr Wilcox on the lawn while we left her to get rooms, and was still speaking about him when Leonard came back to her. This Leonard knew all along. He thought it natural he should be ruined twice. Natural! Could you have contained yourself?'

'It is certainly a very bad business,' said Tibby.

His reply seemed to calm his sister. 'I was afraid that I saw it out of proportion. But you are right outside it, and you must know. In a day or two—or perhaps a week—take whatever steps you think fit. I leave it in your hands.'

She concluded her charge.

'The facts as they touch Meg are all before you,' she added; and Tibby sighed and felt it rather hard that, because of his open mind, he should be empanelled to serve as a juror. He had never been interested in human beings, for which one must blame him, but he had had rather too much of them at Wickham Place. Just as some people cease to attend when books are mentioned, so Tibby's attention wandered when 'personal relations' came under discussion. Ought Margaret to know what Helen knew the Basts to know? Similar questions had vexed him from infancy, and at Oxford he had learned to say that the importance of human beings has been vastly overrated by specialists. The epigram, with its faint whiff of the eighties, meant nothing. But he might have let it off now if his sister had not been ceaselessly beautiful.

'You see, Helen—have a cigarette—I don't see what I'm to do.'

'Then there's nothing to be done. I dare say you are right. Let them marry. There remains the question of compensation.'

'Do you want me to adjudicate that too? Had you not better consult an expert?'

'This part is in confidence,' said Helen. 'It has nothing to do with Meg, and do not mention it to her. The compensation—I do not see who is to pay it if I don't, and I have already decided on the minimum sum. As soon as possible I am placing it to your account, and when I am in Germany you will pay it over for me. I shall never forget your kindness, Tibbikins, if you do this.'

'What is the sum?'

'Five thousand.'

'Good God alive!' said Tibby, and went crimson.

'Now, what is the good of driblets? To go through life having done one thing—to have raised one person from the abyss: not these puny gifts of shillings and blankets—making the grey more grey. No doubt people will think me extraordinary.'

'I don't care a damn what people think!' cried he, heated to unusual manliness of diction. 'But it's half what you have.'

'Not nearly half.' She spread out her hands over her soiled skirt. 'I have far too much, and we settled at Chelsea last spring that three hundred a year is necessary to set a man on his feet. What I give will bring in a hundred and fifty between two. It isn't enough.'

He could not recover. He was not angry or even shocked, and he saw that Helen would still have plenty to live on. But it amazed him to think what haycocks people can make of their lives. His delicate intonations would not work, and he could only blurt out that the five thousand pounds would mean a great deal of bother for him personally.

'I didn't expect you to understand me.'

'I? I understand nobody.'

'But you'll do it?'

'Apparently.'

'I leave you two commissions, then. The first concerns Mr Wilcox, and you are to use your discretion. The second concerns the money, and is to be mentioned to no one, and carried out literally. You will send a hundred pounds on account tomorrow.'

He walked with her to the station, passing through those streets whose serried beauty never bewildered him and never fatigued. The lovely creature raised domes and spires into the cloudless blue, and only the ganglion of vulgarity round Carfax showed how evanescent was the phantom, how faint its claim to represent England. Helen, rehearsing her commission, noticed nothing: the Basts were in her brain, and she retold the crisis in a meditative way, which might have made other men curious. She was seeing whether it would hold. He asked her once why she had taken the Basts right into the heart of Evie's wedding. She stopped like a frightened animal and said, 'Does that seem to you so odd?' Her eyes, the hand laid on the mouth, quite haunted him, until they were absorbed into the figure of St Mary the Virgin, before whom he paused for a moment on the walk home.

It is convenient to follow him in the discharge of his duties. Margaret summoned him the next day. She was terrified at Helen's flight, and he had to say that she had called in at Oxford. Then she said: 'Did she seem worried at any rumour about Henry?' He answered, 'Yes.' 'I knew it was that!' she exclaimed. 'I'll write to her.' Tibby was relieved.

He then sent the cheque to the address that Helen gave him, and stated that later on he was instructed to forward five thousand pounds. An answer came back, very civil and quiet in tone—such an answer as Tibby himself would have given. The cheque was returned, the legacy refused, the writer being in no need of money. Tibby forwarded this to Helen, adding in the fullness of his heart that Leonard Bast seemed somewhat a monumental person after all. Helen's reply was frantic. He was to take no notice. He was to go down at once and say that she commanded acceptance. He went. A scurf of books and china ornaments awaited him. The Basts had just been evicted for not paying their rent, and had wandered no one knew whither. Helen had begun bungling with her money by this time, and had even sold out her shares in the Nottingham and Derby Railway. For some weeks she did nothing. Then she reinvested, and, owing to the good advice of her stockbrokers, became rather richer than she had been before.

Chapter Thirty-one

Houses have their own ways of dying, falling as variously as the generations of men, some with a tragic roar, some quietly, but to an after-life in the city of ghosts, while from others–and thus was the death of Wickham Place–the spirit slips before the body perishes. It had decayed in the spring, disintegrating the girls more than they knew, and causing either to accost unfamiliar regions. By September it was a corpse, void of emotion, and scarcely hallowed by the memories of thirty years of happiness. Through its round-topped doorway passed furniture, and pictures, and books, until the last room was gutted and the last van had rumbled away. It stood for a week or two longer, open-eyed, as if astonished at its own emptiness. Then it fell. Navvies came, and spilt it back into the grey. With their muscles and their beery good temper, they were not the worst of undertakers for a house which had always been human, and had not mistaken culture for an end.

The furniture, with a few exceptions, went down into Hertfordshire, Mr Wilcox having most kindly offered Howards End as a warehouse. Mr Bryce had died abroad–an unsatisfactory affair–and as there seemed little guarantee that the rent would be paid regularly, he cancelled the agreement, and resumed possession himself. Until he relet the house, the Schlegels were welcome to stack their furniture in the garage and lower rooms. Margaret demurred, but Tibby accepted the offer gladly; it saved him from coming to any decision about the future. The plate and the more valuable pictures found a safer home in London, but the bulk of the things went country-ways, and were entrusted to the guardianship of Miss Avery.

Shortly before the move, our hero and heroine were married. They have weathered the storm, and may reasonably expect peace. To have no illusions and yet to love–what stronger surety can a woman find? She had seen her husband's past as well as his heart. She knew her own heart with a thoroughness that commonplace people believe impossible. The heart of Mrs Wilcox was alone hidden, and perhaps it is superstitious to speculate on the feelings of the dead. They were married quietly—really quietly, for as the day approached she refused to go through another Oniton. Her brother gave her away, her aunt, who was out of health, presided over a few colourless refreshments. The Wilcoxes were represented by Charles, who witnessed the marriage settlement, and by Mr Cahill. Paul did send a cablegram. In a few minutes, and without the aid of music, the clergyman made them man and wife, and soon the glass shade had fallen that cuts off married couples from the world. She, a monogamist, regretted the cessation of some of life's innocent odours; he, whose instincts were polygamous, felt morally braced by the change, and less liable to the temptations that had assailed him in the past.

They spent their honeymoon near Innsbruck. Henry knew of a reliable hotel there, and Margaret hoped for a meeting with her sister. In this she was disappointed. As they came south, Helen retreated over the Brenner, and wrote an unsatisfactory postcard from the shores of the Lake of Garda, saying that her plans were uncertain and had better be ignored. Evidently she disliked meeting Henry. Two months are surely enough to accustom an outsider to a situation which a wife has accepted in two days, and Margaret had again to regret her sister's lack of self-control. In a long letter she pointed out the need of charity in sexual matters: so little is known about them; it is hard enough for those who are personally touched to judge; then how futile must be the verdict of Society. 'I don't say there is no standard, for that would destroy morality; only that there can be no standard until our impulses are classified and better understood.' Helen thanked her for her kind letter—rather a curious reply. She moved south again, and spoke of wintering in Naples.

Mr Wilcox was not sorry that the meeting failed. Helen left him time to grow skin over his wound. There were still moments when it pained him. Had he only known that Margaret was awaiting him—Margaret, so lively and intelligent, and yet so submissive—he would have kept himself worthier of her. Incapable of grouping the past, he confused the episode of Jacky with another episode that had taken place in the days of his bachelorhood. The two made one crop of wild oats, for which he was heartily sorry, and he could not see that those oats are of a darker stock which are rooted in another's dishonour. Unchastity and infidelity were as confused to him as to the Middle Ages, his only moral teacher. Ruth (poor old Ruth!) did not enter into his calculations at all, for poor old Ruth had never found him out.

His affection for his present wife grew steadily. Her cleverness gave him no trouble, and, indeed, he liked to see her reading poetry or something about social questions; it distinguished her from the wives of other men. He had only to call, and she clapped the book up and was ready to do what he wished. Then they would argue so jollily, and once or twice she had him in quite a tight corner, but as soon as he grew really serious, she gave in. Man is for war, woman for the recreation of the warrior, but he does not dislike it if she makes a show of fight. She cannot win in a real battle, having no muscles, only nerves. Nerves make her jump out of a moving motor-car, or refuse to be married fashionably. The warrior may well allow her to triumph on such occasions; they move not the imperishable plinth of things that touch his peace.

Margaret had a bad attack of these nerves during the honeymoon. He told her—casually, as was his habit—that Oniton Grange was let. She showed her annoyance, and asked rather crossly why she had not been consulted.

'I didn't want to bother you,' he replied. 'Besides, I have only heard for certain this morning.'

'Where are we to live?' said Margaret, trying to laugh. 'I loved the place extraordinarily. Don't you believe in having a permanent home, Henry?'

He assured her that she misunderstood him. It is home life that distinguishes us from the foreigner. But he did not believe in a damp home.

'This is news. I never heard till this minute that Oniton was damp.'

'My dear girl!'—he flung out his hand—'have you eyes? have you a skin? How could it be anything but damp in such a situation? In the first place, the Grange is on clay, and built where the castle moat must have been; then there's that detestable little river, steaming all night like a kettle. Feel the cellar walls; look up under the eaves. Ask Sir James or anyone. Those Shropshire valleys are notorious. The only possible place for a house in Shropshire is on a hill; but, for my part, I think the country is too far from London, and the scenery nothing special.'

Margaret could not resist saying, 'Why did you go there, then?'

'I—because—' He drew his head back and grew rather angry. 'Why have we come to the Tyrol, if it comes to that? One might go on asking such questions indefinitely.'

One might; but he was only gaining time for a plausible answer. Out it came, and he believed it as soon as it was spoken.

'The truth is, I took Oniton on account of Evie. Don't let this go any further.'

'Certainly not.'

'I shouldn't like her to know that she nearly let me in for a very bad bargain. No sooner did I sign the agreement than she got engaged. Poor little girl! She was so keen on it all, and wouldn't even wait to make proper inquiries about the shooting. Afraid it would get snapped up—just like all of your sex. Well, no harm's done. She has had her country wedding, and I've got rid of my house to some fellows who are starting a preparatory school.'

'Where shall we live, then, Henry? I should enjoy living somewhere.'

'I have not yet decided. What about Norfolk?'

Margaret was silent. Marriage had not saved her from the sense of flux. London was but a foretaste of this nomadic civilization which is altering human nature so profoundly, and throws upon personal relations a stress greater than they have ever borne before. Under cosmopolitanism, if it comes, we shall receive no help from the earth. Trees and meadows and mountains will only be a spectacle, and the binding force that they once exercised on character must be entrusted to Love alone. May Love be equal to the task!

'It is now what?' continued Henry. 'Nearly October. Let us camp for the winter at Ducie Street, and look out for something in the spring.'

'If possible, something permanent. I can't be as young as I was, for these alterations don't suit me.'

'But, my dear, which would you rather have—alterations or rheumatism?'

'I see your point,' said Margaret, getting up. 'If Oniton is really damp, it is impossible, and must be inhabited by little boys. Only, in the spring, let us look before we leap. I will take warning by Evie, and not hurry you. Remember that you have a free hand this time. These endless moves must be bad for the furniture, and are certainly expensive.'

'What a practical little woman it is! What's it been reading? Theo—theo—how much?'

'Theosophy.'

So Ducie Street was her first fate—a pleasant enough fate. The house, being only a little larger than Wickham Place, trained her for the immense establishment that was promised in the spring. They were frequently away, but at home life ran fairly regularly. In the morning Henry went to the business, and his sandwich—a relic this of some prehistoric craving—was always cut by her own hand. He did not rely upon the sandwich for lunch, but liked to have it by him in case he grew hungry at eleven. When he had gone, there was the house to look after, and the servants to humanize, and several kettles of Helen's to keep on the boil. Her conscience pricked her a little about the Basts; she was not sorry to have lost sight of them. No doubt Leonard was worth helping, but being Henry's wife, she preferred to help someone else. As for theatres and discussion societies, they attracted her less and less. She began to 'miss' new movements, and to spend her spare time re-reading or thinking, rather to the concern of her Chelsea friends. They attributed the change to her marriage, and perhaps some deep instinct did warn her not to travel further from her husband than was inevitable. Yet the main cause lay deeper still; she had outgrown stimulants, and was passing from words to things. It was doubtless a pity not to keep up with Wedekind or John, but some closing of the gates is inevitable after thirty, if the mind itself is to become a creative power.

Chapter Thirty-two

She was looking at plans one day in the following spring—they had finally decided to go down into Sussex and build—when Mrs Charles Wilcox was announced.

'Have you heard the news?' Dolly cried, as soon as she entered the room. 'Charles is so ang—I mean he is sure you know about it, or, rather, that you don't know.'

'Why, Dolly!' said Margaret, placidly kissing her. 'Here's a surprise! How are the boys and the baby?'

Boys and the baby were well, and in describing a great row that there had been at the Hilton Tennis Club, Dolly forgot her news. The wrong people had tried to get in. The rector, as representing the older inhabitants, had said—Charles had said—the tax-collector had said—Charles had regretted not saying—and she closed the description with, 'But lucky you, with four courts of your own at Midhurst.'

'It will be very jolly,' replied Margaret.

'Are those the plans? Does it matter me seeing them?'

'Of course not.'

'Charles has never seen the plans.'

'They have only just arrived. Here is the ground floor—no, that's rather difficult. Try the elevation. We are to have a good many gables and a picturesque sky-line.'

'What makes it smell so funny?' said Dolly, after a moment's inspection. She was incapable of understanding plans or maps.

'I suppose the paper.'

'And *which* way up is it?'

'Just the ordinary way up. That's the sky-line, and the part that smells strongest is the sky.'

'Well, ask me another. Margaret—oh—what was I going to say? How's Helen?'

'Quite well.'

'Is she never coming back to England? Everyone thinks it's awfully odd she doesn't.'

'So it is,' said Margaret, trying to conceal her vexation. She was getting rather sore on this point. 'Helen is odd, awfully. She has now been away eight months.'

'But hasn't she any address?'

'A poste restante somewhere in Bavaria is her address. Do write her a line. I will look it up for you.'

'No, don't bother. That's eight months she has been away, surely?'

'Exactly. She left just after Evie's wedding. It would be eight months.'

'Just when baby was born, then?'

'Just so.'

Dolly sighed, and stared enviously round the drawing-room. She was beginning to lose her brightness and good looks. The Charles' were not well off, for Mr Wilcox, having brought up his children with expensive tastes, believed in letting them shift for themselves. After all, he had not treated them generously. Yet another baby was expected, she told Margaret, and they would have to give up the motor. Margaret sympathized, but in a formal fashion, and Dolly little imagined that the step-mother was urging Mr Wilcox to make them a more liberal allowance. She sighed again, and at last the particular grievance was remembered. 'Oh yes,' she cried, 'that is it: Miss Avery has been unpacking your packing-cases.'

'Why has she done that? How unnecessary!'

'Ask another. I suppose you ordered her to.'

'I gave no such orders. Perhaps she was airing the things. She did undertake to light an occasional fire.'

'It was far more than an air,' said Dolly solemnly. 'The floor sounds covered with books. Charles sent me to know what is to be done, for he feels certain you don't know.'

'Books!' cried Margaret, moved by the holy word. 'Dolly, are you serious? Has she been touching our books?'

'Hasn't she, though! What used to be the hall's full of them. Charles thought for certain you knew of it.'

'I am very much obliged to you, Dolly. What can have come over Miss Avery? I must go down about it at once. Some of the books are my brother's, and are quite valuable. She had no right to open any of the cases.'

'I say she's dotty. She was the one that never got married, you know. Oh, I say, perhaps she thinks your books are wedding-presents to herself. Old maids are taken that way sometimes. Miss Avery hates us all like poison ever since her frightful dust-up with Evie.'

'I hadn't heard of that,' said Margaret. A visit from Dolly had its compensations.

'Didn't you know she gave Evie a present last August, and Evie returned it, and then—oh, goloshes! You never read such a letter as Miss Avery wrote.'

'But it was wrong of Evie to return it. It wasn't like her to do such a heartless thing.'

'But the present was so expensive.'

'Why does that make any difference, Dolly?'

'Still, when it costs over five pounds—I didn't see it, but it was a lovely enamel pendant from a Bond Street shop. You can't very well accept that kind of thing from a farm woman. Now, can you?'

'You accepted a present from Miss Avery when you were married.'

'Oh, mine was old earthenware stuff—not worth a halfpenny. Evie's was quite different. You'd have to ask anyone to the wedding who gave you a pendant like that. Uncle Percy and Albert and father and Charles all said it was quite impossible, and when four men agree, what is a girl to do? Evie didn't want to upset the old thing, so thought a sort of joking letter best, and returned the pendant straight to the shop to save Miss Avery trouble.'

'But Miss Avery said—'

Dolly's eyes grew round. 'It was a perfectly awful letter. Charles said it was the letter of a madman. In the end she had the pendant back again from the shop and threw it into the duck-pond.'

'Did she give any reasons?'

'We think she meant to be invited to Oniton, and so climb into society.'

'She's rather old for that,' said Margaret pensively. 'May not she have given the present to Evie in remembrance of her mother?'

'That's a notion. Give everyone their due, eh? Well, I suppose I ought to be toddling. Come along Mr Muff—you want a new coat, but I don't know who'll give it you, I'm sure;' and addressing her apparel with mournful humour, Dolly moved from the room.

Margaret followed her to ask whether Henry knew about Miss Avery's rudeness.

'Oh yes.'

'I wonder, then, why he let me ask her to look after the house.'

'But she's only a farm woman,' said Dolly, and her explanation proved correct. Henry only censured the lower classes when it suited him. He bore with Miss Avery as with Crane—because he could get good value out of them. 'I have patience with a man who knows his job,' he would say, really having patience with the job, and not the man. Paradoxical as it may sound, he had something of the artist about him; he would pass over an insult to his daughter sooner than lose a good charwoman for his wife.

Margaret judged it better to settle the little trouble herself. Parties were evidently ruffled. With Henry's permission, she wrote a pleasant note to Miss Avery, asking her to leave the cases untouched. Then, at the first convenient opportunity, she went down herself, intending to repack her belongings and store them properly in the local warehouse: the plan had been amateurish and a failure. Tibby promised to accompany her, but at the last moment begged to be excused. So, for the second time in her life, she entered the house alone.

Chapter Thirty-three

The day of her visit was exquisite, and the last of unclouded happiness that she was to have for many months. Her anxiety about Helen's extraordinary absence was still dormant, and as for a possible brush with Miss Avery—that only gave zest to the expedition. She had also eluded Dolly's invitation to luncheon. Walking straight up from the station, she crossed the village green and entered the long chestnut avenue that connects it with the church. The church itself stood in the village once. But it there attracted so many worshippers that the devil, in a pet, snatched it from its foundations, and poised it on an inconvenient knoll, three-quarters of a mile away. If this story is true, the chestnut avenue must have been planted by the angels. No more tempting approach could be imagined for the lukewarm Christian, and if he still finds the walk too long, the devil is defeated all the same, Science having built Holy Trinity, a Chapel of Ease, near the Charles', and roofed it with tin.

Up the avenue Margaret strolled slowly, stopping to watch the sky that gleamed through the upper branches of the chestnuts, or to finger the little horseshoes on the lower branches. Why has not England a great mythology? Our folklore has never advanced beyond daintiness, and the greater melodies about our country-side have all issued through the pipes of Greece. Deep and true as the native imagination can be, it seems to have failed here. It has stopped with the witches and the fairies. It cannot vivify one fraction of a summer field, or give names to half a dozen stars. England still waits for the supreme moment of her literature—for the great poet who shall voice her, or, better still, for the thousand little poets whose voices shall pass into our common talk.

At the church the scenery changed. The chestnut avenue opened into a road, smooth but narrow, which led into the untouched country. She followed it for over a mile. Its little hesitations pleased her. Having no urgent destiny, it strolled downhill or up as it wished, taking no trouble about the gradients, nor about the view, which nevertheless expanded. The great estates that throttle the south of Hertfordshire were less obtrusive here, and the appearance of the land was neither aristocratic nor suburban. To define it was difficult, but Margaret knew what it was not: it was not snobbish. Though its contours were slight, there was a touch of freedom in their sweep to which Surrey will never attain, and the distant brow of the Chilterns towered like a mountain. 'Left to itself,' was Margaret's opinion, 'this county would vote Liberal.' The comradeship, not passionate, that is our highest gift as a nation, was promised by it, as by the low brick farm where she called for the key.

But the inside of the farm was disappointing. A most finished young person received her. 'Yes, Mrs Wilcox; no, Mrs Wilcox; oh yes, Mrs Wilcox, auntie received your letter quite duly. Auntie has gone up to your little place at the present moment. Shall I send the servant to direct you?' Followed by: 'Of course, auntie does not generally look after your place; she only does it to oblige a neighbour as something exceptional. It gives her something to do. She spends quite a lot of her time there. My husband says to me sometimes, "Where's auntie?" I say, "Need you ask? She's at Howards End." Yes, Mrs Wilcox. Mrs Wilcox, could I prevail upon you to accept a piece of cake? Not if I cut it for you?'

Margaret refused the cake, but unfortunately this acquired her gentility in the eyes of Miss Avery's niece.

'I cannot let you go on alone. Now don't. You really mustn't. I will direct you myself if it comes to that. I must get my hat. Now'—roguishly—'Mrs Wilcox, don't you move while I'm gone.'

Stunned, Margaret did not move from the best parlour, over which the touch of art nouveau had fallen. But the other rooms looked in keeping, though they conveyed the peculiar sadness of a rural interior. Here had lived an elder race, to which we look back with disquietude. The country which we visit at week-ends was really a home to it, and the graver sides of life, the deaths, the partings, the yearnings for love, have their deepest expression in the heart of the fields. All was not sadness. The sun was shining without. The thrush sang his two syllables on the budding guelder-rose. Some children were playing uproariously in heaps of golden straw. It was the presence of sadness at all that surprised Margaret, and ended by giving her a feeling of completeness. In these English farms, if anywhere, one might see life steadily and see it whole, group in one vision its transitoriness and its eternal youth, connect—connect without bitterness until all men are brothers. But her thoughts were interrupted by the return of Miss Avery's niece, and were so tranquillizing that she suffered the interruption gladly.

It was quicker to go out by the back door, and, after due explanations, they went out by it. The niece was now mortified by innumerable chickens, who rushed up to her feet for food, and by a shameless and maternal sow. She did not know what animals were coming to. But her gentility withered at the touch of the sweet air. The wind was rising, scattering the straw and ruffling the tails of the ducks as they floated in families over Evie's pendant. One of those delicious gales of spring, in which leaves still in bud seem to rustle, swept over the land and then fell silent. 'Georgie,' sang the thrush. 'Cuckoo,' came furtively from the cliff of pine-trees. 'Georgie, pretty Georgie,' and the other birds joined in with nonsense. The hedge was a half-painted picture which would be finished in a few days. Celandines grew on its banks, lords and ladies and primroses in the defended hollows; the wild rose-bushes, still bearing their withered hips, showed also the promise of blossom. Spring had come, clad in no classical garb, yet fairer than all springs; fairer even than she who walks through the myrtles of Tuscany with the graces before her and the zephyr behind.

The two women walked up the lane full of outward civility. But Margaret was thinking how difficult it was to be earnest about furniture on such a day, and the niece was thinking about hats. Thus engaged, they reached Howards End. Petulant cries of 'Auntie!' severed the air. There was no reply, and the front door was locked.

'Are you sure that Miss Avery is up here?' asked Margaret.

'Oh yes, Mrs Wilcox, quite sure. She is here daily.'

Margaret tried to look in through the dining-room window, but the curtain inside was drawn tightly. So were the drawing-room and the hall. The appearance of these curtains was familiar, yet she did not remember them being there on her other visit: her impression was that Mr Bryce had taken everything away. They tried the back. Here again they received no answer, and could see nothing; the kitchen-window was fitted with a blind, while the pantry and scullery had pieces of wood propped up against them, which looked ominously like the lids of packing-cases. Margaret thought of her books, and she lifted up her voice also. At the first cry she succeeded.

'Well, well!' replied someone inside the house. 'If it isn't Mrs Wilcox come at last!'

'Have you got the key, auntie?'

'Madge, go away,' said Miss Avery, still invisible.

'Auntie, it's Mrs Wilcox—'

Margaret supported her. 'Your niece and I have come together—'

'Madge, go away. This is no moment for your hat.'

The poor woman went red. 'Auntie gets more eccentric lately,' she said nervously.

'Miss Avery!' called Margaret. 'I have come about the furniture. Could you kindly let me in?'

'Yes, Mrs Wilcox,' said the voice, 'of course.' But after that came silence. They called again without response. They walked round the house disconsolately.

'I hope Miss Avery is not ill,' hazarded Margaret.

'Well, if you'll excuse me,' said Madge, 'perhaps I ought to be leaving you

now. The servants need seeing to at the farm. Auntie is so odd at times.'
Gathering up her elegancies, she retired defeated, and, as if her departure
had loosed a spring, the front door opened at once.

Miss Avery said, 'Well, come right in, Mrs Wilcox!' quite pleasantly and
calmly.

'Thank you so much,' began Margaret, but broke off at the sight of an
umbrella-stand. It was her own.

'Come right into the hall first,' said Miss Avery. She drew the curtain, and
Margaret uttered a cry of despair. For an appalling thing had happened. The
hall was fitted up with the contents of the library from Wickham Place. The
carpet had been laid, the big work-table drawn up near the window; the
bookcases filled the wall opposite the fireplace, and her father's sword–this
is what bewildered her particularly–had been drawn from its scabbard and
hung naked amongst the sober volumes. Miss Avery must have worked for
days.

'I'm afraid this isn't what we meant,' she began. 'Mr Wilcox and I never
intended the cases to be touched. For instance, these books are my brother's.
We are storing them for him and for my sister, who is abroad. When you
kindly undertook to look after things, we never expected you to do so much.'

'The house has been empty long enough,' said the old woman.

Margaret refused to argue. 'I dare say we didn't explain,' she said civilly.
'It has been a mistake, and very likely our mistake.'

'Mrs Wilcox, it has been mistake upon mistake for fifty years. The house
is Mrs Wilcox's, and she would not desire it to stand empty any longer.'

To help the poor decaying brain, Margaret said:

'Yes, Mrs Wilcox's house, the mother of Mr Charles.'

'Mistake upon mistake,' said Miss Avery. 'Mistake upon mistake.'

'Well, I don't know,' said Margaret, sitting down in one of her own chairs.
'I really don't know what's to be done.' She could not help laughing.

The other said: 'Yes, it should be a merry house enough.'

'I don't know–I dare say. Well, thank you very much, Miss Avery. Yes,
that's all right. Delightful.'

'There is still the parlour.' She went through the door opposite and drew a
curtain. Light flooded the drawing-room and the drawing-room furniture
from Wickham Place. 'And the dining-room.' More curtains were drawn,
more windows were flung open to the spring. 'Then through here—' Miss
Avery continued passing and repassing through the hall. Her voice was lost,
but Margaret heard her pulling up the kitchen blind. 'I've not finished here
yet,' she announced, returning. 'There's still a deal to do. The farm lads will
carry your great wardrobes upstairs, for there is no need to go into expense at
Hilton.'

'It is all a mistake,' repeated Margaret, feeling that she must put her foot
down. 'A misunderstanding. Mr Wilcox and I are not going to live at
Howards End.'

'Oh, indeed. On account of his hay fever?'

'We have settled to build a new home for ourselves in Sussex, and part of
this furniture–my part–will go down there presently.' She looked at Miss

Avery intently, trying to understand the kink in her brain. Here was no maundering old woman. Her wrinkles were shrewd and humorous. She looked capable of scathing wit and also of high but unostentatious nobility.

'You think that you won't come back to live here, Mrs Wilcox, but you will.'

'That remains to be seen,' said Margaret, smiling. 'We have no intention of doing so for the present. We happen to need a much larger house. Circumstances oblige us to give big parties. Of course, some day—one never knows, does one?'

Miss Avery retorted: 'Some day! Tcha! tcha! Don't talk about some day. You are living here now.'

'Am I?'

'You are living here, and have been for the last ten minutes, if you ask me.'

It was a senseless remark, but with a queer feeling of disloyalty Margaret rose from her chair. She felt that Henry had been obscurely censured. They went into the dining-room, where the sunlight poured in upon her mother's cheffonier, and upstairs, where many an old god peeped from a new niche. The furniture fitted extraordinarily well. In the central room—over the hall, the room that Helen had slept in four years ago—Miss Avery had placed Tibby's old bassinette.

'The nursery,' she said.

Margaret turned away without speaking.

At last everything was seen. The kitchen and lobby were still stacked with furniture and straw, but, as far as she could make out, nothing had been broken or scratched. A pathetic display of ingenuity! Then they took a friendly stroll in the garden. It had gone wild since her last visit. The gravel sweep was weedy, and grass had sprung up at the very jaws of the garage. And Evie's rockery was only bumps. Perhaps Evie was responsible for Miss Avery's oddness. But Margaret suspected the the cause lay deeper, and that the girl's silly letter had but loosed the irritation of years.

'It's a beautiful meadow,' she remarked. It was one of those open-air drawing-rooms that have been formed, hundreds of years ago, out of the smaller fields. So the boundary hedge zigzagged down the hill at right angles, and at the bottom there was a little green annex—a sort of powder-closet for the cows.

'Yes, the maidy's well enough,' said Miss Avery, 'for those, that is, who don't suffer from sneezing.' And she cackled maliciously. 'I've seen Charlie Wilcox go out to my lads in hay time—oh, they ought to do this—they mustn't do that—he'd learn them to be lads. And just then the tickling took him. He has it from his father, with other things. There's not one Wilcox that can stand up against a field in June—I laughed fit to burst while he was courting Ruth.'

'My brother gets hay fever too,' said Margaret.

'This house lies too much on the land for them. Naturally, they were glad enough to slip in at first. But Wilcoxes are better than nothing, as I see you've found.'

Margaret laughed.

'They keep a place going, don't they? Yes, it is just that.'

'They keep England going, it is my opinion.'

But Miss Avery upset her by replying: 'Ay, they breed like rabbits. Well, well, it's a funny world. But He who made it knows what He wants in it, I suppose. If Mrs Charlie is expecting her fourth, it isn't for us to repine.'

'They breed and they also work,' said Margaret, conscious of some invitation to disloyalty, which was echoed by the very breeze and by the songs of the birds. 'It certainly is a funny world, but so long as men like my husband and his sons govern it, I think it'll never be a bad one—never really bad.'

'No, better'n nothing,' said Miss Avery, and turned to the wych-elm.

On their way back to the farm she spoke of her old friend much more clearly than before. In the house Margaret had wondered whether she quite distinguished the first wife from the second. Now she said: 'I never saw much of Ruth after her grandmother died, but we stayed civil. It was a very civil family. Old Mrs Howard never spoke against anybody, nor let anyone be turned away without food. Then it was never "Trespassers will be prosecuted" in their land, but would people please not come in? Mrs Howard was never created to run a farm.'

'Had they no men to help them?' Margaret asked.

Miss Avery replied: 'Things went on until there were no men.'

'Until Mr Wilcox came along,' corrected Margaret, anxious that her husband should receive his dues.

'I suppose so; but Ruth should have married a—no disrespect to you to say this, for I take it you were intended to get Wilcox any way, whether she got him first or no.'

'Whom should she have married?'

'A soldier!' exclaimed the old woman. 'Some real soldier.'

Margaret was silent. It was a criticism of Henry's character far more trenchant than any of her own. She felt dissatisfied.

'But that's all over,' she went on. 'A better time is coming now, though you've kept me long enough waiting. In a couple of weeks I'll see your lights shining through the hedge of an evening. Have you ordered in coals?'

'We are not coming,' said Margaret firmly. She respected Miss Avery too much to humour her. 'No. Not coming. Never coming. It has all been a mistake. The furniture must be repacked at once, and I am very sorry, but I am making other arrangements, and must ask you to give me the keys.'

'Certainly, Mrs Wilcox,' said Miss Avery, and resigned her duties with a smile.

Relieved at this conclusion, and having sent her compliments to Madge, Margaret walked back to the station. She had intended to go to the furniture warehouse and give directions for removal, but the muddle had turned out more extensive than she expected, so she decided to consult Henry. It was as well that she did this. He was strongly against employing the local man whom he had previously recommended, and advised her to store in London after all.

But before this could be done an unexpected trouble fell upon her.

Chapter Thirty-four

It was not unexpected entirely. Aunt Juley's health had been bad all the winter. She had had a long series of colds and coughs, and had been too busy to get rid of them. She had scarcely promised her niece 'to really take my tiresome chest in hand,' when she caught a chill and developed acute pneumonia. Margaret and Tibby went down to Swanage. Helen was telegraphed for, and that spring party that after all gathered in that hospitable house had all the pathos of fair memories. On a perfect day, when the sky seemed blue porcelain, and the waves of the discreet little bay beat gentlest of tattoos upon the sand, Margaret hurried up through the rhododendrons, confronted again by the senselessness of Death. One death may explain itself, but it throws no light upon another: the groping inquiry must begin anew. Preachers or scientists may generalize, but we know that no generality is possible about those whom we love; not one heaven awaits them, not even one oblivion. Aunt Juley, incapable of tragedy, slipped out of life with odd little laughs and apologies for having stopped in it so long. She was very weak; she could not rise to the occasion, or realize the great mystery which all agree must await her; it only seemed to her that she was quite done up—more done up than ever before; that she saw and heard and felt less every moment; and that, unless something changed, she would soon feel nothing. Her spare strength she devoted to plans: could not Margaret take some steamer expeditions? were mackerel cooked as Tibby liked them? She worried herself about Helen's absence, and also that she should be the cause of Helen's return. The nurses seemed to think such interests quite natural, and perhaps hers was an average approach to the Great Gate. But Margaret saw Death stripped of any false romance; whatever the idea of Death may contain, the process can be trivial and hideous.

'Important—Margaret dear, take the Lulworth when Helen comes.'

'Helen won't be able to stop, Aunt Juley. She has telegraphed that she can only get away just to see you. She must go back to Germany as soon as you are well.'

'How very odd of Helen! Mr Wilcox—'

'Yes, dear?'

'Can he spare you?'

Henry wished her to come, and had been very kind. Yet again Margaret said so.

Mrs Munt did not die. Quite outside her will, a more dignified power took hold of her and checked her on the downward slope. She returned, without emotion, as fidgety as ever. On the fourth day she was out of danger.

'Margaret—important,' it went on: 'I should like you to have some companion to take walks with. Do try Miss Conder.'

'I have been a litte walk with Miss Conder.'

'But she is not really interesting. If only you had Helen.'

'I have Tibby, Aunt Juley.'

'No, but he has to do his Chinese. Some real companion is what you need. Really, Helen is odd.'

'Helen is odd, very,' agreed Margaret.

'Not content with going abroad, why does she want to go back there at once?'

'No doubt she will change her mind when she sees us. She has not the least balance.'

That was the stock criticism about Helen, but Margaret's voice trembled as she made it. By now she was deeply pained at her sister's behaviour. It may be unbalanced to fly out of England, but to stop away eight months argues that the heart is awry as well as the head. A sick-bed could recall Helen, but she was deaf to more human calls; after a glimpse at her aunt, she would retire into her nebulous life behind some poste restante. She scarcely existed; her letters had become dull and infrequent; she had no wants and no curiosity. And it was all put down to poor Henry's account! Henry, long pardoned by his wife, was still too infamous to be greeted by his sister-in-law. It was morbid, and, to her alarm, Margaret fancied that she could trace the growth of morbidity back in Helen's life for nearly four years. The flight from Oniton; the unbalanced patronage of the Basts; the explosion of grief up on the Downs—all connected with Paul, an insignificant boy whose lips had kissed hers for a fraction of time. Margaret and Mrs Wilcox had feared that they might kiss again. Foolishly: the real danger was reaction. Reaction against the Wilcoxes had eaten into her life until she was scarcely sane. At twenty-five she had an idée fixe. What hope was there for her as an old woman?

The more Margaret thought about it the more alarmed she became. For many months she had put the subject away, but it was too big to be slighted now. There was almost a taint of madness. Were all Helen's actions to be governed by a tiny mishap, such as may happen to any young man or woman? Can human nature be constructed on lines so insignificant? The blundering little encounter at Howards End was vital. It propagated itself where graver intercourse lay barren; it was stronger than sisterly intimacy, stronger than reason or books. In one of her moods Helen had confessed that she still 'enjoyed' it in a certain sense. Paul had faded, but the magic of his caress endured. And where there is enjoyment of the past there may also be reaction—propagation at both ends.

Well, it is odd and sad that our minds should be such seed-beds, and we without power to choose the seed. But man is an odd, sad creature as yet, intent on pilfering the earth, and heedless of the growths within himself. He cannot be bored about psychology. He leaves it to the specialist, which is as if he should leave his dinner to be eaten by a steam-engine. He cannot be bothered to digest his own soul. Margaret and Helen have been more patient, and it is suggested that Margaret has succeeded—so far as success is yet possible. She does understand herself, she has some rudimentary control over her own growth. Whether Helen has succeeded one cannot say.

The day that Mrs Munt rallied Helen's letter arrived. She had posted it at Munich, and would be in London herself on the morrow. It was a disquieting letter, though the opening was affectionate and sane.

> Dearest Meg,
>   Give Helen's love to Aunt Juley. Tell her that I love, and have loved, her ever since I can remember. I shall be in London Thursday.
>   My address will be care of the bankers. I have not yet settled on a hotel, so write or wire to me there and give me detailed news. If Aunt Juley is much better, or if, for a terrible reason, it would be no good my coming down to Swanage, you must not think it odd if I do not come. I have all sorts of plans in my head. I am living abroad at present, and want to get back as quickly as possible. Will you please tell me where our furniture is. I should like to take out one or two books; the rest are for you.
>   Forgive me, dearest Meg. This must read like rather a tiresome letter, but all letters are from your loving
>
>   Helen.

It was a tiresome letter, for it tempted Margaret to tell a lie. If she wrote that Aunt Juley was still in danger her sister would come. Unhealthiness is contagious. We cannot be in contact with those who are in a morbid state without ourselves deteriorating. To 'act for the best' might do Helen good, but would do herself harm, and, at the risk of disaster, she kept her colours flying a little longer. She replied that their aunt was much better, and awaited developments.

Tibby approved of her reply. Mellowing rapidly, he was a pleasanter companion than before. Oxford had done much for him. He had lost his peevishness, and could hide his indifference to people and his interest in food. But he had not grown more human. The years between eighteen and twenty-two, so magical for most, were leading him gently from boyhood to middle age. He had never known young-manliness, that quality which warms the heart till death, and gives Mr Wilcox an imperishable charm. He was frigid, through no fault of his own, and without cruelty. He thought Helen wrong and Margaret right, but the family trouble was for him what a scene behind footlights is for most people. He had only one suggestion to make, and that was characteristic.

'Why don't you tell Mr Wilcox?'

'About Helen?'

'Perhaps he has come across that sort of thing.'

'He would do all he could, but—'

'Oh, you know best. But he is practical.'

It was the student's belief in experts. Margaret demurred for one or two reasons. Presently Helen's answer came. She sent a telegram requesting the address of the furniture, as she would now return at once. Margaret replied, 'Certainly not; meet me at the bankers at four.' She and Tibby went up to London. Helen was not at the bankers, and they were refused her address.

Helen had passed into chaos.

Margaret put her arm round her brother. He was all that she had left, and never had he seemed more unsubstantial.

'Tibby love, what next?'

He replied: 'It is extraordinary.'

'Dear, your judgment's often clearer than mine. Have you any notion what's at the back?'

'None, unless it's something mental.'

'Oh–that!' said Margaret. 'Quite impossible.' But the suggestion had been uttered, and in a few minutes she took it up herself. Nothing else explained. And London agreed with Tibby. The mask fell off the city, and she saw it for what it really is–a caricature of infinity. The familiar barriers, the streets along which she moved, the houses between which she had made her little journeys for so many years, became negligible suddenly. Helen seemed one with grimy trees and the traffic and the slowly-flowing slabs of mud. She had accomplished a hideous act of renunciation and returned to the One. Margaret's own faith held firm. She knew the human soul will be merged, if it be merged at all, with the stars and the sea. Yet she felt that her sister had been going amiss for many years. It was symbolic the catastrophe should come now, on a London afternoon, while rain fell slowly.

Henry was the only hope. Henry was definite. He might know of some paths in the chaos that were hidden from them, and she determined to take Tibby's advice and lay the whole matter in his hands. They must call at his office. He could not well make it worse. She went for a few moments into St Paul's, whose dome stands out of the welter so bravely, as if preaching the gospel of form. But within, St Paul's is as its surroundings–echoes and whispers, inaudible songs, invisible mosaics, wet footmarks crossing and recrossing the floor. Si monumentum requiris, circumspice: it points us back to London. There was no hope of Helen here.

Henry was unsatisfactory at first. That she had expected. He was overjoyed to see her back from Swanage, and slow to admit the growth of a new trouble. When they told him of their search, he only chaffed Tibby and the Schlegels generally, and declared that it was 'just like Helen' to lead her relatives a dance.

'That is what we all say,' replied Margaret. 'But why should it be just like Helen? Why should she be allowed to be so queer, and to grow queerer?'

'Don't ask me. I'm a plain man of business. I live and let live. My advice to you both is, don't worry. Margaret, you've got black marks again under your eyes. You know that's strictly forbidden. First your aunt–then your sister. No, we aren't going to have it. Are we, Theobald?' He rang the bell. 'I'll give you some tea, and then you go straight to Ducie Street. I can't have my girl looking as old as her husband.'

'All the same, you have not quite seen our point,' said Tibby.

Mr Wilcox, who was in good spirits, retorted, 'I don't suppose I ever shall.' He leant back, laughing at the gifted but ridiculous family, while the fire flickered over the map of Africa. Margaret motioned to her brother to go on. Rather diffident, he obeyed her.

'Margaret's point is this,' he said. 'Our sister may be mad.'

Charles, who was working in the inner room, looked round.

'Come in, Charles,' said Margaret kindly. 'Could you help us at all? We are again in trouble.'

'I'm afraid I cannot. What are the facts? We are all mad more or less, you know, in these days.'

'The facts are as follows,' replied Tibby, who had at times a pedantic lucidity. 'The facts are that she has been in England for three days and will not see us. She has forbidden the bankers to give us her address. She refuses to answer questions. Margaret finds her letters colourless. There are other facts, but these are the most striking.'

'She has never behaved like this before, then?' asked Henry.

'Of course not!' said his wife, with a frown.

'Well, my dear, how am I to know?'

A senseless spasm of annoyance came over her. 'You know quite well that Helen never sins against affection,' she said. 'You must have noticed that much in her, surely.'

'Oh yes; she and I have always hit it off together.'

'No, Henry—can't you see?—I don't mean that.'

She recovered herself, but not before Charles had observed her. Stupid and attentive, he was watching the scene.

'I was meaning that when she was eccentric in the past, one could trace it back to the heart in the long-run. She behaved oddly because she cared for someone, or wanted to help them. There's no possible excuse for her now. She is grieving us deeply, and that is why I am sure that she is not well. "Mad" is too terrible a word, but she is not well. I shall never believe it. I shouldn't discuss my sister with you if I thought she was well—trouble you about her, I mean.'

Henry began to grow serious. Ill-health was to him something perfectly definite. Generally well himself, he could not realize that we sink to it by slow gradations. The sick had no rights; they were outside the pale; one could lie to them remorselessly. When his first wife was seized, he had promised to take her down into Hertfordshire, but meanwhile arranged with a nursing-home instead. Helen, too, was ill. And the plan that he sketched out for her capture, clever and well-meaning as it was, drew its ethics from the wolf-pack.

'You want to get hold of her?' he said. 'That's the problem, isn't it? She has got to see a doctor.'

'For all I know she has seen one already.'

'Yes, yes; don't interrupt.' He rose to his feet and thought intently. The genial, tentative host disappeared, and they saw instead the man who had carved money out of Greece and Africa, and bought forests from the natives for a few bottles of gin. 'I've got it,' he said at last. 'It's perfectly easy. Leave it to me. We'll send her down to Howards End.'

'How will you do that?'

'After her books. Tell her that she must unpack them herself. Then you can meet her there.'

'But, Henry, that's just what she won't let me do. It's part of her—whatever it is—never to see me.'

'Of course you won't tell her you're going. When she is there, looking at the cases, you'll just stroll in. If nothing is wrong with her, so much the better. But there'll be the motor round the corner, and we can run her up to a specialist in no time.'

Margaret shook her head. 'It's quite impossible.'

'Why?'

'It doesn't seem impossible to me,' said Tibby; 'it is surely a very tippy plan.'

'It is impossible, because—' She looked at her husband sadly. 'It's not the particular language that Helen and I talk, if you see my meaning. It would do splendidly for other people, whom I don't blame.'

'But Helen doesn't talk,' said Tibby. 'That's our whole difficulty. She won't talk your particular language, and on that account you think she's ill.'

'No, Henry; it's sweet of you, but I couldn't.'

'I see,' he said; 'you have scruples.'

'I suppose so.'

'And sooner than go against them you would have your sister suffer. You could have got her down to Swanage by a word, but you have scruples. And scruples are all very well. I am as scrupulous as any man alive, I hope; but when it is a case like this, when there is a question of madness—'

'I deny it's madness.'

'You said just now—'

'It's madness when I say it, but not when you say it.'

Henry shrugged his shoulders. 'Margaret! Margaret!' he groaned. 'No education can teach a woman logic. Now, my dear, my time is valuable. Do you want me to help you or not?'

'Not in that way.'

'Answer my question. Plain question, plain answer. Do—'

Charles surprised them by interrupting. 'Pater, we may as well keep Howards End out of it,' he said.

'Why, Charles?'

Charles could give no reason; but Margaret felt as if, over tremendous distance, a salutation had passed between them.

'The whole house is at sixes and sevens,' he said crossly. 'We don't want any more mess.'

'Who's "we"?' asked his father. 'My boy, pray, who's "we"?'

'I am sure I beg your pardon,' said Charles. 'I appear always to be intruding.'

By now Margaret wished she had never mentioned her trouble to her husband. Retreat was impossible. He was determined to push the matter to a satisfactory conclusion, and Helen faded as he talked. Her fair, flying hair and eager eyes counted for nothing, for she was ill, without rights, and any of her friends might hunt her. Sick at heart, Margaret joined in the chase. She wrote her sister a lying letter, at her husband's dictation; she said the furniture was all at Howards End, but could be seen on Monday next at

3 p.m., when a charwoman would be in attendance. It was a cold letter, and the more plausible for that. Helen would think she was offended. And on Monday next she and Henry were to lunch with Dolly, and then ambush themselves in the garden.

After they had gone, Mr Wilcox said to his son: 'I can't have this sort of behaviour, my boy. Margaret's too sweet-natured to mind, but I mind for her.'

Charles made no answer.

'Is anything wrong with you, Charles, this afternoon?'

'No, pater; but you may be taking on a bigger business than you reckon.'

'How?'

'Don't ask me.'

Chapter Thirty-five

One speaks of the moods of spring, but the days that are her true children have only one mood: they are all full of the rising and dropping of winds, and the whistling of birds. New flowers may come out, the green embroidery of the hedges increase, but the same heaven broods overhead, soft, thick, and blue, the same figures, seen and unseen, are wandering by coppice and meadow. The morning that Margaret had spent with Miss Avery, and the afternoon she set out to entrap Helen, were the scales of a single balance. Time might never have moved, rain never have fallen, and man alone, with his schemes and ailments, was troubling Nature until he saw her through a veil of tears.

She protested no more. Whether Henry was right or wrong, he was most kind, and she knew of no other standard by which to judge him. She must trust him absolutely. As soon as he had taken up a business, his obtuseness vanished. He profited by the slightest indications, and the capture of Helen promised to be staged as deftly as the marriage of Evie.

They went down in the morning as arranged, and he discovered that their victim was actually in Hilton. On his arrival he called at all the livery-stables in the village, and had a few minutes' serious conversation with the proprietors. What he said, Margaret did not know—perhaps not the truth; but news arrived after lunch that a lady had come by the London train, and had taken a fly to Howards End.

'She was bound to drive,' said Henry. 'There will be her books.'

'I cannot make it out,' said Margaret for the hundredth time.

'Finish your coffee, dear. We must be off.'

'Yes, Margaret, you know you must take plenty,' said Dolly.

Margaret tried, but suddenly lifted her hand to her eyes. Dolly stole glances at her father-in-law which he did not answer. In the silence the motor came round to the door.

'You're not fit for it,' he said anxiously. 'Let me go alone. I know exactly what to do.'

'Oh yes, I am fit,' said Margaret, uncovering her face. 'Only most frightfully worried. I cannot feel that Helen is really alive. Her letters and telegrams seem to have come from someone else. Her voice isn't in them. I don't believe your driver really saw her at the station. I wish I'd never mentioned it. I know that Charles is vexed. Yes, he is—' She seized Dolly's hand and kissed it. 'There, Dolly will forgive me. There. Now we'll be off.'

Henry had been looking at her closely. He did not like this breakdown.

'Don't you want to tidy yourself?'

'Have I time?'

'Yes, plenty.'

She went to the lavatory by the front door, and as soon as the bolt slipped, Mr Wilcox said quietly:

'Dolly, I'm going without her.'

Dolly's eyes lit up with vulgar excitement. She followed him on tip-toe out to the car.

'Tell her I thought it best.'

'Yes, Mr Wilcox, I see.'

'Say anything you like. All right.'

The car started well, and with ordinary luck would have got away. But Porgly-woggles, who was playing in the garden, chose this moment to sit down in the middle of the path. Crane, in trying to pass him, ran one wheel over a bed of wallflowers. Dolly screamed. Margaret, hearing the noise, rushed out hatless, and was in time to jump on the footboard. She said not a single word: he was only treating her as she had treated Helen, and her rage at his dishonesty only helped to indicate what Helen would feel against them. She thought, 'I deserve it: I am punished for lowering my colours.' And she accepted his apologies with a calmness that astonished him.

'I still consider you are not fit for it,' he kept saying.

'Perhaps I was not at lunch. But the whole thing is spread clearly before me now.'

'I was meaning to act for the best.'

'Just lend me your scarf, will you. This wind takes one's hair so.'

'Certainly, dear girl. Are you all right now?'

'Look! My hands have stopped trembling.'

'And have quite forgiven me? Then listen. Her cab should already have arrived at Howards End. (We're a little late, but no matter.) Our first move will be to send it down to wait at the farm, as, if possible, one doesn't want a scene before servants. A certain gentleman'—he pointed at Crane's back—'won't drive in, but will wait a little short of the front gate, behind the laurels. Have you still the keys of the house?'

'Yes.'

'Well, they aren't wanted. Do you remember how the house stands?'

'Yes.'

'If we don't find her in the porch, we can stroll round into the garden. Our object—'

Here they stopped to pick up the doctor.

'I was just saying to my wife, Mansbridge, that our main object is not to frighten Miss Schlegel. The house, as you know, is my property, so it should seem quite natural for us to be there. The trouble is evidently nervous–wouldn't you say so, Margaret?'

The doctor, a very young man, began to ask questions about Helen. Was she normal? Was there anything congenital or hereditary? Had anything occurred that was likely to alienate her from her family?

'Nothing,' answered Margaret, wondering what would have happened if she had added: 'Though she did resent my husband's immorality.'

'She always was highly strung,' pursued Henry, leaning back in the car as it shot past the church. 'A tendency to spiritualism and those things, though nothing serious. Musical, literary, artistic, but I should say normal–a very charming girl.'

Margaret's anger and terror increased every moment. How dare these men label her sister! What horrors lay ahead! What impertinences that shelter under the name of science! The pack was turning on Helen, to deny her human rights, and it seemed to Margaret that all Schlegels were threatened with her. 'Were they normal?' What a question to ask! And it is always those who know nothing about human nature, who are bored by psychology and shocked by physiology, who ask it. However piteous her sister's state, she knew that she must be on her side. They would be mad together if the world chose to consider them so.

It was now five minutes past three. The car slowed down by the farm, in the yard of which Miss Avery was standing. Henry asked her whether a cab had gone past. She nodded, and the next moment they caught sight of it, at the end of the lane. The car ran silently like a beast of prey. So unsuspicious was Helen that she was sitting in the porch, with her back to the road. She had come. Only her head and shoulders were visible. She sat framed in the vine, and one of her hands played with the buds. The wind ruffled her hair, the sun glorified it; she was as she had always been.

Margaret was seated next to the door. Before her husband could prevent her, she slipped out. She ran to the garden gate, which was shut, passed through it, and deliberately pushed it in his face. The noise alarmed Helen. Margaret saw her rise with an unfamiliar movement, and, rushing into the porch, learnt the simple explanation of all their fears–her sister was with child.

'Is the truant all right?' called Henry.

She had time to whisper: 'Oh, my darling—' The keys of the house were in her hand. She unlocked Howards End and thrust Helen into it. 'Yes, all right,' she said, and stood with her back to the door.

Chapter Thirty-six

'Margaret, you look upset!' said Henry.

Mansbridge had followed. Crane was at the gate, and the flyman had stood up on the box. Margaret shook her head at them; she could not speak any more. She remained clutching the keys, as if all their future depended on them. Henry was asking more questions. She shook her head again. His words had no sense. She heard him wonder why she had let Helen in. 'You might have given me a knock with the gate,' was another of his remarks. Presently she heard herself speaking. She, or someone for her, said 'Go away.' Henry came nearer. He repeated, 'Margaret, you look upset again. My dear, give me the keys. What are you doing with Helen?'

'Oh, dearest, do go away, and I will manage it all.'

'Manage what?'

He stretched out his hand for the keys. She might have obeyed if it had not been for the doctor.

'Stop that at least,' she said piteously; the doctor had turned back, and was questioning the driver of Helen's cab. A new feeling came over her; she was fighting for women against men. She did not care about rights, but if men came into Howards End, it should be over her body.

'Come, this is an odd beginning,' said her husband.

The doctor came forward now, and whispered two words to Mr Wilcox—the scandal was out. Sincerely horrified, Henry stood gazing at the earth.

'I cannot help it,' said Margaret. 'Do wait. It's not my fault. Please all four of you to go away now.'

Now the flyman was whispering to Crane.

'We are relying on you to help us, Mrs Wilcox,' said the young doctor. 'Could you go in and persuade your sister to come out?'

'On what grounds?' said Margaret, suddenly looking him straight in the eyes.

Thinking it professional to prevaricate, he murmured something about a nervous breakdown.

'I beg your pardon, but it is nothing of the sort. You are not qualified to attend my sister, Mr Mansbridge. If we require your services, we will let you know.'

'I can diagnose the case more bluntly if you wish,' he retorted.

'You could, but you have not. You are, therefore, not qualified to attend my sister.'

'Come, come, Margaret!' said Henry, never raising his eyes. 'This is a terrible business, an appalling business. It's doctor's orders. Open the door.'

'Forgive me, but I will not.'

'I don't agree.'

Margaret was silent.

'This business is as broad as it's long,' contributed the doctor. 'We had better all work together. You need us, Mrs Wilcox, and we need you.'

'Quite so,' said Henry.

'I do not need you in the least,' said Margaret.

The two men looked at each other anxiously.

'No more does my sister, who is still many weeks from her confinement.'

'Margaret, Margaret!'

'Well, Henry, send your doctor away. What possible use is he now?'

Mr Wilcox ran his eye over the house. He had a vague feeling that he must stand firm and support the doctor. He himself might need support, for there was trouble ahead.

'It all turns on affection now,' said Margaret. 'Affection. Don't you see?' Resuming her usual methods, she wrote the word on the house with her finger. 'Surely you see. I like Helen very much, you not so much. Mr Mansbridge doesn't know her. That's all. And affection, when reciprocated, gives rights. Put that down in your note-book, Mr Mansbridge. It's a useful formula.'

Henry told her to be calm.

'You don't know what you want yourselves,' said Margaret, folding her arms. 'For one sensible remark I will let you in. But you cannot make it. You would trouble my sister for no reason. I will not permit it. I'll stand here all the day sooner.'

'Mansbridge,' said Henry in a low voice, 'perhaps not now.'

The pack was breaking up. At a sign from his master, Crane also went back into the car.

'Now, Henry, you,' she said gently. None of her bitterness had been directed at him. 'Go away now, dear. I shall want your advice later, no doubt. Forgive me if I have been cross. But, seriously, you must go.'

He was too stupid to leave her. Now it was Mr Mansbridge who called in a low voice to him.

'I shall soon find you down at Dolly's,' she called, as the gate at last clanged between them. The fly moved out of the way, the motor backed, turned a little, backed again, and turned in the narrow road. A string of farm carts came up in the middle; but she waited through all, for there was no hurry. When all was over and the car had started, she opened the door. 'Oh, my darling!' she said. 'My darling, forgive me.' Helen was standing in the hall.

Chapter Thirty-seven

Margaret bolted the door on the inside. Then she would have kissed her sister, But Helen, in a dignified voice, that came strangely from her, said:

'Convenient! You did not tell me that the books were unpacked. I have found nearly everything that I want.'

'I told you nothing that was true.'

'It has been a great surprise, certainly. Has Aunt Juley been ill?'

'Helen, you wouldn't think I'd invent that?'

'I suppose not,' said Helen, turning away, and crying a very little. 'But one loses faith in everything after this.'

'We thought it was illness, but even then— I haven't behaved worthily.'

Helen selected another book.

'I ought not to have consulted anyone. What would our father have thought of me?'

She did not think of questioning her sister, nor of rebuking her. Both might be necessary in the future, but she had first to purge a greater crime than any that Helen could have committed–that want of confidence that is the work of the devil.

'Yes, I am annoyed,' replied Helen. 'My wishes should have been respected. I would have gone through this meeting if it was necessary, but after Aunt Juley recovered, it was not necessary. Planning my life, as I now have to do—'

'Come away from those books,' called Margaret. 'Helen, do talk to me.'

'I was just saying that I have stopped living haphazard. One can't go through a great deal of—' she missed out the noun–'without planning one's actions in advance. I am going to have a child in June, and in the first place conversation, discussions, excitement, are not good for me. I will go through them if necessary, but only then. In the second place I have no right to trouble people. I cannot fit in with England as I know it. I have done something that the English never pardon. It would not be right for them to pardon it. So I must live where I am not known.'

'But why didn't you tell me, dearest?'

'Yes,' replied Helen judicially. 'I might have, but decided to wait.'

'I believe you would never have told me.'

'Oh yes, I should. We have taken a flat in Munich.'

Margaret glanced out of the window.

'By "we" I mean myself and Monica. But for her, I am and have been and always wish to be alone.'

'I have not heard of Monica.'

'You wouldn't have. She's an Italian—by birth at least. She makes her living by journalism. I met her originally on Garda. Monica is much the best person to see me through.'

'You are very fond of her, then.'

'She has been extraordinarily sensible with me.'

Margaret guessed at Monica's type—'Italiano Inglesiato' they had named it: the crude feminist of the South, whom one respects but avoids. And Helen had turned to it in her need?

'You must not think that we shall ever meet,' said Helen, with a measured kindness. 'I shall always have a room for you when you can be spared, and the longer you can be with me the better. But you haven't understood yet, Meg, and of course it is very difficult for you. This is a shock to you. It isn't to me, who have been thinking over our futures for many months, and they won't be changed by a slight contretemps, such as this. I cannot live in England.'

'Helen, you've not forgiven me for my treachery. You *couldn't* talk like this to me if you had.'

'Oh, Meg dear, why do we talk at all?' She dropped a book and sighed wearily. Then, recovering herself, she said: 'Tell me, how is it that all the books are down here?'

'Series of mistakes.'

'And a great deal of the furniture has been unpacked.'

'All.'

'Who lives here, then?'

'No one.'

'I suppose you are letting it, though.'

'The house is dead,' said Margaret, with a frown. 'Why worry on about it?'

'But I am interested. You talk as if I had lost all my interest in life. I am still Helen, I hope. Now this hasn't the feel of a dead house. The hall seems more alive even than in the old days, when it held the Wilcoxes' own things.'

'Interested, are you? Very well, I must tell you, I suppose. My husband lent it on condition we—but by a mistake all our things were unpacked, and Miss Avery, instead of—' She stopped. 'Look here, I can't go on like this. I warn you I won't. Helen, why should you be so miserably unkind to me, simply because you hate Henry?'

'I don't hate him now,' said Helen. 'I have stopped being a schoolgirl, and Meg, once again, I'm not being unkind. But as for fitting in with your English life—no, put it out of your head at once. Imagine a visit from me at Ducie Street! It's unthinkable.'

Margaret could not contradict her. It was appalling to see her quietly moving forward with her plans, not bitter or excitable, neither asserting innocence nor confessing guilt, merely desiring freedom and the company of those who would not blame her. She had been through—how much? Margaret did not know. But it was enough to part her from old habits as well as old friends.

'Tell me about yourself,' said Helen, who had chosen her books, and was lingering over the furniture.

'There's nothing to tell.'

'But your marriage has been happy, Meg?'

'Yes, but I don't feel inclined to talk.'

'You feel as I do.'

'Not that, but I can't.'

'No more can I. It is a nuisance, but no good trying.'

Something had come between them. Perhaps it was Society, which henceforward would exclude Helen. Perhaps it was a third life, already potent as a spirit. They could find no meeting-place. Both suffered acutely, and were not comforted by the knowledge that affection survived.

'Look here, Meg, is the coast clear?'

'You mean that you want to go away from me?'

'I suppose so—dear old lady! it isn't any use. I knew we should have nothing to say. Give my love to Aunt Juley and Tibby, and take more yourself than I can say. Promise to come and see me in Munich later.'

'Certainly, dearest.'

'For that is all we can do.'

It seemed so. Most ghastly of all was Helen's common sense: Monica had been extraordinarily good for her.

'I am glad to have seen you and the things.' She looked at the bookcase lovingly, as if she was saying farewell to the past.

Margaret unbolted the door. She remarked: 'The car has gone, and here's your cab.'

She led the way to it, glancing at the leaves and the sky. The spring had never seemed more beautiful. The driver, who was leaning on the gate, called out, 'Please, lady, a message,' and handed her Henry's visiting-card through the bars.

'How did this come?' she asked.

Crane had returned with it almost at once.

She read the card with annoyance. It was covered with instructions in domestic French. When she and her sister had talked she was to come back for the night to Dolly's. 'Il faut dormir sur ce sujet.' While Helen was to be found 'une comfortable chambre à l'hotel.' The final sentence displeased her greatly until she remembered that the Charles' had only one spare room, and so could not invite a third guest.

'Henry would have done what he could,' she interpreted.

Helen had not followed her into the garden. The door once open, she lost her inclination to fly. She remained in the hall, going from bookcase to table. She grew more like the old Helen, irresponsible and charming.

'This *is* Mr Wilcox's house?' she inquired.

'Surely you remember Howards End?'

'Remember? I who remember everything! But it looks to be ours now.'

'Miss Avery was extraordinary,' said Margaret, her own spirits lightening a little. Again she was invaded by a slight feeling of disloyalty. But it brought her relief, and she yielded to it. 'She loved Mrs Wilcox, and would rather furnish her house with our things than think of it empty. In consequence here are all the library books.'

'Not all the books. She hasn't unpacked the Art Books, in which she may show her sense. And we never used to have the sword here.'

'The sword looks well, though.'

'Magnificent.'

'Yes, doesn't it?'

'Where's the piano, Meg?'

'I warehoused that in London. Why?'

'Nothing.'

'Curious, too, that the carpet fits.'

'The carpet's a mistake,' announced Helen. 'I know that we had it in London, but this floor ought to be bare. It is far too beautiful.'

'You still have a mania for under-furnishing. Would you care to come into the dining-room before you start? There's no carpet there.'

They went in, and each minute their talk became more natural.

'Oh, *what* a place for mother's cheffonier!' cried Helen.

'Look at the chairs, though.'

'Oh, look at them! Wickham Place faced north, didn't it?'

'North-west.'

'Anyhow, it is thirty years since any of those chairs have felt the sun. Feel. Their dear little backs are quite warm.'

'But why has Miss Avery made them set to partners? I shall just—'

'Over here, Meg. Put it so that anyone sitting will see the lawn.'

Margaret moved a chair. Helen sat down in it.

'Ye-es. The window's too high.'

'Try a drawing-room chair.'

'No, I don't like the drawing-room so much. The beam has been matchboarded. It would have been so beautiful otherwise.'

'Helen, what a memory you have for some things! You're perfectly right. It's a room that men have spoilt through trying to make it nice for women. Men don't know what we want—'

'And never will.'

'I don't agree. In two thousand years they'll know.'

'But the chairs show up wonderfully. Look where Tibby spilt the soup.'

'Coffee, It was coffee surely.'

Helen shook her head. 'Impossible. Tibby was far too young to be given coffee at that time.'

'Was father alive?'

'Yes.'

'Then you're right and it must have been soup. I was thinking of much later—that unsuccessful visit of Aunt Juley's, when she didn't realize that Tibby had grown up. It was coffee then, for he threw it down on purpose. There was some rhyme, "Tea, coffee—coffee, tea," that she said to him every morning at breakfast. Wait a minute—how did it go?'

'I know—no, I don't. What a detestable boy Tibby was!'

'But the rhyme was simply awful. No decent person could have put up with it.'

'Ah, that greengage tree,' cried Helen, as if the garden was also part of their childhood. 'Why do I connect it with dumb-bells? And there come the chickens. The grass wants cutting. I love yellowhammers—'

Margaret interrupted her. 'I have got it,' she announced.

> '*Tea, tea, coffee, tea,*
> *Or chocolaritee.*'

'That every morning for three weeks. No wonder Tibby was wild.'

'Tibby is moderately a dear now,' said Helen.

'There! I knew you'd say that in the end. Of course he's a dear.'

A bell rang.

'Listen! What's that?'

Helen said, 'Perhaps the Wilcoxes are beginning the siege.'

'What nonsense—listen!'

And the triviality faded from their faces, though it left something behind—the knowledge that they never could be parted because their love was rooted in common things. Explanations and appeals had failed; they had tried for a common meeting-ground, and had only made each other unhappy. And all the time their salvation was lying round them—the past sanctifying the present; the present, with wild heart-throb, declaring that there would after all be a future, with laughter and the voices of children. Helen, still smiling, came up to her sister. She said, 'It is always Meg.' They looked into each other's eyes. The inner life had paid.

Solemnly the clapper tolled. No one was in the front. Margaret went to the kitchen, and struggled between packing-cases to the window. Their visitor was only a little boy with a tin can. And triviality returned.

'Little boy, what do you want?'

'Please, I am the milk.'

'Did Miss Avery send you?' said Margaret, rather sharply.

'Yes, please.'

'Then take it back and say we require no milk.' While she called to Helen, 'No, it's not the siege, but possibly an attempt to provision us against one.'

'But I like milk, cried Helen. 'Why send it away?'

'Do you? Oh, very well. But we've nothing to put it in, and he wants the can.'

'Please, I'm to call in the morning for the can,' said the boy.

'The house will be locked up then.'

'In the morning would I bring eggs, too?'

'Are you the boy whom I saw playing in the stacks last week?'

The child hung his head.

'Well, run away and do it again.'

'Nice little boy,' whispered Helen. 'I say, what's your name? Mine's Helen.'

'Tom.'

That was Helen all over. The Wilcoxes, too, would ask a child its name, but they never told their names in return.

'Tom, this one here is Margaret. And at home we've another called Tibby.'

'Mine are lop-eareds,' replied Tom, supposing Tibby to be a rabbit.

'You're a very good and rather a clever little boy. Mind you come again—Isn't he charming?'

'Undoubtedly,' said Margaret. 'He is probably the son of Madge, and Madge is dreadful. But this place has wonderful powers.'

'What do you mean?'

'I don't know.'

'Because I probably agree with you.'

'It kills what is dreadful and makes what is beautiful live.'

'I do agree,' said Helen, as she sipped the milk. 'But you said that the house was dead not half an hour ago.'

'Meaning that I was dead. I felt it.'

'Yes, the house has a surer life than we, even if it was empty, and, as it is, I can't get over that for thirty years the sun has never shone full on our furniture. After all, Wickham Place was a grave. Meg, I've a startling idea.'

'What is it?'

'Drink some milk to steady you.'

Margaret obeyed.

'No, I won't tell you yet,' said Helen, 'because you may laugh or be angry. Let's go upstairs first and give the rooms an airing.'

They opened window after window, till the inside, too, was rustling to the spring. Curtains blew, picture-frames tapped cheerfully. Helen uttered cries of excitement as she found this bed obviously in its right place, that in its wrong one. She was angry with Miss Avery for not having moved the wardrobes up. 'Then one would see really.' She admired the view. She was the Helen who had written the memorable letters four years ago. As they leant out, looking westward, she said: 'About my idea. Couldn't you and I camp out in this house for the night?'

'I don't think we could well do that,' said Margaret.

'Here are beds, tables, towels—'

'I know; but the house isn't supposed to be slept in, and Henry's suggestion was—'

'I require no suggestions. I shall not alter anything in my plans. But it would give me so much pleasure to have one night here with you. It will be something to look back on. Oh, Meg lovely, do let's!'

'But, Helen, my pet,' said Margaret, 'we can't without getting Henry's leave. Of course, he would give it, but you said yourself that you couldn't visit at Ducie Street now, and this is equally intimate.'

'Ducie Street is his house. This is ours. Our furniture, our sort of people coming to the door. Do let us camp out, just one night, and Tom shall feed us on eggs and milk. Why not? It's a moon.'

Margaret hesitated. 'I feel Charles wouldn't like it,' she said at last. 'Even our furniture annoyed him, and I was going to clear it out when Aunt Juley's illness prevented me. I sympathize with Charles. He feels it's his mother's house. He loves it in rather an untaking way. Henry I could answer for–not Charles.'

'I know he won't like it,' said Helen. 'But I am going to pass out of their lives. What difference will it make in the long run if they say, "And she even spent the night at Howards End"?'

'How do you know you'll pass out of their lives? We have thought that twice before.'

'Because my plans—'

'—which you change in a moment.'

'Then because my life is great and theirs are little,' said Helen, taking fire. 'I know of things they can't know of, and so do you. We *know* that there's poetry. We *know* that there's death. They can only take them on hearsay. We know this is our house, because it feels ours. Oh, they may take the title-deeds and the doorkeys, but for this one night we are at home.'

'It would be lovely to have you once more alone,' said Margaret. 'It may be a chance in a thousand.'

'Yes, and we could talk.' She dropped her voice. 'It won't be a very glorious story. But under that wych-elm–honestly, I see little happiness ahead. Cannot I have this one night with you?'

'I needn't say how much it would mean to me.'

'Then let us.'

'It is no good hesitating. Shall I drive down to Hilton now and get leave?'

'Oh, we don't want leave.'

But Margaret was a loyal wife. In spite of imagination and poetry–perhaps on account of them–she could sympathize with the technical attitude that Henry would adopt. If possible, she would be technical, too. A night's lodging–and they demanded no more–need not involve the discussion of general principles.

'Charles may say no,' grumbled Helen.

'We shan't consult him.'

'Go if you like; I should have stopped without leave.'

It was the touch of selfishness, which was not enough to mar Helen's character, and even added to its beauty. She would have stopped without leave, and escaped to Germany the next morning. Margaret kissed her.

'Expect me back before dark. I am looking forward to it so much. It is like you to have thought of such a beautiful thing.'

'Not a thing, only an ending;' said Helen rather sadly; and the sense of tragedy closed in on Margaret again as soon as she left the house.

She was afraid of Miss Avery. It is disquieting to fulfil a prophecy, however superficially. She was glad to see no watching figure as she drove past the farm, but only little Tom, turning somersaults in the straw.

Chapter Thirty-eight

The tragedy began quietly enough, and, like many another talk, by the man's deft assertion of his superiority. Henry heard her arguing with the driver, stepped out and settled the fellow, who was inclined to be rude, and then led the way to some chairs on the lawn. Dolly, who had not been 'told,' ran out with offers of tea. He refused them, and ordered them to wheel baby's perambulator away, as they desired to be alone.

'But the diddums can't listen; he isn't nine months old,' she pleaded.

'That's not what I was saying,' retorted her father-in-law.

Baby was wheeled out of earshot, and did not hear about the crisis till later years. It was now the turn of Margaret.

'Is it what we feared?' he asked.

'It is.'

'Dear girl,' he began, 'there is a troublesome business ahead of us, and nothing but the most absolute honesty and plain speech will see us through.' Margaret bent her head. 'I am obliged to question you on subjects we'd both prefer to leave untouched. As you know, I am not one of your Bernard Shaws who consider nothing sacred. To speak as I must will pain me, but there are occasions— We are husband and wife, not children. I am a man of the world, and you are a most exceptional woman.'

All Margaret's senses forsook her. She blushed, and looked past him at the Six Hills, covered with spring herbage. Noting her colour, he grew still more kind.

'I see that you feel as I felt when— My poor little wife! Oh, be brave! Just one or two questions, and I have done with you. Was your sister wearing a wedding-ring?'

Margaret stammered a 'No.'

There was an appalling silence.

'Henry, I really came to ask a favour about Howards End.'

'One point at a time. I am now obliged to ask for the name of her seducer.'

She rose to her feet and held the chair between them. Her colour had ebbed, and she was grey. It did not displease him that she should receive his question thus.

'Take your time,' he counselled her. 'Remember that this is far worse for me than for you.'

She swayed; he feared she was going to faint. Then speech came, and she said slowly: 'Seducer? No; I do not know her seducer's name.'

'Would she not tell you?'

'I never even asked her who seduced her,' said Margaret, dwelling on the hateful word thoughtfully.

'That is singular.' Then he changed his mind. 'Natural perhaps, dear girl, that you shouldn't ask. But until his name is known, nothing can be done. Sit down. How terrible it is to see you so upset! I knew you weren't fit for it. I wish I hadn't taken you.'

Margaret answered, 'I like to stand, if you don't mind, for it gives me a pleasant view of the Six Hills.'

'As you like.'

'Have you anything else to ask me, Henry?'

'Next you must tell me whether you have gathered anything. I have often noticed your insight, dear. I only wish my own was as good. You may have guessed something, even though your sister said nothing. The slightest hint would help us.'

'Who is "we"?'

'I thought it best to ring up Charles.'

'That was unnecessary,' said Margaret, growing warmer. 'This news will give Charles disproportionate pain.'

'He has at once gone to call on your brother.'

'That too was unnecessary.'

'Let me explain, dear, how the matter stands. You don't think that I and my son are other than gentlemen? It is in Helen's interests that we are acting. It is still not too late to save her name.'

Then Margaret hit out for the first time. 'Are we to make her seducer marry her?' she asked.

'If possible. Yes.'

'But, Henry, suppose he turned out to be married already? One had heard of such cases.'

'In that case he must pay heavily for his misconduct, and be thrashed within an inch of his life.'

So her first blow missed. She was thankful of it. What had tempted her to imperil both of their lives? Henry's obtuseness had saved her as well as himself. Exhausted with anger, she sat down again, blinking at him as he told her as much as he thought fit. At last she said: 'May I ask you my question now?'

'Certainly, my dear.'

'To-morrow Helen goes to Munich—'

'Well, possibly she is right.'

'Henry, let a lady finish. To-morrow she goes; to-night, with your permission, she would like to sleep at Howards End.'

It was the crisis of his life. Again she would have recalled the words as soon as they were uttered. She had not led up to them with sufficient care. She longed to warn him that they were far more important than he supposed. She saw him weighing them, as if they were a business proposition.

'Why Howards End?' he said at last. 'Would she not be more comfortable, as I suggested, at the hotel?'

Margaret hastened to give him reasons. 'It is an odd request, but you know what Helen is and what women in her state are.' He frowned, and moved irritably. 'She has the idea that one night in your house would give her pleasure and do her good. I think she's right. Being one of those imaginative girls, the presence of all our books and furniture soothes her. This is a fact. It is the end of her girlhood. Her last words to me were, "A beautiful ending."''

'She values the old furniture for sentimental reasons, in fact.'

'Exactly. You have quite understood. It is her last hope of being with it.'

'I don't agree there, my dear! Helen will have her share of the goods wherever she goes—possibly more than her share, for you are so fond of her that you'd give her anything of yours that she fancies, wouldn't you? and I'd raise no objection. I could understand it if it was her old home, because a home, or a house'—he changed the word, designedly; he had thought of a telling point—'because a house in which one has once lived becomes in a sort of way sacred, I don't know why. Associations and so on. Now Helen has no associations with Howards End, though I and Charles and Evie have. I do not see why she wants to stay the night there. She will only catch cold.'

'Leave it that you don't see,' cried Margaret. 'Call it fancy. But realize that fancy is a scientific fact. Helen is fanciful, and wants to.'

Then he surprised her—a rare occurrence. He shot an unexpected bolt. 'If she wants to sleep one night, she may want to sleep two. We shall never get her out of the house, perhaps.'

'Well?' said Margaret, with the precipice in sight. 'And suppose we don't get her out of the house? Would it matter? She would do no one any harm.'

Again the irritated gesture.

'No, Henry,' she panted, receding. 'I didn't mean that. We will only trouble Howards End for this one night. I take her to London to-morrow—'

'Do you intend to sleep in a damp house, too?'

'She cannot be left alone.'

'That's quite impossible! Madness. You must be here to meet Charles.'

'I have already told you that your message to Charles was unnecessary, and I have no desire to meet him.'

'Margaret—my Margaret—'

'What has this business to do with Charles? If it concerns me little, it concerns you less, and Charles not at all.'

'As the future owner of Howards End,' said Mr Wilcox, arching his fingers, 'I should say that it did concern Charles.'

'In what way? Will Helen's condition depreciate the property?'

'My dear, you are forgetting yourself.'

'I think you yourself recommended plain speaking.'

They looked at each other in amazement. The precipice was at their feet now.

'Helen commands my sympathy,' said Henry. 'As your husband, I shall do all for her that I can, and I have no doubt that she will prove more sinned against than sinning. But I cannot treat her as if nothing has happened. I should be false to my position in society if I did.'

She controlled herself for the last time. 'No, let us go back to Helen's request,' she said. 'It is unreasonable, but the request of an unhappy girl.

To-morrow she will go to Germany, and trouble society no longer. To-night she asks to sleep in your empty house—a house which you do not care about, and which you have not occupied for over a year. May she? Will you give my sister leave? Will you forgive her—as you hope to be forgiven, and as you have actually been forgiven? Forgive her for one night only. That will be enough.'

'As I have actually been forgiven—?'

'Never mind for the moment what I mean by that,' said Margaret. 'Answer my question.'

Perhaps some hint of her meaning did dawn on him. If so, he blotted it out. Straight from his fortress he answered: 'I seem rather unaccommodating, but I have some experience of life, and know how one thing leads to another. I am afraid that your sister had better sleep at the hotel. I have my children and the memory of my dear wife to consider. I am sorry, but see that she leaves my house at once.'

'You have mentioned Mrs Wilcox.'

'I beg your pardon?'

'A rare occurrence. In reply, may I mention Mrs Bast?'

'You have not been yourself all day,' said Henry, and rose from his seat with face unmoved. Margaret rushed at him and seized both his hands. She was transfigured.

'Not any more of this!' she cried. 'You shall see the connection if it kills you, Henry! You have had a mistress—I forgave you. My sister has a lover—you drive her from the house. Do you see the connection? Stupid, hypocritical, cruel—oh, contemptible—a man who insults his wife when she's alive and cants with her memory when she's dead. A man who ruins a woman for his pleasure, and casts her off to ruin other men. And gives bad financial advice, and then says he is not responsible. These men are you. You can't recognize them, because you cannot connect. I've had enough of your unweeded kindness. I've spoilt you long enough. All your life you have been spoiled. Mrs Wilcox spoiled you. No one has ever told what you are—muddled, criminally muddled. Men like you use repentance as a blind, so don't repent. Only say to yourself, "What Helen has done, I've done."'

'The two cases are different,' Henry stammered. His real retort was not quite ready. His brain was still in a whirl, and he wanted a little longer.

'In what way different? You have betrayed Mrs Wilcox, Helen only herself. You remain in society, Helen can't. You have had only pleasure, she may die. You have the insolence to talk to me of differences, Henry?'

Oh, the uselessness of it! Henry's retort came.

'I perceive you are attempting blackmail. It is scarcely a pretty weapon for a wife to use against her husband. My rule through life has been never to pay the least attention to threats, and I can only repeat what I said before: I do not give you and your sister leave to sleep at Howards End.'

Margaret loosed his hands. He went into the house, wiping first one and then the other on his handkerchief. For a little she stood looking at the Six Hills, tombs of warriors, breasts of the spring. Then she passed out into what was now the evening.

Chapter Thirty-nine

Charles and Tibby met at Ducie Street, where the latter was staying. Their interview was short and absurd. They had nothing in common but the English language, and tried by its help to express what neither of them understood. Charles saw in Helen the family foe. He had singled her out as the most dangerous of the Schlegels, and, angry as he was, looked forward to telling his wife how right he had been. His mind was made up at once: the girl must be got out of the way before she disgraced them further. If occasion offered she might be married to a villain or, possibly, to a fool. But this was a concession to morality, it formed no part of his main scheme. Honest and hearty was Charles's dislike, and the past spread itself out very clearly before him; hatred is a skilful compositor. As if they were heads in a note-book, he ran through all the incidents of the Schlegel's campaign: the attempt to compromise his brother, his mother's legacy, his father's marriage, the introduction of the furniture, the unpacking of the same. He had not yet heard of the request to sleep at Howards End; that was to be their master-stroke and the opportunity for his. But he already felt that Howards End was the objective, and, though he disliked the house, was determined to defend it.

Tibby, on the other hand, had no opinions. He stood above the conventions: his sister had a right to do what she thought right. It is not difficult to stand above the conventions when we leave no hostages among them; men can always be more unconventional than women, and a bachelor of independent means need encounter no difficulties at all. Unlike Charles, Tibby had money enough; his ancestors had earned it for him, and if he shocked the people in one set of lodgings he had only to move into another. His was the Leisure without sympathy—an attitude as fatal as the strenuous: a little cold culture may be raised on it, but no art. His sisters had seen the family danger, and had never forgotten to discount the gold islets that raised them from the sea. Tibby gave all the praise to himself, and so despised the struggling and the submerged.

Hence the absurdity of the interview; the gulf between them was economic as well as spiritual. But several facts passed: Charles pressed for them with an impertinence that the undergraduate could not withstand. On what date had Helen gone abroad? To whom? (Charles was anxious to fasten the scandal on Germany.) Then, changing his tactics, he said roughly: 'I suppose you realize that you are your sister's protector?'

'In what sense?'

'If a man played about with my sister, I'd send a bullet through him, but perhaps you don't mind.'

'I mind very much,' protested Tibby.

Who d'ye suspect, then? Speak out, man. One always suspects someone.'

'No one. I don't think so.' Involuntarily he blushed. He had remembered the scene in his Oxford rooms.

'You are hiding something,' said Charles. As interviews go, he got the best of this one. 'When you saw her last, did she mention anyone's name? Yes or no!' he thundered, so that Tibby started.

'In my rooms she mentioned some friends, called the Basts—'

'Who are the Basts?'

'People—friends of hers at Evie's wedding.'

'I don't remember. But, by great Scott! I do. My aunt told me about some tag-rag. Was she full of them when you saw her? Is there a man? Did she speak of the man? Or—look here—have you had any dealings with him?'

Tibby was silent. Without intending it, he had betrayed his sister's confidence; he was not enough interested in human life to see where things will lead to. He had a strong regard for honesty, and his word, once given, had always been kept up to now. He was deeply vexed, not only for the harm he had done Helen, but for the flaw he had discovered in his own equipment.

'I see—you are in his confidence. They met at your rooms. Oh, what a family, what a family! God help the poor pater—'

And Tibby found himself alone.

Chapter Forty

Leonard—he could figure at length in a newspaper report, but that evening he did not count for much. The foot of the tree was in shadow, since the moon was still hidden behind the house. But above, to right, to left, down the long meadow the moonlight was streaming. Leonard seemed not a man, but a cause.

Perhaps it was Helen's way of falling in love—a curious way to Margaret, whose agony and whose contempt of Henry were yet imprinted with his image. Helen forgot people. They were husks that had enclosed her emotion. She could pity, or sacrifice herself, or have instincts, but had she ever loved in the noblest way, where man and woman, having lost themselves in sex, desire to lose sex itself in comradeship?

Margaret wondered, but said no word of blame. This was Helen's evening. Troubles enough lay ahead of her—the loss of friends and of social advantages, the agony, the supreme agony, of motherhood, which is even yet not a matter of common knowledge. For the present let the moon shine brightly and the breezes of the spring blow gently, dying away from the gale of the day, and let the earth, who brings increase, bring peace. Not even to herself dare she blame Helen. She could not assess her trespass by any moral code; it was everything or nothing. Morality can tell us that murder is worse then stealing, and group most sins in an order all must approve, but it cannot group Helen. The surer its pronouncements on this point, the surer may we be that morality is not speaking. Christ was evasive when they questioned Him. It is those that cannot connect who hasten to cast the first stone.

This was Helen's evening—won at what cost, and not to be marred by the sorrows of others. Of her own tragedy Margaret never uttered a word.

'One isolates,' said Helen slowly. 'I isolated Mr Wilcox from the other forces that were pulling Leonard downhill. Consequently, I was full of pity, and almost of revenge. For weeks I had blamed Mr Wilcox only, and so, when your letters came—'

'I need never have written them,' sighed Margaret. 'They never shielded Henry. How hopeless it is to tidy away the past, even for others!'

'I did not know that it was your own idea to dismiss the Basts.'

'Looking back, that was wrong of me.'

'Looking back, darling, I know that it was right. It is right to save the man whom one loves. I am less enthusiastic about justice now. But we both thought you wrote at his dictation. It seemed the last touch of his callousness. Being very much wrought up by this time—and Mrs Bast was upstairs. I had not seen her, and had talked for a long time to Leonard—I had snubbed him for no reason, and that should have warned me I was in danger. So when the notes came I wanted us to go to you for an explanation. He said that he guessed the explanation—he knew of it, and you mustn't know. I pressed him to tell me. He said no one must know; it was something to do with his wife. Right up to the end we were Mr Bast and Miss Schlegel. I was going to tell him that he must be frank with me when I saw his eyes, and guessed that Mr Wilcox had ruined him in two ways, not one. I drew him to me. I made him tell me. I felt very lonely myself. He is not to blame. He would have gone on worshipping me. I want never to see him again, though it sounds appalling. I wanted to give him money and feel finished. Oh, Meg, the little that is known about these things!'

She laid her face against the tree.

'The little, too, that is known about growth! Both times it was loneliness, and the night, and panic afterwards. Did Leonard grow out of Paul?'

Margaret did not speak for a moment. So tired was she that her attention had actually wandered to the teeth—the teeth that had been thrust into the tree's bark to medicate it. From where she sat she could see them gleam. She had been trying to count them. 'Leonard is a better growth than madness,' she said. 'I was afraid that you would react against Paul until you went over the verge.'

'I did react until I found poor Leonard. I am steady now. I shan't ever *like* your Henry, dearest Meg, or even speak kindly about him, but all that blinding hate is over. I shall never rave against Wilcoxes any more. I understand how you married him, and you will now be very happy.'

Margaret did not reply.

'Yes,' repeated Helen, her voice growing more tender, 'I do at last understand.'

'Except Mrs Wilcox, dearest; no one understands our little movements.'

'Because in death–I agree.'

'Not quite. I feel that you and I and Henry are only fragments of that woman's mind. She knows everything. She is everything. She is the house, and the tree that leans over it. People have their own deaths as well as their own lives, and even if there is nothing beyond death, we shall differ in our nothingness. I cannot believe that knowledge such as hers will perish with knowledge such as mine. She knew about realities. She knew when people were in love, though she was not in the room. I don't doubt that she knew when Henry deceived her.'

'Good-night, Mrs Wilcox,' called a voice.

'Oh, good-night, Miss Avery.'

'Why should Miss Avery work for us?' Helen murmured.

'Why, indeed?'

Miss Avery crossed the lawn and merged into the hedge that divided it from the farm. An old gap, which Mr Wilcox had filled up, had reappeared, and her track through the dew followed the path that he had turfed over, when he improved the garden and made it possible for games.

'This is not quite our house yet,' said Helen. 'When Miss Avery called, I felt we are only a couple of tourists.'

'We shall be that everywhere, and for ever.'

'But affectionate tourists—'

'But tourists who pretend each hotel is their home.'

'I can't pretend very long,' said Helen. 'Sitting under this tree one forgets, but I know that to-morrow I shall see the moon rise out of Germany. Not all your goodness can alter the facts of the case. Unless you will come with me.'

Margaret thought for a moment. In the past year she had grown so fond of England that to leave it was a real grief. Yet what detained her? No doubt Henry would pardon her outburst, and go on blustering and muddling into a ripe old age. But what was the good? She had just as soon vanish from his mind.

'Are you serious in asking me, Helen? Should I get on with your Monica?'

'You would not, but I am serious in asking you.'

'Still, no more plans now. And no more reminiscences.'

They were silent for a little. It was Helen's evening.

The present flowed by them like a stream. The tree rustled. It had made music before they were born, and would continue after their deaths, but its song was of the moment. The moment had passed. The tree rustled again. Their senses were sharpened, and they seemed to apprehend life. Life passed. The tree rustled again.

'Sleep now,' said Margaret.

The peace of the country was entering into her. It has no commerce with memory, and little with hope. Least of all is it concerned with the hopes of the next five minutes. It is the peace of the present, which passes understanding. Its murmur came 'now,' and 'now' once more as they trod the gravel, and 'now,' as the moonlight fell upon their father's sword. They passed upstairs, kissed, and amidst the endless iterations fell asleep. The house had enshadowed the tree at first, but as the moon rose higher the two disentangled, and were clear for a few moments at midnight. Margaret awoke and looked into the garden. How incomprehensible that Leonard Bast should have won her this night of peace! Was he also part of Mrs Wilcox's mind?

Chapter Forty-one

Far different was Leonard's development. The months after Oniton, whatever minor troubles they might bring him, were all overshadowed by Remorse. When Helen looked back she could philosophize, or she could look into the future and plan for her child. But the father saw nothing beyond his own sin. Weeks afterwards, in the midst of other occupations, he would suddenly cry out, 'Brute—you brute, I couldn't have—' and be rent into two people who held dialogues. Or brown rain would descend, blotting out faces and the sky. Even Jacky noticed the change in him. Most terrible were his sufferings when he awoke from sleep. Sometimes he was happy at first, but grew conscious of a burden hanging to him and weighing down his thoughts when they would move. Or little irons scorched his body. Or a sword stabbed him. He would sit at the edge of his bed, holding his heart and moaning, 'Oh what *shall* I do, whatever *shall* I do?' Nothing brought ease. He could put distance between him and the trespass, but it grew in his soul.

Remorse is not among the eternal verities. The Greeks were right to dethrone her. Her action is too capricious, as though the Erinyes selected for punishment only certain men and certain sins. And of all means to regeneration Remorse is surely the most wasteful. It cuts away healthy tissues with the poisoned. It is a knife that probes far deeper than the evil. Leonard was driven straight through its torments and emerged pure, but enfeebled—a better man, who would never lose control of himself again, but also a smaller man, who had less to control. Nor did purity mean peace. The use of the knife can become a habit as hard to shake off as passion itself, and Leonard continued to start with a cry out of dreams.

He built up a situation that was far enough from the truth. It never occurred to him that Helen was to blame. He forgot the intensity of their talk, the charm that had been lent him by sincerity, the magic of Oniton under darkness and of the whispering river. Helen loved the absolute. Leonard had been ruined absolutely, and had appeared to her as a man apart, isolated from the world. A real man, who cared for adventure and beauty, who desired to live decently and pay his way, who could have travelled more gloriously through life than the Juggernaut car that was crushing him. Memories of Evie's wedding had warped her, the starched servants, the

yards of uneaten food, the rustle of overdressed women, motor-cars oozing
grease on the gravel rubbish on a pretentious band. She had tasted the lees of
this on her arrival: in the darkness, after failure, they intoxicated her. She
and the victim seemed alone in a world of unreality, and she loved him
absolutely, perhaps for half an hour.

In the morning she was gone. The note that she left, tender and hysterical
in tone, and intended to be most kind, hurt her lover terribly. It was as if
some work of art had been broken by him, some picture in the National
Gallery slashed out of its frame. When he recalled her talents and her social
position, he felt that the first passer-by had a right to shoot him down. He
was afraid of the waitress and the porters at the railway-station. He was
afraid at first of his wife, though later he was to regard her with a strange new
tenderness, and to think, 'There is nothing to choose between us, after all.'

The expedition to Shropshire crippled the Basts permanently. Helen in
her flight forgot to settle the hotel bill, and took their return tickets away
with her; they had to pawn Jacky's bangles to get home, and the smash came
a few days afterwards. It is true that Helen offered him five thousand
pounds, but such a sum meant nothing to him. He could not see that the girl
was desperately righting herself, and trying to save something out of the
disaster, if it was only five thousand pounds. But he had to live somehow. He
turned to his family, and degraded himself to a professional beggar. There
was nothing else for him to do.

'A letter from Leonard,' thought Blanche, his sister; 'and after all this
time.' She hid it, so that her husband should not see, and when he had gone
to his work read it with some emotion, and sent the prodigal a little money
out of her dress allowance.

'A letter from Leonard!' said the other sister, Laura, a few days later. She
showed it to her husband. He wrote a cruel, insolent reply, but sent more
money than Blanche, so Leonard soon wrote to him again.

And during the winter the system was developed. Leonard realized that
they need never starve, because it would be too painful for his relatives.
Society is based on the family, and the clever wastrel can exploit this
indefinitely. Without a generous thought on either side, pounds and pounds
passed. The donors disliked Leonard, and he grew to hate them intensely.
When Laura censured his immoral marriage, he thought bitterly, 'She
minds that! What would she say if she knew the truth?' When Blanche's
husband offered him work he found some pretext for avoiding it. He had
wanted work keenly at Oniton, but too much anxiety had shattered him, he
was joining the unemployable. When his brother, the lay-reader, did not
reply to a letter, he wrote again, saying that he and Jacky would come down
to his village on foot. He did not intend this as blackmail. Still, the brother
sent a postal order, and it became part of the system. And so passed his
winter and his spring.

In the horror there are two bright spots. He never confused the past. He
remained alive, and blessed are those who live, if it is only to a sense of
sinfulness. The anodyne of muddledom, by which most men blur and blend
their mistakes, never passed Leonard's lips—

And if I drink oblivion of a day,
So shorten I the stature of my soul.

It is a hard saying, and a hard man wrote it, but it lies at the foot of all character.

And the other bright spot was his tenderness for Jacky. He pitied her with nobility now—not the contemptuous pity of a man who sticks to a woman through thick and thin. He tried to be less irritable. He wondered what her hungry eyes desired—nothing that she could express, or that he or any man could give her. Would she ever receive the justice that is mercy—the justice for by-products that the world is too busy to bestow? She was fond of flowers, generous with money, and not revengeful. If she had borne him a child he might have cared for her. Unmarried, Leonard would never have begged; he would have flickered out and died. But the whole of life is mixed. He had to provide for Jacky, and went down dirty paths that she might have a few feathers and the dishes of food that suited her.

One day he caught sight of Margaret and her brother. He was in St Paul's. He had entered the cathedral partly to avoid the rain and partly to see a picture that had educated him in former years. But the light was bad, the picture ill placed, and Time and Judgment were inside him now. Death alone still charmed him, with her lap of poppies, on which all men shall sleep. He took one glance, and turned aimlessly away towards a chair. Then down the nave he saw Miss Schlegel and her brother. They stood in the fairway of passengers, and their faces were extremely grave. He was perfectly certain that they were in trouble about their sister.

Once outside—and he fled immediately—he wished that he had spoken to them. What was his life? What were a few angry words, or even imprisonment? He had done wrong—that was the true terror. Whatever they might know, he would tell them everything he knew. He re-entered St Paul's. But they had moved in his absence, and had gone to lay their difficulties before Mr Wilcox and Charles.

The sight of Margaret turned remorse into new channels. He desired to confess, and though the desire is proof of a weakened nature, which is about to lose the essence of human intercourse, it did not take an ignoble form. He did not suppose that confession would bring him happiness. It was rather that he yearned to get clear of the tangle. So does the suicide yearn. The impulses are akin, and the crime of suicide lies rather in its disregard for the feelings of those whom we leave behind. Confession need harm no one—it can satisfy that test—and though it was un-English, and ignored by our Anglican cathedral, Leonard had a right to decide upon it.

Moreover, he trusted Margaret. He wanted her hardness now. That cold, intellectual nature of hers would be just, if unkind. He would do whatever she told him, even if he had to see Helen. That was the supreme punishment she would exact. And perhaps she would tell him how Helen was. That was the supreme reward.

He knew nothing about Margaret, not even whether she was married to Mr Wilcox, and tracking her out took several days. That evening he toiled through the wet to Wickham Place, where the new flats were now appearing. Was he also the cause of their move? Were they expelled from society on his account? Thence to a public library, but could find no satisfactory Schlegel in the directory. On the morrow he searched again. He hung about outside Mr Wilcox's office at lunch time, and, as the clerks came out said: 'Excuse me, sir, but is your boss married?' Most of them stared, some said, 'What's that to you?' but one, who had not yet acquired reticence, told him what he wished. Leonard could not learn the private address. That necessitated more trouble with directories and tubes. Ducie Street was not discovered till the Monday, the day that Margaret and her husband went down on their hunting expedition to Howards End.

He called at about four o'clock. The weather had changed, and the sun shone gaily on the ornamental steps—black and white marble in triangles. Leonard lowered his eyes to them after ringing the bell. He felt in curious health: doors seemed to be opening and shutting inside his body, and he had been obliged to sleep sitting up in bed, with his back propped against the wall. When the parlourmaid came he could not see her face; the brown rain had descended suddenly.

'Does Mrs Wilcox live here?' he asked.

'She's out,' was the answer.

'When will she be back?'

'I'll ask,' said the parlourmaid.

Margaret had given instructions that no one who mentioned her name should ever be rebuffed. Putting the door on the chain—for Leonard's appearance demanded this—she went through to the smoking-room, which was occupied by Tibby. Tibby was asleep. He had had a good lunch. Charles Wilcox had not yet rung him up for the distracting interview. He said drowsily: 'I don't know. Hilton. Howards End. Who is it?'

'I'll ask, sir.'

'No, don't bother.'

'They have taken the car to Howards End,' said the parlourmaid to Leonard.

He thanked her, and asked whereabouts that place was.

'You appear to want to know a good deal,' she remarked. But Margaret had forbidden her to be mysterious. She told him against her better judgment that Howards End was in Hertfordshire.

'Is it a village, please?'

'Village! It's Mr Wilcox's private house—at least, it's one of them. Mrs Wilcox keeps her furniture there. Hilton is the village.'

'Yes. And when will they be back?'

'Mr Schlegel doesn't know. We can't know everything, can we?' She shut him out, and went to attend to the telephone, which was ringing furiously.

He loitered away another night of agony. Confession grew more difficult. As soon as possible he went to bed. He watched a patch of moonlight cross the floor of their lodging, and, as sometimes happens when the mind is overtaxed, he fell asleep for the rest of the room, but kept awake for the patch of moonlight. Horrible! Then began one of those disintegrating dialogues.

Part of him said: 'Why horrible? It's ordinary light from the moon.' 'But it moves.' 'So does the moon.' 'But it is a clenched fist.' 'Why not?' 'But it is going to touch me.' 'Let it.' And, seeming to gather motion, the patch ran up his blanket. Presently a blue snake appeared; then another, parallel to it. 'Is there life in the moon?' 'Of course.' 'But I thought it was uninhabited.' 'Not by Time, Death, Judgment, and the smaller snakes.' 'Smaller snakes!' said Leonard indignantly and aloud. 'What a notion!' By a rending effort of the will he woke the rest of the room up. Jacky, the bed, their food, their clothes on the chair, gradually entered his consciousness, and the horror vanished outwards, like a ring that is spreading through water.

'I say, Jacky, I'm going out for a bit.'

She was breathing regularly. The patch of light fell clear of the striped blanket, and began to cover the shawl that lay over her feet. Why had he been afraid? He went to the window, and saw that the moon was descending through a clear sky. He saw her volcanoes, and the bright expanses that a gracious error has named seas. They paled, for the sun, who had lit them up, was coming to light the earth. Sea of Serenity, Sea of Tranquillity, Ocean of the Lunar Storms, merged into one lucent drop, itself to slip into the sempiternal dawn. And he had been afraid of the moon!

He dressed among the contending lights, and went through his money. It was running low again, but enough for a return ticket to Hilton. As it clinked Jacky opened her eyes.

'Hullo, Len! What ho, Len!'

'What ho, Jacky! see you again later.'

She turned over and slept.

The house was unlocked, their landlord being a salesman at Covent Garden. Leonard passed out and made his way down to the station. The train, though it did not start for an hour, was already drawn up at the end of the platform, and he lay down in it and slept. With the first jolt he was in daylight; they had left the gateways of King's Cross, and were under blue sky. Tunnels followed, and after each the sky grew bluer, and from the embankment at Finsbury Park he had his first sight of the sun. It rolled along behind the eastern smokes—a wheel, whose fellow was the descending moon—and as yet it seemed the servant of the blue sky, not its lord. He dozed again. Over Tewin Water it was day. To the left fell the shadow of the embankment and its arches; to the right Leonard saw up into the Tewin Woods and towards the church, with its wild legend of immortality. Six forest trees—that is a fact—grow out of one of the graves in Tewin churchyard. The grave's occupant—that is the legend—is an artist, who declared that if God existed, six forest trees would grow out of her grave. These things in Hertfordshire; and farther afield lay the house of a hermit—Mrs Wilcox had known him—who barred himself up, and wrote prophecies, and gave all he had to the poor. While, powdered in between, were the villas of business men, who saw life more steadily, though with the steadiness of the half-closed eye. Over all the sun was streaming, to all the birds were singing, to all the primroses were yellow, and the speedwell blue, and the country, however they interpreted her, was uttering her cry of 'now'.

She did not free Leonard yet, and the knife plunged deeper into his heart as the train drew up at Hilton. But remorse had become beautiful.

Hilton was asleep, or at the earliest, breakfasting. Leonard noticed the contrast when he stepped out of it into the country. Here men had been up since dawn. Their hours were ruled, not by a London office, but by the movements of the crops and the sun. That they were men of the finest type only the sentimentalist can declare. But they kept to the life of daylight. They are England's hope. Clumsily they carry forward the torch of the sun, until such time as the nation sees fit to take it up. Half clodhopper, half board-school prig, they can still throw back to a nobler stock, and breed yeomen.

At the chalk pit a motor passed him. In it was another type, whom Nature favours—the Imperial. Healthy, ever in motion, it hopes to inherit the earth. It breeds as quickly as the yeoman, and as soundly; strong in the temptation to acclaim it as a super-yeoman, who carries his country's virtue overseas. But the Imperialist is not what he thinks or seems. He is a destroyer. He prepares the way for cosmopolitanism, and though his ambitions may be fulfilled, the earth that he inherits will be grey.

To Leonard, intent on his private sin, there came the conviction of innate goodness elsewhere. It was not the optimism which he had been taught at school. Again and again must the drums tap, and the goblins stalk over the universe before joy can be purged of the superficial. It was rather paradoxical, and arose from his sorrow. Death destroys a man, but the idea of death saves him—that is the best account of it that has yet been given. Squalor and tragedy can beckon to all that is great in us, and strengthen the wings of love. They can beckon; it is not certain that they will, for they are not love's servants. But they can beckon, and the knowledge of this incredible truth comforted him.

As he approached the house all thought stopped. Contradictory notions stood side by side in his mind. He was terrified but happy, ashamed, but had done no sin. He knew the confession: 'Mrs Wilcox, I have done wrong,' but sunrise had robbed its meaning, and he felt rather on a supreme adventure.

He entered a garden, steadied himself against a motor-car that he found in it, found a door open and entered a house. Yes, it would be very easy. From a room to the left he heard voices, Margaret's amongst them. His own name was called aloud, and a man whom he had never seen said, 'Oh, is he there? I am not surprised. I now thrash him within an inch of his life.'

'Mrs Wilcox,' said Leonard, 'I have done wrong.'

The man took him by the collar and cried, 'Bring me a stick.' Women were screaming. A stick, very bright, descended. It hurt him, not where it descended, but in the heart. Books fell over him in a shower. Nothing had sense.

'Get some water,' commanded Charles, who had all through kept very calm. 'He's shamming. Of course I only used the blade. Here, carry him out into the air.'

Thinking that he understood these things, Margaret obeyed him. They laid Leonard, who was dead, on the gravel; Helen poured water over him.

'That's enough,' said Charles.

'Yes, murder's enough,' said Miss Avery, coming out of the house with the sword.

Chapter Forty-two

When Charles left Ducie Street he had caught the first train home, but had no inkling of the newest development until late at night. Then his father, who had dined alone, sent for him, and in very grave tones inquired for Margaret.

'I don't know where she is, pater,' said Charles. 'Dolly kept back dinner nearly an hour for her.'

'Tell me when she comes in.'

Another hour passed. The servants went to bed, and Charles visited his father again, to receive further instructions. Mrs Wilcox had still not returned.

'I'll sit up for her as late as you like, but she can hardly be coming. Isn't she stopping with her sister at the hotel?'

'Perhaps,' said Mr Wilcox thoughtfully—'perhaps.'

'Can I do anything for you sir?'

'Not to-night, my boy.'

Mr Wilcox liked being called sir. He raised his eyes and gave his son more open a look of tenderness than he usually ventured. He saw Charles as little boy and strong man in one. Though his wife had proved unstable his children were left to him.

After midnight he tapped on Charles's door. 'I can't sleep,' he said. 'I had better have a talk with you and get it over.'

He complained of the heat. Charles took him out into the garden, and they paced up and down in their dressing-gowns. Charles became very quiet as the story unrolled; he had known all along that Margaret was as bad as her sister.

'She will feel differently in the morning,' said Mr Wilcox, who had of course said nothing about Mrs Bast. 'But I cannot let this kind of thing continue without comment. I am morally certain that she is with her sister at Howards End. The house is mine—and, Charles, it will be yours—and when I say that no one is to live there, I mean that no one is to live there.' I won't have it. He looked angrily at the moon. 'To my mind this question is connected with something far greater, the rights of property itself.'

'Undoubtedly,' said Charles.

Mr Wilcox lined his arm in his son's, but somehow liked him less as he told him more. 'I don't want you to conclude that my wife and I had anything of the nature of a quarrel. She was only overwrought, as who would not be? I shall do what I can for Helen, but on the understanding that they clear out of the house at once. Do you see? That is a sine qua non.'

'Then at eight to-morrow I may go up in the car?'

'Eight or earlier. Say that you are acting as my representative, and, of course, use no violence, Charles.'

On the morrow, as Charles returned, leaving Leonard dead upon the gravel, it did not seem to him that he had used violence. Death was due to heart disease. His stepmother herself had said so, and even Miss Avery had acknowledged that he only used the flat of the sword. On his way through the village he informed the police, who thanked him, and said there must be an inquest. He found his father in the garden shading his eyes from the sun.

'It has been pretty horrible,' said Charles gravely. 'They were there, and they had the man up there with them too.'

'What—what man?'

'I told you last night. His name was Bast.'

'My God! is it possible?' said Mr Wilcox. 'In your mother's house! Charles, in your mother's house?'

'I know, pater. That was what I felt. As a matter of fact, there is no need to trouble about the man. He was in the last stages of heart disease, and just before I could show him what I thought of him he went off. The police are seeing about it at this moment.'

Mr Wilcox listened attentively.

'I got up there—oh, it couldn't have been more than half-past seven. The Avery woman was lighting a fire for them. They were still upstairs. I waited in the drawing-room. We were all moderately civil and collected, though I had my suspicions. I gave them your message, and Mrs Wilcox said, "Oh yes, I see; yes," in that way of hers.'

'Nothing else?'

'I promised to tell you, "with her love," that she was going to Germany with her sister this evening. That was all we had time for.'

Mr Wilcox seemed relieved.

'Because by then I suppose the man got tired of hiding, for suddenly Mrs Wilcox screamed out his name. I recognized it, and I went for him in the hall. Was I right, pater? I thought things were going a little too far.'

'Right, my dear boy? I don't know. But you would have been no son of mine if you hadn't. Then did he just—just—crumple up as you said?' He shrunk from the simple word.

'He caught hold of the bookcase, which came down over him. So I merely put the sword down and carried him into the garden. We all thought he was shamming. However, he's dead right enough. Awful business!'

'Sword?' cried his father, with anxiety in his voice. 'What sword? Whose sword?'

'A sword of theirs.'

'What were you doing with it?'

'Well, didn't you see, pater, I had to snatch up the first thing handy. I hadn't a riding-whip or stick. I caught him once or twice over the shoulders with the flat of their old German sword.'

'Then what?'

'He pulled over the bookcase, as I said, and fell,' said Charles, with a sigh. It was no fun doing errands for his father, who was never quite satisfied.

'But the real cause was heart disease? Of that you're sure?'

'That or a fit. However, we shall hear more than enough at the inquest on such unsavoury topics.'

They went into breakfast. Charles had a racking headache, consequent on motoring before food. He was also anxious about the future, reflecting that the police must detain Helen and Margaret for the inquest and ferret the whole thing out. He saw himself obliged to leave Hilton. One could not afford to live near the scene of a scandal—it was not fair on one's wife. His comfort was that the pater's eyes were opened at last. There would be a horrible smash up, and probably a separation from Margaret; then they would all start again, more as they had been in his mother's time.

'I think I'll go round to the police-station,' said his father when breakfast was over.

'What for?' cried Dolly, who had still not been 'told.'

'Very well, sir. Which car will you have?'

'I think I'll walk.'

'It's a good half-mile,' said Charles, stepping into the garden. 'The sun's very hot for April. Shan't I take you up, and then, perhaps, a little spin round by Tewin?'

'You go on as if I didn't know my own mind,' said Mr Wilcox fretfully. Charles hardened his mouth. 'You young fellows' one idea is to get into a motor. I tell you, I want to walk: I'm very fond of walking.'

'Oh, all right; I'm about the house if you want me for anything. I thought of not going up to the office to-day, if that is your wish.'

'It is, indeed, my boy,' said Mr Wilcox, and laid a hand on his sleeve.

Charles did not like it; he was uneasy about his father, who did not seem himself this morning. There was a petulant touch about him—more like a woman. Could it be that he was growing old? The Wilcoxes were not lacking in affection; they had it royally, but they did not know how to use it. It was the talent in the napkin, and, for a warm-hearted man, Charles had conveyed very little joy. As he watched his father shuffling up the road, he had a vague regret—a wish that something had been different somewhere—a wish (though he did not express it thus) that he had been taught to say 'I' in his youth. He meant to make up for Margaret's defection, but knew that his father had been very happy with her until yesterday. How had she done it? By some dishonest trick, no doubt—but how?

Mr Wilcox reappeared at eleven, looking very tired. There was to be an inquest on Leonard's body to-morrow, and the police required his son to attend.

'I expected that,' said Charles. 'I shall naturally be the most important witness there.'

Chapter Forty-three

Out of the turmoil and horror that had begun with Aunt Juley's illness and was not even to end with Leonard's death, it seemed impossible to Margaret that healthy life should re-emerge. Events succeeded in a logical, yet senseless, train. People lost their humanity, and took values as arbitrary as those in a pack of playing-cards. It was natural that Henry should do this and cause Helen to do that, and then think her wrong for doing it; natural that she herself should think him wrong; natural that Leonard should want to know how Helen was, and come, and Charles be angry with him for coming—natural, but unreal. In this jangle of causes and effects what had become of their true selves? Here Leonard lay dead in the garden, from natural causes; yet life was a deep, deep river, death a blue sky, life was a house, death a wisp of hay, a flower, a tower, life and death were anything and everything, except this ordered insanity, where the king takes the queen, and the ace the king. Ah, no; there was beauty and adventure behind, such as the man at her feet had yearned for; there was hope this side of the grave; there were truer relationships beyond the limits that fetter us now. As a prisoner looks up and sees stars beckoning, so she, from the turmoil and horror of those days, caught glimpses of the diviner wheels.

And Helen, dumb with fright, but trying to keep calm for the child's sake, and Miss Avery, calm, but murmuring tenderly, 'No one ever told the lad he'll have a child'—they also reminded her that horror is not the end. To what ultimate harmony we tend she did not know, but there seemed great chance that a child would be born into the world, to take the great chances of beauty and adventure that the world offers. She moved through the sunlit garden, gathering narcissi, crimson-eyed and white. There was nothing else to be done; the time for telegrams and anger was over, and it seemed wisest that the hands of Leonard should be folded on his breast and be filled with flowers. Here was the father; leave it at that. Let Squalor be turned into Tragedy, whose eyes are the stars, and whose hands hold the sunset and the dawn.

And even the influx of officials, even the return of the doctor, vulgar and acute, could not shake her belief in the eternity of beauty. After long centuries among the bones and muscles it might be advancing to knowledge of the nerves, but this would never give understanding. One could open the heart to Mr Mansbridge and his sort without discovering its secrets to them, for they wanted everything down in black and white, and black and white was exactly what they were left with.

They questioned her closely about Charles. She never suspected why. Death had come, and the doctor agreed that it was due to heart disease. They asked to see her father's sword. She explained that Charles's anger was natural, but mistaken. Miserable questions about Leonard followed, all of which she answered unfalteringly. Then back to Charles again. 'No doubt Mr Wilcox may have induced death,' she said, 'but if it wasn't one thing it would have been another, as you yourselves know.' At last they thanked her, and took the sword and the body down to Hilton. She began to pick up the books from the floor.

Helen had gone to the farm. It was the best place for her, since she had to wait for the inquest. Though, as if things were not hard enough, Madge and her husband had raised trouble; they did not see why they should receive the offscourings of Howards End. And, of course, they were right. The whole world was going to be right, and amply avenge any brave talk against the conventions. 'Nothing matters,' the Schlegels had said in the past, 'except one's self-respect and that of one's friends.' When the time came, other things mattered terribly. However, Madge had yielded, and Helen was assured of peace for one day and night, and to-morrow she would return to Germany.

As for herself, she determined to go too. No message came from Henry; perhaps he expected her to apologize. Now that she had time to think over her own tragedy, she was unrepentant. She neither forgave him for his behaviour nor wished to forgive him. Her speech to him seemed perfect. She would not have altered a word. It had to be uttered once in a life, to adjust the lopsidedness of the world. It was spoken not only to her husband, but to thousands of men like him—a protest against the inner darkness in high places that comes with a commercial age. Though he would build up his life without hers, she could not apologize. He had refused to connect, on the clearest issue that can be laid before a man, and their love must take the consequences.

No, there was nothing more to be done. They had tried not to go over the precipice, but perhaps the fall was inevitable. And it comforted her to think that the future was certainly inevitable: cause and effect would go jangling forward to some goal doubtless, but to none that she could imagine. At such moments the soul retires within, to float upon the bosom of a deeper stream, and has communion with the dead, and sees the world's glory not diminished, but different in kind to what she has supposed. She alters her focus until trivial things are blurred. Margaret had been tending this way all the winter. Leonard's death brought her to the goal. Alas! that Henry should fade away as reality emerged, and only her love for him should remain clear, stamped with his image like the cameos we rescue out of dreams.

With unfaltering eye she traced his future. He would soon present a healthy mind to the world again, and what did he or the world care if he was rotten at the core? He would grow into a rich, jolly old man, at times a little sentimental about women, but emptying his glass with anyone. Tenacious of power, he would keep Charles and the rest dependent, and retire from business reluctantly and at an advanced age. He would settle down—though she could not realize this. In her eyes Henry was always moving and causing others to move, until the ends of the earth met. But in time he must get too tired to move, and settle down. What next? The inevitable word. The release of the soul to its appropriate Heaven.

Would they meet in it? Margaret believed in immortality for herself. An eternal future had always seemed natural to her. And Henry believed in it for himself. Yet, would they meet again? Are there not rather endless levels beyond the grave, as the theory that he had censured teaches? And his level, whether higher or lower, could it possibly be the same as hers?

Thus gravely meditating, she was summoned by him. He sent up Crane in the motor. Other servants passed like water, but the chauffeur remained, though impertinent and disloyal. Margaret disliked Crane, and he knew it.

'Is it the keys that Mr Wilcox wants?' she asked.

'He didn't say, madam.'

'You haven't any note for me?'

'He didn't say, madam.'

After a moment's thought she locked up Howards End. It was pitiable to see in it the stirrings of warmth that would be quenched for ever. She raked out the fire that was blazing in the kitchen, and spread the coals in the gravelled yard. She closed the windows and drew the curtains. Henry would probably sell the place now.

She was determined not to spare him, for nothing new had happened as far as they were concerned. Her mood might never have altered from yesterday evening. He was standing a little outside Charles's gate, and motioned the car to stop. When his wife got out he said hoarsely: 'I prefer to discuss things with you outside.'

'It will be more appropriate in the road, I am afraid,' said Margaret. 'Did you get my message?'

'What about?'

'I am going to Germany with my sister. I must tell you now that I shall make it my permanent home. Our talk last night was more important than you have realized. I am unable to forgive you and am leaving you.'

'I am extremely tired,' said Henry, in injured tones. 'I have been walking about all the morning, and wish to sit down.'

'Certainly, if you will consent to sit on the grass.'

The Great North Road should have been bordered all its length with glebe. Henry's kind had filched most of it. She moved to the scrap opposite, wherein were the Six Hills. They sat down on the farther side, so that they could not be seen by Charles or Dolly.

'Here are your keys,' said Margaret. She tossed them towards him. They fell on the sunlit slope of grass, and he did not pick them up.

'I have something to tell you,' he said gently.

She knew this superficial gentleness, this confession of hastiness, that was only intended to enhance her admiration of the male.

'I don't want to hear it,' she replied. 'My sister is going to be ill. My life is going to be with her now. We must manage to build up something, she and I and her child.'

'Where are you going?'

'Munich. We start after the inquest, if she is not too ill.'

'After the inquest?'

'Yes.'

'Have you realized what the verdict at the inquest will be?'

'Yes, heart disease.'

'No, my dear; manslaughter.'

Margaret drove her fingers through the grass. The hill beneath her moved as if it was alive.

'Manslaughter,' repeated Mr Wilcox. 'Charles may go to prison. I dare not tell him. I don't know what to do—what to do. I'm broken—I'm ended.'

No sudden warmth arose in her. She did not see that to break him was her only hope. She did not enfold the sufferer in her arms. But all through that day and the next a new life began to move. The verdict was brought in. Charles was committed for trial. It was against all reason that he should be punished, but the law, being made in his image, sentenced him to three years' imprisonment. Then Henry's fortress gave way. He could bear no one but his wife, he shambled up to Margaret afterwards and asked her to do what she could with him. She did what seemed easiest—she took him down to recruit at Howards End.

Chapter Forty-four

Tom's father was cutting the big meadow. He passed again and again amid whirring blades and sweet odours of grass, encompassing with narrowing circles the sacred centre of the field. Tom was negotiating with Helen.

'I haven't any idea,' she replied. 'Do you suppose baby may, Meg?'

Margaret put down her work and regarded them absently. 'What was that?' she asked.

'Tom wants to know whether baby is old enough to play with hay?'

'I haven't the least notion,' answered Margaret, and took up her work again.

'Now, Tom, baby is not to stand; he is not to lie on his face; he is not to lie so that his head wags; he is not to be teased or tickled; and he is not to be cut into two or more pieces by the cutter. Will you be as careful as all that?'

Tom held out his arms.

'That child is a wonderful nursemaid,' remarked Margaret.

'He is fond of baby. That's why he does it!' was Helen's answer. 'They're going to be lifelong friends.'

'Starting at the ages of six and one?'

'Of course. It will be a great thing for Tom.'

'It may be a greater thing for baby.'

Fourteen months had passed, but Margaret still stopped at Howards End.

No better plan had occurred to her. The meadow was being recut, the great red poppies were reopening in the garden. July would follow with the little red poppies among the wheat, August with the cutting of the wheat. These little events would become part of her year after year. Every summer she would fear lest the well should give out, every winter lest the pipes should freeze; every westerly gale might blow the wych-elm down and bring the end of all things, and so she could not read or talk during a westerly gale. The air was tranquil now. She and her sister were sitting on the remains of Evie's rockery, where the lawn merged into the field.

'What a time they all are!' said Helen. 'What can they be doing inside?' Margaret, who was growing less talkative, made no answer. The noise of the cutter came intermittently, like the breaking of waves. Close by them a man was preparing to scythe out one of the dell-holes.

'I wish Henry was out to enjoy this,' said Helen. 'This lovely weather and to be shut up in the house! It's very hard.'

'It has to be,' said Margaret. 'The hay-fever is his chief objection against living here, but he thinks it worth while.'

'Meg, is or isn't he ill? I can't make out.'

'Not ill. Eternally tired. He has worked very hard all his life, and noticed nothing. Those are the people who collapse when they do notice a thing.'

'I suppose he worries dreadfully about his part of the tangle.'

'Dreadfully. That is why I wish Dolly had not come, too, to-day. Still, he wanted them all to come. It has to be.'

'Why does he want them?'

Margaret did not answer.

'Meg, may I tell you something? I like Henry.'

'You'd be odd if you didn't,' said Margaret.

'I usen't to.'

'Usen't!' She lowered her eyes a moment to the black abyss of the past. They had crossed it, always excepting Leonard and Charles. They were building up a new life, obscure, yet gilded with tranquillity. Leonard was dead; Charles had two years more in prison. One usen't always to see clearly before that time. It was different now.

'I like Henry because he does worry.'

'And he likes you because you don't.'

Helen sighed. She seemed humiliated, and buried her face in her hands. After a time she said: 'About love,' a transition less abrupt than it appeared.

Margaret never stopped working.

'I mean a woman's love for a man. I supposed I should hang my life on to that once, and was driven up and down and about as if something was worrying through me. But everything is peaceful now; I seem cured. That Herr Förstmeister, whom Frieda keeps writing about, must be a noble character, but he doesn't see that I shall never marry him or anyone. It isn't shame or mistrust of myself. I simply couldn't. I'm ended. I used to be so dreamy about a man's love as a girl, and think that for good or evil love must be the great thing. But it hasn't been; it has been itself a dream. Do you agree?'

'I do not agree. I do not.'

'I ought to remember Leonard as my lover,' said Helen, stepping down into the field. 'I tempted him, and killed him, and it is surely the least I can do. I would like to throw out all my heart to Leonard on such an afternoon as this. But I cannot. It is no good pretending. I am forgetting him.' Her eyes filled with tears. 'How nothing seems to match–how, my darling, my precious—' She broke off. 'Tommy!'

'Yes, please?'

'Baby's not to try and stand–There's something wanting in me. I see you loving Henry, and understanding him better daily, and I know that death wouldn't part you in the least. But I— Is it some awful appalling, criminal defect?'

Margaret silenced her. She said: 'It is only that people are far more different than is pretended. All over the world men and women are worrying because they cannot develop as they are supposed to develop. Here and there they have the matter out, and it comforts them. Don't fret yourself, Helen. Develop what you have; love your child. I do not love children. I am thankful to have none. I can play with their beauty and charm, but that is all–nothing real, not one scrap of what there ought to be. And others–others go farther still, and move outside humanity altogether. A place, as well as a person, may catch the glow. Don't you see that all this leads to comfort in the end? It is part of the battle against sameness. Differences–eternal differences, planted by God in a single family, so that there may always be colour; sorrow perhaps, but colour in the daily grey. Then I can't have you worrying about Leonard. Don't drag in the personal when it will not come. Forget him.'

'Yes, yes, but what has Leonard got out of life?'

'Perhaps an adventure.'

'Is that enough?'

'Not for us. But for him.'

Helen took up a bunch of grass. She looked at the sorrel, and the red and white and yellow clover, and the quaker grass, and the daisies, and the bents that composed it. She raised it to her face.

'Is it sweetening yet?' asked Margaret.

'No, only withered.'

'It will sweeten to-morrow.'

Helen smiled. 'Oh, Meg, you are a person,' she said. 'Think of the racket and torture this time last year. But now I couldn't stop unhappy if I tried. What a change–and all through you!'

'Oh, we merely settled down. You and Henry learnt to understand one another and to forgive, all through the autumn and the winter.'

'Yes, but who settled us down?'

Margaret did not reply. The scything had begun, and she took off her pince-nez to watch it.

'You!' cried Helen. 'You did it all, sweetest, though you're too stupid to see. Living here was your plan–I wanted you; he wanted you; and everyone said it was impossible, but you knew. Just think of our lives without you,

Meg—I and baby with Monica, revolting by theory, he handed about from Dolly to Evie. But you picked up the pieces, and made us a home. Can't it strike you—even for a moment—that your life has been heroic? Can't you remember the two months after Charles's arrest, when you began to act, and did all?'

'You were both ill at the time,' said Margaret. 'I did the obvious things. I had two invalids to nurse. Here was a house, ready furnished and empty. It was obvious. I didn't know myself it would turn into a permanent home. No doubt I have done a little towards straightening the tangle, but things that I can't phrase have helped me.'

'I hope it will be permanent,' said Helen, drifting away to other thoughts.

'I think so. There are moments when I feel Howards End peculiarly our own.'

'All the same, London's creeping.'

She pointed over the meadow—over eight or nine meadows, but at the end of them was a red dust.

'You see that in Surrey and even Hampshire now,' she continued. 'I can see it from the Purbeck Downs. And London is only part of something else, I'm afraid. Life's going to be melted down, all over the world.'

Margaret knew that her sister spoke truly. Howards End, Oniton, the Purbeck Downs, the Oderberge, were all survivals, and the melting-pot was being prepared for them. Logically, they had no right to be alive. One's hope was in the weakness of logic. Were they possibly the earth beating time?

'Because a thing is going strong now, it need not go strong for ever,' she said. 'This craze for motion has only set in during the last hundred years. It may be followed by a civilization that won't be a movement, because it will rest on the earth. All the signs are against it now, but I can't help hoping, and very early in the morning in the garden I feel that our house is the future as well as the past.'

They turned and looked at it. Their own memories coloured it now, for Helen's child had been born in the central room of the nine. Then Margaret said, 'Oh, take care—!' for something moved behind the window of the hall, and the door opened.

'The conclave's breaking at last. I'll go.'

It was Paul.

Helen retreated with the children far into the field. Friendly voices greeted her. Margaret rose, to encounter a man with a heavy black moustache.

'My father has asked for you,' he said with hostility.

She took her work and followed him.

'We have been talking business,' he continued, 'but I dare say you knew all about it beforehand.'

'Yes, I did.'

Clumsy of movement—for he had spent all his life in the saddle—Paul drove his foot against the paint of the front door. Mrs Wilcox gave a little cry of annoyance. She did not like anything scratched; she stopped in the hall to take Dolly's boa and gloves out of a vase.

Her husband was lying in a great leather chair in the dining-room, and by
his side, holding his hand rather ostentatiously, was Evie. Dolly, dressed in
purple, sat near the window. The room was a little dark and airless; they
were obliged to keep it like this until the carting of the hay. Margaret joined
the family without speaking; the five of them had met already at tea, and she
knew quite well what was going to be said. Averse to wasting her time, she
went on sewing. The clock struck six.

'Is this going to suit everyone?' said Henry in a weary voice. He used the
old phrases, but their effect was unexpected and shadowy. 'Because I don't
want you all coming here later on and complaining that I have been unfair.'

'It's apparently got to suit us,' said Paul.

'I beg your pardon, my boy. You have only to speak, and I will leave the
house to you instead.'

Paul frowned ill-temperedly, and began scratching at his arm. 'As I've
given up the outdoor life that suited me, and I have come home to look after
the business, it's no good my settling down here,' he said at last. 'It's not
really the country, and it's not the town.'

'Very well. Does my arrangement suit you, Evie?'

'Of course, father.'

'And you, Dolly?'

Dolly raised her faded little face, which sorrow could wither but not
steady. 'Perfectly splendidly,' she said. 'I thought Charles wanted it for the
boys, but last time I saw him he said no, because we cannot possibly live in
this part of England again. Charles says we ought to change our name, but I
cannot think what to, for Wilcox just suits Charles and me, and I can't think
of any other name.'

There was a general silence. Dolly looked nervously round, fearing that
she had been inappropriate. Paul continued to scratch his arm.

'Then I leave Howards End to my wife absolutely,' said Henry. 'And let
everyone understand that; and after I am dead let there be no jealousy and no
surprise.'

Margaret did not answer. There was something uncanny in her triumph.
She, who had never expected to conquer anyone, had charged straight
through these Wilcoxes and broken up their lives.

'In consequence, I leave my wife no money,' said Henry. 'That is her own
wish. All that she would have had will be divided among you. I am also
giving you a great deal in my lifetime, so that you may be independent of me.
That is her wish, too. She also is giving away a great deal of money. She
intends to diminish her income by half during the next ten years; she intends
when she dies to leave the house to her—to her nephew, down in the field. Is
all that clear? Does everyone understand?'

Paul rose to his feet. He was accustomed to natives, and a very little shook
him out of the Englishman. Feeling manly and cynical, he said: 'Down in the
field? Oh, come! I think we might have had the whole establishment,
piccaninnies included.'

Mrs Cahill whispered: 'Don't, Paul. You promised you'd take care.'
Feeling a woman of the world, she rose and prepared to take her leave.

Her father kissed her. 'Good-bye, old girl,' he said; 'don't you worry about me.'

'Good-bye, dad.'

Then it was Dolly's turn. Anxious to contribute, she laughed nervously, and said: 'Good-bye, Mr Wilcox. It does seem curious that Mrs Wilcox should have left Margaret Howards End, and yet she get it, after all.'

From Evie came a sharply-drawn breath. 'Good-bye,' she said to Margaret, and kissed her.

And again and again fell the word, like the ebb of a dying sea.

'Good-bye.'

'Good-bye, Dolly.'

'So long, father.'

'Good-bye, my boy; always take care of yourself.'

'Good-bye, Mrs Wilcox.'

'Good-bye.'

Margaret saw their visitors to the gate. Then she returned to her husband and laid her head in his hands. He was pitiably tired. But Dolly's remark had interested her. At last she said: 'Could you tell me, Henry, what was that about Mrs Wilcox having left me Howards End?'

Tranquilly he replied: 'Yes, she did. But that is a very old story. When she was ill and you were so kind to her she wanted to make you some return, and, not being herself at the time, scribbled "Howards End" on a piece of paper. I went into it thoroughly, and, as it was clearly fanciful, I set it aside, little knowing what my Margaret would be to me in the future.'

Margaret was silent. Something shook her life in its inmost recesses, and she shivered.

'I didn't do wrong, did I?' he asked, bending down.

'You didn't, darling. Nothing has been done wrong.'

From the garden came laughter. 'Here they are at last!' exclaimed Henry, disengaging himself with a smile. Helen rushed into the gloom, holding Tom by one hand and carrying her baby on the other. There were shouts of infectious joy.

'The field's cut!' Helen cried excitedly—'the big meadow! We've seen to the very end, and it'll be such a crop of hay as never!'

WEYBRIDGE, 1908–1910.

A PASSAGE TO INDIA

A PASSAGE TO INDIA

To
SYED ROSS MASOOD
and to the seventeen years of our friendship

Mosque

Chapter One

Except for the Marabar Caves—and they are twenty miles off—the city of Chandrapore presents nothing extraordinary. Edged rather than washed by the river Ganges, it trails for a couple of miles along the bank, scarcely distinguishable from the rubbish it deposits so freely. There are no bathing-steps on the river front, as the Ganges happens not to be holy here; indeed there is no river front, and bazaars shut out the wide and shifting panorama of the stream. The streets are mean, the temples ineffective, and though a few fine houses exist they are hidden away in gardens or down alleys whose filth deters all but the invited guest. Chandrapore was never large or beautiful, but two hundred years ago it lay on the road between Upper India, then imperial, and the sea, and the fine houses date from that period. The zest for decoration stopped in the eighteenth century, nor was it ever democratic. There is no painting and scarcely any carving in the bazaars. The very wood seems made of mud, the inhabitants of mud moving. So abased, so monotonous is everything that meets the eye, that when the Ganges comes down it might be expected to wash the excrescence back into the soil. Houses do fall, people are drowned and left rotting, but the general outline of the town persists, swelling here, shrinking there, like some low but indestructible form of life.

Inland, the prospect alters. There is an oval Maidan, and a long sallow hospital. Houses belonging to Eurasians stand on the high ground by the railway station. Beyond the railway—which runs parallel to the river—the land sinks, then rises again rather steeply. On the second rise is laid out the little civil station, and viewed hence Chandrapore appears to be a totally different place. It is a city of gardens. It is no city, but a forest sparsely scattered with huts. It is a tropical pleasaunce washed by a noble river. The toddy palms and neem trees and mangoes and pepul that were hidden behind the bazaars now become visible and in their turn hide the bazaars. They rise from the gardens where ancient tanks nourish them, they burst out of stifling purlieus and unconsidered temples. Seeking light and air, and endowed with more strength than man or his works, they soar above the lower deposit to greet one another with branches and beckoning leaves, and to build a city for the birds. Especially after the rains do they screen what passes below, but at all times, even when scorched or leafless, they glorify the city to the English people who inhabit the rise, so that new-comers cannot believe it to be as meagre as it is described, and have to be driven down to acquire disillusionment. As for the civil station itself, it provokes no emotion. It charms not, neither does it repel. It is sensibly planned, with a red-brick club on its brow, and farther back a grocer's and a cemetery, and the bungalows are disposed along roads that intersect at right angles. It has nothing hideous in it, and only the view is beautiful; it shares nothing with the city except the overarching sky.

The sky too has its changes, but they are less marked than those of the vegetation and the river. Clouds map it up at times, but it is normally a dome of blending tints, and the main tint blue. By day the blue will pale down into white where it touches the white of the land, after sunset it has a new circumference—orange, melting upwards into tenderest purple. But the core of blue persists, and so it is by night. Then the stars hang like lamps from the immense vault. The distance between the vault and them is as nothing to the distance behind them, and that farther distance, though beyond colour, last freed itself from blue.

The sky settles everything—not only climates and seasons but when the earth shall be beautiful. By herself she can do little—only feeble outbursts of flowers. But when the sky chooses, glory can rain into the Chandrapore bazaars or a benediction pass from horizon to horizon. The sky can do this because it is so strong and so enormous. Strength comes from the sun, infused in it daily, size from the prostrate earth. No mountains infringe on the curve. League after league the earth lies flat, heaves a little, is flat again. Only in the south, where a group of fists and fingers are thrust up through the soil, is the endless expanse interrupted. These fists and fingers are the Marabar Hills, containing the extraordinary caves.

Chapter Two

Abandoning his bicycle, which fell before a servant could catch it, the young man sprang up on to the verandah. He was all animation. 'Hamidullah, Hamidullah! am I late?' he cried.

'Do not apologize,' said his host. 'You are always late.'

'Kindly answer my question. Am I late? Has Mahmoud Ali eaten all the food? If so I go elsewhere. Mr Mahmoud Ali, how are you?'

'Thank you, Dr Aziz, I am dying.'

'Dying before your dinner? Oh, poor Mahmoud Ali!'

'Hamidullah here is actually dead. He passed away just as you rode up on your bike.'

'Yes, that is so,' said the other. 'Imagine us both as addressing you from another and a happier world.'

'Does there happen to be such a thing as a hookah in that happier world of yours?'

'Aziz, don't chatter. We are having a very sad talk.'

The hookah had been packed too tight, as was usual in his friend's house, and bubbled sulkily. He coaxed it. Yielding at last, the tobacco jetted up into his lungs and nostrils, driving out the smoke of burning cow dung that had filled them as he rode through the bazaar. It was delicious. He lay in a trance, sensuous but healthy, through which the talk of the two others did not seem particularly sad—they were discussing as to whether or no it is possible to be friends with an Englishman. Mahmoud Ali argued that it was not, Hamidullah disagreed, but with so many reservations that there was no friction between them. Delicious indeed to lie on the broad verandah with the moon rising in front and the servants preparing dinner behind, and no trouble happening.

'Well, look at my own experience this morning.'

'I only contend that it is possible in England,' replied Hamidullah, who had been to that country long ago, before the big rush, and had received a cordial welcome at Cambridge.

'It is impossible here. Aziz! The red-nosed boy has again insulted me in Court. I do not blame him. He was told that he ought to insult me. Until lately he was quite a nice boy, but the others have got hold of him.'

'Yes, they have no chance here, that is my point. They come out intending to be gentlemen, and are told it will not do. Look at Lesley, look at Blakiston, now it is your red-nosed boy, and Fielding will go next. Why, I remember when Turton came out first. It was in another part of the Province. You fellows will not believe me, but I have driven with Turton in his carriage— Turton! Oh yes, we were once quite intimate. He has shown me his stamp collection.'

'He would expect you to steal it now. Turton! But red-nosed boy will be far worse than Turton!'

'I do not think so. They all become exactly the same, not worse, not better. I give any Englishman two years, be he Turton or Burton. It is only the difference of a letter. And I give any Englishwoman six months. All are exactly alike. Do you not agree with me?'

'I do not,' replied Mahmoud Ali, entering into the bitter fun, and feeling both pain and amusement at each word that was uttered. 'For my own part I find such profound differences among our rulers. Red-nose mumbles, Turton talks distinctly, Mrs Turton takes bribes, Mrs Red-nose does not and cannot, because so far there is no Mrs Red-nose.'

'Bribes?'

'Did you not know that when they were lent to Central India over a Canal

Scheme, some Rajah or other gave her a sewing machine in solid gold so that the water should run through his state.'

'And does it?'

'No, that is where Mrs Turton is so skilful. When we poor blacks take bribes, we perform what we are bribed to perform, and the law discovers us in consequence. The English take and do nothing. I admire them.'

'We all admire them. Aziz, please pass me the hookah.'

'Oh, not yet—hookah is so jolly now.'

'You are a very selfish boy.' He raised his voice suddenly, and shouted for dinner. Servants shouted back that it was ready. They meant that they wished it was ready, and were so understood, for nobody moved. Then Hamidullah continued, but with changed manner and evident emotion.

'But take my case—the case of young Hugh Bannister. Here is the son of my dear, my dead friends, the Reverend and Mrs Bannister, whose goodness to me in England I shall never forget or describe. They were father and mother to me, I talked to them as I do now. In the vacations their Rectory became my home. They entrusted all their children to me—I often carried little Hugh about—I took him up to the Funeral of Queen Victoria, and held him in my arms above the crowd.'

'Queen Victoria was different,' murmured Mahmoud Ali.

'I learn now that this boy is in business as a leather merchant at Cawnpore. Imagine how I long to see him and to pay his fare that this house may be his home. But it is useless. The other Anglo-Indians will have got hold of him long ago. He will probably think that I want something, and I cannot face that from the son of my old friends. Oh, what in this country has gone wrong with everything, Vakil Sahib? I ask you.'

Aziz joined in. 'Why talk about the English? Brrrr . . . ! Why be either friends with the fellows or not friends? Let us shut them out and be jolly. Queen Victoria and Mrs Bannister were the only exceptions, and they're dead.'

'No, no, I do not admit that, I have met others.'

'So have I,' said Mahmoud Ali, unexpectedly veering. 'All ladies are far from alike.' Their mood was changed, and they recalled little kindnesses and courtesies. 'She said "Thank you so much" in the most natural way.' 'She offered me a lozenge when the dust irritated my throat.' Hamidullah could remember more important examples of angelic ministration, but the other, who only knew Anglo-India, had to ransack his memory for scraps, and it was not surprising that he should return to 'But of course all this is exceptional. The exception does not prove the rule. The average woman is like Mrs Turton, and, Aziz, you know what she is.' Aziz did not know, but said he did. He too generalized from his disappointments—it is difficult for members of a subject race to do otherwise. Granted the exceptions, he agreed that all Englishwomen are haughty and venal. The gleam passed from the conversation, whose wintry surface unrolled and expanded interminably.

A servant announced dinner. They ignored him. The elder men had reached their eternal politics, Aziz drifted into the garden. The trees smelt sweet–green-blossomed champak–and scraps of Persian poetry came into his head. Dinner, dinner, dinner . . . but when he returned to the house for it, Mahmoud Ali had drifted away in his turn, to speak to his sais. 'Come and see my wife a little then,' said Hamidullah, and they spent twenty minutes behind the purdah. Hamidullah Begum was a distant aunt of Aziz, and the only female relative he had in Chandrapore, and she had much to say to him on this occasion about a family circumcision that had been celebrated with imperfect pomp. It was difficult to get away, because until they had had their dinner she would not begin hers, and consequently prolonged her remarks in case they should suppose she was impatient. Having censured the circumcision, she bethought her of kindred topics, and asked Aziz when he was going to be married.

Respectful but irritated, he answered, 'Once is enough.'

'Yes, he has done his duty,' said Hamidullah. 'Do not tease him so. He carries on his family, two boys and their sister.'

'Aunt, they live most comfortably with my wife's mother, where she was living when she died. I can see them whenever I like. They are such very, very small children.'

'And he sends them the whole of his salary and lives like a low-grade clerk, and tells no one the reason. What more do you require him to do?'

But this was not Hamidullah Begum's point, and having courteously changed the conversation for a few moments she returned and made it. She said, 'What is to become of all our daughters if men refuse to marry? They will marry beneath them, or—' And she began the oft-told tale of a lady of Imperial descent who could find no husband in the narrow circle where her pride permitted her to mate, and had lived on unwed, her age now thirty, and would die unwed, for no one would have her now. While the tale was in progress, it convinced the two men, the tragedy seemed a slur on the whole community; better polygamy almost, than that a woman should die without the joys God has intended her to receive. Wedlock, motherhood, power in the house–for what else is she born, and how can the man who has denied them to her stand up to face her creator and his own at the last day? Aziz took his leave saying 'Perhaps . . . but later . . .'–his invariable reply to such an appeal.

'You mustn't put off what you think right,' said Hamidullah. 'That is why India is in such a plight, because we put off things.' But seeing that his young relative looked worried, he added a few soothing words, and thus wiped out any impression that his wife might have made.

During their absence, Mahmoud Ali had gone off in his carriage leaving a message that he should be back in five minutes, but they were on no account to wait. They sat down to meat with a distant cousin of the house, Mohammed Latif, who lived on Hamidullah's bounty and who occupied the position neither of a servant nor of an equal. He did not speak unless spoken to, and since no one spoke kept unoffended silence. Now and then he belched, in compliment to the richness of the food. A gentle, happy and dishonest old man; all his life he had never done a stroke of work. So long as some one of his relatives had a house he was sure of a home, and it was unlikely that so large a family would all go bankrupt. His wife led a similar existence some hundreds of miles away—he did not visit her, owing to the expense of the railway ticket. Presently Aziz chaffed him, also the servants, and then began quoting poetry, Persian, Urdu, a little Arabic. His memory was good, and for so young a man he had read largely; the themes he preferred were the decay of Islam and the brevity of love. They listened delighted, for they took the public view of poetry, not the private which obtains in England. It never bored them to hear words, words; they breathed them with the cool night air, never stopping to analyse; the name of the poet, Hafiz, Hali, Iqbal, was sufficient guarantee. India—a hundred Indias—whispered outside beneath the indifferent moon, but for the time India seemed one and their own, and they regained their departed greatness by hearing its departure lamented, they felt young again because reminded that youth must fly. A servant in scarlet interrupted him; he was the chuprassi of the Civil Surgeon, and he handed Aziz a note.

'Old Callendar wants to see me at his bungalow,' he said, not rising. 'He might have the politeness to say why.'

'Some case, I daresay.'

'I daresay not, I daresay nothing. He has found out our dinner hour, that's all, and chooses to interrupt us every time, in order to show his power.'

'On the one hand he always does this, on the other it may be a serious case, and you cannot know,' said Hamidullah, considerately paving the way towards obedience. 'Had you not better clean your teeth after pan?'

'If my teeth are to be cleaned, I don't go at all. I am an Indian, it is an Indian habit to take pan. The Civil Surgeon must put up with it. Mohammed Latif, my bike, please.'

The poor relation got up. Slightly immersed in the realms of matter, he laid his hand on the bicycle's saddle, while a servant did the actual wheeling. Between them they took it over a tintack. Aziz held his hands under the ewer, dried them, fitted on his green felt hat, and then with unexpected energy whizzed out of Hamidullah's compound.

'Aziz, Aziz, imprudent boy. . . .' But he was far down the bazaar, riding furiously. He had neither light nor bell nor had he a brake, but what use are such adjuncts in a land where the cyclist's only hope is to coast from face to face, and just before he collides with each it vanishes? And the city was fairly empty at this hour. When his tyre went flat, he leapt off and shouted for a tonga.

He did not at first find one, and he had also to dispose of his bicycle at a friend's house. He dallied furthermore to clean his teeth. But at last he was rattling towards the civil lines, with a vivid sense of speed. As he entered their arid tidiness, depression suddenly seized him. The roads, named after victorious generals and intersecting at right angles, were symbolic of the net Great Britain had thrown over India. He felt caught in their meshes. When he turned into Major Callendar's compound he could with difficulty restrain himself from getting down from the tonga and approaching the bungalow on foot, and this not because his soul was servile but because his feelings—the sensitive edges of him—feared a gross snub. There had been a 'case' last year—an Indian gentleman had driven up to an official's house and been turned back by the servants and been told to approach more suitably—only one case among thousands of visits to hundreds of officials, but its fame spread wide. The young man shrank from a repetition of it. He compromised, and stopped the driver just outside the flood of light that fell across the verandah.

The Civil Surgeon was out.

'But the sahib has left me some message?'

The servant returned an indifferent 'No.' Aziz was in despair. It was a servant whom he had forgotten to tip, and he could do nothing now because there were people in the hall. He was convinced that there was a message, and that the man was withholding it out of revenge. While they argued, the people came out. Both were ladies. Aziz lifted his hat. The first, who was in evening dress, glanced at the Indian and turned instinctively away.

'Mrs Lesley, it *is* a tonga,' she cried.

'Ours?' enquired the second, also seeing Aziz, and doing likewise.

'Take the gifts the gods provide, anyhow,' she screeched, and both jumped in. 'O Tonga wallah, club, club. Why doesn't the fool go?'

'Go, I will pay you to-morrow,' said Aziz to the driver, and as they went off he called courteously, 'You are most welcome, ladies.' They did not reply, being full of their own affairs.

So it had come, the usual thing—just as Mahmoud Ali said. The inevitable snub—his bow ignored, his carriage taken. It might have been worse, for it comforted him somehow that Mesdames Callendar and Lesley should both be fat and weigh the tonga down behind. Beautiful women would have pained him. He turned to the servant, gave him a couple of rupees, and asked again whether there was a message. The man, now very civil, returned the same answer. Major Callendar had driven away half an hour before.

'Saying nothing?'

He had as a matter of fact said, 'Damn Aziz'—words that the servant understood, but was too polite to repeat. One can tip too much as well as too little, indeed the coin that buys the exact truth has not yet been minted.

'Then I will write him a letter.'

He was offered the use of the house, but was too dignified to enter it. Paper and ink were brought on to the verandah. He began: 'Dear Sir,—At your express command I have hastened as a subordinate should—' and then stopped. 'Tell him I have called, that is sufficient,' he said, tearing the protest up. 'Here is my card. Call me a tonga.'

'Huzoor, all are at the club.'

'Then telephone for one down to the railway station.' And since the man hastened to do this he said, 'Enough, enough, I prefer to walk.' He commandeered a match and lit a cigarette. These attentions, though purchased, soothed him. They would last as long as he had rupees, which is something. But to shake the dust of Anglo-India off his feet! To escape from the net and be back among manners and gestures that he knew! He began a walk, an unwonted exercise.

He was an athletic little man, daintily put together, but really very strong. Nevertheless walking fatigued him, as it fatigues everyone in India except the new-comer. There is something hostile in that soil. It either yields, and the foot sinks into a depression, or else it is unexpectedly rigid and sharp, pressing stones or crystals against the tread. A series of these little surprises exhausts; and he was wearing pumps, a poor preparation for any country. At the edge of the civil station he turned into a mosque to rest.

He had always liked this mosque. It was gracious, and the arrangement pleased him. The courtyard—entered through a ruined gate—contained an ablution tank of fresh clear water, which was always in motion, being indeed part of a conduit that supplied the city. The courtyard was paved with broken slabs. The covered part of the mosque was deeper than is usual; its effect was that of an English parish church whose side has been taken out. Where he sat, he looked into three arcades whose darkness was illuminated by a small hanging lamp and by the moon. The front—in full moonlight—had the appearance of marble, and the ninety-nine names of God on the frieze stood out black, as the frieze stood out white against the sky. The contest between this dualism and the contention of shadows within pleased Aziz, and he tried to symbolize the whole into some truth of religion or love. A mosque by winning his approval let loose his imagination. The temple of another creed, Hindu, Christian, or Greek, would have bored him and failed to awaken his sense of beauty. Here was Islam, his own country, more than a Faith, more than a battle-cry, more, much more . . . Islam, an attitude towards life both exquisite and durable, where his body and his thoughts found their home.

His seat was the low wall that bounded the courtyard on the left. The ground fell away beneath him towards the city, visible as a blur of trees, and in the stillness he heard many small sounds. On the right, over in the club, the English community contributed an amateur orchestra. Elsewhere some Hindus were drumming—he knew they were Hindus, because the rhythm was uncongenial to him,—and others were bewailing a corpse—he knew whose, having certified it in the afternoon. There were owls, the Punjab mail . . . and flowers smelt deliciously in the station-master's garden. But the mosque—that alone signified, and he returned to it from the complex appeal of the night, and decked it with meanings the builder had never intended. Some day he too would build a mosque, smaller than this but in perfect taste, so that all who passed by should experience the happiness he felt now. And near it, under a low dome, should be his tomb, with a Persian inscription:

> *Alas, without me for thousands of years*
> *The Rose will blossom and the Spring will bloom,*
> *But those who have secretly understood my heart—*
> *They will approach and visit the grave where I lie.*

He had seen the quatrain on the tomb of a Deccan king and regarded it as profound philosophy—he always held pathos to be profound. The secret understanding of the heart! He repeated the phrase with tears in his eyes, and as he did so one of the pillars of the mosque seemed to quiver. It swayed in the gloom and detached itself. Belief in ghosts ran in his blood, but he sat firm. Another pillar moved, a third, and then an Englishwoman stepped out into the moonlight. Suddenly he was furiously angry and shouted: 'Madam! Madam! Madam!'

'Oh! Oh!' the woman gasped.

'Madam, this is a mosque, you have no right here at all; you should have taken off your shoes; this is a holy place for Moslems.'

'I have taken them off.'

'You have?'

'I left them at the entrance.'

'Then I ask your pardon.'

Still startled, the woman moved out, keeping the ablution tank between them. He called after her, 'I am truly sorry for speaking.'

'Yes, I was right, was I not? If I remove my shoes, I am allowed?'

'Of course, but so few ladies take the trouble, especially if thinking no one is there to see.'

'That makes no difference. God is here.'

'Madam!'

'Please let me go.'

'Oh, can I do you some service now or at any time?'

'No, thank you, really none—good night.'

'May I know your name?'

She was now in the shadow of the gateway, so that he could not see her face, but she saw his, and she said with a change of voice, 'Mrs Moore.'

'Mrs—' Advancing, he found that she was old. A fabric bigger than the mosque fell to pieces, and he did not know whether he was glad or sorry. She was older than Hamidullah Begum, with a red face and white hair. Her voice had deceived him.

'Mrs Moore, I am afraid I startled you. I shall tell my community—our friends—about you. That God is here—very good, very fine indeed. I think you are newly arrived in India.'

'Yes—how did you know?'

'By the way you address me. No, but can I call you a carriage?'

'I have only come from the club. They are doing a play that I have seen in London, and it was so hot.'

'What was the name of the play?'

'*Cousin Kate.*'

'I think you ought not to walk at night alone, Mrs Moore. There are bad characters about and leopards may come across from the Marabar Hills. Snakes also.'

She exclaimed; she had forgotten the snakes.

'For example, a six-spot beetle,' he continued. 'You pick it up, it bites, you die.'

'But you walk about yourself.'

'Oh, I am used to it.'

'Used to snakes?'

They both laughed. 'I'm a doctor,' he said. 'Snakes don't dare bite me.' They sat down side by side in the entrance, and slipped on their evening shoes. 'Please may I ask you a question now? Why do you come to India at this time of year, just as the cold weather is ending?'

'I intended to start earlier, but there was an unavoidable delay.'

'It will soon be so unhealthy for you! And why ever do you come to Chandrapore?'

'To visit my son. He is the City Magistrate here.'

'Oh no, excuse me, that is quite impossible. Our City Magistrate's name is Mr Heaslop. I know him intimately.'

'He's my son all the same,' she said, smiling.

'But, Mrs Moore, how can he be?'

'I was married twice.'

'Yes, now I see, and your first husband died.'

'He did, and so did my second husband.'

'Then we are in the same box,' he said cryptically. 'Then is the City Magistrate the entire of your family now?'

'No, there are the younger ones—Ralph and Stella in England.'

'And the gentleman here, is he Ralph and Stella's half-brother?'

'Quite right.'

'Mrs Moore, this is all extremely strange, because like yourself I have also two sons and a daughter. Is not this the same box with a vengeance?'

'What are their names? Not also Ronny, Ralph, and Stella, surely?'

The suggestion delighted him. 'No, indeed. How funny it sounds! Their names are quite different and will surprise you. Listen, please. I am about to tell you my children's names. The first is called Ahmed, the second is called Karim, the third—she is the eldest—Jamila. Three children are enough. Do not you agree with me?'

'I do.'

They were both silent for a little, thinking of their respective families. She sighed and rose to go.

'Would you care to see over the Minto Hospital one morning?' he enquired. 'I have nothing else to offer at Chandrapore.'

'Thank you, I have seen it already, or I should have liked to come with you very much.'

'I suppose the Civil Surgeon took you.'

'Yes, and Mrs Callendar.'

His voice altered. 'Ah! A very charming lady.'

'Possibly, when one knows her better.'

'What? What? You didn't like her?'

'She was certainly intending to be kind, but I did not find her exactly charming.'

He burst out with: 'She has just taken my tonga without my permission—do you call that being charming?—and Major Callendar interrupts me night after night from where I am dining with my friends and I go at once, breaking up a most pleasant entertainment, and he is not there and not even a message. Is this charming, pray? But what does it matter? I can do nothing and he knows it. I am just a subordinate, my time is of no value, the verandah is good enough for an Indian, yes, yes, let him stand, and Mrs Callendar takes my carriage and cuts me dead . . .'

She listened.

He was excited partly by his wrongs, but much more by the knowledge that someone sympathized with them. It was this that led him to repeat, exaggerate, contradict. She had proved her sympathy by criticizing her fellow-countrywoman to him, but even earlier he had known. The flame that not even beauty can nourish was springing up, and though his words were querulous his heart began to glow secretly. Presently it burst into speech.

'You understand me, you know what others feel. Oh, if others resembled you!'

Rather surprised, she replied: 'I don't think I understand people very well. I only know whether I like or dislike them.'

'Then you are an Oriental.'

She accepted his escort back to the club, and said at the gate that she wished she was a member, so that she could have asked him in.

'Indians are not allowed into the Chandrapore Club even as guests,' he said simply. He did not expatiate on his wrongs now, being happy. As he strolled downhill beneath the lovely moon, and again saw the lovely mosque, he seemed to own the land as much as anyone owned it. What did it matter if a few flabby Hindus had preceded him there, and a few chilly English succeeded?

Chapter Three

The third act of *Cousin Kate* was well advanced by the time Mrs Moore re-entered the club. Windows were barred, lest the servants should see their mem-sahibs acting, and the heat was consequently immense. One electric fan revolved like a wounded bird, another was out of order. Disinclined to return to the audience, she went into the billiard room, where she was greeted by 'I want to see the *real* India,' and her appropriate life came back with a rush. This was Adela Quested, the queer, cautious girl whom Ronny had commissioned her to bring from England, and Ronny was her son, also cautious, whom Miss Quested would probably though not certainly marry, and she herself was an elderly lady.

'I want to see it too, and I only wish we could. Apparently the Turtons will arrange something for next Tuesday.'

'It'll end in an elephant ride, it always does. Look at this evening. *Cousin Kate*! Imagine, *Cousin Kate*! But where have you been off to? Did you succeed in catching the moon in the Ganges?'

The two ladies had happened, the night before, to see the moon's reflection in a distant channel of the stream. The water had drawn it out, so that it had seemed larger than the real moon, and brighter, which had pleased them.

'I went to the mosque, but I did not catch the moon.'

'The angle would have altered—she rises later.'

'Later and later,' yawned Mrs Moore, who was tired after her walk. 'Let me think—we don't see the other side of the moon out here, no.'

'Come, India's not as bad as all that,' said a pleasant voice. 'Other side of the earth, if you like, but we stick to the same old moon.' Neither of them knew the speaker nor did they ever see him again. He passed with his friendly word through red-brick pillars into the darkness.

'We aren't even seeing the other side of the world; that's our complaint,' said Adela. Mrs Moore agreed; she too was disappointed at the dullness of their new life. They had made such a romantic voyage across the Mediterranean and through the sands of Egypt to the harbour of Bombay, to find only a gridiron of bungalows at the end of it. But she did not take the disappointment as seriously as Miss Quested, for the reason that she was forty years older, and had learnt that Life never gives us what we want at the moment that we consider appropriate. Adventures do occur, but not punctually. She said again that she hoped that something interesting would be arranged for next Tuesday.

'Have a drink,' said another pleasant voice. 'Mrs Moore—Miss Quested—have a drink, have two drinks.' They knew who it was this time—the Collector, Mr Turton, with whom they had dined. Like themselves, he had found the atmosphere of *Cousin Kate* too hot. Ronny, he told them, was stage-managing in place of Major Callendar, whom some native subordinate or other had let down, and doing it very well; then he turned to Ronny's other merits, and in quiet, decisive tones said much that was flattering. It wasn't that the young man was particularly good at the games or the lingo, or that he had much notion of the Law, but—apparently a large but—Ronny was dignified.

Mrs Moore was surprised to learn this, dignity not being a quality with which any mother credits her son. Miss Quested learnt it with anxiety, for she had not decided whether she liked dignified men. She tried indeed to discuss this point with Mr Turton, but he silenced her with a good-humoured motion of his hand, and continued what he had come to say. 'The long and the short of it is Heaslop's a sahib; he's the type we want, he's one of us,' and another civilian who was leaning over the billiard table said, 'Hear, hear!' The matter was thus placed beyond doubt, and the Collector passed on, for other duties called him.

Meanwhile the performance ended, and the amateur orchestra played the National Anthem. Conversation and billiards stopped, faces stiffened. It was the Anthem of the Army of Occupation. It reminded every member of the club that he or she was British and in exile. It produced a little sentiment and a useful accession of willpower. The meagre tune, the curt series of demands on Jehovah, fused into a prayer unknown in England, and though they perceived neither Royalty nor Deity they did perceive something, they were strengthened to resist another day. Then they poured out, offering one another drinks.

'Adela, have a drink; mother, a drink.'

They refused—they were weary of drinks—and Miss Quested, who always said exactly what was in her mind, announced anew that she was desirous of seeing the real India.

Ronny was in high spirits. The request struck him as comic, and he called out to another passer-by: 'Fielding! how's one to see the real India?'

'Try seeing Indians,' the man answered, and vanished.

'Who was that?'

'Our schoolmaster—Government College.'

'As if one could avoid seeing them,' sighed Mrs Lesley.

'I've avoided,' said Miss Quested. 'Excepting my own servant, I've scarcely spoken to an Indian since landing.'

'Oh, lucky you.'

'But I want to see them.'

She became the centre of an amused group of ladies. One said, 'Wanting to see Indians! How new that sounds!' Another, 'Natives! why, fancy!' A third, more serious, said, 'Let me explain. Natives don't respect one any the more after meeting one, you see.'

'That occurs after so many meetings.'

But the lady, entirely stupid and friendly, continued: 'What I mean is, I was a nurse before my marriage, and came across them a great deal, so I know. I really do know the truth about Indians. A most unsuitable position for any Englishwoman—I was a nurse in a Native State. One's only hope was to hold sternly aloof.'

'Even from one's patients?'

'Why, the kindest thing one can do to a native is to let him die,' said Mrs Callendar.

'How if he went to heaven?' asked Mrs Moore, with a gentle but crooked smile.

'He can go where he likes as long as he doesn't come near me. They give me the creeps.'

'As a matter of fact I have thought what you were saying about heaven, and that is why I am against Missionaries,' said the lady who had been a nurse. 'I am all for Chaplains, but all against Missionaries. Let me explain.'

But before she could do so, the Collector intervened.

'Do you really want to meet the Aryan Brother, Miss Quested? That can be easily fixed up. I didn't realize he'd amuse you.' He thought a moment. 'You can practically see any type you like. Take your choice. I know the Government people and the landowners, Heaslop here can get hold of the barrister crew, while if you want to specialize on education, we can come down on Fielding.'

'I'm tired of seeing picturesque figures pass before me as a frieze,' the girl explained. 'It was wonderful when we landed, but that superficial glamour soon goes.'

Her impressions were of no interest to the Collector; he was only concerned to give her a good time. Would she like a Bridge Party? He explained to her what that was—not the game, but a party to bridge the gulf between East and West; the expression was his own invention, and amused all who heard it.

'I only want those Indians whom you come across socially—as your friends.'

'Well, we don't come across them socially,' he said, laughing. 'They're full of all the virtues, but we don't, and it's now eleven-thirty, and too late to go into the reasons.'

'Miss Quested, what a name!' remarked Mrs Turton to her husband as they drove away. She had not taken to the new young lady, thinking her ungracious and cranky. She trusted that she hadn't been brought out to marry nice little Heaslop, though it looked like it. Her husband agreed with her in his heart, but he never spoke against an Englishwoman if he could avoid doing so, and he only said that Miss Quested naturally made mistakes. He added: 'India does wonders for the judgment, especially during the hot weather; it has even done wonders for Fielding.' Mrs Turton closed her eyes at this name and remarked that Mr Fielding wasn't pukka, and had better marry Miss Quested, for she wasn't pukka. Then they reached their bungalow, low and enormous, the oldest and most uncomfortable bungalow in the civil station, with a sunk soup plate of a lawn, and they had one drink more, this time of barley water, and went to bed. Their withdrawal from the club had broken up the evening, which, like all gatherings, had an official tinge. A community that bows the knee to a Viceroy and believes that the divinity that hedges a king can be transplanted, must feel some reverence for any viceregal substitute. At Chandrapore the Turtons were little gods; soon they would retire to some suburban villa, and die exiled from glory.

'It's decent of the great man,' chattered Ronny, much gratified at the civility that had been shown to his guests. 'Do you know he's never given a Bridge Party before? Coming on top of the dinner too! I wish I could have arranged something myself, but when you know the natives better you'll realize it's easier for the Burra Sahib than for me. They know him—they know he can't be fooled—I'm still fresh comparatively. No one can even begin to think of knowing this country until he has been in it twenty years.—Hello, the mater! Here's your cloak.—Well: for an example of the mistakes one makes. Soon after I came out I asked one of the Pleaders to have a smoke with me—only a cigarette, mind. I found afterwards that he had sent touts all over the bazaar to announce the fact—told all the litigants, "Oh, you'd better come to my Vakil Mahmoud Ali—he's in with the City Magistrate." Ever since then I've dropped on him in Court as hard as I could. It's taught me a lesson, and I hope him.'

'Isn't the lesson that you should invite all the Pleaders to have a smoke with you?'

'Perhaps, but time's limited and the flesh weak. I prefer my smoke at the club amongst my own sort, I'm afraid.'

'Why not ask the Pleaders to the club?' Miss Quested persisted.

'Not allowed.' He was pleasant and patient, and evidently understood why she did not understand. He implied that he had once been as she, though not for long. Going to the verandah, he called firmly to the moon. His sais answered, and without lowering his head, he ordered his trap to be brought round.

Mrs Moore, whom the club had stupefied, woke up outside. She watched the moon, whose radiance stained with primrose the purple of the surrounding sky. In England the moon had seemed dead and alien; here she was caught in the shawl of night together with earth and all the other stars. A sudden sense of unity, of kinship with the heavenly bodies, passed into the old woman and out, like water through a tank, leaving a strange freshness behind. She did not dislike *Cousin Kate* or the National Anthem, but their note had died into a new one, just as cocktails and cigars had died into invisible flowers. When the mosque, long and domeless, gleamed at the turn of the road, she exclaimed, 'Oh, yes–that's where I got to–that's where I've been.'

'Been there when?' asked her son.

'Between the acts.'

'But, mother, you can't do that sort of thing.'

'Can't mother?' she replied.

'No, really not in this country. It's not done. There's the danger from snakes for one thing. They are apt to lie out in the evening.'

'Ah yes, so the young man there said.'

'That sounds very romantic,' said Miss Quested, who was exceedingly fond of Mrs Moore, and was glad she should have had this little escapade. 'You meet a young man in a mosque, and then never let me know!'

'I was going to tell you, Adela, but something changed the conversation and I forgot. My memory grows deplorable.'

'Was he nice?'

She paused, then said emphatically: 'Very nice.'

'Who was he?' Ronny enquired.

'A doctor. I don't know his name.'

'A doctor? I know of no young doctor in Chandrapore. How odd! What was he like?'

'Rather small, with a little moustache and quick eyes. He called out to me when I was in the dark part of the mosque–about my shoes. That was how we began talking. He was afraid I had them on, but I remembered luckily. He told me about his children, and then we walked back to the club. He knows you well.'

'I wish you had pointed him out to me. I can't make out who he is.'

'He didn't come into the club. He said he wasn't allowed to.'

Thereupon the truth struck him, and he cried 'Oh, good gracious! Not a Mohammedan? Why ever didn't you tell me you'd been talking to a native? I was going all wrong.'

'A Mohammedan! How perfectly magnificent!' exclaimed Miss Quested. 'Ronny, isn't that like your mother? While we talk about seeing the real India, she goes and sees it, and then forgets she's seen it.'

But Ronny was ruffled. From his mother's description he had thought the doctor might be young Muggins from over the Ganges, and had brought out all the comradely emotions. What a mix-up! Why hadn't she indicated by the tone of her voice that she was talking about an Indian? Scratchy and dictatorial, he began to question her. 'He called to you in the mosque, did he? How? Impudently? What was he doing there himself at that time of night?–No, it's not their prayer time.'–This in answer to a suggestion of Miss Quested's, who showed the keenest interest. 'So he called to you over your shoes. Then it was impudence. It's an old trick. I wish you had had them on.'

'I think it was impudence, but I don't know about a trick,' said Mrs Moore. 'His nerves were all on edge–I could tell from his voice. As soon as I answered he altered.'

'You oughtn't to have answered.'

'Now look here,' said the logical girl, 'wouldn't you expect a Mohammedan to answer if you asked him to take off his hat in church?'

'It's different, it's different; you don't understand.'

'I know I don't, and I want to. What is the difference, please?'

He wished she wouldn't interfere. His mother did not signify–she was just a globe-trotter, a temporary escort, who could retire to England with what impressions she chose. But Adela, who meditated spending her life in the country, was a more serious matter; it would be tiresome if she started crooked over the native question. Pulling up the mare, he said, 'There's your Ganges.'

Their attention was diverted. Below them a radiance had suddenly appeared. It belonged neither to water nor moonlight, but stood like a luminous sheaf upon the fields of darkness. He told them that it was where the new sand-bank was forming, and that the dark ravelled bit at the top was the sand, and that the dead bodies floated down that way from Benares, or would if the crocodiles let them. 'It's not much of a dead body that gets down to Chandrapore.'

'Crocodiles down in it too, how terrible!' his mother murmured. The young people glanced at each other and smiled; it amused them when the old lady got these gentle creeps, and harmony was restored between them consequently. She continued: 'What a terrible river! what a wonderful river!' she sighed. The radiance was already altering, whether through shifting of the moon or of the sand; soon the bright sheaf would be gone, and a circlet, itself to alter, be burnished upon the streaming void. The women discussed whether they would wait for the change or not, while the silence broke into patches of unquietness and the mare shivered. On her account they did not wait, but drove on to the City Magistrate's bungalow, where Miss Quested went to bed, and Mrs Moore had a short interview with her son.

He wanted to enquire about the Mohammedan doctor in the mosque. It was his duty to report suspicious characters and conceivably it was some disreputable hakim who had prowled up from the bazaar. When she told him that it was someone connected with the Minto Hospital, he was relieved, and said that the fellow's name must be Aziz, and that he was quite all right, nothing against him at all.

'Aziz! what a charming name!'

'So you and he had a talk. Did you gather he was well disposed?'

Ignorant of the force of this question, she replied, 'Yes, quite, after the first moment.'

'I meant, generally. Did he seem to tolerate us–the brutal conqueror, the sundried bureaucrat, that sort of thing?'

'Oh, yes, I think so, except the Callendars–he doesn't care for the Callendars at all.'

'Oh. So he told you that, did he? The Major will be interested. I wonder what was the aim of the remark.'

'Ronny, Ronny! you're never going to pass it on to Major Callendar?'

'Yes, rather, I must in fact!'

'But, my dear boy—'

'If the Major heard I was disliked by any native subordinate of mine, I should expect him to pass it on to me.'

'But, my dear boy–a private conversation!'

'Nothing's private in India. Aziz knew that when he spoke out, so don't you worry. He had some motive in what he said. My personal belief is that the remark wasn't true.'

'How not true?'

'He abused the Major in order to impress you.'

'I don't know what you mean, dear.'

'It's the educated native's latest dodge. They used to cringe, but the younger generation believe in a show of manly independence. They think it will pay better with the itinerant M.P. But whether the native swaggers or cringes, there's always something behind every remark be makes, always something, and if nothing else he's trying to increase his izzat–in plain Anglo-Saxon, to score. Of course there are exceptions.'

'You never used to judge people like this at home.'

'India isn't home,' he retorted, rather rudely, but in order to silence her he had been using phrases and arguments that he had picked up from older officials, and he did not feel quite sure of himself. When he said 'of course there are exceptions' he was quoting Mr Turton, while 'increasing the izzat' was Major Callendar's own. The phrases worked and were in current use at the club, but she was rather clever at detecting the first from the second hand, and might press him for definite examples.

She only said, 'I can't deny that what you say sounds very sensible, but you really must not hand on to Major Callendar anything I have told you about Doctor Aziz.'

He felt disloyal to his caste, but he promised, adding, 'In return please don't talk about Aziz to Adela.'

'Not talk about him? Why?'

'There you go again, mother–I really can't explain every thing. I don't want Adela to be worried, that's the fact; she'll begin wondering whether we treat the natives properly, and all that sort of nonsense.'

'But she came out to be worried–that's exactly why she's here. She discussed it all on the boat. We had a long talk when we went on shore at

Aden. She knows you in play, as she put it, but not in work, and she felt she must come and look round, before she decided—and before you decided. She is very, very fair-minded.'

'I know,' he said dejectedly.

The note of anxiety in his voice made her feel that he was still a little boy, who must have what he liked, so she promised to do as he wished, and they kissed good night. He had not forbidden her to think about Aziz, however, and she did this when she retired to her room. In the light of her son's comment she reconsidered the scene at the mosque, to see whose impression was correct. Yes, it could be worked into quite an unpleasant scene. The doctor had begun by bullying her, had said Mrs Callendar was nice, and then—finding the ground safe—had changed; he had alternately whined over his grievances and patronized her, had run a dozen ways in a single sentence, had been unreliable, inquisitive, vain. Yes, it was all true, but how false as a summary of the man; the essential life of him had been slain.

Going to hang up her cloak, she found that the tip of the peg was occupied by a small wasp. She had known this wasp or his relatives by day; they were not as English wasps, but had long yellow legs which hung down behind when they flew. Perhaps he mistook the peg for a branch—no Indian animal has any sense of an interior. Bats, rats, birds, insects will as soon nest inside a house as out; it is to them a normal growth of the eternal jungle, which alternately produces houses trees, houses trees. There he clung, asleep, while jackals in the plain bayed their desires and mingled with the percussion of drums.

'Pretty dear,' said Mrs Moore to the wasp. He did not wake, but her voice floated out, to swell the night's uneasiness.

Chapter Four

The Collector kept his word. Next day he issued invitation cards to numerous Indian gentlemen in the neighbourhood, stating that he would be at home in the garden of the club between the hours of five and seven on the following Tuesday, also that Mrs Turton would be glad to receive any ladies of their families who were out of purdah. His action caused much excitement and was discussed in several worlds.

'It is owing to orders from the L.G,' was Mahmoud Ali's explanation. 'Turton would never do this unless compelled. Those high officials are different—they sympathize, the Viceroy sympathizes, they would have us treated properly. But they come too seldom and live too far away. Meanwhile—'

'It is easy to sympathize at a distance,' said an old gentleman with a beard. 'I value more the kind word that is spoken close to my ear. Mr Turton has spoken it, from whatever cause. He speaks, we hear. I do not see why we need discuss it further.' Quotations followed from the Koran.

'We have not all your sweet nature, Nawab Bahadur, nor your learning.'

'The Lieutenant-Governor may be my very good friend, but I give him no trouble.—How do you do, Nawab Bahadur?—Quite well, thank you, Sir Gilbert; how are you?—And all is over. But I can be a thorn in Mr Turton's flesh, and if he asks me I accept the invitation. I shall come in from Dilkusha specially, though I have to postpone other business.'

'You will make yourself chip,' suddenly said a little black man.

There was a stir of disapproval. Who was this illbred upstart, that he should criticize the leading Mohammedan landowner of the district? Mahmoud Ali, though sharing his opinion, felt bound to oppose it. 'Mr Ram Chand!' he said, swaying forward stiffly with his hands on his hips.

'Mr Mahmoud Ali!'

'Mr Ram Chand, the Nawab Bahadur can decide what is cheap without our valuation, I think.'

'I do not expect I shall make myself cheap,' said the Nawab Bahadur to Mr Ram Chand, speaking very pleasantly, for he was aware that the man had been impolite and he desired to shield him from the consequences. It had passed through his mind to reply, 'I expect I shall make myself cheap,' but he rejected this as the less courteous alternative. 'I do not see why we should make ourselves cheap. I do not see why we should. The invitation is worded very graciously.' Feeling that he could not further decrease the social gulf between himself and his auditors, he sent his elegant grandson, who was in attendance on him, to fetch his car. When it came, he repeated all that he had said before, though at greater length, ending up with 'Till Tuesday, then, gentlemen all, when I hope we may meet in the flower gardens of the club.'

This opinion carried great weight. The Nawab Bahadur was a big proprietor and a philanthropist, a man of benevolence and decision. His character among all the communities in the province stood high. He was a straightforward enemy and a staunch friend, and his hospitality was proverbial. 'Give, do not lend; after death who will thank you?' was his favourite remark. He held it a disgrace to die rich. When such a man was prepared to motor twenty-five miles to shake the Collector's hand, the entertainment took another aspect. For he was not like some eminent men, who give out that they will come, and then fail at the last moment, leaving the small fry floundering. If he said he would come, he would come, he would never deceive his supporters. The gentlemen whom he had lectured now urged one another to attend the party, although convinced at heart that his advice was unsound.

He had spoken in the little room near the Courts where the pleaders waited for clients; clients, waiting for pleaders, sat in the dust outside. These had not received a card from Mr Turton. And there were circles even beyond these—people who wore nothing but a loincloth, people who wore not even that, and spent their lives in knocking two sticks together before a scarlet doll—humanity grading and drifting beyond the educated vision, until no earthly invitation can embrace it.

All invitations must proceed from heaven perhaps; perhaps it is futile for men to initiate their own unity, they do but widen the gulfs between them by the attempt. So at all events thought old Mr Graysford and young Mr Sorley, the devoted missionaries who lived out beyond the slaughterhouses, always travelled third on the railways, and never came up to the club. In our Father's house are many mansions, they taught, and there alone will the incompatible multitudes of mankind be welcomed and soothed. Not one shall be turned away by the servants on that verandah, be he black or white, not one shall be kept standing who approaches with a loving heart. And why should the divine hospitality cease here? Consider, with all reverence, the monkeys. May there not be a mansion for the monkeys also? Old Mr Graysford said No, but young Mr Sorley, who was advanced, said Yes; he saw no reason why monkeys should not have their collateral share of bliss, and he had sympathetic discussions about them with his Hindu friends. And the jackals? Jackals were indeed less to Mr Sorley's mind, but he admitted that the mercy of God, being infinite, may well embrace all mammals. And the wasps? He became uneasy during the descent to wasps, and was apt to change the conversation. And oranges, cactuses, crystals and mud? and the bacteria inside Mr Sorley? No, no, this is going too far. We must exclude someone from our gathering, or we shall be left with nothing.

Chapter Five

The Bridge Party was not a success—at least it was not what Mrs Moore and Miss Quested were accustomed to consider a successful party. They arrived early, since it was given in their honour, but most of the Indian guests had arrived even earlier, and stood massed at the farther side of the tennis lawns, doing nothing.

'It is only just five,' said Mrs Turton. 'My husband will be up from his office in a moment and start the thing. I have no idea what we have to do. It's the first time we've every given a party like this at the club. Mr Heaslop, when I'm dead and gone will you give parties like this? It's enough to make the old type of Burra Sahib turn in his grave.'

Ronny laughed deferentially. 'You wanted something not picturesque and we've provided it,' he remarked to Miss Quested. 'What do you think of the Aryan Brother in a topi and spats?'

Neither she nor his mother answered. They were gazing rather sadly over the tennis lawn. No, it was not picturesque; the East, abandoning its secular magnificence, was descending into a valley whose farther side no man can see.

'The great point to remember is that no one who's here matters; those who matter don't come. Isn't that so, Mrs Turton?'

'Absolutely true,' said the great lady, leaning back. She was 'saving herself up,' as she called it—not for anything that would happen that afternoon or even that week, but for some vague future occasion when a high official might come along and tax her social strength. Most of her public appearances were marked by this air of reserve.

Assured of her approbation, Ronny continued: 'The educated Indians will be no good to us if there's a row, it's simply not worth while conciliating them, that's why they don't matter. Most of the people you see are seditious at heart, and the rest 'ld run squealing. The cultivator–he's another story. The Pathan–he's a man if you like. But these people–don't imagine they're India.' He pointed to the dusky line beyond the court, and here and there it flashed a pince-nez or shuffled a shoe, as if aware that he was despising it. European costume had lighted like a leprosy. Few had yielded entirely, but none were untouched. There was a silence when he had finished speaking, on both sides of the court; at least, more ladies joined the English group, but their words seemed to die as soon as uttered. Some kites hovered overhead, impartial, over the kites passed the mass of a vulture, and with an impartiality exceeding all, the sky, not deeply coloured but translucent, poured light from its whole circumference. It seemed unlikely that the series stopped here. Beyond the sky must not there be something that overarches all the skies, more impartial even than they? Beyond which again . . .

They spoke of *Cousin Kate*.

They had tried to reproduce their own attitude to life upon the stage, and to dress up as the middle-class English people they actually were. Next year they would do *Quality Street* or *The Yeomen of the Guard*. Save for this annual incursion, they left literature alone. The men had no time for it, the women did nothing that they could not share with the men. Their ignorance of the Arts was notable, and they lost no opportunity of proclaiming it to one another; it was the Public School attitude, flourishing more vigorously than it can yet hope to do in England. If Indians were shop, the Arts were bad form, and Ronny had repressed his mother when she enquired after his viola; a viola was almost a demerit, and certainly not the sort of instrument one mentioned in public. She noticed now how tolerant and conventional his judgments had become; when they had seen *Cousin Kate* in London together in the past, he had scorned it; now he pretended that it was a good play, in order to hurt nobody's feelings. An 'unkind notice' had appeared in the local paper, 'the sort of thing no white man could have written,' as Mrs Lesley said. The play was praised, to be sure, and so were the stage management and the performance as a whole, but the notice contained the following sentence: 'Miss Derek, though she charmingly looked her part, lacked the necessary experience, and occasionally forgot her words.' This tiny breath of genuine criticism had given deep offence, not indeed to Miss Derek, who was as hard as nails, but to her friends. Miss Derek did not belong to Chandrapore. She was stopping for a fortnight with the McBrydes, the police people, and she had been so good as to fill up a gap in the cast at the last moment. A nice impression of local hospitality she would carry away with her.

'To work, Mary, to work,' cried the Collector, touching his wife on the shoulder with a switch.

Mrs Turton got up awkwardly. 'What do you want me to do? Oh, those purdah women! I never thought any would come. Oh dear!'

A little group of Indian ladies had been gathering in a third quarter of the grounds, near a rustic summer-house in which the more timid of them had already taken refuge. The rest stood with their backs to the company and their faces pressed into a bank of shrubs. At a little distance stood their male relatives, watching the venture. The sight was significant: an island bared by the turning tide, and bound to grow.

'I consider they ought to come over to me.'

'Come along, Mary, get it over.'

'I refuse to shake hands with any of the men, unless it has to be the Nawab Bahadur.'

'Whom have we so far?' He glanced along the line. 'H'm! h'm! much as one expected. We know why he's here, I think—over that contract, and he wants to get the right side of me for Mohurram, and he's the astrologer who wants to dodge the municipal building regulations, and he's that Parsi, and he's—Hullo! there he goes—smash into our hollyhocks. Pulled the left rein when he meant the right. All as usual.'

'They ought never to have been allowed to drive in; it's so bad for them,' said Mrs Turton, who had at last begun her progress to the summer-house, accompanied by Mrs Moore, Miss Quested, and a terrier. 'Why they come at all I don't know. They hate it as much as we do. Talk to Mrs McBryde. Her husband made her give purdah parties until she struck.'

'This isn't a purdah party,' corrected Miss Quested.

'Oh, really,' was the haughty rejoinder.

'Do kindly tell us who these ladies are,' asked Mrs Moore.

'You're superior to them, anyway. Don't forget that. You're superior to everyone in India except one or two of the Ranis, and they're on an equality.'

Advancing, she shook hands with the group and said a few words of welcome in Urdu. She had learnt the lingo, but only to speak to her servants, so she knew none of the politer forms and of the verbs only the imperative mood. As soon as her speech was over, she enquired of her companions, 'Is that what you wanted?'

'Please tell these ladies that I wish we could speak their language, but we have only just come to their country.'

'Perhaps we speak yours a little,' one of the ladies said.

'Why, fancy, she understands!' said Mrs Turton.

'Eastbourne, Piccadilly, High Park Corner,' said another of the ladies.

'Oh yes, they're English-speaking.'

'But now we can talk: how delightful!' cried Adela, her face lighting up.

'She knows Paris also,' called one of the onlookers.

'They pass Paris on the way, no doubt,' said Mrs Turton, as if she was describing the movements of migratory birds. Her manner had grown more distant since she had discovered that some of the group was Westernized, and might apply her own standards to her.

'The shorter lady, she is my wife, she is Mrs Bhattacharya,' the onlooker explained. 'The taller lady, she is my sister, she is Mrs Das.'

The shorter and the taller ladies both adjusted their saris, and smiled.

There was a curious uncertainty about their gestures, as if they sought for a new formula which neither East nor West could provide. When Mrs Bhattacharya's husband spoke, she turned away from him, but she did not mind seeing the other men. Indeed all the ladies were uncertain, cowering, recovering, giggling, making tiny gestures of atonement or despair at all that was said, and alternately fondling the terrier or shrinking from him. Miss Quested now had her desired opportunity; friendly Indians were before her, and she tried to make them talk, but she failed, she strove in vain against the echoing walls of their civility. Whatever she said produced a murmur of deprecation, varying into a murmur of concern when she dropped her pocket-handkerchief. She tried doing nothing, to see what that produced, and they too did nothing. Mrs Moore was equally unsuccessful. Mrs Turton waited for them with a detached expression; she had known what nonsense it all was from the first.

When they took their leave, Mrs Moore had an impulse, and said to Mrs Bhattacharya, whose face she liked, 'I wonder whether you would allow us to call on you some day.'

'When?' she replied, inclining charmingly.

'Whenever is convenient.'

'All days are convenient.'

'Thursday . . .'

'Most certainly.'

'We shall enjoy it greatly, it would be a real pleasure. What about the time?'

'All hours.'

'Tell us which you would prefer. We're quite strangers to your country: we don't know when you have visitors,' said Miss Quested.

Mrs Bhattacharya seemed not to know either. Her gesture implied that she had known, since Thursdays began, that English ladies would come to see her on one of them, and so always stayed in. Everything pleased her, nothing surprised. She added, 'We leave for Calcutta to-day.'

'Oh, do you?' said Adela, not at first seeing the implication. Then she cried, 'Oh, but if you do we shall find you gone.'

Mrs Bhattacharya did not dispute it. But her husband called from the distance, 'Yes, yes, you come to us Thursday.'

'But you'll be in Calcutta.'

'No, no, we shall not.' He said something swiftly to his wife in Bengali. 'We expect you Thursday.'

'Thursday . . .' the woman echoed.

'You can't have done such a dreadful thing as to put off going for our sake?' exclaimed Mrs Moore.

'No, of course not, we are not such people.' He was laughing.

'I believe that you have. Oh, please—it distresses me beyond words.'

Everyone was laughing now, but with no suggestion that they had blundered. A shapeless discussion occurred, during which Mrs Turton retired, smiling to herself. The upshot was that they were to come Thursday, but early in the morning, so as to wreck the Bhattacharya plans as little as possible, and Mr Bhattacharya would send his carriage to fetch them, with servants to point out the way. Did he know where they lived? Yes, of course he knew, he knew everything; and he laughed again. They left among a flutter of compliments and smiles, and three ladies, who had hitherto taken no part in the reception, suddenly shot out of the summer-house like exquisitely coloured swallows, and salaamed them.

Meanwhile the Collector had been going his rounds. He made pleasant remarks and a few jokes, which were applauded lustily, but he knew something to the discredit of nearly every one of his guests, and was consequently perfunctory. When they had not cheated, it was bhang, women, or worse, and even the desirables wanted to get something out of him. He believed that a 'Bridge Party' did good rather than harm, or he would not have given one, but he was under no illusions, and at the proper moment he retired to the English side of the lawn. The impressions he left behind him were various. Many of the guests, especially the humbler and less anglicized, were genuinely grateful. To be addressed by so high an official was a permanent asset. They did not mind how long they stood, or how little happened, and when seven o'clock struck, they had to be turned out. Others were grateful with more intelligence. The Nawab Bahadur, indifferent for himself and for the distinction with which he was greeted, was moved by the mere kindness that must have prompted the invitation. He knew the difficulties. Hamidullah also thought that the Collector had played up well. But others, such as Mahmoud Ali, were cynical; they were firmly convinced that Turton had been made to give the party by his official superiors and was all the time consumed with impotent rage, and they infected some who were inclined to a healthier view. Yet even Mahmoud Ali was glad he had come. Shrines are fascinating, especially when rarely opened, and it amused him to note the ritual of the English club, and to caricature it afterwards to his friends.

After Mr Turton, the official who did his duty best was Mr Fielding, the Principal of the little Government College. He knew little of the district and less against the inhabitants, so he was in a less cynical state of mind. Athletic and cheerful, he romped about, making numerous mistakes which the parents of his pupils tried to cover up, for he was popular among them. When the moment for refreshments came, he did not move back to the English side, but burnt his mouth with gram. He talked to anyone and he ate anything. Amid much that was alien, he learnt that the two new ladies from England had been a great success, and that their politeness in wishing to be Mrs Bhattacharya's guests had pleased not only her but all Indians who heard of it. It pleased Mr Fielding also. He scarcely knew the two new ladies, still he decided to tell them what pleasure thay had given by their friendliness.

He found the younger of them alone. She was looking through a nick in the cactus hedge at the distant Marabar Hills, which had crept near, as was their custom at sunset; if the sunset had lasted long enough, they would have reached the town, but it was swift, being tropical. He gave her his information, and she was so much pleased and thanked him so heartily that he asked her and the other lady to tea.

'I'ld like to come very much indeed, and so would Mrs Moore, I know.'

'I'm rather a hermit, you know.'

'Much the best thing to be in this place.'

'Owing to my work and so on, I don't get up much to the club.'

'I know, I know, and we never get down from it. I envy you being with Indians.'

'Do you care to meet one or two?'

'Very, very, much indeed; it's what I long for. This party to-day makes me so angry and miserable. I think my countrymen out here must be mad. Fancy inviting guests and not treating them properly! You and Mr Turton and perhaps Mr McBryde are the only people who showed any common politeness. The rest make me perfectly ashamed, and it's got worse and worse.'

It had. The Englishmen had intended to play up better, but had been prevented from doing so by their women folk, whom they had to attend, provide with tea, advise about dogs, etc. When tennis began, the barrier grew impenetrable. It had been hoped to have some sets between East and West, but this was forgotten, and the courts were monopolized by the usual club couples. Fielding resented it too, but did not say so to the girl, for he found something theoretical in her outburst. Did she care about Indian music? he enquired; there was an old professor down at the College, who sang.

'Oh, just what we wanted to hear. And do you know Doctor Aziz?'

'I know all about him. I don't know him. Would you like him asked too?'

'Mrs Moore says he is so nice.'

'Very well, Miss Quested. Will Thursday suit you?'

'Indeed it will, and that morning we go to this Indian lady's. All the nice things are coming Thursday.'

'I won't ask the City Magistrate to bring you. I know he'll be busy at that time.'

'Yes, Ronny is always hard-worked,' she replied, contemplating the hills. How lovely they suddenly were! But she couldn't touch them. In front, like a shutter, fell a vision of her married life. She and Ronny would look into the club like this every evening, then drive home to dress; they would see the Lesleys and the Callendars and the Turtons and the Burtons, and invite them and be invited by them, while the true India slid by unnoticed. Colour would remain—the pageant of birds in the early morning, brown bodies, white turbans, idols whose flesh was scarlet or blue—and movement would remain as long as there were crowds in the bazaar and bathers in the tanks. Perched up on the seat of a dogcart, she would see them. But the force that lies behind colour and movement would escape her even more effectually than it did now. She would see India always as a frieze, never as a spirit, and she assumed that it was a spirit of which Mrs Moore had had a glimpse.

And sure enough they did drive away from the club in a few minutes, and they did dress, and to dinner came Miss Derek and the McBrydes, and the menu was: Julienne soup full of bullety bottled peas, pseudo-cottage bread, fish full of branching bones, pretending to be plaice, more bottled peas with the cutlets, trifle, sardines on toast: the menu of Anglo-India. A dish might be added or subtracted as one rose or fell in the official scale, the peas might rattle less or more, the sardines and the vermouth be imported by a different firm, but the tradition remained; the food of exiles, cooked by servants who did not understand it. Adela thought of the young men and women who had come out before her, P. & O. full after P. & O. full, and had been set down to the same food and the same ideas, and been snubbed in the same good-humoured way until they kept to the accredited themes and began to snub others. 'I should never get like that,' she thought, for she was young herself; all the same she knew that she had come up against something that was both insidious and tough, and against which she needed allies. She must gather around her at Chandrapore a few people who felt as she did, and she was glad to have met Mr Fielding and the Indian lady with the unpronounceable name. Here at all events was a nucleus; she should know much better where she stood in the course of the next two days.

Miss Derek—she companioned a Maharani in a remote Native State. She was genial and gay and made them all laugh about her leave, which she had taken because she felt she deserved it, not because the Maharani said she might go. Now she wanted to take the Maharaja's motor-car as well; it had gone to a Chiefs' Conference at Delhi, and she had a great scheme for burgling it at the junction as it came back in the train. She was also very funny about the Bridge Party—indeed she regarded the entire peninsula as a comic opera. 'If one couldn't see the laughable side of these people one 'ld be done for,' said Miss Derek. Mrs McBryde—it was she who had been the nurse—ceased not to exclaim, 'Oh, Nancy, how topping! Oh, Nancy, how killing! I wish I could look at things like that.' Mr McBryde did not speak much; he seemed nice.

When the guests had gone, and Adela gone to bed, there was another interview between mother and son. He wanted her advice and support—while resenting interference. 'Does Adela talk to you much?' he began. 'I'm so driven with work, I don't see her as much as I hoped, but I hope she finds things comfortable.'

'Adela and I talk mostly about India. Dear, since you mention it, you're quite right—you ought to be more alone with her than you are.'

'Yes, perhaps, but then people 'ld gossip.'

'Well, they must gossip sometime! Let them gossip.'

'People are so odd out here, and it's not like home—one's always facing the footlights, as the Burra Sahib said. Take a silly little example: when Adela went out to the boundary of the club compound, and Fielding followed her. I saw Mrs Callendar notice it. They notice everything, until they're perfectly sure you're their sort.'

'I don't think Adela 'll ever be quite their sort—she's much too individual.'

'I know, that's so remarkable about her,' he said thoughtfully. Mrs Moore thought him rather absurd. Accustomed to the privacy of London, she could not realize that India, seemingly so mysterious, contains none, and that consequently the conventions have greater force. 'I suppose nothing's on her mind,' he continued.

'Ask her, ask her yourself, my dear boy.'

'Probably she's heard tales of the heat, but of course I should pack her off to the Hills every April—I'm not one to keep a wife grilling in the Plains.'

'Oh, it wouldn't be the weather.'

'There's nothing in India but the weather, my dear mother; it's the Alpha and Omega of the whole affair.'

'Yes, as Mr McBryde was saying, but it's much more the Anglo-Indians themselves who are likely to get on Adela's nerves. She doesn't think they behave pleasantly to Indians, you see.'

'What did I tell you?' he exclaimed, losing his gentle manner. 'I knew it last week. Oh, how like a woman to worry over a side-issue!'

She forgot about Adela in her surprise. 'A side-issue, a side-issue?' she repeated. 'How can it be that?'

'We're not out here for the purpose of behaving pleasantly!'

'What do you mean?'

'What I say. We're out here to do justice and keep the peace. Them's my sentiments. India isn't a drawing-room.'

'Your sentiments are those of a god,' she said quietly, but it was his manner rather than his sentiments that annoyed her.

Trying to recover his temper, he said, 'India likes gods.'

'And Englishmen like posing as gods.'

'There's no point in all this. Here we are, and we're going to stop, and the country's got to put up with us, gods or no gods. Oh, look here,' he broke out, rather pathetically, 'what do you and Adela want me to do? Go against my class, against all the people I respect and admire out here? Lose such power as I have for doing good in this country because my behaviour isn't pleasant? You neither of you understand what work is, or you 'ld never talk such eyewash. I hate talking like this, but one must occasionally. It's morbidly sensitive to go on as Adela and you do. I noticed you both at the club to-day—after the Collector had been at all that trouble to amuse you. I am out here to work, mind, to hold this wretched country by force. I'm not a missionary or a Labour Member or a vague sentimental sympathetic literary man. I'm just a servant of the Government; it's the profession you wanted me to choose myself, and that's that. We're not pleasant in India, and we don't intend to be pleasant. We've something more important to do.'

He spoke sincerely. Every day he worked hard in the court trying to decide which of two untrue accounts was the less untrue, trying to dispense justice fearlessly, to protect the weak against the less weak, the incoherent against the plausible, surrounded by lies and flattery. That morning he had convicted a railway clerk of overcharging pilgrims for their tickets, and a Pathan of attempted rape. He expected no gratitude, no recognition for this, and both clerk and Pathan might appeal, bribe their witnesses more effectually in the interval, and get their sentences reversed. It was his duty. But he did expect sympathy from his own people, and except from new-comers he obtained it. He did think he ought not to be worried about 'Bridge Parties' when the day's work was over and he wanted to play tennis with his equals or rest his legs upon a long chair.

He spoke sincerely, but she could have wished with less gusto. How Ronny revelled in the drawbacks of his situation! How he did rub it in that he was not in India to behave pleasantly, and derived positive satisfaction therefrom! He reminded her of his public-schooldays. The traces of young-man humanitarianism had sloughed off, and he talked like an intelligent and embittered boy. His words without his voice might have impressed her, but when she heard the self-satisfied lilt of them, when she saw the mouth moving so complacently and competently beneath the little red nose, she felt, quite illogically, that this was not the last word on India. One touch of regret—not the canny substitute but the true regret from the heart—would have made him a different man, and the British Empire a different institution.

'I'm going to argue, and indeed dictate,' she said, clinking her rings. 'The English *are* out here to be pleasant.'

'How do you make that out, mother?' he asked, speaking gently again, for he was ashamed of his irritability.

'Because India is part of the earth. And God has put us on the earth in order to be pleasant to each other. God . . . is . . . love.' She hesitated, seeing how much he disliked the argument, but something made her go on. 'God has put us on earth to love our neighbours and to show it, and He is omnipresent, even in India, to see how we are succeeding.'

He looked gloomy, and a little anxious. He knew this religious strain in her, and that it was a symptom of bad health; there had been much of it when his step-father died. He thought, 'She is certainly ageing, and I ought not to be vexed with anything she says.'

'The desire to behave pleasantly satisfies God. . . . The sincere if impotent desire wins His blessing. I think every one fails, but there are so many kinds of failure. Good will and more good will and more good will. Though I speak with the tongues of . . .'

He waited until she had done, and then said gently, 'I quite see that. I suppose I ought to get off to my files now, and you 'll be going to bed.'

'I suppose so, I suppose so.' They did not part for a few minutes, but the conversation had become unreal since Christianity had entered it. Ronny approved of religion as long as it endorsed the National Anthem, but he objected when it attempted to influence his life. Then he would say in respectful yet decided tones, 'I don't think it does to talk about these things, every fellow has to work out his own religion,' and any fellow who heard him muttered, 'Hear!'

Mrs Moore felt that she had made a mistake in mentioning God, but she found him increasingly difficult to avoid as she grew older, and he had been constantly in her thoughts since she entered India, though oddly enough he satisfied her less. She must needs pronounce his name frequently, as the greatest she knew, yet she had never found it less efficacious. Outside the arch there seemed always an arch, beyond the remotest echo a silence. And she regretted afterwards that she had not kept to the real serious subject that had caused her to visit India—namely the relationship between Ronny and Adela. Would they, or would they not, succeed in becoming engaged to be married?

Chapter Six

Aziz had not gone to the Bridge Party. Immediately after his meeting with Mrs Moore he was diverted to other matters. Several surgical cases came in, and kept him busy. He ceased to be either outcaste or poet, and became the medical student, very gay, and full of details of operations which he poured into the shrinking ears of his friends. His profession fascinated him at times, but he required it to be exciting, and it was his hand, not his mind, that was scientific. The knife he loved and used skilfully, and he also liked pumping in the latest serums. But the boredom of régime and hygiene repelled him, and after inoculating a man for enteric, he would go away and drink unfiltered water himself. 'What can you expect from the fellow?' said dour Major Callendar. 'No grits, no guts.' But in his heart he knew that if Aziz and not he had operated last year on Mrs Graysford's appendix, the old lady would probably have lived. And this did not dispose him any better towards his subordinate.

There was a row the morning after the mosque—they were always having rows. The Major, who had been up half the night, wanted damn well to know why Aziz had not come promptly when summoned.

'Sir, excuse me, I did. I mounted my bike, and it bust in front of the Cow Hospital. So I had to find a tonga.'

'Bust in front of the Cow Hospital, did it? And how did you come to be there?'

'I beg your pardon?'

'Oh Lord, oh Lord! When I live here'—he kicked the gravel—'and you live there—not ten minutes from me—and the Cow Hospital is right ever so far away the other side of you—*there*—then how did you come to be passing the Cow Hospital on the way to me? Now do some work for a change.'

He strode away in a temper, without waiting for the excuse, which as far as it went was a sound one: the Cow Hospital was in a straight line between Hamidullah's house and his own, so Aziz had naturally passed it. He never realized that the educated Indians visited one another constantly, and were weaving, however painfully, a new social fabric. Caste 'or something of the sort' would prevent them. He only knew that no one ever told him the truth, although he had been in the country for twenty years.

Aziz watched him go with amusement. When his spirits were up he felt that the English are a comic institution, and he enjoyed being misunderstood by them. But it was an amusement of the emotions and nerves, which an accident or the passage of time might destroy; it was apart from the fundamental gaiety that he reached when he was with those whom he trusted. A disobliging simile involving Mrs Callendar occurred to his fancy. 'I must tell that to Mahmoud Ali, it'll make him laugh,' he thought. Then he got to work. He was competent and indispensable, and he knew it. The simile passed from his mind while he exercised his professional skill.

During these pleasant and busy days, he heard vaguely that the Collector was giving a party, and that the Nawab Bahadur said every one ought to go to it. His fellow-assistant, Doctor Panna Lal, was in ecstasies at the prospect, and was urgent that they should attend it together in his new tum-tum. The arrangement suited them both. Aziz was spared the indignity of a bicycle or the expense of hiring, while Dr Panna Lal, who was timid and elderly, secured someone who could manage his horse. He could manage it himself, but only just, and he was afraid of the motors and of the unknown turn into the club grounds. 'Disaster may come,' he said politely, 'but we shall at all events get there safe, even if we do not get back.' And with more logic: 'It will, I think, create a good impression should two doctors arrive at the same time.'

But when the time came, Aziz was seized with a revulsion, and determined not to go. For one thing his spell of work, lately concluded, left him independent and healthy. For another, the day chanced to fall on the anniversary of his wife's death. She had died soon after he had fallen in love with her; he had not loved her at first. Touched by Western feeling, he disliked union with a woman whom he had never seen; moreover, when he did see her, she disappointed him, and he begat his first child in mere animality. The change began after its birth. He was won by her love for him, by a loyalty that implied something more than submission, and by her efforts to educate herself against that lifting of the purdah that would come in the next generation if not in theirs. She was intelligent, yet had old-fashioned grace. Gradually he lost the feeling that his relatives had chosen wrongly for him. Sensuous enjoyment—well, even if he had had it, it would have dulled in a year, and he had gained something instead, which seemed to increase the longer they lived together. She became the mother of a son . . . and in giving him a second son she died. Then he realized what he had lost, and that no woman could ever take her place; a friend would come nearer to her than another woman. She had gone, there was no one like her, and what is that uniqueness but love? He amused himself, he forgot her at times: but at other times he felt that she had sent all the beauty and joy of the world into Paradise, and he meditated suicide. Would he meet her beyond the tomb? Is there such a meeting-place? Though orthodox, he did not know. God's unity was indubitable and indubitably announced, but on all other points he wavered like the average Christian; his belief in the life to come would pale to a hope, vanish, reappear, all in a single sentence or a dozen heart-beats, so that the corpuscles of his blood rather than he seemed to decide which opinion he should hold, and for how long. It was so with all his opinions. Nothing stayed, nothing passed that did not return; the circulation was ceaseless and kept him young, and he mourned his wife the more sincerely because he mourned her seldom.

It would have been simpler to tell Dr Lal that he had changed his mind about the party, but until the last minute he did not know that he had changed it; indeed, he didn't change it, it changed itself. Unconquerable aversion welled. Mrs Callendar, Mrs Lesley—no, he couldn't stand them in his sorrow: they would guess it—for he dowered the British matron with strange insight—and would delight in torturing him, they would mock him to their husbands. When he should have been ready, he stood at the Post Office, writing a telegram to his children, and found on his return that Dr Lal had called for him, and gone on. Well, let him go on, as befitted the coarseness of his nature. For his own part, he would commune with the dead.

And unlocking a drawer, he took out his wife's photograph. He gazed at it, and tears spouted from his eyes. He thought, 'How unhappy I am!' But because he really was unhappy, another emotion soon mingled with his self-pity: he desired to remember his wife and could not. Why could he remember people whom he did not love? They were always so vivid to him, whereas the more he looked at this photograph, the less he saw. She had eluded him thus, ever since they had carried her to her tomb. He had known that she would pass from his hands and eyes, but had thought she could live in his mind, not realizing that the very fact that we have loved the dead increases their unreality, and that the more passionately we invoke them the further they recede. A piece of brown cardboard and three children—that was all that was left of his wife. It was unbearable, and he thought again, 'How unhappy I am!' and became happier. He had breathed for an instant the mortal air that surrounds Orientals and all men, and he drew back from it with a gasp, for he was young. 'Never, never shall I get over this,' he told himself. 'Most certainly my career is a failure, and my sons will be badly brought up.' Since it was certain, he strove to avert it, and looked at some notes he had made on a case at the hospital. Perhaps some day a rich person might require this particular operation, and he gain a large sum. The notes interesting him on their own account, he locked the photograph up again. Its moment was over, and he did not think about his wife any more.

After tea his spirits improved, and he went round to see Hamidullah. Hamidullah had gone to the party, but his pony had not, so Aziz borrowed it, also his friend's riding breeches and polo mallet. He repaired to the Maidan. It was deserted except at its rim, where some bazaar youths were training. Training for what? They would have found it hard to say, but the word had got into the air. Round they ran, weedy and knock-kneed—the local physique was wretched—with an expression on their faces not so much of determination as of a determination to be determined. 'Maharajah, salaam,' he called for a joke. The youths stopped and laughed. He advised them not to exert themselves. They promised they would not, and ran on.

Riding into the middle, he began to knock the ball about. He could not play, but his pony could, and he set himself to learn, free from all human tension. He forgot the whole damned business of living as he scurried over the brown platter of the Maidan, with the evening wind on his forehead, and the encircling trees soothing his eyes. The ball shot away towards a stray subaltern who was also practising; he hit it back to Aziz and called, 'Send it along again.'

'All right.'

The new-comer had some notion of what to do, but his horse had none, and forces were equal. Concentrated on the ball, they somehow became fond of one another, and smiled when they drew rein to rest. Aziz liked soldiers—they either accepted you or swore at you, which was preferable to the civilian's hauteur—and the subaltern liked anyone who could ride.

'Often play?' he asked.

'Never.'

'Let's have another chukker.'

As he hit, his horse bucked and off he went, cried, 'Oh God!' and jumped on again. 'Don't you ever fall off?'

'Plenty.'

'Not you.'

They reined up again, the fire of good fellowship in their eyes. But it cooled with their bodies, for athletics can only raise a temporary glow. Nationality was returning, but before it could exert its poison they parted, saluting each other. 'If only they were all like that,' each thought.

Now it was sunset. A few of his co-religionists had come to the Maidan, and were praying with their faces towards Mecca. A Brahminy Bull walked towards them, and Aziz, though disinclined to pray himself, did not see why they should be bothered with the clumsy and idolatrous animal. He gave it a tap with his polo mallet. As he did so, a voice from the road hailed him: it was Dr Panna Lal, returning in high distress from the Collector's party.

'Dr Aziz, Dr Aziz, where you been? I waited ten full minutes' time at your house, then I went.'

'I am so awfully sorry—I was compelled to go to the Post Office.'

One of his own circle would have accepted this as meaning that he had changed his mind, an event too common to merit censure. But Dr Lal, being of low extraction, was not sure whether an insult had not been intended, and he was further annoyed because Aziz had buffeted the Brahminy Bull. 'Post Office? Do you not send your servants?' he said.

'I have so few—my scale is very small.'

'Your servant spoke to me. I saw your servant.'

'But, Dr Lal, consider. How could I send my servant when you were coming: you come, we go, my house is left alone, my servant comes back perhaps, and all my portable property has been carried away by bad characters in the meantime. Would you have that? The cook is deaf—I can never count on my cook—and the boy is only a little boy. Never, never do I and Hassan leave the house at the same time together. It is my fixed rule.' He said all this and much more out of civility, to save Dr Lal's face. It was not offered as truth and should not have been criticized as such. But the other demolished it—an easy and ignoble task. 'Even if this so, what prevents leaving a chit saying where you go?' and so on. Aziz detested ill breeding, and made his pony caper. 'Farther away, or mine will start out of sympathy,' he wailed, revealing the true source of his irritation. 'It has been so rough and wild this afternoon. It spoiled some most valuable blossoms in the club garden, and had to be dragged back by four men. English ladies and gentlemen looking on, and the Collector Sahib himself taking a note. But, Dr Aziz, I'll not take up your valuable time. This will not interest you, who have so many engagements and telegrams. I am just a poor old doctor who thought right to pay my respects when I was asked and where I was asked. Your absence, I may remark, drew commentaries.'

'They can damn well comment.'

'It is fine to be young. Damn well! Oh, very fine. Damn whom?'

'I go or not as I please.'

'Yet you promise me, and then fabricate this tale of a telegram. Go forward, Dapple.'

They went, and Aziz had a wild desire to make an enemy for life. He could do it so easily by galloping near them. He did it. Dapple bolted. He thundered back on to the Maidan. The glory of his play with the subaltern remained for a little, he galloped and swooped till he poured with sweat, and until he returned the pony to Hamidullah's stable he felt the equal of any man. Once on his feet, he had creeping fears. Was he in bad odour with the powers that be? Had he offended the Collector by absenting himself? Dr Panna Lal was a person of no importance, yet was it wise to have quarrelled even with him? The complexion of his mind turned from human to political. He thought no longer, 'Can I get on with people?' but 'Are they stronger than I?' breathing the prevalent miasma.

At his home a chit was awaiting him, bearing the Government stamp. It lay on his table like a high explosive, which at a touch might blow his flimsy bungalow to bits. He was going to be cashiered because he had not turned up at the party. When he opened the note, it proved to be quite different; an invitation from Mr Fielding, the Principal of Government College, asking him to come to tea the day after to-morrow. His spirits revived with violence. They would have revived in any case, for he possessed a soul that could suffer but not stifle, and led a steady life beneath his mutability. But this invitation gave him particular joy, because Fielding had asked him to tea a month ago, and he had forgotten about it—never answered, never gone, just forgotten And here came a second invitation, without a rebuke or even an allusion to his slip. Here was true courtesy—the civil deed that shows the good heart—and snatching up his pen he wrote an affectionate reply, and hurried back for news to Hamidullah's. For he had never met the Principal, and believed that the one serious gap in his life was going to be filled. He longed to know everything about the splendid fellow—his salary, preferences, antecedents, how best one might please him. But Hamidullah was still out, and Mahmoud Ali, who was in, would only make silly rude jokes about the party.

Chapter Seven

This Mr Fielding had been caught by India late. He was over forty when he entered that oddest portal, the Victoria Terminus at Bombay, and–having bribed a European ticket inspector–took his luggage into the compartment of his first tropical train. The journey remained in his mind as significant. Of his two carriage companions one was a youth, fresh to the East like himself, the other a seasoned Anglo-Indian of his own age. A gulf divided him from either; he had seen too many cities and men to be the first or to become the second. New impressions crowded on him, but they were not the orthodox new impressions; the past conditioned them, and so it was with his mistakes. To regard an Indian as if he were an Italian is not, for instance, a common error, nor perhaps a fatal one, and Fielding often attempted analogies between this peninsula and that other, smaller and more exquisitely shaped, that stretches into the classic waters of the Mediterranean.

His career, though scholastic, was varied, and had included going to the bad and repenting thereafter. By now he was a hard-bitten, good-tempered, intelligent fellow on the verge of middle age, with a belief in education. He did not mind whom he taught; public schoolboys, mental defectives and policemen, had all come his way, and he had no objection to adding Indians. Through the influence of friends, he was nominated Principal of the little college at Chandrapore, liked it, and assumed he was a success. He did succeed with his pupils, but the gulf between himself and his countrymen, which he had noticed in the train, widened distressingly. He could not at first see what was wrong. He was not unpatriotic, he always got on with Englishmen in England, all his best friends were English, so why was it not the same out here? Outwardly of the large shaggy type, with sprawling limbs and blue eyes, he appeared to inspire confidence until he spoke. Then something in his manner puzzled people and failed to allay the distrust which his profession naturally inspired. There needs must be this evil of brains in India, but woe to him through whom they are increased! The feeling grew that Mr Fielding was a disruptive force, and rightly, for ideas are fatal to caste, and he used ideas by that most potent method–interchange. Neither a missionary nor a student, he was happiest in the give-and-take of a private conversation. The world, he believed, is a globe of men who are trying to reach one another and can best do so by the help of good will plus culture and intelligence–a creed ill suited to Chandrapore, but he had come out too late to lose it. He had no racial feeling–not because he was superior to his brother civilians, but because he had matured in a different atmosphere, where the herd-instinct does not flourish. The remark that did him most harm at the club was a silly aside to the effect that the so-called white races are really pinko-grey. He only said this to be cheery, he did not realize that 'white' has no more to do with a colour than 'God save the King' with a god, and that it is the height of impropriety to consider what it does connote. The pinko-grey male whom he addressed was subtly scandalized; his sense of insecurity was awoken, and he communicated it to the rest of the herd.

Still, the men tolerated him for the sake of his good heart and strong body; it was their wives who decided that he was not a sahib really. They disliked him. He took no notice of them, and this, which would have passed without comment in feminist England, did him harm in a community where the male is expected to be lively and helpful. Mr Fielding never advised one about dogs or horses, or dined, or paid his midday calls, or decorated trees for one's children at Christmas, and though he came to the club, it was only to get his tennis or billiards, and to go. This was true. He had discovered that it is possible to keep in with Indians and Englishmen, but that he who would also keep in with Englishwomen must drop the Indians. The two wouldn't combine. Useless to blame either party, useless to blame them for blaming one another. It just was so, and one had to choose. Most Englishmen preferred their own kinswomen, who, coming out in increasing numbers, made life on the home pattern yearly more possible. He had found it convenient and pleasant to associate with Indians and he must pay the price. As a rule no Englishwoman entered the College except for official functions, and if he invited Mrs Moore and Miss Quested to tea, it was because they were new-comers who would view everything with an equal if superficial eye, and would not turn on a special voice when speaking to his other guests.

The College itself had been slapped down by the Public Works Department, but its grounds included an ancient garden and a garden-house, and here he lived for much of the year. He was dressing after a bath when Dr Aziz was announced. Lifting up his voice, he shouted from the bedroom, 'Please make yourself at home.' The remark was unpremeditated, like most of his actions; it was what he felt inclined to say.

To Aziz it had a very definite meaning. 'May I really, Mr Fielding? It's very good of you,' he called back; 'I like unconventional behaviour so extremely.' His spirits flared up, he glanced round the living-room. Some luxury in it, but no order—nothing to intimidate poor Indians. It was also a very beautiful room, opening into the garden through three high arches of wood. 'The fact is I have long wanted to meet you,' he continued. 'I have heard so much about your warm heart from the Nawab Bahadur. But where is one to meet in a wretched hole like Chandrapore?' He came close up to the door. 'When I was greener here, I'll tell you what. I used to wish you to fall ill so that we could meet that way.' They laughed, and encouraged by his success he began to improvise. 'I said to myself, How does Mr Fielding look this morning? Perhaps pale. And the Civil Surgeon is pale too, he will not be able to attend upon him when the shivering commences. I should have been sent for instead. Then we would have had jolly talks, for you are a celebrated student of Persian poetry.'

'You know me by sight, then.'

'Of course, of course. You know me?'

'I know you very well by name.'

'I have been here such a short time, and always in the bazaar. No wonder you have never seen me, and I wonder you know my name. I say, Mr Fielding?'

'Yes?'

'Guess what I look like before you come out. That will be a kind of game.'

'You're five feet nine inches high,' said Fielding, surmising this much through the ground glass of the bedroom door.

'Jolly good. What next? Have I not a venerable white beard?'

'Blast!'

'Anything wrong?'

'I've stamped on my last collar stud.'

'Take mine, take mine.'

'Have you a spare one?'

'Yes, yes, one minute.'

'Not if you're wearing it yourself.'

'No, no, one in my pocket.' Stepping aside, so that his outline might vanish, he wrenched off his collar, and pulled out of his shirt the back stud, a gold stud, which was part of a set that his brother-in-law had brought him from Europe. 'Here it is,' he cried.

'Come in with it if you don't mind the unconventionality.'

'One minute again.' Replacing his collar, he prayed that it would not spring up at the back during tea. Fielding's bearer, who was helping him to dress, opened the door for him.

'Many thanks.' They shook hands smiling. He began to look round, as he would have with any old friend. Fielding was not surprised at the rapidity of their intimacy. With so emotional a people it was apt to come at once or never, and he and Aziz, having heard only good of each other, could afford to dispense with preliminaries.

'But I always thought that Englishmen kept their rooms so tidy. It seems that this is not so. I need not be so ashamed.' He sat down gaily on the bed; then, forgetting himself entirely, drew up his legs and folded them under him. 'Everything ranged coldly on shelves was what *I* thought.—I say, Mr Fielding, is the stud going to go in?'

'I hae ma doots.'

'What's that last sentence, please? Will you teach me some new words and so improve my English?'

Fielding doubted whether 'everything ranged coldly on shelves' could be improved. He was often struck with the liveliness with which the younger generation handled a foreign tongue. They altered the idiom, but they could say whatever they wanted to say quickly; there were none of the babuisms ascribed to them up at the club. But then the club moved slowly; it still declared that few Mohammedans and no Hindus would eat at an Englishman's table, and that all Indian ladies were in impenetrable purdah. Individually it knew better; as a club it declined to change.

'Let me put in your stud. I see . . . the shirt back's hole is rather small and to rip it wider a pity.'

'Why in hell does one wear collars at all?' grumbled Fielding as he bent his neck.

'We wear them to pass the Police.'

'What's that?'

'If I'm biking in English dress—starch collar, hat with ditch—they take no notice. When I wear a fez, they cry, "Your lamp's out!" Lord Curzon did not consider this when he urged natives of India to retain their picturesque costumes.—Hooray! Stud's gone in.—Sometimes I shut my eyes and dream I have splendid clothes again and am riding into battle behind Alamgir. Mr Fielding, must not India have been beautiful then, with the Mogul Empire at its height and Alamgir reigning at Delhi upon the Peacock Throne?'

'Two ladies are coming to tea to meet you—I think you know them.'

'Meet me? I know no ladies.'

'Not Mrs Moore and Miss Quested?'

'Oh yes—I remember.' The romance at the mosque had sunk out of his consciousness as soon as it was over. 'An excessively aged lady; but will you please repeat the name of her companion?'

'Miss Quested.'

'Just as you wish.' He was disappointed that other guests were coming, for he preferred to be alone with his new friend.

'You can talk to Miss Quested about the Peacock Throne if you like—she's artistic, they say.'

'Is she a Post Impressionist?'

'Post Impressionism, indeed! Come along to tea. This world is getting too much for me altogether.'

Aziz was offended. The remark suggested that he, an obscure Indian, had no right to have heard of Post Impressionism—a privilege reserved for the Ruling Race, that. He said stiffly, 'I do not consider Mrs Moore my friend, I only met her accidentally in my mosque,' and was adding 'a single meeting is too short to make a friend,' but before he could finish the sentence the stiffness vanished from it, because he felt Fielding's fundamental good will. His own went out to it, and grappled beneath the shifting tides of emotion which can alone bear the voyager to an anchorage but may also carry him across it on to the rocks. He was safe really—as safe as the shore-dweller who can only understand stability and supposes that every ship must be wrecked, and he had sensations the shore-dweller cannot know. Indeed, he was sensitive rather than responsive. In every remark he found a meaning, but not always the true meaning, and his life though vivid was largely a dream. Fielding, for instance, had not meant that Indians are obscure, but that Post Impressionism is; a gulf divided his remark from Mrs Turton's 'Why, they speak English,' but to Aziz the two sounded alike. Fielding saw that something had gone wrong, and equally that it had come right, but he didn't fidget, being an optimist where personal relations were concerned, and their talk rattled on as before.

'Besides the ladies I am expecting one of my assistants–Narayan Godbole.'

'Oho, the Deccani Brahman!'

'He wants the past back too, but not precisely Alamgir.'

'I should think not. Do you know what Deccani Brahmans say: That England conquered India from them–from them, mind, and not from the Moguls. Is not that like their cheek? They have even bribed it to appear in text-books, for they are so subtle and immensely rich. Professor Godbole must be quite unlike all other Deccani Brahmans from all I can hear say. A most sincere chap.'

'Why don't you fellows run a club in Chandrapore, Aziz?'

'Perhaps–some day . . . just now I see Mrs Moore and–what's her name–coming.'

How fortunate that it was an 'unconventional' party, where formalities are ruled out! On this basis Aziz found the English ladies easy to talk to, he treated them like men. Beauty would have troubled him, for it entails rules of its own, but Mrs Moore was so old and Miss Quested so plain that he was spared this anxiety. Adela's angular body and the freckles on her face were terrible defects in his eyes, and he wondered how God could have been so unkind to any female form. His attitude towards her remained entirely straightforward in consequence.

'I want to ask you something, Dr Aziz,' she began. 'I heard from Mrs Moore how helpful you were to her in the mosque, and how interesting. She learnt more about India in those few minutes' talk with you than in the three weeks since we landed.'

'Oh, please do not mention a little thing like that. Is there anything else I may tell you about my country?'

'I want you to explain a disappointment we had this morning; it must be some point of Indian etiquette.'

'There honestly is none,' he replied. 'We are by nature a most informal people.'

'I am afraid we must have made some blunder and given offence,' said Mrs Moore.

'That is even more impossible. But may I know the facts?'

'An Indian lady and gentleman were to send their carriage for us this morning at nine. It has never come. We waited and waited and waited; we can't think what happened.'

'Some misunderstanding,' said Fielding, seeing at once that it was the type of incident that had better not be cleared up.

'Oh no, it wasn't that,' Miss Quested persisted. 'They even gave up going to Calcutta to entertain us. We must have made some stupid blunder, we both feel sure.'

'I wouldn't worry about that.'

'Exactly what Mr Heaslop tells me,' she retorted, reddening a little. 'If one doesn't worry, how's one to understand?'

The host was inclined to change the subject, but Aziz took it up warmly, and on learning fragments of the delinquents' name pronounced that they were Hindus.

'Slack Hindus—they have no idea of society; I know them very well because of a doctor at the hospital. Such a slack, unpunctual fellow! It is as well you did not go to their house, for it would give you a wrong idea of India. Nothing sanitary. I think for my own part they grew ashamed of their house and that is why they did not send.'

'That's a notion,' said the other man.

'I do so hate mysteries,' Adela announced.

'We English do.'

'I dislike them not because I'm English, but from my own personal point of view,' she corrected.

'I like mysteries but I rather dislike muddles,' said Mrs Moore.

'A mystery is a muddle.'

'Oh, do you think so, Mr Fielding?'

'A mystery is only a high-sounding term for a muddle. No advantage in stirring it up, in either case. Aziz and I know well that India's a muddle.'

'India's— Oh, what an alarming idea!'

'There'll be no muddle when you come to see me,' said Aziz, rather out of his depth. 'Mrs Moore and everyone—I invite you all—oh, please.'

The old lady accepted: she still thought the young doctor excessively nice; moreover, a new feeling, half languor, half excitement, bade her turn down any fresh path. Miss Quested accepted out of adventure. She also liked Aziz, and believed that when she knew him better he would unlock his country for her. His invitation gratified her, and she asked him for his address.

Aziz thought of his bungalow with horror. It was a detestable shanty near a low bazaar. There was practically only one room in it, and that infested with small black flies. 'Oh, but we will talk of something else now,' he exclaimed. 'I wish I lived here. See this beautiful room! Let us admire it together for a little. See those curves at the bottom of the arches. What delicacy! It is the architecture of Question and Answer. Mrs Moore, you are in India; I am not joking.' The room inspired him. It was an audience hall built in the eighteenth century for some high official, and though of wood had reminded Fielding of the Loggia de' Lanzi at Florence. Little rooms, now Europeanized, clung to it on either side, but the central hall was unpapered and unglassed, and the air of the garden poured in freely. One sat in public—on exhibition, as it were—in full view of the gardeners who were screaming at the birds and of the man who rented the tank for the cultivation of water chestnut. Fielding let the mango trees too—there was no knowing who might not come in—and his servants sat on his steps night and day to discourage thieves. Beautiful certainly, and the Englishman had not spoilt it, whereas Aziz in an occidental moment would have hung Maude Goodmans on the walls. Yet there was no doubt to whom the room really belonged. . . .

'I am doing justice here. A poor widow who has been robbed comes along and I give her fifty rupees, to another a hundred, and so on and so on. I should like that.'

Mrs Moore smiled, thinking of the modern method as exemplified in her son. 'Rupees don't last for ever, I'm afraid,' she said.

'Mine would. God would give me more when he saw I gave. Always be giving, like the Nawab Bahadur. My father was the same, that is why he died poor.' And pointing about the room he peopled it with clerks and officials, all benevolent because they lived long ago. 'So we would sit giving for ever—on a carpet instead of chairs, that is the chief change between now and then, but I think we would never punish anyone.'

The ladies agreed.

'Poor criminal, give him another chance. It only makes a man worse to go to prison and be corrupted.' His face grew very tender—the tenderness of one incapable of administration, and unable to grasp that if the poor criminal is let off he will again rob the poor widow. He was tender to everyone except a few family enemies whom he did not consider human: on these he desired revenge. He was even tender to the English; he knew at the bottom of his heart that they could not help being so cold and odd and circulating like an ice stream through his land. 'We punish no one, no one,' he repeated, 'and in the evening we will give a great banquet with a nautch and lovely girls shall shine on every side of the tank with fireworks in their hands, and all shall be feasting and happiness until the next day, when there shall be justice as before—fifty rupees, a hundred, a thousand—till peace comes. Ah, why didn't we live in that time?—But are you admiring Mr Fielding's house? Do look how the pillars are painted blue, and the verandah's pavilions—what do you call them?—that are above us inside are blue also. Look at the carving on the pavilions. Think of the hours it took. Their little roofs are curved to imitate bamboo. So pretty—and the bamboos waving by the tank outside. Mrs Moore! Mrs Moore!'

'Well?' she said, laughing.

'You remember the water by our mosque? It comes down and fills this tank—a skilful arrangement of the Emperors. They stopped here going down into Bengal. They loved water. Wherever they went they created fountains, gardens, hammams. I was telling Mr Fielding I would give anything to serve them.'

He was wrong about the water, which no Emperor, however skilful, can cause to gravitate uphill; a depression of some depth together with the whole of Chandrapore lay between the mosque and Fielding's house. Ronny would have pulled him up, Turton would have wanted to pull him up, but restrained himself. Fielding did not even want to pull him up; he had dulled his craving for verbal truth and cared chiefly for truth of mood. As for Miss Quested, she accepted everything Aziz said as true verbally. In her ignorance, she regarded him as 'India,' and never surmised that his outlook was limited and his method inaccurate, and that no one is India.

He was now much excited, chattering away hard, and even saying damn when he got mixed up in his sentences. He told them of his profession, and of the operations he had witnessed and performed, and he went into details that scared Mrs Moore, though Miss Quested mistook them for proofs of his broad-mindedness; she had heard such talk at home in advanced academic circles, deliberately free. She supposed him to be emancipated as well as reliable, and placed him on a pinnacle which he could not retain. He was high enough for the moment, to be sure, but not on any pinnacle. Wings bore him up, and flagging would deposit him.

The arrival of Professor Godbole quieted him somewhat, but it remained his afternoon. The Brahman, polite and enigmatic, did not impede his eloquence, and even applauded it. He took his tea at a little distance from the outcasts, from a low table placed slightly behind him, to which he stretched back, and as it were encountered food by accident; all feigned indifference to Professor Godbole's tea. He was elderly and wizen with a grey moustache and grey-blue eyes, and his complexion was as fair as a European's. He wore a turban that looked like pale purple macaroni, coat, waistcoat, dhoti, socks with clocks. The clocks matched the turban, and his whole appearance suggested harmony—as if he had reconciled the products of East and West, mental as well as physical, and could never be discomposed. The ladies were interested in him, and hoped that he would supplement Dr Aziz by saying something about religion. But he only ate—ate and ate, smiling, never letting his eyes catch sight of his hand.

Leaving the Mogul Emperors, Aziz turned to topics that could distress no one. He described the ripening of the mangoes, and how in his boyhood he used to run out in the Rains to a big mango grove belonging to an uncle and gorge there. 'Then back with water streaming over you and perhaps rather a pain inside. But I did not mind. All my friends were paining with me. We have a proverb in Urdu: "What does unhappiness matter when we are all unhappy together?" which comes in conveniently after mangoes. Miss Quested, do wait for mangoes. Why not settle altogether in India?'

'I'm afraid I can't do that,' said Adela. She made the remark without thinking what it meant. To her, as to the three men, it seemed in key with the rest of the conversation, and not for several minutes—indeed, not for half an hour—did she realize that it was an important remark, and ought to have been made in the first place to Ronny.

'Visitors like you are too rare.'

'They are indeed,' said Professor Godbole. 'Such affability is seldom seen. But what can we offer to detain them?'

'Mangoes, mangoes.'

They laughed. 'Even mangoes can be got in England now,' put in Fielding. 'They ship them in ice-cold rooms. You can make India in England apparently, just as you can make England in India.'

'Frightfully expensive in both cases,' said the girl.

'I suppose so.'

'And nasty.'

But the host wouldn't allow the conversation to take this heavy turn. He turned to the old lady, who looked flustered and put out—he could not imagine why—and asked about her own plans. She replied that she should like to see over the College. Everyone immediately rose, with the exception of Professor Godbole, who was finishing a banana.

'Don't you come too, Adela; you dislike institutions.'

'Yes, that is so,' said Miss Quested, and sat down again.

Aziz hesitated. His audience was splitting up. The more familiar half was going, but the more attentive remained. Reflecting that it was an 'unconventional' afternoon, he stopped.

Talk went on as before. Could one offer the visitors unripe mangoes in a fool? 'I speak now as a doctor: no.' Then the old man said, 'But I will send you up a few healthy sweets. I will give myself that pleasure.'

'Miss Quested, Professor Godbole's sweets are delicious,' said Aziz sadly, for he wanted to send sweets too and had no wife to cook them. 'They will give you a real Indian treat. Ah, in my poor position I can give you nothing.'

'I don't know why you say that, when you have so kindly asked us to your house.'

He thought again of his bungalow with horror. Good heavens, the stupid girl had taken him at his word! What was he to do? 'Yes, all that is settled,' he cried. 'I invite you all to see me in the Marabar Caves.'

'I shall be delighted.'

'Oh, that is a most magnificent entertainment compared to my poor sweets. But has not Miss Quested visited our caves already?'

'No. I've not even heard of them.'

'Not heard of them?' both cried. 'The Marabar Caves in the Marabar Hills?'

'We hear nothing interesting up at the club. Only tennis and ridiculous gossip.'

The old man was silent, perhaps feeling that it was unseemly of her to criticize her race, perhaps fearing that if he agreed she would report him for disloyalty. But the young man uttered a rapid 'I know.'

'Then tell me everything you will, or I shall never understand India. Are they the hills I sometimes see in the evening? What are these caves?'

Aziz undertook to explain, but it presently appeared that he had never visited the caves himself—had always been 'meaning' to go, but work or private business had prevented him, and they were so far. Professor Godbole chaffed him pleasantly. 'My dear young sir, the pot and the kettle! Have you ever heard of that useful proverb?'

'Are they large caves?' she asked.

'No, not large.'

'Do describe them, Professor Godbole.'

'It will be a great honour.' He drew up his chair and an expression of tension came over his face. Taking the cigarette box, she offered to him and to Aziz, and lit up herself. After an impressive pause he said: 'There is an entrance in the rock which you enter, and through the entrance is the cave.'

'Something like the caves at Elephanta?'

'Oh no, not at all; at Elephanta there are sculptures of Siva and Parvati. There are no sculptures at Marabar.'

'They are immensely holy, no doubt,' said Aziz, to help on the narrative.

'Oh no, oh no.'

'Still, they are ornamented in some way.'

'Oh no.'

'Well, why are they so famous? We all talk of the famous Marabar Caves. Perhaps that is our empty brag.'

'No, I should not quite say that.'

'Describe them to this lady, then.'

'It will be a great pleasure.' He forewent the pleasure, and Aziz realized that he was keeping back something about the caves. He realized because he often suffered from similar inhibitions himself. Sometimes, to the exasperation of Major Callendar, he would pass over the one relevant fact in a position, to dwell on the hundred irrelevant. The Major accused him of disingenuousness, and was roughly right, but only roughly. It was rather that a power he couldn't control capriciously silenced his mind. Godbole had been silenced now; no doubt not willingly, he was concealing something. Handled subtly, he might regain control and announce that the Marabar Caves were–full of stalactites, perhaps; Aziz led up to this, but they weren't.

The dialogue remained light and friendly, and Adela had no conception of its underdrift. She did not know that the comparatively simple mind of the Mohammedan was encountering Ancient Night. Aziz played a thrilling game. He was handling a human toy that refused to work–he knew that much. If it worked, neither he nor Professor Godbole would be the least advantaged, but the attempt enthralled him and was akin to abstract thought. On he chattered, defeated at every move by an opponent who would not even admit that a move had been made, and further than ever from discovering what, if anything, was extraordinary about the Marabar Caves.

Into this Ronny dropped.

With an annoyance he took no trouble to conceal, he called from the garden: 'What's happened to Fielding? Where's my mother?'

'Good evening!' she replied coolly.

'I want you and mother at once. There's to be polo.'

'I thought there was to be no polo.'

'Everything's altered. Some soldier men have come in. Come along and I'll tell you about it.'

'Your mother will return shortly, sir,' said Professor Godbole, who had risen with deference. 'There is but little to see at our poor college.'

Ronny took no notice, but continued to address his remarks to Adela; he had hurried away from his work to take her to see the polo, because he thought it would give her pleasure. He did not mean to be rude to the two men, but the only link he could be conscious of with an Indian was the official, and neither happened to be his subordinate. As private individuals he forgot them.

Unfortunately Aziz was in no mood to be forgotten. He would not give up the secure and intimate note of the last hour. He had not risen with Godbole, and now, offensively friendly, called from his seat, 'Come along up and join us, Mr Heaslop; sit down till your mother turns up.'

Ronny replied by ordering one of Fielding's servants to fetch his master at once.

'He may not understand that. Allow me—' Aziz repeated the order idiomatically.

Ronny was tempted to retort; he knew the type; he knew all the types, and this was the spoilt Westernized. But he was a servant of the Government, it was his job to avoid 'incidents,' so he said nothing, and ignored the provocation that Aziz continued to offer. Aziz was provocative. Everything he said had an impertinent flavour or jarred. His wings were failing, but he refused to fall without a struggle. He did not mean to be impertinent to Mr Heaslop, who had never done him harm, but here was an Anglo-Indian who must become a man before comfort could be regained. He did not mean to be greasily confidential to Miss Quested, only to enlist her support; nor to be loud and jolly towards Professor Godbole. A strange quartette—he fluttering to the ground, she puzzled by the sudden ugliness, Ronny fuming, the Brahman observing all three, but with downcast eyes and hands folded, as if nothing was noticeable. A scene from a play, thought Fielding, who now saw them from the distance across the garden grouped among the blue pillars of his beautiful hall.

'Don't trouble to come, mother,' Ronny called; 'we're just starting.' Then he hurried to Fielding, drew him aside and said with pseudo-heartiness, 'I say, old man, do excuse me, but I think perhaps you oughtn't to have left Miss Quested alone.'

'I'm sorry, what's up?' replied Fielding, also trying to be genial.

'Well . . . I'm the sun-dried bureaucrat, no doubt; still, I don't like to see an English girl left smoking with two Indians.'

'She stopped, as she smokes, by her own wish, old man.'

'Yes, that's all right in England.'

'I really can't see the harm.'

'If you can't see, you can't see. . . . Can't you see that fellow's a bounder?' Aziz flamboyant, was patronizing Mrs Moore.

'He isn't a bounder,' protested Fielding. 'His nerves are on edge, that's all.'

'What should have upset his precious nerves?'

'I don't know. He was all right when I left.'

'Well, it's nothing I've said,' said Ronny reassuringly. 'I never even spoke to him.'

'Oh well, come along now, and take your ladies away; the catastrophe over.'

'Fielding . . . don't think I'm taking it badly, or anything of that sort. . . . I suppose you won't come on to the polo with us? We should all be delighted.'

'I'm afraid I can't, thanks all the same. I'm awfully sorry you feel I've been remiss. I didn't mean to be.'

So the leave-taking began. Every one was cross or wretched. It was as if irritation exuded from the very soil. Could one have been so petty on a Scotch moor or an Italian alp? Fielding wondered afterwards. There seemed no reserve of tranquillity to draw upon in India. Either none, or else tranquillity swallowed up everything, as it appeared to do for Professor Godbole. Here was Aziz all shoddy and odious, Mrs Moore and Miss

Quested both silly, and he himself and Heaslop both decorous on the surface, but detestable really, and detesting each other.

'Good-bye, Mr Fielding, and thank you so much. . . . What lovely College buildings!'

'Good-bye, Mrs Moore.'

'Good-bye Mr Fielding. Such an interesting afternoon. . . .'

'Good-bye, Miss Quested.'

'Good-bye, Dr Aziz.'

'Good-bye, Mrs Moore.'

'Good-bye, Dr Aziz.'

'Good-bye, Miss Quested.' He pumped her hand up and down to show that he felt at ease. 'You'll jolly jolly well not forget those caves, won't you? I'll fix the whole show up in a jiffy.'

'Thank you. . . .'

Inspired by the devil to a final effort, he added, 'What a shame you leave India so soon! Oh, do reconsider your decision, do stay.'

'Good-bye, Professor Godbole,' she continued, suddenly agitated. 'It's a shame we never heard you sing.'

'I may sing now,' he replied, and did.

His thin voice rose, and gave out one sound after another. At times there seemed rhythm, at times there was the illusion of a Western melody. But the ear, baffled repeatedly, soon lost any clue, and wandered in a maze of noises, none harsh or unpleasant, none intelligible. It was the song of an unknown bird. Only the servants understood it. They began to whisper to one another. The man who was gathering water chestnut came naked out of the tank, his lips parted with delight, disclosing his scarlet tongue. The sounds continued and ceased after a few moments as casually as they had begun—apparently half through a bar, and upon the subdominant.

'Thanks so much: what was that?' asked Fielding.

'I will explain in detail. It was a religious song. I placed myself in the position of a milkmaiden. I say to Shri Krishna, "Come! come to me only." The god refuses to come. I grow humble and say: "Do not come to me only. Multiply yourself into a hundred Krishnas, and let one go to each of my hundred companions, but one, O Lord of the Universe, come to me." He refuses to come. This is repeated several times. The song is composed in a raga appropriate to the present hour, which is the evening.'

'But He comes in some other song, I hope?' said Mrs Moore gently.

'Oh no, he refuses to come,' repeated Godbole, perhaps not understanding her question. 'I say to Him, Come, come, come, come, come, come. He neglects to come.'

Ronny's steps had died away, and there was a moment of absolute silence. No ripple disturbed the water, no leaf stirred.

Chapter Eight

Although Miss Quested had known Ronny well in England, she felt well advised to visit him before deciding to be his wife. India had developed sides of his character that she had never admired. His self-complacency, his censoriousness, his lack of subtlety, all grew vivid beneath a tropic sky; he seemed more indifferent than of old to what was passing in the minds of his fellows, more certain that he was right about them or that if he was wrong it didn't matter. When proved wrong, he was particularly exasperating; he always managed to suggest that she needn't have bothered to prove it. The point she made was never the relevant point, her arguments conclusive but barren, she was reminded that he had expert knowledge and she none, and that experience would not help her because she could not interpret it. A Public School, London University, a year at a crammer's, a particular sequence of posts in a particular province, a fall from a horse and a touch of fever were presented to her as the only training by which Indians and all who reside in their country can be understood; the only training she could comprehend, that is to say, for of course above Ronny there stretched the higher realms of knowledge, inhabited by Callendars and Turtons, who had been not one year in the country but twenty and whose instincts were superhuman. For himself he made no extravagant claims; she wished he would. It was the qualified bray of the callow official, the 'I am not perfect, but—' that got on her nerves.

How gross he had been at Mr Fielding's—spoiling the talk and walking off in the middle of the haunting song! As he drove them away in the tum-tum, her irritation became unbearable, and she did not realize that much of it was directed against herself. She longed for an opportunity to fly out at him, and since he felt cross too, and they were both in India, an opportunity soon occurred. They had scarcely left the College grounds before she heard him say to his mother, who was with him on the front seat, 'What was that about caves?' and she promptly opened fire.

'Mrs Moore, your delightful doctor has decided on a picnic, instead of a party in his house; we are to meet him out there—you, myself, Mr Fielding, Professor Godbole—exactly the same party.'

'Out where?' asked Ronny.

'The Marabar Caves.'

'Well, I'm blessed,' he murmured after a pause. 'Did he descend to any details?'

'He did not. If you had spoken to him, we could have arranged them.'

He shook his head laughing.

'Have I said anything funny?'

'I was only thinking how the worthy doctor's collar climbed up his neck.'

'I thought you were discussing the caves.'

'So I am. Aziz was exquisitely dressed, from tie-pin to spats, but he had forgotten his back collar-stud, and there you have the Indian all over: inattention to detail; the fundamental slackness that reveals the race. Similarly, to "meet" in the caves as if they were the clock at Charing Cross, when they're miles from a station and each other.'

'Have you been to them?'

'No, but I know all about them, naturally.'

'Oh naturally!'

'Are you too pledged to this expedition, mother?'

'Mother is pledged to nothing,' said Mrs Moore, rather unexpectedly. 'Certainly not to this polo. Will you drive up to the bungalow first, and drop me there, please? I prefer to rest.'

'Drop me too,' said Adela. 'I don't want to watch polo either, I'm sure.'

'Simpler to drop the polo,' said Ronny. Tired and disappointed, he quite lost self-control, and added in a loud lecturing voice, 'I won't have you messing about with Indians any more! If you want to go to the Marabar Caves, you'll go under British auspices.'

'I've never heard of these caves, I don't know what or where they are,' said Mrs Moore, 'but I really can't have'—she tapped the cushion beside her—'so much quarrelling and tiresomeness!'

The young people were ashamed. They dropped her at the bungalow and drove on together to the polo, feeling it was the least they could do. Their crackling bad humour left them, but the heaviness of their spirit remained; thunderstorms seldom clear the air. Miss Quested was thinking over her own behaviour, and didn't like it at all. Instead of weighing Ronny and herself, and coming to a reasoned conclusion about marriage, she had incidentally, in the course of a talk about mangoes, remarked to mixed company that she didn't mean to stop in India. Which meant that she wouldn't marry Ronny: but what a way to announce it, what a way for a civilized girl to behave! She owed him an explanation, but unfortunately there was nothing to explain. The 'thorough talk' so dear to her principles and temperament had been postponed until too late. There seemed no point in being disagreeable to him and formulating her complaints against his character at this hour of the day, which was the evening. . . . The polo took place on the Maidan near the entrance of Chandrapore city. The sun was already declining and each of the trees held a premonition of night. They walked away from the governing group to a distant seat, and there, feeling that it was his due and her own, she forced out of herself the undigested remark: 'We must have a thorough talk, Ronny, I'm afraid.'

'My temper's rotten, I must apologize,' was his reply. 'I didn't mean to order you and mother about, but of course the way those Bengalis let you down this morning annoyed me, and I don't want that sort of thing to keep happening.'

'It's nothing to do with them that I . . .'

'No, but Aziz would make some similar muddle over the caves. He meant nothing by the invitation, I could tell by his voice: it's just their way of being pleasant.'

'It's something very different, nothing to do with caves, that I wanted to talk over with you.' She gazed at the colourless grass. 'I've finally decided we are not going to be married, my dear boy.'

The news hurt Ronny very much. He had heard Aziz announce that she would not return to the country, but had paid no attention to the remark, for he never dreamt that an Indian could be a channel of communication between two English people. He controlled himself and said gently, 'You never said we should marry, my dear girl; you never bound either yourself or me—don't let this upset you.'

She felt ashamed. How decent he was! He might force his opinions down her throat, but did not press her to an 'engagement,' because he believed, like herself, in the sanctity of personal relationships: it was this that had drawn them together at their first meeting, which had occurred among the grand scenery of the English Lakes. Her ordeal was over, but she felt it should have been more painful and longer. Adela will not marry Ronny. It seemed slipping away like a dream. She said, 'But let us discuss things; it's all so frightfully important, we mustn't make false steps. I want next to hear your point of view about me—it might help us both.'

His manner was unhappy and reserved. 'I don't much believe in this discussing—besides, I'm so dead with all this extra work Mohurram's bringing, if you'll excuse me.'

'I only want everything to be absolutely clear between us, and to answer any questions you care to put to me on my conduct.'

'But I haven't got any questions. You've acted within your rights, you were quite right to come out and have a look at me doing my work, it was an excellent plan, and anyhow it's no use talking further—we should only get up steam.' He felt angry and bruised; he was too proud to tempt her back, but he did not consider that she had behaved badly, because where his compatriots were concerned he had a generous mind.

'I suppose that there is nothing else; it's unpardonable of me to have given you and your mother all this bother,' said Miss Quested heavily, and frowned up at the tree beneath which they were sitting. A little green bird was observing her, so brilliant and neat that it might have hopped straight out of a shop. On catching her eye it closed its own, gave a small skip and prepared to go to bed. Some Indian wild bird. 'Yes, nothing else,' she repeated, feeling that a profound and passionate speech ought to have been delivered by one or both of them. 'We've been awfully British over it, but I suppose that's all right.'

'As we are British, I suppose it is.'

'Anyhow we've not quarrelled, Ronny.'

'Oh, that would have been too absurd. Why should we quarrel?'

'I think we shall keep friends.'

'I know we shall.'

'Quite so.'

As soon as they had exchanged this admission, a wave of relief passed through them both, and then transformed itself into a wave of tenderness, and passed back. They were softened by their own honesty, and began to feel lonely and unwise. Experiences, not character, divided them; they were not dissimilar, as humans go; indeed, when compared with the people who stood nearest to them in point of space they became practically identical. The Bhil who was holding an officer's polo pony, the Eurasian who drove the Nawab Bahadur's car, the Nawab Bahadur himself, the Nawab Bahadur's debauched grandson—none would have examined a difficulty so frankly and coolly. The mere fact of examination caused it to diminish. Of course they were friends, and for ever. 'Do you know what the name of that green bird up above us is?' she asked, putting her shoulder rather nearer to his.

'Bee-eater.'

'Oh no, Ronny, it has red bars on its wings.'

'Parrot,' he hazarded.

'Good gracious no.'

The bird in question dived into the dome of the tree. It was of no importance, yet they would have liked to identify it, it would somehow have solaced their hearts. But nothing in India is identifiable, the mere asking of a question causes it to disappear or to merge in something else.

'McBryde has an illustrated bird book,' he said dejectedly. 'I'm no good at all at birds, in fact I'm useless at any information outside my own job. It's a great pity.'

'So am I. I'm useless at everything.'

'What do I hear?' shouted the Nawab Bahadur at the top of his voice, causing both of them to start. 'What most improbable statement have I heard? An English lady useless? No, no, no, no, no.' He laughed genially, sure, within limits, of his welcome.

'Hallo, Nawab Bahadur! Been watching the polo again?' said Ronny tepidly.

'I have, sahib, I have.'

'How do you do?' said Adela, likewise pulling herself together. She held out her hand. The old gentleman judged from so wanton a gesture that she was new to his country, but he paid little heed. Women who exposed their face became by that one act so mysterious to him that he took them at the valuation of their men folk rather than at his own. Perhaps they were not immoral, and anyhow they were not his affair. On seeing the City Magistrate alone with a maiden at twilight, he had borne down on them with hospitable intent. He had a new little car, and wished to place it at their disposal; the City Magistrate would decide whether the offer was acceptable.

Ronny was by this time rather ashamed of his curtness to Aziz and Godbole, and here was an opportunity of showing that he could treat Indians with consideration when they deserved it. So he said to Adela, with the same sad friendliness that he had employed when discussing the bird, 'Would half an hour's spin entertain you at all?'

'Oughtn't we to get back to the bungalow.'

'Why?' He gazed at her.

'I think perhaps I ought to see your mother and discuss future plans.'

'That's as you like, but there's no hurry, is there?'

'Let me take you to the bungalow, and first the little spin,' cried the old man, and hastened to the car.

'He may show you some aspect of the country I can't, and he's a real loyalist. I thought you might care for a bit of a change.'

Determined to give him no more trouble, she agreed, but her desire to see India had suddenly decreased. There had been a factitious element in it.

How should they seat themselves in the car? The elegant grandson had to be left behind. The Nawab Bahadur got up in front, for he had no intention of neighbouring an English girl. 'Despite my advanced years, I am learning to drive,' he said. 'Man can learn everything if he will but try.' And fore-seeing a further difficulty, he added, 'I do not do the actual steering. I sit and ask my chauffeur questions, and thus learn the reason for everything that is done before I do it myself. By this method serious and I may say ludicrous accidents, such as befell one of my compatriots during that delightful reception at the English Club, are avoided. Our good Panna Lal! I hope, sahib, that great damage was not done to your flowers. Let us have our little spin down the Gangavati road. Half one league onwards!' He fell asleep.

Ronny instructed the chauffeur to take the Marabar road rather than the Gangavati, since the latter was under repair, and settled himself down beside the lady he had lost. The car made a burring noise and rushed along a chaussée that ran upon an embankment above melancholy fields. Trees of a poor quality bordered the road, indeed the whole scene was inferior, and suggested that the country-side was too vast to admit of excellence. In vain did each item in it call out, 'Come, come.' There was not enough god to go round. The two young people conversed feebly and felt unimportant. When the darkness began, it seemed to well out of the meagre vegetation, entirely covering the fields each side of them before it brimmed over the road. Ronny's face grew dim—an event that always increased her esteem for his character. Her hand touched his, owing to a jolt, and one of the thrills so frequent in the animal kingdom passed between them, and announced that all their difficulties were only a lovers' quarrel. Each was too proud to increase the pressure, but neither withdrew it, and a spurious unity descended on them, as local and temporary as the gleam that inhabits a firefly. It would vanish in a moment, perhaps to reappear, but the darkness is alone durable. And the night that encircled them, absolute as it seemed, was itself only a spurious unity, being modified by the gleams of day that leaked up round the edges of the earth, and by the stars.

They gripped . . . bump, jump, a swerve, two wheels lifted in the air, brakes on, bump with tree at edge of embankment, standstill. An accident. A slight one. Nobody hurt. The Nawab Bahadur awoke. He cried out in Arabic, and violently tugged his beard.

'What's the damage?' enquired Ronny, after the moment's pause that he permitted himself before taking charge of a situation. The Eurasian, inclined to be flustered, rallied to the sound of his voice, and, every inch an

Englishman, replied, 'You give me five minutes' time, I'll take you any damn anywhere.'

'Frightened, Adela?' He released her hand.

'Not a bit.'

'I consider not to be frightened the height of folly,' cried the Nawab Bahadur quite rudely.

'Well, it's all over now, tears are useless,' said Ronny, dismounting. 'We had some luck butting that tree.'

'All over . . . oh yes, the danger is past, let us smoke cigarettes, let us do anything we please. Oh yes . . . enjoy ourselves–oh my merciful God . . .' His words died into Arabic again.

'Wasn't the bridge. We skidded.'

'We didn't skid,' said Adela, who had seen the cause of the accident, and thought everyone must have seen it too. 'We ran into an animal.'

A loud cry broke from the old man: his terror was disproportionate and ridiculous.

'An animal?'

'A large animal rushed up out of the dark on the right and hit us.'

'By Jove, she's right,' Ronny exclaimed. 'The paint's gone.'

'By Jove, sir, your lady is right,' echoed the Eurasian. Just by the hinges of the door was a dent, and the door opened with difficulty.

'Of course I'm right. I saw its hairy back quite plainly.'

'I say, Adela, what was it?'

'I don't know the animals any better than the birds here–too big for a goat.'

'Exactly, too big for a goat . . .' said the old man.

Ronny said, 'Let's go into this; let's look for its tracks.'

'Exactly; you wish to borrow this electric torch.'

The English people walked a few steps back into the darkness, united and happy. Thanks to their youth and upbringing, they were not upset by the accident. They traced back the writhing of the tyres to the source of their disturbance. It was just after the exit from a bridge; the animal had probably come up out of the nullah. Steady and smooth ran the marks of the car, ribbons neatly nicked with lozenges, then all went mad. Certainly some external force had impinged, but the road had been used by too many objects for any one track to be legible, and the torch created such high lights and black shadows that they could not interpret what it revealed. Moreover, Adela in her excitement knelt and swept her skirts about, until it was she if anyone who appeared to have attacked the car. The incident was a great relief to them both. They forgot their abortive personal relationship, and felt adventurous as they muddled about in the dust.

'I believe it was a buffalo,' she called to their host, who had not accompanied them.

'Exactly.'

'Unless it was a hyena.'

Ronny approved this last conjecture. Hyenas prowl in nullahs and headlights dazzle them.

'Excellent, a hyena,' said the Indian with an angry irony and a gesture at the night. 'Mr Harris!'

'Half a mo-ment. Give me ten minutes' time.'

'Sahib says hyena.'

'Don't worry Mr Harris. He saved us from a nasty smash. Harris, well done!'

'A smash, sahib, that would not have taken place had he obeyed and taken us Gangavati side, instead of Marabar.'

'My fault that. I told him to come this way because the road's better. Mr Lesley has made it pukka right up to the hills.'

'Ah, now I begin to understand.' Seeming to pull himself together, he apologized slowly and elaborately for the accident. Ronny murmured, 'Not at all,' but apologies were his due, and should have started sooner: because English people are so calm at a crisis, it is not to be assumed that they are unimportant. The Nawab Bahadur had not come out very well.

At that moment a large car approached from the opposite direction. Ronny advanced a few steps down the road, and with authority in his voice and gesture stopped it. It bore the inscription 'Mudkul State' across its bonnet. All friskiness and friendliness, Miss Derek sat inside.

'Mr Heaslop, Miss Quested, what are you holding up an innocent female for?'

'We've had a breakdown.'

'But how putrid!'

'We ran into a hyena!'

'How absolutely rotten!'

'Can you give us a lift?'

'Yes, indeed.'

'Take me too,' said the Nawab Bahadur.

'Heh, what about me?' cried Mr Harris.

'Now what's all this? I'm not an omnibus,' said Miss Derek with decision. 'I've a harmonium and two dogs in here with me as it is. I'll take three of you if one'll sit in front and nurse a pug. No more.'

'I will sit in front,' said the Nawab Bahadur.

'Then hop in: I've no notion who you are.'

'Heh no, what about my dinner? I can't be left alone all the night.' Trying to look and feel like a European, the chauffeur interposed aggressively. He still wore a topi, despite the darkness, and his face, to which the Ruling Race had contributed little beyond bad teeth, peered out of it pathetically, and seemed to say, 'What's it all about? Don't worry me so, you blacks and whites. Here I am, stuck in damn India same as you, and you got to fit me in better than this.'

'Nussu will bring you out some suitable dinner upon a bicycle,' said the Nawab Bahadur, who had regained his usual dignity. 'I shall despatch him with all possible speed. Meanwhile, repair my car.'

They sped off, and Mr Harris, after a reproachful glance, squatted down upon his hams. When English and Indians were both present, he grew self-conscious, because he did not know to whom he belonged. For a little he was vexed by opposite currents in his blood, then they blended, and he belonged to no one but himself.

But Miss Derek was in tearing spirits. She had succeeded in stealing the Mudkul car. Her Maharajah would be awfully sick, but she didn't mind, he could sack her if he liked. 'I don't believe in these people letting you down,' she said. 'If I didn't snatch like the devil, I should be nowhere. He doesn't want the car, silly fool! Surely it's to the credit of his State I should be seen about in it at Chandrapore during my leave. He ought to look at it that way. Anyhow he's got to look at it that way. My Maharani's different—my Maharani's a dear. That's her fox terrier, poor little devil. I fished them out both with the driver. Imagine taking dogs to a Chiefs' Conference! As sensible as taking Chiefs, perhaps.' She shrieked with laughter. 'The harmonium—the harmonium's my little mistake, I own. They rather had me over the harmonium. I meant it to stop on the train. Oh lor'!'

Ronny laughed with restraint. He did not approve of English people taking service under the Native States, where they obtain a certain amount of influence, but at the expense of the general prestige. The humorous triumphs of a free lance are of no assistance to an administrator, and he told the young lady that she would outdo Indians at their own game if she went on much longer.

'They always sack me before that happens, and then I get another job. The whole of India seethes with Maharanis and Ranis and Begums who clamour for such as me.'

'Really. I had no idea.'

'How could you have any idea, Mr Heaslop? What should he know about Maharanis, Miss Quested? Nothing. At least I should hope not.'

'I understand those big people are not particularly interesting,' said Adela, quietly, disliking the young woman's tone. Her hand touched Ronny's again in the darkness, and to the animal thrill there was now added a coincidence of opinion.

'Ah, there you're wrong. They're priceless.'

'I would scarcely call her wrong,' broke out the Nawab Bahadur, from his isolation on the front seat, whither they had relegated him. 'A Native State, a Hindu State, the wife of a ruler of a Hindu State, may beyond doubt be a most excellent lady, and let it not be for a moment supposed that I suggest anything against the character of Her Highness and Maharani of Mudkul. But I fear she will be uneducated, I fear she will be superstitious. Indeed, how could she be otherwise? What opportunity of education has such a lady had? Oh, superstition is terrible, terrible! oh, it is the great defect in our Indian character!'—and as if to point his criticism, the lights of the civil station appeared on a rise to the right. He grew more and more voluble. 'Oh, it is the duty of each and every citizen to shake superstition off, and though I have little experience of Hindu States, and none of this particular one, namely Mudkul (the Ruler, I fancy, has a salute of but eleven guns)—yet I cannot imagine that they have been as successful as British India, where we see reason and orderliness spreading in every direction, like a most health-giving flood!'

Miss Derek said 'Golly!'

Undeterred by the expletive, the old man swept on. His tongue had been loosed and his mind had several points to make. He wanted to endorse Miss Quested's remark that big people are not interesting, because he was bigger himself than many an independent chief; at the same time, he must neither remind nor inform her that he was big, lest she felt she had committed a discourtesy. This was the groundwork of his oration; worked in with it was his gratitude to Miss Derek for the lift, his willingness to hold a repulsive dog in his arms, and his general regret for the trouble he had caused the human race during the evening. Also he wanted to be dropped near the city to get hold of his cleaner, and to see what mischief his grandson was up to. As he wove all these anxieties into a single rope, he suspected that his audience felt no interest, and that the City Magistrate fondled either maiden behind the cover of the harmonium, but good breeding compelled him to continue; it was nothing to him if they were bored, because he did not know what boredom is, and it was nothing to him if they were licentious, because God has created all races to be different. The accident was over, and his life, equally useful, distinguished, happy, ran on as before and expressed itself in streams of well-chosen words.

When this old geyser left them, Ronny made no comment, but talked lightly about polo; Turton had taught him that it is sounder not to discuss a man at once, and he reserved what he had to say on the Nawab's character until later in the evening. His hand, which he had removed to say good-bye, touched Adela's again; she caressed it definitely, he responded, and their firm and mutual pressure surely meant something. They looked at each other when they reached the bungalow, for Mrs Moore was inside it. It was for Miss Quested to speak, and she said nervously, 'Ronny, I should like to take back what I said on the Maidan.' He assented, and they became engaged to be married in consequence.

Neither had foreseen such a consequence. She had meant to revert to her former condition of important and cultivated uncertainty, but it had passed out of her reach at its appropriate hour. Unlike the green bird or the hairy animal, she was labelled now. She felt humiliated again, for she deprecated labels, and she felt too that there should have been another scene between her lover and herself at this point, something dramatic and lengthy. He was pleased instead of distressed, he was surprised, but he had really nothing to say. What indeed is there to say? To be or not to be married, that was the question, and they had decided it in the affirmative.

'Come along and let's tell the mater all this'—opening the perforated zinc door that protected the bungalow from the swarms of winged creatures. The noise woke the mater up. She had been dreaming of the absent children who were so seldom mentioned, Ralph and Stella, and did not at first grasp what was required of her. She too had become used to thoughtful procrastination, and felt alarmed when it came to an end.

When the announcement was over, he made a gracious and honest remark. 'Look here, both of you, see India if you like and as you like—I know I made myself rather ridiculous at Fielding's, but . . . it's different now. I wasn't quite sure of myself.'

'My duties here are evidently finished, I don't want to see India now; now for my passage back,' was Mrs Moore's thought. She reminded herself of all that a happy marriage means, and of her own happy marriages, one of which had produced Ronny. Adela's parents had also been happily married, and excellent it was to see the incident repeated by the younger generation. On and on! the number of such unions would certainly increase as education spread and ideals grew loftier, and characters firmer. But she was tired by her visit to Government College, her feet ached, Mr Fielding had walked too fast and far, the young people had annoyed her in the tum-tum, and given her to suppose they were breaking with each other, and though it was all right now she could not speak as enthusiastically of wedlock or of anything as she should have done. Ronny was suited, now she must go home and help the others, if they wished. She was past marrying herself, even unhappily; her function was to help others, her reward to be informed that she was sympathetic. Elderly ladies must not expect more than this.

They dined alone. There was much pleasant and affectionate talk about the future. Later on they spoke of passing events, and Ronny reviewed and recounted the day from his own point of view. It was a different day from the women's, because while they had enjoyed themselves or thought, he had worked. Mohurram was approaching, and as usual the Chandrapore Mohammedans were building paper towers of a size too large to pass under the branches of a certain pepul tree. One knew what happened next; the tower stuck, a Mohammedan climbed up the pepul and cut the branch off, the Hindus protested, there was a religious riot, and Heaven knew what, with perhaps the troops sent for. There had been deputations and conciliation committees under the auspices of Turton, and all the normal work of Chandrapore had been hung up. Should the procession take another route, or should the towers be shorter? The Mohammedans offered the former, the Hindus insisted on the latter. The Collector had favoured the Hindus, until he suspected that they had artificially bent the tree nearer the ground. They said it sagged naturally. Measurements, plans, an official visit to the spot. But Ronny had not disliked his day, for it proved that the British were necessary to India; there would certainly have been bloodshed without them. His voice grew complacent again; he was here not to be pleasant but to keep the peace, and now that Adela had promised to be his wife, she was sure to understand.

'What does our old gentleman of the car think?' she asked, and her negligent tone was exactly what he desired.

'Our old gentleman is helpful and sound, as he always is over public affairs. You've seen in him our show Indian.'

'Have I really?'

'I'm afraid so. Incredible, aren't they, even the best of them? They're all—they all forget their back collar studs sooner or later. You've had to do with three sets of Indians to-day, the Bhattacharyas, Aziz, and this chap, and it really isn't a coincidence that they've all let you down.'

'I like Aziz, Aziz is my real friend,' Mrs Moore interposed.

'When the animal runs into us the Nawab loses his head, deserts his unfortunate chauffeur, intrudes upon Miss Derek . . . no great crimes, no great crimes, but no white man would have done it.'

'What animal?'

'Oh, we had a small accident on the Marabar road. Adela thinks it was a hyena.'

'An accident?' she cried.

'Nothing; no one hurt. Our excellent host awoke much rattled from his dreams, appeared to think it was our fault, and chanted exactly, exactly.'

Mrs Moore shivered, 'A ghost!' But the idea of a ghost scarcely passed her lips. The young people did not take it up, being occupied with their own outlooks, and deprived of support it perished, or was reabsorbed into the part of the mind that seldom speaks.

'Yes, nothing criminal,' Ronny summed up, 'but there's the native, and there's one of the reasons why we don't admit him to our clubs, and how a decent girl like Miss Derek can take service under natives puzzles me. . . . But I must get on with my work. Krishna!' Krishna was the peon who should have brought the files from his office. He had not turned up, and a terrific row ensued. Ronny stormed, shouted, howled, and only the experienced observer could tell that he was not angry, did not much want the files, and only made a row because it was the custom. Servants, quite understanding, ran slowly in circles, carrying hurricane lamps. Krishna the earth, Krishna the stars replied, until the Englishman was appeased by their echoes, fined the absent peon eight annas, and sat down to his arrears in the next room.

'Will you play Patience with your future mother-in-law, dear Adela, or does it seem too tame?'

'I should like to–I don't feel a bit excited–I'm just glad it's settled up at last, but I'm not conscious of vast changes. We are all three the same people still.'

'That's much the best feeling to have.' She dealt out the first row of 'demon.'

'I suppose so,' said the girl thoughtfully.

'I feared at Mr Fielding's that it might be settled the other way . . . black knave on a red queen. . . .' They chatted gently about the game.

Presently Adela said: 'You heard me tell Aziz and Godbole I wasn't stopping in their country. I didn't mean it, so why did I say it? I feel I haven't been–frank enough, attentive enough, or something. It's as if I got everything out of proportion. You have been so very good to me, and I meant to be good when I sailed, but somehow I haven't been. . . . Mrs Moore, if one isn't absolutely honest, what is the use of existing?'

She continued to lay out her cards. The words were obscure, but she understood the uneasiness that produced them. She had experienced it twice herself, during her own engagements–this vague contrition and doubt. All had come right enough afterwards and doubtless would this time–marriage makes most things right enough. 'I wouldn't worry,' she said. 'It's partly the odd surroundings; you and I keep on attending to trifles instead of what's important; we are what the people here call "new."'

'You mean that my bothers are mixed up with India?'

'India's—' She stopped.

'What made you call it a ghost?'

'Call what a ghost?'

'The animal thing that hit us. Didn't you say "Oh, a ghost," in passing?'

'I couldn't have been thinking of what I was saying.'

'It was probably a hyena, as a matter of fact.'

'Ah, very likely.'

And they went on with their Patience. Down in Chandrapore the Nawab Bahadur waited for his car. He sat behind his town house (a small unfurnished building which he rarely entered) in the midst of the little court that always improvises itself round Indians of position. As if turbans were the natural product of darkness a fresh one would occasionally froth to the front, incline itself towards him, and retire. He was preoccupied, his diction was appropriate to a religious subject. Nine years previously, when first he had had a car, he had driven it over a drunken man and killed him, and the man had been waiting for him ever since. The Nawab Bahadur was innocent before God and the Law, he had paid double the compensation necessary; but it was no use, the man continued to wait in an unspeakable form, close to the scene of his death. None of the English people knew of this, nor did the chauffeur; it was a racial secret communicable more by blood than speech. He spoke now in horror of the particular circumstances; he had led others into danger, he had risked the lives of two innocent and honoured guests. He repeated, 'If I had been killed, what matter? It must happen sometime; but they who trusted me—' The company shuddered and invoked the mercy of God. Only Aziz held aloof, because a personal experience restrained him: was it not by despising ghosts that he had come to know Mrs Moore? 'You know, Nureddin,' he whispered to the grandson–an effeminate youth whom he seldom met, always liked, and invariably forgot–'you know, my dear fellow, we Moslems simply must get rid of these superstitions, or India will never advance. How long must I hear of the savage pig upon the Marabar Road?' Nureddin looked down. Aziz continued: 'Your grandfather belongs to another generation, and I respect and love the old gentleman, as you know. I say nothing against him, only that it is wrong for us, because we are young. I want you to promise me–Nureddin, are you listening?–not to believe in Evil Spirits, and if I die (for my health grows very weak) to bring up my three children to disbelieve in them too.' Nureddin smiled, and a suitable answer rose to his pretty lips, but before he could make it the car arrived, and his grandfather took him away.

The game of Patience up in the civil lines went on longer than this. Mrs Moore continued to murmur 'Red ten on a black knave,' Miss Quested to assist her, and to intersperse among the intricacies of the play details about the hyena, the engagement, the Maharani of Mudkul, the Bhattacharyas, and the day generally, whose rough desiccated surface acquired as it receded a definite outline, as India itself might, could it be viewed from the moon. Presently the players went to bed, but not before other people had woken up elsewhere, people whose emotions they could not share, and whose existence they ignored. Never tranquil, never perfectly dark, the night wore itself away, distinguished from other nights by two or three blasts of wind, which seemed to fall perpendicularly out of the sky and to bounce back into it, hard and compact, leaving no freshness behind them: the hot weather was approaching.

Chapter Nine

Aziz fell ill as he foretold—slightly ill. Three days later he lay abed in his bungalow, pretending to be very ill. It was a touch of fever, which he would have neglected if there was anything important at the hospital. Now and then he groaned and thought he should die, but did not think so for long, and a very little diverted him. It was Sunday, always an equivocal day in the East, and an excuse for slacking. He could hear church bells as he drowsed, both from the civil station and from the missionaries out beyond the slaughter house—different bells and rung with different intent, for one set was calling firmly to Anglo-India, and the other feebly to mankind. He did not object to the first set; the other he ignored, knowing their inefficiency. Old Mr Graysford and young Mr Sorley made converts during a famine, because they distributed food; but when times improved they were naturally left alone again, and though surprised and aggrieved each time this happened, they never learnt wisdom. 'No Englishman understands us except Mr Fielding,' he thought; 'but how shall I see him again? If he entered this room the disgrace of it would kill me.' He called to Hassan to clear up, but Hassan, who was testing his wages by ringing them on the step of the verandah, found it possible not to hear him; heard and didn't hear, just as Aziz had called and hadn't called. 'That's India all over . . . how like us . . . there we are . . .' He dozed again, and his thoughts wandered over the varied surface of life.

Gradually they steadied upon a certain spot—the Bottomless Pit according to missionaries, but he had never regarded it as more than a dimple, Yes, he did want to spend an evening with some girls, singing and all that, the vague jollity that would culminate in voluptuousness. Yes, that was what he did want. How could it be managed? If Major Callendar had been an Indian, he would have remembered what young men are, and granted two or three days' leave to Calcutta without asking questions. But the Major assumed either that his subordinates were made of ice, or that they repaired to the Chandrapore bazaars—disgusting ideas both. It was only Mr Fielding who—

'Hassan!'

The servant came running.

'Look at those flies, brother;' and he pointed to the horrible mass that hung from the ceiling. The nucleus was a wire which had been inserted as a homage to electricity. Electricity had paid no attention, and a colony of eye-flies had come instead and blackened the coils with their bodies.

'Huzoor, those are flies.'

'Good, good, they are, excellent, but why have I called you?'

'To drive them elsewhere,' said Hassan, after painful thought.

'Driven elsewhere, they always return.'

'Huzoor.'

'You must make some arrangement against flies; that is why you are my servant,' said Aziz gently.

Hassan would call the little boy to borrow the stepladder from Mahmoud Ali's house; he would order the cook to light the Primus stove and heat water; he would personally ascend the steps with a bucket in his arms, and dip the end of the coil into it.

'Good, very good. Now what have you to do?'

'Kill flies.'

'Good. Do it.'

Hassan withdrew, the plan almost lodged in his head, and began to look for the little boy. Not finding him, his steps grew slower, and he stole back to his post on the verandah, but did not go on testing his rupees, in case his master heard them clink. On twittered the Sunday bells; the East had returned to the East via the suburbs of England, and had become ridiculous during the detour.

Aziz continued to think about beautiful women.

His mind here was hard and direct, though not brutal. He had learnt all he needed concerning his own constitution many years ago, thanks to the social order into which he had been born, and when he came to study medicine he was repelled by the pedantry and fuss with which Europe tabulates the facts of sex. Science seemed to discuss everything from the wrong end. It didn't interpret his experiences when he found them in a German manual, because by being there they ceased to be his experiences. What he had been told by his father or mother or had picked up from servants—it was information of that sort that he found useful, and handed on as occasion offered to others.

But he must not bring any disgrace on his children by some silly escapade. Imagine if it got about that he was not respectable! His professional position too must be considered, whatever Major Callendar thought. Aziz upheld the proprieties, though he did not invest them with any moral halo, and it was here that he chiefly differed from an Englishman. His conventions were social. There is no harm in deceiving society as long as she does not find you out, because it is only when she finds you out that you have harmed her; she is not like a friend or God, who are injured by the mere existence of unfaithfulness. Quite clear about this, he meditated what type of lie he should tell to get away to Calcutta, and had thought of a man there who could be trusted to send him a wire and a letter that he could show to Major Callendar, when the noise of wheels was heard in his compound. Someone had called to enquire. The thought of sympathy increased his fever, and with a sincere groan he wrapped himself in his quilt.

'Aziz, my dear fellow, we are greatly concerned,' said Hamidullah's voice. One, two, three, four bumps, as people sat down upon his bed.

'When a doctor falls ill it is a serious matter,' said the voice of Mr Syed Mohammed, the assistant engineer.

'When an engineer falls ill, it is equally important,' said the voice of Mr Haq, a police inspector.

'Oh yes, we are all jolly important, our salaries prove it.'

'Dr Aziz took tea with our Principal last Thursday afternoon,' piped Rafi, the engineer's nephew. 'Professor Godbole, who also attended, has sickened too, which seems rather a curious thing, sir, does it not?'

Flames of suspicion leapt up in the breast of each man. 'Humbug!' exclaimed Hamidullah, in authoritative tones, quenching them.

'Humbug, most certainly,' echoed the others, ashamed of themselves. The wicked schoolboy, having failed to start a scandal, lost confidence and stood up with his back to the wall.

'Is Professor Godbole ill?' enquired Aziz, penetrated by the news. 'I am sincerely sorry.' Intelligent and compassionate, his face peeped out of the bright crimson folds of the quilt. 'How do you do, Mr Syed Mohammed, Mr Haq? How very kind of you to enquire after my health! How do you do, Hamidullah? But you bring me bad news. What is wrong with him, the excellent fellow?'

'Why don't you answer, Rafi? You're the great authority,' said his uncle.

'Yes, Rafi's the great man,' said Hamidullah, rubbing it in. 'Rafi is the Sherlock Holmes of Chandrapore. Speak up, Rafi.'

Less than the dust, the schoolboy murmured the word 'Diarrhoea,' but took courage as soon as it had been uttered, for it improved his position. Flames of suspicion shot up again in the breasts of his elders, though in a different direction. Could what was called diarrhoea really be an early case of cholera?

'If this is so, this is a very serious thing: this is scarcely the end of March. Why have I not been informed?' cried Aziz.

'Dr Panna Lal attends him, sir.'

'Oh yes, both Hindus; there we have it; they hang together like flies and keep everything dark. Rafi, come here. Sit down. Tell me all the details. Is there vomiting also?'

'Oh yes indeed, sir, and the serious pains.'

'That settles it. In twenty-four hours he will be dead.'

Everybody looked and felt shocked, but Professor Godbole had diminished his appeal by linking himself with a co-religionist. He moved them less than when he had appeared as a suffering individual. Before long they began to condemn him as a source of infection. 'All illness proceeds from Hindus,' Mr Haq said. Mr Syed Mohammed had visited religious fairs, at Allahabad and at Ujjain, and described them with biting scorn. At Allahabad there was flowing water, which carried impurities away, but at Ujjain the little river Sipra was banked up, and thousands of bathers deposited their germs in the pool. He spoke with disgust of the hot sun, the cowdung and marigold flowers, and the encampment of saddhus, some of whom strode stark naked through the streets. Asked what was the name of the chief idol at Ujjain, he replied that he did not know, he had disdained to enquire, he really could not waste his time over such trivialities. His outburst took some time, and in his excitement he fell into Punjabi (he came from that side) and was unintelligible.

Aziz liked to hear his religion praised. It soothed the surface of his mind, and allowed beautiful images to form beneath. When the engineer's noisy tirade was finished, he said, 'That is exactly my own view.' He held up his hand, palm outward, his eyes began to glow, his heart to fill with tenderness. Issuing still farther from his quilt, he recited a poem by Ghalib. It had no connection with anything that had gone before, but it came from his heart and spoke to theirs. They were overwhelmed by its pathos; pathos, they agreed, is the highest quality in art; a poem should touch the hearer with a sense of his own weakness, and should institute some comparison between mankind and flowers. The squalid bedroom grew quiet; the silly intrigues, the gossip, the shallow discontent were stilled, while words accepted as immortal filled the indifferent air. Not as a call to battle, but as a calm assurance came the feeling that India was one; Moslem; always had been; an assurance that lasted until they looked out of the door. Whatever Ghalib had felt, he had anyhow lived in India, and this consolidated it for them: he had gone with his own tulips and roses, but tulips and roses do not go. And the sister kingdoms of the north—Arabia, Persia, Ferghana, Turkestan—stretched out their hands as he sang, sadly, because all beauty is sad, and greeted ridiculous Chandrapore, where every street and house was divided against itself, and told her that she was a continent and a unity.

Of the company, only Hamidullah had any comprehension of poetry. The minds of the others were inferior and rough. Yet they listened with pleasure, because literature had not been divorced from their civilization. The police inspector, for instance, did not feel that Aziz had degraded himself by reciting, nor break into the cheery guffaw with which an Englishman averts the infection of beauty. He just sat with his mind empty, and when his thoughts, which were mainly ignoble, flowed back into it they had a pleasant freshness. The poem had done no 'good' to anyone, but it was a passing reminder, a breath from the divine lips of beauty, a nightingale between two worlds of dust. Less explicit than the call to Krishna, it voiced our loneliness nevertheless, our isolation, our need for the Friend who never comes yet is not entirely disproved. Aziz it left thinking about women again, but in a different way: less definite, more intense. Sometimes poetry had this effect on him, sometimes it only increased his local desires, and he never knew beforehand which effect would ensue: he could discover no rule for this or for anything else in life.

Hamidullah had called in on his way to a worrying committee of notables, nationalist in tendency, where Hindus, Moslems, two Sikhs, two Parsis, a Jain, and a Native Christian tried to like one another more than came natural to them. As long as someone abused the English, all went well, but nothing constructive had been achieved, and if the English were to leave India, the committee would vanish also. He was glad that Aziz, whom he loved and whose family was connected with his own, took no interest in politics, which ruin the character and career, yet nothing can be achieved without them. He thought of Cambridge–sadly, as of another poem that had ended. How happy he had been there, twenty years ago! Politics had not mattered in Mr and Mrs Bannister's rectory. There, games, work, and pleasant society had interwoven, and appeared to be sufficient substructure for a national life. Here all was wirepulling and fear. Messrs Syed Mohammed and Haq–he couldn't even trust them, although they had come in his carriage, and the schoolboy was a scorpion. Bending down, he said, 'Aziz, Aziz, my dear boy, we must be going, we are already late. Get well quickly, for I do not know what our little circle would do without you.'

'I shall not forget those affectionate words,' replied Aziz.

'Add mine to them,' said the engineer.

'Thank you, Mr Syed Mohammed, I will.'

'And mine,' 'And, sir accept mine,' cried the others, stirred each according to his capacity towards goodwill. Little ineffectual unquenchable flames! The company continued to sit on the bed and to chew sugar-cane, which Hassan had run for into the bazaar, and Aziz drank a cup of spiced milk. Presently there was the sound of another carriage. Dr Panna Lal had arrived, driven by horrid Mr Ram Chand. The atmosphere of a sick-room was at once re-established, and the invalid retired under his quilt.

'Gentlemen, you will excuse, I have come to enquire by Major Callendar's orders,' said the Hindu, nervous of the den of fanatics into which his curiosity had called him.

'Here he lies,' said Hamidullah, indicating the prostrate form.

'Dr Aziz, Dr Aziz, I come to enquire.'

Aziz presented an expressionless face to the thermometer.

'Your hand also, please.' He took it, gazed at the flies on the ceiling, and finally announced 'Some temperature.'

'I think not much,' said Ram Chand, desirous of fomenting trouble.

'Some; he should remain in bed,' repeated Dr Panna Lal, and shook the thermometer down, so that its altitude remained for ever unknown. He loathed his young colleague since the disasters with Dapple, and he would have liked to do him a bad turn and report to Major Callendar that he was shamming. But he might want a day in bed himself soon,–besides, though Major Callendar always believed the worst of natives, he never believed them when they carried tales about one another. Sympathy seemed the safer course. 'How is stomach?' he enquired, 'how head?' And catching sight of the empty cup, he recommended a milk diet.

'This is a great relief to us, it is very good of you to call, Doctor Sahib,' said Hamidullah, buttering him up a bit.

'It is only my duty.'

'We know how busy you are.'

'Yes, that is true.'

'And how much illness there is in the city.'

The doctor suspected a trap in this remark; if he admitted that there was or was not illness, either statement might be used against him. 'There is always illness,' he replied, 'and I am always busy—it is a doctor's nature.'

'He has not a minute, he is due double sharp at Government College now,' said Ram Chand.

'You attend Professor Godbole there perhaps?'

The doctor looked professional and was silent.

'We hope his diarrhoea is ceasing.'

'He progresses, but not from diarrhoea.'

'We are in some anxiety over him—he and Dr Aziz are great friends. If you could tell us the name of his complaint we should be grateful to you.'

After a cautious pause he said, 'Haemorrhoids.'

'And so much, my dear Rafi, for your cholera,' hooted Aziz, unable to restrain himself.

'Cholera, cholera, what next, what now?' cried the doctor, greatly fussed. 'Who spreads such untrue reports about my patients?'

Hamidullah pointed to the culprit.

'I hear cholera, I hear bubonic plague, I hear every species of lie. Where will it end, I ask myself sometimes. This city is full of misstatements, and the originators of them ought to be discovered and punished authoritatively.'

'Rafi, do you hear that? Now why do you stuff us up with all this humbug?'

The schoolboy murmured that another boy had told him, also that the bad English grammar the Government obliged them to use often gave the wrong meaning for words, and so led scholars into mistakes.

'That is no reason you should bring a charge against a doctor,' said Ram Chand.

'Exactly, exactly,' agreed Hamidullah, anxious to avoid an unpleasantness. Quarrels spread so quickly and so far, and Messrs Syed Mohammed and Haq looked cross, and ready to fly out. 'You must apologize properly, Rafi, I can see your uncle wishes it,' he said. 'You have not yet said that you are sorry for the trouble you have caused this gentleman by your carelessness.'

'It is only a boy,' said Dr Panna Lal, appeased.

'Even boys must learn,' said Ram Chand.

'Your own son failing to pass the lowest standard, I think,' said Syed Mohammed suddenly.

'Oh, indeed? Oh yes, perhaps. He has not the advantage of a relative in the Prosperity Printing Press,'

'Nor you the advantage of conducting their cases in the Courts any longer.'

Their voices rose. They attacked one another with obscure allusions and had a silly quarrel. Hamidullah and the doctor tried to make peace between them. In the midst of the din someone said, 'I say! Is he ill or isn't he ill?' Mr Fielding had entered unobserved. All rose to their feet, and Hassan, to do an Englishman honour, struck with a sugar-cane at the coil of flies.

Aziz said, 'Sit down,' coldly. What a room! What a meeting! Squalor and ugly talk, the floor strewn with fragments of cane and nuts, and spotted with ink, the pictures crooked upon the dirty walls, no punkah! He hadn't meant to live like this or among these third-rate people. And in his confusion he thought only of the insignificant Rafi, whom he had laughed at, and allowed to be teased. The boy must be sent away happy, or hospitality would have failed, along the whole line.

'It is good of Mr Fielding to condescend to visit our friend,' said the police inspector. 'We are touched by this great kindness.'

'Don't talk to him like that, he doesn't want it, and he doesn't want three chairs; he's not three Englishmen,' he flashed. 'Rafi, come here. Sit down again. I'm delighted you could come with Mr Hamidullah, my dear boy; it will help me to recover, seeing you.'

'Forgive my mistakes,' said Rafi, to consolidate himself.

'Well, are you ill, Aziz, or aren't you?' Fielding repeated.

'No doubt Major Callendar has told you that I am shamming.'

'Well, are you?' The company laughed, friendly and pleased. 'An Englishman at his best,' they thought; 'so genial.'

'Enquire from Dr Panna Lal.'

'You're sure I don't tire you by stopping?'

'Why, no! There are six people present in my small room already. Please remain seated, if you will excuse the informality.' He turned away and continued to address Rafi, who was terrified at the arrival of his Principal, remembered that he had tried to spread slander about him, and yearned to get away.

'He is ill and he is not ill,' said Hamidullah, offering a cigarette. 'And I suppose that most of us are in that same case.'

Fielding agreed; he and the pleasant sensitive barrister got on well. They were fairly intimate and beginning to trust each other.

'The whole world looks to be dying, still it doesn't die, so we must assume the existence of a beneficent Providence.'

'Oh, that is true, how true!' said the policeman, thinking religion had been praised.

'Does Mr Fielding think it's true?'

'Think which true? The world isn't dying. I'm certain of that!'

'No, no—the existence of Providence.'

'Well, I don't believe in Providence.'

'But how then can you believe in God?' asked Syed Mohammed.

'I don't believe in God.'

A tiny movement as of 'I told you so!' passed round the company, and Aziz looked up for an instant, scandalized. 'Is it correct that most are atheists in England now?' Hamidullah enquired.

'The educated thoughtful people? I should say so, though they don't like the name. The truth is that the West doesn't bother much over belief and disbelief in these days. Fifty years ago, or even when you and I were young, much more fuss was made.'

'And does not morality also decline?'

'It depends what you call—yes, yes, I suppose morality does decline.'

'Excuse the question, but if this is the case, how is England justified in holding India?'

There they were! Politics again. 'It's a question I can't get my mind on to,' he replied. 'I'm out here personally because I needed a job. I cannot tell you why England is here or whether she ought to be here. It's beyond me.'

'Well-qualified Indians also need jobs in the educational.'

'I guess they do; I got in first,' said Fielding, smiling.

'Then excuse me again—is it fair an Englishman should occupy one when Indians are available? Of course I mean nothing personally. Personally we are delighted you should be here, and we benefit greatly by this frank talk.'

There is only one answer to a conversation of this type: 'England holds India for her good.' Yet Fielding was disinclined to give it. The zeal for honesty had eaten him up. He said, 'I'm delighted to be here too–that's my answer, there's my only excuse. I can't tell you anything about fairness. It mayn't have been fair I should have been born. I take up some other fellow's air, don't I, whenever I breathe? Still, I'm glad it's happened, and I'm glad I'm out here. However big a badmash one is–if one's happy in consequence, that is some justification.'

The Indians were bewildered. The line of thought was not alien to them, but the words were too definite and bleak. Unless a sentence paid a few compliments to Justice and Morality in passing, its grammar wounded their ears and paralysed their minds. What they said and what they felt were (except in the case of affection) seldom the same. They had numerous mental conventions and when these were flouted they found it very difficult to function. Hamidullah bore up best. 'And those Englishmen who are not delighted to be in India–have they no excuse?' he asked.

'None. Chuck 'em out.'

'It may be difficult to separate them from the rest,' he laughed.

'Worse than difficult, wrong,' said Mr Ram Chand. 'No Indian gentleman approves chucking out as a proper thing. Here we differ from those other nations. We are so spiritual.'

'Oh that is true, how true!' said the police inspector.

'Is it true, Mr Haq? I don't consider us spiritual. We can't co-ordinate, we can't co-ordinate, it only comes to that. We can't keep engagements, we can't catch trains. What more than this is the so-called spirituality of India? You and I ought to be at the Committee of Notables, we're not; our friend Dr Lal ought to be with his patients, he isn't. So we go on, and so we shall continue to go, I think, until the end of time.'

'It is not the end of time, it is scarcely ten-thirty, ha, ha!' cried Dr Panna Lal, who was again in confident mood. 'Gentlemen, if I may be allowed to say a few words, what an interesting talk, also thankfulness and gratitude to Mr Fielding in the first place teaches our sons and gives them all the great benefits of his experience and judgment—'

'Dr Lal!'

'Dr Aziz?'

'You sit on my leg.'

'I beg pardon, but some might say your leg kicks.'

'Come along, we tire the invalid in either case,' said Fielding, and they filed out–four Mohammedans, two Hindus and the Englishman. They stood on the verandah while their conveyances were summoned out of various patches of shade.

'Aziz has a high opinion of you, he only did not speak because of his illness.'

'I quite understand,' said Fielding, who was rather disappointed with his call. The Club comment, 'making himself cheap as usual,' passed through his mind. He couldn't even get his horse brought up. He had liked Aziz so much at their first meeting, and had hoped for developments.

Chapter Ten

The heat had leapt forward in the last hour, the street was deserted as if a catastrophe had cleaned off humanity during the inconclusive talk. Opposite Aziz' bungalow stood a large unfinished house belonging to two brothers, astrologers, and a squirrel hung head-downwards on it, pressing its belly against burning scaffolding and twitching a mangy tail. It seemed the only occupant of the house, and the squeals it gave were in tune with the infinite, no doubt, but not attractive except to other squirrels. More noises came from a dusty tree, where brown birds creaked and floundered about looking for insects; another bird, the invisible coppersmith, had started his 'ponk ponk.' It matters so little to the majority of living beings what the minority, that calls itself human, desires or decides. Most of the inhabitants of India do not mind how India is governed. Nor are the lower animals of England concerned about England, but in the tropics the indifference is more prominent, the inarticulate world is closer at hand and readier to resume control as soon as men are tired. When the seven gentlemen who had held such various opinions inside the bungalow came out of it, they were aware of a common burden, a vague threat which they called 'the bad weather coming.' They felt that they could not do their work, or would not be paid enough for doing it. The space between them and their carriages, instead of being empty, was clogged with a medium that pressed against their flesh, the carriage cushions scalded their trousers, their eyes pricked, domes of hot water accumulated under their head-gear and poured down their cheeks. Salaaming feebly, they dispersed for the interior of other bungalows, to recover their self-esteem and the qualities that distinguished them from each other.

All over the city and over much of India the same retreat on the part of humanity was beginning, into cellars, up hills, under trees. April, herald of horrors, is at hand. The sun was returning to his kingdom with power but without beauty—that was the sinister feature. If only there had been beauty! His cruelty would have been tolerable then. Through excess of light, he failed to triumph, he also; in his yellowy-white overflow not only matter, but brightness itself lay drowned. He was not the unattainable friend, either of men or birds or other suns, he was not the eternal promise, the never-withdrawn suggestion that haunts our consciousness; he was merely a creature, like the rest, and so debarred from glory.

Chapter Eleven

Although the Indians had driven off, and Fielding could see his horse standing in a small shed in the corner of the compound, no one troubled to bring it to him. He started to get it himself, but was stopped by a call from the house. Aziz was sitting up in bed, looking dishevelled and sad. 'Here's your home,' he said sardonically. 'Here's the celebrated hospitality of the East. Look at the flies. Look at the chunam coming off the walls. Isn't it jolly? Now I suppose you want to be off, having seen an Oriental interior.'

'Anyhow, you want to rest.'

'I can rest the whole day, thanks to worthy Dr Lal. Major Callendar's spy, I suppose you know, but this time it didn't work. I am allowed to have a slight temperature.'

'Callendar doesn't trust anyone, English or Indian: that's his character, and I wish you weren't under him; but you are, and that's that.'

'Before you go, for you are evidently in a great hurry, will you please unlock that drawer? Do you see a piece of brown paper at the top?'

'Yes.'

'Open it.'

'Who is this?'

'She was my wife. You are the first Englishman she has ever come before. Now put her photograph away.'

He was astonished, as a traveller who suddenly sees, between the stones of the desert, flowers. The flowers have been there all the time, but suddenly he sees them. He tried to look at the photograph, but in itself it was just a woman in a sari, facing the world. He muttered, 'Really, I don't know why you pay me this great compliment, Aziz, but I do appreciate it.'

'Oh, it's nothing, she was not a highly educated woman or even beautiful, but put it away. You would have seen her, so why should you not see her photograph?'

'You would have allowed me to see her?'

'Why not? I believe in the purdah, but I should have told her you were my brother, and she would have seen you. Hamidullah saw her, and several others.'

'Did she think they were your brothers?'

'Of course not, but the word exists and is convenient. All men are my brothers, and as soon as one behaves as such he may see my wife.'

'And when the whole world behaves as such, there will be no more purdah?'

'It is because you can say and feel such a remark as that, that I show you the photograph,' said Aziz gravely. 'It is beyond the power of most men. It is because you behave well while I behave badly that I show it you. I never expected you to come back just now when I called you. I thought, "He has certainly done with me; I have insulted him." Mr Fielding, no one can ever realize how much kindness we Indians need, we do not even realize it ourselves. But we know when it has been given. We do not forget, though we may seem to. Kindness, more kindness, and even after that more kindness. I assure you it is the only hope.' His voice seemed to arise from a dream. Altering it, yet still deep below his normal surface, he said, 'We can't build up India except on what we feel. What is the use of all these reforms, and Conciliation Committees for Mohurram, and shall we cut the tazia short or shall we carry it another route, and Councils of Notables and official parties where the English sneer at our skins?'

'It's beginning at the wrong end, isn't it? I know, but institutions and the governments don't.' He looked again at the photograph. The lady faced the world at her husband's wish and her own, but how bewildering she found it, the echoing contradictory world!

'Put her away, she is of no importance, she is dead,' said Aziz gently. 'I showed her to you because I have nothing else to show. You may look round the whole of my bungalow now, and empty everything. I have no other secrets, my three children live away with their grandmamma, and that is all.'

Fielding sat down by the bed, flattered at the trust reposed in him, yet rather sad. He felt old. He wished that he too could be carried away on waves of emotion. The next time they met, Aziz might be cautious and standoffish. He realized this, and it made him sad that he should realize it. Kindness, kindness, and more kindness—yes, that he might supply, but was that really all that the queer nation needed? Did it not also demand an occasional intoxication of the blood? What had he done to deserve this outburst of confidence, and what hostage could he give in exchange? He looked back at his own life. What a poor crop of secrets it had produced! There were things in it that he had shown to no one, but they were so uninteresting, it wasn't worth while lifting a purdah on their account. He'd been in love, engaged to be married, lady broke it off, memories of her and thoughts about her had kept him from other women for a time; then indulgence, followed by repentance and equilibrium. Meagre really except the equilibrium, and Aziz didn't want to have that confided to him—he would have called it 'everything ranged coldly on shelves.'

'I shall not really be intimate with this fellow,' Fielding thought, and then 'nor with anyone.' That was the corollary. And he had to confess that he really didn't mind, that he was content to help people, and like them as long as they didn't object, and if they objected pass on serenely. Experience can do much, and all that he had learnt in England and Europe was an assistance to him, and helped him towards clarity, but clarity prevented him from experiencing something else.

'How did you like the two ladies you met last Thursday?' he asked.

Aziz shook his head distastefully. The question reminded him of his rash remark about the Marabar Caves.

'How do you like Englishwomen generally?'

'Hamidullah liked them in England. Here we never look at them. Oh no, much too careful. Let's talk of something else.'

'Hamidullah's right: they are much nicer in England. There's something that doesn't suit them out here.'

Aziz after another silence said, 'Why are you not married?'

Fielding was pleased that he had asked. 'Because I have more or less come through without it,' he replied. 'I was thinking of telling you a little about myself some day if I can make it interesting enough. The lady I liked wouldn't marry me—that is the main point, but that's fifteen years ago and now means nothing.'

'But you haven't children.'

'None.'

'Excuse the following question: have you any illegitimate children?'

'No. I'ld willingly tell you if I had.'

'Then your name will entirely die out.'

'It must.'

'Well.' He shook his head. 'This indifference is what the Oriental will never understand.'

'I don't care for children.'

'Caring has nothing to do with it,' he said impatiently.

'I don't feel their absence, I don't want them weeping around my death-bed and being polite about me afterwards, which I believe is the general notion. I'd far rather leave a thought behind me than a child. Other people can have children. No obligation, with England getting so chock-a-block and overrunning India for jobs.'

'Why don't you marry Miss Quested?'

'Good God! why, the girl's a prig.'

'Prig, prig? Kindly explain. Isn't that a bad word?'

'Oh, I don't know her, but she struck me as one of the more pathetic products of Western education. She depresses me.'

'But prig, Mr Fielding? How's that?'

'She goes on and on as if she's at a lecture—trying ever so hard to understand India and life, and occasionally taking a note.'

'I thought her so nice and sincere.'

'So she probably is,' said Fielding, ashamed of his roughness: any suggestion that he should marry always does produce overstatements on the part of the bachelor, and a mental breeze. 'But I can't marry her if I wanted to, for she has just become engaged to the City Magistrate.'

'Has she indeed? I am so glad!' he exclaimed with relief, for this exempted him from the Marabar expedition: he would scarcely be expected to entertain regular Anglo-Indians.

'It's the old mother's doing. She was afraid her dear boy would choose for himself, so she brought out the girl on purpose, and flung them together until it happened.'

'Mrs Moore did not mention that to me among her plans.'

'I may have got it wrong–I'm out of club gossip. But anyhow they're engaged to be married.'

'Yes, you're out of it, my poor chap,' he smiled. 'No Miss Quested for Mr Fielding. However, she was not beautiful. She has practically no breasts, if you come to think of it.'

He smiled too, but found a touch of bad taste in the reference to a lady's breasts.

'For the City Magistrate they shall be sufficient perhaps, and he for her. For you I shall arrange a lady with breasts like mangoes. . . .'

'No, you won't.'

'I will not really, and besides your position makes it dangerous for you.' His mind had slipped from matrimony to Calcutta. His face grew grave. Fancy if he had persuaded the Principal to accompany him there, and then got him into trouble! And abruptly he took up a new attitude towards his friend, the attitude of the protector who knows the dangers of India and is admonitory. 'You can't be too careful in every way, Mr Fielding; whatever you say or do in this damned country there is always some envious fellow on the look-out. You may be surprised to know that there were at least three spies sitting here when you came to enquire. I was really a good deal upset that you talked in that fashion about God. They will certainly report it.'

'To whom?'

'That's all very well, but you spoke against morality also, and you said you had come to take other people's jobs. All that was very unwise. This is an awful place for scandal Why, actually one of your own pupils was listening.'

'Thanks for telling me that; yes, I must try and be more careful. If I'm interested, I'm apt to forget myself. Still, it doesn't do real harm.'

'But speaking out may get you into trouble.'

'It's often done so in the past.'

'There, listen to that! But the end of it might be that you lost your job.'

'If I do, I do. I shall survive it. I travel light.'

'Travel light! You are a most extraordinary race,' said Aziz, turning away as if he were going to sleep, and immediately turning back again. 'Is it your climate, or what?'

'Plenty of Indians travel light too–saddhus and such. It's one of the things I admire about your country. Any man can travel light until he has a wife or children. That's part of my case against marriage. I'm a holy man minus the holiness. Hand that on to your three spies, and tell them to put it in their pipes.'

Aziz was charmed and interested, and turned the new idea over in his mind. So this was why Mr Fielding and a few others were so fearless! They had nothing to lose. But he himself was rooted in society and Islam. He belonged to a tradition which bound him, and he had brought children into the world, the society of the future. Though he lived so vaguely in this flimsy bungalow, nevertheless he was placed, placed.

'I can't be sacked from my job, because my job's Education. I believe in teaching people to be individuals, and to understand other individuals. It's the only thing I do believe in. At Government College, I mix it up with trigonometry, and so on. When I'm a saddhu, I shall mix it up with something else.'

He concluded his manifesto, and both were silent. The eye-flies became worse than ever and danced close up to their pupils, or crawled into their ears. Fielding hit about wildly. The exercise made him hot, and he got up to go.

'You might tell your servant to bring my horse. He doesn't seem to appreciate my Urdu.'

'I know. I gave him orders not to. Such are the tricks we play on unfortunate Englishmen. Poor Mr Fielding! But I will release you now. Oh dear! With the exception of yourself and Hamidullah, I have no one to talk to in this place. You like Hamidullah, don't you?'

'Very much.'

'Do you promise to come at once to us when you are in trouble?'

'I never can be in trouble.'

'There goes a queer chap, I trust he won't come to grief,' thought Aziz, left alone. His period of admiration was over, and he reacted towards patronage. It was difficult for him to remain in awe of anyone who played with all his cards on the table. Fielding, he discovered on closer acquaintance, was truly warm-hearted and unconventional, but not what can be called wise. That frankness of speech in the presence of Ram Chand, Rafi and Co. was dangerous and inelegant. It served no useful end.

But they were friends, brothers. That part was settled, their compact had been subscribed by the photograph, they trusted one another, affection had triumphed for once in a way. He dropped off to sleep amid the happier memories of the last two hours—poetry of Ghalib, female grace, good old Hamidullah, good Fielding, his honoured wife and dear boys. He passed into a region where these joys had no enemies but bloomed harmoniously in an eternal garden, or ran down watershoots of ribbed marble, or rose into domes whereunder were inscribed, black against white, the ninety-nine attributes of God.

Caves

Chapter Twelve

The Ganges, though flowing from the foot of Vishnu and through Siva's hair, is not an ancient stream. Geology, looking further than religion, knows of a time when neither the river nor the Himalayas that nourished it existed, and an ocean flowed over the holy places of Hindustan. The mountains rose, their debris silted up the ocean, the gods took their seats on them and contrived the river, and the India we call immemorial came into being. But India is really far older. In the days of the prehistoric ocean the southern part of the peninsula already existed, and the high places of Dravidia have been land since land began, and have seen on the one side the sinking of a continent that joined them to Africa, and on the other the upheaval of the Himalayas from a sea. They are older than anything in the world. No water has ever covered them, and the sun who has watched them for countless aeons may still discern in their outlines forms that were his before our globe was torn from his bosom. If flesh of the sun's flesh is to be touched anywhere, it is here, among the incredible antiquity of these hills.

Yet even they are altering. As Himalayan India rose, this India, the primal, has been depressed, and is slowly re-entering the curve of the earth. It may be that in aeons to come an ocean will flow here too, and cover the sun-born rocks with slime. Meanwhile the plain of the Ganges encroaches on them with something of the sea's action. They are sinking beneath the newer lands. Their main mass is untouched, but at the edge their outposts have been cut off and stand knee-deep, throat-deep, in the advancing soil. There is something unspeakable in these outposts. They are like nothing else in the world, and a glimpse of them makes the breath catch. They rise abruptly, insanely, without the proportion that is kept by the wildest hills elsewhere, they bear no relation to anything dreamt or seen. To call them 'uncanny' suggests ghosts, and they are older than all spirit. Hinduism has scratched and plastered a few rocks, but the shrines are unfrequented, as if pilgrims, who generally seek the extraordinary, had here found too much of it. Some saddhus did once settle in a cave, but they were smoked out, and even Buddha, who must have passed this way down to the Bo Tree of Gya, shunned a renunciation more complete than his own, and has left no legend of struggle or victory in the Marabar.

The caves are readily described. A tunnel eight feet long, five feet high, three feet wide, leads to a circular chamber about twenty feet in diameter. This arrangement occurs again and again throughout the group of hills, and this is all, this is a Marabar Cave. Having seen one such cave, having seen two, having seen three, four, fourteen, twenty-four, the visitor returns to Chandrapore uncertain whether he has had an interesting experience or a dull one or any experience at all. He finds it difficult to discuss the caves, or to keep them apart in his mind, for the pattern never varies, and no carving, not even a bees'-nest or a bat distinguishes one from another. Nothing, nothing attaches to them, and their reputation—for they have one—does not depend upon human speech. It is as if the surrounding plain or the passing birds have taken upon themselves to exclaim 'extraordinary,' and the word has taken root in the air, and been inhaled by mankind.

They are dark caves. Even when they open towards the sun, very little light penetrates down the entrance tunnel into the circular chamber. There is little to see, and no eye to see it, until the visitor arrives for his five minutes, and strikes a match. Immediately another flame rises in the depths of the rock and moves towards the surface like an imprisoned spirit: the walls of the circular chamber have been most marvellously polished. The two flames approach and strive to unite, but cannot, because one of them breathes air, the other stone. A mirror inlaid with lovely colours divides the lovers, delicate stars of pink and grey interpose, exquisite nebulae, shadings fainter than the tail of a comet or the midday moon, all the evanescent life of the granite, only here visible. Fists and fingers thrust above the advancing soil—here at last is their skin, finer than any covering acquired by the animals, smoother than windless water, more voluptuous than love. The radiance increases, the flames touch one another, kiss, expire. The cave is dark again, like all the caves.

Only the wall of the circular chamber has been polished thus. The sides of the tunnel are left rough, they impinge as an afterthought upon the internal perfection. An entrance was necessary, so mankind made one. But elsewhere, deeper in the granite, are there certain chambers that have no entrances? Chambers never unsealed since the arrival of the gods. Local report declares that these exceed in number those that can be visited, as the dead exceed the living—four hundred of them, four thousand or million. Nothing is inside them, they were sealed up before the creation of pestilence or treasure; if mankind grew curious and excavated, nothing, nothing would be added to the sum of good or evil. One of them is rumoured within the boulder that swings on the summit of the highest of the hills; a bubble-shaped cave that has neither ceiling nor floor, and mirrors its own darkness in every direction infinitely. If the boulder falls and smashes, the cave will smash too—empty as an Easter egg. The boulder because of its hollowness sways in the wind, and even moves when a crow perches upon it: hence its name and the name of its stupendous pedestal: the Kawa Dol.

Chapter Thirteen

These hills look romantic in certain lights and at suitable distances, and seen of an evening from the upper verandah of the club they caused Miss Quested to say conversationally to Miss Derek that she should like to have gone, that Dr Aziz at Mr Fielding's had said he would arrange something, and that Indians seem rather forgetful. She was overheard by the servant who offered them vermouths. This servant understood English. And he was not exactly a spy, but he kept his ears open, and Mahmoud Ali did not exactly bribe him, but did encourage him to come and squat with his own servants, and would happen to stroll their way when he was there. As the story travelled, it accreted emotion and Aziz learnt with horror that the ladies were deeply offended with him, and had expected an invitation daily. He thought his facile remark had been forgotten. Endowed with two memories, a temporary and a permanent, he had hitherto relegated the caves to the former. Now he transferred them once for all, and pushed the matter through. They were to be a stupendous replica of the tea party. He began by securing Fielding and old Godbole, and then commissioned Fielding to approach Mrs Moore and Miss Quested when they were alone—by this device Ronny, their official protector, could be circumvented. Fielding didn't like the job much; he was busy, caves bored him, he foresaw friction and expense, but he would not refuse the first favour his friend had asked from him, and did as required. The ladies accepted. It was a little inconvenient in the present press of their engagements, still, they hoped to manage it after consulting Mr Heaslop. Consulted, Ronny raised no objection, provided Fielding undertook full responsibility for their comfort. He was not enthusiastic about the picnic, but, then, no more were the ladies—no one was enthusiastic, yet it took place.

Aziz was terribly worried. It was not a long expedition—a train left Chandrapore just before dawn, another would bring them back for tiffin—but he was only a little official still, and feared to acquit himself dishonourably. He had to ask Major Callendar for half a day's leave, and be refused because of his recent malingering; despair; renewed approach of Major Callendar through Fielding, and contemptuous snarling permission. He had to borrow cutlery from Mahmoud Ali without inviting him. Then there was the question of alcohol; Mr Fielding, and perhaps the ladies, were drinkers, so must he provide whisky-sodas and ports? There was the problem of transport from the wayside station of Marabar to the caves. There was the problem of Professor Godbole and his food, and of Professor Godbole and other people's food—two problems, not one problem. The

Professor was not a very strict Hindu—he would take tea, fruit, soda-water and sweets, whoever cooked them, and vegetables and rice if cooked by a Brahman; but not meat, not cakes lest they contained eggs, and he would not allow anyone else to eat beef: a slice of beef upon a distant plate would wreck his happiness. Other people might eat mutton, they might eat ham. But over ham Aziz' own religion raised its voice: he did not fancy other people eating ham. Trouble after trouble encountered him, because he had challenged the spirit of the Indian earth, which tries to keep men in compartments.

At last the moment arrived.

His friends thought him most unwise to mix himself up with English ladies, and warned him to take every precaution against unpunctuality. Consequently he spent the previous night at the station. The servants were huddled on the platform, enjoined not to stray. He himself walked up and down with old Mohammed Latif, who was to act as major-domo. He felt insecure and also unreal. A car drove up, and he hoped Fielding would get out of it, to lend him solidity. But it contained Mrs Moore, Miss Quested, and their Goanese servant. He rushed to meet them, suddenly happy. 'But you've come, after all. Oh how very very kind of you!' he cried. 'This is the happiest moment in all my life.'

The ladies were civil. It was not the happiest moment in their lives, still, they looked forward to enjoying themselves as soon as the bother of the early start was over. They had not seen him since the expedition was arranged, and they thanked him adequately.

'You don't require tickets—please stop your servant. There are no tickets on the Marabar branch line; it is its peculiarity. You come to the carriage and rest till Mr Fielding joins us. Did you know you are to travel purdah? Will you like that?'

They replied that they should like it. The train had come in, and a crowd of dependents were swarming over the seats of the carriage like monkeys. Aziz had borrowed servants from his friends, as well as bringing his own three, and quarrels over precedence were resulting. The ladies' servant stood apart, with a sneering expression on his face. They had hired him while they were still globe-trotters, at Bombay. In a hotel or among smart people he was excellent, but as soon as they consorted with anyone whom he thought second-rate he left them to their disgrace.

The night was still dark, but had acquired the temporary look that indicates its end. Perched on the roof of a shed, the station-master's hens began to dream of kites instead of owls. Lamps were put out, in order to save the trouble of putting them out later; the smell of tobacco and the sound of spitting arose from third-class passengers in dark corners; heads were unshrouded, teeth cleaned on the twigs of a tree. So convinced was a junior official that another sun would rise, that he rang a bell with enthusiasm. This upset the servants. They shrieked that the train was starting, and ran to both ends of it to intercede. Much had still to enter the purdah carriage—a box bound with brass, a melon wearing a fez, a towel containing guavas, a step-ladder and a gun. The guests played up all right. They had no race-consciousness—Mrs Moore was too old, Miss Quested too new—and they behaved to Aziz as to any young man who had been kind to them in the country. This moved him deeply. He had expected them to arrive with Mr Fielding, instead of which they trusted themselves to be with him a few moments alone.

'Send back your servant,' he suggested. 'He is unnecessary. Then we shall all be Moslems together.'

'And he is such a horrible servant. Antony, you can go; we don't want you,' said the girl impatiently.

'Master told me to come.'

'Mistress tells you to go.'

'Master says, keep near the ladies all the morning.'

'Well, your ladies won't have you.' She turned to the host. 'Do get rid of him, Dr Aziz!'

'Mohammed Latif!' he called.

The poor relative exchanged fezzes with the melon, and peeped out of the window of the railway carriage, whose confusion he was superintending.

'Here is my cousin, Mr Mohammed Latif. Oh no, don't shake hands. He is an Indian of the old-fashioned sort, he prefers to salaam. There, I told you so. Mohammed Latif, how beautifully you salaam. See, he hasn't understood; he knows no English.'

'You spick lie,' said the old man gently.

'I spick a lie! Oh, jolly good. Isn't he a funny old man? We will have great jokes with him later. He does all sorts of little things. He is not nearly as stupid as you think, and awfully poor. It's lucky ours is a large family.' He flung an arm round the grubby neck. 'But you get inside, make yourselves at home; yes, you lie down.' The celebrated Oriental confusion appeared at last to be at an end. 'Excuse me, now I must meet our other two guests!'

He was getting nervous again, for it was ten minutes to the time. Still, Fielding was an Englishman, and they never do miss trains, and Godbole was a Hindu and did not count, and, soothed by this logic, he grew calmer as the hour of departure approached. Mohammed Latif had bribed Antony not to come. They walked up and down the platform, talking usefully. They agreed that they had overdone the servants, and must leave two or three behind at Marabar station. And Aziz explained that he might be playing one or two practical jokes at the caves—not out of unkindness, but to make the guests laugh. The old man assented with slight sideway motions of the head: he was always willing to be ridiculed, and he bade Aziz not spare him. Elated by his importance, he began an indecent anecdote.

'Tell me another time, brother, when I have more leisure, for now, as I have already explained, we have to give pleasure to non-Moslems. Three will be Europeans, one a Hindu, which must not be forgotten. Every attention must be paid to Professor Godbole, lest he feel that he is inferior to my other guests.'

'I will discuss philosophy with him.'

'That will be kind of you; but the servants are even more important. We must not convey an impression of disorganization. It can be done, and I expect you to to it . . .'

A shriek from the purdah carriage. The train had started.

'Merciful God!' cried Mohammed Latif. He flung himself at the train, and leapt on to the footboard of a carriage. Aziz did likewise. It was an easy feat, for a branch-line train is slow to assume special airs. 'We're monkeys, don't worry,' he called, hanging on to a bar and laughing. Then he howled, 'Mr Fielding! Mr Fielding!'

There were Fielding and old Godbole, held up at the level-crossing. Appalling catastrophe! The gates had been closed earlier than usual. They leapt from their tonga; they gesticulated, but what was the good. So near and yet so far! As the train joggled past over the points, there was time for agonized words.

'Bad, bad, you have destroyed me.'

'Godbole's pujah did it,' cried the Englishman.

The Brahman lowered his eyes, ashamed of religion. For it was so: he had miscalculated the length of a prayer.

'Jump on, I must have you,' screamed Aziz, beside himself.

'Right, give a hand.'

'He's not to, he'll kill himself,' Mrs Moore protested. He jumped, he failed, missed his friend's hand, and fell back on to the line. The train rumbled past. He scrambled on to his feet, and bawled after them, 'I'm all right, you're all right, don't worry,' and then they passed beyond range of his voice.

'Mrs Moore, Miss Quested, our expedition is a ruin.' He swung himself along the footboard, almost in tears.

'Get in, get in; you'll kill yourself as well as Mr Fielding. I see no ruin.'

'How is that? Oh, explain to me!' he said piteously, like a child.

'We shall be all Moslems together now, as you promised.'

She was perfect as always, his dear Mrs Moore. All the love for her he had felt at the mosque welled up again, the fresher for forgetfulness. There was nothing he would not do for her. He would die to make her happy.

'Get in, Dr Aziz, you make us giddy,' the other lady called. 'If they're so foolish as to miss the train, that's their loss, not ours.'

'I am to blame. I am the host.'

'Nonsense, go to your carriage. We're going to have a delightful time without them.'

Not perfect like Mrs Moore, but very sincere and kind. Wonderful ladies, both of them, and for one precious morning his guests. He felt important and competent. Fielding was a loss personally, being a friend, increasingly dear, yet if Fielding had come, he himself would have remained in leading-strings. 'Indians are incapable of responsibility,' said the officials, and Hamidullah sometimes said so too. He would show those pessimists that they were wrong. Smiling proudly, he glanced outward at the country, which was still invisible except as a dark movement in the darkness; then upwards at the sky, where the stars of the sprawling Scorpion had begun to pale. Then he dived through a window into a second-class carriage.

'Mohammed Latif, by the way, what is in these caves, brother? Why are we all going to see them?'

Such a question was beyond the poor relative's scope. He could only reply that God and the local villagers knew, and that the latter would gladly act as guides.

Chapter Fourteen

Most of life is so dull that there is nothing to be said about it, and the books and talk that would describe it as interesting are obliged to exaggerate, in the hope of justifying their own existence. Inside its cocoon of work or social obligation, the human spirit slumbers for the most part, registering the distinction between pleasure and pain, but not nearly as alert as we pretend. There are periods in the most thrilling day during-which nothing happens, and though we continue to exclaim, 'I do enjoy myself,' or, 'I am horrified,' we are insincere. 'As far as I feel anything, it is enjoyment, horror'—it's no more than that really, and a perfectly adjusted organism would be silent.

It so happened that Mrs Moore and Miss Quested had felt nothing acutely for a fortnight. Ever since Professor Godbole had sung his queer little song, they had lived more or less inside cocoons, and the difference between them was that the elder lady accepted her own apathy, while the younger resented hers. It was Adela's faith that the whole stream of events is important and interesting, and if she grew bored she blamed herself severely and compelled her lips to utter enthusiasms. This was the only insincerity in a character otherwise sincere, and it was indeed the intellectual protest of her youth. She was particularly vexed now because she was both in India and engaged to be married, which double event should have made every instant sublime.

India was certainly dim this morning, though seen under the auspices of Indians. Her wish had been granted, but too late. She could not get excited over Aziz and his arrangements. She was not the least unhappy or depressed, and the various odd objects that surrounded her—the comic 'purdah' carriage, the piles of rugs and bolsters, the rolling melons, the scent of sweet oils, the ladder, the brass-bound box, the sudden irruption of Mahmoud Ali's butler from the lavatory with tea and poached eggs upon a tray—they were all new and amusing, and led her to comment appropriately, but they wouldn't bite into her mind. So she tried to find comfort by reflecting that her main interest would henceforward be Ronny.

'What a nice cheerful servant! What a relief after Antony!'

'They startle one rather. A strange place to make tea in,' said Mrs Moore, who had hoped for a nap.

'I want to sack Antony. His behaviour on the platform has decided me.'

Mrs Moore thought that Antony's better self would come to the front at Simla. Miss Quested was to be married at Simla; some cousins, with a house looking straight on to Thibet, had invited her.

'Anyhow, we must get a second servant, because at Simla you will be at the hotel, and I don't think Ronny's Baldeo . . .' She loved plans.

'Very well, you get another servant, and I'll keep Antony with me. I am used to his unappetizing ways. He will see me through the Hot Weather.'

'I don't believe in the Hot Weather. People like Major Callendar who always talk about it—it's in the hope of making one feel inexperienced and small, like their everlasting, "I've been twenty years in this country."'

'I believe in the Hot Weather, but never did I suppose it would bottle me up as it will.' For owing to the sage leisureliness of Ronny and Adela, they could not be married till May, and consequently Mrs Moore could not return to England immediately after the wedding, which was what she had hoped to do. By May a barrier of fire would have fallen across India and the adjoining sea, and she would have to remain perched up in the Himalayas waiting for the world to get cooler.

'I won't be bottled up,' announced the girl. 'I've no patience with these women here who leave their husbands grilling in the plains. Mrs McBryde hasn't stopped down once since she married; she leaves her quite intelligent husband alone half the year, and then's surprised she's out of touch with him.'

'She has children, you see.'

'Oh yes, that's true,' said Miss Quested, disconcerted.

'It is the children who are the first consideration. Until they are grown up, and married off. When that happens one has again the right to live for oneself—in the plains or the hills, as suits.'

'Oh yes, you're perfectly right. I never thought it out.'

'If one has not become too stupid and old.' She handed her empty cup to the servant.

'My idea now is that my cousins shall find me a servant in Simla, at all events to see me through the wedding, after which Ronny means to reorganize his staff entirely. He does it very well for a bachelor; still, when he is married no doubt various changes will have to be made—his old servants won't want to take their orders from me, and I don't blame them.'

Mrs Moore pushed up the shutters and looked out. She had brought Ronny and Adela together by their mutual wish, but really she could not advise them further. She felt increasingly (vision or nightmare?) that, though people are important, the relations between them are not, and that in particular too much fuss has been made over marriage; centuries of carnal embracement, yet man is no nearer to understanding man. And to-day she felt this with such force that it seemed itself a relationship, itself a person who was trying to take hold of her hand.

'Anything to be seen of the hills?'

'Only various shades of the dark.'

'We can't be far from the place where my hyena was.' She peered into the timeless twilight. The train crossed a nullah. 'Pomper, pomper, pomper,' was the sound that the wheels made as they trundled over the bridge, moving very slowly. A hundred yards on came a second nullah, then a third, suggesting the neighbourhood of higher ground. 'Perhaps this is mine; anyhow, the road runs parallel with the railway.' Her accident was a pleasant memory; she felt in her dry, honest way that it had given her a good shake up, and taught her Ronny's true worth. Then she went back to her plans; plans had been a passion with her from girlhood. Now and then she paid tribute to the present, said how friendly and intelligent Aziz was, ate a guava, couldn't eat a fried sweet, practised her Urdu on the servant; but her thoughts ever veered to the manageable future, and to the Anglo-Indian life she had decided to endure. And as she appraised it with its adjuncts of Turtons and Burtons, the train accompanied her sentences, 'pomper, pomper,' the train half asleep, going nowhere in particular and with no passenger of importance in any of its carriages, the branch-line train, lost on a low embankment between dull fields. Its message—for it had one—avoided her well-equipped mind. Far away behind her, with a shriek that meant business, rushed the Mail, connecting up important towns such as Calcutta and Lahore, where interesting events occur and personalities are developed. She understood that. Unfortunately, India has few important towns. India is the country, fields, fields, then hills, jungle, hills, and more fields. The branch line stops, the road is only practicable for cars to a point, the bullock-carts lumber down the side tracks, paths fray out into the cultivation, and disappear near a splash of red paint. How can the mind take hold of such a country? Generations of invaders have tried, but they remain in exile. The important towns they build are only retreats, their quarrels the malaise of men who cannot find their way home. India knows of their trouble. She knows of the whole world's trouble, to its uttermost depth. She calls 'Come' through her hundred mouths, through objects ridiculous and august. But come to what? She has never defined. She is not a promise, only an appeal.

'I will fetch you from Simla when it's cool enough. I will unbottle you in fact,' continued the reliable girl. 'We then see some of the Mogul stuff—how appalling if we let you miss the Taj!—and then I will see you off at Bombay. Your last glimpse of this country really shall be interesting.' But Mrs Moore had fallen asleep, exhausted by the early start. She was in rather low health, and ought not to have attempted the expedition, but had pulled herself together in case the pleasure of the others should suffer. Her dreams were of the same texture, but there it was her other children who were wanting something, Stella and Ralph, and she was explaining to them that she could not be in two families at once. When she awoke, Adela had ceased to plan, and leant out of a window, saying, 'They're rather wonderful.'

Astonishing even from the rise of the civil station, here the Marabar were gods to whom earth is a ghost. Kawa Dol was nearest. It shot up in a single slab, on whose summit one rock was poised—if a mass so great can be called one rock. Behind it, recumbent, were the hills that contained the other caves, isolated each from his neighbour by broad channels of the plain. The assemblage, ten in all, shifted a little as the train crept past them, as if observing its arrival.

'I'ld not have missed this for anything,' said the girl, exaggerating her enthusiasm. 'Look, the sun's rising—this'll be absolutely magnificent—come quickly—look. I wouldn't have missed this for anything. We should never have seen it if we'd stuck to the Turtons and their eternal elephants.'

As she spoke, the sky to the left turned angry orange. Colour throbbed and mounted behind a pattern of trees, grew in intensity, was yet brighter, incredibly brighter, strained from without against the globe of the air. They awaited the miracle. But at the supreme moment, when night should have died and day lived, nothing occurred. It was as if virtue had failed in the celestial fount. The hues in the east decayed, the hills seemed dimmer though in fact better lit, and a profound disappointment entered with the morning breeze. Why, when the chamber was prepared, did the bridegroom not enter with trumpets and shawms, as humanity expects? The sun rose without splendour. He was presently observed trailing yellowish behind the trees, or against insipid sky, and touching the bodies already at work in the fields.

'Ah, that must be the false dawn—isn't it caused by dust in the upper layers of the atmosphere that couldn't fall down during the night? I think Mr McBryde said so. Well, I must admit that England has it as regards sunrises. Do you remember Grasmere?'

'Ah, dearest Grasmere!' Its little lakes and mountains were beloved by them all. Romantic yet manageable, it sprang from a kindlier planet. Here an untidy plain stretched to the knees of the Marabar.

'Good morning, good morning, put on your topis,' shouted Aziz from farther down the train. 'Put on your topis at once, the early sun is highly dangerous for heads. I speak as a doctor.'

'Good morning, good morning, put on your own.'

'Not for my thick head,' he laughed, banging it and holding up pads of his hair.

'Nice creature he is,' murmured Adela.

'Listen—Mohammed Latif says "Good morning" next.' Various pointless jests.

'Dr Aziz, what's happened to your hills? The train has forgotten to stop.'

'Perhaps it is a circular train and goes back to Chandrapore without a break. Who knows!'

Having wandered off into the plain for a mile, the train slowed up against an elephant. There was a platform too, but it shrivelled into insignificance. An elephant, waving her painted forehead at the morn! 'Oh, what a surprise!' called the ladies politely. Aziz said nothing, but he nearly burst with pride and relief. The elephant was the one grand feature of the picnic, and God alone knew what he had gone through to obtain her. Semi-official, she was best approached through the Nawab Bahadur, who was best approached through Nureddin, but he never answered letters, but his mother had great influence with him and was a friend of Hamidullah Begum's, who had been excessively kind and had promised to call on her provided the broken shutter of the purdah carriage came back soon enough from Calcutta. That an elephant should depend from so long and so slender a string filled Aziz with content, and with humorous appreciation of the East, where the friends of friends are a reality, where everything gets done sometime, and sooner or later every one gets his share of happiness. And Mohammed Latif was likewise content, because two of the guests had missed the train, and consequently he could ride on the howdah instead of following in a cart, and the servants were content because an elephant increased their self-esteem, and they tumbled out the luggage into the dust with shouts and bangs, issuing orders to one another, and convulsed with goodwill.

'It takes an hour to get there, an hour to get back, and two hours for the caves, which we will call three,' said Aziz, smiling charmingly. There was suddenly something regal about him. 'The train back is at eleven-thirty, and you will be sitting down to your tiffin in Chandrapore with Mr Heaslop at exactly your usual hour, namely, one-fifteen. I know everything about you. Four hours—quite a small expedition—and an hour extra for misfortunes, which occur somewhat frequently among my people. My idea is to plan everything without consulting you; but you, Mrs Moore, or Miss Quested, you are at any moment to make alterations if you wish, even if it means giving up the caves. Do you agree? Then mount this wild animal.'

The elephant had knelt, grey and isolated, like another hill. They climbed up the ladder, and he mounted shikar fashion, treading first on the sharp edge of the heel and then into the looped-up tail. When Mohammed Latif followed him, the servant who held the end of the tail let go of it according to previous instructions, so that the poor relative slipped and had to cling to the netting over the buttocks. It was a little piece of court buffoonery, and distressed only the ladies, whom it was intended to divert. Both of them disliked practical jokes. Then the beast rose in two shattering movements, and poised them ten feet above the plain. Immediately below was the scurf of life that an elephant always collects round its feet—villagers, naked babies. The servants flung crockery into tongas. Hassan annexed the stallion intended for Aziz, and defied Mahmoud Ali's man from its altitude. The Brahman who had been hired to cook for Professor Godbole was planted under an acacia tree, to await their return. The train, also hoping to return, wobbled away through the fields, turning its head this way and that like a centipede. And the only other movement to be seen was a movement as of antennae, really the counterpoises of the wells which rose and fell on their pivots of mud all over the plain and dispersed a feeble flow of water. The scene was agreeable rather than not in the mild morning air, but there was little colour in it, and no vitality.

As the elephant moved towards the hills (the pale sun had by this time saluted them to the base, and pencilled shadows down their creases) a new quality occurred, a spiritual silence which invaded more senses than the ear. Life went on as usual, but had no consequences, that is to say, sounds did not echo or thoughts develop. Everything seemed cut off at its root, and therefore infected with illusion. For instance, there were some mounds by the edge of the track, low, serrated, and touched with whitewash. What were these mounds—graves, breasts of the goddess Parvati? The villagers beneath gave both replies. Again, there was a confusion about a snake which was never cleared up. Miss Quested saw a thin, dark object reared on end at the farther side of a watercourse, and said, 'A snake!' The villagers agreed, and Aziz explained: yes, a black cobra, very venomous, who had reared himself up to watch the passing of the elephant. But when she looked through Ronny's field-glasses, she found it wasn't a snake, but the withered and twisted stump of a toddy-palm. So she said, 'It isn't a snake.' The villagers contradicted her. She had put the word into their minds, and they refused to abandon it. Aziz admitted that it looked like a tree through the glasses, but insisted that it was a black cobra really, and improvised some rubbish about protective mimicry. Nothing was explained, and yet there was no romance. Films of heat, radiated from the Kawa Dol precipices, increased the confusion. They came at irregular intervals and moved capriciously. A patch of field would jump as if it was being fried, and then lie quiet. As they drew closer the radiation stopped.

The elephant walked straight at the Kawa Dol as if she would knock for admission with her forehead, then swerved, and followed a path round its base. The stones plunged straight into the earth, like cliffs into the sea, and while Miss Quested was remarking on this, and saying that it was striking, the plain quietly disappeared, peeled off, so to speak, and nothing was to be seen on either side but the granite, very dead and quiet. The sky dominated as usual, but seemed unhealthily near, adhering like a ceiling to the summits of the precipices. It was as if the contents of the corridor had never been changed. Occupied by his own munificence, Aziz noticed nothing. His guests noticed a little. They did not feel that it was an attractive place or quite worth visiting, and wished it could have turned into some Mohammedan object, such as a mosque, which their host would have appreciated and explained. His ignorance became evident, and was really rather a drawback. In spite of his gay, confident talk, he had no notion how to treat this particular aspect of India; he was lost in it without Professor Godbole, like themselves.

The corridor narrowed, then widened into a sort of tray. Here, more or less, was their goal. A ruined tank held a little water which would do for the animals, and close above the mud was punched a black hole—the first of the caves. Three hills encircled the tray. Two of them pumped out heat busily, but the third was in shadow, and here they camped.

'A horrid, stuffy place really,' murmured Mrs Moore to herself.

'How quick your servants are!' Miss Quested exclaimed. For a cloth had already been laid, with a vase of artificial flowers in its centre, and Mahmoud Ali's butler offered them poached eggs and tea for the second time.

'I thought we would eat this before our caves, and breakfast after.'

'Isn't this breakfast?'

'This breakfast? Did you think I should treat you so strangely?' He had been warned that English people never stop eating, and that he had better nourish them every two hours until a solid meal was ready.

'How very well it is all arranged.'

'That you shall tell me when I return to Chandrapore. Whatever disgraces I bring upon myself, you remain my guests.' He spoke gravely now. They were dependent on him for a few hours, and he felt grateful to them for placing themselves in such a position. All was well so far; the elephant held a fresh cut bough to her lips, the tonga shafts stuck up into the air, the kitchen-boy peeled potatoes, Hassan shouted, and Mohammed Latif stood as he ought, with a peeled switch in his hand. The expedition was a success, and it was Indian; an obscure young man had been allowed to show courtesy to visitors from another country, which is what all Indians long to do—even cynics like Mahmoud Ali—but they never have the chance. Hospitality had been achieved, they were 'his' guests; his honour was involved in their happiness, and any discomfort they endured would tear his own soul.

Like most Orientals, Aziz overrated hospitality, mistaking it for intimacy, and not seeing that it is tainted with the sense of possession. It was only when Mrs Moore or Fielding was near him that he saw further, and knew that it is more blessed to receive than to give. These two had strange and beautiful effects on him—they were his friends, his for ever, and he theirs for ever; he loved them so much that giving and receiving became one. He loved them even better than the Hamidullahs, because he had surmounted obstacles to meet them, and this stimulates a generous mind. Their images remained somewhere in his soul up to his dying day, permanent additions. He looked at her now as she sat on a deck-chair, sipping his tea, and had for a moment a joy that held the seeds of its own decay, for it would lead him to think, 'Oh, what more can I do for her?' and so back to the dull round of hospitality. The black bullets of his eyes filled with soft expressive light, and he said, 'Do you ever remember our mosque, Mrs Moore?'

'I do, I do,' she said, suddenly vital and young.

'And how rough and rude I was, and how good you were.'

'And how happy we both were.'

'Friendships last longest that begin like that, I think. Shall I ever entertain your other children?'

'Do you know about the others? She will never talk about them to me,' said Miss Quested, unintentionally breaking a spell.

'Ralph and Stella, yes, I know everything about them. But we must not forget to visit our caves. One of the dreams of my life is accomplished in having you both here as my guests. You cannot imagine how you have honoured me. I feel like the Emperor Babur.'

'Why like him?' she enquired, rising.

'Because my ancestors came down with him from Afghanistan. They joined him at Herat. He also had often no more elephants than one, none sometimes, but he never ceased showing hospitality. When he fought or hunted or ran away, he would always stop for a time among hills, just like us; he would never let go of hospitality and pleasure, and if there was only a little food, he would have it arranged nicely, and if only one musical instrument, he would compel it to play a beautiful tune. I take him as my ideal. He is the poor gentleman, and he became a great king.'

'I thought another Emperor is your favourite—I forget the name—you mentioned him at Mr Fielding's: what my book calls Aurangzebe.'

'Alamgir? Oh yes, he was of course the more pious. But Babur—never in his whole life did he betray a friend, so I can only think of him this morning. And you know how he died? He laid down his life for his son. A death far more difficult than battle. They were caught in the heat. They should have gone back to Kabul for the bad weather, but could not for reasons of state, and at Agra Humayun fell sick. Babur walked round the bed three times, and said, 'I have borne it away,' and he did bear it away; the fever left his son and came to him instead, and he died. That is why I prefer Babur to Alamgir. I ought not to do so, but I do. However, I mustn't delay you. I see you are ready to start.'

'Not at all,' she said, sitting down by Mrs Moore again. 'We enjoy talk like this very much.' For at last he was talking about what he knew and felt, talking as he had in Fielding's garden-house; he was again the Oriental guide whom they appreciated.

'I always enjoy conversing about the Moguls. It is the chief pleasure I know. You see, those first six emperors were all most wonderful men, and as soon as one of them is mentioned, no matter which, I forget everything else in the world except the other five. You could not find six such kings in all the countries of the earth, not, I mean, coming one after the other—father, son.'

'Tell us something about Akbar.'

'Ah, you have heard the name of Akbar. Good. Hamidullah—whom you shall meet—will tell you that Akbar is the greatest of all. I say, "Yes, Akbar is very wonderful, but half a Hindu; he was not a true Moslem," which makes Hamidullah cry, "No more was Babur, he drank wine." But Babur always repented afterwards, which makes the entire difference, and Akbar never repented of the new religion he invented instead of the Holy Koran.'

'But wasn't Akbar's new religion very fine? It was to embrace the whole of India.'

'Miss Quested, fine but foolish. You keep your religion, I mine. That is the best. Nothing embraces the whole of India, nothing, nothing, and that was Akbar's mistake.'

'Oh, do you feel that, Dr Aziz?' she said thoughtfully. 'I hope you're not right. There will have to be something universal in this country—I don't say religion, for I'm not religious, but something, or how else are barriers to be broken down?'

She was only recommending the universal brotherhood he sometimes dreamed of, but as soon as it was put into prose it became untrue.

'Take my own case,' she continued—it was indeed her own case that had animated her. 'I don't know whether you happen to have heard, but I'm going to marry Mr Heaslop.'

'On which my heartiest congratulations.'

'Mrs Moore, may I put our difficulty to Dr Aziz—I mean our Anglo-Indian one?'

'It is your difficulty, not mine, my dear.'

'Ah, that's true. Well, by marrying Mr Heaslop, I shall become what is known as an Anglo-Indian.'

He held up his hand in protest. 'Impossible. Take back such a terrible remark.'

'But I shall; it's inevitable. I can't avoid the label. What I do hope to avoid is the mentality. Women like—' She stopped, not quite liking to mention names; she would boldly have said 'Mrs Turton and Mrs Callendar' a fortnight ago. 'Some women are so—well, ungenerous and snobby about Indians, and I should feel too ashamed for words if I turned like them, but—and here's my difficulty—there's nothing special about me, nothing specially good or strong, which will help me to resist my environment and avoid becoming like them. I've most lamentable defects. That's why I want Akbar's "universal religion" or the equivalent to keep me decent and sensible. Do you see what I mean?'

Her remarks pleased him, but his mind shut up tight because she had alluded to her marriage. He was not going to be mixed up in that side of things. 'You are certain to be happy with any relative of Mrs Moore's,' he said with a formal bow.

'Oh, my happiness—that's quite another problem. I want to consult you about this Anglo-Indian difficulty. Can you give me any advice?'

'You are absolutely unlike the others, I assure you. You will never be rude to my people.'

'I am told we all get rude after a year.'

'Then you are told a lie,' he flashed, for she had spoken the truth and it touched him on the raw; it was itself an insult in these particular circumstances. He recovered himself at once and laughed, but her error broke up their conversation—their civilization it had almost been—which scattered like the petals of a desert flower, and left them in the middle of the hills. 'Come along,' he said, holding out a hand to each. They got up a little reluctantly, and addressed themselves to sightseeing.

The first cave was tolerably convenient. They skirted the puddle of water, and then climbed up over some unattractive stones, the sun crashing on their backs. Bending their heads, they disappeared one by one into the interior of the hills. The small black hole gaped where their varied forms and colours had momentarily functioned. They were sucked in like water down a drain. Bland and bald rose the precipices; bland and glutinous the sky that connected the precipices; solid and white, a Brahminy kite flapped between the rocks with a clumsiness that seemed intentional. Before man, with his itch for the seemly, had been born, the planet must have looked thus. The kite flapped away. . . . Before birds, perhaps. . . . And then the hole belched and humanity returned.

A Marabar cave had been horrid as far as Mrs Moore was concerned, for she had nearly fainted in it, and had some difficulty in preventing herself from saying so as soon as she got into the air again. It was natural enough: she had always suffered from faintness, and the cave had become too full, because all their retinue followed them. Crammed with villagers and servants, the circular chamber began to smell. She lost Aziz and Adela in the dark, didn't know who touched her, couldn't breathe, and some vile naked thing struck her face and settled on her mouth like a pad. She tried to regain the entrance tunnel, but an influx of villagers swept her back. She hit her head. For an instant she went mad, hitting and gasping like a fanatic. For not only did the crush and stench alarm her; there was also a terrifying echo.

Professor Godbole had never mentioned an echo; it never impressed him, perhaps. There are some exquisite echoes in India; there is the whisper round the dome at Bijapur; there are the long, solid sentences that voyage through the air at Mandu, and return unbroken to their creator. The echo in a Marabar cave is not like these, it is entirely devoid of distinction. Whatever is said, the same monotonous noise replies, and quivers up and down the walls until it is absorbed into the roof. 'Boum' is the sound as far as the human alphabet can express it, or 'bou-oum,' or 'ou-boum,'–utterly dull. Hope, politeness, the blowing of a nose, the squeak of a boot, all produce 'boum.' Even the striking of a match starts a little worm coiling, which is too small to complete a circle but is eternally watchful. And if several people talk at once, an overlapping howling noise begins, echoes generate echoes, and the cave is stuffed with a snake composed of small snakes, which writhe independently.

After Mrs Moore all the others poured out. She had given the signal for the reflux. Aziz and Adela both emerged smiling and she did not want him to think his treat was a failure, so smiled too. As each person emerged she looked for a villain, but none was there, and she realized that she had been among the mildest individuals, whose only desire was to honour her, and that the naked pad was a poor little baby, astride its mother's hip. Nothing evil had been in the cave, but she had not enjoyed herself; no, she had not enjoyed herself, and she decided not to visit a second one.

'Did you see the reflection of his match–rather pretty?' asked Adela.

'I forget . . .'

'But he says this isn't a good cave, the best are on the Kawa Dol.'

'I don't think I shall go on to there. I dislike climbing.'

'Very well, let's sit down again in the shade until breakfast's ready.'

'Ah, but that'll disappoint him so; he has taken such trouble. You should go on; you don't mind.'

'Perhaps I ought to,' said the girl, indifferent to what she did, but desirous of being amiable.

The servants, etc., were scrambling back to the camp, pursued by grave censures from Mohammed Latif. Aziz came to help the guests over the rocks. He was at the summit of his powers, vigorous and humble, too sure of himself to resent criticism, and he was sincerely pleased when he heard they were altering his plans. 'Certainly, Miss Quested, so you and I will go together, and leave Mrs Moore here, and we will not be long, yet we will not hurry, because we know that will be her wish.'

'Quite right. I'm sorry not to come too, but I'm a poor walker.'

'Dear Mrs Moore, what does anything matter so long as you are my guests? I am very glad you are *not* coming, which sounds strange, but you are treating me with true frankness, as a friend.'

'Yes, I am your friend,' she said, laying her hand on his sleeve, and thinking, despite her fatigue, how very charming, how very good, he was, and how deeply she desired his happiness. 'So may I make another suggestion? Don't let so many people come with you this time. I think you may find it more convenient.'

'Exactly, exactly,' he cried, and, rushing to the other extreme, forbade all except one guide to accompany Miss Quested and him to the Kawa Dol. 'Is that all right?' he enquired.

'Quite right, now enjoy yourselves, and when you come back tell me all about it.' And she sank into the deck-chair.

If they reached the big pocket of caves, they would be away nearly an hour. She took out her writing-pad, and began, 'Dear Stella, Dear Ralph,' then stopped, and looked at the queer valley and their feeble invasion of it. Even the elephant had become a nobody. Her eye rose from it to the entrance tunnel. No, she did not wish to repeat that experience. The more she thought over it, the more disagreeable and frightening it became. She minded it much more now than at the time. The crush and the smells she could forget, but the echo began in some indescribable way to undermine her hold on life. Coming at a moment when she chanced to be fatigued, it had managed to murmur, 'Pathos, piety, courage—they exist, but are identical, and so is filth. Everything exists, nothing has value.' If one had spoken vileness in that place, or quoted lofty poetry, the comment would have been the same—'ou-boum.' If one had spoken with the tongues of angels and pleaded for all the unhappiness and misunderstanding in the world, past, present, and to come, for all the misery men must undergo whatever their opinion and position, and however much they dodge or bluff—it would amount to the same, the serpent would descend and return to the ceiling. Devils are of the North, and poems can be written about them, but no one could romanticize the Marabar because it robbed infinity and eternity of their vastness, the only quality that accommodates them to mankind.

She tried to go on with her letter, reminding herself that she was only an elderly woman who had got up too early in the morning and journeyed too far, that the despair creeping over her was merely her despair, her personal weakness, and that even if she got a sunstroke and went mad the rest of the world would go on. But suddenly, at the edge of her mind, Religion appeared, poor little talkative Christianity, and she knew that all its divine words from 'Let there be Light' to 'It is finished' only amounted to 'boum.' Then she was terrified over an area larger than usual; the universe, never comprehensible to her intellect, offered no repose to her soul, the mood of the last two months took definite form at last, and she realized that she didn't want to write to her children, didn't want to communicate with anyone, not even with God. She sat motionless with horror, and, when old Mohammed Latif came up to her, thought he would notice a difference. For a time she thought, 'I am going to be ill,' to comfort herself, then she surrendered to the vision. She lost all interest, even in Aziz, and the affectionate and sincere words that she had spoken to him seemed no longer hers but the air's.

Chapter Fifteen

Miss Quested and Aziz and a guide continued the slightly tedious expedition. They did not talk much, for the sun was getting high. The air felt like a warm bath into which hotter water is trickling constantly, the temperature rose and rose, the boulders said, 'I am alive,' the small stones answered, 'I am almost alive.' Between the chinks lay the ashes of little plants. They meant to climb to the rocking-stone on the summit, but it was too far, and they contented themselves with the big group of caves. *En route* for these, they encountered several isolated caves, which the guide persuaded them to visit, but really there was nothing to see; they lit a match, admired its reflection in the polish, tested the echo and came out again. Aziz was 'pretty sure they should come on some interesting old carvings soon,' but only meant he wished there were some carvings. His deeper thoughts were about the breakfast. Symptoms of disorganization had appeared as he left the camp. He ran over the menu: an English breakfast, porridge and mutton chops, but some Indian dishes to cause conversation, and pan afterwards. He had never liked Miss Quested as much as Mrs Moore, and had little to say to her, less than ever now that she would marry a British official.

Nor had Adela much to say to him. If his mind was with the breakfast, hers was mainly with her marriage. Simla next week, get rid of Antony, a view of Thibet, tiresome wedding bells, Agra in October, see Mrs Moore comfortably off from Bombay—the procession passed before her again, blurred by the heat, and then she turned to the more serious business of her life at Chandrapore. There were real difficulties here—Ronny's limitations and her own—but she enjoyed facing difficulties, and decided that if she could control her peevishness (always her weak point), and neither rail against Anglo-India nor succumb to it, their married life ought to be happy and profitable. She mustn't be too theoretical; she would deal with each problem as it came up, and trust to Ronny's common sense and her own. Luckily, each had abundance of common sense and good will.

But as she toiled over a rock that resembled an inverted saucer, she thought, 'What about love?' The rock was nicked by a double row of footholds, and somehow the question was suggested by them. Where had she seen footholds before? Oh yes, they were the pattern traced in the dust by the wheels of the Nawab Bahadur's car. She and Ronny—no, they did not love each other.

'Do I take you too fast?' enquired Aziz, for she had paused, a doubtful expression on her face. The discovery had come so suddenly that she felt like a mountaineer whose rope had broken. Not to love the man one's going to marry! Not to find it out till this moment! Not even to have asked oneself the question until now! Something else to think out. Vexed rather than appalled, she stood still, her eyes on the sparkling rock. There was esteem and animal contact at dusk, but the emotion that links them was absent. Ought she to break her engagement off? She was inclined to think not—it would cause so much trouble to others; besides, she wasn't convinced that love is necessary to a successful union. If love is everything, few marriages would survive the honeymoon. 'No, I'm all right, thanks,' she said, and, her emotions well under control, resumed the climb, though she felt a bit dashed. Aziz held her hand, the guide adhered to the surface like a lizard and scampered about as if governed by a personal centre of gravity.

'Are you married, Dr Aziz?' she asked, stopping again, and frowning.

'Yes, indeed, do come and see my wife'—for he felt it more artistic to have his wife alive for a moment.

'Thank you,' she said absently.

'She is not in Chandrapore just now.'

'And have you children?'

'Yes, indeed, three,' he replied in firmer tones.

'Are they a great pleasure to you?'

'Why, naturally, I adore them,' he laughed.

'I suppose so.' What a handsome little Oriental he was, and no doubt his wife and children were beautiful too, for people usually get what they already possess. She did not admire him with any personal warmth, for there was nothing of the vagrant in her blood, but she guessed he might attract women of his own race and rank, and she regretted that neither she nor Ronny had physical charm. It does make a difference in a relationship—beauty, thick hair, a fine skin. Probably this man had several wives—Mohammedans always insist on their full four, according to Mrs Turton. And having no one else to speak to on that eternal rock, she gave rein to the subject of marriage and said in her honest, decent, inquisitive way: 'Have you one wife or more than one?'

The question shocked the young man very much. It challenged a new conviction of his community, and new convictions are more sensitive than old. If she had said, 'Do you worship one god or several?' he would not have objected. But to ask an educated Indian Moslem how many wives he has—appalling, hideous! He was in trouble how to conceal his confusion. 'One, one in my own particular case,' he sputtered, and let go of her hand. Quite a number of caves were at the top of the track, and thinking, 'Damn the English even at their best,' he plunged into one of them to recover his balance. She followed at her leisure, quite unconscious that she had said the wrong thing, and not seeing him, she also went into a cave, thinking with half her mind 'sight-seeing bores me,' and wondering with the other half about marriage.

Chapter Sixteen

He waited in his cave a minute, and lit a cigarette so that he could remark on rejoining her, 'I bolted in to get out of the draught,' or something of the sort. When he returned, he found the guide, alone, with his head on one side. He had heard a noise, he said, and then Aziz heard it too: the noise of a motor-car. They were now on the outer shoulder of the Kawa Dol, and by scrambling twenty yards they got a glimpse of the plain. A car was coming towards the hills down the Chandrapore road. But they could not get a good view of it, because the precipitous bastion curved at the top, so that the base was not easily seen and the car disappeared as it came nearer. No doubt it would stop almost exactly beneath them, at the place where the pukka road degenerated into a path, and the elephant had turned to sidle into the hills.

He ran back, to tell the strange news to his guest.

The guide explained that she had gone into a cave.

'Which cave?'

He indicated the group vaguely.

'You should have kept her in sight, it was your duty,' said Aziz severely. 'Here are twelve caves at least. How am I to know which contains my guest? Which is the cave I was in myself?'

The same vague gesture. And Aziz, looking again, could not even be sure he had returned to the same group. Caves appeared in every direction—it seemed their original spawning place—and the orifices were always the same size. He thought, 'Merciful Heavens, Miss Quested is lost,' then pulled himself together, and began to look for her calmly.

'Shout!' he commanded.

When they had done this for awhile, the guide explained that to shout is useless, because a Marabar cave can hear no sound but its own. Aziz wiped his head, and sweat began to stream inside his clothes. The place was so confusing; it was partly a terrace, partly a zigzag, and full of grooves that led this way and that like snaketracks. He tried to go into every one, but he never knew where he had started. Caves got behind caves or confabulated in pairs, and some were at the entrance of a gully.

'Come here!' he called gently, and when the guide was in reach, he struck him in the face for a punishment. The man fled, and he was left alone. He thought, 'This is the end of my career, my guest is lost.' And then he discovered the simple and sufficient explanation of the mystery.

Miss Quested wasn't lost. She had joined the people in the car—friends of hers, no doubt, Mr Heaslop perhaps. He had a sudden glimpse of her, far down the gully—only a glimpse, but there she was quite plain, framed between rocks, and speaking to another lady. He was so relieved that he did not think her conduct odd. Accustomed to sudden changes of plan, he supposed that she had run down the Kawa Dol impulsively, in the hope of a little drive. He started back alone towards his camp, and almost at once caught sight of something which would have disquieted him very much a moment before: Miss Quested's field glasses. They were lying at the verge of a cave, half-way down an entrance tunnel. He tried to hang them over his shoulder, but the leather strap had broken, so he put them into his pocket instead. When he had gone a few steps, he thought she might have dropped something else, so he went back to look. But the previous difficulty recurred: he couldn't identify the cave. Down in the plain he heard the car starting; however, he couldn't catch a second glimpse of that. So he scrambled down the valley-face of the hill towards Mrs Moore, and here he was more successful: the colour and confusion of his little camp soon appeared, and in the midst of it he saw an Englishman's topi, and beneath it—oh joy!—smiled not Mr Heaslop, but Fielding.

'Fielding! Oh, I have so wanted you!' he cried, dropping the 'Mr' for the first time.

And his friend ran to meet him, all so pleasant and jolly, no dignity, shouting explanations and apologies about the train. Fielding had come in the newly arrived car—Miss Derek's car—that other lady was Miss Derek. Chatter, chatter, all the servants leaving their cooking to listen. Excellent Miss Derek! She had met Fielding by chance at the post office, said, 'Why haven't you gone to the Marabar?' heard how he missed the train, offered to run him there and then. Another nice English lady. Where was she? Left with car and chauffeur while Fielding found camp. Car couldn't get up—no, of course not—hundreds of people must go down to escort Miss Derek and show her the way. The elephant in person. . . .

'Aziz, can I have a drink?'

'Certainly not.' He flew to get one.

'Mr Fielding!' called Mrs Moore, from her patch of shade; they had not spoken yet, because his arrival had coincided with the torrent from the hill.

'Good morning again!' he cried, relieved to find all well.

'Mr Fielding, have you seen Miss Quested?'

'But I've only just arrived. Where is she?'

'I do not know.'

'Aziz! Where have you put Miss Quested to?'

Aziz, who was returning with a drink in his hand, had to think for a moment. His heart was full of new happiness. The picnic, after a nasty shock or two, had developed into something beyond his dreams, for Fielding had not only come, but brought an uninvited guest. 'Oh, she's all right,' he said; 'she went down to see Miss Derek. Well, here's luck! Chin-chin!'

'Here's luck, but chin-chin I do refuse,' laughed Fielding, who detested the phrase. 'Here's to India!'

'Here's luck, and here's to England!'

Miss Derek's chauffeur stopped the cavalcade which was starting to escort his mistress up, and informed it that she had gone back with the other young lady to Chandrapore; she had sent him to say so. She was driving herself.

'Oh yes, that's quite likely,' said Aziz. 'I knew they'd gone for a spin.'

'Chandrapore? The man's made a mistake,' Fielding exclaimed.

'Oh no, why?' He was disappointed, but made light of it; no doubt the two young ladies were great friends. He would prefer to give breakfast to all four; still, guests must do as they wish, or they become prisoners. He went away cheerfully to inspect the porridge and the ice.

'What's happened?' asked Fielding, who felt at once that something had gone queer. All the way out Miss Derek had chattered about the picnic, called it an unexpected treat, and said that she preferred Indians who didn't invite her to their entertainments to those who did it. Mrs Moore sat swinging her foot, and appeared sulky and stupid. She said: 'Miss Derek is most unsatisfactory and restless, always in a hurry, always wanting something new; she will do anything in the world except go back to the Indian lady who pays her.'

Fielding, who didn't dislike Miss Derek, replied: 'She wasn't in a hurry when I left her. There was no question of returning to Chandrapore. It looks to me as if Miss Quested's in the hurry.'

'Adela?—she's never been in a hurry in her life,' said the old lady sharply.

'I say it'll prove to be Miss Quested's wish, in fact I know it is,' persisted the schoolmaster. He was annoyed—chiefly with himself. He had begun by missing a train—a sin he was never guilty of—and now that he did arrive it was to upset Aziz' arrangements for the second time. He wanted someone to share the blame, and frowned at Mrs Moore rather magisterially. 'Aziz is a charming fellow,' he announced.

'I know,' she answered, with a yawn.

'He has taken endless trouble to make a success of our picnic.'

They knew one another very little, and felt rather awkward at being drawn together by an Indian. The racial problem can take subtle forms. In their case it had induced a sort of jealousy, a mutual suspicion. He tried to goad her enthusiasm; she scarcely spoke. Aziz fetched them to breakfast.

'It is quite natural about Miss Quested,' he remarked, for he had been working the incident a little in his mind, to get rid of its roughnesses. 'We were having an interesting talk with our guide, then the car was seen, so she decided to go down to her friend.' Incurably inaccurate, he already thought that this was what had occurred. He was inaccurate because he was sensitive. He did not like to remember Miss Quested's remark about polygamy, because it was unworthy of a guest, so he put it from his mind, and with it the knowledge that he had bolted into a cave to get away from her. He was inaccurate because he desired to honour her, and—facts being entangled—he had to arrange them in her vicinity, as one tidies the ground after extracting a weed. Before breakfast was over, he had told a good many lies. 'She ran to her friend, I to mine,' he went on, smiling. 'And now I am with my friends and they are with me and each other, which is happiness.'

Loving them both, he expected them to love each other. They didn't want to. Fielding thought with hostility, 'I knew these women would make trouble,' and Mrs Moore thought, 'This man, having missed the train, tries to blame us'; but her thoughts were feeble; since her faintness in the cave she was sunk in apathy and cynicism. The wonderful India of her opening weeks, with its cool nights and acceptable hints of infinity, had vanished.

Fielding ran up to see one cave. He wasn't impressed. Then they got on the elephant and the picnic began to unwind out of the corridor and escaped under the precipice towards the railway station, pursued by stabs of hot air. They came to the place where he had quitted the car. A disagreeable thought now struck him, and he said: 'Aziz, exactly where and how did you leave Miss Quested?'

'Up there.' He indicated the Kawa Dol cheerfully.

'But how—' A gully, or rather a crease, showed among the rocks at this place; it was scurfy with cactuses. 'I suppose the guide helped her.'

'Oh, rather, most helpful.'

'Is there a path off the top?'

'Millions of paths, my dear fellow.'

Fielding could see nothing but the crease. Everywhere else the glaring granite plunged into the earth.

'But you saw them get down safe?'

'Yes, yes, she and Miss Derek, and go off in the car.'

'Then the guide came back to you?'

'Exactly. Got a cigarette?'

'I hope she wasn't ill,' pursued the Englishman. The crease continued as a nullah across the plain, the water draining off this way towards the Ganges.

'She would have wanted me, if she was ill, to attend her.'

'Yes, that sounds sense.'

'I see you're worrying, let's talk of other things,' he said kindly. 'Miss Quested was always to do what she wished, it was our arrangement. I see you are worrying on my account, but really I don't mind, I never notice trifles.'

'I do worry on your account. I consider they have been impolite!' said Fielding, lowering his voice. 'She had no right to dash away from your party, and Miss Derek had no right to abet her.'

So touchy as a rule, Aziz was unassailable. The wings that uplifted him did not falter, because he was a Mogul emperor who had done his duty. Perched on his elephant, he watched the Marabar Hills recede, and saw again, as provinces of his kingdom, the grim untidy plain, the frantic and feeble movements of the buckets, the white shrines, the shallow graves, the suave sky, the snake that looked like a tree. He had given his guests as good a time as he could, and if they came late or left early that was not his affair. Mrs Moore slept, swaying against the rods of the howdah, Mohammed Latif embraced her with efficiency and respect, and by his own side sat Fielding, whom he began to think of as 'Cyril.'

'Aziz, have you figured out what this picnic will cost you?'

'Sh! my dear chap, don't mention that part. Hundreds and hundreds of rupees. The completed account will be too awful; my friends' servants have robbed me right and left, and as for an elephant, she apparently eats gold. I can trust you not to repeat this. And M.L.—please employ initials, he listens–is far the worst of all.'

'I told you he's no good.'

'He is plenty of good for himself; his dishonesty will ruin me.'

'Aziz, how monstrous!'

'I am delighted with him really, he has made my guests comfortable; besides, it is my duty to employ him, he is my cousin. If money goes, money comes. If money stays, death comes. Did you ever hear that useful Urdu proverb? Probably not, for I have just invented it.'

'My proverbs are: A penny saved is a penny earned; A stitch in time saves nine; Look before you leap; and the British Empire rests on them. You will never kick us out, you know, until you cease employing M.L.'s and such.'

'Oh, kick you out? Why should I trouble over that dirty job? Leave it to the politicians. . . . No, when I was a student I got excited over your damned countrymen, certainly; but if they'll let me get on with my profession and not be too rude to me officially, I really don't ask for more.'

'But you do; you take them to a picnic.'

'This picnic is nothing to do with English or Indian; it is an expedition of friends.'

So the cavalcade ended, partly pleasant, partly not; the Brahman cook was picked up, the train arrived, pushing its burning throat over the plain, and the twentieth century took over from the sixteenth. Mrs Moore entered her carriage, the three men went to theirs, adjusted the shutters, turned on the electric fan and tried to get some sleep. In the twilight, all resembled corpses, and the train itself seemed dead though it moved–a coffin from the scientific north which troubled the scenery four times a day. As it left the Marabars, their nasty little cosmos disappeared, and gave place to the Marabars seen from a distance, finite and rather romantic. The train halted once under a pump, to drench the stock of coal in its tender. Then it caught sight of the main line in the distance, took courage, and bumped forward, rounded the civil station, surmounted the level-crossing (the rails were scorching now), and clanked to a standstill. Chandrapore, Chandrapore! The expedition was over.

And as it ended, as they sat up in the gloom and prepared to enter ordinary life, suddenly the long drawn strangeness of the morning snapped. Mr Haq, the Inspector of Police, flung open the door of their carriage and said in shrill tones: 'Dr Aziz, it is my highly painful duty to arrest you.'

'Hullo, some mistake,' said Fielding, at once taking charge of the situation.

'Sir, they are my instructions. I know nothing.'

'On what charge do you arrest him?'

'I am under instructions not to say.'

'Don't answer me like that. Produce your warrant.'

'Sir, excuse me, no warrant is required under these particular circumstances. Refer to Mr McBryde.'

'Very well, so we will. Come along, Aziz, old man; nothing to fuss about, some blunder.'

'Dr Aziz, will you kindly come?–a closed conveyance stands in readiness.'

The young man sobbed—his first sound—and tried to escape out of the opposite door on to the line.

'That will compel me to use force,' Mr Haq wailed.

'Oh, for God's sake—' cried Fielding, his own nerves breaking under the contagion, and pulled him back before a scandal started, and shook him like a baby. A second later, and he would have been out, whistles blowing, a man-hunt. . . . 'Dear fellow, we're coming to McBryde together, and enquire what's gone wrong—he's a decent fellow, it's all unintentional . . . he'll apologize. Never, never act the criminal.'

'My children and my name!' he gasped, his wings broken.

'Nothing of the sort. Put your hat straight and take my arm. I'll see you through.'

'Ah, thank God, he comes,' the Inspector exclaimed.

They emerged into the midday heat, arm in arm. The station was seething. Passengers and porters rushed out of every recess, many Government servants, more police. Ronny escorted Mrs Moore. Mohammed Latif began wailing. And before they could make their way through the chaos, Fielding was called off by the authoritative tones of Mr Turton, and Aziz went on to prison alone.

Chapter Seventeen

The Collector had watched the arrest from the interior of the waiting-room, and throwing open its perforated doors of zinc, he was now revealed like a god in a shrine. When Fielding entered the doors clapped to, and were guarded by a servant, while a punkah, to mark the importance of the moment, flapped dirty petticoats over their heads. The Collector could not speak at first. His face was white, fanatical, and rather beautiful—the expression that all English faces were to wear at Chandrapore for many days. Always brave and unselfish, he was now fused by some white and generous heat; he would have killed himself, obviously, if he had thought it right to do so. He spoke at last. 'The worst thing in my whole career has happened,' he said. 'Miss Quested has been insulted in one of the Marabar caves.'

'Oh no, oh no, no,' gasped the other, feeling sickish.

'She escaped—by God's grace.'

'Oh no, no, but not Aziz . . . not Aziz . . .'

He nodded.

'Absolutely impossible, grotesque.'

'I called you to preserve you from the odium that would attach to you if you were seen accompanying him to the Police Station,' said Turton, paying no attention to his protest, indeed scarcely hearing it.

He repeated 'Oh no,' like a fool. He couldn't frame other words. He felt that a mass of madness had arisen and tried to overwhelm them all; it had to be shoved back into its pit somehow, and he didn't know how to do it, because he did not understand madness: he had always gone about sensibly and quietly until a difficulty came right. 'Who lodges this infamous charge?' he asked, pulling himself together.

'Miss Derek and—the victim herself. . . .' He nearly broke down, unable to repeat the girl's name.

'Miss Quested herself definitely accuses him of—'

He nodded and turned his face away.

'Then she's mad.'

'I cannot pass that last remark,' said the Collector, waking up to the knowledge that they differed, and trembling with fury. 'You will withdraw it instantly. It is the type of remark you have permitted yourself to make ever since you came to Chandrapore.'

'I'm excessively sorry, sir; I certainly withdraw it unconditionally.' For the man was half mad himself.

'Pray, Mr Fielding, what induced you to speak to me in such a tone?'

'The news gave me a very great shock, so I must ask you to forgive me. I cannot believe that Dr Aziz is guilty.'

He slammed his hand on the table. 'That—that is a repetition of your insult in an aggravated form.'

'If I may venture to say so, no,' said Fielding, also going white, but sticking to his point. 'I make no reflection on the good faith of the two ladies, but the charge they are bringing against Aziz rests upon some mistake, and five minutes will clear it up. The man's manner is perfectly natural; besides, I know him to be incapable of infamy.'

'It does indeed rest upon a mistake,' came the thin, biting voice of the other. 'It does indeed. I have had twenty-five years' experience of this country'—he paused, and 'twenty-five years' seemed to fill the waiting-room with their staleness and ungenerosity—'and during those twenty-five years I have never known anything but disaster result when English people and Indians attempt to be intimate socially. Intercourse, yes. Courtesy, by all means. Intimacy—never, never. The whole weight of my authority is against it. I have been in charge at Chandrapore for six years, and if everything has gone smoothly, if there has been mutual respect and esteem, it is because both peoples kept to this simple rule. New-comers set our traditions aside, and in an instant what you see happens, the work of years is undone and the good name of my District ruined for a generation. I—I—can't see the end of this day's work, Mr Fielding. You, who are imbued with modern ideas—no doubt you can. I wish I had never lived to see its beginning, I know that. It is the end of me. That a lady, that a young lady engaged to my most valued subordinate—that she—an English girl fresh from England—that I should have lived—'

Involved in his own emotions, he broke down. What he had said was both dignified and pathetic, but had it anything to do with Aziz? Nothing at all, if Fielding was right. It is impossible to regard a tragedy from two points of view, and whereas Turton had decided to avenge the girl, he hoped to save the man. He wanted to get away and talk to McBryde, who had always been friendly to him, was on the whole sensible, and could, anyhow, be trusted to keep cool.

'I came down particularly on your account—while poor Heaslop got his mother away. I regarded it as the most friendly thing I could do. I meant to tell you that there will be an informal meeting at the club this evening to discuss the situation, but I am doubtful whether you will care to come. Your visits there are always infrequent.'

'I shall certainly come, sir, and I am most grateful to you for all the trouble you have taken over me. May I venture to ask—where Miss Quested is.'

He replied with a gesture; she was ill.

'Worse and worse, appalling,' he said feelingly.

But the Collector looked at him sternly, because he was keeping his head. He had not gone mad at the phrase 'an English girl fresh from England,' he had not rallied to the banner of race. He was still after facts, though the herd had decided on emotion. Nothing enrages Anglo-India more than the lantern of reason if it is exhibited for one moment after its extinction is decreed. All over Chandrapore that day the Europeans were putting aside their normal personalities and sinking themselves in their community. Pity, wrath, heroism, filled them, but the power of putting two and two together was annihilated.

Terminating the interview, the Collector walked on to the platform. The confusion there was revolting. A chuprassi of Ronny's had been told to bring up some trifles belonging to the ladies, and was appropriating for himself various articles to which he had no right; he was a camp follower of the angry English. Mohammed Latif made no attempt to resist him. Hassan flung off his turban, and wept. All the comforts that had been provided so liberally were rolled about and wasted in the sun. The Collector took in the situation at a glance, and his sense of justice functioned though he was insane with rage. He spoke the necessary word, and the looting stopped. Then he drove off to his bungalow and gave rein to his passions again. When he saw the coolies asleep in the ditches or the shopkeepers rising to salute him on their little platforms, he said to himself: 'I know what you're like at last; you shall pay for this, you shall squeal.'

Chapter Eighteen

Mr McBryde, the District Superintendent of Police, was the most reflective and best educated of the Chandrapore officials. He had read and thought a good deal, and, owing to a somewhat unhappy marriage, had evolved a complete philosophy of life. There was much of the cynic about him, but nothing of the bully; he never lost his temper or grew rough, and he received Aziz with courtesy, was almost reassuring. 'I have to detain you until you get bail,' he said, 'but no doubt your friends will be applying for it, and of course they will be allowed to visit you, under regulations. I am given certain information, and have to act on it–I'm not your judge.' Aziz was led off weeping. Mr McBryde was shocked at his downfall, but no Indian ever surprised him, because he had a theory about climatic zones. The theory ran: 'All unfortunate natives are criminals at heart, for the simple reason that they live south of latitude 30. They are not to blame, they have not a dog's chance–we should be like them if we settled here.' Born at Karachi, he seemed to contradict his theory, and would sometimes admit as much with a sad, quiet smile.

'Another of them found out,' he thought, as he set to work to draft his statement to the Magistrate.

He was interrupted by the arrival of Fielding.

He imparted all he knew without reservations. Miss Derek had herself driven in the Mudkul car about an hour ago, she and Miss Quested both in a terrible state. They had gone straight to his bungalow where he happened to be, and there and then he had taken down the charge and arranged for the arrest at the railway station.

'What is the charge, precisely?'

'That he followed her into the cave and made insulting advances. She hit at him with her field-glasses: he pulled at them and the strap broke, and that is how she got away. When we searched him just now, they were in his pocket.'

'Oh no, oh no, no; it'll be cleared up in five minutes,' he cried again.

'Have a look at them.'

The strap had been newly broken, the eye-piece was jammed. The logic of evidence said 'Guilty.'

'Did she say any more?'

'There was an echo that appears to have frightened her. Did you go into those caves?'

'I saw one of them. There was an echo. Did it get on her nerves?'

'I couldn't worry her overmuch with questions. She'll have plenty to go through in the witness-box. They don't bear thinking about, these next weeks. I wish the Marabar Hills and all they contain were at the bottom of the sea. Evening after evening one saw them from the club, and they were just a harmless name. . . . Yes, we start already.' For a visiting card was brought; Vakil Mahmoud Ali, legal adviser to the prisoner, asked to be allowed to see him. McBryde sighed, gave permission, and continued: 'I heard some more from Miss Derek–she is an old friend of us both and talks freely; well–her account is that you went off to locate the camp, and almost at once she heard stones falling on the Kawa Dol and saw Miss Quested running straight down the face of a precipice. Well. She climbed up a sort of gully to her, and found her practically done for–her helmet off—'

'Was a guide not with her?' interrupted Fielding.

'No. She had got among some cactuses. Miss Derek saved her life coming just then–she was beginning to fling herself about. She helped her down to the car. Miss Quested couldn't stand the Indian driver, cried, "Keep him away"–and it was that that put our friend on the track of what had happened. They made straight for our bungalow, and are there now. That's the story as far as I know it yet. She sent the driver to join you. I think she behaved with great sense.'

'I suppose there's no possibility of my seeing Miss Quested?' he asked suddenly.

'I hardly think that would do. Surely.'

'I was afraid you'ld say that. I should very much like to.'

'She is in no state to see anyone. Besides, you don't know her well.'

'Hardly at all. . . . But you see I believe she's under some hideous delusion, and that that wretched boy is innocent.'

The policeman started in surprise, and a shadow passed over his face, for he could not bear his dispositions to be upset. 'I had no idea that was in your mind,' he said, and looked for support at the signed deposition, which lay before him.

'Those field-glasses upset me for a minute, but I've thought since: it's impossible that, having attempted to assault her, he would put her glasses into his pocket.'

'Quite possible, I'm afraid; when an Indian goes bad, he goes not only very bad, but very queer.'

'I don't follow.'

'How should you? When you think of crime you think of English crime. The psychology here is different. I dare say you'll tell me next that he was quite normal when he came down from the hill to greet you. No reason he should not be. Read any of the Mutiny records; which, rather than the Bhagavad Gita, should be your Bible in this country. Though I'm not sure that the one and the other are not closely connected. Am I not being beastly? But, you see, Fielding, as I've said to you once before, you're a schoolmaster, and consequently you come across these people at their best. That's what puts you wrong. They can be charming as boys. But I know them as they really are, after they have developed into men. Look at this, for instance.' He held up Aziz' pocket-case. 'I am going through the contents. They are not edifying. Here is a letter from a friend who apparently keeps a brothel.'

'I don't want to hear his private letters.'

'It'll have to be quoted in Court, as bearing on his morals. He was fixing up to see women at Calcutta.'

'Oh, that'll do, that'll do.'

McBryde stopped, naïvely puzzled. It was obvious to him that any two sahibs ought to pool all they knew about any Indian, and he could not think where the objection came in.

'I dare say you have the right to throw stones at a young man for doing that, but I haven't. I did the same at his age.'

So had the Superintendent of Police, but he considered that the conversation had taken a turn that was undesirable. He did not like Fielding's next remark either.

'Miss Quested really cannot be seen? You do know that for a certainty?'

'You have never explained to me what's in your mind here. Why on earth do you want to see her?'

'On the off chance of her recanting before you send in that report and he's committed for trial, and the whole thing goes to blazes. Old man, don't argue about this, but do of your goodness just ring up your wife or Miss Derek and enquire. It'll cost you nothing.'

'It's no use ringing up them,' he replied, stretching out for the telephone. 'Callendar settles a question like that, of course. You haven't grasped that she's seriously ill.'

'He's sure to refuse, it's all he exists for,' said the other desperately.

The expected answer came back: the Major would not hear of the patient being troubled.

'I only wanted to ask her whether she is certain, dead certain, that it was Aziz who followed her into the cave.'

'Possibly my wife might ask her that much.'

'But *I* wanted to ask her. I want someone who believes in him to ask her.'

'What difference does that make?'

'She is among people who disbelieve in Indians.'

'Well, she tells her own story, doesn't she?'

'I know, but she tells it to you.'

McBryde raised his eyebrows, murmuring: 'A bit too finespun. Anyhow, Callendar won't hear of you seeing her. I'm sorry to say he gave a bad account just now. He says that she is by no means out of danger.'

They were silent. Another card was brought into the office–Hamidullah's. The opposite army was gathering.

'I must put this report through now, Fielding.'

'I wish you wouldn't.'

'How can I not?'

'I feel that things are rather unsatisfactory as well as most disastrous. We are heading for a most awful smash. I can see your prisoner, I suppose.'

He hesitated. 'His own people seem in touch with him all right.'

'Well, when he's done with them.'

'I wouldn't keep you waiting; good heavens, you take precedence of any Indian visitor, of course. I meant what's the good. Why mix yourself up with pitch?'

'I say he's innocent—'

'Innocence or guilt, why mix yourself up? What's the good?'

'Oh, good, good,' he cried, feeling that every earth was being stopped. 'One's got to breathe occasionally, at least I have. I mayn't see her, and now I mayn't see him. I promised him to come up here with him to you, but Turton called me off before I could get two steps.'

'Sort of all-white thing our Collector would do,' he muttered sentimentally. And trying not to sound patronizing, he stretched his hand over the table, and said: 'We shall all have to hang together, old man, I'm afraid. I'm your junior in years, I know, but very much your senior in service; you don't happen to know this poisonous country as well as I do, and you must take it from me that the general situation is going to be nasty at Chandrapore during the next few weeks, very nasty indeed.'

'So I have just told you.'

'But at a time like this there's no room for—well—personal views. The man who doesn't toe the line is lost.'

'I see what you mean.'

'No, you don't see entirely. He not only loses himself, he weakens his friends. If you leave the line, you leave a gap in the line. These jackals'—he pointed at the lawyers' cards—'are looking with all their eyes for a gap.'

'Can I visit Aziz?' was his answer.

'No.' Now that he knew of Turton's attitude, the policeman had no doubts. 'You may see him on a magistrate's order, but on my own responsibility I don't feel justified. It might lead to more complications.'

He paused, reflecting that if he had been either ten years younger or ten years longer in India, he would have responded to McBryde's appeal. The bit between his teeth, he then said, 'To whom do I apply for an order?'

'City Magistrate.'

'That sounds comfortable!'

'Yes, one can't very well worry poor Heaslop.'

More 'evidence' appeared at this moment—the tabledrawer from Aziz' bungalow, borne with triumph in a corporal's arms.

'Photographs of women. Ah!'

'That's his wife,' said Fielding, wincing.

'How do you know that?'

'He told me.'

McBryde gave a faint, incredulous smile, and started rummaging in the drawer. His face became inquisitive and slightly bestial. 'Wife indeed, I know those wives!' he was thinking. Aloud he said: 'Well, you must trot off now, old man, and the Lord help us, the Lord help us all. . . .'

As if his prayer had been heard, there was a sudden rackety-dacket on a temple bell.

Chapter Nineteen

Hamidullah was the next stage. He was waiting outside the Superintendent's office, and sprang up respectfully when he saw Fielding. To the Englishman's passionate 'It's all a mistake,' he answered, 'Ah, ah, has some evidence come?'

'It will come,' said Fielding, holding his hand.

'Ah, yes, Mr Fielding; but when once an Indian has been arrested, we do not know where it will stop.' His manner was deferential. 'You are very good to greet me in this public fashion, I appreciate it; but, Mr Fielding, nothing convinces a magistrate except evidence. Did Mr McBryde make any remark when my card came in? Do you think my application annoyed him, will prejudice him against my friend at all? If so, I will gladly retire.'

'He's not annoyed, and if he was, what does it matter?'

'Ah, it's all very well for you to speak like that, but we have to live in this country.'

The leading barrister of Chandrapore, with the dignified manner and Cambridge degree, had been rattled. He too loved Aziz, and knew he was calumniated; but faith did not rule his heart, and he prated of 'policy' and 'evidence' in a way that saddened the Englishman. Fielding, too, had his anxieties—he didn't like the field-glasses or the discrepancy over the guide—but he relegated them to the edge of his mind, and forbade them to infect its core. Aziz *was* innocent, and all action must be based on that, and the people who said he was guilty were wrong, and it was hopeless to try to propitiate them. At the moment when he was throwing in his lot with Indians, he realized the profundity of the gulf that divided him from them. They always do something disappointing. Aziz had tried to run away from the police, Mohammed Latif had not checked the pilfering. And now Hamidullah!—instead of raging and denouncing, he temporized. Are Indians cowards? No, but they are bad starters and occasionally jib. Fear is everywhere; the British Raj rests on it; the respect and courtesy Fielding himself enjoyed were unconscious acts of propitiation. He told Hamidullah to cheer up, all would end well; and Hamidullah did cheer up, and became pugnacious and sensible. McBryde's remark, 'If you leave the line, you leave a gap in the line,' was being illustrated.

'First and foremost, the question of bail . . .'

Application must be made this afternoon. Fielding wanted to stand surety. Hamidullah thought the Nawab Bahadur should be approached.

'Why drag in him, though?'

To drag in everyone was precisely the barrister's aim. He then suggested that the lawyer in charge of the case would be a Hindu; the defence would then make a wider appeal. He mentioned one or two names—men from a distance who would not be intimidated by local conditions—and said he should prefer Amritrao, a Calcutta barrister, who had a high reputation professionally and personally, but who was notoriously anti-British.

Fielding demurred; this seemed to him going to the other extreme. Aziz must be cleared, but with a minimum of racial hatred. Amritrao was loathed at the club. His retention would be regarded as a political challenge.

'Oh no, we must hit with all our strength. When I saw my friend's private papers carried in just now in the arms of a dirty policeman, I said to myself, "Amritrao is the man to clear up this."'

There was a lugubrious pause. The temple bell continued to jangle harshly. The interminable and disastrous day had scarcely reached its afternoon. Continuing their work, the wheels of Dominion now propelled a messenger on a horse from the Superintendent to the Magistrate with an official report of arrest. 'Don't complicate, let the cards play themselves' entreated Fielding, as he watched the man disappear into dust. 'We're bound to win, there's nothing else we can do. She will never be able to substantiate the charge.'

This comforted Hamidullah, who remarked with complete sincerity, 'At a crisis, the English are really unequalled.'

'Good-bye, then, my dear Hamidullah (we must drop the 'Mr' now). Give Aziz my love when you see him, and tell him to keep calm, calm, calm. I shall go back to the College now. If you want me, ring me up; if you don't, don't, for I shall be very busy.'

'Good-bye, my dear Fielding, and you actually are on our side against your own people?'

'Yes. Definitely.'

He regretted taking sides. To slink through India unlabelled was his aim. Henceforward he would be called 'anti-British,' 'seditious'—terms that bored him, and diminished his utility. He foresaw that besides being a tragedy, there would be a muddle; already he saw several tiresome little knots, and each time his eye returned to them, they were larger. Born in freedom, he was not afraid of muddle, but he recognized its existence.

This section of the day concluded in a queer vague talk with Professor Godbole. The interminable affair of the Russell's Viper was again in question. Some weeks before, one of the masters at the College, an unpopular Parsi, had found a Russell's Viper nosing round his class-room. Perhaps it had crawled in of itself, but perhaps it had not, and the staff still continued to interview their Principal about it, and to take up his time with their theories. The reptile is so poisonous that he did not like to cut them short, and this they knew. Thus when his mind was bursting with other troubles and he was debating whether he should compose a letter of appeal to Miss Quested, he was obliged to listen to a speech which lacked both basis and conclusion, and floated through air. At the end of it Godbole said, 'May I now take my leave?'—always an indication that he had not come to his point yet. 'Now I take my leave, I must tell you how glad I am to hear that after all you succeeded in reaching the Marabar. I feared my unpunctuality had prevented you, but you went (a far pleasanter method) in Miss Derek's car. I hope the expedition was a successful one.'

'The news has not reached you yet, I can see.'

'Oh yes.'

'No; there has been a terrible catastrophe about Aziz.'

'Oh yes. That is all round the College.'

'Well, the expedition where that occurs can scarcely be called a successful one,' said Fielding, with an amazed stare.

'I cannot say. I was not present.'

He stared again—a most useless operation, for no eye could see what lay at the bottom of the Brahman's mind, and yet he had a mind and a heart too, and all his friends trusted him, without knowing why. 'I am most frightfully cut up,' he said.

'So I saw at once on entering your office. I must not detain you, but I have a small private difficulty on which I want your help; I am leaving your service shortly, as you know.'

'Yes, alas!'

'And am returning to my birthplace in Central India to take charge of education there. I want to start a High School there on sound English lines, that shall be as like Government College as possible.'

'Well?' he sighed, trying to take an interest.

'At present there is only vernacular education at Mau. I shall feel it my duty to change all that. I shall advise His Highness to sanction at least a High School in the Capital, and if possible another in each pargana.'

Fielding sunk his head on his arms; really, Indians were sometimes unbearable.

'The point—the point on which I desire your help is this: what name should be given to the school?'

'A name? A name for a school?' he said, feeling sickish suddenly, as he had done in the waiting-room.

'Yes, a name, a suitable title, by which it can be called, by which it may be generally known.'

'Really—I have no names for schools in my head. I can think of nothing but our poor Aziz. Have you grasped that at the present moment he is in prison?'

'Oh yes. Oh no, I do not expect an answer to my question now. I only meant that when you are at leisure, you might think the matter over, and suggest two or three alternative titles for schools. I had thought of the 'Mr Fielding High School,' but failing that, the 'King-Emperor George the Fifth.''

'Godbole!'

The old fellow put his hands together, and looked sly and charming.

'Is Aziz innocent or guilty?'

'That is for the Court to decide. The verdict will be in strict accordance with the evidence, I make no doubt.'

'Yes, yes, but your personal opinion. Here's a man we both like, generally esteemed; he lives here quietly doing his work. Well, what's one to make of it? Would he or would he not do such a thing?'

'Ah, that is rather a different question from your previous one, and also more difficult: I mean difficult in our philosophy. Dr Aziz is a most worthy young man, I have a great regard for him; but I think you are asking me whether the individual can commit good actions or evil actions, and that is rather difficult for us.' He spoke without emotion and in short tripping syllables.

'I ask you: did he do it or not? Is that plain? I know he didn't, and from that I start. I mean to get at the true explanation in a couple of days. My last notion is that it's the guide who went round with them. Malice on Miss Quested's part—it couldn't be that, though Hamidullah thinks so. She has certainly had some appalling experience. But you tell me, oh no—because good and evil are the same.'

'No, not exactly, please, according to our philosophy. Because nothing can be performed in isolation. All perform a good action, when one is performed, and when an evil action is performed, all perform it. To illustrate my meaning, let me take the case in point as an example.

'I am informed that an evil action was performed in the Marabar Hills, and that a highly esteemed English lady is now seriously ill in consequence. My answer to that is this: that action was performed by Dr Aziz.' He stopped and sucked in his thin cheeks. 'It was performed by the guide.' He stopped again. 'It was performed by you.' Now he had an air of daring and of coyness. 'It was performed by me.' He looked shyly down the sleeve of his own coat. 'And by my students. It was even performed by the lady herself. When evil occurs, it expresses the whole of the universe. Similarly when good occurs.'

'And similarly when suffering occurs, and so on and so forth, and everything is anything and nothing something,' he muttered in his irritation, for he needed the solid ground.

'Excuse me, you are now again changing the basis of our discussion. We were discussing good and evil. Suffering is merely a matter for the individual. If a young lady has sunstroke, that is a matter of no significance to the universe. Oh no, not at all. Oh no, not the least. It is an isolated matter, it only concerns herself. If she thought her head did not ache, she would not be ill, and that would end it. But it is far otherwise in the case of good and evil. They are not what we think them, they are what they are, and each of us has contributed to both.'

'You're preaching that evil and good are the same.'

'Oh no, excuse me once again. Good and evil are different, as their names imply. But, in my own humble opinion, they are both of them aspects of my Lord. He is present in the one, absent in the other, and the difference between presence and absence is great, as great as my feeble mind can grasp. Yet absence implies presence, absence is not non-existence, and we are therefore entitled to repeat, "Come, come, come, come."' And in the same breath, as if to cancel any beauty his words might have contained, he added, 'But did you have time to visit any of the interesting Marabar antiquities?'

Fielding was silent, trying to meditate and rest his brain.

'Did you not even see the tank by the usual camping ground?' he nagged.

'Yes, yes,' he answered distractedly, wandering over half a dozen things at once.

'That is good, then you saw the Tank of the Dagger.' And he related a legend which might have been acceptable if he had told it at the tea-party a fortnight ago. It concerned a Hindu Rajah who had slain his own sister's son, and the dagger with which he performed the deed remained clamped to his hand until in the course of years he came to the Marabar Hills, where he was thirsty and wanted to drink but saw a thirsty cow and ordered the water to be offered to her first, which, when done, 'dagger fell from his hand, and to commemorate miracle he built Tank.' Professor Godbole's conversations frequently culminated in a cow. Fielding received this one in gloomy silence.

In the afternnoon he obtained a permit and saw Aziz, but found him unapproachable through misery. 'You deserted me,' was the only coherent remark. He went away to write his letter to Miss Quested. Even if it reached her, it would do no good, and probably the McBrydes would withhold it. Miss Quested did pull him up short. She was such a dry, sensible girl, and quite without malice: the last person in Chandrapore wrongfully to accuse an Indian.

Chapter Twenty

Although Miss Quested had not made herself popular with the English, she brought out all that was fine in their character. For a few hours an exalted emotion gushed forth, which the women felt even more keenly than the men, if not for so long. 'What can we do for our sister?' was the only thought of Mesdames Callendar and Lesley, as they drove through the pelting heat to enquire. Mrs Turton was the only visitor admitted to the sick-room. She came out ennobled by an unselfish sorrow. 'She is my own darling girl,' were the words she spoke, and then, remembering that she had called her 'not pukka' and resented her engagement to young Heaslop, she began to cry. No one had ever seen the Collector's wife cry. Capable of tears—yes, but always reserving them for some adequate occasion, and now it had come. Ah, why had they not all been kinder to the stranger, more patient, given her not only hospitality but their hearts? The tender core of the heart that is so seldom used—they employed it for a little, under the stimulus of remorse. If all is over (as Major Callendar implied), well, all is over, and nothing can be done, but they retained some responsibility in her grievous wrong that they couldn't define. If she wasn't one of them, they ought to have made her one, and they could never do that now, she had passed beyond their invitation. 'Why don't one think more of other people?' sighed pleasure-loving Miss Derek. These regrets only lasted in their pure form for a few hours. Before sunset, other considerations adulterated them, and the sense of guilt (so strangely connected with our first sight of any suffering) had begun to wear away.

People drove into the club with studious calm—the jog-trot of country gentlefolk between green hedgerows, for the natives must not suspect that they were agitated. They exchanged the usual drinks, but everything tasted different, and then they looked out at the palisade of cactuses stabbing the purple throat of the sky; they realized that they were thousands of miles from any scenery that they understood. The club was fuller than usual, and several parents had brought their children into the rooms reserved for adults, which gave the air of the Residency at Lucknow. One young mother—a brainless but most beautiful girl—sat on a low ottoman in the smoking-room with her baby in her arms; her husband was away in the district, and she dared not return to her bungalow in case the 'niggers attacked.' The wife of a small railway official, she was generally snubbed; but this evening, with her abundant figure and masses of corn-gold hair, she symbolized all that is worth fighting and dying for; more permanent a symbol, perhaps, than poor Adela. 'Don't worry, Mrs Blakiston, those drums are only Mohurram,' the men would tell her. 'Then they've started,' she moaned, clasping the infant and rather wishing he would not blow bubbles down his chin at such a moment as this. 'No, of course not, and anyhow, they're not coming to the club.' 'And they're not coming to the Burra Sahib's bungalow either, my dear, and that's where you and your baby'll sleep tonight,' answered Mrs Turton, towering by her side like Pallas Athene, and determining in the future not to be such a snob.

The Collector clapped his hands for silence. He was much calmer than when he had flown out at Fielding. He was indeed always calmer when he addressed several people than in a *tête-à-tête*. 'I want to talk specially to the ladies,' he said. 'Not the least cause for alarm. Keep cool, keep cool. Don't go out more than you can help, don't go into the city, don't talk before your servants. That's all.'

'Harry, is there any news from the city?' asked his wife, standing at some distance from him, and also assuming her public-safety voice. The rest were silent during the august colloquy.

'Everything absolutely normal.'

'I gathered as much. Those drums are merely Mohurram, of course.'

'Merely the preparations for it—the Procession is not till next week.'

'Quite so, not till Monday.'

'Mr McBryde's down there disguised as a Holy Man,' said Mrs Callendar.

'That's exactly the sort of thing that must not be said,' he remarked, pointing at her. 'Mrs Callendar, be more careful than that, please, in these times.'

'I . . . well, I . . .' She was not offended, his severity made her feel safe.

'Any more questions? Necessary questions.'

'Is the—where is he—' Mrs Lesley quavered.

'Jail. Bail has been refused.'

Fielding spoke next. He wanted to know whether there was an official bulletin about Miss Quested's health, or whether the grave reports were due to gossip. His question produced a bad effect, partly because he had pronounced her name; she, like Aziz, was always referred to by a periphrasis.

'I hope Callendar may be able to let us know how things are going before long.'

'I fail to see how that last question can be termed a necessary question,' said Mrs Turton.

'Will all ladies leave the smoking-room now, please?' he cried, clapping his hands again. 'And remember what I have said. We look to you to help us through a difficult time, and you can help us by behaving as if everything is normal. It is all I ask. Can I rely on you?'

'Yes, indeed, oh indeed,' they chorused out of peaked, anxious faces. They moved out, subdued yet elated, Mrs Blakiston in their midst like a sacred flame. His simple words had reminded them that they were an outpost of Empire. By the side of their compassionate love for Adela another sentiment sprang up which was to strangle it in the long run. Its first signs were prosaic and small. Mrs Turton made her loud, hard jokes at bridge, Mrs Lesley began to knit a comforter.

When the smoking-room was clear, the Collector sat on the edge of a table, so that he could dominate without formality. His mind whirled with contradictory impulses. He wanted to avenge Miss Quested and punish Fielding, while remaining scrupulously fair. He wanted to flog every native that he saw, but to do nothing that would lead to a riot or to the necessity for military intervention. The dread of having to call in the troops was vivid to him; soldiers put one thing straight, but leave a dozen others crooked, and they love to humiliate the civilian administration. One soldier was in the room this evening—a stray subaltern from a Gurkha regiment; he was a little drunk, and regarded his presence as providential. The Collector sighed. There seemed nothing for it but the old weary business of compromise and moderation. He longed for the good old days when an Englishman could satisfy his own honour and no questions asked afterwards. Poor young Heaslop had taken a step in this direction, by refusing bail, but the Collector couldn't feel this was wise of poor young Heaslop. Not only would the Nawab Bahadur and others be angry, but the Government of India itself also watches—and behind it is that caucus of cranks and cravens, the British Parliament. He had constantly to remind himself that, in the eyes of the law, Aziz was not yet guilty, and the effort fatigued him.

The others, less responsible, could behave naturally. They had started speaking of 'women and children'—that phrase that exempts the male from sanity when it has been repeated a few times. Each felt that all he loved best in the world was at stake, demanded revenge, and was filled with a not unpleasing glow, in which the chilly and half-known features of Miss Quested vanished, and were replaced by all that is sweetest and warmest in the private life. 'But it's the women and children,' they repeated, and the Collector knew he ought to stop them intoxicating themselves, but he hadn't the heart. 'They ought to be compelled to give hostages,' etc. Many of the said women and children were leaving for the Hill Station in a few days, and the suggestion was made that they should be packed off at once in a special train.

'*And* a jolly suggestion,' the subaltern cried. 'The army's got to come in sooner or later. (A special train was in his mind inseparable from troops.) This would never have happened if Barabas Hill was under military control. Station a bunch of Gurkhas at the entrance of the cave was all that was wanted.'

'Mrs Blakiston was saying if only there were a few Tommies,' remarked someone.

'English no good,' he cried, getting his loyalties mixed. 'Native troops for this country. Give me the sporting type of native, give me Gurkhas, give me Rajputs, give me Jats, give me the Punjabi, give me Sikhs, give me Marathas, Bhils, Afridis and Pathans, and really if it comes to that, I don't mind if you give me the scums of the bazaars. Properly led, mind. I'd lead them anywhere—'

The Collector nodded at him pleasantly, and said to his own people: 'Don't start carrying arms about. I want everything to go on precisely as usual, until there's cause for the contrary. Get the womenfolk off to the hills, but do it quietly, and for Heaven's sake no more talk of special trains. Never mind what you think or feel. Possibly I have feelings too. One isolated Indian has attempted—is charged with an attempted crime.' He flipped his forehead hard with his finger-nail, and they all realized that he felt as deeply as they did, and they loved him, and determined not to increase his difficulties. 'Act upon that fact until there are more facts,' he concluded. 'Assume every Indian is an angel.'

They murmured, 'Right you are, so we will. . . . Angels. . . . Exactly. . . .' From the subaltern: 'Exactly what I said. The native's all right if you get him alone. Lesley! Lesley! You remember the one I had a knock with on your Maidan last month. Well, he was all right. Any native who plays polo is all right. What you've got to stamp on is these educated classes, and, mind, I do know what I'm talking about this time.'

The smoking-room door opened, and let in a feminine buzz. Mrs Turton called out, 'She's better,' and from both sections of the community a sigh of joy and relief rose. The Civil Surgeon, who had brought the good news, came in. His cumbrous, pasty face looked ill-tempered. He surveyed the company, saw Fielding crouched below him on an ottoman, and said, 'H'm!' Everyone began pressing him for details. 'No one's out of danger in this country as long as they have a temperature,' was his answer. He appeared to resent his patient's recovery, and no one who knew the old Major and his ways was surprised at this.

'Squat down, Callendar; tell us all about it.'

'Take me some time to do that.'

'How's the old lady?'

'Temperature.'

'My wife heard she was sinking.'

'So she may be. I guarantee nothing. I really can't be plagued with questions, Lesley.'

'Sorry, old man.'

'Heaslop's just behind me.'

At the name of Heaslop a fine and beautiful expression was renewed on every face. Miss Quested was only a victim, but young Heaslop was a martyr; he was the recipient of all the evil intended against them by the country they had tried to serve; he was bearing the sahib's cross. And they fretted because they could do nothing for him in return; they felt so craven sitting on softness and attending the course of the law.

'I wish to God I hadn't given my jewel of an assistant leave. I'ld cut my tongue out first. To feel I'm responsible, that's what hits me. To refuse, and then give in under pressure. That is what I did, my sons, that is what I did.'

Fielding took his pipe from his mouth and looked at it thoughtfully. Thinking him afraid, the other went on: 'I understood an Englishman was to accompany the expedition. That is why I gave in.'

'No one blames you, my dear Callendar,' said the Collector, looking down. 'We are all to blame in the sense that we ought to have seen the expedition was insufficiently guaranteed, and stopped it. I knew about it myself; we lent our car this morning to take the ladies to the station. We are all implicated in that sense, but not an atom of blame attaches to you personally.'

'I don't feel that. I wish I could. Responsibility is a very awful thing, and I've no use for the man who shirks it.' His eyes were directed on Fielding. Those who knew that Fielding had undertaken to accompany and missed the early train were sorry for him; it was what is to be expected when a man mixes himself up with natives; always ends in some indignity. The Collector, who knew more, kept silent, for the official in him still hoped that Fielding would toe the line. The conversation turned to women and children again, and under its cover Major Callendar got hold of the subaltern, and set him on to bait the schoolmaster. Pretending to be more drunk than he really was, he began to make semi-offensive remarks.

'Heard about Miss Quested's servant?' reinforced the Major.

'No, what about him?'

'Heaslop warned Miss Quested's servant last night never to lose sight of her. Prisoner got hold of this and managed to leave him behind. Bribed him. Heaslop has just found out the whole story, with names and sums–a well-known pimp to those people gave the money, Mohammed Latif by name. So much for the servant. What about the Englishman–our friend here? How did they get rid of him? Money again.'

Fielding rose to his feet, supported by murmurs and exclamations, for no one yet suspected his integrity.

'Oh, I'm being misunderstood, apologies,' said the Major offensively. 'I didn't mean they bribed Mr Fielding.'

'Then what do you mean?'

'They paid the other Indian to make you late–Godbole. He was saying his prayers. I know those prayers!'

'That's ridiculous . . .' He sat down again, trembling with rage; person after person was being dragged into the mud.

Having shot this bolt, the Major prepared the next. 'Heaslop also found out something from his mother. Aziz paid a herd of natives to suffocate her in a cave. That was the end of her, or would have been only she got out. Nicely planned, wasn't it? Neat. Then he could go on with the girl. He and she and a guide, provided by the same Mohammed Latif. Guide now can't be found. Pretty.' His voice broke into a roar. 'It's not the time for sitting down. It's the time for action. Call in the troops and clear the bazaars.'

The Major's outbursts were always discounted, but he made everyone uneasy on this occasion. The crime was even worse than they had supposed–the unspeakable limit of cynicism, untouched since 1857. Fielding forgot his anger on poor old Godbole's behalf, and became thoughtful; the evil was propagating in every direction, it seemed to have an existence of its own, apart from anything that was done or said by individuals, and he understood better why both Aziz and Hamidullah had been inclined to lie down and die. His adversary saw that he was in trouble, and now ventured to say, 'I suppose nothing that's said inside the club will go outside the club?' winking the while at Lesley.

'Why should it?' responded Lesley.

'Oh, nothing. I only heard a rumour that a certain member here present has been seeing the prisoner this afternoon. You can't run with the hare and hunt with the hounds, at least not in this country.'

'Does anyone here present want to?'

Fielding was determined not to be drawn again. He had something to say, but it should be at his own moment. The attack failed to mature, because the Collector did not support it. Attention shifted from him for a time. Then the buzz of women broke out again. The door had been opened by Ronny.

The young man looked exhausted and tragic, also gentler than usual. He always showed deference to his superiors, but now it came straight from his heart. He seemed to appeal for their protection in the insult that had befallen him, and they, in instinctive homage, rose to their feet. But every human act in the East is tainted with officialism, and while honouring him they condemned Aziz and India. Fielding realized this, and he remained seated. It was an ungracious, a caddish thing to do, perhaps an unsound thing to do, but he felt he had been passive long ennugh, and that he might be drawn into the wrong current if he did not make a stand. Ronny, who had not seen him, said in husky tones, 'Oh please–please all sit down, I only want to listen what has been decided.'

'Heaslop, I'm telling them I'm against any show of force,' said the Collector apologetically. 'I don't know whether you will feel as I do, but that is how I am situated. When the verdict is obtained, it will be another matter.'

'You are sure to know best; I have no experience, I can't tell.'

'How is your mother, old boy?'

'Better, thank you. I wish everyone would sit down.'

'Some have never got up,' the young soldier said.

'And the Major brings us an excellent report of Miss Quested,' Turton went on.

'I do, I do, I'm satisfied.'

'You thought badly of her earlier, did you not, Major? That's why I refused bail.'

Callendar laughed with friendly inwardness, and said, 'Heaslop, Heaslop, next time bail's wanted, ring up the old doctor before giving it; his shoulders are broad, and, speaking in the strictest confidence, don't take the old doctor's opinion too seriously. He's a blithering idiot, we can always leave it at that, but he'll do the little he can towards keeping in quod the—' He broke off with affected politeness. 'Oh, but he has one of his friends here.'

The subaltern called, 'Stand up, you swine.'

'Mr Fielding, what has prevented you from standing up?' said the Collector, entering the fray at last. It was the attack for which Fielding had waited, and to which he must reply.

'May I make a statement, sir?'

'Certainly.'

Seasoned and self-contained, devoid of the fervours of nationality or youth, the schoolmaster did what was for him a comparatively easy thing. He stood up and said, 'I believe Dr Aziz to be innocent.'

'You have a right to hold that opinion if you choose, but pray is that any reason why you should insult Mr Heaslop?'

'May I conclude my statement?'

'Certainly.'

'I am waiting for the verdict of the courts. If he is guilty I resign from my service, and leave India. I resign from the club now.'

'Hear, hear!' said voices, not entirely hostile, for they liked the fellow for speaking out.

'You have not answered my question. Why did you not stand when Mr Heaslop entered?'

'With all deference, sir, I am not here to answer questions, but to make a personal statement, and I have concluded it.'

'May I ask whether you have taken over charge of this District?'

Fielding moved towards the door.

'One moment, Mr Fielding. You are not to go yet, please. Before you leave the club, from which you do very well to resign, you will express some detestation of the crime, and you will apologize to Mr Heaslop.'

'Are you speaking to me officially, sir?'

The Collector, who never spoke otherwise, was so infuriated that he lost his head. He cried, 'Leave this room at once, and I deeply regret that I demeaned myself to meet you at the station. You have sunk to the level of your associates; you are weak, weak, that is what is wrong with you—'

'I want to leave the room, but cannot while this gentleman prevents me,' said Fielding lightly; the subaltern had got across his path.

'Let him go,' said Ronny, almost in tears.

It was the only appeal that could have saved the situation. Whatever Heaslop wished must be done. There was a slight scuffle at the door, from which Fielding was propelled, a little more quickly than is natural, into the room where the ladies were playing cards. 'Fancy if I'd fallen or got angry,' he thought. Of course he was a little angry. His peers had never offered him violence or called him weak before, besides Heaslop had heaped coals of fire on his head. He wished he had not picked the quarrel over poor suffering Heaslop, when there were cleaner issues at hand.

However, there it was, done, muddled through, and to cool himself and regain mental balance he went on to the upper verandah for a moment, where the first object he saw was the Marabar Hills. At this distance and hour they leapt into beauty; they were Monsalvat, Walhalla, the towers of a cathedral, peopled with saints and heroes, and covered with flowers. What miscreant lurked in them, presently to be detected by the activities of the law? Who was the guide, and had he been found yet? What was the 'echo' of which the girl complained? He did not know, but presently he would know. Great is information, and she shall prevail. It was the last moment of the light, and as he gazed at the Marabar Hills they seemed to move graciously towards him like a queen, and their charm became the sky's. At the moment they vanished they were everywhere, the cool benediction of the night descended, the stars sparkled, and the whole universe was a hill. Lovely, exquisite moment—but passing the Englishman with averted face and on swift wings. He experienced nothing himself; it was as if someone had told him there was such a moment, and he was obliged to believe. And he felt dubious and discontented suddenly, and wondered whether he was really and truly successful as a human being. After forty years' experience, he had learnt to manage his life and make the best of it on advanced European lines, had developed his personality, explored his limitations, controlled his passions—and he had done it all without becoming either pedantic or worldly. A creditable achievement, but as the moment passed, he felt he ought to have been working at something else the whole time,—he didn't know at what, never would know, never could know, and that was why he felt sad.

Chapter Twenty-one

Dismissing his regrets, as inappropriate to the matter in hand, he accomplished the last section of the day by riding off to his new allies. He was glad that he had broken with the club, for he would have picked up scraps of gossip there, and reported them down in the city, and he was glad to be denied this opportunity. He would miss his billiards, and occasional tennis, and cracks with McBryde, but really that was all, so light did he travel. At the entrance of the bazaars, a tiger made his horse shy—a youth dressed up as a tiger, the body striped brown and yellow, a mask over the face. Mohurram was working up. The city beat a good many drums, but seemed good-tempered. He was invited to inspect a small tazia—a flimsy and frivolous erection, more like a crinoline than the tomb of the grandson of the Prophet, done to death at Kerbela. Excited children were pasting coloured paper over its ribs. The rest of the evening he spent with the Nawab Bahadur, Hamidullah, Mahmoud Ali, and others of the confederacy. The campaign was also working up. A telegram had been sent to the famous Amritrao, and his acceptance received. Application for bail was to be renewed—it could not well be withheld now that Miss Quested was out of danger. The conference was serious and sensible, but marred by a group of itinerant musicians, who were allowed to play in the compound. Each held a large earthenware jar, containing pebbles, and jerked it up and down in time to a doleful chant. Distracted by the noise, he suggested their dismissal, but the Nawab Bahadur vetoed it; he said that musicians, who had walked many miles, might bring good luck.

Late at night, he had an inclination to tell Professor Godbole of the tactical and moral error he had made in being rude to Heaslop, and to hear what he would say. But the old fellow had gone to bed, and slipped off unmolested to his new job in a day or two: he always did possess the knack of slipping off.

Chapter Twenty-two

Adela lay for several days in the McBrydes' bungalow. She had been touched by the sun, also hundreds of cactus spines had to be picked out of her flesh. Hour after hour Miss Derek and Mrs McBryde examined her through magnifying glasses, always coming on fresh colonies, tiny hairs that might snap off and be drawn into the blood if they were neglected. She lay passive beneath their fingers, which developed the shock that had begun in the cave. Hitherto she had not much minded whether she was touched or not: her senses were abnormally inert and the only contact she anticipated was that of mind. Everything now was transferred to the surface of her body, which began to avenge itself, and feed unhealthily. People seemed very much alike, except that some would come close while others kept away. 'In space things touch, in time things part,' she repeated to herself while the thorns were being extracted—her brain so weak that she could not decide whether the phrase was a philosophy or a pun.

They were kind to her, indeed over-kind, the men too respectful, the women too sympathetic; whereas Mrs Moore, the only visitor she wanted, kept away. No one understood her trouble, or knew why she vibrated between hard commonsense and hysteria. She would begin a speech as if nothing particular had happened. 'I went into this detestable cave,' she would say dryly, 'and I remember scratching the wall with my finger-nail, to start the usual echo, and then as I was saying there was this shadow, or sort of shadow, down the entrance tunnel, bottling me up. It seemed like an age, but I suppose the whole thing can't have lasted thirty seconds really. I hit at him with the glasses, he pulled me round the cave by the strap, it broke, I escaped, that's all. He never actually touched me once. It all seems such nonsense.' Then her eyes would fill with tears. 'Naturally I'm upset, but I shall get over it.' And then she would break down entirely, and the women would feel she was one of themselves and cry too, and men in the next room murmur: 'Good God, good God!' No one realized that she thought tears vile, a degradation more subtle than anything endured in the Marabar, a negation of her advanced outlook and the natural honesty of her mind. Adela was always trying to 'think the incident out,' always reminding herself that no harm had been done. There was 'the shock,' but what is that? For a time her own logic would convince her, then she would hear the echo again, weep, declare she was unworthy of Ronny, and hope her assailant would get the maximum penalty. After one of these bouts, she longed to go out into the bazaars and ask pardon from everyone she met, for she felt in some vague way that she was leaving the world worse than she found it. She felt that it was her crime, until the intellect, reawakening, pointed out to her that she was inaccurate here, and set her again upon her sterile round.

If only she could have seen Mrs Moore! The old lady had not been well either, and was disinclined to come out, Ronny reported. And consequently the echo flourished, raging up and down like a nerve in the faculty of her hearing, and the noise in the cave, so unimportant intellectually, was prolonged over the surface of her life. She had struck the polished wall—for no reason—and before the comment had died away, he followed her, and the climax was the falling of her field-glasses. The sound had spouted after her when she escaped, and was going on still like a river that gradually floods the plain. Only Mrs Moore could drive it back to its source and seal the broken reservoir. Evil was loose . . . she could even hear it entering the lives of others. . . . And Adela spent days in this atmosphere of grief and depression. Her friends kept up their spirits by demanding holocausts of natives, but she was too worried and weak to do that.

When the cactus thorns had all been extracted, and her temperature fallen to normal, Ronny came to fetch her away. He was worn with indignation and suffering, and she wished she could comfort him; but intimacy seemed to caricature itself, and the more they spoke the more wretched and self-conscious they became. Practical talk was the least painful, and he and McBryde now told her one or two things which they had concealed from her during the crisis, by the doctor's orders. She learnt for the first time of the Mohurram troubles. There had nearly been a riot. The last day of the festival, the great procession left its official route, and tried to enter the civil station, and a telephone had been cut because it interrupted the advance of one of the larger paper towers. McBryde and his police had pulled the thing straight—a fine piece of work. They passed on to another and very painful subject: the trial. She would have to appear in court, identify the prisoner, and submit to cross-examination by an Indian lawyer.

'Can Mrs Moore be with me?' was all she said.

'Certainly, and I shall be there myself,' Ronny replied. 'The case won't come before me; they've objected to me on personal grounds. It will be at Chandrapore—we thought at one time it would be transferred elsewhere.'

'Miss Quested realizes what all that means, though,' said McBryde sadly. 'The case will come before Das.'

Das was Ronny's assistant—own brother to the Mrs Bhattacharya whose carriage had played them false last month. He was courteous and intelligent, and with the evidence before him could only come to one conclusion; but that he should be judge over an English girl had convulsed the station with wrath, and some of the women had sent a telegram about it to Lady Mellanby, the wife of the Lieutenant-Governor.

'I must come before someone.'

'That's—that's the way to face it. You have the pluck, Miss Quested.' He grew very bitter over the arrangements, and called them 'the fruits of democracy.' In the old days an Englishwoman would not have had to appear, nor would any Indian have dared to discuss her private affairs. She would have made her deposition, and judgment would have followed. He apologized to her for the condition of the country, with the result that she gave one of her sudden little shoots of tears. Ronny wandered miserably about the room while she cried, treading upon the flowers of the Kashmir carpet that so inevitably covered it or drumming on the brass Benares bowls. 'I do this less every day, I shall soon be quite well,' she said, blowing her nose and feeling hideous. 'What I need is something to do. That is why I keep on with this ridiculous crying.'

'It's not ridiculous, we think you wonderful,' said the policeman very sincerely. 'It only bothers us that we can't help you more. Your stopping here—at such a time—is the greatest honour this house—' He too was overcome with emotion. 'By the way, a letter came here for you while you were ill,' he continued. 'I opened it, which is a strange confession to make, Will you forgive me? The circumstances are peculiar. It is from Fielding.'

'Why should he write to me?'

'A most lamentable thing has happened. The defence got hold of him.'

'He's a crank, a crank,' said Ronny lightly.

'That's your way of putting it, but a man can be a crank without being a cad. Miss Quested had better know how be behaved to you. If you don't tell her, somebody else will.' He told her. 'He is now the mainstay of the defence, I needn't add. He is the one righteous Englishman in a horde of tyrants. He receives deputations from the bazaar, and they all chew betel nut and smear one another's hands with scent. It is not easy to enter into the mind of such a man. His students are on strike—out of enthusiasm for him they won't learn their lessons. If it weren't for Fielding one would never have had the Mohurram trouble. He has done a very grave disservice to the whole community. The letter lay here a day or two, waiting till you were well enough, then the situation got so grave that I decided to open it in case it was useful to us.'

'Is it?' she said feebly.

'Not at all. He only has the impertinence to suggest you have made a mistake.'

'Would that I had!' She glanced through the letter, which was careful and formal in its wording. 'Dr Aziz is innocent,' she read. Then her voice began to tremble again. 'But think of his behaviour to you, Ronny. When you had already to bear so much for my sake! It was shocking of him. My dear, how can I repay you? How can one repay when one has nothing to give? What is the use of personal relationships when everyone brings less and less to them? I feel we ought all to go back into the desert for centuries and try and get good. I want to begin at the beginning. All the things I thought I'd learnt are just a hindrance, they're not knowledge at all. I'm not fit for personal relationships. Well, let's go, let's go. Of course Mr Fielding's letter doesn't count; he can think and write what he likes, only he shouldn't have been rude to you when you had so much to bear. That's what matters. . . . I don't want your arm, I'm a magnificent walker, so don't touch me, please.'

Mrs McBryde wished her an affectionate good-bye—a woman with whom she had nothing in common and whose intimacy oppressed her. They would have to meet now, year after year, until one of their husbands was super-annuated. Truly Anglo-India had caught her with a vengeance, and perhaps it served her right for having tried to take up a line of her own. Humbled yet repelled, she gave thanks. 'Oh, we must help one another, we must take the rough with the smooth,' said Mrs McBryde. Miss Derek was there too, still making jokes about her comic Maharajah and Rani. Required as a witness at the trial, she had refused to send back the Mudkul car; they would be frightfully sick. Both Mrs McBryde and Miss Derek kissed her, and called her by her Christian name. Then Ronny drove her back. It was early in the morning, for the day, as the hot weather advanced, swelled like a monster at both ends, and left less and less room for the movements of mortals.

As they neared his bungalow, he said: 'Mother's looking forward to seeing you, but of course she's old, one mustn't forget that. Old people never take things as one expects, in my opinion.' He seemed warning her against approaching disappointment, but she took no notice. Her friendship with Mrs Moore was so deep and real that she felt sure it would last, whatever else happened. 'What can I do to make things easier for you? it's you who matter,' she sighed.

'Dear old girl to say so.'

'Dear old boy.' Then she cried: 'Ronny, she isn't ill too?'

He reassured her; Major Callendar was not dissatisfied.

'But you'll find her—irritable. We are an irritable family. Well, you'll see for yourself. No doubt my own nerves are out of order, and I expected more from mother when I came in from the office than she felt able to give. She is sure to make a special effort for you; still, I don't want your home-coming to be a disappointing one. Don't expect too much.'

The house came in sight. It was a replica of the bungalow she had left. Puffy, red, and curiously severe, Mrs Moore was revealed upon a sofa. She didn't get up when they entered, and the surprise of this roused Adela from her own troubles.

'Here you are both back,' was the only greeting.

Adela sat down and took her hand. It withdrew, and she felt that just as others repelled her, so did she repel Mrs Moore.

'Are you all right? You appeared all right when I left,' said Ronny, trying not to speak crossly, but he had instructed her to give the girl a pleasant welcome, and he could not but feel annoyed.

'I am all right,' she said heavily. 'As a matter of fact I have been looking at my return ticket. It is interchangeable, so I have a much larger choice of boats home than I thought.'

'We can go into that later, can't we?'

'Ralph and Stella may be wanting to know when I arrive.'

'There is plenty of time for all such plans. How do you think our Adela looks?'

'I am counting on you to help me through; it is such a blessing to be with you again, everyone else is a stranger,' said the girl rapidly.

But Mrs Moore showed no inclination to be helpful. A sort of resentment emanated from her. She seemed to say: 'Am I to be bothered for ever?' Her

Christian tenderness had gone, or had developed into a hardness, a just irritation against the human race; she had taken no interest at the arrest, asked scarcely any questions, and had refused to leave her bed on the awful last night of Mohurram, when an attack was expected on the bungalow.

'I know it's all nothing; I must be sensible, I do try—' Adela continued, working again towards tears. 'I shouldn't mind if it had happened anywhere else; at least I really don't know where it did happen.'

Ronny supposed that he understood what she meant: she could not identify or describe the particular cave, indeed almost refused to have her mind cleared up about it, and it was recognized that the defence would try to make capital out of this during the trial. He reassured her: the Marabar caves were notoriously like one another; indeed, in the future they were to be numbered in sequence with white paint.

'Yes, I mean that, at least not exactly; but there is this echo that I keep on hearing.'

'Oh, what of the echo?' asked Mrs Moore, paying attention to her for the first time.

'I can't get rid of it.'

'I don't suppose you ever will.'

Ronny had emphasized to his mother that Adela would arrive in a morbid state, yet she was being positively malicious.

'Mrs Moore, what is this echo?'

'Don't you know?'

'No—what is it? oh, do say! I felt you would be able to explain it . . . this will comfort me so. . . .'

'If you don't know, you don't know, I can't tell you.'

'I think you're rather unkind not to say.'

'Say, say, say,' said the old lady bitterly. 'As if anything can be said! I have spent my life in saying or in listening to sayings; I have listened too much. It is time I was left in peace. Not to die,' she added sourly. 'No doubt you expect me to die, but when I have seen you and Ronny married, and seen the other two and whether they want to be married—I'll retire then into a cave of my own.' She smiled, to bring down her remark into ordinary life and thus add to its bitterness. 'Somewhere where no young people will come asking questions and expecting answers. Some shelf.'

'Quite so, but meantime a trial is coming on,' said her son hotly, 'and the notion of most of us is that we'd better pull together and help one another through, instead of being disagreeable. Are you going to talk like that in the witness-box?'

'Why should I be in the witness-box?'

'To confirm certain points in our evidence.'

'I have nothing to do with your ludicrous law courts,' she said, angry. 'I will not be dragged in at all.'

'I won't have her dragged in, either; I won't have any more trouble on my account,' cried Adela, and again took the hand, which was again withdrawn. 'Her evidence is not the least essential.'

'I thought she would want to give it. No one blames you, mother, but the

fact remains that you dropped off at the first cave, and encouraged Adela to
go on with him alone, whereas if you'd been well enough to keep on too
nothing would have happened. He planned it, I know. Still, you fell into his
trap just like Fielding and Antony before you. . . . Forgive me for speaking so
plainly, but you've no right to take up this high and mighty attitude about
law courts. If you're ill, that's different; but you say you're all right and you
seem so, in which case I thought you'ld want to take your part, I did really.'

'I'll not have you worry her whether she's well or ill,' said Adela, leaving
the sofa and taking his arm; then dropped it with a sigh and sat down again.
But he was pleased she had rallied to him and surveyed his mother
patronizingly. He had never felt easy with her. She was by no means the dear
old lady outsiders supposed, and India had brought her into the open.

'I shall attend your marriage, but not your trial,' she informed them,
tapping her knee; she had become very restless, and rather ungraceful.
'Then I shall go to England.'

'You can't go to England in May, as you agreed.'

'I have changed my mind.'

'Well, we'd better end this unexpected wrangle,' said the young man,
striding about. 'You appear to want to be left out of everything, and that's
enough.'

'My body, my miserable body,' she sighed. 'Why isn't it strong? Oh, why
can't I walk away and be gone? Why can't I finish my duties and be gone?
Why do I get headaches and puff when I walk? And all the time this to do and
that to do and this to do in your way and that to do in her way, and everything
sympathy and confusion and bearing one another's burdens. Why can't this
be done and that be done in my way and they be done and I at peace? Why
has anything to be done, I cannot see. Why all this marriage, marriage? . . .
The human race would have become a single person centuries ago if
marriage was any use. And all this rubbish about love, love in a church, love
in a cave, as if there is the least difference, and I held up from my business
over such trifles!'

'What do you want?' he said, exasperated. 'Can you state it in simple
language? If so, do.'

'I want my pack of patience cards.'

'Very well, get them.'

He found, as he expected, that the poor girl was crying. And, as always, an
Indian close outside the window, a mali in this case, picking up sounds.
Much upset, he sat silent for a moment, thinking over his mother and her
senile intrusions. He wished he had never asked her to visit India, or become
under any obligation to her.

'Well, my dear girl, this isn't much of a home-coming,' he said at last. 'I
had no idea she had this up her sleeve.'

Adela had stopped crying. An extraordinary expression was on her face,
half relief, half horror. She repeated, 'Aziz, Aziz.'

They all avoided mentioning that name. It had become synonymous with
the power of evil. He was 'the prisoner,' 'the person in question,' 'the defence,' and the sound of it now rang out like the first note of new symphony.

'Aziz . . . have I made a mistake?'

'You're over-tired,' he cried, not much surprised.

'Ronny, he's innocent; I made an awful mistake.'

'Well, sit down anyhow.' He looked round the room, but only two sparrows were chasing one another. She obeyed and took hold of his hand. He stroked it and she smiled, and gasped as if she had risen to the surface of the water, then touched her ear.

'My echo's better.'

'That's good. You'll be perfectly well in a few days, but you must save yourself up for the trial. Das is a very good fellow, we shall all be with you.'

'But Ronny, dear Ronny, perhaps there oughtn't to be any trial.'

'I don't quite know what you're saying, and I don't think you do.'

'If Dr Aziz never did it he ought to be let out.'

A shiver like impending death passed over Ronny. He said hurriedly, 'He was let out—until the Mohurram riot, when he had to be put in again.' To divert her, he told her the story, which was held to be amusing. Nureddin had stolen the Nawab Bahadur's car and driven Aziz into a ditch in the dark. Both of them had fallen out, and Nureddin had cut his face open. Their wailing had been drowned by the cries of the faithful, and it was quite a time before they were rescued by the police. Nureddin was taken to the Minto Hospital, Aziz restored to prison, with an additional charge against him of disturbing the public peace. 'Half a minute,' he remarked when the anecdote was over, and went to the telephone to ask Callendar to look in as soon as he found it convenient, because she hadn't borne the journey well.

When he returned, she was in a nervous crisis, but it took a different form—she clung to him, and sobbed, 'Help me to do what I ought. Aziz is good, You heard your mother say so.'

'Heard what?'

'He's good; I've been so wrong to accuse him.'

'Mother never said so.'

'Didn't she?' she asked, quite reasonable, open to every suggestion anyway.

'She never mentioned that name once.'

'But, Ronny, I heard her.'

'Pure illusion. You can't be quite well, can you, to make up a thing like that.'

'I suppose I can't. How amazing of me!'

'I was listening to all she said, as far as it could be listened to; she gets very incoherent.'

'When her voice dropped she said it—towards the end, when she talked about love—love—I couldn't follow, but just then she said: "Doctor Aziz never did it."'

'Those words?'

'The idea more than the words.'

'Never, never, my dear girl. Complete illusion. His name was not mentioned by anyone. Look here—you are confusing this with Fielding's letter.'

'That's it, that's it,' she cried, greatly relieved. I knew I'd heard his name somewhere. I am so grateful to you for clearing this up—it's the sort of mistake that worries me, and proves I'm neurotic.'

'So you won't go saying he's innocent again, will you? for every servant I've got is a spy.' He went to the window. The mali had gone, or rather had turned into two small children—impossible they should know English, but he sent them packing. 'They all hate us,' he explained. 'It'll be all right after the verdict, for I will say this for them, they do accept the accomplished fact; but at present they're pouring out money like water to catch us tripping, and a remark like yours is the very thing they look out for. It would enable them to say it was a put-up job on the part of us officials. You see what I mean.'

Mrs Moore came back, with the same air of ill-temper, and sat down with a flump by the card-table. To clear the confusion up, Ronny asked her point-blank whether she had mentioned the prisoner. She could not understand the question and the reason of it had to be explained. She replied: 'I never said his name,' and began to play patience.

'I thought you said, "Aziz is an innocent man," but it was in Mr Fielding's letter.'

'Of course he is innocent,' she answered indifferently: it was the first time she had expressed an opinion on the point.

'You see, Ronny, I was right,' said the girl.

'You were not right, she never said it.'

'But she thinks it.'

'Who cares what she thinks?'

'Red nine on black ten—' from the card-table.

'She can think, and Fielding too, but there's such a thing as evidence, I suppose.'

'I know, but—'

'Is it again my duty to talk?' asked Mrs Moore, looking up. 'Apparently, as you keep interrupting me.'

'Only if you have anything sensible to say.'

'Oh, how tedious . . . trivial . . .' and as when she had scoffed at love, love, love, her mind seemed to move towards them from a great distance and out of darkness. 'Oh, why is everything still my duty? when shall I be free from your fuss? Was he in the cave and were you in the cave and on and on . . . and Unto us a Son is born, unto us a Child is given . . . and am I good and is he bad and are we saved? . . . and ending everything the echo.'

'I don't hear it so much,' said Adela, moving towards her. 'You send it away, you do nothing but good, you are so good.'

'I am not good, no, bad.' She spoke more calmly and resumed her cards, saying as she turned them up, 'A bad old woman, bad, bad, detestable. I used to be good with the children growing up, also I meet this young man in his mosque, I wanted him to be happy. Good, happy, small people. They do not exist, they were a dream. . . . But I will not help you to torture him for what he never did. There are different ways of evil and I prefer mine to yours.'

'Have you any evidence in the prisoner's favour?' said Ronny in the tones of the just official. 'If so, it is your bounden duty to go into the witness-box for him instead of for us. No one will stop you.'

'One knows people's characters, as you call them,' she retorted disdainfully, as if she really knew more than character but could not impart it. 'I have heard both English and Indians speak well of him, and I felt it isn't the sort of thing he would do.'

'Feeble, mother, feeble.'

'Most feeble.'

'And most inconsiderate to Adela.'

Adela said: 'It would be so appalling if I was wrong. I should take my own life.'

He turned on her with: 'What was I warning you just now? You know you're right, and the whole station knows it.'

'Yes, he . . . This is very, very awful. I'm as certain as ever he followed me . . . only, wouldn't it be possible to withdraw the case? I dread the idea of giving evidence more and more, and you are all so good to women here and you have so much more power than in England—look at Miss Derek's motor-car. Oh, of course it's out of the question, I'm ashamed to have mentioned it; please forgive me.'

'That's all right,' he said inadequately. 'Of course I forgive you, as you call it. But the case has to come before a magistrate now; it really must, the machinery has started.'

'She has started the machinery; it will work to its end.'

Adela inclined towards tears in consequence of this unkind remark, and Ronny picked up the list of steamship sailings with an excellent notion in his head. His mother ought to leave India at once: she was doing no good to herself or to anyone else there.

Chapter Twenty-three

Lady Mellanby, wife to the Lieutenant-Governor of the Province, had been gratified by the appeal addressed to her by the ladies of Chandrapore. She could not do anything—besides, she was sailing for England; but she desired to be informed if she could show sympathy in any other way. Mrs Turton replied that Mr Heaslop's mother was trying to get a passage, but had delayed too long, and all the boats were full; could Lady Mellanby use her influence? Not even Lady Mellanby could expand the dimensions of a P. and O., but she was a very, very nice woman, and she actually wired offering the unknown and obscure old lady accommodation in her own reserved cabin. It was like a gift from heaven; humble and grateful, Ronny could not but reflect that there are compensations for every woe. His name was familiar at Government House owing to poor Adela, and now Mrs Moore would stamp it on Lady Mellanby's imagination, as they journeyed across the Indian Ocean and up the Red Sea. He had a return of tenderness for his mother—as we do for our relatives when they receive conspicuous and unexpected honour. She was not negligible, she could still arrest the attention of a high official's wife.

So Mrs Moore had all she wished; she escaped the trial, the marriage, and the hot weather; she would return to England in comfort and distinction, and see her other children. At her son's suggestion, and by her own desire, she departed. But she accepted her good luck without enthusiasm. She had come to that state where the horror of the universe and its smallness are both visible at the same time—the twilight of the double vision in which so many elderly people are involved. If this world is not to our taste, well, at all events there is Heaven, Hell, Annihilation—one or other of those large things, that huge scenic background of stars, fires, blue or black air. All heroic endeavour, and all that is known as art, assumes that there is such a background, just as all practical endeavour, when the world is to our taste, assumes that the world is all. But in the twilight of the double vision, a spiritual muddledom is set up for which no high-sounding words can be found; we can neither act nor refrain from action, we can neither ignore nor respect Infinity. Mrs Moore had always inclined to resignation. As soon as she landed in India it seemed to her good, and when she saw the water flowing through the mosque-tank, or the Ganges, or the moon, caught in the shawl of night with all the other stars, it seemed a beautiful goal and an easy one. To be one with the universe! So dignified and simple. But there was always some little duty to be performed first, some new card to be turned up from the diminishing pack and placed, and while she was pottering about, the Marabar struck its gong.

What had spoken to her in that scoured-out cavity of the granite? What dwelt in the first of the caves? Something very old and very small. Before time, it was before space also. Something snub-nosed, incapable of generosity—the undying worm itself. Since hearing its voice, she had not entertained one large thought, she was actually envious of Adela. All this fuss over a frightened girl! Nothing had happened, 'and if it had,' she found herself thinking with the cynicism of a withered priestess, 'if it had, there are worse evils than love.' The unspeakable attempt presented itself to her as love: in a cave, in a church—Boum, it amounts to the same. Visions are supposed to entail profundity, but— Wait till you get one, dear reader! The abyss also may be petty, the serpent of eternity made of maggots; her constant thought was: 'Less attention should be paid to my future daughter-in-law and more to me, there is no sorrow like my sorrow,' although when the attention was paid she rejected it irritably.

Her son couldn't escort her to Bombay, for the local situation continued acute, and all officials had to remain at their posts. Antony couldn't come either, in case he never returned to give his evidence. So she travelled with no one who could remind her of the past. This was a relief. The heat had drawn back a little before its next advance, and the journey was not unpleasant. As she left Chandrapore the moon, full again, shone over the Ganges and touched the shrinking channels into threads of silver, then veered and looked into her window. The swift and comfortable mail-train slid with her through the night, and all the next day she was rushing through Central India, through landscapes that were baked and bleached but had not the hopeless melancholy of the plain. She watched the indestructible life of man and his changing faces, and the houses he has built for himself and God, and they appeared to her not in terms of her own trouble but as things to see. There was, for instance, a place called Asirgarh which she passed at sunset and identified on a map—an enormous fortress among wooded hills. No one had ever mentioned Asirgarh to her, but it had huge and noble bastions and to the right of them was a mosque. She forgot it. Ten minutes later, Asirgarh reappeared. The mosque was to the left of the bastions now. The train in its descent through the Vindyas had described a semicircle round Asirgarh. What could she connect it with except its own name? Nothing; she knew no one who lived there. But it had looked at her twice and seemed to say: 'I do not vanish.' She woke in the middle of the night with a start, for the train was falling over the western cliff. Moonlit pinnacles rushed up at her like the fringes of a sea; then a brief episode of plain, the real sea, and the soupy dawn of Bombay. 'I have not seen the right places,' she thought, as she saw embayed in the platforms of the Victoria Terminus the end of the rails that had carried her over a continent and could never carry her back. She would never visit Asirgarh or the other untouched places; neither Delhi nor Agra nor the Rajputana cities nor Kashmir, nor the obscurer marvels that had sometimes shone through men's speech: the bilingual rock of Girnar, the statue of Shri Belgola, the ruins of Mandu and Hampi, temples of Khajraha, gardens of Shalimar. As she drove through the huge city which the West has built and abandoned with a gesture of despair, she longed to stop, though it was only Bombay, and disentangle the hundred Indias that passed each other in its streets. The feet of the horses moved her on, and presently the boat sailed and thousands of coco-nut palms appeared all round the anchorage and climbed the hills to wave her farewell. 'So you thought an echo was India; you took the Marabar caves as final?' they laughed. 'What have we in common with them, or they with Asirgarh? Good-bye!' Then the steamer rounded Colaba, the continent swung about, the cliff of the Ghats melted into the haze of a tropic sea. Lady Mellanby turned up and advised her not to stand in the heat: 'We are safely out of the frying-pan,' said Lady Mellanby, 'it will never do to fall into the fire.'

Chapter Twenty-four

Making sudden changes of gear, the heat accelerated its advance after Mrs Moore's departure until existence had to be endured and crime punished with the thermometer at a hundred and twelve. Electric fans hummed and spat, water splashed on to screens, ice clinked, and outside these defences, between a greyish sky and a yellowish earth, clouds of dust moved hesitatingly. In Europe life retreats out of the cold, and exquisite fireside myths have resulted—Balder, Persephone—but here the retreat is from the source of life, the treacherous sun, and no poetry adorns it because disillusionment cannot be beautiful. Men yearn for poetry though they may not confess it; they desire that joy shall be graceful and sorrow august and infinity have a form, and India fails to accommodate them. The annual helter-skelter of April, when irritability and lust spread like a canker, is one of her comments on the orderly hopes of humanity. Fish manage better; fish, as the tanks dry, wriggle into the mud and wait for the rains to uncake them. But men try to be harmonious all the year round, and the results are occasionally disastrous. The triumphant machine of civilization may suddenly hitch and be immobilized into a car of stone, and at such moments the destiny of the English seems to resemble their predecessors', who also entered the country with intent to refashion it, but were in the end worked into its pattern and covered with its dust.

Adela, after years of intellectualism, had resumed her morning kneel to Christianity. There seemed no harm in it, it was the shortest and easiest cut to the unseen, and she could tack her troubles on to it. Just as the Hindu clerks asked Lakshmi for an increase in pay, so did she implore Jehovah for a favourable verdict. God who saves the King will surely support the police. Her deity returned a consoling reply, but the touch of her hands on her face started prickly heat, and she seemed to swallow and expectorate the same insipid clot of air that had weighed on her lungs all the night. Also the voice of Mrs Turton disturbed her. 'Are you ready, young lady?' it pealed from the next room.

'Half a minute,' she murmured. The Turtons had received her after Mrs Moore left. Their kindness was incredible, but it was her position not her character that moved them; she was the English girl who had had the terrible experience, and for whom too much could not be done. No one, except Ronny, had any idea of what passed in her mind, and he only dimly, for where there is officialism every human relationship suffers. In her sadness she said to him, 'I bring you nothing but trouble; I was right on the Maidan, we had better just be friends,' but he protested, for the more she suffered the more highly he valued her. Did she love him? This question was somehow draggled up with the Marabar, it had been in her mind as she entered the fatal cave. Was she capable of loving anyone?

'Miss Quested, Adela, what d'ye call yourself, it's half-past seven; we ought to think of starting for that Court when you feel inclined.'

'She's saying her prayers,' came the Collector's voice.

'Sorry, my dear; take your time. . . . Was your chhota hazri all right?'

'I can't eat; might I have a little brandy?' she asked, deserting Jehovah.

When it was brought, she shuddered, and said she was ready to go.

'Drink it up; not a bad notion, a peg.'

'I don't think it'll really help me, Burra Sahib.'

'You sent brandy down to the Court, didn't you, Mary?'

'I should think I did, champagne too.'

'I'll thank you this evening, I'm all to pieces now,' said the girl, forming each syllable carefully as if her trouble would diminish if it were accurately defined. She was afraid of reticence, in case something that she herself did not perceive took shape beneath it, and she had rehearsed with Mr McBryde in an odd, mincing way her terrible adventure in the cave, how the man had never actually touched her but dragged her about, and so on. Her aim this morning was to announce, meticulously, that the strain was appalling, and she would probably break down under Mr Amritrao's cross-examination and disgrace her friends. 'My echo has come back again badly,' she told them.

'How about aspirin?'

'It is not a headache, it is an echo.'

Unable to dispel the buzzing in her ears, Major Callendar had diagnosed it as a fancy, which must not be encouraged. So the Turtons changed the subject. The cool little lick of the breeze was passing over the earth, dividing night from day; it would fail in ten minutes, but they might profit by it for their drive down into the city.

'I am sure to break down,' she repeated.

'You won't,' said the Collector, his voice full of tenderness.

'Of course she won't, she's a real sport.'

'But Mrs Turton . . .'

'Yes, my dear child?'

'If I do break down, it is of no consequence. It would matter in some trials, not in this. I put it to myself in the following way: I can really behave as I like, cry, be absurd, I am sure to get my verdict, unless Mr Das is most frightfully unjust.'

'You're bound to win,' he said calmly, and did not remind her that there was bound to be an appeal. The Nawab Bahadur had financed the defence, and would ruin himself sooner than let an 'innocent Moslem perish,' and other interests, less reputable, were in the background too. The case might go up from court to court, with consequences that no official could foresee. Under his very eyes, the temper of Chandrapore was altering. As his car turned out of the compound, there was a tap of silly anger on its paint—a pebble thrown by a child. Some larger stones were dropped near the mosque. In the Maidan, a squad of native police on motor cycles waited to escort them through the bazaars. The Collector was irritated and muttered, 'McBryde's an old woman'; but Mrs Turton said, 'Really, after Mohurram a show of force will do no harm; it's ridiculous to pretend they don't hate us, do give up that farce.' He replied in an odd, sad voice, 'I don't hate them, I don't know why,' and he didn't hate them; for if he did, he would have had to condemn his own career as a bad investment. He retained a contemptuous affection for the pawns he had moved about for so many years, they must be worth his pains. 'After all, it's our women who make everything more difficult out here,' was his inmost thought, as he caught sight of some obscenities upon a long blank wall, and beneath his chivalry to Miss Quested resentment lurked, waiting its day—perhaps there is a grain of resentment in all chivalry. Some students had gathered in front of the City Magistrate's Court—hysterical boys whom he would have faced if alone, but he told the driver to work round to the rear of the building. The students jeered, and Rafi (hiding behind a comrade that he might not be identified) called out the English were cowards.

They gained Ronny's private room, where a group of their own sort had collected. None were cowardly, all nervy, for queer reports kept coming in. The Sweepers had just struck, and half the commodes of Chandrapore remained desolate in consequence–only half, and Sweepers from the District, who felt less strongly about the innocence of Dr Aziz, would arrive in the afternoon, and break the strike, but why should the grotesque incident occur? And a number of Mohammedan ladies had sworn to take no food until the prisoner was acquitted; their death would make little difference, indeed, being invisible, they seemed dead already, nevertheless it was disquieting. A new spirit seemed abroad, a rearrangement, which no one in the stern little band of whites could explain. There was a tendency to see Fielding at the back of it: the idea that he was weak and cranky had been dropped. They abused Fielding vigorously: he had been seen driving up with the two counsels, Amritrao and Mahmoud Ali; he encouraged the Boy Scout movement for seditious reasons; he received letters with foreign stamps on them, and was probably a Japanese spy. This morning's verdict would break the renegade, but he had done his country and the Empire incalculable disservice. While they denounced him, Miss Quested lay back with her hands on the arms of her chair and her eyes closed, reserving her strength. They noticed her after a time, and felt ashamed of making so much noise.

'Can we do nothing for you?' Miss Derek said.

'I don't think so, Nancy, and I seem able to do nothing for myself.'

'But you're strictly forbidden to talk like that; you're wonderful.'

'Yes indeed,' came the reverent chorus.

'My old Das is all right,' said Ronny, starting a new subject in low tones.

'Not one of them's all right,' contradicted Major Callendar.

'Das is, really.'

'You mean he's more frightened of acquitting than convicting, because if he acquits he'll lose his job,' said Lesley with a clever little laugh.

Ronny did mean that, but he cherished 'illusions' about his own subordinates (following the finer traditions of his service here), and he liked to maintain that his old Das really did possess moral courage of the Public School brand. He pointed out that–from one point of view–it was good that an Indian was taking the case. Conviction was inevitable; so better let an Indian pronounce it, there would be less fuss in the long run. Interested in the argument, he let Adela become dim in his mind.

'In fact, you disapprove of the appeal I forwarded to Lady Mellanby,' said Mrs Turton with considerable heat. 'Pray don't apologize, Mr Heaslop; I am accustomed to being in the wrong.'

'I didn't mean that . . .'

'All right. I said don't apologize.'

'Those swine are always on the look-out for a grievance,' said Lesley, to propitiate her.

'Swine, I should think so,' the Major echoed. 'And what's more, I'll tell you what. What's happened is a damn good thing really, barring of course its application to present company. It'll make them squeal and it's time they did squeal. I've put the fear of God into them at the hospital anyhow. You should see the grandson of our so-called leading loyalist.' He tittered brutally as he described poor Nureddin's present appearance. 'His beauty's gone, five upper teeth, two lower and a nostril. . . . Old Panna Lal brought him the looking-glass yesterday and he blubbered. . . . I laughed; I laughed, I tell you, and so would you; that used to be one of these buck niggers, I thought, now he's all septic; damn him, blast his soul—er—I believe he was unspeakably immoral—er—' He subsided, nudged in the ribs, but added, 'I wish I'd had the cutting up of my late assistant too; nothing's too bad for these people.'

'At last some sense is being talked,' Mrs Turton cried, much to her husband's discomfort.

'That's what I say; I say there's not such a thing as cruelty after a thing like this.'

'Exactly, and remember it afterwards, you men. You're weak, weak, weak. Why, they ought to crawl from here to the caves on their hands and knees whenever an Englishwoman's in sight, they oughtn't to be spoken to, they ought to be spat at, they ought to be ground into the dust, we've been far too kind with our Bridge Parties and the rest.'

She paused. Profiting by her wrath, the heat had invaded her. She subsided into a lemon squash, and continued between the sips to murmur, 'Weak, weak.' And the process was repeated. The issues Miss Quested had raised were so much more important than she was herself that people inevitably forgot her.

Presently the case was called.

Their chairs preceded them into the Court, for it was important that they should look dignified. And when the chuprassies had made all ready, they filed into the ramshackly room with a condescending air, as if it was a booth at a fair. The Collector made a small official joke as he sat down, at which his entourage smiled, and the Indians, who could not hear what he said, felt that some new cruelty was afoot, otherwise the sahibs would not chuckle.

The Court was crowded and of course very hot, and the first person Adela noticed in it was the humblest of all who were present, a person who had no bearing officially upon the trial: the man who pulled the punkah. Almost naked, and splendidly formed, he sat on a raised platform near the back, in the middle of the central gangway, and he caught her attention as she came in, and he seemed to control the proceedings. He had the strength and beauty that sometimes come to flower in Indians of low birth. When that strange race nears the dust and is condemned as untouchable, then nature remembers the physical perfection that she accomplished elsewhere, and throws out a god—not many, but one here and there, to prove to society how little its categories impress her. This man would have been notable anywhere: among the thin-hammed, flat-chested mediocrities of Chandrapore he stood out as divine, yet he was of the city, its garbage had nourished him, he would end on its rubbish heaps. Pulling the rope towards him, relaxing it rhythmically, sending swirls of air over others, receiving none himself, he seemed apart from human destinies, a male fate, a winnower of souls. Opposite him, also on a platform, sat the little assistant magistrate, cultivated, self-conscious, and conscientious. The punkah wallah was none of these things: he scarcely knew that he existed and did not understand why the Court was fuller than usual, indeed he did not know that it was fuller than usual, didn't even know he worked a fan, though he thought he pulled a rope. Something in his aloofness impressed the girl from middle-class England, and rebuked the narrowness of her sufferings. In virtue of what had she collected this roomful of people together? Her particular brand of opinions, and the suburban Jehovah who sanctified them—by what right did they claim so much importance in the world, and assume the title of civilization? Mrs Moore—she looked round, but Mrs Moore was far away on the sea; it was the kind of question they might have discussed on the voyage out before the old lady had turned disagreeable and queer.

While thinking of Mrs Moore she heard sounds, which gradually grew more distinct. The epoch-making trial had started, and the Superintendent of Police was opening the case for the prosecution.

Mr McBryde was not at pains to be an interesting speaker; he left eloquence to the defence, who would require it. His attitude was, 'Everyone knows the man's guilty, and I am obliged to say so in public before he goes to the Andamans.' He made no moral or emotional appeal, and it was only by degrees that the studied negligence of his manner made itself felt, and lashed part of the audience to fury. Laboriously did he describe the genesis of the picnic. The prisoner had met Miss Quested at an entertainment given by the Principal of Government College, and had there conceived his intentions concerning her: prisoner was a man of loose life, as documents found upon him at his arrest would testify, also his fellow-assistant, Dr Panna Lal, was in a position to throw light on his character, and Major Callendar himself would speak. Here Mr McBryde paused. He wanted to keep the proceedings as clean as possible, but Oriental Pathology, his favourite theme, lay around him, and he could not resist it. Taking off his spectacles, as was his habit before enunciating a general truth, he looked into them sadly, and remarked that the darker races are physically attracted by the fairer, but not *vice versa*—not a matter for bitterness this, not a matter for abuse, but just a fact which any scientific observer will confirm.

'Even when the lady is so uglier than the gentleman?'

The comment fell from nowhere, from the ceiling perhaps. It was the first interruption, and the Magistrate felt bound to censure it. 'Turn that man out,' he said. One of the native policemen took hold of a man who had said nothing, and turned him out roughly. Mr McBryde resumed his spectacles and proceeded. But the comment had upset Miss Quested. Her body resented being called ugly, and trembled.

'Do you feel faint, Adela?' asked Miss Derek, who tended her with loving indignation.

'I never feel anything else, Nancy. I shall get through, but it's awful, awful.'

This led to the first of a series of scenes. Her friends began to fuss around her, and the Major called out, 'I must have better arrangements than this made for my patient; why isn't she given a seat on the platform? She gets no air.'

Mr Das looked annoyed and said: 'I shall be happy to accommodate Miss Quested with a chair up here in view of the particular circumstances of her health.' The chuprassies passed up not one chair but several, and the entire party followed Adela on to the platform, Mr Fielding being the only European who remained in the body of the hall.

'That's better,' remarked Mrs Turton, as she settled herself.

'Thoroughly desirable change for several reasons,' replied the Major.

The Magistrate knew that he ought to censure this remark, but did not dare to. Callendar saw that he was afraid, and called out authoritatively, 'Right, McBryde, go ahead now; sorry to have interrupted you.'

'Are you all right yourselves?' asked the Superintendent.

'We shall do, we shall do.'

'Go on, Mr Das, we are not here to disturb you,' said the Collector patronizingly. Indeed, they had not so much disturbed the trial as taken charge of it.

While the prosecution continued, Miss Quested examined the hall—timidly at first, as though it would scorch her eyes. She observed to left and right of the punkah man many a half-known face. Beneath her were gathered all the wreckage of her silly attempt to see India—the people she had met at the Bridge Party, the man and his wife who hadn't sent their carriage, the old man who would lend his car, various servants, villagers, officials, and the prisoner himself. There he sat—strong, neat little Indian with very black hair, and pliant hands. She viewed him without special emotion. Since they last met, she had elevated him into a principle of evil, but now he seemed to be what he had always been—a slight acquaintance. He was negligible, devoid of significance, dry like a bone, and though he was 'guilty' no atmosphere of sin surrounded him. 'I suppose he *is* guilty. Can I possibly have made a mistake?' she thought. For this question still occurred to her intellect, though since Mrs Moore's departure it had ceased to trouble her conscience.

Pleader Mahmoud Ali now arose, and asked with ponderous and ill-judged irony whether his client could be accommodated on the platform too: even Indians felt unwell sometimes, though naturally Major Callendar did not think so, being in charge of a Government Hospital. 'Another example of their exquisite sense of humour,' sang Miss Derek. Ronny looked at Mr Das to see how he would handle the difficulty, and Mr Das became agitated, and snubbed Pleader Mahmoud Ali severely.

'Excuse me—' It was the turn of the eminent barrister from Calcutta. He was a fine-looking man, large and bony, with grey closely cropped hair. 'We object to the presence of so many European ladies and gentlemen upon the platform,' he said in an Oxford voice. 'They will have the effect of intimidating our witnesses. Their place is with the rest of the public in the body of the hall. We have no objection to Miss Quested remaining on the platform, since she has been unwell; we shall extend every courtesy to her throughout, despite the scientific truths revealed to us by the District Superintendent of Police; but we do object to the others.'

'Oh, cut the cackle and let's have the verdict,' the Major growled.

The distinguished visitor gazed at the Magistrate respectfully.

'I agree to that,' said Mr Das, hiding his face desperately in some papers. 'It was only to Miss Quested that I gave permission to sit up here. Her friends should be so excessively kind as to climb down.'

'Well done, Das, quite sound,' said Ronny with devastating honesty.

'Climb down, indeed, what incredible impertinence!' Mrs Turton cried.

'Do come quietly, Mary,' murmured her husband.

'Hi! my patient can't be left unattended.'

'Do you object to the Civil Surgeon remaining, Mr Amritrao?'

'I should object. A platform confers authority.'

'Even when it's one foot high; so come along all,' said the Collector, trying to laugh.

'Thank you very much, sir,' said Mr Das, greatly relieved. 'Thank you, Mr Heaslop; thank you ladies all.'

And the party, including Miss Quested, descended from its rash eminence. The news of their humiliation spread quickly, and people jeered outside. Their special chairs followed them. Mahmoud Ali (who was quite silly and useless with hatred) objected even to these; by whose authority had special chairs been introduced, why had the Nawab Bahadur not been given one? etc. People began to talk all over the room, about chairs ordinary and special, strips of carpet, platforms one foot high.

But the little excursion had a good effect on Miss Quested's nerves. She felt easier now that she had seen all the people who were in the room. It was like knowing the worst. She was sure now that she should come through 'all right'—that is to say, without spiritual disgrace, and she passed the good news on to Ronny and Mrs Turton. They were too much agitated with the defeat to British prestige to be interested. From where she sat, she could see the renegade Mr Fielding. She had had a better view of him from the platform, and knew that an Indian child perched on his knee. He was watching the proceedings, watching her. When their eyes met, he turned his away, as if direct intercourse was of no interest to him.

The Magistrate was also happier. He had won the battle of the platform, and gained confidence. Intelligent and impartial, he continued to listen to the evidence, and tried to forget that later on he should have to pronounce a verdict in accordance with it. The Superintendent trundled steadily forward: he had expected these outbursts of insolence—they are the natural gestures of an inferior race, and he betrayed no hatred of Aziz, merely an abysmal contempt.

The speech dealt at length with the 'prisoner's dupes,' as they were called—Fielding, the servant Antony, the Nawab Bahadur. This aspect of the case had always seemed dubious to Miss Quested, and she had asked the police not to develop it. But they were playing for a heavy sentence, and wanted to prove that the assault was premeditated. And in order to illustrate the strategy, they produced a plan of the Marabar Hills, showing the route that the party had taken, and the 'Tank of the Dagger' where they had camped.

The Magistrate displayed interest in archaeology.

An elevation of a specimen cave was produced; it was lettered 'Buddhist Cave.'

'Not Buddhist, I think, Jain. . . .'

'In which cave is the offence alleged, the Buddhist or the Jain?' asked Mahmoud Ali, with the air of unmasking a conspiracy.

'All the Marabar caves are Jain.'

'Yes, sir; then in which Jain cave?'

'You will have an opportunity of putting such questions later.'

Mr McBryde smiled faintly at their fatuity. Indians invariably collapse over some such point as this. He knew that the defence had some wild hope of establishing an alibi, that they had tried (unsuccessfully) to identify the guide, and that Fielding and Hamidullah had gone out to the Kawa Dol and paced and measured all one moonlit night. 'Mr Lesley says they're Buddhist, and he ought to know if anyone does. But may I call attention to the shape?' And he described what had occurred there. Then he spoke of Miss Derek's arrival, of the scramble down the gully, of the return of the two ladies to Chandrapore, and of the document Miss Quested signed on her arrival, in which mention was made of the field-glasses. And then came the culminating evidence: the discovery of the field-glasses on the prisoner. 'I have nothing to add at present,' he concluded, removing his spectacles. 'I will now call my witnesses. The facts will speak for themselves. The prisoner is one of those individuals who have led a double life. I dare say his degeneracy gained upon him gradually. He has been very cunning at concealing, as is usual with the type, and pretending to be a respectable member of society, getting a Government position even. He is now entirely vicious and beyond redemption, I am afraid. He behaved most cruelly, most brutally, to another of his guests, another English lady. In order to get rid of her, and leave him free for his crime, he crushed her into a cave among his servants. However, that is by the way.'

But his last words brought on another storm, and suddenly a new name, Mrs Moore, burst on the court like a whirlwind. Mahmoud Ali had been enraged, his nerves snapped; he shrieked like a maniac, and asked whether his client was charged with murder as well as rape, and who was this second English lady.

'I don't propose to call her.'

'You don't because you can't, you have smuggled her out of the country; she is Mrs Moore, she would have proved his innocence, she was on our side, she was poor Indians' friend.'

'You could have called her yourself,' cried the Magistrate. 'Neither side called her, neither must quote her as evidence.'

'She was kept from us until too late—I learn too late—this is English justice, here is your British Raj. Give us back Mrs Moore for five minutes only, and she will save my friend, she will save the name of his sons; don't rule her out, Mr Das; take back those words as you yourself are a father; tell me where they have put her, oh, Mrs Moore. . . .'

'If the point is of any interest, my mother should have reached Aden,' said Ronny dryly; he ought not to have intervened, but the onslaught had startled him.

'Imprisoned by you there because she knew the truth.' He was almost out of his mind, and could be heard saying above the tumult: 'I ruin my career, no matter; we are all to be ruined one by one.'

'This is no way to defend your case,' counselled the Magistrate.

'I am not defending a case, nor are you trying one. We are both of us slaves.'

'Mr Mahmoud Ali, I have already warned you, and unless you sit down I shall exercise my authority.'

'Do so; this trial is a farce, I am going.' And he handed his papers to Amritrao and left, calling from the door histrionically yet with intense passion, 'Aziz, Aziz—farewell for ever.' The tumult increased, the invocation of Mrs Moore continued, and people who did not know what the syllables meant repeated them like a charm. They became Indianized into Esmiss Esmoor, they were taken up in the street outside. In vain the Magistrate threatened and expelled. Until the magic exhausted itself, he was powerless.

'Unexpected,' remarked Mr Turton.

Ronny furnished the explanation. Before she sailed, his mother had taken to talk about the Marabar in her sleep, especially in the afternoon when servants were on the verandah, and her disjointed remarks on Aziz had doubtless been sold to Mahmoud Ali for a few annas: that kind of thing never ceases in the East.

'I thought they'd try something of the sort. Ingenious.' He looked into their wide-open mouths. 'They get just like over their religion,' he added calmly. 'Start and can't stop. I'm sorry for your old Das, he's not getting much of a show.'

'Mr Heaslop, how disgraceful dragging in your dear mother,' said Miss Derek, bending forward.

'It's just a trick, and they happened to pull it off. Now one sees why they had Mahmoud Ali—just to make a scene on the chance. It is his speciality.' But he disliked it more than he showed. It was revolting to hear his mother travestied into Esmiss Esmoor, a Hindu goddess.

Esmiss Esmoor
Esmiss Esmoor
Esmiss Esmoor
Esmiss Esmoor. . . .

'Ronny—'
'Yes, old girl?'

'Isn't it all queer.'

'I'm afraid it's very upsetting for you.'

'Not the least. I don't mind it.'

'Well, that's good.'

She had spoken more naturally and healthily than usual. Bending into the middle of her friends, she said: 'Don't worry about me, I'm much better than I was; I don't feel the least faint; I shall be all right, and thank you all, thank you, thank you for your kindness.' She had to shout her gratitude, for the chant, Esmiss Esmoor, went on.

Suddenly it stopped. It was as if the prayer had been heard, and the relics exhibited. 'I apologize for my colleague,' said Mr Amritrao, rather to everyone's surprise. 'He is an intimate friend of our client, and his feelings have carried him away.'

'Mr Mahmoud Ali will have to apologize in person,' the Magistrate said.

'Exactly, sir, he must. But we had just learnt that Mrs Moore had important evidence which she desired to give. She was hurried out of the country by her son before she could give it; and this unhinged Mr Mahmoud Ali—coming as it does upon an attempt to intimidate our only other European witness, Mr Fielding. Mr Mahmoud Ali would have said nothing had not Mrs Moore been claimed as a witness by the police.' He sat down.

'An extraneous element is being introduced into the case,' said the Magistrate. 'I must repeat that as a witness Mrs Moore does not exist. Neither you, Mr Amritrao, nor, Mr McBryde, you, have any right to surmise what that lady would have said. She is not here, and consequently she can say nothing.'

'Well, I withdraw my reference,' said the Superintendent wearily. 'I would have done so fifteen minutes ago if I had been given the chance. She is not of the least importance to me.'

'I have already withdrawn it for the defence.' He added with forensic humour: 'Perhaps you can persuade the gentlemen outside to withdraw it too,' for the refrain in the street continued.

'I am afraid my powers do not extend so far,' said Das, smiling.

So peace was restored, and when Adela came to give her evidence the atmosphere was quieter than it had been since the beginning of the trial. Experts were not surprised. There is no stay in your native. He blazes up over a minor point, and has nothing left for the crisis. What he seeks is a grievance, and this he had found in the supposed abduction of an old lady. He would now be less aggrieved when Aziz was deported.

But the crisis was still to come.

Adela had always meant to tell the truth and nothing but the truth, and she had rehearsed this as a difficult task—difficult, because her disaster in the cave was connected, though by a thread, with another part of her life, her engagement to Ronny. She had thought of love just before she went in, and had innocently asked Aziz what marriage was like, and she supposed that her question had roused evil in him. To recount this would have been incredibly painful, it was the one point she wanted to keep obscure; she was willing to give details that would have distressed other girls, but this story of her private failure she dared not allude to, and she dreaded being examined in public in case something came out. But as soon as she rose to reply, and heard the sound of her own voice, she feared not even that. A new and unknown sensation protected her, like magnificent armour. She didn't think what had happened, or even remember in the ordinary way of memory, but she returned to the Marabar Hills, and spoke from them across a sort of darkness to Mr McBryde. The fatal day recurred, in every detail, but now she was of it and not of it at the same time, and this double relation gave it indescribable splendour. Why had she thought the expedition 'dull'? Now the sun rose again, the elephant waited, the pale masses of the rock flowed round her and presented the first cave; she entered, and a match was reflected in the polished walls–all beautiful and significant, though she had been blind to it at the time. Questions were asked, and to each she found the exact reply; yes, she had noticed the 'Tank of the Dagger,' but not known its name; yes, Mrs Moore had been tired after the first cave and sat in the shadow of a great rock, near the dried-up mud. Smoothly the voice in the distance proceeded, leading along the paths of truth, and the airs from the punkah behind her wafted her on. . . .

'. . . the prisoner and the guide took you on to the Kawa Dol, no one else being present?'

'The most wonderfully shaped of those hills. Yes.' As she spoke, she created the Kawa Dol, saw the niches up the curve of the stone, and felt the heat strike her face. And something caused her to add: 'No one else was present to my knowledge. We appeared to be alone.'

'Very well, there is a ledge half-way up the hill, or broken ground rather, with caves scattered near the beginning of a nullah.'

'I know where you mean.'

'You went alone into one of those caves?'

'That is quite correct.'

'And the prisoner followed you.'

'Now we've got 'im,' from the Major.

She was silent. The court, the place of question, awaited her reply. But she could not give it until Aziz entered the place of answer.

'The prisoner followed you, didn't he?' he repeated in the monotonous tones that they both used; they were employing agreed words throughout, so that this part of the proceedings held no surprises.

'May I have half a minute before I reply to that, Mr McBryde?'

'Certainly.'

Her vision was of several caves. She saw herself in one, and she was also outside it, watching its entrance, for Aziz to pass in. She failed to locate him. It was the doubt that had often visited her, but solid and attractive, like the hills, 'I am not—' Speech was more difficult than vision. 'I am not quite sure.'

'I beg your pardon?' said the Superintendent of Police.

'I cannot be sure . . .'

'I didn't catch that answer.' He looked scared, his mouth shut with a snap. 'You are on that landing, or whatever we term it, and you have entered a cave. I suggest to you that the prisoner followed you.'

She shook her head.

'What do you mean, please?'

'No,' she said in a flat, unattractive voice. Slight noises began in various parts of the room, but no one yet understood what was occurring except Fielding. He saw that she was going to have a nervous breakdown and that his friend was saved.

'What is that, what are you saying? Speak up, please.' The Magistrate bent forward.

'I'm afraid I have made a mistake.'

'What nature of mistake?'

'Dr Aziz never followed me into the cave.'

The Superintendent slammed down his papers, then picked them up and said calmly: 'Now, Miss Quested, let us go on. I will read you the words of the deposition which you signed two hours later in my bungalow.'

'Excuse me, Mr McBryde, you cannot go on. I am speaking to the witness myself. And the public will be silent. If it continues to talk, I have the court cleared. Miss Quested, address your remarks to me, who am the Magistrate in charge of the case, and realize their extreme gravity. Remember you speak on oath, Miss Quested.'

'Dr Aziz never—'

'I stop these proceedings on medical grounds,' cried the Major on a word from Turton, and all the English rose from their chairs at once, large white figures behind which the little magistrate was hidden. The Indians rose too, hundreds of things went on at once, so that afterwards each person gave a different account of the catastrophe.

'You withdraw the charge? Answer me,' shrieked the representative of Justice.

Something that she did not understand took hold of the girl and pulled her through. Though the vision was over, and she had returned to the insipidity of the world, she remembered what she had learnt. Atonement and confession—they could wait. It was in hard prosaic tones that she said, 'I withdraw everything.'

'Enough—sit down. Mr McBryde, do you wish to continue in the face of this?'

The Superintendent gazed at his witness as if she was a broken machine, and said, 'Are you mad?'

'Don't question her, sir; you have no longer the right.'

'Give me time to consider—'

'Sahib, you will have to withdraw; this becomes a scandal,' boomed the Nawab Bahadur suddenly from the back of the court.

'He shall not,' shouted Mrs Turton against the gathering tumult. 'Call the other witnesses; we're none of us safe—' Ronny tried to check her, and she gave him an irritable blow, then screamed insults at Adela.

The Superintendent moved to the support of his friends, saying nonchalantly to the Magistrate as he did so, 'Right, I withdraw.'

Mr Das rose, nearly dead with the strain. He had controlled the case, just controlled it. He had shown that an Indian can preside. To those who could hear him he said, 'The prisoner is released without one stain on his character; the question of costs will be decided elsewhere.'

And then the flimsy framework of the court broke up, the shouts of derision and rage culminated, people screamed and cursed, kissed one another, wept passionately. Here were the English, whom their servants protected, there Aziz fainted in Hamidullah's arms. Victory on this side, defeat on that—complete for one moment was the antithesis. Then life returned to its complexities, person after person struggled out of the room to their various purposes, and before long no one remained on the scene of the fantasy but the beautiful naked god. Unaware that anything unusual had occurred, he continued to pull the cord of his punkah, to gaze at the empty dais and the overturned special chairs, and rhythmically to agitate the clouds of descending dust.

Chapter Twenty-five

Miss Quested had renounced her own people. Turning from them, she was drawn into a mass of Indians of the shopkeeping class, and carried by them towards the public exit of the court. The faint, indescribable smell of the bazaars invaded her, sweeter than a London slum, yet more disquieting: a tuft of scented cotton wool, wedged in an old man's ear, fragments of pan between his black teeth, odorous powders, oils—the Scented East of tradition, but blended with human sweat as if a great king had been entangled in ignominy and could not free himself, or as if the heat of the sun had boiled and fried all the glories of the earth into a single mess. They paid no attention to her. They shook hands over her shoulder, shouted through her body—for when the Indian does ignore his rulers, he becomes genuinely unaware of their existence. Without part in the universe she had created, she was flung against Mr Fielding.

'What do you want here?'

Knowing him for her enemy, she passed on into the sunlight without speaking.

He called after her, 'Where are you going, Miss Quested?'

'I don't know.'

'You can't wander about like that. Where's the car you came in?'

'I shall walk.'

'What madness . . . there's supposed to be a riot on . . . the police have struck, no one knows what'll happen next. Why don't you keep to your own people?'

'Ought I to join them?' she said, without emotion. She felt emptied, valueless; there was no more virtue in her.

'You can't, it's too late. How are you to get round to the private entrance now? Come this way with me—quick—I'll put you into my carriage.'

'Cyril, Cyril, don't leave me,' called the shattered voice of Aziz.

'I'm coming back. . . . This way, and don't argue.' He gripped her arm. 'Excuse manners, but I don't know anyone's position. Send my carriage back any time to-morrow, if you please.'

'But where am I to go in it?'

'Where you like. How should I know your arrangements?'

The victoria was safe in a quiet side lane, but there were no horses, for the sais, not expecting the trial would end so abruptly, had led them away to visit a friend. She got into it obediently. The man could not leave her, for the confusion increased, and spots of it sounded fanatical. The main road through the bazaars was blocked, and the English were gaining the civil station by by-ways; they were caught like caterpillars, and could have been killed off easily.

'What—what have you been doing?' he cried suddenly. 'Playing a game, studying life, or what?'

'Sir, I intend these for you, sir,' interrupted a student, running down the lane with a garland of jasmine on his arm.

'I don't want the rubbish; get out.'

'Sir, I am a horse, we shall be your horses,' another cried as he lifted the shafts of the victoria into the air.

'Fetch my sais, Rafi; there's a good chap.'

'No, sir, this is an honour for us.'

Fielding wearied of his students. The more they honoured him the less they obeyed. They lassoed him with jasmine and roses, scratched the splash-board against a wall, and recited a poem, the noise of which filled the lane with a crowd.

'Hurry up, sir; we pull you in a procession.' And, half affectionate, half impudent, they bundled him in.

'I don't know whether this suits you, but anyhow you're safe,' he remarked. The carriage jerked into the main bazaar, where it created some sensation. Miss Quested was so loathed in Chandrapore that her recantation was discredited, and the rumour ran that she had been stricken by the Deity in the middle of her lies. But they cheered when they saw her sitting by the heroic Principal (some addressed her as Mrs Moore!), and they garlanded her to match him. Half gods, half guys, with sausages of flowers round their necks, the pair were dragged in the wake of Aziz' victorious landau. In the applause that greeted them some derision mingled. The English always stick together! That was the criticism. Nor was it unjust. Fielding shared it himself, and knew that if some misunderstanding occurred, and an attack was made on the girl by his allies, he would be obliged to die in her defence. He didn't want to die for her, he wanted to be rejoicing with Aziz.

Where was the procession going? To friends, to enemies, to Aziz' bungalow, to the Collector's bungalow, to the Minto Hospital where the Civil Surgeon would eat dust and the patients (confused with prisoners) be released, to Delhi, Simla. The students thought it was going to Government College. When they reached a turning, they twisted the victoria to the right, ran it by side lanes down a hill and through a garden gate into the mango plantation, and, as far as Fielding and Miss Quested were concerned, all was peace and quiet. The trees were full of glossy foliage and slim green fruit, the tank slumbered; and beyond it rose the exquisite blue arches of the garden-house. 'Sir, we fetch the others; sir, it is a somewhat heavy load for our arms,' were heard. Fielding took the refugee to his office, and tried to telephone to McBryde. But this he could not do; the wires had been cut. All his servants had decamped. Once more he was unable to desert her. He assigned her a couple of rooms, provided her with ice and drinks and biscuits, advised her to lie down, and lay down himself—there was nothing else to do. He felt restless and thwarted as he listened to the retreating sounds of the procession, and his joy was rather spoilt by bewilderment. It was a victory, but such a queer one.

At that moment Aziz was crying, 'Cyril, Cyril . . .' Crammed into a carriage with the Nawab Bahadur, Hamidullah, Mahmoud Ali, his own little boys, and a heap of flowers, he was not content; he wanted to be surrounded by all who loved him. Victory gave no pleasure, he had suffered too much. From the moment of his arrest he was done for, he had dropped like a wounded animal; he had despaired, not through cowardice, but because he knew that an Englishwoman's word would always outweigh his own. 'It is fate,' he said; and, 'It is fate,' when he was imprisoned anew after Mohurram. All that existed, in that terrible time, was affection, and affection was all that he felt in the first painful moments of his freedom. 'Why isn't Cyril following? Let us turn back.' But the procession could not turn back. Like a snake in a drain, it advanced down the narrow bazaar towards the basin of the Maidan, where it would turn about itself, and decide on its prey.

'Forward, forward,' shrieked Mahmoud Ali, whose every utterance had become a yell. 'Down with the Collector, down with the Superintendent of Police.'

'Mr Mahmoud Ali, this is not wise,' implored the Nawab Bahadur: he knew that nothing was gained by attacking the English, who had fallen into their own pit and had better be left there; moreover, he had great possessions and deprecated anarchy.

'Cyril, again you desert,' cried Aziz.

'Yet some orderly demonstration is necessary,' said Hamidullah, 'otherwise they will still think we are afraid.'

'Down with the Civil Surgeon . . . rescue Nureddin.'

'Nurredin?'

'They are torturing him.'

'Oh, my God . . .'—for this, too, was a friend.

'They are not. I will not have my grandson made an excuse for an attack on the hospital,' the old man protested.

'They are. Callendar boasted so before the trial. I heard through the tatties; he said, "I have tortured that nigger."'

'Oh, my God, my God. . . . He called him a nigger, did he?'

'They put pepper instead of antiseptic on the wounds.'

'Mr Mahmoud Ali, impossible; a little roughness will not hurt the boy, he needs discipline.'

'Pepper. Civil Surgeon said so. They hope to destroy us one by one; they shall fail.'

The new injury lashed the crowd to fury. It had been aimless hitherto, and had lacked a grievance. When they reached the Maidan and saw the sallow arcades of the Minto they shambled towards it howling. It was near midday. The earth and sky were insanely ugly, the spirit of evil again strode abroad. The Nawab Bahadur alone struggled against it, and told himself that the rumour must be untrue. He had seen his grandson in the ward only last week. But he too was carried forward over the new precipice. To rescue, to maltreat Major Callendar in revenge, and then was to come the turn of the civil station generally.

But disaster was averted, and averted by Dr Panna Lal.

Dr Panna Lal had offered to give evidence for the prosecution in the hope of pleasing the English, also because he hated Aziz. When the case broke down, he was in a very painful position. He saw the crash coming sooner than most people, slipped from the court before Mr Das had finished, and drove Dapple off through the bazaars, in flight from the wrath to come. In the hospital he should be safe, for Major Callendar would protect him. But the Major had not come, and now things were worse than ever, for here was a mob, entirely desirous of his blood, and the orderlies were mutinous and would not help him over the back wall, or rather hoisted him and let him drop back, to the satisfaction of the patients. In agony he cried, 'Man can but die the once,' and waddled across the compound to meet the invasion, salaaming with one hand and holding up a pale yellow umbrella in the other. 'Oh, forgive me,' he whined as he approached the victorious landau. 'Oh, Dr Aziz, forgive the wicked lies I told.' Aziz was silent, the others thickened their throats and threw up their chins in token of scorn. 'I was afraid, I was mislaid,' the suppliant continued. 'I was mislaid here, there, and everywhere as regards your character. Oh, forgive the poor old hakim who gave you milk when ill! Oh, Nawab Bahadur, whoever merciful, is it my poor little dispensary you require? Take every cursed bottle.' Agitated, but alert, he saw them smile at his indifferent English, and suddenly he started playing the buffoon, flung down his umbrella, trod through it, and struck himself upon the nose. He knew what he was doing, and so did they. There was nothing pathetic or eternal in the degradation of such a man. Of ignoble origin, Dr Panna Lal possessed nothing that could be disgraced, and he wisely decided to make the other Indians feel like kings, because it would put them into better tempers. When he found they wanted Nureddin, he skipped like a goat, he scuttled like a hen to do their bidding, the hospital was saved, and to the end of his life he could not understand why he had not obtained promotion on the morning's work. 'Promptness, sir, promptness similar to you,' was the argument he employed to Major Callendar when claiming it.

When Nureddin emerged, his face all bandaged, there was a roar of relief as though the Bastille had fallen. It was the crisis of the march, and the Nawab Bahadur managed to get the situation into hand. Embracing the young man publicly, he began a speech about Justice, Courage, Liberty, and

Prudence, ranged under heads, which cooled the passion of the crowd. He further announced that he should give up his British-conferred title, and live as a private gentleman, plain Mr Zulfiqar, for which reason he was instantly proceeding to his country seat. The landau turned, the crowd accompanied it, the crisis was over. The Marabar caves had been a terrible strain on the local administration; they altered a good many lives and wrecked several careers, but they did not break up a continent or even dislocate a district.

'We will have rejoicings to-night,' the old man said. 'Mr Hamidullah, I depute you to bring out our friends Fielding and Amritrao, and to discover whether the latter will require special food. The others will keep with me. We shall not go out to Dilkusha until the cool of the evening, of course. I do not know the feelings of other gentlemen; for my own part, I have a slight headache, and I wish I had thought to ask our good Panna Lal for aspirin.'

For the heat was claiming its own. Unable to madden, it stupefied, and before long most of the Chandrapore combatants were asleep. Those in the civil station kept watch a little, fearing an attack, but presently they too entered the world of dreams—that world in which a third of each man's life is spent, and which is thought by some pessimists to be a premonition of eternity.

Chapter Twenty-six

Evening approached by the time Fielding and Miss Quested met and had the first of their numerous curious conversations. He had hoped, when he woke up, to find someone had fetched her away, but the College remained isolated from the rest of the universe. She asked whether she could have 'a sort of interview,' and, when he made no reply, said, 'Have you any explanation of my extraordinary behaviour?'

'None,' he said curtly. 'Why make such a charge if you were going to withdraw it?'

'Why, indeed.'

'I ought to feel grateful to you, I suppose, but—'

'I don't expect gratitude. I only thought you might care to hear what I have to say.'

'Oh, well,' he grumbled, feeling rather schoolboyish. 'I don't think a discussion between us is desirable. To put it frankly, I belong to the other side in this ghastly affair.'

'Would it not interest you to hear my side?'

'Not much.'

'I shouldn't tell you in confidence, of course. So you can hand on all my remarks to your side, for there is one great mercy that has come out of all to-day's misery: I have no longer any secrets. My echo has gone—I call the buzzing sound in my ears an echo. You see, I have been unwell ever since that expedition to the caves, and possibly before it.'

The remark interested him rather; it was what he had sometimes suspected himself. 'What kind of illness?' he enquired.

She touched her head at the side, then shook it.

'That was my first thought, the day of the arrest: hallucination.'

'Do you think that would be so?' she asked with great humility. 'What should have given me an hallucination?'

'One of three things certainly happened in the Marabar,' he said, getting drawn into a discussion against his will. 'One of four things. Either Aziz is guilty, which is what your friends think; or you invented the charge out of malice, which is what my friends think; or you have had an hallucination. I'm very much inclined'—getting up and striding about—'now that you tell me that you felt unwell before the expedition—it's an important piece of evidence—I believe that you yourself broke the strap of the field-glasses; you were alone in that cave the whole time.'

'Perhaps. . . .'

'Can you remember when you first felt out of sorts?'

'When I came to tea with you there, in that garden-house.'

'A somewhat unlucky party. Aziz and old Godbole were both ill after it too.'

'I was not ill—it is far too vague to mention: it is all mixed up with my private affairs. I enjoyed the singing . . . but just about then a sort of sadness began that I couldn't detect at the time . . . no, nothing as solid as sadness: living at half pressure expresses it best. Half pressure. I remember going on to polo with Mr Heaslop at the Maidan. Various other things happened—it doesn't matter what, but I was under par for all of them. I was certainly in that state when I saw the caves, and you suggest (nothing shocks or hurts me)—you suggest that I had an hallucination there, the sort of thing—though in an awful form—that makes some women think they've had an offer of marriage when none was made.'

'You put it honestly, anyhow.'

'I was brought up to be honest; the trouble is it gets me nowhere.'

Liking her better, he smiled and said, 'It'll get us to heaven.'

'Will it?'

'If heaven existed.'

'Do you not believe in heaven, Mr Fielding, may I ask?' she said, looking at him shyly.

'I do not. Yet I believe that honesty gets us there.'

'How can that be?'

'Let us go back to hallucinations. I was watching you carefully through your evidence this morning, and if I'm right, the hallucination (what you call half pressure—quite as good a word) disappeared suddenly.'

She tried to remember what she had felt in court, but could not; the vision disappeared whenever she wished to interpret it. 'Events presented themselves to me in their logical sequence,' was what she said, but it hadn't been that at all.

'My belief—and of course I was listening carefully, in hope you would make some slip—my belief is that poor McBryde exorcised you. As soon as he asked you a straightforward question, you gave a straightforward answer, and broke down.'

'Exorcise in that sense. I thought you meant I'd seen a ghost.'

'I don't go to that length!'

'People whom I respect very much believe in ghosts,' she said rather sharply. 'My friend Mrs Moore does.'

'She's an old lady.'

'I think you need not be impolite to her, as well as to her son.'

'I did not intend to be rude. I only meant it is difficult, as we get on in life, to resist the supernatural. I've felt it coming on me myself. I still jog on without it, but what a temptation, at forty-five, to pretend that the dead live again; one's own dead; no one else's matter.'

'Because the dead don't live again.'

'I fear not.'

'So do I.'

There was a moment's silence, such as often follows the triumph of rationalism. Then he apologized handsomely enough for his behaviour to Heaslop at the club.

'What does Dr Aziz say of me?' she asked, after another pause.

'He—he has not been capable of thought in his misery, naturally he's very bitter,' said Fielding, a little awkward, because such remarks as Aziz had made were not merely bitter, they were foul. The underlying notion was, 'It disgraces me to have been mentioned in connection with such a hag.' It enraged him that he had been accused by a woman who had no personal beauty; sexually, he was a snob. This had puzzled and worried Fielding. Sensuality, as long as it is straightforward, did not repel him, but this derived sensuality—the sort that classes a mistress among motor-cars if she is beautiful, and among eye-flies if she isn't—was alien to his own emotions, and he felt a barrier between himself and Aziz whenever it arose. It was, in a new form, the old, old trouble that eats the heart out of every civilization: snobbery, the desire for possessions, creditable appendages; and it is to escape this rather than the lusts of the flesh that saints retreat into the Himalayas. To change the subject, he said, 'But let me conclude my analysis. We are agreed that he is not a villain and that you are not one, and we aren't really sure that it was an hallucination. There's a fourth possibility which we must touch on: was it somebody else?'

'The guide.'

'Exactly, the guide. I often think so. Unluckily Aziz hit him on the face, and he got a fright and disappeared. It is most unsatisfactory, and we hadn't the police to help us, the guide was of no interest to them.'

'Perhaps it was the guide,' she said quietly; the question had lost interest for her suddenly.

'Or could it have been one of that gang of Pathans who have been drifting through the district?'

'Someone who was in another cave, and followed me when the guide was looking away? Possibly.'

At that moment Hamidullah joined them, and seemed not too pleased to find them closeted together. Like everyone else in Chandrapore, he could make nothing of Miss Quested's conduct. He had overheard their last remark. 'Hullo, my dear Fielding,' he said. 'So I run you down at last. Can you come out at once to Dilkusha?'

'At once?'

'I hope to leave in a moment, don't let me interrupt,' said Adela.

'The telephone has been broken; Miss Quested can't ring up her friends,' he explained.

'A great deal has been broken, more than will ever be mended,' said the other. 'Still, there should be some way of transporting this lady back to the civil lines. The resources of civilization are numerous.' He spoke without looking at Miss Quested, and he ignored the slight movement she made towards him with her hand.

Fielding, who thought the meeting might as well be friendly, said, 'Miss Quested has been explaining a little about her conduct of this morning.'

'Perhaps the age of miracles has returned. One must be prepared for everything, our philosophers say.'

'It must have seemed a miracle to the onlookers,' said Adela, addressing him nervously. 'The fact is that I realized before it was too late that I had made a mistake, and had just enough presence of mind to say so. That is all my extraordinary conduct amounts to.'

'All it amounts to, indeed,' he retorted, quivering with rage but keeping himself in hand, for he felt she might be setting another trap. 'Speaking as a private individual, in a purely informal conversation, I admired your conduct, and I was delighted when our warm-hearted students garlanded you. But, like Mr Fielding, I am surprised; indeed, surprise is too weak a word. I see you drag my best friend into the dirt, damage his health and ruin his prospects in a way you cannot conceive owing to your ignorance of our society and religion, and then suddenly you get up in the witness-box: "Oh no, Mr McBryde, after all I am not quite sure, you may as well let him go." Am I mad? I keep asking myself. Is it a dream, and if so, when did it start? And without doubt it is a dream that has not yet finished. For I gather you have not done with us yet, and it is now the turn of the poor old guide who conducted you round the caves.'

'Not at all, we were only discussing possibilities,' interposed Fielding.

'An interesting pastime, but a lengthy one. There are one hundred and seventy million Indians in this notable peninsula, and of course one or other of them entered the cave. Of course some Indian is the culprit, we must never doubt that. And since, my dear Fielding, these possibilities will take you some time'—here he put his arm over the Englishman's shoulder and swayed him to and fro gently—'don't you think you had better come out to the Nawab Bahadur's—or I should say to Mr Zulfiqar's, for that is the name he now requires us to call him by.'

'Gladly, in a minute . . .'

'I have just settled my movements,' said Miss Quested. 'I shall go to the Dak Bungalow.'

'Not the Turtons?' said Hamidullah, goggle-eyed. 'I thought you were their guest.'

The Dak Bungalow of Chandrapore was below the average, and certainly servantless. Fielding, though he continued to sway with Hamidullah, was thinking on independent lines, and said in a moment: 'I have a better idea than that, Miss Quested. You must stop here at the College. I shall be away at least two days, and you can have the place entirely to yourself, and make your plans at your convenience.'

'I don't agree at all,' said Hamidullah, with every symptom of dismay. 'The idea is a thoroughly bad one. There may quite well be another demonstration to-night, and suppose an attack is made on the College. You would be held responsible for this lady's safety, my dear fellow.'

'They might equally attack the Dak Bungalow.'

'Exactly, but the responsibility there ceases to be yours.'

'Quite so. I have given trouble enough.'

'Do you hear? The lady admits it herself. It's not an attack from our people I fear—you should see their orderly conduct at the hospital; what we must guard against is an attack secretly arranged by the police for the purpose of discrediting you. McBryde keeps plenty of roughs for this purpose, and this would be the very opportunity for him.'

'Never mind. She is not going to the Dak Bungalow,' said Fielding. He had a natural sympathy for the down-trodden—that was partly why he rallied from Aziz—and had become determined not to leave the poor girl in the lurch. Also, he had a new-born respect for her, consequent on their talk. Although her hard schoolmistressy manner remained, she was no longer examining life, but being examined by it; she had become a real person.

'Then where is she to go? We shall never have done with her!' For Miss Quested had not appealed to Hamidullah. If she had shown emotion in court, broke down, beat her breast, and invoked the name of God, she would have summoned forth his imagination and generosity—he had plenty of both. But while relieving the Oriental mind, she had chilled it, with the result that he could scarcely believe she was sincere, and indeed from his standpoint she was not. For her behaviour rested on cold justice and honesty; she had felt, while she recanted, no passion of love for those whom she had wronged. Truth is not truth in that exacting land unless there go with it kindness and more kindness and kindness again, unless the Word that was with God also is God. And the girl's sacrifice—so creditable according to Western notions—was rightly rejected, because, though it came from her heart, it did not include her heart. A few garlands from students was all that India ever gave her in return.

'But where is she to have her dinner, where is she to sleep? I say here, here, and if she is hit on the head by roughs, she is hit on the head. That is my contribution. Well, Miss Quested?'

'You are very kind. I should have said yes, I think, but I agree with Mr Hamidullah. I must give no more trouble to you. I believe my best plan is to return to the Turtons, and see if they will allow me to sleep, and if they turn me away I must go to the Dak. The Collector would take me in, I know, but

Mrs Turton said this morning that she would never see me again.' She spoke without bitterness, or, as Hamidullah thought, without proper pride. Her aim was to cause the minimum of annoyance.

'Far better stop here than expose yourself to insults from that preposterous woman.'

'Do you find her preposterous? I used to. I don't now.'

'Well, here's our solution,' said the barrister, who had terminated his slightly minatory caress and strolled to the window. 'Here comes the City Magistrate. He comes in a third-class band-ghari for purposes of disguise, he comes unattended, but here comes the City Magistrate.'

'At last,' said Adela sharply, which caused Fielding to glance at her.

'He comes, he comes, he comes. I cringe. I tremble.'

'Will you ask him what he wants, Mr Fielding?'

'He wants you, of course.'

'He may not even know I'm here.'

'I'll see him first, if you prefer.'

When he had gone, Hamidullah said to her bitingly: 'Really, really. Need you have exposed Mr Fielding to this further discomfort? He is far too considerate.' She made no reply, and there was complete silence between them until their host returned.

'He has some news for you,' he said. 'You'll find him on the verandah. He prefers not to come in.'

'Does he tell me to come out to him?'

'Whether he tells you or not, you will go, I think,' said Hamidullah.

She paused, then said, 'Perfectly right,' and then said a few words of thanks to the Principal for his kindness to her during the day.

'Thank goodness, that's over,' he remarked, not escorting her to the verandah, for he held it unnecessary to see Ronny again.

'It was insulting of him not to come in.'

'He couldn't very well after my behaviour to him at the Club. Heaslop doesn't come out badly. Besides, Fate has treated him pretty roughly to-day. He has had a cable to the effect that his mother's dead, poor old soul.'

'Oh, really. Mrs Moore. I'm sorry,' said Hamidullah rather indifferently.

'She died at sea.'

'The heat, I suppose.'

'Presumably.'

'May is no month to allow an old lady to travel in.'

'Quite so. Heaslop ought never to have let her go, and he knows it. Shall we be off?'

'Let us wait until the happy couple leave the compound clear . . . they really are intolerable dawdling there. Ah well, Fielding, you don't believe in Providence, I remember. I do. This is Heaslop's punishment for abducting our witness in order to stop us establishing our alibi.'

'You go rather too far there. The poor old lady's evidence could have had no value, shout and shriek Mahmoud Ali as he will. She couldn't see through the Kawa Dol even if she had wanted to. Only Miss Quested could have saved him.'

'She loved Aziz, he says, also India, and he loved her.'

'Love is of no value in a witness, as a barrister ought to know. But I see there is about to be an Esmiss Esmoor legend at Chandrapore, my dear Hamidullah, and I will not impede its growth.'

The other smiled, and looked at his watch. They both regretted the death, but they were middle-aged men, who had invested their emotions elsewhere, and outbursts of grief could not be expected from them over a slight acquaintance. It's only one's own dead who matter. If for a moment the sense of communion in sorrow came to them, it passed. How indeed is it possible for one human being to be sorry for all the sadness that meets him on the face of the earth, for the pain that is endured not only by men, but by animals and plants, and perhaps by the stones? The soul is tired in a moment, and in fear of losing the little she does understand, she retreats to the permanent lines which habit or chance have dictated, and suffers there. Fielding had met the dead woman only two or three times, Hamidullah had seen her in the distance once, and they were far more occupied with the coming gathering at Dilkusha, the 'victory' dinner, for which they would be most victoriously late. They agreed not to tell Aziz about Mrs Moore till the morrow, because he was fond of her, and the bad news might spoil his fun.

'Oh, this is unbearable!' muttered Hamidullah. For Miss Quested was back again.

'Mr Fielding, has Ronny told you of this new misfortune?'

He bowed.

'Ah me!' She sat down, and seemed to stiffen into a monument.

'Heaslop is waiting for you, I think.'

'I do so long to be alone. She was my best friend, far more to me than to him. I can't bear to be with Ronny ... I can't explain ... Could you do me the very great kindness of letting me stop after all?'

Hamidullah swore violently in the vernacular.

'I should be pleased, but does Mr Heaslop wish it?'

'I didn't ask him, we are too much upset—it's so complex, not like what unhappiness is supposed to be. Each of us ought to be alone, and think. Do come and see Ronny again.'

'I think he should come in this time,' said Fielding, feeling that this much was due to his own dignity. 'Do ask him to come.'

She returned with him. He was half miserable, half arrogant—indeed, a strange mix-up—and broke at once into uneven speech. 'I came to bring Miss Quested away, but her visit to the Turtons has ended, and there is no other arrangement so far, mine are bachelor quarters now—'

Fielding stopped him courteously. 'Say no more, Miss Quested stops here. I only wanted to be assured of your approval. Miss Quested, you had better send for your own servant if he can be found, but I will leave orders with mine to do all they can for you, also I'll let the Scouts know. They have guarded the College ever since it was closed, and may as well go on. I really think you'll be as safe here as anywhere. I shall be back Thursday.'

Meanwhile Hamidullah, determined to spare the enemy no incidental pain, had said to Ronny: 'We hear, sir, that your mother has died. May we ask where the cable came from?'

'Aden.'

'Ah, you were boasting she had reached Aden, in court.'

'But she died on leaving Bombay,' broke in Adela. 'She was dead when they called her name this morning. She must have been buried at sea.'

Somehow this stopped Hamidullah, and he desisted from his brutality, which had shocked Fielding more than anyone else. He remained silent while the details of Miss Quested's occupation of the College were arranged, merely remarking to Ronny, 'It is clearly to be understood, sir, that neither Mr Fielding nor any of us are responsible for this lady's safety at Government College,' to which Ronny agreed. After that, he watched the semi-chivalrous behavings of the three English with quiet amusement; he thought Fielding had been incredibly silly and weak, and he was amazed by the younger people's want of proper pride. When they were driving out to Dilkusha, hours late, he said to Amritrao, who accompanied them: 'Mr Amritrao, have you considered what sum Miss Quested ought to pay as compensation?'

'Twenty thousand rupees.'

No more was then said, but the remark horrified Fielding. He couldn't bear to think of the queer honest girl losing her money and possibly her young man too. She advanced into his consciousness suddenly. And, fatigued by the merciless and enormous day, he lost his usual sane view of human intercourse, and felt that we exist not in ourselves, but in terms of each others' minds—a notion for which logic offers no support and which had attacked him only once before, the evening after the catastrophe, when from the verandah of the club he saw the fists and fingers of the Marabar swell until they included the whole night sky.

Chapter Twenty-seven

'Aziz, are you awake?'

'No, so let us have a talk; let us dream plans for the future.'

'I am useless at dreaming.'

'Good night then, dear fellow.'

The Victory Banquet was over, and the revellers lay on the roof of plain Mr Zulfiqar's mansion, asleep, or gazing through mosquito nets at the stars. Exactly above their heads hung the constellation of the Lion, the disc of Regulus so large and bright that it resembled a tunnel, and when this fancy was accepted all the other stars seemed tunnels too.

'Are you content with our day's work, Cyril?' the voice on his left continued.

'Are you?'

'Except that I ate too much. "How is stomach, how head?"—I say, Panna

Lal and Callendar'll get the sack.'

'There'll be a general move at Chandrapore.'

'And you'll get promotion.'

'They can't well move me down, whatever their feelings.'

'In any case we spend our holidays together, and visit Kashmir, possibly Persia, for I shall have plenty of money. Paid to me on account of the injury sustained by my character,' he explained with cynical calm. 'While with me you shall never spend a single pie. This is what I have always wished, and as the result of my misfortunes it has come.'

'You have won a great victory . . .' began Fielding.

'I know, my dear chap, I know; your voice need not become so solemn and anxious. I know what you are going to say next: Let, oh let Miss Quested off paying, so that the English may say, "Here is a native who has actually behaved like a gentleman; if it was not for his black face we would almost allow him to join our club." The approval of your compatriots no longer interests me, I have become anti-British, and ought to have done so sooner, it would have saved me numerous misfortunes.'

'Including knowing me.'

'I say, shall we go and pour water on to Mohammed Latif's face? He is so funny when this is done to him asleep.'

The remark was not a question but a full-stop. Fielding accepted it as such and there was a pause, pleasantly filled by a little wind which managed to brush the top of the house. The banquet, though riotous, had been agreeable, and now the blessings of leisure—unknown to the West, which either works or idles—descended on the motley company. Civilization strays about like a ghost here, revisiting the ruins of empire, and is to be found not in great works of art or mighty deeds, but in the gestures well-bred Indians make when they sit or lie down. Fielding, who had dressed up in native costume, learnt from his excessive awkwardness in it that all his motions were makeshifts, whereas when the Nawab Bahadur stretched out his hand for food or Nureddin applauded a song, something beautiful had been accomplished which needed no development. This restfulness of gesture—it is the Peace that passeth Understanding, after all, it is the social equivalent of Yoga. When the whirring of action ceases, it becomes visible, and reveals a civilization which the West can disturb but will never acquire. The hand stretches out for ever, the lifted knee has the eternity though not the sadness of the grave. Aziz was full of civilization this evening, complete, dignified, rather hard, and it was with diffidence that the other said: 'Yes, certainly you must let off Miss Quested easily. She must pay all your costs, that is only fair, but do not treat her like a conquered enemy.'

'Is she wealthy? I depute you to find out.'

'The sums mentioned at dinner when you all got so excited—they would ruin her, they are perfectly preposterous. Look here . . .'

'I am looking, though it gets a bit dark. I see Cyril Fielding to be a very nice chap indeed and my best friend, but in some ways a fool. You think that by letting Miss Quested off easily I shall make a better reputation for myself and Indians generally. No, no. It will be put down to weakness and the attempt to gain promotion officially. I have decided to have nothing more to do with British India, as a matter of fact. I shall seek service in some Moslem State, such as Hyderabad, Bhopal, where Englishmen cannot insult me any more. Don't counsel me otherwise.'

'In the course of a long talk with Miss Quested . . .'

'I don't want to hear your long talks.'

'Be quiet. In the course of a long talk with Miss Quested I have begun to understand her character. It's not an easy one, she being a prig. But she is perfectly genuine and very brave. When she saw she was wrong, she pulled herself up with a jerk and said so. I want you to realize what that means. All her friends around her, the entire British Raj pushing her forward. She stops, sends the whole thing to smithereens. In her place I should have funked it. But she stopped, and almost did she become a national heroine, but my students ran us down a side street before the crowd caught flame. Do treat her considerately. She really mustn't get the worst of both worlds. I know what all these'—he indicated the shroud 'will want, but you mustn't listen to them. Be merciful. Act like one of your six Mogul Emperors, or all the six rolled into one.'

'Not even Mogul Emperors showed mercy until they received an apology.'

'She'll apologize if that's the trouble,' he cried, sitting up. 'Look, I'll make you an offer. Dictate to me whatever form of words you like, and this time tomorrow I'll bring it back signed. This is not instead of any public apology she may make you in law. It's an addition.'

' "Dear Dr Aziz, I wish you had come into the cave; I am an awful old hag, and it is my last chance." Will she sign that?'

'Well good night, good night, it's time to go to sleep, after that.'

'Good night, I suppose it is.'

'Oh, I wish you wouldn't make that kind of remark,' he continued after a pause. 'It is the one thing in you I can't put up with.'

'I put up with all things in you, so what is to be done?'

'Well, you hurt me by saying it; good night.'

There was silence, then dreamily but with deep feeling the voice said: 'Cyril, I have had an idea which will satisfy your tender mind: I shall consult Mrs Moore.'

Opening his eyes, and beholding thousands of stars, he could not reply, they silenced him.

'Her opinion will solve everything; I can trust her so absolutely. If she advises me to pardon this girl, I shall do so. She will counsel me nothing against my real and true honour, as you might.'

'Let us discuss that to-morrow morning.'

'Is it not strange? I keep on forgetting she has left India. During the shouting of her name in court I fancied she was present. I had shut my eyes, I confused myself on purpose to deaden the pain. Now this very instant I forgot again. I shall be obliged to write. She is now far away, well on her way towards Ralph and Stella.'

'To whom?'

'To those other children.'

'I have not heard of other children.'

'Just as I have two boys and a girl, so has Mrs Moore. She told me in the mosque.'

'I knew her so slightly.'

'I have seen her but three times, but I know she is an Oriental.'

'You are so fantastic. . . . Miss Quested, you won't treat her generously; while over Mrs Moore there is this elaborate chivalry. Miss Quested anyhow behaved decently this morning, whereas the old lady never did anything for you at all, and it's pure conjecture that she would have come forward in your favour, it only rests on servants' gossip. Your emotions never seem in proportion to their objects, Aziz.'

'Is emotion a sack of potatoes, so much the pound, to be measured out? Am I a machine? I shall be told I can use up my emotions by using them, next.'

'I should have thought you could. It sounds common sense. You can't eat your cake and have it, even in the world of the spirit.'

'If you are right, there is no point in any friendship; it all comes down to give and take, or give and return, which is disgusting, and we had better all leap over this parapet and kill ourselves. Is anything wrong with you this evening that you grow so materialistic?'

'Your unfairness is worse than my materialism.'

'I see. Anything further to complain of?' He was good-tempered and affectionate but a little formidable. Imprisonment had made channels for his character, which would never fluctuate as widely now as in the past. 'Because it is far better you put all your difficulties before me, if we are to be friends for ever. You do not like Mrs Moore, and are annoyed because I do; however, you will like her in time.'

When a person, really dead, is supposed to be alive, an unhealthiness infects the conversation. Fielding could not stand the tension any longer and blurted out: 'I'm sorry to say Mrs Moore's dead.'

But Hamidullah, who had been listening to all their talk, and did not want the festive evening spoilt, cried from the adjoining bed: 'Aziz, he is trying to pull your leg; don't believe him, the villain.'

'I do not believe him,' said Aziz; he was inured to practical jokes, even of this type.

Fielding said no more. Facts are facts, and everyone would learn of Mrs Moore's death in the morning. But it struck him that people are not really dead until they are felt to be dead. As long as there is some misunderstanding about them, they possess a sort of immortality. An experience of his own confirmed this. Many years ago he had lost a great friend, a woman, who believed in the Christian heaven, and assured him that after the changes and chances of this mortal life they would meet in it again. Fielding was a blank, frank atheist, but he respected every opinion his friend held: to do this is essential in friendship. And it seemed to him for a time that the dead awaited him, and when the illusion faded it left behind it an emptiness that was almost guilt: 'This really is the end,' he thought, 'and I gave her the final blow.' He had tried to kill Mrs Moore this evening, on the roof of the Nawab

Bahadur's house; but she still eluded him, and the atmosphere remained tranquil. Presently the moon rose—the exhausted crescent that precedes the sun—and shortly after men and oxen began their interminable labour, and the gracious interlude, which he had tried to curtail, came to its natural conclusion.

Chapter Twenty-eight

Dead she was—committed to the deep while still on the southward track, for the boats from Bombay cannot point towards Europe until Arabia has been rounded; she was further in the tropics than ever achieved while on shore, when the sun touched her for the last time and her body was lowered into yet another India—the Indian Ocean. She left behind her sore discomfort, for a death gives a ship a bad name. Who was this Mrs Moore? When Aden was reached, Lady Mellanby cabled, wrote, did all that was kind, but the wife of a Lieutenant-Governor does not bargain for such an experience; and she repeated: 'I had only seen the poor creature for a few hours when she was taken ill; really this has been needlessly distressing, it spoils one's home-coming.' A ghost followed the ship up the Red Sea, but failed to enter the Mediterranean. Somewhere about Suez there is always a social change: the arrangements of Asia weaken and those of Europe begin to be felt, and during the transition Mrs Moore was shaken off. At Port Said the grey blustery north began. The weather was so cold and bracing that the passengers felt it must have broken in the land they had left, but it became hotter steadily there in accordance with its usual law.

The death took subtler and more lasting shapes in Chandrapore. A legend sprang up that an Englishman had killed his mother for trying to save an Indian's life—and there was just enough truth in this to cause annoyance to the authorities. Sometimes it was a cow that had been killed—or a crocodile with the tusks of a boar had crawled out of the Ganges. Nonsense of this type is more difficult to combat than a solid lie. It hides in rubbish heaps and moves when no one is looking. At one period two distinct tombs containing Esmiss Esmoor's remains were reported: one by the tannery, the other up near the goods station. Mr McBryde visited them both and saw signs of the beginning of a cult—earthenware saucers and so on. Being an experienced official, he did nothing to irritate it, and after a week or so, the rash died down. 'There's propaganda behind all this,' he said, forgetting that a hundred years ago, when Europeans still made their home in the country-side and appealed to its imagination, they occasionally became local demons after death—not a whole god, perhaps, but part of one, adding an epithet or gesture to what already existed, just as the gods contribute to the great gods, and they to the philosophic Brahm.

Ronny reminded himself that his mother had left India at her own wish, but his conscience was not clear. He had behaved badly to her, and he had either to repent (which involved a mental overturn), or to persist in unkindness towards her. He chose the latter course. How tiresome she had been with her patronage of Aziz! What a bad influence upon Adela! And now she still gave trouble with ridiculous 'tombs,' mixing herself up with natives. She could not help it, of course, but she had attempted similar exasperating expeditions in her lifetime, and he reckoned it against her. The young man had much to worry him–the heat, the local tension, the approaching visit of the Lieutenant-Governor, the problems of Adela–and threading them all together into a grotesque garland were these Indianizations of Mrs Moore. What does happen to one's mother when she dies? Presumably she goes to heaven, anyhow she clears out. Ronny's religion was of the sterilized Public School brand, which never goes bad, even in the tropics. Wherever he entered, mosque, cave, or temple, he retained the spiritual outlook of the Fifth Form, and condemned as 'weakening' any attempt to understand them. Pulling himself together, he dismissed the mater from his mind. In due time he and his half-brother and -sister would put up a tablet to her in the Northamptonshire church where she had worshipped, recording the dates of her birth and death and the fact that she had been buried at sea. This would be sufficient.

And Adela–she would have to depart too; he hoped she would have made the suggestion herself ere now. He really could not marry her–it would mean the end of his career. Poor lamentable Adela. . . . She remained at Government College, by Fielding's courtesy–unsuitable and humiliating, but no one would receive her at the civil station. He postponed all private talk until the award against her was decided. Aziz was suing her for damages in the sub-judge's court. Then he would ask her to release him. She had killed his love, and it had never been very robust; they would never have achieved betrothal but for the accident to the Nawab Bahadur's car. She belonged to the callow academic period of his life which he had out-grown–Grasmere, serious talks and walks, that sort of thing.

Chapter Twenty-nine

The visit of the Lieutenant-Governor of the Province formed the next stage in the decomposition of the Marabar. Sir Gilbert, though not an enlightened man, held enlightened opinions. Exempted by a long career in the Secretariate from personal contact with the peoples of India, he was able to speak of them urbanely, and to deplore racial prejudice. He applauded the outcome of the trial, and congratulated Fielding on having taken 'the broad, the sensible, the only possible charitable view from the first. Speaking confidentially . . .' he proceeded. Fielding deprecated confidences, but Sir Gilbert insisted on imparting them; the affair had been 'mishandled by certain of our friends up the hill' who did not realize that 'the hands of the clock move forward, not back,' etc., etc. One thing he could guarantee: the Principal would receive a most cordial invitation to rejoin the club, and he begged, nay commanded him, to accept. He returned to his Himalayan altitudes well satisfied; the amount of money Miss Quested would have to pay, the precise nature of what had happened in the caves–these were local details, and did not concern him.

Fielding found himself drawn more and more into Miss Quested's affairs. The College remained closed and he ate and slept at Hamidullah's, so there was no reason she should not stop on if she wished. In her place he would have cleared out, sooner than submit to Ronny's half-hearted and distracted civilities, but she was waiting for the hour-glass of her sojourn to run through. A house to live in, a garden to walk in during the brief moment of the cool–that was all she asked, and he was able to provide them. Disaster had shown her her limitations, and he realized now what a fine loyal character she was. Her humility was touching. She never repined at getting the worst of both worlds; she regarded it as the due punishment of her stupidity. When he hinted to her that a personal apology to Aziz might be seemly, she said sadly: 'Of course. I ought to have thought of it myself, my instincts never help me. Why didn't I rush up to him after the trial? Yes, of course I will write him an apology, but please will you dictate it?' Between them they concocted a letter, sincere, and full of moving phrases, but it was not moving as a letter. 'Shall I write another?' she enquired. 'Nothing matters if I can undo the harm I have caused. I can do this right, and that right; but when the two are put together they come wrong. That's the defect of my character. I have never realized it until now. I thought that if I was just and asked questions I would come through every difficulty.' He replied: 'Our letter is a failure for a simple reason which we had better face: you have no real affection for Aziz, or Indians generally.' She assented. 'The first time I saw you, you were wanting to see India, not Indians, and it occurred to me: Ah, that won't take us far. Indians know whether they are liked or not–they cannot be fooled here. Justice never satisfies them, and that is why the British Empire rests on sand.' Then he said: 'Do I like anyone, though?' Presumably she liked Heaslop, and he changed the subject, for this side of her life did not concern him.

His Indian friends were, on the other hand, a bit above themselves. Victory, which would have made the English sanctimonious, made them aggressive. They wanted to develop an offensive, and tried to do so by discovering new grievances and wrongs, many of which had no existence. They suffered from the usual disillusion that attends warfare. The aims of battle and the fruits of conquest are never the same; the latter have their value and only the saint rejects them, but their hint of immortality vanishes as soon as they are held in the hand. Although Sir Gilbert had been courteous, almost obsequious, the fabric he represented had in no wise bowed its head. British officialism remained, as all-pervading and as unpleasant as the sun; and what was next to be done against it was not very obvious, even to Mahmoud Ali. Loud talk and trivial lawlessness were attempted, and behind them continued a genuine but vague desire for education. 'Mr Fielding, we must all be educated promptly.'

Aziz was friendly and domineering. He wanted Fielding to 'give in to the East,' as he called it, and live in a condition of affectionate dependence upon it. 'You can trust me, Cyril.' No question of that, and Fielding had no roots among his own people. Yet he really couldn't become a sort of Mohammed Latif. When they argued about it something racial intruded—not bitterly, but inevitably, like the colour of their skins: coffee-colour versus pinko-grey. And Aziz would conclude: 'Can't you see that I'm grateful to you for your help and want to reward you?' And the other would retort: 'If you want to reward me, let Miss Quested off paying.'

The insensitiveness about Adela displeased him. It would, from every point of view, be right to treat her generously, and one day he had the notion of appealing to the memory of Mrs Moore. Aziz had this high and fantastic estimate of Mrs Moore. Her death had been a real grief to his warm heart; he wept like a child and ordered his three children to weep also. There was no doubt that he respected and loved her. Fielding's first attempt was a failure. The reply was: 'I see your trick. I want revenge on them. Why should I be insulted and suffer and the contents of my pockets read and my wife's photograph taken to the police station? Also I want the money—to educate my little boys, as I explained to her.' But he began to weaken, and Fielding was not ashamed to practise a little necromancy. Whenever the question of compensation came up, he introduced the dead woman's name. Just as other propagandists invented her a tomb, so did he raise a questionable image of her in the heart of Aziz, saying nothing that he believed to be untrue, but producing something that was probably far from the truth. Aziz yielded suddenly. He felt it was Mrs Moore's wish that he should spare the woman who was about to marry her son, that it was the only honour he could pay her, and he renounced with a passionate and beautiful outburst the whole of the compensation money, claiming only costs. It was fine of him, and, as he foresaw, it won him no credit with the English. They still believed he was guilty, they believed it to the end of their careers, and retired Anglo-Indians in Tunbridge Wells or Cheltenham still murmur to each other: 'That Marabar case which broke down because the poor girl couldn't face giving her evidence—that was another bad case.'

When the affair was thus officially ended, Ronny, who was about to be transferred to another part of the Province, approached Fielding with his usual constraint and said: 'I wish to thank you for the help you have given Miss Quested. She will not of course trespass on your hospitality further; she has as a matter of fact decided to return to England. I have just arranged about her passage for her. I understand she would like to see you.'

'I shall go round at once.'

On reaching the College, he found her in some upset. He learnt that the engagement had been broken by Ronny. 'Far wiser of him,' she said pathetically. 'I ought to have spoken myself, but I drifted on wondering what would happen. I would willingly have gone on spoiling his life through inertia—one has nothing to do, one belongs nowhere and becomes a public nuisance without realizing it.' In order to reassure him, she added: 'I speak only of India. I am not astray in England. I fit in there—no, don't think I shall do harm in England. When I am forced back there, I shall settle down to some career. I have sufficient money left to start myself, and heaps of friends of my own type. I shall be quite all right.' Then sighing: 'But oh, the trouble I've brought on everyone here. . . . I can never get over it. My carefulness as to whether we should marry or not . . . and in the end Ronny and I part and aren't even sorry. We ought never to have thought of marriage. Weren't you amazed when our engagement was originally announced?'

'Not much. At my age one's seldom amazed,' he said, smiling. 'Marriage is too absurd in any case. It begins and continues for such very slight reasons. The social business props it up on one side, and the theological business on the other, but neither of them are marriage, are they? I've friends who can't remember why they married, no more can their wives. I suspect that it mostly happens haphazard, though afterwards various noble reasons are invented. About marriage I am cynical.'

'I am not. This false start has been all my own fault. I was bringing to Ronny nothing that ought to be brought, that was why he rejected me really. I entered that cave thinking: Am I fond of him? I have not yet told you that, Mr Fielding. I didn't feel justified. Tenderness, respect, personal intercourse—I tried to make them take the place—of—'

'I no longer want love,' he said, supplying the word.

'No more do I. My experiences here have cured me. But I want others to want it.'

'But to go back to our first talk (for I suppose this is our last one)—when you entered that cave, who did follow you, or did no one follow you? Can you now say? I don't like it left in air.'

'Let us call it the guide,' she said indifferently. 'It will never be known. It's as if I ran my finger along that polished wall in the dark, and cannot get further. I am up against something, and so are you. Mrs Moore—she did know.'

'How could she have known what we don't?'

'Telepathy, possibly.'

The pert, meagre word fell to the ground. Telepathy? What an explanation! Better withdraw it, and Adela did so. She was at the end of her spiritual tether, and so was he. Were there worlds beyond which they could never touch, or did all that is possible enter their consciousness? They could not tell. They only realized that their outlook was more or less similar, and found in this a satisfaction. Perhaps life is a mystery, not a muddle; they could not tell. Perhaps the hundred Indias which fuss and squabble so tiresomely are one, and the universe they mirror is one. They had not the apparatus for judging.

'Write to me when you get to England.'

'I shall, often. You have been excessively kind. Now that I'm going, I realize it. I wish I could do something for you in return, but I see you've all you want.'

'I think so,' he replied after a pause. 'I have never felt more happy and

secure out here. I really do get on with Indians, and they do trust me. It's
pleasant that I haven't had to resign my job. It's pleasant to be praised by an
L.-G. Until the next earthquake I remain as I am.'

'Of course this death has been troubling me.'

'Aziz was so fond of her too.'

'But it has made me remember that we must all die: all these personal
relations we try to live by are temporary. I used to feel death selected people,
it is a notion one gets from novels, because some of the characters are usually
left talking at the end. Now "death spares no one" begins to be real.'

'Don't let it become too real, or you'll die yourself. That is the objection to
meditating upon death. We are subdued to what we work in. I have felt the
same temptation, and had to sheer off. I want to go on living a bit.'

'So do I.'

A friendliness, as of dwarfs shaking hands, was in the air. Both man and
woman were at the height of their powers—sensible, honest, even subtle.
They spoke the same language, and held the same opinions, and the variety
of age and sex did not divide them. Yet they were dissatisfied. When they
agreed, 'I want to go on living a bit,' or, 'I don't believe in God,' the words
were followed by a curious backwash as though the universe had displaced
itself to fill up a tiny void, or as though they had seen their own gestures from
an immense height—dwarfs talking, shaking hands and assuring each other
that they stood on the same footing of insight. They did not think they were
wrong, because as soon as honest people think they are wrong instability sets
up. Not for them was an infinite goal behind the stars, and they never sought
it. But wistfulness descended on them now, as on other occasions; the
shadow of the shadow of a dream fell over their clear-cut interests, and
objects never seen again seemed messages from another world.

'And I do like you so very much, if I may say so,' he affirmed.

'I'm glad, for I like you. Let's meet again.'

'We will, in England, if I ever take home leave.'

'But I suppose you're not likely to do that yet.'

'Quite a chance. I have a scheme on now as a matter of fact.'

'Oh, that would be very nice.'

So it petered out. Ten days later Adela went off, by the same route as her
dead friend. The final beat up before the monsoon had come. The country
was stricken and blurred. Its houses, trees and fields were all modelled out of
the same brown paste, and the sea at Bombay slid about like broth against the
quays. Her last Indian adventure was with Antony, who followed her on to
the boat and tried to blackmail her. She had been Mr Fielding's mistress,
Antony said. Perhaps Antony was discontended with his tip. She rang the
cabin bell and had him turned out, but his statement created rather a
scandal, and people did not speak to her much during the first part of the
voyage. Through the Indian Ocean and the Red Sea she was left to herself,
and to the dregs of Chandrapore.

With Egypt the atmosphere altered. The clean sands, heaped on each side
of the canal, seemed to wipe off everything that was difficult and equivocal,
and even Port Said looked pure and charming in the light of a rose-grey

morning. She went on shore there with an American missionary, they walked out to the Lesseps statue, they drank the tonic air of the Levant. 'To what duties, Miss Quested, are you returning in your own country after your taste of the tropics?' the missionary asked. 'Observe, I don't say to what do you turn, but to what do you *re*-turn. Every life ought to contain both a turn and a *re*-turn. This celebrated pioneer (he pointed to the statue) will make my question clear. He turns to the East, he *re*-turns to the West. You can see it from the cute position of his hands, one of which holds a string of sausages.' The missionary looked at her humorously, in order to cover the emptiness of his mind. He had no idea what he meant by 'turn' and 'return,' but he often used words in pairs, for the sake of moral brightness. 'I see,' she replied. Suddenly, in the Mediterranean clarity, she had seen. Her first duty on returning to England was to look up those other children of Mrs Moore's, Ralph and Stella, then she would turn to her profession. Mrs Moore had tended to keep the products of her two marriages apart, and Adela had not come across the younger branch so far.

Chapter Thirty

Another local consequence of the trial was a Hindu-Moslem entente. Loud protestations of amity were exchanged by prominent citizens, and there went with them a genuine desire for a good understanding. Aziz, when he was at the hospital one day, received a visit from rather a sympathetic figure: Mr Das. The magistrate sought two favours from him: a remedy for shingles and a poem for his brother-in-law's new monthly magazine. He accorded both.

'My dear Das, why, when you tried to send me to prison, should I try to send Mr Bhattacharya a poem? Eh? That is naturally entirely a joke. I will write him the best I can, but I thought your magazine was for Hindus.'

'It is not for Hindus, but Indians generally,' he said timidly.

'There is no such person in existence as the general Indian.'

'There was not, but there may be when you have written a poem. You are our hero; the whole city is behind you, irrespective of creed.'

'I know, but will it last?'

'I fear not,' said Das, who had much mental clearness. 'And for that reason, if I may say so, do not introduce too many Persian expressions into the poem, and not too much about the bulbul.'

'Half a sec,' said Aziz, biting his pencil. He was writing out a prescription. 'Here you are. . . . Is not this better than a poem?'

'Happy the man who can compose both.'

'You are full of compliments to-day.'

'I know you bear me a grudge for trying that case,' said the other, stretching out his hand impulsively. 'You are so kind and friendly, but always I detect irony beneath your manner.'

'No, no, what nonsense!' protested Aziz. They shook hands, in a half-embrace that typified the entente. Between people of distant climes there is always the possibility of romance, but the various branches of Indians know too much about each other to surmount the unknowable easily. The approach is prosaic. 'Excellent,' said Aziz, patting a stout shoulder and thinking, 'I wish they did not remind me of cow-dung'; Das thought, 'Some Moslems are very violent.' They smiled wistfully, each spying the thought in the other's heart, and Das, the more articulate, said: 'Excuse my mistakes, realize my limitations. Life is not easy as we know it on the earth.'

'Oh, well, about this poem—how did you hear I sometimes scribbled?' he asked, much pleased, and a good deal moved—for literature had always been a solace to him, something that the ugliness of facts could not spoil.

'Professor Godbole often mentioned it, before his departure for Mau.'

'How did he hear?'

'He too was a poet; do you not divine each other?'

Flattered by the invitation, he got to work that evening. The feel of the pen between his fingers generated bulbuls at once. His poem was again about the decay of Islam and the brevity of love; as sad and sweet as he could contrive, but not nourished by personal experience, and of no interest to these excellent Hindus. Feeling dissatisfied, he rushed to the other extreme, and wrote a satire, which was too libellous to print. He could only express pathos or venom, though most of his life had no concern with either. He loved poetry—science was merely an acquisition, which he laid aside when unobserved like his European dress—and this evening he longed to compose a new song which should be acclaimed by multitudes and even sung in the fields. In what language shall it be written? And what shall it announce? He vowed to see more of Indians who were not Mohammedans, and never to look backward. It is the only healthy course. Of what help, in this latitude and hour, are the glories of Cordova and Samarcand? They have gone, and while we lament them the English occupy Delhi and exclude us from East Africa. Islam itself, though true, throws cross-lights over the path to freedom. The song of the future must transcend creed.

The poem for Mr Bhattacharya never got written, but it had an effect. It led him towards the vague and bulky figure of a mother-land. He was without natural affection for the land of his birth, but the Marabar Hills drove him to it. Half closing his eyes, he attempted to love India. She must imitate Japan. Not until she is a nation will her sons be treated with respect. He grew harder and less approachable. The English, whom he had laughed at or ignored, persecuted him everywhere; they had even thrown nets over his dreams. 'My great mistake has been taking our rulers as a joke,' he said to Hamidullah next day; who replied with a sigh: 'It is far the wisest way to take them, but not possible in the long run. Sooner or later a disaster such as yours occurs, and reveals their secret thoughts about our character. If God himself descended from heaven into their club and said you were innocent, they would disbelieve him. Now you see why Mahmoud Ali and self waste so much time over intrigues and associate with creatures like Ram Chand.'

'I cannot endure committees. I shall go right away.'

'Where to? Turtons and Burtons, all are the same.'

'But not in an Indian state.'

'I believe the Politicals are obliged to have better manners. It amounts to no more.'

'I do want to get away from British India, even to a poor job. I think I could write poetry there. I wish I had lived in Babur's time and fought and written for him. Gone, gone, and not even any use to say "Gone, gone," for it weakens us while we say it. We need a king, Hamidullah; it would make our lives easier. As it is, we must try to appreciate these quaint Hindus. My notion now is to try for some post as doctor in one of their states.'

'Oh, that is going much too far.'

'It is not going as far as Mr Ram Chand.'

'But the money, the money—they will never pay an adequate salary, those savage Rajahs.'

'I shall never be rich anywhere, it is outside my character.'

'If you had been sensible and made Miss Quested pay—'

'I chose not to. Discussion of the past is useless,' he said, with sudden sharpness of tone. 'I have allowed her to keep her fortune and buy herself a husband in England, for which it will be very necessary. Don't mention the matter again.'

'Very well, but your life must continue a poor man's; no holidays in Kashmir for you yet, you must stick to your profession and rise to a highly paid post, not retire to a jungle-state and write poems. Educate your children, read the latest scientific periodicals, compel European doctors to respect you. Accept the consequences of your own actions like a man.'

Aziz winked at him slowly and said: 'We are not in the law courts. There are many ways of being a man; mine is to express what is deepest in my heart.'

'To such a remark there is certainly no reply,' said Hamidullah, moved. Recovering himself and smiling, he said: 'Have you heard this naughty rumour that Mohammed Latif has got hold of?'

'Which?'

'When Miss Quested stopped in the College, Fielding used to visit her . . . rather too late in the evening, the servants say.'

'A pleasant change for her if he did,' said Aziz, making a curious face.

'But you understand my meaning?'

The young man winked again and said: 'Just! Still, your meaning doesn't help me out of my difficulties. I am determined to leave Chandrapore. The problem is, for where? I am determined to write poetry. The problem is, about what? You give me no assistance.' Then, surprising both Hamidullah and himself, he had an explosion of nerves. 'But who does give me assistance? No one is my friend. All are traitors, even my own children. I have had enough of friends.'

'I was going to suggest we go behind the purdah, but your three treacherous children are there, so you will not want too.'

'I am sorry, it is ever since I was in prison my temper is strange; take me, forgive me.'

'Nureddin's mother is visiting my wife now. That is all right, I think.'

'They come before me separately, but not so far together. You had better prepare them for the united shock of my face.'

'No, let us surprise them without warning, far too much nonsense still goes on among our ladies. They pretended at the time of your trial they would give up purdah; indeed, those of them who can write composed a document to that effect, and now it ends in humbug. You know how deeply they all respect Fielding, but not one of them has seen him. My wife says she will, but always when he calls there is some excuse—she is not feeling well, she is ashamed of the room, she has no nice sweets to offer him, only Elephants' Ears, and if I say Elephants' Ears are Mr Fielding's favourite sweet, she replies that he will know how badly hers are made, so she cannot see him on their account. For fifteen years, my dear boy, have I argued with my begum, for fifteen years, and never gained a point, yet the missionaries inform us our women are down-trodden. If you want a subject for a poem, take this: The Indian lady as she is and not as she is supposed to be.'

Chapter Thirty-one

Aziz had no sense of evidence. The sequence of his emotions decided his beliefs, and led to the tragic coolness between himself and his English friend. They had conquered but were not to be crowned. Fielding was away at a conference, and after the rumour about Miss Quested had been with him undisturbed for a few days, he assumed it was true. He had no objection on moral grounds to his friends amusing themselves, and Cyril, being middle-aged, could no longer expect the pick of the female market, and must take his amusement where he could find it. But he resented him making up to this particular woman, whom he still regarded as his enemy; also, why had he not been told? What is friendship without confidences? He himself had told things sometimes regarded as shocking, and the Englishman had listened, tolerant, but surrendering nothing in return.

He met Fielding at the railway station on his return, agreed to dine with him, and then started taxing him by the oblique method, outwardly merry. An avowed European scandal there was—Mr McBryde and Miss Derek. Miss Derek's faithful attachment to Chandrapore was now explained: Mr McBryde had been caught in her room, and his wife was divorcing him. 'That pure-minded fellow. However, he will blame the Indian climate. Everything is our fault really. Now, have I not discovered an important piece of news for you, Cyril?'

'Not very,' said Fielding, who took little interest in distant sins. 'Listen to mine.' Aziz' face lit up. 'At the conference, it was settled. . . .'

'This evening will do for schoolmastery. I should go straight to the Minto now, the cholera looks bad. We begin to have local cases as well as imported.

In fact, the whole of life is somewhat sad. The new Civil Surgeon is the same as the last, but does not dare to be. That is all any administrative change amounts to. All my suffering has won nothing for us. But look here, Cyril, while I remember it. There's gossip about you as well as McBryde. They say that you and Miss Quested became also rather too intimate friends. To speak perfectly frankly, they say you and she have been guilty of impropriety.'

'They would say that.'

'It's all over the town, and may injure your reputation. You know, everyone is by no means your supporter. I have tried all I could to silence such a story.'

'Don't bother. Miss Quested has cleared out at last.'

'It is those who stop in the country, not those who leave it, whom such a story injures. Imagine my dismay and anxiety. I could scarcely get a wink of sleep. First my name was coupled with her and now it is yours.'

'Don't use such exaggerated phrases.'

'As what?'

'As dismay and anxiety.'

'Have I not lived all my life in India? Do I not know what produces a bad impression here?' His voice shot up rather crossly.

'Yes, but the scale, the scale. You always get the scale wrong, my dear fellow. A pity there is this rumour, but such a very small pity—so small that we may as well talk of something else.'

'You mind for Miss Quested's sake, though. I can see from your face.'

'As far as I do mind. I travel light.'

'Cyril, that boastfulness about travelling light will be your ruin. It is raising up enemies against you on all sides, and makes me feel excessively uneasy.'

'What enemies?'

Since Aziz had only himself in mind, he could not reply. Feeling a fool, he became angrier. 'I have given you list after list of the people who cannot be trusted in this city. In your position I should have the sense to know I was surrounded by enemies. You observe I speak in a low voice. It is because I see your sais is new. How do I know he isn't a spy?' He lowered his voice: 'Every third servant is a spy.'

'Now, what is the matter?' he asked, smiling.

'Do you contradict my last remark?'

'It simply doesn't affect me. Spies are as thick as mosquitoes, but it's years before I shall meet the one that kills me. You've something else in your mind.'

'I've not; don't be ridiculous.'

'You have. You're cross with me about something or other.'

Any direct attack threw him out of action. Presently he said: 'So you and Madamsell Adela used to amuse one another in the evening, naughty boy.'

Those drab and high-minded talks had scarcely made for dalliance. Fielding was so startled at the story being taken seriously, and so disliked being called a naughty boy, that he lost his head and cried: 'You little rotter!

Well, I'm damned. Amusement indeed. Is it likely at such a time?'

'Oh, I beg your pardon, I'm sure. The licentious Oriental imagination was at work,' he replied, speaking gaily, but cut to the heart; for hours after his mistake he bled inwardly.

'You see, Aziz, the circumstances . . . also the girl was still engaged to Heaslop, also I never felt . . .'

'Yes, yes; but you didn't contradict what I said, so I thought it was true. Oh dear, East and West. Most misleading. Will you please put your little rotter down at his hospital?'

'You're not offended?'

'Most certainly I am not.'

'If you are, this must be cleared up later on.'

'It has been,' he answered, dignified. 'I believe absolutely what you say, and of that there need be no further question.'

'But the way I said it must be cleared up. I was unintentionally rude. Unreserved regrets.'

'The fault is entirely mine.'

Tangles like this still interrupted their intercourse. A pause in the wrong place, an intonation misunderstood, and a whole conversation went awry. Fielding had been startled, not shocked, but how convey the difference? There is always trouble when two people do not think of sex at the same moment, always mutual resentment and surprise, even when the two people are of the same race. He began to recapitulate his feelings about Miss Quested. Aziz cut him short with: 'But I believe you, I believe. Mohammed Latif shall be severely punished for inventing this.'

'Oh, leave it alone, like all gossip–it's merely one of those half-alive things that try to crowd out real life. Take no notice, it'll vanish, like poor old Mrs Moore's tombs.'

'Mohammed Latif has taken to intriguing. We are already much displeased with him. Will it satisfy you if we send him back to his family without a present?'

'We'll discuss M.L. at dinner.'

His eyes went clotted and hard. 'Dinner. This is most unlucky— I forgot. I have promised to dine with Das.'

'Bring Das to me.'

'He will have invited other friends.'

'You are coming to dinner with me as arranged,' said Fielding, looking away. 'I don't stand this. You are coming to dinner with me. You come.'

They had reached the hospital now. Fielding continued round the Maidan alone. He was annoyed with himself, but counted on dinner to pull things straight. At the post office he saw the Collector. Their vehicles were parked side by side while their servants competed in the interior of the building. 'Good morning; so you are back,' said Turton icily. 'I should be glad if you will put in your appearance at the club this evening.'

'I have accepted re-election, sir. Do you regard it as necessary I should come? I should be glad to be excused; indeed, I have a dinner engagement this evening.'

'It is not a question of your feelings, but of the wish of the Lieutenant-Governor. Perhaps you will ask me whether I speak officially. I do. I shall expect you this evening at six. We shall not interfere with your subsequent plans.'

He attended the grim little function in due course. The skeletons of hospitality rattled–'Have a peg, have a drink.' He talked for five minutes to Mrs Blakiston, who was the only surviving female. He talked to McBryde, who was defiant about his divorce, conscious that he had sinned as a sahib. He talked to Major Roberts, the new Civil Surgeon; and to young Milner, the new City Magistrate; but the more the club changed, the more it promised to be the same thing. 'It is no good,' he thought, as he returned past the mosque, 'we all build upon sand; and the more modern the country gets, the worse'll be the crash. In the old eighteenth century, when cruelty and injustice raged, an invisible power repaired their ravages. Everything echoes now; there's no stopping the echo. The original sound may be harmless, but the echo is always evil.' This reflection about an echo lay at the verge of Fielding's mind. He could never develop it. It belonged to the universe that he had missed or rejected. And the mosque missed it too. Like himself, those shallow arcades provided but a limited asylum. 'There is no God but God' doesn't carry us far through the complexities of matter and spirit; it is only a game with words, really, a religious pun, not a religious truth.

He found Aziz overtired and dispirited, and he determined not to allude to their misunderstanding until the end of the evening; it would be more acceptable then. He made a clean breast about the club–said he had only gone under compulsion, and should never attend again unless the order was renewed. 'In other words, probably never; for I am going quite soon to England.'

'I thought you might end in England,' he said very quietly, then changed the conversation. Rather awkwardly they ate their dinner, then went out to sit in the Mogul garden-house.

'I am only going for a little time. On official business. My service is anxious to get me away from Chandrapore for a bit. It is obliged to value me highly, but does not care for me. The situation is somewhat humorous.'

'What is the nature of the business? Will it leave you much spare time?'

'Enough to see my friends.'

'I expected you to make such a reply. You are a faithful friend. Shall we now talk about something else?'

'Willingly. What subject?'

'Poetry,' he said, with tears in his eyes. 'Let us discuss why poetry has lost the power of making men brave. My mother's father was also a poet, and fought against you in the Mutiny. I might equal him if there was another mutiny. As it is, I am a doctor, who has won a case and has three children to support, and whose chief subject of conversation is official plans.'

'Let us talk about poetry.' He turned his mind to the innocuous subject. 'You people are sadly circumstanced. Whatever are you to write about? You cannot say, "The rose is faded," for evermore. We know it's faded. Yet you can't have patriotic poetry of the "India, my India" type, when it's nobody's India.'

'I like this conversation. It may lead to something interesting.'

'You are quite right in thinking that poetry must touch life. When I knew you first, you used it as an incantation.'

'I was a child when you knew me first. Everyone was my friend then. The Friend: a Persian expression for God. But I do not want to be a religious poet either.'

'I hoped you would be.'

'Why, when you yourself are an atheist?'

'There is something in religion that may not be true, but has not yet been sung.'

'Explain in detail.'

'Something that the Hindus have perhaps found.'

'Let them sing it.'

'Hindus are unable to sing.'

'Cyril, you sometimes make a sensible remark. That will do for poetry for the present. Let us now return to your English visit.'

'We haven't discussed poetry for two seconds,' said the other, smiling.

But Aziz was addicted to cameos. He held the tiny conversation in his hand, and felt it epitomized his problem. For an instant he recalled his wife, and, as happens when a memory is intense, the past became the future, and he saw her with him in a quiet Hindu jungle native state, far away from foreigners. He said: 'I suppose you will visit Miss Quested.'

'If I have time. It will be strange seeing her in Hampstead.'

'What is Hampstead?'

'An artistic and thoughtful little suburb of London—'

'And there she lives in comfort: you will enjoy seeing her. . . . Dear me, I've got a headache this evening. Perhaps I am going to have cholera. With your permission, I'll leave early.'

'When would you like the carriage?'

'Don't trouble—I'll bike.'

'But you haven't got your bicycle. My carriage fetched you—let it take you away.'

'Sound reasoning,' he said, trying to be gay. 'I have not got my bicycle. But I am seen too often in your carriage. I am thought to take advantage of your generosity by Mr Ram Chand.' He was out of sorts and uneasy. The conversation jumped from topic to topic in a broken-backed fashion. They were affectionate and intimate, but nothing clicked tight.

'Aziz, you have forgiven me the stupid remark I made this morning?'

'When you called me a little rotter?'

'Yes, to my eternal confusion. You know how fond I am of you.'

'That is nothing, of course, we all of us make mistakes. In a friendship such as ours a few slips are of no consequence.'

But as he drove off, something depressed him—a dull pain of body or mind, waiting to rise to the surface. When he reached the bungalow he wanted to return and say something very affectionate; instead, he gave the sais a heavy tip, and sat down gloomily on the bed, and Hassan massaged him incompetently. The eye-flies had colonized the top of an almeira; the red stains on the durry were thicker, for Mohammed Latif had slept here during his imprisonment and spat a good deal; the table drawer was scarred where the police had forced it open; everything in Chandrapore was used up, including the air. The trouble rose to the surface now: he was suspicious; he suspected his friend of intending to marry Miss Quested for the sake of her money, and of going to England for that purpose.

'Huzoor?'–for he had muttered.

'Look at those flies on the ceiling. Why have you not drowned them?'

'Huzoor, they return.'

'Like all evil things.'

To divert the conversation, Hassan related how the kitchen-boy had killed a snake, good, but killed it by cutting it in two, bad, because it becomes two snakes.

'When he breaks a plate, does it become two plates?'

'Glasses and a new teapot will similarly be required, also for myself a coat.'

Aziz sighed. Each for himself. One man needs a coat, another a rich wife; each approaches his goal by a clever detour. Fielding had saved the girl a fine of twenty thousand rupees, and now followed her to England. If he desired to marry her, all was explained; she would bring him a larger dowry. Aziz did not believe his own suspicions–better if he had, for then he would have denounced and cleared the situation up. Suspicion and belief could in his mind exist side by side. They sprang from different sources, and need never intermingle. Suspicion in the Oriental is a sort of malignant tumour, a mental malady, that makes him self-conscious and unfriendly suddenly; he trusts and mistrusts at the same time in a way the Westerner cannot comprehend. It is his demon, as the Westerner's is hypocrisy. Aziz was seized by it, and his fancy built a satanic castle, of which the foundation had been laid when he talked at Dilkusha under the stars. The girl had surely been Cyril's mistress when she stopped in the College–Mohammed Latif was right. But was that all? Perhaps it was Cyril who followed her into the cave. . . . No; impossible. Cyril hadn't been on the Kawa Dol at all. Impossible. Ridiculous. Yet the fancy left him trembling with misery. Such treachery–if true–would have been the worst in Indian history; nothing so vile, not even the murder of Afzul Khan by Sivaji. He was shaken, as though by a truth, and told Hassan to leave him.

Next day he decided to take his children back to Mussoorie. They had come down for the trial, that he might bid them farewell, and had stayed on at Hamidullah's for the rejoicings. Major Roberts would give him leave, and during his absence Fielding would go off to England. The idea suited both his beliefs and his suspicions. Events would prove which was right, and preserve, in either case, his dignity.

Fielding was conscious of something hostile, and because he was really fond of Aziz his optimism failed him. Travelling light is less easy as soon as affection is involved. Unable to jog forward in the serene hope that all would come right, he wrote an elaborate letter in the rather modern style: 'It is on my mind that you think me a prude about women. I had rather you thought anything else of me. If I live impeccably now, it is only because I am well on the forties—a period of revision. In the eighties I shall revise again. And before the nineties come—I shall be revised! But, alive or dead, I am absolutely devoid of morals. Do kindly grasp this about me.' Aziz did not care for the letter at all. It hurt his delicacy. He liked confidences, however gross, but generalizations and comparisons always repelled him. Life is not a scientific manual. He replied coldly, regretting his inability to return from Mussoorie before his friend sailed: 'But I must take my poor little holiday while I can. All must be economy henceforward, all hopes of Kashmir have vanished for ever and ever. When you return I shall be slaving far away in some new post.'

And Fielding went, and in the last gutterings of Chandrapore—heaven and earth both looking like toffee—the Indian's bad fancies were confirmed. His friends encouraged them, for though they had liked the Principal, they felt uneasy at his getting to know so much about their private affairs. Mahmoud Ali soon declared that treachery was afoot. Hamidullah murmured, 'Certainly of late he no longer addressed us with his former frankness,' and warned Aziz 'not to expect too much—he and she are, after all, both members of another race.' 'Where are my twenty thousand rupees?' he thought. He was absolutely indifferent to money—not merely generous with it, but promptly paying his debts when he could remember to do so—yet these rupees haunted his mind, because he had been tricked about them, and allowed them to escape overseas, like so much of the wealth of India. Cyril would marry Miss Quested—he grew certain of it, all the unexplained residue of the Marabar contributing. It was the natural conclusion of the horrible senseless picnic, and before long he persuaded himself that the wedding had actually taken place.

Chapter Thirty-two

Egypt was charming—a green strip of carpet and walking up and down it four sorts of animals and one sort of man. Fielding's business took him there for a few days. He re-embarked at Alexandria—bright blue sky, constant wind, clean low coast-line, as against the intricacies of Bombay. Crete welcomed him next with the long snowy ridge of its mountains, and then came Venice. As he landed on the piazzetta a cup of beauty was lifted to his lips, and he drank with a sense of disloyalty. The buildings of Venice, like the mountains of Crete and the fields of Egypt, stood in the right place, whereas in poor India everything was placed wrong. He had forgotten the beauty of form among idol temples and lumpy hills; indeed, without form, how can there be beauty? Form stammered here and there in a mosque, became rigid through nervousness even, but oh these Italian churches! San Giorgio standing on the island which could scarcely have risen from the waves without it, the Salute holding the entrance of a canal which, but for it, would not be the Grand Canal! In the old undergraduate days he had wrapped himself up in the many-coloured blanket of St Mark's, but something more precious than mosaics and marbles was offered to him now: the harmony between the works of man and the earth that upholds them, the civilization that has escaped muddle, the spirit in a reasonable form, with flesh and blood subsisting. Writing picture post-cards to his Indian friends, he felt that all of them would miss the joys he experienced now, the joys of form, and that this constituted a serious barrier. They would see the sumptuousness of Venice, not its shape, and though Venice was not Europe, it was part of the Mediterranean harmony. The Mediterranean is the human norm. When men leave that exquisite lake, whether through the Bosphorus or the Pillars of Hercules, they approach the monstrous and extraordinary; and the southern exit leads to the strangest experience of all. Turning his back on it yet again, he took the train northward, and tender romantic fancies that he thought were dead for ever, flowered when he saw the buttercups and daisies of June.

Temples

Chapter Thirty-three

Some hundreds of miles westward of the Marabar Hills, and two years later in time, Professor Narayan Godbole stands in the presence of God. God is not born yet—that will occur at midnight—but He has also been born centuries ago, nor can He ever be born, because He is the Lord of the Universe, who transcends human processes. He is, was not, is not, was. He and Professor Godbole stood at opposite ends of the same strip of carpet.

> *Tukaram, Tukaram,*
> *Thou art my father and mother and everybody.*
> *Tukaram, Tukaram,*
> *Thou art my father and mother and everybody.*
> *Tukaram, Tukaram,*
> *Thou art my father and mother and everybody.*
> *Tukaram, Tukaram,*
> *Thou art my father and mother and everybody.*
> *Tukaram. . . .*

This corridor in the palace at Mau opened through other corridors into a courtyard. It was of beautiful hard white stucco, but its pillars and vaulting could scarcely be seen behind coloured rags, iridescent balls, chandeliers of opaque pink glass, and murky photographs framed crookedly. At the end was the small but famous shrine of the dynastic cult, and the God to be born was largely a silver image the size of a teaspoon. Hindus sat on either side of the carpet where they could find room, or overflowed into the adjoining corridors and the courtyard—Hindus, Hindus only, mild-featured men, mostly villagers, for whom anything outside their villages passed in a dream.

They were the toiling ryot, whom some call the real India. Mixed with them sat a few tradesmen out of the little town, officials, courtiers, scions of the ruling house. Schoolboys kept inefficient order. The assembly was in a tender, happy state unknown to an English crowd, it seethed like a beneficent potion. When the villagers broke cordon for a glimpse of the silver image, a most beautiful and radiant expression came into their faces, a beauty in which there was nothing personal, for it caused them all to resemble one another during the moment of its indwelling, and only when it was withdrawn did they revert to individual clods. And so with the music. Music there was, but from so many sources that the sum-total was untrammelled. The braying banging crooning melted into a single mass which trailed round the palace before joining the thunder. Rain fell at intervals throughout the night.

It was the turn of Professor Godbole's choir. As Minister of Education, he gained this special honour. When the previous group of singers dispersed into the crowd, he pressed forward from the back, already in full voice, that the chain of sacred sounds might be uninterrupted. He was barefoot and in white, he wore a pale blue turban; his gold pince-nez had caught in a jasmine garland, and lay sideways down his nose. He and the six colleagues who supported him clashed their cymbals, hit small drums, droned upon a portable harmonium, and sang:

> *Tukaram, Tukaram,*
> *Thou art my father and mother and everybody.*
> *Tukaram, Tukaram,*
> *Thou art my father and mother and everybody.*
> *Tukaram, Tukaram. . . .*

They sang not even to the God who confronted them, but to a saint; they did not one thing which the non-Hindu would feel dramatically correct; this approaching triumph of India was a muddle (as we call it), a frustration of reason and form. Where was the God Himself, in whose honour the congregation had gathered? Indistinguishable in the jumble of His own altar, huddled out of sight amid images of inferior descent, smothered under rose-leaves, overhung by oleographs, outblazed by golden tablets representing the Rajah's ancestors, and entirely obscured, when the wind blew, by the tattered foliage of a banana. Hundreds of electric lights had been lit in His honour (worked by an engine whose thumps destroyed the rhythm of the hymn). Yet His face could not be seen. Hundreds of His silver dishes were piled around Him with the minimum of effect. The inscriptions which the poets of the State had composed were hung where they could not be read, or had twitched their drawing-pins out of the stucco, and one of them (composed in English to indicate His universality) consisted, by an unfortunate slip of the draughtsman, of the words, 'God si Love.'

God si Love. Is this the final message of India?

> *Tukaram, Tukaram . . .,*

continued the choir, reinforced by a squabble behind the purdah curtain, where two mothers tried to push their children at the same moment to the front. A little girl's leg shot out like an eel. In the courtyard, drenched by the rain, the small Europeanized band stumbled off into a waltz. 'Nights of Gladness' they were playing. The singers were not perturbed by this rival, they lived beyond competition. It was long before the tiny fragment of Professor Godbole that attended to outside things decided that his pince-nez was in trouble, and that until it was adjusted he could not choose a new hymn. He laid down one cymbal, with the other he clashed the air, with his free hand he fumbled at the flowers round his neck. A colleague assisted him. Singing into one another's grey moustaches, they disentangled the chain from the tinsel into which it had sunk. Godbole consulted the music-book, said a word to the drummer, who broke rhythm, made a thick little blur of sound, and produced a new rhythm. This was more exciting, the inner images it evoked more definite, and the singers' expressions became fatuous and languid. They loved all men, the whole universe, and scraps of their past, tiny splinters of detail, emerged for a moment to melt into the universal warmth. Thus Godbole, though she was not important to him, remembered an old woman he had met in Chandrapore days. Chance brought her into his mind while it was in this heated state, he did not select her, she happened to occur among the throng of soliciting images, a tiny splinter, and he impelled her by his spiritual force to that place where completeness can be found. Completeness, not reconstruction. His senses grew thinner, he remembered a wasp seen he forgot where, perhaps on a stone. He loved the wasp equally, he impelled it likewise, he was imitating God. And the stone where the wasp clung—could he . . . no, he could not, he had been wrong to attempt the stone, logic and conscious effort had seduced, he came back to the strip of red carpet and discovered that he was dancing upon it. Up and down, a third of the way to the altar and back again, clashing his cymbals, his little legs twinkling, his companions dancing with him and each other. Noise, noise, the Europeanized band louder, incense on the altar, sweat, the blaze of lights, wind in the bananas, noise, thunder, eleven-fifty by his wrist-watch, seen as he threw up his hands and detached the tiny reverberation that was his soul. Louder shouts in the crowd. He danced on. The boys and men who were squatting in the aisles were lifted forcibly and dropped without changing their shapes into the laps of their neighbours. Down the path thus cleared advanced a litter.

It was the aged ruler of the state, brought against the advice of his physicians to witness the Birth ceremony.

No one greeted the Rajah, nor did he wish it; this was no moment for human glory. Nor could the litter be set down, lest it defiled the temple by becoming a throne. He was lifted out of it while its feet remained in air, and deposited on the carpet close to the altar, his immense beard was straightened, his legs tucked under him, a paper containing red powder was placed in his hand. There he sat, leaning against a pillar, exhausted with illness, his eyes magnified by many unshed tears.

He had not to wait long. In a land where all else was unpunctual, the hour of the Birth was chronometrically observed. Three minutes before it was due, a Brahman brought forth a model of the village of Gokul (the Bethlehem in that nebulous story) and placed it in front of the altar. The model was on a wooden tray about a yard square; it was of clay, and was gaily blue and white with streamers and paint. Here, upon a chair too small for him and with a head too large, sat King Kansa, who is Herod, directing the murder of some Innocents, and in a corner, similarly proportioned, stood the father and mother of the Lord, warned to depart in a dream. The model was not holy, but more than a decoration, for it diverted men from the actual image of the God, and increased their sacred bewilderment. Some of the villagers thought the Birth had occurred, saying with truth that the Lord must have been born, or they could not see Him. But the clock struck midnight, and simultaneously the rending note of the conch broke forth, followed by the trumpeting of elephants; all who had packets of powder threw them at the altar, and in the rosy dust and incense, and clanging and shouts, Infinite Love took upon itself the form of SHRI KRISHNA, and saved the world. All sorrow was annihilated, not only for Indians, but for foreigners, birds, caves, railways, and the stars; all became joy, all laughter; there had never been disease nor doubt, misunderstanding, cruelty, fear. Some jumped in the air, others flung themselves prone and embraced the bare feet of the universal lover; the women behind the purdah slapped and shrieked; the little girl slipped out and danced by herself, her black pigtails flying. Not an orgy of the body; the tradition of that shrine forbade it. But the human spirit had tried by a desperate contortion to ravish the unknown, flinging down science and history in the struggle, yes, beauty herself. Did it succeed? Books written afterwards say 'Yes.' But how, if there is such an event, can it be remembered afterwards? How can it be expressed in anything but itself? Not only from the unbeliever are mysteries hid, but the adept himself cannot retain them. He may think, if he chooses, that he has been with God, but as soon as he thinks it, it becomes history, and falls under the rules of time.

A cobra of papier-mâché now appeared on the carpet, also a wooden cradle swinging from a frame. Professor Godbole approached the latter with a red silk napkin in his arms. The napkin was God, not that it was, and the image remained in the blur of the altar. It was just a napkin, folded into a shape which indicated a baby's. The Professor dandled it and gave it to the Rajah, who, making a great effort, said, 'I name this child Shri Krishna,' and tumbled it into the cradle. Tears poured from his eyes, because he had seen the Lord's salvation. He was too weak to exhibit the silk baby to his people, his privilege in former years. His attendants lifted him up, a new path was cleared through the crowd, and he was carried away to a less sacred part of the palace. There, in a room accessible to Western science by an outer staircase, his physician, Dr Aziz, awaited him. His Hindu physician, who had accompanied him to the shrine, briefly reported his symptoms. As the ecstasy receded, the invalid grew fretful. The bumping of the steam engine that worked the dynamo disturbed him, and he asked for what reason it had been introduced into his home. They replied that they would enquire, and administered a sedative.

Down in the sacred corridors, joy had seethed to jollity. It was their duty to play various games to amuse the newly born God, and to simulate his sports with the wanton dairymaids of Brindaban. Butter played a prominent part in these. When the cradle had been removed, the principal nobles of the state gathered together for an innocent frolic. They removed their turbans, and one put a lump of butter on his forehead, and waited for it to slide down his nose into his mouth. Before it could arrive, another stole up behind him, snatched the melting morsel, and swallowed it himself. All laughed exultantly at discovering that the divine sense of humour coincided with their own. 'God si love!' There is fun in heaven. God can play practical jokes upon Himself, draw chairs away from beneath His own posteriors, set His own turbans on fire, and steal His own petticoats when He bathes. By sacrificing good taste, this worship achieved what Christianity has shirked: the inclusion of merriment. All spirit as well as all matter must participate in salvation, and if practical jokes are banned, the circle is incomplete. Having swallowed the butter, they played another game which chanced to be graceful: the fondling of Shri Krishna under the similitude of a child. A pretty red and gold ball is thrown, and he who catches it chooses a child from the crowd, raises it in his arms, and carries it round to be caressed. All stroke the darling creature for the Creator's sake, and murmur happy words. The child is restored to his parents, the ball thrown on, and another child becomes for a moment the World's Desire. And the Lord bounds hither and thither through the aisles, chance, and the sport of chance, irradiating little mortals with His immortality. . . . When they had played this long enough—and being exempt from boredom, they played it again and again, they played it again and again—they took many sticks and hit them together, whack smack, as though they fought the Pandava wars, and threshed and churned with them, and later on they hung from the roof of the temple, in a net, a great black earthenware jar, which was painted here and there with red, and wreathed with dried figs. Now came a rousing sport. Springing up, they struck at the jar with their sticks. It cracked, broke, and a mass of greasy rice and milk poured on to their faces. They ate and smeared one another's mouths, and dived between each other's legs for what had been pashed upon the carpet. This way and that spread the divine mess, until the line of schoolboys, who had somewhat fended off the crowd, broke for their share. The corridors, the courtyard, were filled with benign confusion. Also the flies awoke and claimed their share of God's bounty. There was no quarrelling, owing to the nature of the gift, for blessed is the man who confers it on another, he imitates God. And those 'imitations,' those 'substitutions,' continued to flicker through the assembly for many hours, awaking in each man, according to his capacity, an emotion that he would not have had otherwise. No definite image survived; at the Birth it was questionable whether a silver doll or a mud village, or a silk napkin, or an intangible spirit, or a pious resolution, had been born. Perhaps all these things! Perhaps none! Perhaps all birth is an allegory! Still, it was the main event of the religious year. It caused strange thoughts. Covered with grease and dust, Professor Godbole had once more developed the life of his spirit. He had, with increasing vividness, again seen Mrs Moore, and round her faintly clinging forms of trouble. He was a Brahman, she Christian, but it made no difference, it made no difference whether she was a trick of his memory or a telepathic appeal. It was his duty, as it was his desire, to place himself in the position of the God and to love her, and to place himself in her position and to say to the God, 'Come, come, come, come.' This was all he could do. How inadequate! But each according to his own capacities, and he knew that his own were small. 'One old Englishwoman and one little, little wasp,' he thought, as he stepped out of the temple into the grey of a pouring wet morning. 'It does not seem much, still it is more than I am myself.'

Chapter Thirty-four

Dr Aziz left the palace at the same time. As he returned to his house—which stood in a pleasant garden further up the main street of the town—he could see his old patron paddling and capering in the slush ahead. 'Hullo!' he called, and it was the wrong remark, for the devotee indicated by circular gestures of his arms that he did not desire to be disturbed. He added, 'Sorry,' which was right, for Godbole twisted his head till it didn't belong to his body, and said in a strained voice that had no connection with his mind: 'He arrived at the European Guest House perhaps—at least possibly.'

'Did he? Since when?'

But time was too definite. He waved his arm more dimly and disappeared. Aziz knew who 'he' was—Fielding—but he refused to think about him, because it disturbed his life, and he still trusted the floods to prevent him from arriving. A fine little river issued from his garden gate and gave him much hope. It was impossible that anyone could get across from Deora in such weather as this. Fielding's visit was official. He had been transferred from Chandrapore, and sent on a tour through Central India to see what the remoter states were doing with regard to English education. He had married, he had done the expected with Miss Quested, and Aziz had no wish to see him again.

'Dear old Godbole,' he thought, and smiled. He had no religious curiosity, and had never discovered the meaning of this annual antic, but he was well assured that Godbole was a dear old man. He had come to Mau through him and remained on his account. Without him he could never have grasped problems so totally different from those of Chandrapore. For here the cleavage was between Brahman and non-Brahman; Moslems and English were quite out of the running, and sometimes not mentioned for days. Since Godbole was a Brahman, Aziz was one also for purposes of intrigue: they would often joke about it together. The fissures in the Indian soil are infinite: Hinduism, so solid from a distance, is riven into sects and

clans, which radiate and join, and change their names according to the aspect
from which they are approached. Study it for years with the best teachers,
and when you raise your head, nothing they have told you quite fits. Aziz,
the day of his inauguration, had remarked: 'I study nothing, I
respect'—making an excellent impression. There was now a minimum of
prejudice against him. Nominally under a Hindu doctor, he was really chief
medicine man to the court. He had to drop inoculation and such Western
whims, but even at Chandrapore his profession had been a game, centring
round the operating table, and here in the backwoods he let his instruments
rust, ran his little hospital at half steam, and caused no undue alarm.

His impulse to escape from the English was sound. They had frightened
him permanently, and there are only two reactions against fright: to kick and
scream on committees, or to retreat to a remote jungle, where the sahib
seldom comes. His old lawyer friends wanted him to stop in British India
and help agitate, and might have prevailed, but for the treachery of Fielding.
The news had not surprised him in the least. A rift had opened between
them after the trial when Cyril had not joined in his procession; those
advocacies of the girl had increased it; then came the post-cards from
Venice, so cold, so unfriendly that all agreed that something was wrong; and
finally, after a silence, the expected letter from Hampstead. Mahmoud Ali
was with him at the time. 'Some news that will surprise you. I am to marry
someone whom you know. . . .' He did not read further. 'Here it comes,
answer for me—' and he threw it to Mahmoud Ali. Subsequent letters he
destroyed unopened. It was the end of a foolish experiment. And though
sometimes at the back of his mind he felt that Fielding had made sacrifices
for him, it was now all confused with his genuine hatred of the English. 'I am
an Indian at last,' he thought, standing motionless in the rain.

Life passed pleasantly, the climate was healthy so that the children could
be with him all the year round, and he had married again—not exactly a
marriage, but he liked to regard it as one—and he read his Persian, wrote
his poetry, had his horse, and sometimes got some shikar while the good
Hindus looked the other way. His poems were all on one topic—Oriental
womanhood. 'The purdah must go,' was their burden, 'otherwise we shall
never be free.' And he declared (fantastically) that India would not have
been conquered if women as well as men had fought at Plassy. 'But we do not
show our women to the foreigner'—not explaining how this was to be
managed, for he was writing a poem. Bulbuls and roses would still persist,
the pathos of defeated Islam remained in his blood and could not be expelled
by modernities. Illogical poems—like their writer. Yet they struck a true
note: there cannot be a mother-land without new homes. In one poem—the
only one funny old Godbole liked—he had skipped over the mother-land
(whom he did not truly love) and gone straight to internationality. 'Ah, that
is bhakti; ah, my young friend, that is different and very good. Ah, India,
who seems not to move, will go straight there while the other nations waste
their time. May I translate this particular one into Hindi? In fact, it might be
rendered into Sanskrit almost, it is so enlightened. Yes, of course, all your
other poems are very good too. His Highness was saying to Colonel Maggs

last time he came that we are proud of you'—simpering slightly.

Colonel Maggs was the Political Agent for the neighbourhood and Aziz' dejected opponent. The Criminal Investigation Department kept an eye on Aziz ever since the trial—they had nothing actionable against him, but Indians who have been unfortunate must be watched, and to the end of his life he remained under observation, thanks to Miss Quested's mistake. Colonel Maggs learnt with concern that a suspect was coming to Mau, and, adopting a playful manner, rallied the old Rajah for permitting a Moslem doctor to approach his sacred person. A few years ago, the Rajah would have taken the hint, for the Political Agent then had been a formidable figure, descending with all the thunders of Empire when it was most inconvenient, turning the polity inside out, requiring motor-cars and tiger-hunts, trees cut down that impeded the view from the Guest House, cows milked in his presence, and generally arrogating the control of internal affairs. But there had been a change of policy in high quarters. Local thunders were no longer endorsed, and the group of little states that composed the agency discovered this and began comparing notes with fruitful result. To see how much, or how little, Colonel Maggs would stand, became an agreeable game at Mau, which was played by all the departments of State. He had to stand the appointment of Dr Aziz. The Rajah did not take the hint, but replied that Hindus were less exclusive than formerly, thanks to the enlightened commands of the Viceroy, and he felt it his duty to move with the times.

Yes, all had gone well hitherto, but now, when the rest of the state was plunged in its festival, he had a crisis of a very different sort. A note awaited him at his house. There was no doubt that Fielding had arrived overnight, nor much doubt that Godbole knew of his arrival, for the note was addressed to him, and he had read it before sending it on to Aziz, and had written in the margin, 'Is not this delightful news, but unfortunately my religious duties prevent me from taking any action.' Fielding announced that he had inspected Mudkul (Miss Derek's former preserve), that he had nearly been drowned at Deora, that he had reached Mau according to time-table, and hoped to remain there two days, studying the various educational innovations of his old friend. Nor had he come alone. His wife and her brother accompanied him. And then the note turned into the sort of note that always did arrive from the State Guest House. Wanting something. No eggs. Mosquito nets torn. When would they pay their respects to His Highness? Was it correct that a torchlight procession would take place? If so, might they view it? They didn't want to give trouble, but if they might stand in a balcony, or if they might go out in a boat. . . . Aziz tore the note up. He had had enough of showing Miss Quested native life. Treacherous hideous harridan! Bad people altogether. He hoped to avoid them, though this might be difficult, for they would certainly be held up for several days at Mau. Down country, the floods were even worse, and the pale grey faces of lakes had appeared in the direction of the Asirgarh railway station.

Chapter Thirty-five

Long before he discovered Mau, another young Mohammedan had retired there—a saint. His mother said to him, 'Free prisoners.' So he took a sword and went up to the fort. He unlocked a door, and the prisoners streamed out and resumed their previous occupations, but the police were too much annoyed and cut off the young man's head. Ignoring its absence, he made his way over the rocks that separate the fort and the town, killing policemen as he went, and he fell outside his mother's house, having accomplished her orders. Consequently there are two shrines to him to-day—that of the Head above, and that of the Body below—and they are worshipped by the few Mohammedans who live near, and by Hindus also. 'There is no God but God'; that symmetrical injunction melts in the mild airs of Mau; it belongs to pilgrimages and universities, not to feudalism and agriculture. When Aziz arrived, and found that even Islam was idolatrous, he grew scornful, and longed to purify the place, like Alamgir. But soon he didn't mind, like Akbar. After all, this saint had freed prisoners, and he himself had lain in prison. The Shrine of the Body lay in his own garden and produced a weekly crop of lamps and flowers, and when he saw them he recalled his sufferings. The Shrine of the Head made a nice short walk for the children. He was off duty the morning after the great pujah, and he told them to come. Jemila held his hand. Ahmed and Karim ran in front, arguing what the body looked like as it came staggering down, and whether they would have been frightened if they met it. He didn't want them to grow up superstitious, so he rebuked them, and they answered yes father, for they were well brought up, but, like himself, they were impervious to argument, and after a polite pause they continued saying what their natures compelled them to say.

A slim, tall eight-sided building stood at the top of the slope, among some bushes. This was the Shrine of the Head. It had not been roofed, and was indeed merely a screen. Inside it crouched a humble dome, and inside that, visible through a grille, was a truncated gravestone, swathed in calico. The inner angles of the screen were cumbered with bees' nests, and a gentle shower of broken wings and other aerial oddments kept falling, and had strewn the damp pavement with their flue. Ahmed, apprized by Mohammed Latif of the character of the bee, said, 'They will not hurt us, whose lives are chaste,' and pushed boldly in; his sister was more cautious. From the shrine they went to a mosque, which, in size and design, resembled a fire-screen; the arcades of Chandrapore had shrunk to a flat piece of ornamental stucco, with protuberances at either end to suggest minarets. The funny little thing didn't even stand straight, for the rock on which it had been put was slipping down the hill. It, and the shrine, were a strange outcome of the protests of Arabia.

They wandered over the old fort, now deserted, and admired the various views. The scenery, according to their standards, was delightful—the sky grey and black, bellyfuls of rain all over it, the earth pocked with pools of water and slimy with mud. A magnificent monsoon—the best for three years, the tanks already full, bumper crops possible. Out towards the river (the route by which the Fieldings had escaped from Deora) the downpour had been enormous, the mails had to be pulled across by ropes. They could just see the break in the forest trees where the gorge came through, and the rocks above that marked the site of the diamond mine, glistening with wet. Close beneath was the suburban residence of the Junior Rani, isolated by floods, and Her Highness, lax about purdah, to be seen paddling with her handmaidens in the garden and waving her sari at the monkeys on the roof. But better not look close beneath, perhaps—nor towards the European Guest House either. Beyond the Guest House rose another grey-green gloom of hills, covered with temples like little white flames. There were over two hundred gods in that direction alone, who visited each other constantly, and owned numerous cows, and all the betel-leaf industry, besides having shares in the Asirgarh motor omnibus. Many of them were in the palace at this moment, having the time of their lives; others, too large or proud to travel, had sent symbols to represent them. The air was thick with religion and rain.

Their white shirts fluttering, Ahmed and Karim ran about over the fort, shrieking with joy. Presently they intersected a line of prisoners, who were looking aimlessly at an old bronze gun. 'Which of you is to be pardoned?' they asked. For to-night was the procession of the Chief God, when He would leave the palace, escorted by the whole power of the State, and pass by the Jail, which stood down in the town now. As He did so, troubling the waters of our civilization, one prisoner would be released, and then He would proceed to the great Mau tank that stretched as far as the Guest House garden, where something else would happen, some final or subsidiary apotheosis, after which He would submit to the experience of sleep. The Aziz family did not grasp as much as this, being Moslem, but the visit to the Jail was common knowledge. Smiling, with downcast eyes, the prisoners discussed with the gentry their chances of salvation. Except for the irons on their legs they resembled other men, nor did they feel different. Five of them, who had not yet been brought to trial, could expect no pardon, but all who had been convicted were full of hope. They did not distinguish between the God and the Rajah in their minds, both were too far above them; but the guard was better educated, and ventured to enquire after His Highness's health.

'It always improves,' replied the medicine man. As a matter of fact, the Rajah was dead, the ceremony overnight had overtaxed his strength. His death was being concealed lest the glory of the festival were dimmed. The Hindu physician, the Private Secretary, and a confidential servant remained with the corpse, while Aziz had assumed the duty of being seen in public, and misleading people. He had liked the ruler very much, and might not prosper under his successor, yet he could not worry over such problems yet, for he was involved in the illusion he helped to create. The children continued to run about, hunting for a frog to put in Mohammed Latif's bed, the little fools. Hundreds of frogs lived in their own garden, but they must needs catch one up on the fort. They reported two topis below. Fielding and his brother-in-law, instead of resting after their journey, were climbing the slope to the saint's tomb!

'Throw stones?' asked Karim.

'Put powdered glass in their pan?'

'Ahmed, come here for such wickedness.' He raised his hand to smite his firstborn, but allowed it to be kissed instead. It was sweet to have his sons with him at this moment, and to know they were affectionate and brave. He pointed out that the Englishmen were State guests, so must not be poisoned, and received, as always, gentle yet enthusiastic assent to his words.

The two visitors entered the octagon, but rushed out at once pursued by some bees. Hither and thither they ran, beating their heads; the children shrieked with derision, and out of heaven, as if a plug had been pulled, fell a jolly dollop of rain. Aziz had not meant to greet his former friend, but the incident put him into an excellent temper. He felt compact and strong. He shouted out, 'Hullo, gentlemen, are you in trouble?'

The brother-in-law exclaimed; a bee had got him.

'Lie down in a pool of water, my dear sir—here are plenty. Don't come near me. . . . I cannot control them, they are State bees; complain to His Highness of their behaviour.' There was no real danger, for the rain was increasing. The swarm retired to the shrine. He went up to the stranger and pulled a couple of stings out of his wrist, remarking, 'Come, pull yourself together and be a man.'

'How do you do, Aziz, after all this time? I heard you were settled in here,' Fielding called to him, but not in friendly tones. 'I suppose a couple of stings don't signify.'

'Not the least. I'll send an embrocation over to the Guest House. I heard you were settled in there.'

'Why have you not answered my letters?' he asked, going straight for the point, but not reaching it, owing to buckets of rain. His companion, new to the country, cried, as the drops drummed on his topi, that the bees were renewing their attack. Fielding checked his antics rather sharply, then said: 'Is there a short cut down to our carriage? We must give up our walk. The weather's pestilential.'

'Yes. That way.'

'Are you not coming down yourself?'

Aziz sketched a comic salaam; like all Indians, he was skilful in the slighter impertinences. 'I tremble, I obey,' the gesture said, and it was not lost upon Fielding. They walked down a rough path to the road—the two men first; the brother-in-law (boy rather than man) next, in a state over his arm, which hurt; the three Indian children last, noisy and impudent—all six wet through.

'How goes it, Aziz?'

'In my usual health.'

'Are you making anything out of your life here?'

'How much do you make out of yours?'

'Who is in charge of the Guest House?' he asked, giving up his slight effort to recapture their intimacy, and growing more official; he was older and sterner.

'His Highness's Private Secretary, probably.'

'Where is he, then?'

'I don't know.'

'Because not a soul's been near us since we arrived.'

'Really.'

'I wrote beforehand to the Durbar, and asked if a visit was convenient. I was told it was, and arranged my tour accordingly; but the Guest House servants appear to have no definite instructions, we can't get any eggs, also my wife wants to go out in the boat.'

'There are two boats.'

'Exactly, and no oars.'

'Colonel Maggs broke the oars when here last.'

'All four?'

'He is a most powerful man.'

'If the weather lifts, we want to see your torchlight procession from the water this evening,' he pursued. 'I wrote to Godbole about it, but he has taken no notice; it's a place of the dead.'

'Perhaps your letter never reached the Minister in question.'

'Will there be any objection to English people watching the procession?'

'I know nothing at all about the religion here. I should never think of watching it myself.'

'We had a very different reception both at Mudkul and Deora, they were kindness itself at Deora, the Maharajah and Maharani wanted us to see everything.'

'You should never have left them.'

'Jump in, Ralph'—they had reached the carriage.

'Jump in, Mr Quested, and Mr Fielding.'

'Who on earth is Mr Quested?'

'Do I mispronounce that well known name? Is he not your wife's brother?'

'Who on earth do you suppose I've married?'

'I'm only Ralph Moore,' said the boy, blushing, and at that moment there fell another pailful of the rain, and made a mist round their feet. Aziz tried to withdraw, but it was too late.

'Quested? Quested? Don't you know that my wife was Mrs Moore's daughter?'

He trembled, and went purplish grey; he hated the news, hated hearing the name Moore.

'Perhaps this explains your odd attitude?'

'And pray what is wrong with my attitude?'

'The preposterous letter you allowed Mahmoud Ali to write for you.'

'This is a very useless conversation, I consider.'

'However did you make such a mistake?' said Fielding, more friendly than before, but scathing and scornful. 'It's almost unbelievable. I should think I wrote you half a dozen times, mentioning my wife by name. Miss Quested! What an extraordinary notion!' From his smile, Aziz guessed that Stella was beautiful. 'Miss Quested is our best friend, she introduced us, but . . . what an amazing notion. Aziz, we must thrash this misunderstanding out later on. It is clearly some devilry of Mahmoud Ali's. He knows perfectly well I married Miss Moore. He called her 'Heaslop's sister' in his insolent letter to me.'

The name woke furies in him. 'So she is, and here is Heaslop's brother, and you his brother-in-law, and good-bye.' Shame turned into a rage that brought back his self-respect. 'What does it matter to me who you marry? Don't trouble me here at Mau is all I ask. I do not want you, I do not want one of you in my private life, with my dying breath I say it. Yes, yes, I made a foolish blunder; despise me and feel cold. I thought you married my enemy. I never read your letter. Mahmoud Ali deceived me. I thought you'd stolen my money, but'—he clapped his hands together, and his children gathered round him—'it's as if you stole it. I forgive Mahmoud Ali all things, because he loved me.' Then pausing, while the rain exploded like pistols, he said, 'My heart is for my own people henceforward,' and turned away. Cyril followed him through the mud, apologizing, laughing a little, wanting to argue and reconstruct, pointing out with irrefragable logic that he had married, not Heaslop's betrothed, but Heaslop's sister. What difference did it make at this hour of the day? He had built his life on a mistake, but he had built it. Speaking in Urdu, that the children might understand, he said: 'Please do not follow us, whomever you marry. I wish no Englishman or Englishwoman to be my friend.'

He returned to the house excited and happy. It had been an uneasy, uncanny moment when Mrs Moore's name was mentioned, stirring memories. 'Esmiss Esmoor . . .'—as though she was coming to help him. She had always been so good, and that youth whom he had scarcely looked at was her son, Ralph Moore, Stella and Ralph, whom he had promised to be kind to, and Stella had married Cyril.

Chapter Thirty-six

All the time the palace ceased not to thrum and tumtum. The revelation was over, but its effect lasted, and its effect was to make men feel that the revelation had not yet come. Hope existed despite fulfilment, as it will be in heaven. Although the God had been born, His procession—loosely supposed by many to be the birth—had not taken place. In normal years, the middle hours of this day were signalized by performances of great beauty in the private apartments of the Rajah. He owned a consecrated troupe of men and boys, whose duty it was to dance various actions and meditations of his faith before him. Seated at his ease, he could witness the Three Steps by which the Saviour ascended the universe to the discomfiture of Indra, also the death of the dragon, the mountain that turned into an umbrella, and the saddhu who (with comic results) invoked the God before dining. All culminated in the dance of the milkmaidens before Krishna, and in the still greater dance of Krishna before the milkmaidens, when the music and the musicians swirled through the dark blue robes of the actors into their tinsel crowns, and all became one. The Rajah and his guests would then forget that this was a dramatic performance, and would worship the actors. Nothing of the sort could occur to-day, because death interrupts. It interrupted less here than in Europe, its pathos was less poignant, its irony less cruel. There were two claimants to the throne, unfortunately, who were in the palace now and suspected what had happened, yet they made no trouble, because religion is a living force to the Hindus, and can at certain moments fling down everything that is petty and temporary in their natures. The festival flowed on, wild and sincere, and all men loved each other, and avoided by instinct whatever could cause inconvenience or pain.

Aziz could not understand this, any more than an average Christian could. He was puzzled that Mau should suddenly be purged from suspicion and self-seeking. Although he was an outsider, and excluded from their rites, they were always particularly charming to him at this time; he and his household received small courtesies and presents, just because he was outside. He had nothing to do all day, except to send the embrocation over to the Guest House, and towards sunset he remembered it, and looked round his house for a local palliative, for the dispensary was shut. He found a tin of ointment belonging to Mohammed Latif, who was unwilling it should be removed, for magic words had been spoken over it while it was being boiled down, but Aziz promised that he would bring it back after application to the stings: he wanted an excuse for a ride.

The procession was beginning to form as he passed the palace. A large crowed watched the loading of the State palanquin, the prow of which protruded in the form of a silver dragon's head through the lofty half-opened door. Gods, big and little, were getting aboard. He averted his eyes, for he never knew how much he was supposed to see, and nearly collided with the Minister of Education. 'Ah, you might make me late'—meaning that the touch of a non-Hindu would necessitate another bath; the words were spoken without moral heat. 'Sorry,' said Aziz. The other smiled, and again mentioned the Guest House party, and when he heard that Fielding's wife was not Miss Quested after all, remarked 'Ah, no, he married the sister of Mr Heaslop. Ah, exactly, I have known that for over a year'—also without heat. 'Why did you not tell me? Your silence plunged me into a pretty pickle.' Godbole, who had never been known to tell anyone anything, smiled again, and said in deprecating tones: 'Never be angry with me. I am, as far as my limitations permit, your true friend; besides, it is my holy festival.' Aziz always felt like a baby in that strange presence, a baby who unexpectedly receives a toy. He smiled also, and turned his horse into a lane, for the crush increased. The Sweepers' Band was arriving. Playing on sieves and other emblems of their profession, they marched straight at the gate of the palace with the air of a victorious army. All other music was silent, for this was ritually the moment of the Despised and Rejected; the God could not issue from his temple until the unclean Sweepers played their tune, they were the spot of filth without which the spirit cannot cohere. For an instant the scene was magnificent. The doors were thrown open, and the whole court was seen inside, barefoot and dressed in white robes; in the fairway stood the Ark of the Lord, covered with cloth of gold and flanked by peacock fans and by stiff circular banners of crimson. It was full to the brim with statuettes and flowers. As it rose from the earth on the shoulders of its bearers, the friendly sun of the monsoons shone forth and flooded the world with colour, so that the yellow tigers painted on the palace walls seemed to spring, and pink and green skeins of cloud to link up the upper sky. The palanquin moved. . . . The lane was full of State elephants, who would follow it, their howdahs empty out of humility. Aziz did not pay attention to these sanctities, for they had no connection with his own; he felt bored, slightly cynical, like his own dear Emperor Babur, who came down from the north and found in Hindustan no good fruit, no fresh water or witty conversation, not even a friend.

The lane led quickly out of the town on to high rocks and jungle. Here he drew rein and examined the great Mau tank, which lay exposed beneath him to its remotest curve. Reflecting the evening clouds, it filled the nether-world with an equal splendour, so that earth and sky leant toward one another, about to clash in ecstasy. He spat, cynical again, more cynical than before. For in the centre of the burnished circle a small black blot was advancing–the Guest House boat. Those English had improvised something to take the place of oars, and were proceeding in their work of patrolling India. The sight endeared the Hindus by comparison, and looking back at the milk-white hump of the palace, he hoped that they would enjoy carrying their idol about, for at all events it did not pry into other people's lives. This pose of 'seeing India' which had seduced him to Miss Quested at Chandrapore was only a form of ruling India; no sympathy lay behind it; he knew exactly what was going on in the boat as the party gazed at the steps down which the image would presently descend, and debated how near they might row without getting into trouble officially.

He did not give up his ride, for there would be servants at the Guest House whom he could question; a little information never comes amiss. He took the path by the sombre promontory that contained the royal tombs. Like the palace, they were of snowy stucco, and gleamed by their internal light, but their radiance grew ghostly under approaching night. The promontory was covered with lofty trees, and the fruit-bats were unhooking from the boughs and making kissing sounds as they grazed the surface of the tank; hanging upside down all the day, they had grown thirsty. The signs of the contented Indian evening multiplied; frogs on all sides, cow-dung burning eternally; a flock of belated hornbills overhead, looking like winged skeletons as they flapped across the gloaming. There was death in the air, but not sadness; a compromise had been made between destiny and desire, and even the heart of man acquiesced.

The European Guest House stood two hundred feet above the water, on the crest of a rocky and wooded spur that jutted from the jungle. By the time Aziz arrived, the water had paled to a film of mauve-grey, and the boat vanished entirely. A sentry slept in the Guest House porch, lamps burned in the cruciform of the deserted rooms. He went from one room to another, inquisitive, and malicious. Two letters lying on the piano rewarded him, and he pounced and read them promptly. He was not ashamed to do this. The sanctity of private correspondence has never been ratified by the East. Moreover, Mr McBryde had read all his letters in the past, and spread their contents. One letter—the more interesting of the two—was from Heaslop to Fielding. It threw light on the mentality of his former friend, and it hardened him further against him. Much of it was about Ralph Moore, who appeared to be almost an imbecile. 'Hand on my brother whenever suits you. I write to you because he is sure to make a bad bunderbust.' Then: 'I quite agree—life is too short to cherish grievances, also I'm relieved you feel able to come into line with the Oppressors of India to some extent. We need all the support we can get. I hope that next time Stella comes my way she will bring you with her, when I will make you as comfortable as a bachelor can—it's certainly time we met. My sister's marriage to you coming after my mother's death and my own difficulties did upset me, and I was unreasonable. It is about time we made it up properly, as you say—let us leave it at faults on both sides. Glad about your son and heir. When next any of you write to Adela, do give her some sort of message from me, for I should like to make my peace with her too. You are lucky to be out of British India at the present moment. Incident after incident, all due to propaganda, but we can't lay our hands on the connecting thread. The longer one lives here, the more certain one gets that everything hangs together. My personal opinion is, it's the Jews.'

Thus far the red-nosed boy. Aziz was distracted for a moment by blurred sounds coming from over the water; the procession was under way. The second letter was from Miss Quested to Mrs Fielding. It contained one or two interesting touches. The writer hoped that 'Ralph will enjoy his India more than I did mine,' and appeared to have given him money for this purpose—'my debt which I shall never repay in person.' What debt did Miss Quested imagine she owed the country? He did not relish the phrase. Talk of Ralph's health. It was all 'Stella and Ralph,' even 'Cyril' and 'Ronny'—all so friendly and sensible, and written in a spirit he could not command. He envied the easy intercourse that is only possible in a nation whose women are free. These five people were making up their little difficulties, and closing their broken ranks against the alien. Even Heaslop was coming in. Hence the strength of England, and in a spurt of temper he hit the piano, and since the notes had swollen and stuck together in groups of threes, he produced a remarkable noise.

'Oh, oh, who is that?' said a nervous and respectful voice; he could not remember where he had heard its tones before. Something moved in the twilight of an adjoining room. He replied, 'State doctor, ridden over to enquire, very little English,' slipped the letters into his pocket, and to show that he had free entry to the Guest House, struck the piano again.

Ralph Moore came into the light.

What a strange-looking youth, tall, prematurely aged, the big blue eyes faded with anxiety, the hair impoverished and tousled! Not a type that is often exported imperially. The doctor in Aziz thought, 'Born of too old a mother,' the poet found him rather beautiful.

'I was unable to call earlier owing to pressure of work. How are the celebrated bee-stings?' he asked patronizingly.

'I—I was resting, they thought I had better; they throb rather.'

His timidity and evident 'newness' had complicated effects on the malcontent. Speaking threateningly, he said, 'Come here, please, allow me to look.' They were practically alone, and he could treat the patient as Callendar had treated Nureddin.

'You said this morning—'

'The best of doctors make mistakes. Come here, please, for the diagnosis under the lamp. I am pressed for time.'

'Aough—'

'What is the matter, pray?'

'Your hands are unkind.'

He started and glanced down at them. The extraordinary youth was right, and he put them behind his back before replying with outward anger: 'What the devil have my hands to do with you? This is a most strange remark. I am a qualified doctor, who will not hurt you.'

'I don't mind pain, there is no pain.'

'No pain?'

'Not really.'

'Excellent news,' sneered Aziz.

'But there is cruelty.'

'I have brought you some salve, but how to put it on in your present nervous state becomes a problem,' he continued, after a pause.

'Please leave it with me.'

'Certainly not. It returns to my dispensary at once.' He stretched forward, and the other retreated to the farther side of a table. 'Now, do you want me to treat your stings, or do you prefer an English doctor? There is one at Asirgarh. Asirgarh is forty miles away, and the Ringnod dam broken. Now you see how you are placed. I think I had better see Mr Fielding about you; this is really great nonsense, your present behaviour.'

'They are out in a boat,' he replied, glancing about him for support.

Aziz feigned intense surprise. 'They have not gone in the direction of Mau, I hope. On a night like this the people become most fanatical.' And, as if to confirm him, there was a sob, as though the lips of a giant had parted; the procession was approaching the Jail.

'You should not treat us like this,' he challenged, and this time Aziz was checked, for the voice, though frightened, was not weak.

'Like what?'

'Dr Aziz, we have done you no harm.'

'Aha, you know my name, I see. Yes, I am Aziz. No, of course your great friend Miss Quested did me no harm at the Marabar.'

Drowning his last words, all the guns of the State went off. A rocket from the Jail garden gave the signal. The prisoner had been released, and was kissing the feet of the singers. Rose-leaves fall from the houses, sacred spices and coco-nut are brought forth. . . . It was the half-way moment; the God had extended His temple, and paused exultantly. Mixed and confused in their passage, the rumours of salvation entered the Guest House. They were startled and moved on to the porch, drawn by the sudden illumination. The bronze gun up on the fort kept flashing, the town was a blur of light, in which the houses seemed dancing, and the palace waving little wings. The water below, the hills and sky above, were not involved as yet; there was still only a little light and song struggling among the shapeless lumps of the universe. The song became audible through much repetition; the choir was repeating and inverting the names of deities.

> *Radhakrishna Radhakrishna,*
> *Radhakrishna Radhakrishna,*
> *Krishnaradha Radhakrishna,*
> *Radhakrishna Radhakrishna,*

they sang, and woke the sleeping sentry in the Guest House; he leant upon his iron-tipped spear.

'I must go back now, good night,' said Aziz, and held out his hand, completely forgetting that they were not friends, and focusing his heart on something more distant than the caves, something beautiful. His hand was taken, and then he remembered how detestable he had been, and said gently, 'Don't you think me unkind any more?'

'No.'

'How can you tell, you strange fellow?'

'Not difficult, the one thing I always know.'

'Can you always tell whether a stranger is your friend?'

'Yes.'

'Then you are an Oriental.' He unclasped as he spoke, with a little shudder. Those words—he had said them to Mrs Moore in the mosque in the beginning of the cycle, from which, after so much suffering, he had got free. Never be friends with the English! Mosque, caves, mosque, caves. And here he was starting again. He handed the magic ointment to him. 'Take this, think of me when you use it. I shall never want it back. I must give you one little present, and it is all I have got; you are Mrs Moore's son.'

'I am that,' he murmured to himself; and a part of Aziz' mind that had been hidden seemed to move and force its way to the top.

'But you are Heaslop's brother also, and alas, the two nations cannot be friends.'

'I know. Not yet.'

'Did your mother speak to you about me?'

'Yes.' And with a swerve of voice and body that Aziz did not follow he added, 'In her letters, in her letters. She loved you.'

'Yes, your mother was my best friend in all the world.' He was silent, puzzled by his own great gratitude. What did this eternal goodness of Mrs Moore amount to? To nothing, if brought to the test of thought. She had not borne witness in his favour, nor visited him in the prison, yet she had stolen to the depths of his heart, and he always adored her. 'This is our monsoon, the best weather,' he said, while the lights of the procession waved as though embroidered on an agitated curtain. 'How I wish she could have seen them, our rains. Now is the time when all things are happy, young and old. They are happy out there with their savage noise, though we cannot follow them; the tanks are all full so they dance, and this is India. I wish you were not with officials, then I would show you my country, but I cannot. Perhaps I will just take you out on the water now, for one short half-hour.'

Was the cycle beginning again? His heart was too full to draw back. He must slip out in the darkness, and do this one act of homage to Mrs Moore's son. He knew where the oars were—hidden to deter the visitors from going out—and he brought the second pair, in case they met the other boat; the Fieldings had pushed themselves out with long poles, and might get into difficulties, for the wind was rising.

Once on the water, he became easy. One kind action was with him always a channel for another, and soon the torrent of his hospitality gushed forth and he began doing the honours of Mau and persuading himself that he understood the wild procession, which increased in lights and sounds as the complications of its ritual developed. There was little need to row, for the freshening gale blew them in the direction they desired. Thorns scratched the keel, they ran into an islet and startled some cranes. The strange temporary life of the August flood-water bore them up and seemed as though it would last for ever.

The boat was a rudderless dinghy. Huddled up in the stern, with the spare pair of oars in his arms, the guest asked no questions about details. There was presently a flash of lightning, followed by a second flash—little red scratches on the ponderous sky. 'Was that the Rajah?' he asked.

'What—what do you mean?'

'Row back.'

'But there's no Rajah—nothing—'

'Row back, you will see what I mean.'

Aziz found it hard work against the advancing wind. But he fixed his eyes on the pin of light that marked the Guest House and backed a few strokes. 'There . . .'

Floating in the darkness was a king, who sat under a canopy, in shining royal robes. . . .

'I can't tell you what that is, I'm sure,' he whispered. 'His Highness is dead. I think we should go back at once.'

They were close to the promontory of the tombs, and had looked straight into the chhatri of the Rajah's father through an opening in the trees. That was the explanation. He had heard of the image—made to imitate life at enormous expense—but he had never chanced to see it before, though he frequently rowed on the lake. There was only one spot from which it could be seen, and Ralph had directed him to it. Hastily he pulled away, feeling that his companion was not so much a visitor as a guide. He remarked, 'Shall we go back now?'

'There is still the procession.'

'I'd rather not go nearer—they have such strange customs, and might hurt you.'

'A little nearer.'

Aziz obeyed. He knew with his heart that this was Mrs Moore's son, and indeed until his heart was involved he knew nothing. 'Radhakrishna Radhakrishna Radhakrishna Radhakrishna Krishnaradha,' went the chant, then suddenly changed, and in the interstice he heard, almost certainly, the syllables of salvation that had sounded during his trial at Chandrapore.

'Mr Moore, don't tell anyone that the Rajah is dead. It is a secret still, I am supposed not to say. We pretend he is alive until after the festival, to prevent unhappiness. Do you want to go still nearer?'

'Yes.'

He tried to keep the boat out of the glare of the torches that began to star the other shore. Rockets kept going off, also the guns. Suddenly, closer than he had calculated, the palanquin of Krishna appeared from behind a ruined wall, and descended the carven glistening watersteps. On either side of it the singers tumbled, a woman prominent, a wild and beautiful young saint with flowers in her hair. She was praising God without attributes—thus did she apprehend Him. Others praised Him without attributes, seeing Him in this or that organ of the body or manifestation of the sky. Down they rushed to the foreshore and stood in the small waves, and a sacred meal was prepared, of which those who felt worthy partook. Old Godbole detected the boat, which was drifting in on the gale, and he waved his arms—whether in wrath or joy Aziz never discovered. Above stood the secular power of Mau—elephants, artillery, crowds—and high above them a wild tempest started, confined at first to the upper regions of the air. Gusts of wind mixed darkness and light, sheets of rain cut from the north, stopped, cut from the south, began rising from below, and across them struggled the singers, sounding every note but terror, and preparing to throw God away, God Himself, (not that God can be thrown) into the storm. Thus was He thrown year after year, and were others thrown—little images of Ganpati, baskets of ten-day corn, tiny tazias after Mohurram—scapegoats, husks, emblems of passage; a passage not easy, not now, not here, not to be apprehended except when it is unattainable: the God to be thrown was an emblem of that.

The village of Gokul reappeared upon its tray. It was the substitute for the silver image, which never left its haze of flowers; on behalf of another symbol, it was to perish. A servitor took it in his hands, and tore off the blue and white streamers. He was naked, broad-shouldered, thin-waisted—the Indian body again triumphant—and it was his hereditary office to close the gates of salvation. He entered the dark waters, pushing the village before him, until the clay dolls slipped off their chairs and began to gutter in the rain, and King Kansa was confounded with the father and mother of the Lord. Dark and solid, the little waves sipped, then a great wave washed and then English voices cried 'Take care!'

The boats had collided with each other.

The four outsiders flung out their arms and grappled, and, with oars and poles sticking out, revolved like a mythical monster in the whirlwind. The worshippers howled with wrath or joy, as they drifted forward helplessly against the servitor. Who awaited them, his beautiful dark face expressionless, and as the last morsels melted on his tray, it struck them.

The shock was minute, but Stella, nearest to it, shrank into her husband's arms, then reached forward, then flung herself against Aziz, and her motions capsized them. They plunged into the warm, shallow water, and rose struggling into a tornado of noise. The oars, the sacred tray, the letters of Ronny and Adela, broke loose and floated confusedly. Artillery was fired, drums beaten, the elephants trumpeted, and drowning all an immense peal of thunder, unaccompanied by lightning, cracked like a mallet on the dome.

That was the climax, as far as India admits of one. The rain settled in steadily to its job of wetting everybody and everything through, and soon spoiled the cloth of gold on the palanquin and the costly disc-shaped banners. Some of the torches went out, fireworks didn't catch, there began to be less singing, and the tray returned to Professor Godbole, who picked up a fragment of the mud adhering and smeared it on his forehead without much ceremony. Whatever had happened had happened, and while the intruders picked themselves up, the crowds of Hindus began a desultory move back into the town. The image went back too, and on the following day underwent a private death of its own, when some curtains of magenta and green were lowered in front of the dynastic shrine. The singing went on even longer . . . ragged edges of religion . . . unsatisfactory and undramatic tangles. . . . 'God si love.' Looking back at the great blur of the last twenty-four hours, no man could say where was the emotional centre of it, any more than he could locate the heart of a cloud.

Chapter Thirty-seven

Friends again, yet aware that they could meet no more, Aziz and Fielding went for their last ride in the Mau jungles. The floods had abated and the Rajah was officially dead, so the Guest House party were departing next morning, as decorum required. What with the mourning and the festival, the visit was a failure. Fielding had scarcely seen Godbole, who promised every day to show him over the King-Emperor George Fifth High School, his main objective, but always made some excuse. This afternoon Aziz let out what had happened: the King-Emperor had been converted into a granary, and the Minister of Education did not like to admit this to his former Principal. The school had been opened only last year by the Agent to the Governor-General, and it still flourished on paper; he hoped to start it again before its absence was remarked and to collect its scholars before they produced children of their own. Fielding laughed at the tangle and waste of energy, but he did not travel as lightly as in the past; education was a continuous concern to him, because his income and the comfort of his family depended on it. He knew that few Indians think education good in itself, and he deplored this now on the widest grounds. He began to say something heavy on the subject of Native States, but the friendliness of Aziz distracted him. This reconciliation was a success, anyhow. After the funny shipwreck there had been no more nonsense or bitterness, and they went back laughingly to their old relationship as if nothing had happened. Now they rode between jolly bushes and rocks. Presently the ground opened into full sunlight and they saw a grassy slope bright with butterflies, also a cobra, which crawled across doing nothing in particular, and disappeared among some custard-apple trees. There were round white clouds in the sky, and white pools on the earth; the hills in the distance were purple. The scene was as park-like as England, but did not cease being queer. They drew rein, to give the cobra elbow-room, and Aziz produced a letter that he wanted to send to Miss Quested. A charming letter. He wanted to thank his old enemy for her fine behaviour two years back: perfectly plain was it now that she had behaved well. 'As I fell into our largest Mau tank under circumstances our other friends will relate, I thought how brave Miss Quested was, and decided to tell her so, despite my imperfect English. Through you I am happy here with my children instead of in a prison, of that I make no doubt. My children shall be taught to speak of you with the greatest affection and respect.'

'Miss Quested will be greatly pleased. I am glad you have seen her courage at last.'

'I want to do kind actions all round and wipe out the wretched business of the Marabar for ever. I have been so disgracefully hasty, thinking you meant to get hold of my money: as bad a mistake as the cave itself.'

'Aziz, I wish you would talk to my wife. She too believes that the Marabar is wiped out.'

'How so?'

'I don't know, perhaps she might tell you, she won't tell me. She has ideas I don't share—indeed, when I'm away from her I think them ridiculous. When I'm with her, I suppose because I'm fond of her, I feel different, I feel half dead and half blind. My wife's after something. You and I and Miss Quested are, roughly speaking, not after anything. We jog on as decently as we can, you a little in front—a laudable little party. But my wife is not with us.'

'What are you meaning? Is Stella not faithful to you, Cyril? This fills me with great concern.'

Fielding hesitated. He was not quite happy about his marriage. He was passionate physically again—the final flare-up before the clinkers of middle age—and he knew that his wife did not love him as much as he loved her, and he was ashamed of pestering her. But during the visit to Mau the situation had improved. There seemed a link between them at last—that link outside either participant that is necessary to every relationship. In the language of theology, their union had been blessed. He could assure Aziz that Stella was not only faithful to him, but likely to become more so; and trying to express what was not clear to himself, he added dully that different people had different points of view. 'If you won't talk about the Marabar to Stella, why won't you talk to Ralph? He is a wise boy really. And (same metaphor) he rides a little behind her, though with her.'

'Tell him also, I have nothing to say to him, but he is indeed a wise boy and has always one Indian friend. I partly love him because he brought me back to you to say good-bye. For this is good-bye, Cyril, though to think about it will spoil or ride and make us sad.'

'No, we won't think about it.' He too felt that this was their last free intercourse. All the stupid misunderstandings had been cleared up, but socially they had no meeting-place. He had thrown in his lot with Anglo-India by marrying a countrywoman, and he was acquiring some of its limitations, and already felt surprise at his own past heroism. Would he to-day defy all his own people for the sake of a stray Indian? Aziz was a memento, a trophy, they were proud of each other, yet they must inevitably part. And, anxious to make what he could of this last afternoon, he forced himself to speak intimately about his wife, the person most dear to him. He said: 'From her point of view, Mau has been a success. It calmed her—both of them suffer from restlessness. She found something soothing, some solution of her queer troubles here.' After a silence—myriads of kisses around them as the earth drew the water in—he continued: 'Do you know anything about this Krishna business?'

'My dear chap, officially they call it Gokul Ashtami. All the State offices are closed, but how else should it concern you and me?'

'Gokul is the village where Krishna was born—well, more or less born, for there's the same hovering between it and another village as between Bethlehem and Nazareth. What I want to discover is its spiritual side, if it has one.'

'It is useless discussing Hindus with me. Living with them teaches me no more. When I think I annoy them, I do not. When I think I don't annoy them, I do. Perhaps they will sack me for tumbling on to their dolls'-house; on the other hand, perhaps they will double my salary. Time will prove. Why so curious about them?'

'It's difficult to explain. I never really understood or liked them, except an occasional scrap of Godbole. Does the old fellow still say "Come, come?"'

'Oh, presumably.'

Fielding sighed, opened his lips, shut them, then said with a little laugh, 'I can't explain, because it isn't in words at all, but why do my wife and her brother like Hinduism, though they take no interest in its forms? They won't talk to me about this. They know I think a certain side of their lives is a mistake, and are shy. That's why I wish you would talk to them, for at all events you're Oriental.'

Aziz refused to reply. He didn't want to meet Stella and Ralph again, knew they didn't want to meet him, was incurious about their secrets, and felt good old Cyril to be a bit clumsy. Something—not a sight, but a sound—flitted past him, and caused him to re-read his letter to Miss Quested. Hadn't he wanted to say something else to her? Taking out his pen, he added: 'For my own part, I shall henceforth connect you with the name that is very sacred in my mind, namely, Mrs Moore.' When he had finished, the mirror of the scenery was shattered, the meadow disintegrated into butterflies. A poem about Mecca—the Caaba of Union—the thorn-bushes where pilgrims die before they have seen the Friend—they flitted next; he thought of his wife; and then the whole semi-mystic, semi-sensuous overturn, so characteristic of his spiritual life, came to end like a landslip and rested in its due place, and he found himself riding in the jungle with his dear Cyril.

'Oh, shut up,' he said. 'Don't spoil our last hour with foolish questions. Leave Krishna alone, and talk about something sensible.'

They did. All the way back to Mau they wrangled about politics. Each had hardened since Chandrapore, and a good knock about proved enjoyable. They trusted each other, although they were going to part, perhaps because they were going to part. Fielding had 'no further use for politeness,' he said, meaning that the British Empire really can't be abolished because it's rude. Aziz retorted, 'Very well, and we have no use for you,' and glared at him with abstract hate. Fielding said: 'Away from us, Indians go to seed at once. Look at the King-Emperor High School! Look at you, forgetting your medicine and going back to charms. Look at your poems.'—'Jolly good poems, I'm getting published Bombay side.'—'Yes, and what do they say? Free our women and India will be free. Try it, my lad. Free your own lady in the first place, and see who'll wash Ahmed Karim and Jamila's faces. A nice situation!'

Aziz grew more excited. He rose in his stirrups and pulled at his horse's head in the hope it would rear. Then he should feel in a battle. He cried: 'Clear out, all you Turtons and Burtons. We wanted to know you ten years back—now it's too late. If we see you and sit on your committees, it's for political reasons, don't you make any mistake.' His horse did rear. 'Clear out, clear out, I say. Why are we put to so much suffering? We used to blame you, now we blame ourselves, we grow wiser. Until England is in difficulties we keep silent, but in the next European war—aha, aha! Then is our time.' He paused, and the scenery, though it smiled, fell like a gravestone on any human hope. They cantered past a temple to Hanuman—God so loved the world that he took monkey's flesh upon him—and past a Saivite temple, which invited to lust, but under the semblance of eternity, its obscenities bearing no relation to those of our flesh and blood. They splashed through butterflies and frogs; great trees with leaves like plates rose among the brushwood. The divisions of daily life were returning, the shrine had almost shut.

'Who do you want instead of the English? The Japanese?' jeered Fielding, drawing rein.

'No, the Afghans. My own ancestors.'

'Oh, your Hindu friends will like that, won't they?'

'It will be arranged–a conference of Oriental statesmen.'

'It will indeed be arranged.'

'Old story of "We will rob every man and rape every woman from Peshawar to Calcutta," I suppose, which you get some nobody to repeat and then quote every week in the *Pioneer* in order to frighten us into retaining you! We know!' Still he couldn't quite fit in Afghans at Mau, and, finding he was in a corner, made his horse rear again until he remembered that he had, or ought to have, a mother-land. Then he shouted: 'India shall be a nation! No foreigners of any sort! Hindu and Moslem and Sikh and all shall be one! Hurrah! Hurrah for India! Hurrah! Hurrah!'

India a nation! What an apotheosis! Last comer to the drab nineteenth-century sisterhood! Waddling in at this hour of the world to take her seat! She, whose only peer was the Holy Roman Empire, she shall rank with Guatemala and Belgium perhaps! Fielding mocked again. And Aziz in an awful rage danced this way and that, not knowing what to do, and cried: 'Down with the English anyhow. That's certain. Clear out, you fellows, double quick, I say. We may hate one another, but we hate you most. If I don't make you go, Ahmed will, Karim will, if it's fifty five-hundred years we shall get rid of you, yes, we shall drive every blasted Englishman into the sea, and then'–he rode against him furiously–'and then,' he concluded, half kissing him, 'you and I shall be friends.'

'Why can't we be friends now?' said the other, holding him affectionately. 'It's what I want. It's what you want.'

But the horses didn't want it–they swerved apart; the earth didn't want it, sending up rocks through which riders must pass single file; the temples, the tank, the jail, the palace, the birds, the carrion, the Guest House, that came into view as they issued from the gap and saw Mau beneath: they didn't want it, they said in their hundred voices, 'No, not yet,' and the sky said, 'No, not there.'

Weybridge, 1924.